A Crown of Cobwebs

J. Darris Mitchell

INDIES UNITED PUBLISHING HOUSE, LLC

This book represents hours and hours of work done by the author as well as many other people he both loves and respects. Don't steal it. If you are interested in sharing it contact the author and he will be happy to assist you. It violates the sacred bond of writer and reader to reproduce or reprint any part of this book without the author's written permission, except for brief quotations in critical reviews. In other words, reprinting or reproducing this book is illegal. It's totally OK to let a friend read this copy, but please direct them to the website so they can purchase the rest of the series themselves and thus help the author and those in his life put food on their tables.

Thank you.

A CROWN OF COBWEBS
Version 1.0
Copyright © 2020 by J. Darris Mitchell
Published July 2020
by Indies United Publishing House, LLC

This is a work of fiction. All of the characters, events and organizations are either imagined by the author or used fictitiously.

ISBN: 978-1-64456-152-2
Library of Congress Control Number: 2020932485

INDIES UNITED PUBLISHING HOUSE, LLC
P.O. BOX 3071
QUINCY, IL 62305-3071
www.indiesunited.net

Other Works by
J. Darris Mitchell

INTERSTELLAR SPRING

Fireflies and Cosmos

Diamondcrabs and Mangoes

Iceoaks and Warblers

Interstellar Sunrise
A podcast and prequel to the Interstellar Spring Saga

THE WILD LANDS

The Wild Man

This one's for Cole

BOOK 1

An Engagement of Abominations

Chapter 1

Adrianna

On the day of her wedding, the spider princess wore a silk dress for her webmother, dagger for her fiancé, and a scowl because she couldn't help herself. Adrianna Morticia scowled at the rickety rope bridge beneath her feet and the cursed castle ahead of her, floating above a caldera of lava. She scowled at her long-dead ancestors, who got her into this mess when they lost a castle they'd help build millennia ago. She scowled because seven generations of spiderfolk had lived in caves instead of the castle, snatching up unwary mortals so that one day, the eighth daughter of the eighth daughter could stand in front of The Lich and a bunch of draconic mongrels and marry some monstrous bastard she didn't even know to fulfill a pact she hadn't even made, take back a castle she'd never been to and prevent a war that no one— least of all the spider princess—wanted. Adrianna also scowled because her feet ached.

For every step of her Path of Cleansing the spider princess wore black shoes with daggers for heels. They were horribly uncomfortable, even for a princess of the spiderfolk. Adrianna wanted to hurl the shoes into the lava below the rope bridge along with her white dress.

The spider princess took a deep breath and tried to calm down. Her abdominal vents felt stifled in the silk dress, despite the airholes she'd woven into the fabric, but she didn't want to destroy it. Her webmother's face when she saw it would make the time it took to spin the thing worth it.

It's going to be fine, she told herself. She would marry the prince of the castle, war would be prevented and her webmother would be appeased. Then some knight in shining armor would come along and slay Adrianna and spill her ichor all over her ancestral home and the prince could go back to whatever he was doing before a swarm of spiderfolk invaded the castle he'd lived in his entire life and forced him to marry a waif of a princess. Adrianna had always wanted to be a hero, now she'd probably be killed by one.

Adrianna sighed and continued across the rope bridge towards the crumbling castle. It had been symmetrical once, it must have been, but right now it looked as if some rampaging demigod had smashed half of it away along with Adrianna's dreams of enjoying her twenties and thirties. Inside the castle was a cathedral that her ancestors had designed and built. In that cathedral, the interior of which Adrianna had never seen, she was to marry a man whose ancestors had broken their pact and forced the spiderfolk underground for millennia. Her webmother had told her that this was her birthright, that her destiny was to take back her family's inheritance by marrying a stranger.

The inheritance, Krag's Doom as the current inhabitants styled the castle, floated above the volcano because of a spell purported to have taken thirteen sorcerers thirteen months to cast. Eruptions from times past had spewed magma that had cooled on the bottom of the castle like roots or, in her eyes, the legs of a massive spider. She watched as one of lava legs seemed to take a step towards her before collapsing into segments and falling away into the pool of molten lava below. Adrianna felt like her legs were going to do the same thing.

She made it across the rickety rope bridge without incident. The doors to the castle opened.

A mess of arachnid eyes, clicking chelicera and grasping pedipalps greeted her. *Etterqueen,* Adrianna cursed in her head. She'd have preferred the door to be answered by one of the draconic mongrels—flamehearts, her tutors said the army of draconic women called themselves—instead of her own sister.

'Adrianna, finally! Just like the spider princess to be late to her own wedding. We thought you'd finally decided to eat that thrall of a boyfriend of yours and let him fertilize your egg sack.'

'Asakusa is *not* my boyfriend, Lutecia. And I am *not* late. This wedding wasn't supposed to happen for decades yet." Adrianna replied.

'The castle won't last decades, something you'd have noticed if you'd been here to help prepare instead of waiting for the last possible moment to arrive. And I'm Ismina, you insect, don't you know the face of your own sister?'

Adrianna blanched. She *didn't* know the face of her sisters. She had left home when she was nine years old, at her webmother's insistence, and never come home. Adrianna had seven sisters, and each of their bodies were variations on a theme: human and spider monstrosity. Only Adrianna was gifted with a human face and a human body, and only when she Folded away her spider form. As eighth daughter of a Mortician, the ability to Fold into a true human form (except for her abdominal vents) was her gift. The problem was that, as the only one of her sisters with a passably human form, she was expected to marry someone outside the species and procreate.

She had accepted that—her tutors in S'kar-Vozi had drilled it into her daily—but she'd thought she had more time. Krag's Doom had lasted millennia, surely it could have lasted another century. But Adrianna knew enough of architecture to know that it couldn't have. One of the halls had collapsed into the lava below. If another did, the spell holding it up might become unbalanced and topple the entire thing into the volcano. If that happened the Valkannas would burn the entire Archipelago in their rage and the Morticians' chance of moving to the surface would literally go up in smoke. She was doing *good* by agreeing to this marriage, good for her family, good for the people of S'kar-Vozi she'd spent the last decade with, and good for the Valkannas. It was probably the most noble thing she'd do with her entire life, and yet she felt horrible.

She wanted to be a *hero*, not princess of the spiderfolk. She'd worked hard to earn her meager reputation in S'kar-Vozi, harder than most because of what she was, and that would all be undone with this marriage. Humans could stomach spiderfolk, Adrianna had proven that, but she'd lose what credibility she had if her husband was… well, a Valkanna.

'I'm sorry, Ismina,' Adrianna said, confused and embarrassed. She had been *certain* this was Lutecia.

'I *am* Lutecia you roach,' Lutecia laughed, a gesture that involved far too many mouthparts. 'Now come here and let me fix your hair. You have exoskeleton showing.' Lutecia had a human torso, four human arms and four spider legs. Every inch of her was covered in coarse, spider hair and her face was an absolute wreck. Ismina was identical except she had spider arms and human legs. They had pulled the name trick on Adrianna every day of her life for nine years. And they had been the nice ones. Her sisters had spent the first nine years of Adrianna's life torturing her (spider legs would grow back in a molt, something Adrianna's sisters proved to her), trying to get her killed by creatures that made it inside their subterranean complex of caves ('No Webmother, I don't know how the Deurg-Demon got past our webs'), and (like many older siblings) ruthlessly insulting and berating her until she believed all of the horrible things they said.

They were right really, Adrianna was disgusting for a spiderfolk. She was skinny, bony more like, with black eyes (only six of them when she wasn't Folded), a pert nose and a small mouth. Her bony body felt far more comfortable under black leather armor than a silk dress. Her hair was her only attractive feature. White and silky, it hung to her waist when it wasn't tied up. Other than that, she was as her sisters had taught her, a bony wretch of a human. At least they respected her in her spider form. To insult *that* body would be to insult their own webmother.

'The dress isn't terrible,' Lutecia said. That was about as close to a compliment as any of her sisters had ever given her.

'Thank you, this is the eighth version.'

Lutecia nodded in approval as her four arms fussed with Adrianna's hair. Adrianna could feel her skin tighten as Lutecia pulled her long white hair into an elaborate pattern of braids.

'And you followed mother's design?'

Adrianna nodded. The dress would see her through the night. It would Unfold with her, and when the marriage was done and consummated, it would hold the eggs. Adrianna shuddered at the thought.

'Nervous?' Lutecia chittered. 'I was too on my wedding day, long ago as it was, but you needn't be. The bedding takes less time than the ceremony, and then there's always breakfast in bed. Herman *was* delicious.'

'Don't be so cruel, Lutecia,' said another of Adrianna's sisters. Marliana, Adrianna knew, the oldest. Her face was pretty enough but it was stuck on the abdomen of a fat brown tarantula the size of a war-pig. She crawled down a wall of the castle and went about raising the hem of Adrianna's dress to reveal her thighs.

Adrianna had made the dress to *not* reveal as much skin as her webmother had insisted, but of course, she wouldn't get to make that decision. She hadn't made *any* decisions for the wedding. She'd been doing her best to willfully ignore the whole thing for as long as she had been able. She'd been hoping to ignore it for years, but the crumbling walls and worn-through pillars of the room around them spoke of the urgency of the needed repairs to the castle.

'You know pretty Adrianna won't be feasting upon her husband's ichor. She's soft,' Marliana said, prodding Adrianna in the thigh with a barbed leg. 'And he's tough. Even your little band of—what are you, questers? — wouldn't be a match for Prince Valkanna.'

'We're *adventurers*, Marliana, and we've made a name for ourselves in the free city of S'kar-vozi.' Adrianna wanted to say more, that Magnus himself had sent them on a quest to rescue a family of shipwrecked islanders, but the dress and the weight of what Marliana said took her breath away. *My friends didn't come?* The wedding would start at sunset, which was only a few minutes away. Her friends should have been here already.

'Yes, we've heard of you. Even up here at Krag's Doom we've heard of the Slaves to the Spider Princess,' Marliana said, her voice laden with venom. 'A little much, considering our webmother is still alive and you're not yet married. Did you order them to stay away, or are they as scared of your family as you are?'

Adrianna scowled. Marliana was goading her. She wouldn't let it get to her; not today, there was enough else on her web. And it wasn't like she'd actually *invited* them. Right now, surrounded by her sisters, she wished she had, but she *couldn't*.

It would have been a disaster.

Ebbo would have been a liability with all the magick around, and that was if her sisters didn't try to eat him. Clayton didn't do well around heat, but he had been so supportive. She should have at least shown him her dress. And Asakusa… Adrianna fumed as she thought of the Gatekeeper's thrall. *He* should be here! He'd been avoiding her, spending the last month under an umbrella on the beach, rubbing ointment on his Corruption and refusing to talk about the wedding. And why? The contract that allowed him to open Gates to the Ways of the Undead meant he couldn't be cornered. Not by her webmother or her soon-to-be oathfather.

Sure, she didn't invite them, but they hadn't been invited to the sea witch's seaweed palace either, nor to the gnoll stronghold to drive out the cannibals. Her friends were heroes! They saved people they hadn't known from dire threats, so why not Adrianna? She was a princess, after all, much as she hated to admit it. She knew they couldn't save her, though. Not from two families as dangerous as the Morticians and Valkannas. But they could have come to say good-bye.

That was why she was in such a foul mood. The fate of two ancient families had conspired to ruin her life, and her friends weren't even here to joke about *what* she was marrying. Adrianna shuddered at the thought, earning a curse from Marliana as the claws at the tips of her tarantula arms worked at her hem. As much as Adrianna hated to admit it, she wasn't in a bad mood because of *who* her fiancé was. By all accounts, he was rich, handsome, and a sharp dresser. He treated his servants well enough, cared for his family, and *actually agreed* to marry a skinny spider princess, and yet, the idea of marrying *what* he was made her stomach churn.

It did not much help her mood that the groom to be was a dragon.

Chapter 2

Ebbo

On the day Ebbo Brandyoak stepped out from under his oak tree of a home and into adventure, he never thought he'd find himself strolling toward a Gate to the Ways of the Dead, but he had to look casual if he was going to pinch some magick before Adrianna's wedding. He needed to hurry, but he had time to score, especially in the bustling Farmer's Market. Ebbo definitely didn't need any magick, he just really wanted some; really, really bad. That desire, scratching at the back of his mind like a cat teasing a wounded bird, kept his keen eyes on distracted shoppers and his hands in unguarded pockets.

Ebbo sniffed at the air. Nutmeg, thyme, curry. He wrinkled his nose at the smell of raw sewage from Bog's Bay. Apple and barley cobbler, roast corn. Then he smelled it: magick. The smell of magick was different to every islander. Some of them, the lucky ones, hardly noticed it at all, but to Ebbo it smelled of acorn mash and cold well water, of cinnamon scones like his gran used to make and Ol' Burba's smokeleaf. The familiar smell of magic wafted from a crowd of shoppers gathered around an elvish bard with swept-back yellow hair playing an accordion.

Ebbo went to work.

He ignored the humans. Most of them worked and lived in the free city of S'kar-Vozi and wouldn't have two pieces of silver in their pockets. Ebbo's fellow short-statured islanders weren't much better targets. Those with coins would be tourists from the Co-op, the co-operative of farms spread out across the Archipelago that had flourished in the last few decades, and Ebbo didn't want to steal from them. It would be like stealing from his own family, and besides, islanders that lived in the Co-op didn't use magick, period. Ebbo told himself that wasn't one of the reasons he left, but he knew that for the lie that it was.

A dwarf drank from a stone flagon filled with acorn brandy. Ebbo recognized the smell; it had been brewed by his family on Strong Oak Isle. Liquor wasn't magick, but the dwarf looked as if he'd been charmed by the potent drink all the same. Ebbo reached past the dwarf's beard without tickling it, under his chain mail without clinking it, and found a few coppers in a purse. Coppers, basically worthless, but practically useful.

Ebbo took the stolen coins to the bard's tip jar and let them drop in with a clink. He felt for any paper packets or vials in the jar, but again found only coin. The bard languidly watched Ebbo check the jar. His neutral gaze was enough to tell Ebbo he shouldn't have bothered to check for magick. Elves cared little for anything that couldn't make music. Coins were as beneath their notice as islanders were. If there had been something in tip that the elf could use to augment his accordion, he wouldn't have let a skinny islander get so close.

Ebbo sniffed the air again. It was strong magick, possibly draconic. That should have meant something to Ebbo, he was sure, but he couldn't get over the potency of the aroma. Ebbo sniffed again and withdrew his hand from the tip jar, but he had lingered too long.

'Watch where you're putting your hands, you curly-headed little twerp,' a blue skinned woman yelled. She had slimy gills on her neck, fins on her head, and an axe strapped over her green robe. Probably a warrior from the Cthult of Cthulu. Ebbo should have tried her pocket instead of the elf's tip jar. Too late, she'd alerted her band and they came for the islander.

'If I catch you, I'll smash your head like one of your rotten pumpkins!' said a warrior with a mustache the color of kelp. He shrugged off a robe, revealing hard muscles and tattooed blue skin that had been greased up with stinking fish oil. Ebbo vanished into the crowd, reminding himself that he had a wedding to get to.

It was easy for Ebbo to slip away. He was half the height of most of the shoppers, and his bare feet could move soundlessly over the multicolored cobblestones. His mop of hair was curly and blond, almost silver, a fairly uncommon color, but the hood of his home-spun tunic was a greyish green and hid his hair easily enough. The ornate dagger at his belt might have let the Cthultists identify him, but he kept it hidden under his cloak as he stepped from shadow to shadow almost without thinking, staying in the peripheries of the larger shoppers all around him. He couldn't be blamed for checking their pockets for magick. Big people could be painfully oblivious.

He smelled it again. He was getting closer.

One day, Ebbo thought as he made his way toward a bearded man in a sky-blue robe who positively reeked of magick, he wouldn't have to worry about Cthultists or anyone else roughing him up. He would be as famous as Vecnos, the only islander anyone knew by name. That Vecnos was an infamous assassin who killed those who dared insult his name didn't bother Ebbo in the slightest. Better than being seen as a meal, as most islanders were.

Ebbo silently approached the robed man and sniffed at his pockets. The smell of magick was overpowering. Definitely draconic. Ebbo hadn't done anything this strong since he'd met Adrianna. The thought snapped him back to the wedding. He had to hurry. If it wasn't for Adrianna, he might have Transcended and left his body in a comatose state, like so many islanders had. Because of the spider princess and a bowl of soup, he'd come back from the brink and learned his limits. Magick was just something fun to pass the time. Ebbo knew he could quit it if he wanted to. He wouldn't Transcend. Not Ebbo Brandyoak.

Carefully, Ebbo wrapped his fingers around the envelope in the old man's pocket. It radiated potency, but that just meant it would last him a long time. Ebbo began to slowly withdraw the envelope when the pocket snapped shut on his hand.

Ebbo pulled, but he couldn't remove his hand from the pocket. It was as if the sleeve of his tunic had been stitched to the pocket of the robe. As the owner of the blue robe turned to face the tiny pickpocket, Ebbo realized with growing dread that he was trapped. He didn't know if he was more afraid of the bearded old man—a wizard! Ebbo realized—or of Adrianna Morticia, the spider princess whose wedding he was supposed to be crashing.

Chapter 3

Clayton

Clayton Steelheart rubbed his fingers on the collar of a purple hemp shirt. The organic cloth felt smooth as silk. The color was rich as sunset. He briefly wondered if purple was too garish for a wedding, but he silenced the thought. At least it wasn't white.

'How much?'

'Three gold coins,' the shopkeeper said and smiled demurely at him. Her look said she'd do anything to make him happy. Her charms were wasted on him, though, for Clayton Steelheart was not a man, but a golem.

'*Three* gold coins?' Clayton balked. 'I'll give you one, just because the size is right and I'm in a hurry.' The golem held the shirt up to his chest. He'd have to bulk up just slightly to fill it out, but that would only take a few Heartbeats, and he'd been saving up plenty for this particular adventure.

The golem's body currently consisted of about a ton of clay and was held together by an artificer's surprisingly well-made steel heart. He was named by said artificer, one Leopold the Grimy, whose work was not known to last much longer than his warrantees, and thus had him to thank for the rather nail-on-the-head sort of name. It wouldn't do for a wizard, even a lowly artificer with a title like "the Grimy," to forget which golem was which. Clayton sometimes wondered what his name could have been if his mother had named him.

Maybe the woman who animated the piece of steel with Heartbeats that could move clay like a sculptor's hands might have named him something like Quartz Chestsong or Chert Sandson. Leopold had called him Clayton, and that was how the women of the brothel where he worked had known him since he had gained sentience three years ago.

'Just because you're a free golem doesn't mean the clothes are free,' the shopkeeper said. There were disadvantages to his newfound fame, then.

'Two,' Clayton countered. He *had* to have the shirt for the wedding.

The shopkeeper nodded distractedly. She looked past Clayton into the bustling market.

Clayton focused the silica crystals on the back of his head. It was hard to make out much without spending the Heartbeats to concentrate the silica into another set of eyes, but the golem could see enough.

A man who stunk of magick was spinning in a circle. Behind him, lightning flashed. Clayton could smell a faint hint of brimstone blowing past his clay skin.

'Halfing's gonna get it, he is,' the shopkeep said with a vicious grin.

Clayton didn't fault her for it. Islanders, especially those addicted to magick, stole anything from anyone.

'They don't like to be called that,' Clayton said distractedly as he put the gold pieces down on the counter, and then pulled the shirt on over his bare, sculpted chest. While most golems looked like lumpy, unfinished, vaguely human shapes, Clayton had learned he could spend a few Heartbeats to form his body into an anatomically correct sculpture. The muscles didn't make him any stronger, but they looked good with his strong jaw and perfectly molded cheekbones.

Clayton made his way through the crowd and toward the wizard. Glowing runes swirled behind him. Clayton recognized those runes. They were *not* coming from the wizard.

The wizard slowly turned around to look for Ebbo, and not seeing him, continued to turn like a dog chasing its tail. Ebbo's hand was stuck in the wizard's pocket. The robe had to be imbued with magic; there was no way the wizard's craggy old fingers could have held the thief's hand so tightly.

'Excuse me,' Clayton said, causing the wizard to stop his spinning with his back to the lightning and swirling runes. Ebbo had already drawn the ire of the wizard; hopefully Asakusa's Gate would escape his notice.

'This *old man* won't let go of my hand!' Ebbo said, as if he'd been standing at the wizard's side this entire time.

'This *halfling* is attempting to pick my pocket,' the wizard said and indignantly thumped his staff on the cobblestones. His pocket still clutched the islander's hand quite tightly.

Clayton cleared his throat, a strange thing for golem to do. 'There's no reason to use profanity, Mr.—'

'I am Dandel the Dire, Ambassador to the Floral Plane for Magnus the Fecund, and Advisor in Magicks to the Great and Powerful Artificer, Susannah!'

'You mean the hippie dwarf gardener who can only grow like seven crops, and the wizard stupid enough to trap herself in the body of a seven-year-old girl?' Ebbo asked a bit too innocently.

Clayton forced a smile at Dandel. Ebbo wasn't making this any easier.

'What the young islander means to say is that there appears to be a misunderstanding. Perhaps your lovely blue robe has malfunctioned and snagged the boy by mistake,' Clayton said. He was all charm with wizards. The women of the Red Underoo had taught him that. Old, powerful men liked their ego stroked more than younger men did certain body parts.

'*This* robe was made by Master Seamstress Zultana! Do you question her craftsmanship over the word of this ruffian?' Dandel asked, growing impetuous.

This isn't good, Clayton thought. The shoppers of the market were starting to notice the argument and were beginning to take bets. There was nothing tourists liked to watch more than a good street fight. But if tourists noticed *them*, they were going to notice Asakusa's Gate, and if they noticed *that*, the rumors would reach the Nine in the Ringwall before the wedding had even begun, whether by Dandel's tongue or a thousand others.

Behind Dandel the Dire, black lightning shot out of the thrall's fingers and fueled a swirling circle of arcane runes. Asakusa was framed by the Gate. His too-long black hair, normally in his face, whipped about in the stinking wind. The silver rivets and spikes on his leather jacket caught bolts of lightning. His heavy black boots were planted firmly beside his weapon: *Byergen,* the stone hammer. Clayton smirked. *Now there's someone who knows how to dress.* Not that Clayton would be caught dead in leather.

Through the Gate, Clayton could see the souls of the dead. They cracked boulders with blunt tools and stacked them into a low bridge that crossed a different path made of crushed stone. Other souls—these ones mostly skinny islanders—shuffled along the path beneath the bridge. The view through the Gate shifted, as if the world therein pivoted. Clayton saw a road elevated in a grey sky and bordered by jagged cliffs. The High Path, Clayton knew. It was the path they needed to take if they were to arrive at the wedding on time.

Asakusa had spent weeks mapping this particular path through the Gates.

It was not easy nor particularly advisable to travel long distances outside of established and well-tested teleportation spells, but those spells were difficult to perform and besides, people were no more willing to teleport someone to Krag's Doom—a cursed castle built atop a volcanic island and home to a family of dragons—than they were to take a boat there. Most magick could be tracked, and the kind that couldn't was expensive. Asakusa's path through the Gates couldn't be traced but it came with its downsides. The first of which being the thrall's Corrupted right hand. The tips of Asakusa's fingernails burned like black candles as lightning shot from them, holding the Gate open. Ribbons of muscle slowly inched up his arm, crawling out from the black flames and digging into Asakusa's skin like hungry, legless centipedes.

A pity, Clayton thought. He had rather liked the look of Asakusa's last Corruption. This one seemed a bit...slimier. They had to hurry.

'I only mean to say that I know this young man, and that I don't see what could possibly compel him to go picking anyone's pocket when he has a *perfectly good job.*' Clayton said the last few words with a glare pointed at Ebbo.

'This hooligan insults acquaintances of mine. Susannah is a powerful mage who has brought magick to thousands, and Magnus's *gardening* keeps this city fed! Neither of them are worthy of the insults of a magick-addicted pickpocket.'

'I'm not addicted!' Ebbo said.

'Then why haven't you let go of the packet of crushed dragon scales in my pocket?' Dandel said, smirking into the moment of silence that followed. 'Master Seamstress Zultana made this pocket so that no one but the wearer of the robe could remove anything in a closed hand. All you had to do to earn your freedom was to let go, but your addiction wouldn't allow it. However,' Dandel crouched down, getting in Ebbo's face, 'you are in luck. I have been tasked with helping little island people like you. That's what you like to be called, correct? Little island people?'

Clayton could see when Ebbo released the little package, for the robe relaxed its grip on his hand. He was free. Not a moment too soon, Clayton thought.

'It's islanders,' Ebbo said. His attention was still on the pocket.

'See, it is as I said. But I was serious about my offer, islander. Let me help you. I have magick, and much more than a few scales.'

He was from the Half-way Home, then. A place that took islanders for 'rehabilitation' before they Transcended. A scam if there ever was one. It was funded by Vecnos and thus probably used as a front, or something worse. Visions of islanders on tables, staring at the ceiling with sightless eyes while their blood was drained, flashed in Clayton's mind. It was just a rumor, but a persistent one. Clayton found his opinion of the wizard souring.

'Dander, was it? Look, we really must be going,' Clayton said, seeing Ebbo lick his lips.

'I don't know who your master is, golem, but he needs to recast his recognition spells,' the wizard said, deciding in the end to ignore the islander and focus on the ton of clay. 'My hat alone should cue you as to who I am.'

Indeed, Dandel's hat was embroidered with stars and comets and was quite clearly a custom job. Perhaps it really was embroidered by the great Zultana herself. Clayton put its worth at more than what a woman would make in a year at the Red Underoo. He decided he was quite finished with this wizard.

'I'll have you know I have no master. I am Clayton Steelheart, the Free Golem,' Clayton said.

Clayton didn't particularly mind being recognized as a golem. His face, despite the chiseled features most women swooned over, was quite obviously made of mud. But when Clayton introduced himself, and the wizard laughed his wheezy wizard laugh in response, the golem gave up on earning his respect.

'Come on!' Asakusa shouted. The lightning was really cracking now, and from the Gate blew a hot wind that stank so strongly of brimstone, one could actually smell it over the spices of the market and the unclean funk of Bog's Bay.

'Is that a Gate to the Ways of the Dead?' Dandel asked, noticing the smell of brimstone and thus at least demonstrating he was a local. 'Who are you wretches?'

'I already told you my name.' Clayton clenched his fists and began hardening them by drawing the moisture out of his knuckles, one Heartbeat at a time. He continued, 'This is Ebbo Brandyoak of Strong Oak Island, and our colleague who is waiting so patiently for this conversation to end is Asakusa Sangrekana, thrall to a Gatekeeper whose name is nearly impossible to pronounce. We are running late for the wedding of our dear friend and spider princess, Adrianna Morticia, so I must ask you a final time: please step aside.'

'But that's not allowed in the city!' Dandel blurted.

'Seeing as how we're standing in the Free City of S'Kar-Vozi, where there is no king, no mayor, and no laws, I don't see how you can *allow* us to do a berry-picking thing,' Ebbo said.

'There may be no laws, but there are certain *obligations* that must be honored!'

'Obligations we understand,' Clayton said smoothly. 'For example, I feel obliged to inform you that if you do not step aside, I will punch you in the head.'

'The Gate's shifting!' Asakusa said, his voice tight with exertion, his forearm already consumed by the writhing worms of muscle.

Ebbo looked between Asakusa, Clayton, and Dandel's pocket. *Cursed islander!* Clayton thought.

'There's *no way* a smart-talking golem, a magick-addict, and a Gatekeeper's thrall got invited to *that* wedding. Who did you say you were?' Dandel said.

The crystal on the end of his staff glowed a musky yellow and smoked from its facets. It matched the yellow embroidery of his robes perfectly. It took many wizards years to get the colors just right. Dandel probably thought it made him appear to be quite the forbidding character.

Clayton didn't buy it. And he *knew* the fool wizard was intentionally forgetting their names.

'I can't hold it!' Asakusa shouted. The crawling tendrils were past his elbow and moving faster.

'Get him!' Ebbo said, and lunged for Dandel's pocket.

Dandel, not expecting Ebbo to strike at all, began to mumble a spell.

Clayton swung his fist, now hardened to stone, right into Dandel' smug face.

Dandel proved to be a more powerful wizard than most, for Clayton's fingers shattered before they could so much as touch the wizard.

Dandel snorted, obviously expecting such brutality. However, Clayton had the last laugh, for the wizard was as unaccustomed to fighting a sentient golem as anyone else. Dandel's magick only accounted for the stone fist, and not the river of clay that came spurting at his face. Changing Clayton's form always cost a him a number of Heartbeats equal to the mass of the clay that was changed, so this maneuver cost close to a hundred of them. They pounded out of his steel heart like it was a snare drum, leaving in less than a second despite having taken minutes of sitting completely still to accumulate. No other golem could do this: accumulate Heartbeats. Clayton often wondered what that meant and if his cache of Heartbeats were responsible for his unique cognitive abilities, but now was not the time for idle speculation.

In that moment Ebbo reached his hand into the wizard's pocket. With a flick of his wrist, the envelope of crushed dragon scales shot out of the pocket. *Well, bake me in a kiln, Ebbo's sticky fingers got the magick out of the wizard's pocket without closing his hand, Clayton thought.* The islander withdrew his hand just as Clayton's moist punch sent the wizard tumbling down the street.

Ebbo snatched the packet out of the air, then stuck the envelope of crushed dragon scales in his satchel and ran for the Gate.

'Clayton, come on!' Asakusa said. The Corruption had worked its way past his elbow and was heading for his shoulder. It was spreading far too fast, and they still had to open the Gate on the other end of the Path. Clayton stole a glance back at Dandel.

The wizard was pushing himself to his feet, his robe dusting him off a bit too enthusiastically. Robes like that weren't any cheaper than pointy hats with stars and moons, and in S'Kar-Vozi, a city without laws, money meant power.

But that was a problem for another day. Clayton used one of the spider princess's silk threads he carried to suck up as much clay as possible from Dandel's face—expending close to another hundred Heartbeats in the process —then the golem ran through the Gate and into certain doom. *

Chapter 4

Asakusa

According to Asakusa's calculations, they had nine minutes before the High Path shifted away from Krag's Doom. They could make the walk in six. Asakusa grabbed *Byergen*, the stone hammer, with his Corrupted arm and began to drag it down the path toward Adrianna. 'This way,' he said.

'Just a moment. I could go with a bit of good, packed clay. I seemed to have left a bit of my fist on that wizard.'

Veins of clay spread out from Clayton's feet, tasting the ground like hungry pumpkin vines.

'We don't have time. And besides, don't take anything from here. There's always a price for shortcuts,' Asakusa said, not stopping.

The veins of clay pumped back into Clayton's body to the steady pulse of his Heartbeats. The golem harrumphed at his now baggy purple shirt.

As they walked, Asakusa took out some ointment and began to rub it on his Corrupted arm. It had no effect. Asakusa took another vial from the bandolier strapped across his chest. The balm therein also did nothing. He grabbed another and another, but the Corruption ignored each in turn.

Not good. The ointment was all that kept Asakusa from sacrificing his body to the Gatekeeper.

'It's spreading faster than news of a pie cook-off,' Ebbo said. Asakusa rolled his eyes—now was no time for jokes—but the islander was right. The Corruption had never worked its way so far up Asakusa's arm. It was already to his shoulder. The sleeve of his leather jacket was tearing at the seam. Some of the worms of his Corruption grasped tentatively at the silver studs and spikes. Hopefully, Adrianna would like the look.

'Should we run, maybe?' Clayton asked.

'No. I timed it so we wouldn't have to run,' Asakusa said, dragging *Byergen*, the stone hammer, behind him. When your weapon was an un-liftable hammer, it was hard to run anywhere.

'Well I would've much preferred a bit of a quick walk to all that drama in the market!' Clayton said. 'That was a terrible place to open the Gate. That Dandel was quite rude, and I think he might actually know some of the people he said he did.'

'That's easy for you to say. You don't get tired and only have to take half as many steps,' Ebbo said.

'Keep your voices down. And the market wouldn't have been a problem if you hadn't tried to get more drug money,' Asakusa hissed. Asakusa tolerated Ebbo because the islander *had* saved Asakusa plenty of times, but his addiction was pathetic. And that he'd tried to score before walking the Ways of the Dead baffled Asakusa. Didn't he realize they had to get to the wedding in time to stop it?

Clayton, Asakusa, and Ebbo walked along a path that ran along the very top of a range of mountains. Immediately to their left and right were steep drops that ended far below. They could see for leagues. Spreading out on both sides of the mountain range were hundreds of stone paths. Some were straight, others sinuous. Some crossed deep chasms or elevated over other paths on simple stone arches; at some junctions, five or even six bridges were stacked on top of each other. The souls of the dead shuffled along the paths. Some of the paths were quite crowded, while others seemed to have been made for a single soul. Empty paths were being torn apart by moaning ghosts while red-fleshed, horned demons urged them to work faster with the cracks of whips. A single castle towered in the distance, far below the mountain range they were on. It looked cruel and pointy, like the landscape had melted all but the worst parts of it. A frightening number of the roads seemed to pass through that castle. Asakusa grimaced. He knew the woman who called that castle home.

'I wasn't trying to get any drug money!' Ebbo said.

'No, you were trying to get drugs, and you succeeded,' Clayton said.

Ebbo grimaced. 'I wasn't after any drugs.'

'Haven't you heard any of the creation myths? Magick sticks to clay quite well, and you stink,' Clayton said with a frown.

'Magick is not drugs, and besides, I can quit anytime that I'd like. I simply don't want to. There's no long-term side effects,' Ebbo said.

'No islander has used magick long enough to find out if there are long-term side effects,' Asakusa said.

'So perhaps I snort a wee bit of pixie dust, lick a cursed toad every now and then. It's just a bit of fun,' Ebbo said. 'It's not like I've traded my flesh to a demon.'

'Snorting magick and my infernal pact are completely different. I don't have a choice anymore. I have to use this power until I die. You don't.' Asakusa quickened his pace, grunting as he pulled the hammer along. 'And don't talk so loud. You two aren't supposed to be here.'

Asakusa could open the Gates to the Ways of Dead because he'd traded his flesh to a demonic Gatekeeper. What the Gatekeeper had failed to realize —not being of the material plane, and therefore not privy to the events of the last century—was that the thriving Farmer's Market in S'kar-Vozi made it much easier for humans to get the rare varieties of herbs necessary to heal demonic Corruption. Asakusa's contract had stipulated that one could cure oneself with "the proper herb." But apparently, no one had cured themselves from even one Corruption before Asakusa. The trick was that each Corruption needed herbs from different corners of the Archipelago. A thrall was to travel between the Gates, trying to gather ingredients. That would be the thrall's demise, for the farther one travelled between the Gates, the faster a Corruption spread. A demon's deal, to be sure, but Asakusa had outsmarted the Gatekeeper by simply shopping at the Farmer's Market. Asakusa had bought as many varieties of herbs as he could afford, taken them to a witch, and paid her to make a balm out of each one. One had worked, the witch had a new business, and Asakusa was healed. Or so he thought he had.

A tiny worm was already working its way onto Asakusa's chest, like a maggot searching for shelter after having its meal stolen by a condor.

Maggots. That was the best way to describe what was on Asakusa's arm.

Each Corruption had a theme. This one seemed to be muscles made of maggots. Each of Asakusa's fingers was made of boneless worms that ended in one of his flickering fingernails. His hand and arm looked like they were wrapped in black cords of muscle, but each ribbon of meat inched and pulsed of its own accord, as if they were only tolerating Asakusa's command and teamwork in general until they could find something better to eat—be it another entity or more of Asakusa.

'Why is it spreading so fast?' Asakusa said to himself, trying to ignore Clayton and Ebbo's bickering. Clayton was going on about using weaker magick, but Ebbo wouldn't give up what he had in his pocket. He could be so disgusting. Asakusa wouldn't have tolerated him, except that Adrianna had saved him… so Asakusa put up with him. Fortunately, they were well above most of the Ways of the Dead. No one should be able to hear them.

'Can't you two keep your voices down? Someone's going to hear—'

Too late. A Gate sprung into existence directly in front of them. This Gate was made of wood with black iron hinges. That meant it belonged to demon, not a thrall.

A corpulent, fat-tongued frog stepped through. It was Byorginkyatulk—Tulk, as he insisted his material clients call him. Asakusa's Gatekeeper. The demon who had a lease on his flesh.

'You said I could pass this way,' Asakusa said, thankful Ebbo and Clayton had stopped their argument and replaced it with nervous stares.

'Isssh that any way to ssshay hello?' Tulk said. His long tongue didn't fit inside of his mouth, so he slurred his "s's" horribly. 'You assshked a queshtion, Ashhakussha, I am here to anshhwer it. Oh, hey, guysssh,' he said to Ebbo and Clayton.

Ebbo nodded, smiling nervously.

'How are you, good demon?' Clayton said, bowing.

'I'm good, can't complain, unlike those poor souls,' Tulk said, butchering the word "souls" and gesturing to the decidedly ghost-like individuals laboring to build bridges and paths, and the souls walking upon them.

'We're kind of in a hurry,' Asakusa said.

'Walk and talk, then,' Tulk said, his Gate vanishing as soon as the door closed.

Asakusa clenched his teeth but nodded. They'd already lost a minute, and Tulk would chat them to death if he let them. He started walking

'Why's the Corruption spreading so fast? Is it because they're here too?'

'No. Your fingernails should shield them if they're close,' Tulk said. Sometimes Asakusa wondered if he intentionally chose "s" words just to put off his clients.

Asakusa glanced at his fingernails. They were the only thing that stayed the same between each Corruption. They burned like black candles when walking the Ways of the Dead, and they cast a shadow that made Asakusa invisible to the demons of the realm.

'Then why?'

Tulk smiled and shrugged. 'Fine print. You want me to show you the legalese?'

'No,' Asakusa said and hurried on.

'Shuuit yourshhelf.' Tulk opened a Gate, stepped through, and vanished. Asakusa knew he wouldn't be gone for long.

'Asa,' Clayton began, his voice dripping with concern, 'you didn't tell us you renegotiated your contract.'

'The High Path was the only way to make it to the wedding. Krag's Doom doesn't have any regular paths through it, doesn't fit into anyone's beliefs about the afterlife. Besides, I couldn't have asked Adrianna for money for a boat. She'd have figured it out.'

'It's just a wedding,' Clayton said, even though the golem had been more excited than anyone when Asakusa came to them with a plan on how to get there. 'Don't misunderstand me, I was terribly offended when Adrianna failed to invite us, and you know I'd give my left leg to see her in that dress, but still... those maggoty things don't look good.'

'I made this choice because I had to,' Asakusa said, his expression darkening. 'You know I'm not good with... with words. Or whatever. I have to *show* her.'

'Show her what? What *exactly* are your plans once we get there?' Ebbo said.

Asakusa flushed. 'Why did you try to rob a wizard right before we go save her? You told us you were getting clean!'

Two bat-like creatures screeched and flew off from the side of the High Path.

'I thought you said to keep it down,' Ebbo said.

'We've all seen what happens, Ebbo. You can't deny that,' Clayton said, his voice low.

'Old Burba used to say just because the fire's not bright, doesn't mean the oven's not hot.' Ebbo said.

'And when an oven falls into a stupor and starves to death, or is dumped in Bog's Bay just because it's taking up room, what does Burba say then?' Asakusa said. He was being too loud, he knew he was, but Ebbo could be so infuriating.

Ebbo stopped walking, his eyes wide, his bottom lip quivering. 'You'd...if I Transcended, you'd dump me in Bog's Bay?'

'What happens to islanders who abuse magick is not transcendence, it's overdose,' Asakusa said.

Ebbo's frown deepened.

'Oh, now look what you've gone and done,' Clayton said to Asakusa. 'Of course, we wouldn't drop you in Bog's Bay,' he said, turning to Ebbo. 'I'd stuff Hama's pies down your throat for a year if I had to, but please don't make me. I'm not one for choosing a good pie.'

Ebbo nodded. Talking of food usually calmed him. 'I *was* clean, but I just fell off the boat. Maybe if I can stay with one of you, I can get back on.'

'Of course. Just give me whatever you took from Dandel before I punched him.'

'I didn't take anything,' Ebbo said too quickly.

'I *told* you, I can smell it on you,' Clayton said.

'That's just from what I *already* had. It leaves something behind. That's what you're sensing, I bet.'

Clayton rolled his eyes, a gesture he'd learned watching Asakusa.

'Well, I hope you brought a change of clothes for your grand reveal,' Clayton said, looking at Asakusa's torn sleeve.

'It won't matter at all if we don't make it in time to stop the wedding,' Asakusa said, holding up his Corrupted arm and stopping his companions.

'Well then, why ever did you bother to stop us?' Ebbo said.

Asakusa dragged his Stone Hammer forward with his left hand and flexed his right fist, sending a ripple of activity across the maggots.

'We've been noticed.'

Chapter 5

Clayton

To say they came from the sky would be to sell short the geography of the Ways of the Dead. A dozen demons flew toward the trio, of that much Clayton felt certain, for the hiss of their flapping wings grew louder—from a shrill buzz to the sound of an animal dying from too many insect stings. But as they flew, the demons flickered in and out of existence, one second appearing in the corner of one's vision, the next filling one's sight, their horrible teeth wide in a gaping smile that Clayton could not turn away from, no matter how hard he tried. The only thing that seemed consistent in this place were the stone pathways and the shambling souls walking upon them.

Ebbo yelped and tried to run further down the path, but Clayton grabbed him by the back of his shirt and held him with the group.

'I don't suppose they have any weak spots?' Clayton asked.

'Crush their skulls,' Asakusa answered.

The demons looked like broken skeletons. Broken skeletons wrapped in tight, torn leather that bled from wounds inflicted by their own jagged bones.

'They look about as nice as stale beer and flat bread,' Ebbo said.

Clayton couldn't help but smile at Ebbo's tasteless joke, but Asakusa only snorted.

As the demons approached, their bodies coalesced into more predictable patterns. They may not have been made of what the wizards called matter, but being in the presence of it would force their bodies to follow its rules. Something the demons were no doubt counting on.

A pair of them were suddenly close enough to attack. They raked their claws across Clayton's chest, tearing open his shirt.

'Do you bastards know how much fair-trade hemp costs?' the golem screamed.

Another of the demons swooped down at Asakusa. Asakusa lifted his stone hammer from the ground, and with a swooping uppercut smashed one of the demon's lower jaws up through its head. Its body followed its crushed-in face as it tumbled down the jagged cliffs that bordered the High Path.

Three of the skeletal demons attacked Ebbo. Two of them fell into a squabble over the plump islander, but before Clayton could stop the third, it snatched up Ebbo in its claws and was flying away.

'Asakusa!' Clayton called, pointing at their struggling friend.

Asakusa nodded, made an arcane gesture with his maggoty arm, and opened a Gate.

How odd it was, Clayton thought, to see the Gate open from this side. He was accustomed to seeing the twisted runes that made the Gates frame stone paths and shambling souls. Now, he saw blue water lapping at a calm shore. He smelled sweet flowers. He heard a baliset noodling along. A stark contrast to the glowing red runes that framed the Gate. Asakusa emerged from another Gate farther down the beach. He ran for the islander, dragging his hammer through the sand.

The demon hurtled through the Gate with Ebbo in its claws. It turned and shrieked for its demonic brethren to follow. Ebbo tried to reach for his dagger, but he was held tight in the demon's grip.

Asakusa intercepted the demon and struck it with his hammer. Its head exploded, teeth shooting everywhere in spectacular effect. Then Asakusa was leaping through a Gate, holding Ebbo with his Corrupted arm.

'Another's getting through!' Clayton shouted.

Asakusa hit the ground and used his maggoty fist to break his fall. Ebbo had crawled onto his back and away from the maggots.

'You need to defend yourself,' Asakusa said to the islander.

'I'll be fine, Clayton's here. Just go! I think that was Shellbeach! I have a cousin there.'

Asakusa nodded at Clayton, and then opened a portal back to the beach he'd used as a shortcut to save Ebbo. No longer could the sounds of the novice baliset player be heard, though she might have future as a singer, for her shrieks of terror were well above high C.

The portal closed behind him and Asakusa vanished, leaving Ebbo and Clayton behind in the Ways of the Dead. A hundred more skeletal demons were on the horizon. They'd be to the High Path in no time at all.

'Whenever you're ready to fight is fine!' Clayton yelled as he clobbered a demon with one of the bricks from the path. It tumbled down the jagged cliffs.

'Right!' Ebbo said, fumbling at the dagger on his belt. *Deondadel* was a fine weapon, made by elves in times of old. Its shining blade would surely make the demons think twice about feasting on an islander. But Ebbo's fingers couldn't seem to open the clasp, despite it being attuned to its master.

Clayton smashed another demon with another brick.

Another demon snatched up Ebbo.

'Ebbo! If you don't do something, I won't be able to save you!'

Clayton could see him trying and failing to open the magickal clasp. After a moment, he reached for another pocket. Clayton watched as Ebbo brought a reddish powder to his nose. A Gate appeared in the sky above him. A demon hurtled through, followed by Asakusa. The maggots had made it to his neck. No doubt his chest was corrupted underneath his black leather jacket. His hammer crashed into the demon, sending bone fragments everywhere.

Ebbo inhaled the crushed dragon scales. He undid the clasp to his dagger as easily as his father would pull a carrot from his garden and jammed it up into the creature's groin. The demon shrieked, as vulnerable to crotch shots as just about anything else, and dropped Ebbo.

'Wind, hot like summer days,' Ebbo mumbled as he fell, 'the smell of grandmother lighting a stove with that wizard's fool matches, the ground coming up like... like...' he snapped from his reverie, 'actually, that doesn't look so good.'

Just before Ebbo struck the ground, Clayton dove beneath him. Ebbo landed with a loud squelch. He pushed himself out of the golem's backside, dirty but unharmed.

Clayton stood back up, then healed himself. Instead of defending them with his dagger, Ebbo watched in amazement as clay pumped into the crater the islander had created in his friend's body. First, veins of clay formed in time to Clayton's Heartbeats, then bones of clay, clay muscles, and finally a smooth layer of brown skin. Clayton punched the ground, and chunks of black obsidian stuck to his fist. In time to his Heartbeats, they reoriented themselves into spikes on his knuckles. Doing all that had cost more than a thousand heartbeats. It was a good thing Clayton had so many stored up when this mission began.

'Asakusa said not to use anything!' Ebbo said

'I'm just borrowing them until we leave,' Clayton said.

Ebbo brandished his elven dagger and faced the circling demons. There were now over a hundred in the empty sky, reeling like gulls, shrieking and trading places in puffs of smoke and fire.

'I'm just glad those scales were un-cut,' Ebbo said. 'I feel like I should be terrified, but I just keep thinking those demons look like the little red parrots I used to feed, back on Strong Oak Isle.'

Asakusa stepped from a Gate and appeared next to Clayton.

'If I open any more Gates, I won't have the flesh needed to open the one at Krag's Doom,' Asakusa said, his voice cool, though Clayton could see fear creeping into the thrall's face. Maggots had torn a seam on the side of his jacket. A few longer ones wriggled through a hole at his armpit.

'I'm not doing great either. I already had to rebuild once, plus it's hot here, and if I lose too much moisture, my Heartbeats won't go as far,' Clayton said.

'We're going to be fine. We always are,' Ebbo said, clutching his knife and looking at the demons.

'You can't just say that,' Asakusa said. The flock of demons drew closer and closer, closing in like impatient, monstrous vultures on a not-quite-dead corpse. And then, 'You snorted the scales!'

'The clasp was jammed! How the huckleberry was I supposed to get it open?'

'The tremors are that bad?' Clayton said.

'You're lucky we're about to die. It sounds like you're just a few fairy wings away from an overdose,' Asakusa said.

'No one ever overdoses on fairy wings, that's why people *do* fairy wings! You think I'd be snorting dragon scales if I had those?'

'Now is not the time to be comparing magicks!' Clayton said and swung a fist at a demon that dove at the party. He missed. The demons drew closer. Clayton sighed. Not ever getting to see Adrianna's dress was now the least of his problems. They were in the eye of a hurricane of demons. Clayton couldn't quite convince himself that not being alive would spare him from eternal torment.

Asakusa gripped his stone hammer.

Clayton raised his fists, his knuckles jagged with black obsidian and bits of bone.

'Curse it, Ebbo, this is all your fault!' Asakusa said.

Clayton should've said something, he knew he should've, but he was a little distracted by the maelstrom of skeletons and leathery flesh all around them.

'So, wait, I'm about to die for no good reason because I agreed to your dumb plan, and this is all my fault?' Ebbo said.

'No!' Asakusa said, lashing out with his Corrupted hand and ripping a demon's ribcage from the storm. 'We're about to die because we had to try to stop the wedding. Adrianna doesn't *love* him. She doesn't want to get married at all! She wants to keep adventuring with us.'

'I'm sorry. Look, I'm high as huckleberries right now, but I feel like I'm missing something.' Ebbo said. 'Who cares who she marries? It's not like she'd marry any of us.'

The demons were circling closer and closer, forcing the trio to push their backs against each other, but they weren't attacking. Clayton had been on enough quests to recognize when minions were stalling. The boss was on its way. This fight would be over soon then, one way or the other. That wasn't what held Clayton's attention, though. He couldn't believe what Ebbo had just said.

'Ebbo, isn't it obvious?' Clayton said.

'What's obvious?' Ebbo said, slashing at the skeletal claw of a demon reaching for him.

'Tell him, Asakusa.'

'Tell me what?'

'Now's not the time!' Asakusa said.

Clayton couldn't control himself any longer. 'Asakusa has a crush on Adrianna!' Clayton said, glee in his voice despite their imminent demise. Oh, it felt good to share a secret on one's death bed.

'But, she's the spider princess,' Ebbo said.

'I know,' Asakusa said.

'And way out of your league,' Ebbo said.

'I know!'

'Then why are we even here?' Ebbo said.

'Because... because I love her!' Asakusa said. Clayton could hear tears in his voice.

And then, the demons screeched and began to reel away. As they flew off, they flickered in and out of existence, until they were gone. Clayton couldn't believe it! But then flames erupted from below and a huge demon— his arms big as trees, his torso as tall as the High Path itself—emerged as if he'd been waiting on a knee this entire time.

In one hand the demon held a trident, black as coal, and in the other a cage made of bone and filled with flies. Though the spaces between the bone cage were wide enough for an islander to easily fit through, the flies seemed to like it. They flew in and out, an angry buzzing mass.

The demon had two horns on his head. Each was big enough to impale all three of the adventurers, so long as Ebbo was impaled last, as he was too small to be pushed down to the base of the horn. The demon's flesh was red as blood. His eyes were black. A goatee rimmed his mouth and drew

Clayton's attention to his unsettlingly human teeth. The demon flicked his forked tongue, threw back his head and laughed. As he did, his muscled red chest heaved, and the mountains beneath Clayton's feet shook. Around his neck, the demon wore a gold chain that was perpetually melting. Each drop fell onto his red flesh and sizzled into nothing before reappearing as one of the links.

He looked down at the adventurers. It was not a kind look.

Chapter 6

Asakusa

'Who dares trespass in the Realm of the Demon King?' the Demon King boomed. His mouth and the words did not line up. When he spoke, his tongue wagged back and forth and his jaw worked, but the sounds came from inside Asakusa's head. It was a low and sinister voice, a voice Asakusa recognized as the voice of his own father. He wondered what nightmares Ebbo and Clayton heard.

'I am Asakusa Sangrekana, thrall to the Gatekeeper Byorginkyatulk.'

'Show me your flesh, thrall!' the Demon King boomed, and the maggots on Asakusa's arms obeyed. They all stood on end. Most of them were short things, not much longer than a digit on a finger, but a few were more than a foot long. All of them whipped back and forth with such vigor that they tore through Asakusa's jacket, exploding it away.

Ebbo looked like he wanted to barf, and for once Asakusa didn't blame him. His Corruption had never spread so far. Asakusa's entire arm, much of his neck, his chest, and both his legs were covered in the maggots. Only his left arm, feet, and face were free of them.

'You are free to come and go along the High Path, as your pact allows. But who are these that travel my roads without paying their toll?'

'We are going to a wedding,' Ebbo said.

The Demon King laughed. It was a deep, horrible sound, like an avalanche burying a village of bears.

'And whose wedding requires one to walk the High Path?'

'We are guests of honor at the wedding of Her Highness the Spider Princess Adrianna Morticia and the Dragon Prince Richard Valkanna,' Clayton Steelheart said. Asakusa was impressed that Clayton's voice didn't shake, but then, it never did. Clayton certainly had a gift with words. Asakusa knew that he didn't. His own voice shook if he spent too long haggling for a snabbage in the market.

The Demon King stopped laughing at that. '*You* got invitations to that wedding? I don't believe it.'

'It's true, your Unholiness,' a voice gurgled, and beside Asakusa stood Tulk.

Though Asakusa had seen Tulk countless times, the demon's appearance never ceased to disgust him. He looked like a fat frog with too many jagged teeth. His eyes bugged out and his tongue was too big, and yet—unlike the Demon King—he used it to speak. Asakusa found himself wishing Tulk would do the dissonant whispers thing like The Demon King did. Instead he had to listen to the Gatekeeper's slurred S's and quick, snorty laugh.

'These are the ones I told you about, Oh Vicious One,' Tulk said. *Onesssh*, it sounded like, and there was that laugh, really a series of grunts, delivered past his fat frog tongue.

'I thought they would be... I don't know... cooler-looking,' the Demon King said.

Tulk shrugged. 'You ripped my thrall's coat. He's normally the cool one of the group.'

'He's got the maggots Corruption? That's gross,' the Demon King said. His voice spoke deep inside Asakusa's skull as his tongue wagged back and forth. 'Why didn't you give him the lizard scales, or the curse of machinery? That's a cool one.'

'I wanted him to look bad at the wedding. I was thinking if it goes poorly, he'll have to bail and come back through here. Although, after the flesh he spent in that fight...' Tulk shrugged. It was not an attractive gesture for the fat frog.

'Nice,' the Demon King said, and nodded, 'but what about these other two? I mean, one's a worthless halfling and this guy is a what... a golem? Do we have jurisdiction over golems?'

'We prefer to be called islanders,' Ebbo mumbled. Thankfully, the Demon King ignored him.

'No rules on constructs, Oh Lord of Souls. I can't make a contract with one per se, as they don't technically have an afterlife, but I've talked with Kyertrixin about some pretty clever forms of eternal labor. She thinks they could lay the pitch for the roads by hand. It would get all in their clay, see?'

'I thought golems were taller. His clothes are all baggy,' the Demon King said.

'I spent much of my clay fighting the demons, Your Unholiness,' Clayton said. He was indeed about a foot shorter than when the fight had begun.

The Demon King and Tulk laughed at that.

'You call those demons?' *thosshe demonsssh?* Tulk said with his long tongue. 'Those aren't demons.'

'Those are but the insects of this realm. Animated by the human souls of your dead brethren who lost their way long before they came to walks the Ways of the Dead,' the Demon King said.

'I'm not human,' Clayton said.

'Technically, neither am I,' Ebbo chimed in.

'Oh, shut the Hell up. You were about to get your asses handed to you by a bunch of mosquiters.'

'Mosquitoes, sir,' Tulk said.

'Whatever,' the Demon King said, then turned to the adventurers three, his voice again booming with the weight of ten thousand's men's hearts. 'Take this to the wedding, and I won't flay the three of you with my trident. I'd take it myself, but the duties of the Demon King do not allow me to leave these paths for personal matters. Also, it's not an open bar.' The Demon King cleared his throat. 'And yet no wedding of a Spider Queen shall pass without the gift of the Flies of the Abyss!'

The Demon King put the bone cage down. The flies buzzed angrily as the cage shrank to a small enough size for a human to be able hold it.

'These flies feed on the suffering of humans and will bring misery and horror to an otherwise cheerful dungeon,' The Demon King said. 'They will give birth to seven generations of seven generations of flies. They will be a plague upon your earth before returning here to bite the eyes of the travelers. They're also a great snack. Also, can you tell them that the invitation was cute, and I'm sorry I didn't RSVP?'

'Wait, I'm confused. If those demons we were fighting were mosquitoes, then how are the flies, like, actual flies?' Ebbo said.

'SILENCE!' boomed the Demon King, his voice was so powerful it shook the High Path and one of the mountains crumbled away into nothing. Inside were the sleeping forms of men and women. Demons descended upon them, cracking whips as the souls began to stack the rocks into yet another path.

'Take my gift and send my unholy blessing. Return here, and suffer seven lifetimes of pain. Obviously halflings count as people, and I guess we have some plans for you too, tiny golem.'

'As you command,' Asakusa said and bowed formally.

The Demon King laughed, and a gate opened. This one was far more elaborate than the ones Asakusa made, more elaborate even than Tulk's wood door. Rather than lightning and cryptic runes that seemed to tear a hole in space, the Demon King's power was such that a door as big as a castle appeared, made of some horrible wood with the faces of people in its grain, framed in brick, and crawling with runes that Asakusa dared not read. The gates swung open, and there was the white castle that would soon be Adrianna's prison.

'Come on, we don't have much time,' Asakusa said.

Ebbo followed quickly.

Clayton let the shards from his fists drop back to the ground, and then stepped through the Gate of the Demon King.

Chapter 7

Adrianna

The slitted eyes of flamehearts and the many eyes of spiderfolk watched as Adrianna's black stilettos clacked up the white marble steps and into the cathedral. She felt stifled in the dress; her sister had tied her hair so tightly that even her abdomen vents had closed, though admittedly, it could be the situation that was causing her to feel this way. Her fiancé's family had stolen the castle from The Morticians in a horrible war, millennia ago. Today it would be theirs again. All Adrianna had to do was say yes to the monster at the altar.

She found herself wishing that she didn't have to enter the cathedral in her human form. A skinny girl in a big dress with elaborate hair would not be very intimidating, even with daggers poking from the hidden pockets in her dress.

She looked around desperately for her friends, for Ebbo, for Clayton. Please, Asakusa, be inside, ready to open a Gate for me, Adrianna thought, even though she wasn't sure if she'd step through it even if it was there. She saw only her old family, her new one, and him.

He stood there, in human form, with his winning smile and pointy teeth. The Prince Richard Valkanna. That was what it said on the invitations. She didn't know much else about him, besides that he was a fire-breathing dragon. In fact, this was the first time Adrianna had even laid her six eyes upon Prince Valkanna. She didn't know if she was disappointed or relieved. This marriage had been arranged seven generations ago, pretty much as soon as the Morticians had lost the place. Finally standing here, it was obvious why her webmother wanted it back so badly.

The thin pillars were classic Mortician Architecture, the spiderweb motif still obvious despite how worn and cracked they were. Adrianna could see bright silver silk in some of the cracks, newly spun to keep the place together while the Morticians fixed it up, though Viriana had made some aesthetic choices as well.

Enchanted spiders continually weaving webs into silken tapestries was a signature Mortician effect. Even in the subterranean caves where Adrianna had spent her childhood, her mother had spiders weaving tapestries. These were different, though. These tapestries acknowledged the draconic inhabitants of the castle, for the spiders wove pictures of dragons ravaging villages, dragons incinerating knights, dragons eating mortals foolish enough to call themselves kings. They matched the chipped sculptures of spiders consuming lesser species—as both the Morticians and Valkannas thought of pretty much everyone—quite nicely.

Still, to Adrianna, it felt like a spider palace that had been dressed up to look like a dragon lived there, and then dumped above a volcano. But that floating-above-a-volcano bit was the detail adventurers remembered most, and why it was known as Krag's Doom and not Widow's Peak in the history books. That sort of magic couldn't be performed except by the Valkanna's most trusted warlocks, their highest paid sorcerers, or the realm's most gullible wizards. That floating trick was why they were here. The Valkannas were broke and didn't have the retinue of warlocks they once did. If Krag's Doom wasn't repaired before it cracked in half, the floating spell would push it apart like a stack of blocks.

Adrianna stepped inside the Cathedral. The doors slammed shut behind her.

For the last two thousand years, the brides of the Valkannas had walked meekly to the altar with their hair done up neatly. For two thousand years, a Valkanna had stood at the altar, smiling with their pointy teeth, smug in their human glamour as their wives-to-be walked down the aisle to die.

Maybe concubine-to-be was a better term.

For the Valkanna blood was strong. Valkannas didn't need to breed with female dragons for their children to be born true. Stranger still, only males were born as true dragons. Females were born as eggs that hatched into draconic half-breeds and were raised to serve in the Valkanna army as flamehearts. Yet a mongrel daughter was the best a mother could hope for, because every mother of a true dragon had died in childbirth. Adrianna was the first woman in two thousand years to know anything but fear of birthing a fire-breathing reptile. Morticians didn't carry their babies in their gut like a spinning mammal.

Adrianna didn't want to think about breeding. She didn't think she'd have to think about it for fifty years! She was here to marry the heir to the castle. The ceremony would be performed by the Lich, and then it would be done. At that point, Adrianna reasoned, the dragon king would get the repairs to the castle he needed, Adrianna's mother would move in and never leave, and Adrianna could murder her husband in his sleep if he so much as looked at her wrong. Neither dragons nor spiderfolk had much of a history of respecting the order of succession, and Lucien Valkanna, Richard's father, might live for a thousand years yet, so losing his eldest son might not bother him so long as he kept his castle.

She looked at him, Richard Valkanna, her husband-to-be, with murder in her eyes. He looked back at her and smiled. And for just a moment his glamour faded, and she saw what he truly was: a dragon. He was big, bigger than a giant, bigger than some of the mortal's gods. In Adrianna's spiderform, her torso was still human-sized. In the prince's dragon form, he could swallow her torso in one gulp and crunch her abdomen like a meat pie. His wings spanned almost half of the cathedral. And the heat pouring off him, even from this distance, was intense. The flamehearts hooded their eyes as the heat washed over them, and then it was gone, and the groom was hidden inside his glamour once more. No need to tie up his hair, no need to so much as say an incantation. Killing him would be harder than she realized. Impossible, she kept thinking and telling herself not to think. He will be impossible to kill, especially with Adrianna's weapons of choice: daggers and a whip.

There had to be a way out of this. Even if she didn't have to carry his young inside her, the sick monster might make her try. Adrianna's eyes searched for something, anything—a trap door, some sort of crystalline dragon-slaying ice sword, one of Asakusa's Gates waiting for her—but what she saw ensured she would not leave, not until the ceremony was over and her family's inheritance restored.

Adrianna's webmother poked her head out into the aisle.

Adrianna sighed. She loved her mom. In an instant, she was painfully aware of how much she'd missed her since being sent off to school. Adrianna felt like she'd been gone a long time, and she had, more than half of her short life, but in terms of a female spiderfolk's lifespan, it had been a blink. And yet, Viriana's age was starting to show. The spider queen needed glasses to see, and the six little circles of glass glinted from the fireballs that the flamehearts apparently couldn't control when they were drunk. Her mom's hair wasn't all there anymore, either. It was a secret of the Morticians that they didn't grey; they went bald.

When Adrianna was a little girl and still lived in the caves, her webmother would spend each morning attaching silk to her own scalp to hide her age. The strands were white and as thin as normal hair, but they could not be used to Fold her body away like Adrianna's hair still could. Six of her mother's appendages rested on the floor, but two of her spider legs and her human hands worked nervously in the familiar spinning patterns she'd taught to Adrianna and all of her sisters. That was to be expected, though. After all, her mom was over six hundred years old.

But still, the human part of her body looked amazing. Her figure, unlike Adrianna's, was like something out of a Paladin's 'holy book.' Milk-white skin over human curves. Adrianna was thinner, bonier really, and so tan after years on the surface (a flaw her sisters had already pounced upon while working on her dress and hair). Their skin and face were the same, though. Most mortals wouldn't put Viriana's age over thirty and were far more likely to think Adrianna and Viriana cursed sisters, rather than daughter and mother, but then most mortals didn't dare guess the age of the Spider Queen.

She had been so excited when Adrianna had agreed to the wedding. It was destined to be, of course. She was the eighth daughter of the eighth daughter, eight generations back, but Adrianna still remembered her mother's excitement when she'd told Adrianna of the wedding on her sixth hatchday. Viriana had said she could have convinced the Valkannas to go for another daughter, if Adrianna insisted—everyone knew they were low on funds and the castle was badly in need of repairs that only the Morticians could perform—but Adrianna knew from the look on her mother's face that she had wanted Adrianna to be the One all along.

She hadn't been able to say no then, and she hadn't been able to say no when she received her mom's message by parrot sixty-three days ago.

While Adrianna had worked on her dress and lamented her lost decades of freedom, her mom had been here, overseeing the first round of repairs to the castle and spending way too much time decorating. In addition to the animated tapestries of dragons in the hall, there were tapestries in the cathedral as well. Tapestries of Adrianna and Prince Valkanna, holding hands, hugging, locked in passionate embrace…making love in dragon and spider form?

Adrianna looked away from the tapestry of the spider and dragon having sex to her mom, who only cocked three of her eyes and winked two of them. Adrianna sighed. Hopefully the guests weren't familiar with the anatomy of the cursed, but she could tell by the looks from both sides of the aisle that indeed, most of the guests knew exactly what the tapestries meant. At least they were somewhat tasteful—there was no dragon-dong, thank the Etterqueen—and the workmanship was exquisite.

Her webmother nodded, and Adrianna sighed. It was time.

The spider princess looked once more at the dozens of female draconic mongrels on her right, then at the hundreds of her spiderfolk brothers on her left. Neither side looked happy to be here. Surely the flamehearts didn't like the idea of sharing their home with Adrianna's brothers and cousins any more than her own family liked it when foolish warriors ventured into their caves, looking for glory. She wondered if the flamehearts were expected to sacrifice themselves for their dragon lords as readily as the male spiderfolk were expected to die for their spider queen. It sure felt like it. She could feel the tension between the two families. There was only one way to release it.

Adrianna started down the aisle, toward Richard Valkanna and her inescapable future. As she walked, she let down her hair. As she loosened each braid, she felt the tiny threads that ran through her nervous system loosen with it. Without the strands keeping her appendages in place, Adrianna's true spiderform Unfolded from the magick space it inhabited when her hair was tied up. One braid on her left, and a spider leg appeared as if from nowhere; a matching braid on her right and a matching leg. The spider princess walked down the aisle, carefully letting each piece of her immaculately done-up hair down in turn. One by one, spider legs appeared out of thin air until Adrianna's hair hung loose and all the way to her black spider abdomen. Her human head, arms and torso were unchanged, but now —instead of human legs—she had a black hairy spider abdomen with eight segmented spider limbs. The red hourglass on her abdomen was currently obscured by the white silk of her dress.

Her spiderfolk brothers, driven by hormones as they were, gasped and clicked their chelicera in excitement. Judging from the lack of fireballs, the draconic flamehearts' collective breath had been taken away. Adrianna ignored them all.

Tears came to all six of her mother's eyes when she saw Adrianna in her spider form. One of Adrianna's seven sisters, Sabiana, passed her a silk hanky.

Sabiana had shown Adrianna that her hair could be used to immobilize her body as well as transform it. Once, Sabiana had done Adriana's hair in cruelly tight braids and left her to drown in a chamber flooding with sea water. Adrianna would not have escaped without her enchanted dagger, *Bloodweaver*. It had taken a year for her hair to grow long enough for her to properly Fold again after that particular incident. Currently (and whenever their webmother was around), Sabiana played the part of doting older sister. She had her hair up and her spiderform Folded away, but unlike Adrianna, her shoulders, arms and upper half of her face were decidedly arachnid. Their mother had often reminded the eight sisters that Adrianna's human face and body had power in the world above their warren of caves of tunnels that her older sisters did not.

Beauty had an unfair power in this world, as it does in many others. The truth of that hit her when she saw Richard.

His eyes were dark and brooding, yet they held a spark in their depths that dared her to stoke it like a flame. His hair was long and slicked back, but unlike the human glamours of the two dragon groomsmen to the side of him, it was in a tight ponytail that didn't show any of the characteristic spikes until past his shoulders, a good look. He had a beard. It was black as his hair, and perhaps a bit pointy for Adrianna's taste. She was accustomed to the more rounded dwarven beards and the clean cheeks of islanders, rather than this more devilish style, but the dragon prince wore it well. He had broad shoulders that filled out his suit quite nicely. The suit was dark red suit with golden scales faintly stitched onto it. An effect Adrianna hated to admit she thought was kind of cool, but was mostly too much. Her mother no doubt loved it, and Adrianna could already imagine her mom telling her that at least he cared about how he looked. He wore a sword in a jeweled scabbard and a ceremonial dagger. Adrianna had a matching one next to her whip.

Adrianna had come of age in S'kar-vozi, amongst humans and mostly humanoid tutors. She slept and ate in her human form, fought and had her first kiss as a human, but as she walked down the aisle, she relished the freedom of her true body. Such power she felt as her eight legs moved her forward. As she neared the altar, she lifted herself up off the ground (as her webmother had insisted she do). She hadn't anticipated the dress to split and reveal her still human thighs—her sister must have tucked a braid in her hair while hemming the dress—but she gyrated all the same. She did it, and judging from the reaction of the crowded cathedral, she looked good doing it. Her thighs were glorious. Her calves, though hidden beneath tight white silk, were nonetheless spectacular, and of course her sister had discreetly slit the dress so that it split perfectly to show her garters. The dress was beautiful, high-collared and done in fine silken lace. She was a princess and would one day be a queen, but as she appeared to float down the aisle with her white hair flowing freely, her spider legs hidden beneath the dress, and her hair discreetly tied to make her front-most legs still appear to be human, she was the image of a goddess.

At least, that's what her webmother said everyone would think.

Adrianna reached back and found the last little braid, hidden beneath the rest of her white hair. She untied it, and coarse spider hair Unfolded from her human legs, transforming her completely into what most humans described as a spider centaur. Let's see how the dragon prince likes that, Adrianna thought and smirked.

She lowered herself a bit when she came to rest beside the dragon prince, but she did not let her frontmost feet touch the ground. She'd been on them long enough, and besides, her fiancé was already dark and handsome. Might as well not let him be taller than her until she had to.

The Lich stood before them and gravely pulled back his hood, revealing a skull with skin pulled tight across it and dark eye sockets that glowed with an unblinking yellow light from within.

Etterqueen's weavings, this was really going to happen.

Adrianna looked back at the assembly of what any normal human would call abominations one last time. Nope. He definitely wasn't here.

She couldn't believe it.

Asakusa hadn't made it.

Chapter 8

Asakusa

'It's ridiculous, though, you must admit.'

'I won't admit a damn thing,' Asakusa mumbled, and then turned his back on Clayton and continued to pace.

They were standing at the top of a tall staircase made of a solidified lava flow. It looked slick and treacherous. Traversing such a stair in boots would have been difficult, yet Asakusa was sure Adrianna had done it in heels—with grace, speed and probably a fair amount of cursing.

'Ok, but it is funny,' Ebbo Brandyoak said. 'You took us thousands of leagues away from S'Kar-Vozi, but you didn't take us far enough. We might as well be back home, perusing the shelves at Old Glass Eye's shop, maybe finding some old salve she'd forgotten about with latent magical properties. But instead we're here, doomed as it were, dooooomed,' Ebbo said, gesturing at the lake of lava between them and Krag's Doom. There was nothing but a worn-out rope bridge to get across. Clayton weighed over a ton, Asakusa had a hammer that couldn't be lifted except to attack, and they were supposed to carry a cage of flies across.

'And besides,' Ebbo went on, 'telling Adrianna how you felt would've way been easier than being torn to shreds by these monsters. How long have you liked her?'

'I don't know what you're talking about,' Asakusa said. Three years, two months, and six days. That was also how long they'd known each other.

'If you didn't want her to get married, you probably should have said so,' Ebbo said. 'You know she cares way too much about what other people think. Who knows? Maybe she cares about you, too!'

Asakusa stopped pacing long enough to glare at the islander.

'He has a point, though,' Clayton said. 'Women prefer a certain amount of directness. It's one of the things they like about men: men are disposable and therefore capable of far greater risks.'

'And more hilarious spectacles!' Ebbo said. 'Like almost getting eaten by demons while trying to break up a wedding you could have said something about literally any time in the last six months!'

'No, I could not have. By the time she even told me, she had already finished making most of her dress!'

'That was her second dress; she digested it and redid it four more times,' Clayton said.

'That's not the point,' Asakusa growled.

'The point is you don't have enough flesh left to get us across that bridge, let alone out of here, and you still don't have the guts to tell her how you really feel!' Ebbo said.

'I could make a bridge. I do have one of Adrianna's threads,' Clayton said, 'though I was hoping to save the Heartbeats for whatever happens inside.'

Asakusa ignored him. He said, 'The point is that she hated making that dress. She complained about it constantly. Every time I asked her why she had to do this now, she didn't have a good reason. She'd just talk about a castle her family didn't need. I mean, I get it, Krag's Doom is famous, but why do the spiderfolk even want it? Seems like it would be smarter to let it crumble and just wipe out the Valkannas once and for all. If Adrianna's family had made an alliance with the Nine in the Ringwall, we could've beat them.'

'But then, why didn't you say anything?' Clayton said.

Asakusa scowled. It was times like this that Clayton reminded Asakusa that his head really was filled with clay.

'Because if she cared about it enough to give up her whole life the moment her mom sent a parrot, who I am to intervene? I'm just some nobody who traded his soul to try and save his sister, and I couldn't even do that. I'm a failure, and a loser, and she's freaking amazing,' Asakusa said.

'Well, doesn't matter much now. As soon as that wedding's over, we'll be eaten by like a hundred dragons or a thousand spiders. Or I will, anyway.' Ebbo crossed his arms and frowned. 'Everything eats the islander first.'

'Pity,' said Asakusa, turning to Ebbo and keeping his voice level, hoping Clayton wouldn't notice. 'To think, how magical that wedding is going to be.'

Ebbo was halfway across the bridge before he even looked down. His bare feet grasped the rope with his toes. He didn't need the rickety boards at all.

'I think we'll be alright,' Ebbo said, turning back when he'd made it about two-thirds of the way. 'Come on.'

'You always do this,' Asakusa shouted as Ebbo returned.

'Do what? Save your butts?' Ebbo said.

'You scout ahead and act like it's safe, and you forget Clayton is a golem.'

'This one's a magick rope. No doubt enchanted so the flamehearts can cross the bridge. Do I need to spell it out? It will be fine,' Ebbo said, walking back with his toes wrapped around the rope.

'Really, Asa, you don't need to make a big deal about this,' Clayton said.

'No, Clayton, it is a big deal. His head is not in the mission. He's over there thinking about drugs, and he forgets you're a golem and almost gets us killed.'

'You can't kill a golem. That's what's so great about us,' Clayton said.

'You said to go ahead, and I'm ahead. What do you want from me?' Ebbo said.

Asakusa took a deep breath. 'We've been over this. You need to go across the bridge, sneak in, find the cathedral and determine the best place for us to bust in there. Clayton and I will figure out an alternative route, hopefully that doesn't need a Gate or many Heartbeats, and be there soon. And tell us if it's that part of the ceremony that's like "speak now, or forever hold your peace." The plan hasn't changed at all!'

'Except for the fifty-foot gap,' Ebbo said, 'and that I never actually agreed to infiltrate anything.'

'You know how much magick is in there? Dragons and spiderfolk practically bleed magick,' Asakusa said.

'That's what the Demon King said inside my brain!' Ebbo said.

'What you said earlier was intentional!' Clayton said. 'We've talked about this. You have to stop enabling. You can't be against his habits until they benefit you.'

'He would've figured it out,' Asakusa said. Curse it. He hated Clayton's guilt trips.

'Yeah, I would have figured it out... Wait, exactly how much magic are we talking here?'

Chapter 9

Adrianna

The Lich was an old family friend. It had resurrected Adrianna's great-great-great-grandmother Sita after she was killed by the Just Knights, an order that stood for a level of gleaming goodliness rarely even tried for in the poor excuse for politics in the modern world. Thus, the Lich's unliving corpse was somewhere between 2,006 and 2,766 years old—older than Krag's Doom, almost as old as the Mortician name.

The ceremony seemed about that outdated.

The Lich's shrunken leather strip of a tongue worked through the ancient dialect of Necromantic like an old leather shoe being torn apart by zombies. Adrianna recognized most of the nouns and verbs: 'death, eternal bonds, against all foes, kill, suffering, death, knives, death, death, and eternal death.' It was the adverbs she had trouble with. Based on the suffixes, they were mostly about pain, but the tones were far more screamy than her professors' dead languages had been. Adrianna nodded along as best as she could. Even if she couldn't understand everything that was said, she felt the power of the spell drawing her and Richard Valkanna closer together. Once completed, nothing could break the magick bond the Lich was creating, except for death itself.

Adrianna stole a glance at the dragon prince. His brown eyes were waiting for her. In this light, they were flecked with golden sparks and were beyond stunning. He smiled at her for just a moment before the Lich screeched at them both. The sound of a thousand people screaming to their deaths.

'PLEASE!' it shrieked. 'DO NOT INTERRUPT.'

It went back to reading from its book bound of human skin. The Lich's empty eye sockets, sunken deep into its leathery skull, twinkled with a yellow light as it read the cursed scripture. Adrianna could see both flamehearts on the groom's side and spiderfolk on her own side nodding off. On the other hand, her mother and soon-to-be oathfather were listening in rapt attention. It was their castle, after all; the flamehearts and spiderfolk were just there to protect it with their lives.

Adrianna couldn't see directly behind her, even with her six eyes open, so she stole a glance back at the door, drawing a horrible rasping hiss from the Lich and an angry click from her mother.

No one was there.

Her mother nodded.

Adrianna bit her lip, but she nodded as well.

There was no going back.

The Spider Princess would claim her birthright and get the hell out of here, if she could. And if she couldn't? Would she sacrifice the rest of her life to, to what? To honor her family's horrible legacy?

It's not like she was going to convince them that the juices from sentient creatures didn't taste good.

Why am I going through with this?

The Lich shrieked, and Adrianna knew it was time to draw her dagger. The hilt was the body of a beautiful orb weaver spider. Her eight legs came to a point to make the blade.

Bloodweaver, the dagger was called.

Never had the weapon found a substance it could not cut through. It was her birthright as much as the castle was, and just like the castle, *Bloodweaver* sometimes seemed more important to her family than she was. And Adrianna was just supposed to give it away because of some ancient ritual? For the Etterqueen's sake, she'd spent more time with *Bloodweaver* than she had her own mother!

It was just one of the thousands of things that Adrianna was supposed to give up: her freedom, her friends, Hama's pies, the smell of spices fighting with the stench of Bog's Bay, fantastic shopping, and monster hunting—all for life in a hot castle in the middle of nowhere? AND she was supposed to give up her dagger?

For what, for duty?

The Etterqueen could take her duty.

The Lich shrieked again, impatiently.

But there was no way out... and it was better than the two families starting a war that would surely consume the entire Archipelago. Since she was six years old, Adrianna had known this was her fate. She'd just thought she'd have more time... but she didn't. Her time living as a human had been amazing. She'd miss it. She'd miss being a hero, she'd miss defeating flesh-hungry monsters instead of having dinner with them, she'd miss the look in Ebbo's eyes when she saved yet another islander. But that was all over.

Let's get this thing over with, Adrianna thought, then drew her blade and stabbed the legs of *Bloodweaver* into her own hand.

Chapter 10

Ebbo

Ebbo Brandyoak scampered across the rope bridge before him. A few of the planks were fakes. He could tell which ones quite easily with his sensitive toes. A big person would have almost certainly broken through and died or just barely caught themselves before they tumbled to their doom. Ebbo was not a big person.

He made it to the end of the bridge, cracked his toes in satisfaction, and went to the door of the castle.

Ebbo ventured just a pinch of dragon scales as he stepped around the spider trapdoor at the end of the bridge—Adrianna had taught him to look for the telltale sign of twiggy hinges—and put his ear to the door.

Some creature was shrieking from within. That would be the Lich. His voice sounds worse than his name, Ebbo thought. The islander was glad there was only a single undying sorcerer of death in the whole of the Archipelago.

He sniffed at cracks in the weir wood door and gasped. He'd expected to smell magic, of course, but what he smelled sobered him up immediately.

It was Adrianna's blood.

Ebbo panicked. He pounded on the door.

'Let me in!' he shouted in a moment of blind bravery.

He seemed to remember something about Adrianna's blood and the wedding ritual. She'd need to use her dagger to share her blood, or something…but Ebbo had found dehydrated mermaid fins that day, and well, most of his memories were swimmingly unclear.

'What are you doing?' Asakusa yelled across the chasm.

'The flies! Throw me the flies!' Ebbo shouted.

Clayton obliged the islander. He hurled the cage of flies across the chasm. Ebbo managed to get his body under the cage, thus breaking the cage's fall instead of the cage itself.

The door to the castle was creaking open. Two hairy legs that ended in hooked barbs stuck out, then two more.

Ebbo felt himself pale. He didn't fight spiders. That was one of the perks of being friends with Adrianna.

He fumbled at the latch on the cage of flies. Fortunately, the dragon scales kept his fingers steady. He opened the cage and released the flies.

'Flies of Hell, carry me over the wall!' Ebbo shouted to the fat white flies. They had spots on their abdomens to make them look like tiny winged skulls with compound eyes.

The flies all flew directly into Ebbo's face. He screamed as they bit at his eyelids.

'This isn't working!' When he opened his mouth, they flew inside and bit his lips and tongue as he gagged.

Ebbo stumbled backwards and tumbled into the spider-pit.

Chapter 11

Clayton

When Ebbo unleashed the flies, Clayton had said that perhaps the islander had a plan, and cautioned Asakusa to wait.

Asakusa had not listened.

He ran across the rickety rope bridge, dragging his hammer behind him and breaking slats as he went. He made it nearly halfway before his foot broke through a slat and fell through the bridge. His corrupted, worm-like fingers caught the rope as he fell, slithering around it and holding Asakusa tight. It seemed Tulk didn't want him falling to his death.

'Perhaps I should just—' Clayton said.

'I'm fine! Adventurers break slats all the time,' Asakusa shouted petulantly, but he couldn't get back up onto the unbroken slats.

Clayton acted before Asakusa could think about opening another Gate.

He hurled one of his fists across the chasm, then used his Heartbeats to pump clay across the strand of silk anchored inside the fist. It took more Heartbeats to move clay away from his body on one of the spider princess's threads, but Clayton had been saving them for a reason. The golem grabbed the ground he was standing on with his other hand and pumped the rest of his body out onto the silk strand. The clay bridge thickened around the silk as his body shrunk, stretching across the chasm until there was just a hand on each side, holding a thick clay-covered thread. A pulsating lump worked its way across the strand—Clayton's steel heart. When his heart made it above the thrall, he reached a skinny arm down and unceremoniously grabbed Asakusa by the uncorrupted scruff of his neck. After another thousand Heartbeats, both Asakusa and Clayton's heart were across.

'I could have taken a Gate,' Asakusa said, but Clayton could hear the unspoken gratitude in the thrall's voice.

'Get...the door!' Clayton said, currently just a mouth and a puddle. Huge spider legs, thick as clubs, were dragging a struggling, Ebbo-sized sack inside the castle, but Asakusa was too late. The door shut with an ominous click.

Asakusa slammed his hammer into the ground, shaking the floating island in the center of the volcano.

'Can't...turn back... now,' Clayton said. With each Heartbeat, more and more of his clay coalesced around his steel heart, bringing the golem's human form back together. So far, he was just a lumpy head connected to two feet. That bridge maneuver had cost him over thousands of Heartbeats, but that couldn't be helped. He'd get them back with time.

Though time was something they were currently short on.

Chapter 12

Ebbo

When Ebbo came to a few minutes later, all he could see was white. He could tell it had only been a few minutes, because he was still high on the dragon scales, and the Lich was still shrieking, though his voice was much louder. *I must be inside Krag's Doom,* Ebbo reasoned. There were other voices, too.

'Is a gift for *her,* ennit?' said a voice that sounded like it had far too many moving parts in its mouth. A spiderfolk's voice, to be sure.

'Why would one of *your* messengers fall in a spider pit?' hissed someone whose breath stank of brimstone. One of the draconic women, then. Flamehearts, Adrianna called them.

Ebbo tried to reach for his dagger but found himself restrained.

'Why would anyone bring flies for a dragon?'

'I'm sure they didn't bring them for you to eat!'

Something pounded at the door. The spiderfolk and the flameheart stopped arguing.

'You hear that?'

'O' course I heard that. How could I not hear that?'

'I didn't know you had ears.'

'Says the reptile with holes in the side of her head.'

Something pounded again. It was louder this time. The dragon scales conjured images of orcs, giant squid, and the snake people who used to come to Strong Oak Isle and steal islanders from their families.

Ebbo had to escape, but his fingers could find no way through the web. His toes, though; maybe his toes…

Chapter 13

Asakusa

Asakusa smashed through the door to the castle with the third blow of *Byergen*, the stone hammer.

The doors flew off their hinges and crashed to the floor — well, almost. Beneath one of the doors was the crushed body of a spiderfolk, beneath the other an unmoving flameheart. The spider's body cracked and hissed as Asakusa walked over it and into the antechamber.

Clayton trudged in behind him. He'd formed his legs, but not his arms. His face was a rough version of his usual stunningly handsome features. With every second, he expended more Heartbeats to bring his body back together.

'That bridge was longer than I realized,' Clayton was saying. 'I'm down to less than than half of my reserves of Heartbeats. I'll need a good week-long vacation after this, and in the meantime, I would appreciate minimizing the theatrics—'

'She wasn't kidding about this place,' Asakusa said. All around them, cracked pillars thin as bones rose to the ceiling before scattering into filaments thin as web. Most of these tiny strands were broken, but some glowed like silver. On the walls, glowing silver spiders pulled threads from tapestries of… Adrianna. In them, she was wearing far less than her usual neck-high, black padded armor.

Asakusa swallowed. She looked good.

'I found Ebbo,' Clayton said. His mud toes wrapped around a thread of silk.

Asakusa heard the click of a heavy door being closed.

He was not surprised to see the silk thread went underneath the door.

'That idiot just—'

'I know,' Clayton said. 'But come on. At least we can listen in now.

Chapter 14

Ebbo

The hinges were extremely rusty, but this was no problem for Ebbo, as he was quite adept at moving hinges. He pushed open the door without a sound and scooted inside.

Adrianna stood next to some handsome cranberry in a red dragon-scale suit, presumably the groom. The Lich stood before them both. He looked about as horrible as he sounded. Adrianna's back was to Ebbo, but he could see she was holding her knife over her other hand. That's right! She was supposed to offer her blood, so she hadn't been in any real danger, well, not any danger beyond signing her life away to a dragon.

There was a gust that sucked the door shut with a loud clack. Every eye in the cathedral turned from Adrianna to Ebbo. Despite there only being about a hundred flamehearts and a few hundred spiderfolk, Ebbo found thousands of eyes, both slitted and arachnid, looking at him.

He smiled.

'Sorry I'm late,' the islander said and made for the row second from the back of the Cathedral, on the bride's side. The seat closest to the back held a single, massive brown spider. It dabbed at its eyes with a silk hanky. Ebbo sat down next to five spiders with human eyes. They were about his size, jumpers no doubt. They scooted over and clicked their pedipalps distastefully while they hissed 'late' at him in the common tongue.

The Lich shrieked, then resumed reading from his book. Ebbo took a deep breath as all the eyes left him and turned back toward the bleeding bride. They'd forgotten all about his quiet intrusion almost as soon as they'd noticed it.

One of Adrianna's back legs was tapping. Ebbo looked down. She'd left a thread at the doorway; it was vibrating with her coded message. Ebbo reached a toe out to the thread and felt the coded letters.

'W...A...T......R......U......D...U...I...N...G?' Adrianna tapped.

'Rescuing you!' Ebbo tapped back.

'N...O!' Adrianna replied.

Chapter 15

Adrianna

Somehow, every head in the Cathedral turning to look at Adrianna was far worse than when they'd simply been looking at her in the first place.

Great. Just great. Ebbo was here, which meant that the pounding they'd all heard was Asakusa getting ready to interrupt the whole thing, just like she'd told him *not* to. Well, she'd never actually said that, but she'd certainly thought it. Unfortunately, Asakusa wasn't here yet, which meant she'd have to hear the groom's vows.

'Friend of yours?' Richard Valkanna whispered.

The Lich shrieked at him. Then he shrieked more politely for the dragon prince to begin his vows. It was forbidden to speak out of turn during the ceremony. To do so risked being turned into a skeleton slave of the Lich. The only words that wouldn't come from the Lich's leathery tongue would be the bride and groom's vows. During their vows, they could say anything they wanted. That was part of what made the ritual so strong, that illusion of freedom, as Adrianna liked to think of it. It truly was forbidden to interrupt. Adrianna seemed to remember some of the groom's draconic ancestors using the time to simply list all the duties of their bride-to-be, if they didn't die birthing a son. Adrianna's grandmother had used her vows to one of her eight husbands to explain which body parts her daughter would eat first. The honesty and cruelty of these statements had only served to strengthen the bond the Lich wove.

The prince cleared his throat and began, revealing a voice too low, too smooth, and entirely too sexy.

'Adrianna Morticia, it is a pleasure to meet you. And this *is* the first time we've met,' he said, raising an eyebrow at the attended masses so fiercely, it seemed for a moment to be a spiked horn. Adrianna supposed it really *was* a horn. His transformation was different than hers. While her legs were Folded away, his dragonform manifested... Adrianna found she didn't know exactly how dragon glamour worked. Her tutors in S'kar-Vozi had never taught her, but then, she'd never asked. She'd spent most of her time trying to ignore the fact that one day—in the *far future,* she'd always told herself—she'd marry a dragon.

'When my father first told me of our betrothal, I was eight years old, and I have to admit that the idea of marrying a spider princess was not something I was particularly excited about.'

Nervous laughter from the far back of the Cathedral. Ebbo's nervous laughter.

'I was given your used handkerchiefs, and told to learn your scent: Lilac,' the prince said. 'I read from your discarded children's books. I was taught the songs you loved. My father taught me that if you ever moved against me, I would be able to use the magick of memory against you.'

It was then, after this horrifying admission of power he might possess over her, that Richard Valkanna smiled.

It was also at that moment that Adrianna began to feel Ebbo's frantic tapping in one of her back legs again. She stole a glance and earned a piercing shriek from the Lich. Ebbo's leg was out in the aisle and his toes were manipulating her silk thread, sending her a message she didn't want to hear.

'Asakusa here. Loves you. Oops. Not supposed to say that,' Ebbo's toes said.

'2...L...8'

'2 L8? Oh, too late. I get it.'

Ebbo and Clayton were both far more adept at sending messages on Adrianna's silk threads than she was. She could understand the code just fine, but tapping it out was not something she could do with her spider legs. They couldn't gesture independently like her human appendages could. Her spider parts always moved in sync, a symptom of how her nervous system functioned.

'This guy is creepy. Let's go,' Ebbo tapped with his toes.

Adrianna ignored him.

Richard was smiling at her. His smile was wonderful, even if his teeth were pointy. Fires burned in his dark eyes. He seemed to be able to tell that she wasn't paying attention, something few people noticed when all her six of her eyes were open.

Adrianna smiled for him to continue.

'When I found out that manipulating you was what my father wanted me to do with all that stuff, I threw it all away. It was the hardest thing I'd ever done. I had learned to love the teensy-weensy spider, Little Miss Muffet, and even the Seven Sultry Spinners.'

'Asakusa made us take the High Path. We met the Demon King. He's kind of a big eh,' Ebbo said over the thread.

'2 L8!' Adrianna tapped back in a skitter of legs. The gesture made her look flustered to her family, and probably aroused to the stupid dragons. Why couldn't they all just shut up and let her listen to Richard? He'd read Seven Sultry Spinners... and *liked it?*

She nodded at Richard again, who had glanced towards the back door, as had many in the back of the cathedral.

There had been the sound of wood breaking, some shouting, and a grunt. The tails of the dragons began to flick. When the sounds did not continue, everyone turned back to the prince, a bit disappointed. It seemed the flamehearts were as accustomed to leaping into battle to protect their superiors as the spiderfolk males were. *The only difference to any of them was that they might get a chance to die drunk today,* Adrianna thought bitterly. She didn't really know her brothers—she hadn't seen them for over a decade, after all—but she didn't want them to die over an interruption to her wedding.

'I didn't want to have that kind of power over you because I was beginning to fall in love. You see, when I was fifteen, I began to receive daily reports about you.'

That caught her attention and stopped her mind from wandering. Whatever the hell Ebbo was talking about on the thread could wait. The Valkannas had daily reports on her? And he was talking about them at *their wedding?*

'I know, it's unsettling, but listen. I'm glad I got those reports, because without them, I never would have learned about how amazing you are. I never would have learned about your bravery, or kindness, or generosity. Because of those reports, I want to use our families, yours and mine, for good.'

'You've made your point. This charade has gone on long enough,' Richard's father, Lucien, hissed from the front row. The Lich shrieked fiercely at him. The old man's tail flicked and his wings unfurled from nowhere, but he sat back down. It seemed even the king of the dragons didn't want to push the Lich's patience.

The Lich gestured for Richard to continue. Vows were sacred things, and an integral part of the oath they were making. Their words, along with drawing their own blood, served for consent in this ancient, depraved ritual.

'I heard about when you saved those orphans from that coven of Blood-hags. That was so brave. I know that blood magic is especially powerful against you, as your threads of silk are made of your blood. I heard about when you defeated that horde of orcs to reopen the sea routes for the halflings' pumpkin season. You didn't even take the Piebelly's youngest child, as they'd promised the sirens, and was your right. You took a *pig* and shared it with your friends!'

'That was pretty epic,' Ebbo tapped. 'Even if we do prefer to be called islanders. Also, Clayton says your dress is super beautiful.'

'He's here?' Adrianna said out loud and turned around, only to cause the Lich to shriek and her future oath-father to ruffle his wings.

'No, Adrianna, I've had tabs on you. That's what I'm saying,'

If Richard hadn't misinterpreted her shout, someone might have noticed the pair of tiny feet in the aisle, toes wiggling in totally separate patterns. Ebbo had a thread to Clayton, then.

The Etterqueen take them! The pair were far more attuned to their feet and vibrations than Adrianna was. They could really gab over a nice, taut thread. It totally creeped out Adrianna that they used part of her body—essentially her solidified blood—to gossip, but then, she'd taught them how. She'd just never expected them to be so adept at it. Ebbo had probably tapped out a matrix of the design of the dress, and sent it to Clayton.

She focused on Richard.

He was on one knee.

Never, not once in any of the weddings past, had a dragon prince ever taken a knee for his wife. It was akin to admitting she was an equal. Dragons knelt only for their own blood, their fathers, not the string of mothers who'd died in childbirth, and not the wives they knew they'd kill if they sired a son. Adrianna's breath caught in her abdomen. Tears threatened to come from the corners of her six eyes. Here they were, at a marriage they'd been forced into, and Valkanna—Richard, rather—was actually making it about *them?* Adrianna had never heard of anything so romantic!

'I will not rule this kingdom as my father did. He raised me to control you, but I won't do it. We'll rule as you see fit, together. A Dark Queen and King no longer, but shining ones! The flamehearts will support our mission, for they know my uncle and cousins see them as an impure army, while I see them as they are: my sisters, aunts, cousins, and the fiercest warriors in the Archipelago.'

Nods and gouts of fire from the flamehearts. It seemed what Richard said was true. That was impressive. Adrianna knew her brothers even less than she knew her sisters. There were just so many of them, and they were so *fragile.* Her mother had taught her long ago that it wouldn't do to get attached.

Adrianna thought Richard's father had probably taught him something similar, and yet he seemed to have earned the flamehearts' respect all the same.

'I know this is crazy, but people have gotten married for far sillier reasons,' Richard said. 'Our parents need us to have children eventually, which I'm no rush to do until we, uh… talk about the specifics. I don't exactly want you to die birthing a son, and I don't want to be eaten so you can have a daughter, either. Neither of our parents procreated in the first century of their lives, so we shouldn't have to either. So, what do you say? How 'bout it, will you marry me?'

Adrianna was breathless. She had been prepared to sacrifice her freedom for her webmother. As she'd journeyed here, she'd toyed with the idea of murdering her husband, or running away, or turning her sisters against him. Never once did she think he'd actually feel like she did, like he'd been forced into this crazy wedding because a castle was more important to his family than he was.

Richard smiled up at her, then blushed, scales flickering across his face as he reached for his belt.

'Err… sorry, I forgot the important bit,' he said, and drew a beautiful dagger. The golden hilt was a dragon's body, the tiny guard its jaws, and the silver blade its tongue. It was as beautiful as Adrianna's own blade, more beautiful in that she'd never seen it before, and she knew it would take days just to appreciate the detail of the craftsmanship.

'This is *Flametongue*. It burns those it stabs, and it's pretty smoking wicked.' Richard drew the blade across the palm of his hand, drawing red blood and making a sizzle of flames. 'Doesn't cauterize the wound unless you will it to.

'With my blood, I thee wed,' Richard said, and with those words, Adrianna felt her own exposed blood prickle.

There was actually pretty strong applause from the flamehearts, even a few whoops and cheers. More evidence that Richard actually cared about them, and that they thought for themselves more than the spiderfolk males did.

In the back of her mind, she still heard Ebbo's secret communication to her. He was saying something about Clayton being just legs and how Ebbo needed to give him a 'hand.' Humor was lost over the thread. This was what she leaving behind? Misadventures with her weird friends? They'd had fun together, she'd always look back at the times fondly, but maybe it was time to move on. And maybe she could still go on adventures.

And maybe that's what this would be: a grand adventure. They'd get married and try to change their families, somehow end up having a bunch of kids—an army, if their parents had their way.

Maybe she'd be able to have a son that lived longer than a few decades. Maybe, with the Valkanna blood, she could hatch a daughter that didn't need to eat her father's flesh to survive. They might be able to have a normal family —well, normal as a spider dragon could be. Adrianna found the idea warmed her heart in a way she'd never expected. And Richard… she still couldn't believe he liked Seven Sultry Spiders. One couldn't lie about something like that. There would be no point. She had only ever met one other person who'd liked that story, and the asshole was trying to ruin her wedding after kissing her and then friend-zoning her for like four years!

The Lich was staring at her with the unblinking yellow lights that glowed deep in its eye sockets. It was time for her vows. Time for her to say whatever she wanted, without interruption. Then, their blood would be joined and the ritual would be complete. Adrianna found, for the first time in her entire life, that the idea of that wasn't so terrible.

'I had a big speech prepared too,' she said, sure Ebbo's toes were twitching and transmitting everything she said to Clayton who was probably narrating for Asakusa.

'But what you said was so brave, and sweet, and *honest,* that forget it.' Adrianna tossed her notes aside.

'I was going to say how this was my duty. That I was scared, but that this would be better. I was going to try to strike fear of change into all of your hearts, but I can see now I don't need to. I… there's no reason *not* to marry you. I'm scared as hell, but you're right. Together we can make the world a better place. We have to do this. Times are changing. We need to adapt or perish.'

'Adapt or perish. I like it,' Richard said, drawing a shriek from the Lich.

'So yeah, this is crazy, but let's do it. At least you're not scared to tell me how you feel!' Adrianna said, stealing a glance at Ebbo, who would relay the jab to Clayton, who'd tell Asakusa.

She looked Richard in the eye. 'I cannot believe we are going to do this.'

'Me neither. Burn our parents.' The Lich looked annoyed, but for once, didn't shriek. Both their parents, the ancient spiny red dragon and the beautiful spider queen, bristled at this, but neither said a thing. Adrianna knew they wouldn't. They wanted the ritual completed and the families bound, so repairs could begin in earnest on the castle.

'The Etterqueen take them. With this blood, I thee wed.'

The spiderfolk clapped their many hands in respectful confusion. Adrianna knew her brothers, cousins, and nephews wouldn't have much of an opinion about the particulars of their vows. She just didn't know any of them very well. She hadn't been home to their caves in more than ten years. The spiderfolk that directly served her webmother might have some inkling of how their lives might be changing, but those that served her sisters were probably brainwashed to think Adrianna was worse than the mortals. The flamehearts were applauding louder than the spiderfolk, despite the fact that they had considerably less hands to clap.

When Adrianna said the last line of her vows, she felt her dagger pulse in her hand, and motes of light emerged from Richard's bloody palm.

They traded daggers, each spinning the weapon, then extending it to their partner hilt first. If they stabbed each other at this point, it would be sixty-six years bad luck, a bad honeymoon for sure, but they didn't.

Adrianna took Richard's blade, and he took hers.

Adrianna felt giddy. It felt good in her hands, heavier than her blade for sure, thicker too, but the weight felt *right*, like this was the new woman she was going to become.

Richard held her dagger delicately. It looked thin and dainty in his thick hands. His glamour flickered with his excitement, and his scales appeared in the reflection of the blade made of the eight spider legs. It looked pretty, spinning slick with his claws, too.

They both tucked their daggers into their belts and reached out their hands.

The ritual was almost complete.

She'd drawn her blood for his vows.

He'd drawn his blood for hers.

Now they would unite their bloodlines and seal the pact their families had been fighting for and against for eight generations…

Chapter 16

Adrianna

The doors to the cathedral smashed open.

'I object!' Asakusa marched in, dragging his hammer behind him. His corrupted arm, chest, and neck pulsed with black maggots.

Gross, Adrianna found herself thinking, *but also cool.*

Asakusa raised his hammer with his uncorrupted arm and slammed it to the ground, severing Ebbo's chatter still vibrating through Adrianna's feet.

On either side of the aisle, pews were kicked back as flamehearts drew curved swords and the spiderfolk unveiled daggers hidden in silk purses.

'Our weddings don't have that part!' roared Richard's ancient father as he transformed into an equally ancient red dragon.

The Lich shrieked.

'On what grounds?' Adrianna's mom demanded.

'Grounds? What do you mean, grounds?' Asakusa asked.

The Lich shrieked again and pointed a skeletal finger at Asakusa. No one was supposed to interrupt the bride and groom.

'Why are you here?' Adrianna demanded. At this, the Lich regarded Adrianna with a hiss and flipped through his book. After a moment, he nodded begrudgingly. Or it seemed begrudging. The yellow motes of light deep in his eye sockets dimmed, and his cheek muscles tightened just a bit. Adrianna knew she had a right to have her questions answered before they completed the blood oath. She had paid attention when her tutors had gone over the parts of the ritual that allowed her to actually express herself.

The flamehearts and spiderfolk relaxed their grips on their weapons. Though they were obviously spoiling for a fight, they wouldn't risk interrupting the ceremony against the Lich's wishes. He probably wouldn't turn one the leaders of the Valkannas or Mortician families into skeleton slaves, but he wouldn't hesitate to necrify a less important flameheart or spiderfolk.

'You don't want to marry that guy! You don't even know him!' Asakusa said.

'I do now, and I know he cares about me because he *said so!*'

Asakusa's jaw dropped open.

'But you know that I... I mean, *I* care...' Asakusa said, scratching the back of his head with his Corrupted hand.

'Care about what, Asakusa?' Adrianna said.

'You!'

'You what?'

'I care.'

'Damnit, Asakusa *this* is why I'm getting married! Why can't you just *say it?*'

'I...um... I care about *you.* Especially. And I want you to... you know... be happy. We can leave right now with Ebbo and Clayton...'

Richard's father looked at the Lich. The Lich nodded.

'The rules of the wedding ritual state it is forbidden to steal the bride,' Lucien said. 'Flamehearts, defend our prince!' The rest of the flamehearts drew their weapons.

Asakusa didn't lift *Byergen*—he couldn't unless he was attacking—but he gripped its handle and spit at his attackers.

'I can tell them to stand down. Let him walk out of here alive,' Richard whispered to Adrianna. 'They respect me far more than my father.'

The Lich looked between them and started flipping through his book. It seemed even he needed to consult the particulars of the ancient ceremony.

'My mom would never allow it. Not if he doesn't propose,' Adrianna said, shaking her head.

'You love him?' Richard said.

Adrianna shrugged. 'He's my friend. I don't want him to die.' The spider princess felt the truth of that statement as soon she said it. She liked Asakusa. He was brave, and fearless when fighting for others. He was incredibly loyal and used his powers over the Gates to help the less fortunate at the cost of his own flesh. She always told herself that she'd wished he'd kissed her more than once. Adrianna supposed she could've made the next move, but she'd grown up a transforming spider centaur in a city of humans. She'd lacked the confidence, but now, she felt a little relieved that they'd only shared that one kiss. Richard seemed to be perfect. He'd overcome a dark family history and a bizarre childhood, he had the respect of his flameheart sisters, and he exuded self-confidence in a way that Asakusa simply didn't. And yet, the idea of Asakusa being murdered at her wedding made her stomach churn. No matter what else he was, Asakusa was her *friend*. He'd saved her life more times than she could count. He'd held her hair back when she'd gotten sick from eating too much spiced vegetable soup. He sucked with words, and he couldn't hide his disgust when she spit on her meat to digest it before swallowing it, and he could be mean to Ebbo—but for all his faults, he was her friend. Her only human friend, really. She wouldn't let him die today. She couldn't.

'Marry me, and he won't.'

Adrianna smiled and looked at Richard. 'You make it sound so easy.'

'It is. Marry me. Fulfill your destiny. Your friend lives. We fix the world, I mean really fix it—no more of these little charity cases you've been doing, but structurally. Think about it: my sisters and your brothers, flamehearts and spiderfolk, working together. We could stop killing the mortals.' Richard was smiling his confident smile, but his eyes were heavy with emotion. Steaming, actually. Tears, Adrianna realized. He *wanted* this wedding to work. He'd obviously thought about it far more than Adrianna had. But then, of course he had. He'd grown up in a castle that was literally falling to pieces. He'd seen mortals abandon babies—*his sisters*—at the foot of the volcano to die or be forgotten. He should have been a bitter, manipulative person, but he wasn't.

'We could stop the mortals from killing each other,' Adrianna said.

Richard laughed. 'That'll be the day.'

The flamehearts were tightening their circle around Asakusa. Some of the spiderfolk were climbing the pillars in the cathedral.

'Dragon scales!' a flameheart hissed, brandishing a packet near the back of the room.

'Those are mine!' someone called out from the among the spiderfolk. Adrianna recognized the voice as Ebbo's. No one else did.

'Part of the agreement is to stop using each other's kind for magic,' Richard's father said, growing to his full form. 'If you spiders are to stay in *our castle*, we have to know you won't suck our blood at night.'

'Quiet, Lucien,' Adrianna's webmother said. 'You need our help securing Krag's Doom as much as repairing it.' She eyed Asakusa.

'Mom, Asakusa's just a friend, and it's *not* like he's trying to marry me,' Adrianna said, glancing at Asakusa and watching his skin flush a deeper red than Richard's jacket.

'Quiet, girl!' roared Richard's father. 'One of your guests dares consume the body of a dragon in *my castle?*'

'It's hardly your castle, thief,' tutted Adrianna's mom.

They both fell silent as the Lich raised his bony finger and pointed it at one, then the other. It seemed he would tolerate the flamehearts quelling an interruption, but not the bickering of the soon to be oath-laws.

'Come on, all this over a few scales? This is crazy. You guys shed them, right?' Adrianna said.

'And you think that makes it okay? People have hunted and killed my sisters just for their scales and horns,' Richard said. The smile was still on his face but the fire in his eyes was no longer inviting. It blazed with anger now, like old coals reawakened. Adrianna knew the look. One did not grow up as part of a cursed family without getting a chip on one's shoulder.

'Oh, like you've never eaten spider legs,' Adrianna replied, perhaps a bit petulantly. Honestly, she was relieved the handsome, broad-shouldered prince wasn't perfect. He was defensive about his family, just like Adrianna.

The Lich looked between the pair of them. He wanted to complete the ritual as much as anyone, despite Asakusa's interruption.

'That's different. There's like millions of you people,' Richard said. That was true. A single brood of spiderfolk could hatch into *thousands* of brothers, but that didn't make it any less rude.

'What do you mean, *you people?*'

'The hordes of spiderfolk.'

'So, what? There's hordes of us, so we're worth less than you?'

'That's not what I said. And how can you be mad? The reports said you and your sisters all ate your own fathers!'

'We had to. There's too much magick in a female spiderfolk's body to survive without the flesh of her father.'

The argument might have lasted longer if the groom's family hadn't started breathing fireballs at Adrianna's friends.

Chapter 17

Asakusa

A flameheart spread its stumpy wings, then jumped at Asakusa.

Asakusa lifted his hammer and spun it up into his attacker's face. The uppercut sent the flameheart's jaw up through its eyes and out the top of his skull.

Three more flamehearts attacked.

Again, Asakusa lifted *Byergen* and forced the stone hammer into motion. *Byergen* was too heavy to carry. It rested on the ground unless called upon for battle. But once awakened, its momentum kept its stone head moving through its foes. Asakusa crippled all three of the flamehearts.

A flameheart threw a dog-sized spider at Asakusa.

'Ahhh!' Asakusa screamed as he tried to slow his stone hammer and stop it from killing the member of Adrianna's family. He might have succeeded, but his Corrupted arm flexed horribly, seized his weapon, and it swung into the spider's abdomen with uncomfortable gusto. With a terrible *squelch*, the hammer struck the spider. Its abdomen cracked, streaming white goo as it careened into a fat red dragon prince whom the flamehearts had been plying with dead birds and rodents throughout the evening. The glutton screamed. A low-pitched yodel, rich with terror.

His suitors attacked the spider, naturally.

Three burly and barrel-chested spiderfolk ran to their comrade's defense. *It is best to think of their faces as nothing more than six eyes above handlebar mustaches*, Asakusa thought. The details of what was below the mustache, a twisted combination of human and arachnid mouthparts, was too horrible to look at. Better to focus on their six tattooed arms. Each of the trio of spiderfolk's eighteen arms was covered in thick external muscle, a rarity for the normally exoskeleton clad race. Their tattoos were mostly portraits of them killing things.

As they made their way through the crowd, they were able to punch quite a lot of people.

And that was how an entire room of flamehearts and spiderfolk managed to forget about Asakusa interrupting the wedding.

Chapter 18

Adrianna

'Adrianna!' Asakusa yelled. 'Come with us!'

Adrianna wished it was so simple.

Jumping spiders the size of skulls leapt up into the air, grabbing winged flamehearts, who rained fire down on half of the guests. The jumpers were too small to hurt the flamehearts. Instead, they wrapped impossibly strong strands of silk around their appendages. The spiders' larger compatriots then hauled the snagged flamehearts down to the ground, where they could be pummeled and stabbed more conveniently. The spiders that missed the jump were knocked back to the ground with well-aimed punches.

Adrianna didn't know how to feel. When she was a girl and their caves were attacked, her brothers had died by the hundreds while defending their home. They'd all been taught—Adrianna, her sisters, and *especially* her brothers—that they must be willing to sacrifice for the Mortician family. At least this time they had a buzz.

Only she, Richard and the Lich were still motionless. The Lich held his book open, its magick enveloping them, a bubble of calm in a cathedral of chaos.

Richard smiled at her. 'Your mistress seems to be quite the handful.'

Adrianna looked from the brawl to the dagger in her hand.

'It's just that I've never met you, you know?'

Around them, the guests released years of pent-up frustration. Adrianna figured the flamehearts had much the same status as her spiderfolk brothers. Accustomed to being used as disposable infantry and little else, a wedding presented little more than a hope to get drunk before dying in one of their better's battles. Fire and webs were everywhere. Once dry, the web was flammable, so the spiderfolk couldn't keep any of the dragons restrained, but it burned slowly and came out as a liquid, so the spiders were able to use it to protect themselves from flameheart breath.

'I won't force you to be exclusive,' Richard said, shrugging his broad shoulders.

Damnit, does he have to be this good? Adrianna thought. She wanted to join the fray, stab a few flamehearts and get out of here, but she couldn't. All they had to do to complete the wedding ritual was join their blood. If they did, would the fighting really stop?

'I want to know the Adrianna that's *not* in the daily briefings,' Richard continued, speaking quickly, trying to hold Adrianna's attention. 'I want to know *why*. Why Hama's pies? Why watch the cinnamon boats unload? I want to know if there's ever going to be an eighth Sultry Spider.'

Adrianna smiled despite how unbelievably creepy it was that he knew all this stuff about her. He seemed nice, nicer than a spider princess could ask for, and if they completed the ritual, the fighting would stop. Maybe.

I have to decide, she thought, looking at the cursed families once more. In that moment the room seemed frozen in time, like a master's painting about the absurdity of violence.

The guests had proceeded to the hand-to-hand portion of the melee. Their webs and flames proven ineffective, daggers and scimitars would have to suffice. Most of the battle was on the floor, though some spiderfolk swung from pillars into flamehearts still trying to use their flight as an advantage. She'd been taught not to care about her spiderfolk brothers. Adrianna could see that the deaths of the flamehearts hurt Richard far more than the deaths of her family hurt her.

Adrianna spotted Ebbo, running amongst fat spider legs and flameheart tails, slicing madly with his elven dagger in one hand, robbing guests with the other. He dodged every swing of a sword simply by not being noticed amongst the chaos. He used the relative safety that unvisibility gave him to sniff at the vials and packets he filched. He discarded some, smiled wildly at others.

The little islander really has a problem.

Clayton had found some grave dirt and had reconstituted himself into a ball a bit bigger than Ebbo. He rolled around smashing into things, gradually working his way through a crowd of stumbling creatures and broken pews up to Adrianna. The ball of dirt had a mouth that stayed near the top and complimented Adrianna's dress as it approached.

Flamehearts attacked Asakusa from every angle, but the worm-like strands of Corrupted flesh caught their weapons and held them just long enough for the whirling stone hammer to crash into their bodies, breaking their ribs like bags of champagne flutes.

But there were too many.

One of the flamehearts got her tail around Asakusa's neck, and two more stabbed him in the gut with their scimitars. He faltered, nearly dropping his hammer as he struggled to breathe.

'No!' Adrianna screamed. The moment was broken. Adrianna lunged toward Asakusa.

Richard stopped her. He had her by the wrist.

'You really love him,' Richard said. Adrianna could hear the incredulity in his voice. His grip was firm, but not painful. He looked frustrated, not angry.

'Let me go!' Adrianna said. He was strong, impossibly strong, stronger than the spider princess. No longer did a human hand hold her own. Scaly red talons held her now.

Adrianna grabbed her silk whip with her free hand, whipped it around the neck of one of the flamehearts that had stabbed Asakusa, and yanked her into the other one.

The one choking Asakusa roared and fell backwards, pulling him to the ground with her. There was some shoving, a scream, and then Ebbo was helping Asakusa to his feet. His blade was dirty with the blood of the flameheart he'd stabbed. He licked the blade, then spit the blood back out. No magick, then.

'Open your hand and we complete the ritual,' Richard said.

'I'm not marrying you while I watch my friends die!' Adrianna said.

'If we don't marry, our parents will continue to use your brothers and my sisters as little more than meat shields. They care only for the castle. We can end the feud between Valkanna and Morticia for good. Surely the lives of your kin are worth than the life of a single mortal!'

Adrianna was shocked. She hated to admit it, but she'd never thought of her brothers the same way Richard thought of his sisters. The spiderfolk were people, of course, but her brothers were so easily controlled by a female's pheromones that sometimes they seemed more like animals, especially to a scared little girl whose sisters had been intent on torturing her with fear. Adrianna felt a pang of guilt, and for a moment would've respected Richard — if his clawed hand wasn't holding her tight.

'He's *not* just some mortal,' Adrianna said, trying and failing to pull her hand free.

'He is nothing to us. Keep him—I don't care—but join our blood *and complete the ritual*. We will fix this broken world and give it to our children.'

'He's my friend, you cockroach. Now let me go!' Adrianna said.

Richard's pleading smile slipped into a scowl.

Adrianna's free arms and two of her legs attacked. At this point, Richard was still mostly in human form, but his wings and tail appeared and managed to parry her stabbing daggers well enough. He didn't, however, manage to block her knee as Adrianna rocketed it into his crotch.

In human form no longer, Richard roared in pain and flew away. The enormous red dragon sprayed a breath of flame at Adrianna that was far larger than the flamehearts' little fireballs. It would have incinerated her and her dress, but the flames wicked into the blade Richard had given her. The tongue of the dragon-dagger grew brighter, and smoke poured from its eyes. But when the fire stopped, the blade returned to shiny silver. *Flametongue* hadn't even gotten warm.

'Nice move, Adrianna, now let's go,' Ebbo said. He'd managed to get safely behind her before Richard had unleashed his fire breath. 'The dirt Clayton found is mostly humus. He's barely holding it together with pulverized bone. Asakusa's hurt, and that guy's a sour blueberry if I've ever met one.'

Richard flew about the room, lifting up spiderfolk and dropping them onto each other. She watched one of her brothers' bodies fall into another brother and break at the seams, squirting white goo like a donut stacked atop another donut and struck with a closed fist. Spiderfolk exoskeletons were quite weak to blunt impact. The bastard knew exactly how to hurt her family. She'd seen such violence happen before, of course, and old instincts kicked in.

'Let's get the hell out of here. Come on, Mom!' Adrianna yelled.

'Are you kidding? I haven't felt like this since my 300's!' Adrianna's webmother wielded two whips that lashed and snapped at the jaws of Richard's father, whose gnarled and bony black dragon form had more spines and spikes than skin. He seemed unable to get his dragon breath to rise to the occasion, so was striking at her with his claws. She caught and deflected his blows in poetic rhythm, meeting him, parrying him, urging him to go faster and slower to match her dexterity and grace.

Adrianna's heart sunk. Her mom didn't really care about her; Adrianna was just a means to an end. The key to the castle. Now that Viriana was back in Krag's Doom and had discovered she could hold her own against the dragon king, Adrianna was irrelevant.

'I think she's going to be fine,' Ebbo said, then reached into his pocket. 'Here, leave her a rolly of Mellow Leaf. It's a great smoke after an, err... exertion.'

Adrianna thought her mother's dismissal of her would've broke her heart, if not for the islander's wink. She loved her friends; they'd accepted in her in a way her family never would. They couldn't die because of her.

'Let's get out of this tangled web.'

Adrianna ran for Asakusa.

Asakusa no longer possessed the strength to lift his hammer. He clung to it, struggling just to keep his grip on the handle. So long as he didn't let go, he couldn't be knocked down.

His Corrupted arm moved with its own energy. It jerked him about, catching weapons, deflecting blows, protecting him like an overzealous dog with the corpse of a prized chipmunk.

Adrianna had seen his Corruption act of its own volition, but never like this. Asakusa really had sacrificed a lot to get here. Adrianna knew how those Gates worked. To travel anything further than a few fields took a lot of energy, and he'd come hundreds of leagues. He shouldn't have sacrificed so much of his flesh. But then, that was Asakusa. Adrianna knew he'd give anything to defend her. She owed him the same protection.

Adrianna moved through attackers, knocking flamehearts aside with cracks of her whip. Those who got too close, got stabbed. With her extra legs, she bundled Asakusa up onto her abdomen.

'He's hurt pretty bad,' Ebbo said from her abdomen. She hadn't even noticed he'd climbed onto her back, spinning islander. 'I'll stuff the wound with milk nettle to stop the acid, but he's going to need bandaging.'

Mending wounds was something Adrianna had more than enough practice with. She went to work, but with two of her arms stitching up Asakusa, Adrianna had no choice but to run. In this form she was faster, but she needed four legs on the ground for balance.

'Where's Clayton?'

'Clearing a path,' Ebbo said.

Clayton rolled down the aisle, knocking spiderfolk and flamehearts aside as he made for the door.

'Right,' Adrianna said and scurried forward on her four legs. They easily scuttled over the burned corpses of spiderfolk and the flamehearts, whose bodies lay still, either poisoned or suffocated with web. Adrianna found herself wondering what Richard would think of his dead relatives. He really did care more for his sisters than she did her brothers.

Her wedding was ruined. Asakusa's grand, dorky entrance had been like water to hot oil.

There would be no peace between their families. Their parents would send wave after wave of their mongrel offspring at each other until there wasn't anyone left to die. Then they'd just make more. Richard didn't really think he could stop all this, did he?

It didn't matter, Adrianna realized with growing dread. Her fiancé was about to kill one of her friends.

'Clayton, no!' Adrianna said.

Richard landed, blocking the doors. His great red wings unfurled as he breathed in. He roared as he exhaled a great gout of flame that sent pews flying back and burned every spiderfolk within range to a crisp.

Later, Adrianna would feel guilty she hadn't even thought of them. She'd been trained not to. What caught her breath in her throat was Clayton Steelheart.

Perhaps Clayton would have been safe if he'd stayed as a ball, but not knowing about the dagger, he'd formed himself into a wall to protect Adrianna. It did almost nothing to stop the furnace that came from Richard's mouth. The wall dried and cracked immediately. Bits from the top blew away, then holes opened up, and then the golem was nothing but a pile of dust blowing away from a charred steel heart.

Adrianna held up her dagger and shielded her friends from the inferno.

Most of them.

Two of them.

Not Clayton.

Good ol' Clayton Steelheart, who could walk on the bottom of the ocean but couldn't stand arid climates.

'A well-made toy. I'll have to get you another one,' Richard said, his voice just as low and rich despite now coming from the toothy grin of a red dragon. Smoke curled from his nostrils. 'Marry me.'

'No,' she said, thinking of Clayton asking about her dress *a thousand times*, Clayton demanding that they go and rescue a prostitute's son despite her having no money to pay them, Clayton convincing her that Ebbo had been worth saving. Twisted as it made Adrianna feel, she could forgive someone killing her brothers, in her lifetime thousands had died—but there was only one Clayton.

Adrianna cracked her whip and wrapped it around Richard's jaws, snapping his mouth shut. 'You may be hotter than anyone I've ever lain six eyes on and charming as roadside sorcerer, but you're a brute and a creep. Now get out of my way!'

Adrianna cracked the whip loose, then snapped it into one of the dragon's slitted eyes. He roared and grabbed at his face, stumbling about and shattering a window. Ethereal spiders began to re-spin the stained glass, even as Richard crashed into another one.

'Get Clayton. I'll hold him off,' Adrianna said.

Asakusa grunted and rolled off her back. Ebbo landed soundlessly and scurried to the lump that the golem had been reduced to. The islander dug through the ashes and found Clayton's heart. It was blackened and hot. Ebbo picked it up, but had to drop it, blowing on his hands as the steel heart fell to the ground with an empty clang. Ebbo opened his satchel and put the burned heart in all the same. Adrianna wished to the Etterqueen that Clayton's heart was still beating.

Richard leapt twenty feet, his body being near that length, and hurtled toward Adrianna.

She stepped to the side, dodging his teeth and claws but getting struck by his tail. She went sprawling. Her abdomen righted itself and then spun her torso around to match. She used the momentum to flick her whip at Richard's face.

This time, though, the dragon was ready. Richard held his wrist up and allowed the whip to wrap around it. Then, held like a toothpick in his dragon claws, he used her dagger on her weapon.

Bloodweaver cut the whip like a piece of string.

Furious, Adrianna attacked again, but Richard struck at the whip and shortened it by a finger length. 'Never forget, I was trained to be your master,' the dragon growled. 'You got in a lucky hit, but you will not get another. You have done nothing that I cannot forgive. Marry me and this all ends.'

'You killed Clayton!' Adrianna screamed, tears streaming from her six eyes. She struck again and again, a blur of strikes. Richard met each lash with her own dagger, protecting himself and forcing her to draw closer.

He was as good as he said.

'Come on, Adrianna,' Asakusa said from the door to the Cathedral. Ebbo had got him conscious again. Good.

'I'll meet you outside,' Adrianna said, thinking only of Clayton. The spider princess, all eight appendages now free, rushed the remaining distance, daggers in two hands, the dragon dagger *Flametongue* in a third. Her wounded palm, she held tightly in a fist.

'Marry me!' Richard roared, then became human again and drew— unsurprisingly—a flaming sword. He brought it down toward Adrianna's skull with both hands.

Adrianna deflected the blow to the ground with the dragon dagger. The blow was strong enough to smash the stone floor. Richard was the real deal. And he wasn't holding back.

He had returned to human form, which gave Adrianna a size advantage. She'd take it.

She pressed forward, three arms a flurry of strikes, her legs offering an occasional kick to keep him off-balance. He was fast, but her cuts got through. They always did. Adrianna Morticia might not hit hard, but she always hit.

His thrusts were much stronger, probably strong enough to incapacitate her, not that Adrianna wanted to test that theory. She moved between his blows, letting him attack so she could parry as the hot ichor in his veins boiled with rage.

He was weakening, Adrianna could tell. His grin grew wider, his eyes fiercer. He wouldn't last much longer. A man couldn't outlast a spider princess, after all, even if this one happened to be a dragon.

Adrianna almost had him. She would paralyze him to stop his blood from flowing, and then force his father and the flamehearts to leave Krag's Doom. Her mom could pick up the mess. She would come back to kill her fiancé if she couldn't find an artificer to fix Clayton.

But then Richard faltered. He fell forward onto *Flametongue*, the dagger he'd traded her in the ceremony. The blade sunk into his chest.

He roared. Smoke billowed from his throat, but the inferno Adrianna had expected did not come. *Flametongue* glowed in her hands, absorbing the dragon's power.

'Damn,' Richard grunted. 'You're pretty tough.'

'I get it from my mom.'

'Sexy, comparing yourself to your mom.' Richard spit acid that incinerated when it hit the ground.

Adrianna snorted. 'Are we done here?'

'Marry me. Last time I ask nicely.'

'Look, maybe some other time, okay? I'm not really feeling it, what with you and your sisters trying to incinerate my friends, our families killing each other, and the dagger in your chest.'

'Fine, but don't say I didn't warn you. Open communication is a pillar of our relationship.'

'There is no relationship—' Adrianna tried to say, but was cut off as Richard grabbed her by the hair.

He wrapped his fingers through her long straight hair, her hair that she always kept tied up, her hair that she had to keep up just to be in her human form, her hair that wasn't really hair. He yanked once, hard, and Adrianna felt her hands drop the other daggers and her back legs spasm.

'Almost got it,' Richard said, then moved his fingers through her hair. He wrapped it in complex patterns, then made a fist behind her head. As Richard clenched his fist, Adrianna unclenched hers. He was pulling on the nerve strands she used to Fold her body. It was a horrible sensation, her body being jerked about like a marionette—worse even than when her sister had used her hair to immobilize her and leave her to drown, if only because it was so unexpected. She clenched her teeth as tears came to her eyes.

'I told you, I know everything about you. All your strengths. All your weaknesses.' Adrianna wanted the dragon prince to sound cruel and heartless as he held her immobilized, but instead his voice faltered. 'This doesn't change anything. I still want to remake the world with you as my queen,' Richard said. Then he pulled down on her hair, and she brought her hand up involuntarily. Adrianna couldn't close her own fingers. The wound on her hand still bled freely. She was terrified of this monster, terrified of the knowledge he had over her. If—no, *when* she broke free, there would be no *if* —she would make him suffer for this. She would cut out his venom sacks and take his fire breath, she would tear holes in his wings so he'd never fly again, she would—

'With this blood, I thee wed,' Richard said, his voice formal with dutiful resignation.

He touched his palm to hers.

When their blood touched, it was unlike anything Adrianna had ever experienced. Hot power flowed through her, from her palm, up her arm, to her heart, then *everywhere.* It was the most pleasurable thing she'd ever experienced. The Lich's magick made her nostrils smoke and her heart pound in her abdomen. That the dragon prince had forced her to do it made her feel sick.

Richard didn't seem to be any more prepared for her blood. His anger and rage and smoke seemed to melt away, until he was just a man in a torn suit, vulnerable as the next, better-looking than most, breathing way too hard and looking completely overwhelmed with sensuous pleasure.

Nothing could be heard except for the Lich's shriek. He screamed and screamed, drawing no breath, never stopping the screeching wall of sound.

Flameheart and spiderfolk alike dropped their weapons and clutched their ears, earholes, or sensitive hairs.

From the bride's dagger came a spider made of shadow, from the groom's, a dragon of smoke. Spider and dragon fought with claw and fang until the dragon fell back. The spider climbed upon the dragon's belly and sunk her fangs into its neck, but at that moment the dragon bit the spider, and the two began to make love. Finally, they dissipated into smoke and shadow.

At least, that was what Adrianna's mother said was happening, but whoever had designed the illusion perhaps didn't know much of either spider or dragon anatomy, because to Adrianna it never really looked like they stopped fighting.

Adrianna, free from the shock of heat in her veins, pulled the dagger out of Richard's chest. He let go of her hand and fell backwards with a self-satisfied grin.

'You bastard. You spinning bastard,' Adrianna said as flamehearts rushed to help their fallen prince.

Then the spider princess turned and ran.

She ran out of the cathedral to find Asakusa had fallen unconscious again. Ebbo was sobbing and pounding Clayton's heart. 'I can't hear his pulse! Asakusa needs to restart it with his hammer, but he passed out.'

'Come on,' Adrianna said, and spun herself a parachute. She pulled Asakusa onto the back of her abdomen, and once Ebbo climbed up with Clayton's heart, she leapt from the rim of the volcano. Her friends rode atop her spider abdomen and weighed her down, some of them nothing but a heart she cared for.

The parachute opened. They caught a thermal and soared up over the rim of the volcano, and then down its steep edge toward the ocean.

They glided for nearly a league before Ebbo spotted an islander's fishing boat.

Adrianna managed to crash into the boat, only spilling Ebbo overboard. She snagged him with her whip before he sank and pulled him into the tiny boat. Seeing another islander calmed the fisherman somewhat, for when Ebbo asked for safe passage, the islander quickly agreed.

Adrianna looked back at Krag's Doom only once. No one was coming after them. Not any of the winged flamehearts, nor any of her sisters. The spider princess and dragon prince had completed the ritual. No one cared that the bride had escaped. The Morticians and Valkanas were united, not in love, but in oath. Neither family would abandon the castle. That was the point of all this, after all.

Adrianna's only consolation was that the groom was stuck with her webmother.

She had more pressing concerns, though. Her family could take care of themselves, but the stitches on Asakusa's wound had torn open. Ebbo was clearly coming down off his magick, as he was turning his pockets out again and again, feeling at wet packets and asking the islander whose boat they were in if there were any mermaids around.

Adrianna picked up Clayton's steel heart. His pulse was weak, but it was there.

Adrianna took a deep breath, then she laughed. She laughed so hard that tears came from her six eyes. They were hurt, leagues away from home, and were probably going to eaten by the Kraken, but they were alive! She would get them out of this. She'd gotten them out of far worse.

'Why are you laughing?' Ebbo said.

'Because it looks like I'll be spending my honeymoon with Asakusa after all.'

'You mean—'

'We completed the marriage. I tried to stop it, but Richard knew me too well.'

Ebbo looked between his two unconscious friends and scratched his head.

Finally, he said, 'I don't think either of them will find this very funny.'

BOOK 2

A Tropic of Skeletons

Chapter 19

Ebbo

Throwing his best friend's still-ticking heart overboard was not the most difficult thing Ebbo Brandyoak had to do this thirteenth of Mur. Holding onto the rope wrapped around the heart as mermaids sang a song of enchantment was a far more demanding task for the short-statured islander. How badly Ebbo wanted to jump overboard and swim for the mermaids. They were beings of almost pure magick; at least, that's what the sailors' stories said.

Ebbo really wanted to lick one.

Adrianna Morticia seemed less than interested in the mermaids and their song.

'I *cannot* believe that Richard spinning *Valkanna* made me complete the wedding ceremony! And even worse, he almost made me *like him!* He must have found out about my hair from my spinning sisters. And to think I was ready to give up on adventuring and settle down!'

'We'd never give up… on you,' Asakusa wheezed.

Typical. The thrall was terrible with words unless he was on the verge of death. Though maybe 'verge of death' didn't currently apply. The Corruption maggots covering much of his body seemed to be fixing up his wounds. If the Corruption spread any further, it risked completely covering Asakusa's body, but the thrall wouldn't die from that. Well, his body wouldn't, anyway.

Maybe it is *a good time to woo her*, Ebbo thought.

Too bad clumsy-tongued Asakusa flubbed his one chance to be romantic at the wedding. Ebbo could already see the writing on the wall. Their relationship had as much future as a dandelion in a tomato patch.

Adrianna rowed with her two human arms while her spider legs skittered back and forth nervously.

'We need to get back to S'kar-Vozi and talk to the Nine. Tell them the spinning Valkannas and my sisters are allied. I don't know how they did it, but I'm sure that's what happened. The city will have to be ready in case they invade. Please tell me you've found a mineral deposit.'

'The Nine are way out of our league,' Ebbo said. 'I mean, I'd love to get Vecnos to sign my dagger, but honestly, we're still up-and-comers. And your mom seemed nice. She's not going to invade anything. And no. No ton of clay for the old Steelheart yet.' Ebbo tried to focus on the vibrations coming up from the rope, instead of Adrianna's latest, greatest plan or the mermaids with their enchantingly luscious song.

'*You're* an up-and-comer. We've been doing this since before Clayton pointed you out to Adrianna and you started messing everything up,' Asakusa scoffed. He was looking better. The Corruption maggots were working on his wound, knitting it together, healing him. It would be kind of cool if it wasn't so creepy.

'What we need is a reason to introduce ourselves that doesn't sound like a conspiracy theory. Something so crazy that if we told Krouche le Douche, he'd take us straight to Ringwall,' Adrianna said as one of her spider appendages came up to stroke her chin.

Strawberries, Ebbo thought, he definitely preferred her human form.

'And proof, too. Whatever it is, we need to make sure we bring back a piece of it,' Asakusa said.

Visions of monstrous teeth and horrible claws, jawbones and hipbones and tailbones flicked through Ebbo's mind.

'I should, uh… really be focusing.'

Though that was proving to be a difficult task.

As Ebbo felt for specific vibrations through the rope with his toes, his eyes kept drifting to the mermaids. There were four of them on a boulder. Three of them had hair the color of the sea, braided with shells and lengths of exotic kelp. Two of them had tails like fantastically voluptuous dolphins, the third had chitinous growths that sparkled a shade of orange more brilliant than any coat of dragon scales, but it was the fourth who set Ebbo's own heart a-pumping. She had a purple tail, silver hair, fair skin, and was gloriously topless.

But that wasn't why Ebbo liked her.

Ebbo had seen stouter bellies on the attractively short islanders back home on Strong Oak Isle. What set Ebbo's heart a-pounding was the purple mermaid's song. She led the others in a slow melody sung in rounds. Their voices were beautiful, hers achingly so. Ebbo could feel the purple mermaid's music deep in his chest, begging him to rescue her and let her feed him oysters.

That it was an obviously magickal effect in no way diminished Ebbo's desire to swim to the woman. If their voices were this laden with magick, a lock of their hair or some of the goo scraped from their gills would get him high for days.

'Cover your ears,' Asakusa Sangrekana said, and then fell into a coughing fit. Ebbo thought he was hamming it up. Sure, his Corruption covered more than half of his body, and yes, he'd been stabbed in the gut, but the maggots were knitting together over his wound quite nicely. Ebbo hadn't seen any blood for at least twenty minutes. He didn't know how all that would affect the deal Asakusa made with Gatekeeper who granted him his powers, but that was a problem for another time.

'Rest now, Asa. Ebbo has found mineral deposits for Clayton a dozen times. We'll be fine,' Adrianna said. Every time Ebbo looked at the spider princess, he had to look again. He simply could not get used to seeing her in a charred wedding dress instead of her usual padded black leather armor. It didn't much help that her hair was currently down and her spider body Unfolded. Thus, Ebbo was sharing a boat with a spider centaur wearing a wedding dress.

'You *are* taking care of Clayton, right, Ebbo?' she said. 'Because I need some time to think of how we're going to slay a monster important enough to merit us an audience with the Nine when Clayton doesn't have a body and Asakusa can't use any Gates.'

'I can use Gates. Just not many... and not the convenient ones,' Asakusa protested.

'Of course I'm taking care of Clayton,' Ebbo said. 'He's the only one of you that shows me any berry-picking respect.' The rope fell slack. That meant the steel heart had sunk to the sea floor. The islander whose boat they had commandeered had been right about the depth, then. Deep enough for Ebbo to drown, certainly, but not so deep as to hide the Kraken.

'Anything yet?' Adrianna said.

Ebbo's sensitive toes felt the heart bump against a particularly pointy bit of staghorn coral. He jerked it free.

'Nope, just sand.' Ebbo had been terrified when Richard Valkanna had blasted Clayton's heart at Adrianna's wedding. In the chaos of that moment, he hadn't been able to hear it pumping at all. If he were to lose Clayton... Ebbo took a deep breath. He would be fine. He'd lost his clay, but that had happened before. Adrianna had listened and heard a heartbeat coming from the steel heart, and that was all that mattered. Ebbo had heard it too, once they were away from the brawl the wedding had become. If he thought it sounded off, well, he was still coming down off the crushed dragon scales.

He tried to still his trembling toes as the mermaids went into another round. Ebbo could normally identify all sorts of materials through the vibration of a rope, but the mermaids were making it difficult.

Maybe they know where to find decent clay! Ebbo thought.

'Thanks for nothing.' Asakusa fell back with a grunt of pain.

Ebbo *knew* he was faking it. He just wanted Adrianna to take pity on him while he insulted poor Ebbo.

'There won't be any clay this far out from the shore,' Mipple said. Mipple was the islander whose boat they had landed in when they'd escaped Adrianna's wedding by silken parachute. He was helping Adrianna row, despite being a fifth her size.

'Should we go closer to shore, then?' Ebbo glanced at the gorgeous purple mermaid. Her smoldering eyes looked across the sea at him, begging him to come closer, to smell her hair, touch her body, inhale the magick that she laced through her music.

'No! We both know the halfing's no match for the sirens,' Asakusa said.

Ebbo found that extremely annoying. Here Asakusa was, Corrupted beyond anything he had ever seen before, with a stab wound being held together from said Corruption, clinging to consciousness, just so he could make racial slurs and stop the islander from relaxing with a bit of magick?

'Now, princess, I agreed to let you use my boat without so much as a question about what you fellows are doing here, because I figured you needed to get away from Krag's Doom. The least you could do, which is more than enough, would be to consider not permitting your fellows to use that kind of language so freely,' Mipple said, not at all confidently.

It was difficult for islanders to tell people to stop being impolite, because it was their nature to be very polite, and asking someone to stop saying something was not polite at all.

Ebbo had figured that Mipple hadn't complained about them taking over his little voyage because Asakusa was crawling with demonic maggots, Adrianna was a magic spider centaur armed with daggers and a whip, and Ebbo had threatened the man with a glowing knife the second they'd crashed into his boat, but he supposed it could be out of some misplaced sense of kindness. Islanders were like that.

'I apologize for my friend. He's not well,' Adrianna said with a polite nod toward Asakusa's Corrupted flesh.

Despite Mipple looking pouty, he didn't say anything to the thrall or the black maggoty muscles that covered his arm, pulsing and burrowing underneath each other.

Asakusa was the only one in the tiny rowboat with any kind of room, mostly because he was gross. Adrianna hadn't yet tied up her hair and Folded her spider form away, so the decidedly arachnid lower half of her body took up half the boat, and Ebbo—being an islander—just barely sort of managed to stay out of everybody's way.

Mipple looked away with classic islander deference. *Poor guy,* Ebbo thought. Adrianna shot a scowl at Asakusa so fierce, the maggots seemed to try to escape it.

'If there's clay on the seafloor closer to the shore, we need to get closer,' Adrianna said. 'We need Clayton back in action and a plan on how to make introductions to the Nine. If we can't find anything worth slaying on the way home, he probably knows an escort one of them prefers or something. Etterqueen, I hope my webmother is alright.'

'She'll be fine,' Asakusa said. 'She doesn't exactly have weaknesses.'

'Oh, and I do?'

'No, that's not what I meant. I mean, because your mom's bald.'

'Mixed company?' Adrianna said, raising her two human hands and two spider appendages in frustration as she gestured at Mipple.

Mipple balked at that. 'I am known for my secret-keeping abilities. Why, my great-aunt has a recipe for cherry pie, and with just a touch of lemon—' He slapped his hands to his mouth.

'Don't tell anyone her mom has fake pubic hair, or we'll kill you,' Ebbo said, waggling his dagger and giggling at his deception. 'Plus, her shiny new oath-laws are probably going to be on us any minute, and you're not exactly a fast rower. Make for the clay deposits! I still feel nothing but sand down there.'

Asakusa sat up straighter. The maggots really were working wonders on his wound. 'If we get any closer to those mermaids, Ebbo might jump.'

Adrianna rolled her six eyes. 'He's not going to jump.' She looked at Ebbo. 'You're not going to jump.' It wasn't a question. 'But something's weird about them. We've tangled with mermaids before. Usually they use the siren song to enchant—'

'Which is working, by the way,' Ebbo said, grinning and then cursing himself. Would've been better to not let that slip.

'But then one usually slips up onto the boat and starts slitting throats.' Adrianna's casual tone of voice did little for poor Mipple's nerves, who started peering into the murky water even more neurotically than he was already looking at his unexpected passengers.

'Don't worry about them, Mipple. Worry about us.'

Mipple nodded and looked at Ebbo's hand, casually tossing his dagger.

Ebbo would never hurt another islander. But he also didn't like the others threatening the little guys; it just didn't feel right. Better to come from one of their own. Plus, he'd prefer that Mipple think of him as a bully rather than a magick addict.

Not that he was addicted.

Mipple looked from Ebbo to the spider princess in her wedding dress, sort of grumbled about his lunch, and rowed. 'You'll have to be ready, Miss. Your friend was right. I have earplugs, but their song pulls heavy on the hearts of some islanders. Enchanting it is, like the smell of apple pie, if ya see my reckoning.'

Mipple was right. As they moved closer to the mermaids, Ebbo found it harder and harder to resist their song. He tried to think of Clayton, of all they'd been through together, but the melody was like something from the Green Acorn—Ebbo's favorite tavern back home—only with harmonies unlike anything an islander could sing. The sound enveloped him like the sea. And the words! He didn't know the words, and yet he *understood*. The mermaids wanted him to help them escape, to swim far away with them and their song in all its glory, to taste their oysters, to feel their hands running through his curly hair. It was a song of forbidden love and lustful taboos, of passions fulfilled and desires sated in faraway lands. It was positively rife with magick, and the most wonderful thing he had ever heard. If he could just get a bit closer...

'Ebbo, don't make me come after you!' Adrianna shouted, but he hardly heard her.

He was too busy jumping overboard.

As a rule, islanders didn't much know how to swim. That was why most rarely left their islands. Ebbo was no different. He flailed his arms and gasped for air but quickly found himself underwater. He'd nearly drowned many times, that was one of the chief perils of travelling in the Archipelago and not knowing how to swim, but this time was different.

Ebbo felt his fear and panic diminish as he sank deeper and deeper beneath the sea. The pressure of the water didn't feel so bad; his lungs burned, yes, but he knew that pain would soon go away. For the song echoing through the water told him that the purple-tailed, silver-haired mermaid was swimming toward him, still singing her song.

Despite not seeing her enter the water, she swam around him now, an angel in profile, her mouth closed in a demure smile. That was weird—up close her skin seemed less like porcelain, and more... rotten? She reached out a hand. That too was odd; Ebbo hadn't noticed her long, skeletal fingers from the boat.

The song of escape was louder, more urgent, and yet this mermaid wasn't singing. Ebbo paddled backwards, going nowhere. The mermaid turned to him. The other half of her face was nothing but fleshless bone! Needle-like teeth ran in a hideous line all through her cheek. Her one eye was entirely black—and entirely loveless. The other was an empty socket framed by yellow bone.

Raspberries! Ebbo cursed to himself.

Asakusa had been right. Ebbo had fallen for her wiles! He didn't know what was worse, his imminent death at the hands of this now-silent and decidedly less attractive mermaid, or the fact that if he was saved, the crushed dragon scales in his pocket were going to take forever to dry.

Ebbo reached for his dagger and swung at the mermaid, but she was too fast. She dodged the blade easily. That about exhausted the halfling's underwater prowess, but no matter. He felt true ecstasy before he slipped into unconsciousness. He just barely noticed a tentacle wrap around his neck, but he didn't really mind.

Chapter 20

Adrianna

Adrianna hauled Ebbo out of the water with her whip. Once she could see his head, two of her spider legs reached overboard and—drawing the rakes of a mermaid's claws—hauled the waterlogged islander back into the rowboat.

'Spinning islanders,' Adrianna cursed. She noted Ebbo still held the rope with his toes. There were reasons she kept him around.

Mipple didn't complain, either because his earplugs were working or because the mermaid was slamming into the rowboat. 'They don't usually ram the boat! And when they do, they don't use their pretty faces!'

'That's not a mermaid, or not anymore, anyway,' Ebbo sputtered. 'She's a corpse!'

The mermaids, all four of them, were still on their rock, while this other one smashed against Adrianna's tiny commandeered ship.

The other mermaids kept singing, begging the rowboat and its riders to come closer. Though their tune had changed. Adrianna recognized hunger in the harmonies, a minor chord that sounded of desperation. The mermaids were trapped. They were hoping to be rescued.

The magick of their music had little effect on Adrianna, and almost none on Asakusa. Each had magick of their own, but Ebbo, whose magick (if you could even call it that) was decidedly more pedestrian, hadn't stood a chance. Well, and then there was his addiction. That certainly hadn't helped.

Adrianna felt confident that she could defeat a mermaid… from a proper ship, after a nap, and if it was the living variety. Out here, with the waves rocking the tiny boat and her silk stores depleted from spinning the parachute and not having time to eat it and digest it back into her ichor, she wasn't so sure. She kept it at bay with her whip, and with *Flametongue*—the dagger her husband had given her for their wedding—yet the boat was still moving toward the rocky shore. 'You're sure it was undead?'

'If you mean *not-alive*, then yes, I'm sure!' Ebbo said, fumbling with his pockets.

'You're positive, Ebbo? It's not a magickal hallucination or whatever?'

'Boysenberries, it doesn't work like that! Why in all the bramble thickets would I use magick if it made me see yellow skeletons?'

That caused Adrianna to gasp through her air vents. This mermaid could be just the break they were looking for! Well, if it didn't kill them and turn them into undead skeletons like it was obviously trying to do. 'You're sure it was *yellow?*'

'It's gonna sink our ship and feed us to the Kraken, and you're worried about what *color* it is?' Mipple shouted, either in terror or to compensate for the earplugs.

'The Kraken's just a bunch of superstitious nonsense,' Adrianna said as she cracked her whip at the surface of the water, trying and failing to keep the mermaid from striking the ship. She'd seen plenty of mermaids in her day and had to admit this specimen was proving to be a weird one. They pretty much stuck to the 'lure in sailors with their siren song and kill the ones who didn't go for it' shtick. Never did they ram their heads repeatedly against a boat. Too bad she couldn't see it to confirm what Ebbo had said. The water was too murky. If it really was yellow, then this was bad, worse even than her sisters.

'And this isn't a ship,' Ebbo said between coughs of water.

'It's gonna sink like one! And the Kraken *is* real. Hardly anyone believes in the monsters that live around Krag's Doom either, but I got a whole mess of them in my boat!'

'Good for you. It's good to see an islander stand up for himself,' Ebbo said.

'I'm standing up to *you*!' Mipple said.

'The rope!' Asakusa shouted.

Ebbo looked down and raised his eyebrows as the rope that he'd managed to keep hold of with his toes was now rapidly being pulled overboard.

'Clayton!' Ebbo said, and snatched at the rope with his right foot, then his left, then fell forward and grasped at it with his hands. He failed at each of the four attempts.

Adrianna tried next, stamping at the rope with the clawed ends of her spider legs, but they were far less adept at fine tasks, and the rope ran between them like a snake through a grove of hairy bamboo.

'I... got it,' Asakusa grunted and caught the rope. It was moving so fast, it cut him. The rope turned red for a few feet before stopping in his hand. The boat lurched away from the rocky shore. The smell of blood drove the mermaid mad. Rather, the skeletal mermaid. It was seeming less and less likely that it was a regular mermaid, what with the pieces of its rotten flesh sloughing off into the water.

Asakusa's other arm, the Corrupted one, grabbed the side of the boat and held him back. The maggots crawled down from his arm to his hand and fingers. There seemed to be an endless supply of them, for despite his fingers dividing and thickening, no part of his arm was exposed. Instead more ribbons of black, writhing muscle were underneath. Asakusa held onto the rope with one hand and the boat with the other, until the wooden side of the boat cracked, then gave way, and he toppled forward and into the water.

'Asakusa!' Adrianna yelled.

'Good riddance!' said Mipple.

Ebbo, in a gesture that warmed Adrianna's heart with the power of friendship, grabbed Asakusa's legs—and was promptly pulled into the water.

Adrianna acted quickly. She snapped her silk whip around the islander's ankle.

Immediately she felt resistance.

Split second to decide.

Adrianna was big in her spider form, big enough to maybe haul up whatever fish had snagged Clayton's heart, but could she do it before Ebbo ran out of air and Asakusa tried to open a damned Gate? She also *really* wanted to mess up that mer-corpse.

She made a tiny silk balloon of air, armed herself with daggers in seven of her eight appendages (she'd sewn pockets into her wedding dress), and dove into the sea.

Adrianna let herself get pulled deeper underwater. As she descended, she scanned the waters for the mermaid. If it really was undead… well… that was something of note. There'd been no undead in the Archipelago—except for the Lich—for at least a hundred years. Surely the Nine in the Ringwall would notice that. And if there were yellow bones, well, a spider princess didn't attend the best of the dark schools and drop out their final year without knowing what yellow bones signified.

As if in response to her thoughts, the mermaid attacked Adrianna.

It was immediately obvious that it wasn't a mermaid, not anymore. Its tail was rotten and looked to have been eaten away by the various scavengers of the sea. Its face, when it came to bite Adrianna's neck, was more than half-gone, no doubt left smeared up on the rowboat above. What was left was all skeleton—glorious, yellow skeleton. This was Adrianna's chance!

If she had been in her human form, perhaps the creature would have been a threat, but as a spider armed with daggers galore, she was a maelstrom of stabbing blades. They didn't do much, though. Even though each wound knocked away more rotten flesh, the skeletal core of the mermaid fought on until Adrianna stabbed it in the eye socket, cracking its skull. Only then did it fall still and start to drift apart as Adrianna was pulled deeper below.

She took the skull with her and turned her attention to the depths.

Through the murk, Adrianna saw that Asakusa had managed to bring the rope to his chest, where the maggots had taken hold of it as well as Ebbo. So, they'd both be dragged into the waiting jaws of the giant clam, or hyper-intelligent cuttlefish, or whatever was taking shape ahead of him.

Whatever it was, it seemed to have arms that were raveling the rope around broad, brown shoulders. Adrianna couldn't see much through the murk—a bicep, a snatch of rope, a chiseled jaw. Wait a minute, Adrianna knew that chiseled jaw!

Ebbo seemed to recognize him too. 'Clayton!' he tried to call out and only succeeded in swallowing a mouthful of water.

Adrianna used her whip, still wrapped around Ebbo's ankle, to pull the halfling to her. She gave him her bubble of air. He pointed and almost cheered again as the form of her old friend, Clayton Steelheart, took shape amidst the ocean currents. Clayton's body reformed in time to the thumping rhythm of his steel heart until he was fully formed.

Clayton gave her a thumbs-up, then pointed at Asakusa and shook his head. Even through the murk and the maggots, Adrianna could still see the Dark Key glowing in his hand. It had been buried in Asakusa's flesh when he had become a thrall and agreed to trade his body to Byorginkyatulk for the right to pass through the Gates to the Ways of the Dead.

Asakusa had opened a Gate, damn him! All they'd needed to do was swim back to the surface. An entirely possible task now that the skeletal mermaid had been defeated, but of course, Asakusa had to go and further risk his life. Sometimes it seemed like he just couldn't help it. Like he thought the best thing a friend could do was sacrifice.

Still, now that he'd gone and opened the Gate, Adrianna would use it. It wasn't as if her lingering would serve any purpose. The maggots on Asakusa's Corrupted arm rippled, his fingertips ignited like dark candles, and then lightning shot from his fingers and a Gate opened up in front of them. Through the Gate, Adrianna could see another, nearly identical one. It opened up on a sandy beach by a green hill. Between the two was a span of inky blackness framed in crumbling brick.

Clayton marched through the Gate. Adrianna hurried through, not wanting it to be open a second longer than necessary, taking Ebbo with her. Finally, Asakusa followed.

Adrianna had been through the Ways of the Dead more than once, but never underwater. Instead of paths and bridges everywhere, they found themselves in a tunnel of bricks filled with inky, viscous water. Through holes formed by missing bricks, Adrianna could see strange, moving lights. Nothing else could be seen except another Gate a few armlengths ahead of them. Clayton had already marched through it.

Adrianna, her lungs burning but not nearly as strongly as her curiosity, peered through a hole in the tunnel. Crawling about, illuminated by the glowing bodies of squids and fish, were lobsters big as men, starfish the size of tree stumps. They all wandered in the same unerring, listless way of those who walked the Ways of the Dead above the sea. Some of the fish seemed to be following unseen paths as well. Did these souls also trudge to their afterlife, as Asakusa said the souls of the thinking did? Did that mean these creatures—squids, lobsters, even *starfish*, could conceive of an afterlife? Adrianna had never seen anything other than humanoids on the paths above the sea. Were these creatures the ocean's equivalent?

An eel certainly seemed to think so. It tried to force its way into their tunnel, and when it found it couldn't fit, crackled with lightning. Adrianna held up her dragon dagger, and it absorbed the energy as easily as it had her husband's attack back at the wedding. Those same flames that had nearly killed Clayton.

And then they were through, and Clayton was pulling them out of the water and onto a white, sandy beach. He was going to be okay! Ebbo was coughing up water and Asakusa wasn't breathing, but that was business as usual.

Adrianna leaned over Asakusa, sniffed out his pulse, and then used her teeth to inject him with a tiny amount of venom. Asakusa sat up, clutching at his chest and breathing fast. He looked at Adrianna, her mouth still open from administering Death's Stolen Kiss, as it was called, and blushed.

Foolish boy.

His Corruption had spread even further. Now everything but Asakusa's head and left arm were covered in black, writhing maggots, but at least he was alive. He rolled away from her, coughing out seawater.

'You saved us!' Ebbo said, sounding genuinely impressed. Adrianna loved that about Ebbo, that no matter how many times she saved the little halfling, he still thanked her like she'd just brought him a pie.

'Clayton, thank the Etterqueen you're alright!' Adrianna said.

'More than alright. Looks like the big guy's happy to see us,' Asakusa said, still sitting on the beach and currently eye level with the anatomically correct golem.

'I do apologize,' Clayton said as the clay penis melted into his crotch. 'I tend to get excited when I save my friends from certain death, and that mermaid song was rather enchanting. Reminded me of a melody that the women of the Red Underoo used to sing before they would have their way with me.'

'And you couldn't feel it a bit, yeah-yeah-yeah,' Ebbo said, then he laughed and laughed.

Adrianna smiled too. Clay's pulse had been so faint, and the dents on his heart had looked severe, but here he was! In the flesh, or the clay, or whatever.

'Where are we?' Adrianna said, brandishing the yellow skull with one of her daggers stabbed through its eye.

'Where did you get that oh-berries-I'm-gonna-be-sick.' Ebbo barfed, not his proudest moment but far from his worse. Adrianna used the opportunity to pull some of the hair and the last bits of flesh off of the skull.

'I used the Gate with the cheapest price,' Asakusa said, sounding smug. 'But I, uh... I have no idea where we are.'

'Well, we *were* twenty feet below a perfectly functional rowboat and a few days from S'kar-Vozi, where we need to go, so we can show the Nine this skull,' Adrianna said.

'Wait, did I miss something? Did we rescue Adrianna from the wedding or not?' Clayton scratched his head, and then noticed he was still naked, if lacking genitals. Clothes sculpted themselves from his clay, in time to his heartbeats. 'How long was I out?' Clayton said.

'We succeeded,' Ebbo said.

'No, we definitely did *not*,' Asakusa said.

Clayton cocked his head to the side. Adrianna smiled like she was going to explain, then didn't. Asakusa looked annoyed, and Clayton desperate for gossip, but Ebbo simply nodded at her once. Ebbo understood; he hated explaining himself.

'What matters is that we get back to S'kar-Vozi and show Krouche le Douche this skull,' Adrianna said, brandishing the skull. She had still not removed it from the dagger she'd stabbed it with. 'Then we'll meet the Nine in the Ringwall, tell them about my family, go on a proper mission, and things can get back to normal. Or you know, as normal as your life can be when your job is to save innocent lives from monsters. And you were just out for an hour.'

'I think I know where we are, but we're leagues away from where we were,' Ebbo said, sounding confused as only an islander could. 'If I'm not mistaken, those two hills in the shape of a kitten's ears mark this place as Berry Berry Isle! Famous for its berry preserves!'

Islanders prided themselves on knowing the various goods and crafts that came from the Farm—the cooperative of islander-run farms and artisanal crafts made on the hundreds of islands in the Archipelago.

'I think I have a cousin here,' Ebbo said.

The islander set out for a curling trail of smoke rising from a field of brambles, as if nothing worse had happened than having a picnic beset by ants. Ebbo followed the trail of smoke to a house built atop a nearby hill that was covered so thickly in raspberries, Adrianna could smell them over the sea.

Chapter 21

Ebbo

A week later and Ebbo, Adrianna, and Asakusa were completely sick of raspberries. Even Clayton was complaining about them getting everywhere.

'You know, I thought it was a versatile flavor, but it's really not.' Ebbo looked up at the five-hundred-foot cliffs on either side of the narrow entrance to Bog's Bay. He was somewhat surprised to find himself feeling relieved to see the somewhat terrifying passage; it felt like coming home. They'd spent the last four days travelling back to S'kar-Vozi by ship laden with berries in all their forms: fresh, jellied, jarred and dried. Ebbo could really go for one of the city's infamous apple barley crumbles. *Blueberries,* he thought, he'd settle for a bowl of snabbage soup!

'I couldn't believe those fish sandwiches,' Asakusa said and scoffed, about the closest he ever got to a laugh.

Though Ebbo had spent the voyage trying to keep as far away from Asakusa as he possibly could—what with the constant stream of insults coupled with a just plain nasty Corruption—the islander could tell that the thrall was doing better. The wound was finally holding, although the Corruption hadn't abated at all. Despite Adrianna's plan to go to the Nine in the Ringwall, she had paid close attention to the Corruption. They'd have to take care of it soon.

'Which ones? Raw tuna and raspberry preserves, or pickled herring and pickled raspberries. Yech!' Ebbo laughed. He was surprised how happy he was to have Asakusa healthy again, considering that the cursed thrall used half of his breaths to insult poor Ebbo.

'I thought the fish was good,' Adrianna said, 'and at least it smelled better than Bog's Bay does right now.'

She was certainly right about that. The clockwork sewer system that allowed S'kar-Vozi to have indoor plumbing was the envy of just about everyone who'd *never* smelled the bay where the waste was dumped.

Ebbo and Asakusa nodded at her and tried not to roll their watering eyes. It *was* good fish, but it was never pleasant for Ebbo to watch Adrianna eat. Maybe he was happy that Asakusa was doing better because the thrall was the only other one in the party who actually ate normal food. Adrianna only consumed meat, and she didn't really eat it but *drank it,* and Clayton ate mud through his feet.

'So was the clay. Good, even grains. It was generous of them to let me spend some time in their mud bath. Too bad about the cape,' Clayton said.

Truly, *Clayton* was why Ebbo was in a good enough mood to put up with Asakusa. He was thankful and all that Adrianna and Asakusa had saved his life, but he shuddered to think what would have happened if Clayton hadn't been okay. There was no man kinder than Clayton Steelheart, the only free golem in the free city of S'kar-Vozi. In Ebbo's eyes, Clayton was practically their glorious mascot, and more importantly, Ebbo's best friend.

'Too bad you spend so much time on sculpting your mud shoulders, you wouldn't want to cover them up with *actual* clothing,' Ebbo said. 'You look like someone left a dried-up sea sponge in a puddle.'

'Well, forgive me for not being built to wear a pillowcase with majesty. And I'll have you know that hemp is *actual* clothing. It's more durable than your halfling-cloth and hangs better.'

'Did you just—' Asakusa started to say, but was cut off by the irate islander.

'You just called me a halfling, you insensitive dirt bag!' Ebbo said.

Clayton rolled his eyes, but his smile didn't falter. 'Oh, come on, that's only been a bad word for a decade, and cot-on sounds strange.'

'Oh, whatever. You're a glorified cleaning spell who hasn't even been alive for a decade. I've seen dented suits of armor with more personality than you. Leopold the Grimy should have named you Mudbrains Bleedingheart; at least then maybe we'd have known enough to warn you from jumping in front of a fire-breathing dragon. You don't even like going to the islands in the south because the air is too dry!' Ebbo said with a smirk.

'I was *trying* to protect the princess!' Clayton splayed his fingers on his chest in offense.

'It was sweet,' Adrianna said. 'If unnecessary.'

'And stupid,' Asakusa said. 'You failed to notice that the dagger Valkanna gave her absorbs fire. Maybe Ebbo's right. Mudbrains is about as accurate as Clayton.'

Ebbo squealed with laughter. It was rare that Asakusa insulted anyone except the islander. Oh, boysenberries, it was good to have Clayton back.

'I was a little busy saving all of your fleshy rumps,' Clayton said with a huff. 'And you can bet I won't forget now that it's her dagger instead of her husband's.'

That sobered them all, and for a time no one said a thing, though it could have just been that they were busy holding their breath.

Chapter 22

Adrianna

It took Adrianna's breath away every time she sailed into Bog's Bay, and it wasn't just the stench.

She loved this place—well, not the Bay specifically, but S'kar-Vozi at large—and how so many different kinds of people could work together despite no official rules stopping them from eating each other.

Even the crew of the merchant ship they were aboard was a marvel of interspecies tolerance. The ship's witch, who continued to fill their sails with wind until they docked, didn't threaten to boil the islanders alive, and in turn they didn't threaten her with pitchforks. It was a peace, of sorts, and it said something about the Berry Island operation that the islanders there could afford a wind witch. Not long ago, islanders couldn't have afforded—let alone dared—to hire someone that sounded so nefarious, but then, times were changing.

S'kar-Vozi itself was a testament to change. The city was a hodgepodge of architectural styles. Most were borrowed or ripped off from the old dwarven and elven masterpieces, but done in lumber, a material that humans were far better at working than either of the elder races. Apartments crowded out alleys as they grew higher and higher, shoving each other to the side, wrestling with each other like spiders vying to make a web close to a torch. Those rich enough to invest in imported stone—anything to get away from the coarse, black, volcanic rock that made up the bedrock of the entire Archipelago—were often forced to change colors halfway up, because as others built, they often bought stone from the same exorbitantly priced quarry.

Today, Adrianna looked past the hodgepodge of construction and demolition, up and up and up and up, all the way to the very top of the city, to the structure where the very richest lived. The Ringwall.

The Ringwall was made of a single piece of white stone. It had no mortar or lines upon its perfectly smooth surface, nor could anyone—armed with enchanted weapons, powered-up scrolls, or whatever else—mar its white stone. The Ringwall spread from one side of S'kar-Vozi all the way to the other. A half-circle that, together with the black cliffs, completely surrounded S'kar-Vozi except for the single cleft they'd sailed through on the far side of Bog's Bay.

No one knew who made the Ringwall. For that matter, no one exactly knew *what* made it, or when. Obviously, it was older than S'kar-Vozi's scant century of history. The VanChamps claimed their elven ancestors built it, but seeing as how the incestual elven twins managed to cling to their place in the Ringwall by selling cheap baubles to tourists, this was generally not believed beyond the people who'd only recently purchased a soon-to-malfunction bauble. The Ringwall had simply been there—a perfect structure for defense, complete with nine separate strongholds with holes pre-drilled for door hinges—when Bolden sailed into Bog's Bay a hundred years ago, armed only with his trusty shovel and sledge hammer, and started to build. Why no one had sought to live beneath this looming, ominous monstrosity was a mystery to most humans and painfully obvious to other races. Though, now that the Ringwall looked down upon the richest and fastest growing city in the Archipelago, those other races were just as eager to move in as any human.

If Adrianna had her way, soon they'd be meeting with someone who actually lived there.

The ship docked, and—after helping unload the cargo as the islanders had asked in exchange for passage—they disembarked.

'Alright. First things first. What do we do, just plop that yellow skull of yours on Krouche le Douche's desk?' Ebbo asked.

'First we need to take care of those... *things*,' Clayton said, gesturing disdainfully at Asakusa's squiggling maggots.

'Agreed,' Adrianna said. 'Let's get you a balm, and then we'll talk to le Douche.'

'I'm fine. Really,' Asakusa said a bit petulantly. 'Seltrayis always has *something* that works. And Krouche is on the way to her shop.'

'Asa, we should get the balm first,' Adrianna said. Part of her wanted to agree with him, the same part that wanted to be a hero at all costs; she tried to ignore it.

'The Corruption won't spread as long as I don't open a Gate, and the sooner you tell Krouche about the skull, the sooner we can tell the Nine about your, uh...'

'Freaky weird marriage?' Ebbo said.

'Yeah. That. But seriously, I'm fine. No, wait!' Asakusa reached out with his Corrupted hand. The maggots felt at the air. 'There's a Gate going straight to Seltrayis. I can take it. It'll be faster than us walking. If you really want me to get the balm as soon as possible, that's the best way.'

'No!' Adrianna, Ebbo and Clayton all shouted at once.

'Asa, please don't. We're a team. You know I hate it when you try to be a martyr,' Adrianna said.

'I'm not being a martyr. I have, like, a whole other arm and leg before I lose my body.'

'No!' Adrianna found it incredibly frustrating when Asakusa got like this. 'Just… look, if you really think it won't matter, we'll go to Krouche's together, and then we'll get your balm. Please don't take a Gate. I'd rather stick together for a while. I missed you dinguses.'

Asakusa nodded. 'Fine.'

'We missed you too, six-eyes!' Ebbo said back.

Adrianna smiled. She loved her friends. They were the only people who teased a spider princess — well, besides her sisters, and they had always taken teasing way too far.

'Speaking of splitting up for stupid reasons… can't you just give that dagger back, and you won't be married anymore?' Ebbo looked up at Adrianna.

Adrianna shrugged and looked from Ebbo to Asakusa and his Corruption. She wanted to say that everything was fine, that she'd tied her white hair up in elaborate braids and Folded away her arachnid body because they were about to go on another adventure. But she couldn't say that. Not to her friends. Her wedding meant that sometime, probably sometime *soon*, someone — most likely either her husband or her spinning sisters — was going to come and fetch her and drag her home. Before that happened, she needed — more than anything — to make sure her friends, namely Asakusa, were going to be safe from whatever an alliance between her family and the Valkannas meant.

But she didn't say any of that. They knew it already. They'd been over it on the spinning boat ride over. All Adrianna could do was look at Asakusa' Corruption, and wonder how Ebbo could think of *anything* besides the Corruption on the thrall's chest. It hadn't spread any further on his body during the boat ride, but it hadn't retreated either. That, its stubbornness to heal itself without a balm from Asakusa's witchy friend, made a pit of dread in Adrianna's stomach. Well, not her stomach, but in the glands that produced the acids she regurgitated on her food before eating.

Adrianna hoped that Asakusa was right, and that Seltrayis could sort him out. And if not, if somehow coming to her wedding had doomed him... Adrianna's hand came to rest on the aforementioned dagger.

'Those shadows meant something too, right? That you completed the marriage,' Asakusa said.

'We said our vows to each other's open wounds, traded the daggers as dowries, and sealed it with our blood. It's done. Only one of our deaths would end it, or the Lich dying, I guess.'

'So let's kill him!' Ebbo said.

'The Lich? No way! He was like a father to me—well, a dead, mostly desiccated father, but still,' Adrianna said.

'But shouldn't Valkanna be chasing you down?' Asakusa said. 'I know I would.'

'I have no idea. I mean... honestly, the wedding's not even about Richard and me. It's about uniting the families. They're probably glad I'm not there. Richard was the only one there who seemed to actually care about what I thought.'

'But he *made* you open your palm,' Ebbo said. 'I saw him grab your hair and yank you around like a puppet.'

'What *I want* is not important,' Adrianna said, the same thing she'd told herself every time her sisters had tormented her as a little girl before she'd gone away to the free city. 'Not to the Lich. He's conducted plenty of weddings against mortal's wills. Why should I be any different?'

'It seems fairly important to me,' Clayton said. 'How did he know what strands of hair to pull? I've seen plenty of baddies grab you by the hair, and none of them have done *that.'*

Ebbo nodded.

'Richard told me that he was trained to be my master. It only makes sense. Look, I'm not saying that it wasn't brave of all of you to come and ... erm... save me. I just wish I would have had some notice. Maybe then we wouldn't have had to get Clayton fresh clay, and take care of...'

Adrianna looked at Asakusa's writhing arm. They *had* to get him the balm.

'What's important now is that we get Asakusa back to full strength, so we're ready for whatever the Nine want us to do.'

'Are you sure you're going to get to keep adventuring with us?'

'The Nine are more powerful than my family. That's one of the reasons I was sent here as a kid. If we're on a mission for them, maybe my mother and sisters will finally show me some respect.'

'And were you going to elaborate on the significance of the yellow skull?' Ebbo said.

'And risk one of you ruining our first monologue from one of the Nine? Definitely not,' Adrianna said, and grinned. She hoped it looked genuine.

These days the nine most powerful people—well, nine most powerful figureheads and their associates, really—lived in the nine mansions carved into the inside of the Ringwall. It was these nine, rather, The Nine, who maintained the free city with their own fortunes. Some of them built magical tools for the defenseless, others exacted vengeance on those without the strength to avenge themselves. One grew the seven sacred crops that kept the city fed. Others (most of the others) did less respectable things. Weapons thief. Potions mogul. The VanChamps.

There was even a renowned assassin who called one of the nine mansions in the Ringwall home. It was said he kept his place in the Ringwall by brutally murdering anyone who so much as implied he didn't deserve it. His name was Vecnos. He was an islander and kind of Ebbo's hero. Adrianna hoped that if they met him, Ebbo would be able to keep his cool.

Honestly, she was a bit concerned about her team embarrassing her. Ebbo might very well try to rob one of them, Clayton took offense at anyone who hadn't heard of him, and Asakusa—well, thralls were never popular to begin with, and this Corruption was especially far along, not to mention hard on the eyes.

The maggots wiggled about constantly, probing at Asakusa as well as anything they touched. Sometimes one would fall away and evaporate into black smoke, but always another would be underneath to replace it. Adrianna tried not to let the severity of the Corruption bother her. But it was hard. After all, it was her fault Asakusa had let it progress so far. She owed it to her friend to heal him.

Hopefully Krouche would be as intrigued by the yellow skull as Adrianna anticipated, and one of the Nine would give them enough of an advance to pay Seltrayis to keep Asakusa in his mortal form a bit longer.

Chapter 23

Adrianna

'Well, if it isn't my favorite little spider princess and her shits-for-brains lackeys!'

'Hi, Krouche, nice to see you too.' Adrianna said. It really wasn't. Despite S'kar-Vozi being a place of true multi-species diversity, Krouche le Douche pushed the limits of what most could comfortably accept. Even to Adrianna, he was a bit much.

Krouche had pitch-black eyes, purple skin, a barbed tail so fat it resembled a prized salami, and two horns, though one was broken and had been for years. Basically, he looked like a bloated purple demon with a creeper's goatee, a greasy ponytail, way too many tattoos that had been washed out by the sun, and a habit of wearing vests that hid none of these details.

Not wanting to cause a panic, Adrianna had stuffed the yellow skull in a bag and endured waiting in line for the bounty broker's presence. Krouche's tiny office was jam-packed with mercs, both notables like Hilde Hoffbrau—the mustachioed, axe-wielding dwarven woman of death—as well as hopefuls like Rollo, the head halfling from the Sober Six, a group of adventurers who'd sworn to find a cure for the addiction to magick so many halflings suffered from. They had a pretty high turnover.

'We're not shit-for-brains!' Clayton said.

'Yeah, apologies, ya gods-damned golem, whatever was a I thinking? I should've said the spider princess and her *two* shits-for-brain lackeys, plus her walking pleasure peer!' Krouche threw back his head and laughed, causing his massive, tattooed gut to ripple.

Clayton sighed. As he'd famously gained consciousness in a brothel, he couldn't exactly deny the label. Plus, there was no point in arguing with Krouche unless one was intent on testing the limits of vulgarity. The team had long ago decided that only Adrianna was to speak to him. Of course, getting them to actually stop talking was much more difficult than getting them to agree to the concept.

'As much as we'd love to banter,'–Adrianna's tone said she'd love anything but—'We're here because we need you to get a message to the Nine.'

'Oh, well, suck my infected cold sores, the spider princess comes back and thinks she's a queen? Where's the husband, by the way? You eat him already? I figured he'd give you heart*burn*!' Krouche laughed, a horrible sound to begin with that had only been made worse from years of smoking mellow leaf, as well as pretty much anything else that would burn.

As planned, Clayton and Asakusa crowded in to block the rest of the mercs from seeing. Ebbo took watch. Already his toes were tapping frantic messages to Adrianna over the silk thread she'd given him.

'Is this some sort of an ultimatum?' Krouche said, though he didn't look at all threatened, only amused.

Adrianna pulled the yellow skull out of her bag, and put it on the table between her and le Douche.

'Actually, I was hoping to make an impression.'

Adrianna had never seen Krouche surprised before.

And he wasn't the only one.

'Rollo and Hilde saw the skull,' Ebbo tapped. 'They look like someone just picked all their gooseberries, and it's totally unfair that they knew what a yellow skull means and you still haven't told me.'

Meanwhile, Krouche mumbled an unintelligible string of obscenities focused on either pleasuring or punishing his various body parts, but finally settled on, 'Finger my holes, are you trying to cause a fucking panic? Where did you get that?'

'Near Krag's Doom. It's from a mermaid.'

'No shit?'

'No shit. And we both know what that means.'

'Sweetie, you have no fucking idea what you just got yourself into, but yeah, yeah, I see the implications of a damn mermaid. I gotta say... this is... well, good on you for finding one and killing it, *Princess.*'

'Are you going to send a parrot or what?'

'I'm sending one, I'm sending one. Don't get your little silk panties in a bunch. In fact, the littlest one of the Nine told me to keep an eye out for exactly this sort of thing. How do those work when you transform, by the way? They like, stretchy or something?'

'Just send the parrot.'

Krouche scowled, but he turned from his desk and went through the single door.

That earned a huge groan from the rest of the assembled mercenaries, bounty hunters and treasure seekers. When Krouche went to his roof to send a parrot, he could be gone for a while, despite the ever-present crowd in his tiny office.

'For the sake of sea, what did you show him?' said a fishman with mucous smeared over his gills so he could breathe. One of the Selkie Brothers? Based on his trident, he certainly looked important.

'It's her business,' Hilde said, nodding once at Adrianna.

Adrianna felt a tug at the silk thread connecting her to Ebbo.

'Black bird,' the islander messaged her. Before she could think what that meant, Krouche's door swung open. Apparently, he'd decided to finish his cigar of mellow leaf behind his desk. Hopefully that meant the yellow skull was as urgent as Adrianna believed it to be. The Selkie brother immediately started coughing and hurried out of the room. Everyone else took a step forward. No one saved spots in Krouche le Douche's office.

'It's sent. I would tell you about some shit I got that's more your level, but it looks like you might've just graduated to the kill-it-or-get-killed league. Soon you'll be scowling like Hilde-fucking-Hoffbrau. Lucky you.'

Hilde Hoffbrau nodded; her scowl didn't falter for a moment.

'When do we go to the Ringwall? Now?' Adrianna stuffed the skull back in her bag.

'One of the Nine will be in touch. In the meantime, looks like you got some unfinished business to attend to.' Krouche nodded at Asakusa's Corruption. 'Be careful with them Gatekeepers, kid. How you think ol' Krouche ended up so fucking fat and purple? I sold my soul and got sold out.'

His hacking laughter followed them out into the street.

Chapter 24

Ebbo

Only one road stayed unchanged through the constant iterations of the free city, so naturally, most people used it.

The Spine—cobbled in flecks of gems and the scraps of the imported multicolored stone that made up the facades of the homes of the very rich— snaked up through the free city of S'kar-Vozi. Higher and higher the road went, up from the tourist district that pushed up against Bog's Bay, through the warehouses that supplied the market, then through a barrio that seemed to be growing less poor and less diverse with each passing day. Higher and higher the Spine of the city rose, past the well-guarded front steps of counting houses, past specialty shops with ambiguously intimidating signs that didn't rely on tourist eyes, past the homes of merchants who'd gambled well in decades past. Up and up and up the Spine went, snaking through an ever-growing city until it reached its end.

Ebbo wondered if this day would end with them drinking tea at the top of it, in the Ringwall itself. He certainly hoped so. Their current conversational partner, Seltrayis—the witch who made the balms that cured Asakusa—kept glaring at him from underneath layers of black rags like she thought he might bite her. Her hair was like dirty straw, her eyes milky, her nose abundant with warts. In other words, she was the real deal. A bona-fide witch. Though Ebbo was quite certain she was magick, he definitely did *not* want to lick her.

'There's nothing I can do for *that.*' Seltrayis pointed at Asakusa's Corruption.

'It's never been a problem before,' Asakusa said.

'Yeah well, apparently *that* Corruption is popular. What'd you do to get the maggots? I thought you said Tulk liked you.'

'He crashed the Spider Princess's wedding,' Ebbo said, pointing a thumb at Asakusa.

Asakusa flushed crimson before saying, 'It's not as severe as the scales were. Give me some of the cream you did for that. I'll be fine.'

Seltrayis shrugged and started digging around in one of her bags. She had a little cart she pushed around with a black cauldron on the top, which she used to brew her potions. Though she was currently using it to brew some sort of fish and shrimp stew. Not an unusual choice of meats for the denizens of S'kar-Vozi, the only choice in fact, but there was a bitter fruit mixed in that the witch called olives, as well as tomato sauce, not a cheap fruit in the free city, as it had to be imported. It smelled quite horrible. Seltrayis had already tried to sell them all a bowl. Ebbo had declined, despite the exotic, expensive ingredients.

She must be good if she can afford to waste imported stuff like this in a nasty soup, he thought.

The only things that grew in the farmland that the druid Magnus managed outside the Ringwall were corn, barley, taters, lush apples, carrots, snabbage, and nonions.

Seltrayis proffered a jar of cream. 'You can have this—consider it a gift for your loyal patronage—but it won't work for the maggots. The scales are made with a fairly common form of demonic energy. These maggots are necrotic.'

'You mean undead?' Clayton said.

Seltrayis nodded. 'Exactly. And the only thing that works to heal necrotic energies is skull blossom.'

'Skull blossom? But that's hardly magick at all. I know guys that cut proper magick herbs with that,' Ebbo said.

'Well, talk to them, then. If they have it this time of year I'll take some too. I was just, uh… cleaned out, as it were,' Seltrayis said, and crossed her arms in a huff.

'Cleaned out? But Seltrayis, you *always* have something for me… I mean, I *started* your business,' Asakusa said. Ugh, Ebbo shuddered. He sounded so pathetic when he was trying to be nice.

'I know, believe me. And I didn't want to, but—well, I couldn't refuse.'

'But how can skull blossom heal if it's not magick?' Adrianna said.

Seltrayis snorted. 'I don't deal in magick. You know what it's like to try to channel a divinity in this town? Between the Ourder of Ouroboros and the Cthult of Cthulu, it's not too wise to talk about anything supernatural that's not a snake or an octopus.'

'Well, what if we went to one of their priests?' Clayton said. 'Members of both congregations frequent the Red Underoo. I'm sure the ladies wouldn't mind alerting me next time one comes by for their services. Clergy are fun to blackmail.'

'It won't work. Part of my contract stipulates that I can't seek holy healing. Not even for regular stuff. If I try it, it'll just accelerate the Corruption,' Asakusa said.

'There has to be something we can do,' Adrianna said.

'Not until autumn,' said a quiet voice from behind. Though barely a whisper, the voice sent shivers to Ebbo's very core. 'Skull blossom doesn't grow anywhere around here. Too hot.'

Ebbo turned around, and despite his sharp islander's eyes, at first he saw only the shadowed alley behind them.

'Who's there?' Asakusa said.

'The man that bought me out. If you'll excuse me,' Seltrayis said, and then pushed her cart away.

'Well where does it grow?' Clayton said. His senses didn't work like the others did. He could probably smell the diminutive figure stepping toward them.

Whoever the person was, he was obviously an islander, for he was hardly a pace high, shorter even than Ebbo. His feet were bare, and his hands rested on twin daggers at his belt. His cloak was the black of deepest shadow, and a hood covered his face. All that Ebbo could see was a mess of dark curly hair, a scowl, and the cutest little button nose he'd ever seen.

It can't be... Ebbo thought, but he took a deep breath, tried to look cool, and said, 'Any islander can tell you that.' Then he stood straighter and sang a poem.

> *'On fallen friends, place a stone,*
> *While they rest skull blossom grows,*
> *Keep it clean, and keep it clear,*
> *Black and white blooms you'll see each year'*

Halfway through the poem, the cloaked figure joined him in song. Though his voice was good and pure as only an islander's could be, he sang in a discordant pitch that chilled Ebbo.

'You... you're Vecnos!' Adrianna said. She sounded about as giddy as Ebbo felt. Or terrified? Ebbo couldn't be sure, he just knew that his stomach was flipping back and forth.

'Astute deduction. And you must be the spider princess and her bumbling henchmen that Krouche told me about.'

'They're not my henchmen,' Adrianna said.

Vecnos clenched his tiny little jaw. 'If you're not henchmen, then what do you prefer to be called?'

'Uh...' Clayton scratched his head.

'Her... friends?' Ebbo said.

'Fine! Fine. Princess, silence your bumbling *friends*, now is the part where you listen.'

Adrianna glanced at them. Ebbo shrugged. He'd been called worse by people far less important than Vecnos. Asakusa looked pissed, and Clayton looked annoyed, but they both nodded at Adrianna.

'Do you want to see the skull?' she said.

Vecnos shook his head. 'I've seen more than I care to. When this is all done, if you're capable, you will have as well.'

'I, uh... I completed the marriage to Richard Valkanna. He's allied with my sisters... I think. They might attack S'kar-Vozi at any minute! I was hoping the skull would get your attention so I could tell the Nine in the Ringwall, I mean, you-'

'Did you not hear me when I said it was the part where you listen?'

Adrianna flinched at his words. Ebbo was awed. Adrianna was easily the greatest fighter he'd ever seen, like *ever*. If she feared the Valkannas and her family, that *meant* something. And Vecnos didn't even want to hear about the hilariously disastrous wedding? Ebbo couldn't decide if that made Vecnos extremely cool or extremely rude.

'I just thought... I mean, two bloodlines united against the mortals. A wedding eight generations in the making. Um... spider dragons?' Adrianna was floundering.

'I have... agents at Krag's Doom. The castle is hardly holding together, and the spider queen can be... persuasive. We're not in any more danger now than we were before your little ceremony. Have you been in touch with Valkanna?'

'What? No!'

Vecnos nodded at that. Ebbo thought the assassin knew something but wasn't saying.

'The Ringwall and the cliffs of Bog's Bay will keep us safe,' Vecnos said.

Ebbo looked up the slanted city to the structure that sat at the top. Vecno's berry-picking *house!*

Vecnos was the first islander to ever claim one of the Ringwall's nine mansions as their home. And now he needed Ebbo's help! Well, Adrianna's probably, and Clayton would certainly lend a hand, and as much as Ebbo liked to complain about Asakusa, he *was* useful in a fight… but if anything needed stealing for some reason, Ebbo was his man!

'As much as I love a good soap drama, I'm a bit more concerned about the horde of undead growing larger as we speak,' the tiny assassin said.

Ebbo, Clayton, and Asakusa's response was much the same. Sputtering, curses, shock and dismay.

'Prickling raspberries, you can't be serious!' Was the closest thing to reason anyone managed.

'Watch your language,' Vecnos snapped at Ebbo.

'A horde? You must be joking. Please be joking?' Adrianna said. 'I just saw the one skeleton. She hadn't even killed her friends yet. We *saved* them!'

'I don't 'joke.' But you're correct. Perhaps I… overstated the facts for dramatic effect. We're simply not sure. Every team we've sent to the Blighted Island hasn't returned.'

'The Blighted Island?' Ebbo said. 'You want us to go the Blighted Island? But… but, it's blighted!'

The scowl Vecnos shot at Ebbo was so far beyond anything Adrianna had ever attempted, it was sort of impressive. But mostly terrifying. Meeting your hero was turning out to be a real mixed bag.

'Why us?' Adrianna said.

Vecnos held up a finger.

'Mostly because you're expendable.'

Another finger.

'Also, because if you do get killed by whatever you find there, it might bring the wrath of the Morticians and—if we're at all lucky—the Valkannas down upon whatever's hiding behind that fog.'

A third finger.

'But mostly because I *just* bought out the last of skull blossom in this market, your friend there is badly in need of it, and the only place it grows with any consistency is exactly where I'm sending you.'

Adrianna and Clayton looked shocked, but Asakusa gritted his teeth and glared at Vecnos. Ebbo had to admit that was kind of an impressive move for the thrall. Vecnos was as scary as he was intimidating, but Asakusa could glare with the best of them.

'But how did you know that we would need skull blossom?' Ebbo said. 'We only just found out!'

'I have ears everywhere, but *especially* in Krouche's office. As soon as I knew you had a yellow skull, I came to Seltrayis.'

'That doesn't explain the skull blossom,' Asakusa said.

'Don't be an idiot. Do you really think that you're the only thrall to face a necrotic Corruption? Your maggots aren't exactly hard to see.'

'But that means… if I had taken a Gate up here, she'd still have the flower,' Asakusa said through gritted teeth.

Vecnos smiled at that. 'I suppose so.'

Ebbo looked at Adrianna. Her eyes were so wide that her other four had fully opened. Poor thing, she would probably blame herself for Asakusa not getting healed fast enough. 'What do you want for the skull blossom? I… if you'll take spidercoin, my family can pay anything you ask…'

Adrianna really was worried about Asakusa. She *never* asked her family for money.

'I'm already one of the nine richest people in the richest city in the Archipelago. Money is meaningless to me. It's favors that I'm after, favors that I trade. For example, I just requested a favor of Fyelna—perhaps you've heard of her?—she's the renowned potions master of the Ringwall and one of my dear friends. Anyway, I asked her to prepare a salve of the skull blossom and send it by parrot to that ship.'

Vecnos stood on his tiptoes to point over the apartments and shops of S'kar-Vozi and all the way down to a ship docked in Bog's Bay. The layout and elevation of the city was such that one could almost always see Bog's Bay so long as one wasn't being robbed in an alley. The ship's banner was a daisy.

'It will leave the next time the bay flushes, which is…' Vecnos glanced up at the quick moon, the smaller of the two celestial bodies that orbited the planet ten times between sunrise and sunset. '…in about forty-five minutes. If you're not on it, the captain has orders to dump the contents of the vial overboard.'

Vecnos smiled.

'This is blackmail,' Asakusa said.

'Blackmail? No. Some would say extortion, but not me. This is exaction. As in, the four of you are about to do *exactly* what I want.'

'We could just walk away from all this,' Adrianna said shakily.

'And risk the thrall's life, any chance at future contacts with any of the Nine, and possibly the fate of the Archipelago? Come on. You're supposed to be the smart one, Adrianna. As I said, I now control all the skull blossom in this city. If you want any, well, I expect you to impress me.'

Vecnos tossed Ebbo a sack of coin and he caught it, preserving what coolness he still had. By the time the islander looked back up, the assassin had stepped back into the shadows of the alley and vanished completely.

'Mulberry milkshakes… he was cool!'

Chapter 25

Adrianna

'Prepare yeselves to disembark. The Kraken's nearly upon us.' The captain of the Daisy Duke was less formidable than his employer, even though he was twice the islander assassin's height. He had spent most of the voyage in stoic silence, but now—with a storm behind them and the ocean seething with hundreds of sea creatures possessed with a desire to destroy— he'd perked right up.

Adrianna found she had preferred him when he was quiet and unconcerned.

'The Kraken's not real!' Asakusa said, rubbing his chest with the last of the balm that Vecnos had sent to the ship. It was much to Adrianna's chagrin that his entire right arm was still Corrupted. Vecnos hadn't provided nearly enough to fully heal him.

'You can thank me crew for thinking such things, thrall,' the captain replied. 'The Kraken's been around for centuries, always hungry, always growing. Vecnos pays us to cull it so it don't get so big as to be able to destroy S'kar-Vozi. Has the bonus of keeping Ragnar's Cthult of Cthulu from getting too zealous as well.'

'How can we help?' Adrianna said, though in truth she didn't know if they could. Underwater fighting wasn't her forte, and Asakusa—despite having healed some of his Corruption—was still far from one hundred percent. But she was more willing than Asakusa, as she had known the Kraken to exist while he had thought it legend.

'You can do as our boss said, and figure out why we ain't ever seen any of you adventurers come back from the Blighted Island. Aye. Send 'em off, before we make contact!' the captain barked to a fish man with silver scales and a wooden oar that replaced his leg below the knee.

'You know, they say there's a tombstone castle out there? Built of the graves of all the elves and orcs that died there a *thousand years ago*.' The fishman took the tarp off a small boat that turned out to be shaped like a dolphin.

'That's stupid. No one's used a stone to mark a grave in the S'kar-Vozi in more than a hundred years,' Asakusa said, not taking his eyes off the storm behind them. Adrianna watched it too. Shark fins and shoals of flying fish broke the surface of the water; beyond them, growing closer by the second, was a great mass of tentacles and a snail shell larger than Adrianna had thought possible.

Adrianna wasn't so sure that the fishman was wrong about the Blighted Island. The part about the elves and orcs checked out—her grandwebmother had been involved in that war—but Adrianna had been taught that the island had been barren for the centuries since. 'Who would have built the thing?' she asked.

'Er... their *ghoooosts*,' said Silverscales with a wave of his webbed fingers.

When Adrianna only raised three eyebrows—she was in her spider form, no point in doing her hair to impress a bunch of crusty sailors when she could just intimidate the silk out of them—he jumped overboard with hardly a splash and made for the kraken. The water turned red and Adrianna feared the worst, but then the fishman popped up, the head of a massive tuna in his hand, before diving back under with a splash of his oar. Apparently, this crew really had faced the Kraken before.

'That's not what I hear,' said Patches as he loaded the dolphin-shaped boat with a waterskin.

Patches was a catman with both splotchy fur and a missing eye whose former socket he kept covered with a bandana, sporting a daisy to match their flag. He'd embroidered it himself and had finally convinced Adrianna to let him repair some tears and do some white webs out of her silk on the back of her leather armor.

'I hear there's a great beast made of the dead bones sleeping beneath the island. It's from a land of flame and hate, so hot that when it exhales, its breath makes the fog that shrouds the place. They say, one day he'll sneeze!' Patches laughed until he coughed, and he coughed until he spit up a hairball.

'Does that mean there's a volcano hidden out there?' Asakusa finally turned from the Kraken to stare into the approaching wall of fog. Adrianna felt like they were getting hemmed in, with the Kraken on one side and the hidden Blighted Island on the other, but Patches seemed unconcerned.

The catman pulled at his whiskers. 'Ya know, that sorta makes sense, but no. I was just making shit up.'

Patches took the hairball, aimed carefully—no easy task with one eye—

and threw it down the gullet of a shark that had come from the teeming waters that currently housed the hundreds of pieces of the Kraken's body. The shark snapped at it and promptly choked to death.

'I hear there's a skeleton ball, and the reason ain't mo adventurers ever returned is that they're all dancing!' That was Cook, the cook. He also played the accordion poorly. For most of the voyage Adrianna had thought it sounded out of tune, but now there was something to it that seemed to bolster her and the crew. A set of harmonies that got everyone working together, so those that dove into the sea to slaughter the closest pieces of the Kraken never seemed to get in the way of the crew on deck firing projectiles. 'Now, on the boat with ye!' Cook said.

'You're sure we can't help?' Adrianna said.

A massive tentacle came up from the water and smashed across the deck of the boat. Dozens of crabs poured off of the tentacle, then all went to tear the rigging of the ship as the rain began to beat down. It seemed the Kraken made its own weather.

Cook laughed. 'We've been doing this for years. Pity you won't be here tomorrow. Nothing tastes as good as me Kraken stew.'

Adrianna nodded. She supposed that she would respect the crew, for she too hated being underestimated. So, not really absolved of the guilt of ditching but not wanting to stay either, she scurried onto the Dolphin. It was much too small for her spider form, so she quickly tied up her hair into two thick, rowed braids. It wasn't perfect, so her legs were still hairy and her hands looked like spider fingers, but it would do.

Asakusa hopped into the boat, and then carefully swung his unliftable hammer in after him. His Corrupted arm easily caught it before it crashed through the bottom of the boat. There were advantages to the malady—demonic strength, for one.

'Maybe it's good the halfling and that dumb golem ditched us,' Asakusa grumbled. 'The four of us wouldn't have fit in this tiny boat.'

'Will you stop it? At least he explained his plan!'

Asakusa looked at Adrianna with hurt in his eyes. Spin him, even with a ship under attack by what some worshipped as a dark god, Asakusa had taken that to be about the wedding.

'Trying to steal more of the balm from *Vecnos* is not a plan!' Asakusa's maggots twitched as if they agreed. 'Neither is running away from this fight. I can beat that thing! *Byergen* can crack that snail shell.'

Adrianna thought that Asakusa might be right—the stone hammer was a formidable weapon—but there was no way of knowing how many Gates he would need to use to get away from the shoals of sea life attacking the crew. It was a relief that the maggots no longer covered his chest, but Adrianna still didn't want him to use any Gates until they'd secured a way to heal him completely.

'We're ready to go!' Adrianna yelled over the rising wind.

Another tentacle came up and crashed into the ship with enough force to crack the deck.

'We got a breach!' the captain yelled, his stoicism breaking into panic.

For a moment Adrianna reconsidered fighting this monster. True, Vecnos had not sent them to fight the Kraken—he hadn't even mentioned it—but if they managed to defeat an aquatic god *and* discover what lay behind the wall of fog that obscured the Blighted Island, well, who wouldn't be impressed with that?

But then the captain brought his axe down on the rope holding the Dolphin above the sea, and it plummeted down and splashed into the water. 'Vecnos ordered us to get you to the Blighted Island! We can't disappoint. We might miss our pickup, though!' An octopus as big as a man crawled onto his back. The captain attacked it with a pair of axes, screaming as he did, 'Die, ye brainless monster, so at least your kin won't be infected! Now paddle, paddle for ye lives!'

Adrianna found that at her feet were two pedals connected to paddles at the rear of the Dolphin.

Adrianna and Asakusa both furiously pumped the pedals, and the Dolphin lurched into motion.

Adrianna craned her neck to watch as the Kraken overwhelmed the ship. The bulk of the beast was a giant squid wrapped around an enormous snail. It threw more and more tentacles at the Daisy Duke, constricting the wooden vessel, squeezing it until it began to pop like an overripe banana. The snail portion of the Kraken simply weighted the ship down, pulling it deeper and deeper into the water while all the crabs and barracudas and sea jellies focused on consuming the crew, who—despite losing their ship—resisted being consumed. Adrianna sighted Patches at the top of the mast, in the crow's nest. He was yelling a message to a black parrot that he then threw into the winds of the storm. It vanished in the dark clouds, and Patches went back to hurling hairballs.

'I can feel a Gate that will get me back on the ship. My hammer can crack that snail's shell.'

'No,' Adrianna said. 'You still aren't healed, and we both know the Gates shift. You might not be able to make it back to me.'

Asakusa looked at her, eyebrows raised so far as to vanish into his long and messy dark hair, but he didn't say anything.

'We have to get you the skull blossom, and they said they've been fighting this thing for years.'

'Doesn't mean they won't lose,' Asakusa said, but he obeyed. Other than crashing her wedding, Asakusa had always respected her orders. And—if she was being honest—she hadn't exactly ordered him to stay away from her wedding.

In moments, the sounds of the battle with Kraken were lost in the fog. With a pitiful and painfully awkward *fap-fap-fap* the Dolphin proceeded toward the Blighted Island.

Chapter 26

Asakusa

They went as straight as they could in the gloom, as the captain had told them to, and before long found themselves on a white beach framed by hills covered in dead trees. Even here, hidden in fog and out at sea, Asakusa could feel when they passed where he could open a Gate. The geography of the Ways of the Dead was always shifting—as that realm rotated differently than the one the Archipelago sat upon on—and yet Asakusa knew that he couldn't open any of them. He could afford the flesh—he wasn't particularly concerned about that—but he didn't want to make Adrianna worry.

Asakusa got out of the boat and reached for his hammer. To lift it, he had to swing it and smash it into the beach. It crashed to shore, sending bits of whitish stone everywhere. 'So you really think that Ebbo stealing from Vecnos will actually *impress* him?'

'Vecnos said that he had bought up all the skull blossom in S'kar-Vozi,' Adrianna said with a sigh. One of her spider legs tapped. Asakusa had been adventuring with Adrianna a long time, and he recognized the gesture for what it was: poorly hidden annoyance. Her rowed braid had come loose but not completely undone, so she now had six appendages instead of two. 'Maybe there's something poetic to Ebbo stealing from him. I mean, Vecnos *is* an assassin. He probably earned his place in the Ring through subterfuge. He might respect someone being able to out-thieve him.'

Despite growing up in S'kar-Vozi, Asakusa didn't really know how Vecnos had come to be one of the Nine. No one did. The islander assassin fiercely guarded his past.

'At least Clayton can contact us with the scrying orb if Ebbo ends up forgetting his half-baked plan and snorting more magick,' Asakusa said.

'Ebbo *cares* about you, Asa, we all do. Clayton will call us for a rescue long before he calls about Ebbo doing any magick.'

'Whatever,' Asakusa grumbled, which was his way of saying that he knew Adrianna was right and that he'd respect her decision-making as the team's chosen leader.

At least Adrianna had left Clayton and Ebbo with a scrying stone. Clayton would *try* to keep Ebbo from doing magick, and the party could still contact each other through Adrianna's mirror and the pricey, rented stone for emergencies. Something about the oddly shaped stones at Asakusa's feet made him think that soon they'd be in an emergency.

Adrianna stepped to shore and attached a thread of silk to the boat, so if the tide came in, it wouldn't get washed away. She walked up the beach, looking for a rock large enough to tether the boat to with her strand of silk. There weren't any. The largest rocks weren't any bigger than Asakusa's head. Most of them were so riddled with holes as to be hollow. Their color was the off-white of bone.

'Are these skulls?' Asakusa said, picking up one of the larger pieces with his Corrupted hand.

Adrianna knelt down and picked up another piece. She nodded. 'It's definitely a skull, or a broken one, anyway. Orc, if my phrenology is right.'

Asakusa dropped the piece of bone and shuddered. He knew she was right. He'd met her when she was still in dark princess school or whatever, and had helped her cram for a test on the skulls of what he knew her mother had raised her to call the 'mortal races.'

'That's weird. A band of orcs hasn't come through the Archipelago in decades, and I'm sure they wouldn't have stopped here to raid. This skull is probably ancient.' Then, in a cheerful tone that belied her upbringing as a dark princess: 'Oh, look, this one's elven.' She picked up another broken skull. It was nearly half the size, and thinner than the orc skull, with high cheekbones. 'And look, dwarf.' Adrianna tossed Asakusa a jaw bone with huge molars, many of them replaced with silver.

He didn't catch it.

'What happened here?' Asakusa said.

'A war.'

'Wars happen all the time in the Archipelago.'

'Not like this one. This one had weapons powerful enough to enslave their makers and damage the blood and the minds of their enemies. The Blighted Island has been like this since before my webmother's time, and she's nearly six hundred and sixty-six. I guess the Lich might know the finer details, but I never asked him. Come on.'

'We're just supposed to go in there and destroy a bunch of yellow skeletons?' Asakusa said, standing amidst this beach of bone. He didn't know how Adrianna could sound so calm at the idea of facing a skeletal horde.

'These skulls are broken… if the Lich was right, they shouldn't be able to animate. Vecnos wants information. We find out what we can, get any flowers we see, and go,' Adrianna said.

Asakusa nodded. He didn't want Adrianna to see how scared he was.

Up the beach they trudged, their feet leaving imprints in sand made of bone. Asakusa's hammer dragged behind them, creating a trench in the scree of the dead. Adrianna tied off the strand of silk connected to the Dolphin to a massive, dead tree. Asakusa hoped that it would still be standing when they came back. He tried not think the word 'if.'

Chapter 27

Asakusa

After not much of a walk past not many trees, the fog give way, though it didn't quell Asakusa's nerves. He never expected to see what lay in the heart of this rotten land, not in a hundred years. In the place of dead trees there were rows and rows of fruiting orchards. There were trees with blue-gray leaves and branches laden with black olives like the witch Seltrayis had put in her stew. Grapes vines wet with dew sparkled in the setting sun. There were vegetables, too: tomatoes, cucumbers, peppers, even rows of halfling leaf. All of it grew from thick black soil.

'It's like what Magnus's gardens must look like,' Asakusa murmured, having grown up dreaming of the powerful druid's edible forests that he grew on the far side of the Ringwall and fed S'kar-Vozi with.

'It's gotta be some kind of illusion. The witch said there was a graveyard here. Where are the tombstones?' Adrianna plucked an orange from a tree and pricked it with some of her venom. It slowly began to turn to mush, like a week's worth of rot compressed into a moment. Asakusa tried not to grin. Still, after all these years, Adrianna was just too cool.

'Illusions don't respond to venom, right?' Asakusa said.

Adrianna shook her head. 'This is real.'

That was almost too much for Asakusa to believe. Some sort of Supreme Sorcerer creating a deadly illusion to distract meddlers, he could at least pretend to understand, but an actual orchard here? How was that even possible?

'I thought we were going to be fighting a bunch of skeletons,' Asakusa said and flexed his Corrupted arm. He preferred brawls to mysteries.

'Someone has to be growing all this... Vecnos must want us to figure out who.'

'Can't we just find the skull blossom and get back to town? As far as we know, we've already survived longer than any other team of adventurers,'

Asakusa said.

'This could be revolutionary for S'kar-Vozi.' Adrianna tugged the lock of hair that had been hanging in her face back into place, and a finger Folded back into its human form. 'Magnus is always going on about recruiting more druids to farm. With this place, maybe he would be able to grow more food without them. We should bring some back some of the soil. I'm sure Vecnos will want to show it to Magnus.'

Asakusa ran his hands through the rich loam and shrugged. 'You think that will be enough to please the little halfling?'

'They really don't like it when you call them that.'

'What? There's not even any here.'

'Yeah, well. No one likes a label.'

Asakusa furrowed his brow and crossed his arms. The leather sleeve of his left arm and the writhing maggots of his right made for quite the contrast. 'You don't snap at Ebbo when he calls me thrall.' He couldn't believe that they had just walked across a beach of broken skulls and found a secret orchard with unseen gardeners, and Adrianna was still defending the little addict.

'Fair point. I can stand up to Ebbo for you, if you'd like.'

Asakusa glared at her. 'No. That's not what I meant.'

'I know what you meant,' Adrianna said, and Asakusa felt his heart plummet into his stomach. She continued. 'And no, I have no idea what Vecnos expects from us. He seemed way more intent on making us know he was in control than actually giving concrete details for the mission, but that's typical for both assassins and the extremely rich and powerful.'

'You sound like you're speaking from experience.'

'I *am*. Spider princess, remember? My nanny was an assassin, and I just married one of the rich and powerful.'

Asakusa tried to keep his face impassive at the mention of Adrianna's new husband, but he could tell by her expression that he'd failed at that.

'I'm just saying I know enough of these types to understand how they work,' Adrianna said. 'What we need to do is find out as much as we can before we find the skull blossom, and then get out of here. We'll tell Vecnos everything we know, and if it's not enough, we'll hope the strings of the web twitch and he makes us come back once you're at full strength and Ebbo and Clayton didn't, uh… ditch us.'

Asakusa nodded. Much as he liked to insult the halfling, he knew Ebbo had his strengths, sneaking around creepy places being high on the list.

The pair walked further into the field. They soon saw past the orchards to a magnificent palace built just at the edge of the fog. Its bottom floor was covered in thick vines. Some of its towers were still under construction, but the others were topped with weeping winged elves and nine-pointed stars, ancient funerary symbols.

'I think this *is* the graveyard. That's a gravestone, right?' Asakusa said, pointing to a rectangle of stone with words etched upon it. Empty rectangles of black earth were all around it. He'd never seen a gravestone before, and yet seeing just that *one*, all by itself, wasn't exactly comforting. A pit was forming in his stomach. Two pits, really—one from always saying the wrong damned thing to Adrianna, and one from the amount of death that seemed to be around them. Asakusa had seen thousands of souls trudge through the Ways of the Dead. He didn't like to be reminded that their corpses had all been left behind to rot in the material realm.

'Some are missing,' Adrianna said, kneeling behind the empty square of black earth. Pale vines with tiny leaves covered the single tombstone. 'This must be skull blossom! How much do we need, exactly? Assuming that we'll need to have your witch or Fyelna make you a balm,' Adrianna said, examining the skull blossom for buds. They wouldn't be able to harvest until dark, of course.

Asakusa grimaced. He was wondering if Vecnos had been lying about having more of the balm. It was just that he'd sent so little. 'We'll need a lot more than what's there.'

'Which means we'll have to keep exploring.'

Asakusa nodded and tried to look like he gave zero shits about walking ever deeper into a massive graveyard with missing gravestones.

They approached the black castle, trying to make out details on the pockmarked and scuffed stone quarried eons ago from somewhere in the Archipelago. Though the rock was familiar, the castle was ominous and haphazard in a way that made Adrianna—the heir to a line of architects— profoundly uneasy. Asakusa could tell because she kept looking at the castle and fidgeting with a thread of silk in her hands. She only did that when trying to figure out the architecture of somewhere that she wanted to break into. Stones cut of different, seemingly random sizes made up the castle's towers and supported the sculpted funerary figures. Noble-looking elves with their ears broken off, rough-hewn orcs that probably looked that way to begin with, dwarves carved with such precision that as they weathered, their beards stayed clear of the forces of nature, so they still looked magnificent despite being made ages ago. But as they drew closer, it was the bricks themselves that drew Asakusa's eye, not the decorations atop them. There were thousands of bricks making up the castle, tens of thousands. Each was a different shade of black, as if each represented a life snuffed out from a different corner of the Archipelago. Some bricks were rough and bare save a single, ragged rune, others had flowing script alive with moss and lichen, and still others were worked with friezes that must have once been magnificent.

'They're all gravestones,' Asakusa said, stopping. He'd never seen one before, and now there were thousands jammed together into a castle. Asakusa doubled down on his own beliefs. Dead bodies should be burned or thrown out to sea. This business with the gravestones lent itself to schemes that were way too creepy.

Adrianna nodded. 'They used them as bricks.' It seemed she'd already figured that out, but of course she had. She was their leader for a reason.

'But that's... that pirate was *right?*' Asakusa felt mixed feelings of terror and disbelief. 'Who would want to live somewhere so creepy?'

'There's only one way to find out,' Adrianna said, raising her hand to strike the heavy wooden door. It was clearly made of the dead trees they'd walked through. The wood was warped and twisted, and Asakusa could make out haunted faces in the grain, though he told himself that his eyes were just playing tricks on him.

'Are you crazy?' Asakusa said and made to stop her, but he was too late.

Adrianna was already laughing.

'You really thought I was going to knock on the door to a gravestone castle, just before we steal a bunch of flowers?'

Asakusa snorted and managed a smile. The Corruption maggots stopped flailing so desperately.

'No, I know you wouldn't. I just thought you'd want to go in there for Vecnos.'

'I'd do it for you,' Adrianna said.

Asakusa looked at her with a thousand questions in his eyes.

'But there's no need,' Adrianna quickly continued, ignoring the questions Asakusa should have asked. 'It's like Ebbo's poem. The skull blossom must be using all these decomposed mortals for fertilizer, and their gravestones as a trellis to climb.'

Asakusa nodded, trying not to look half as nervous as he felt. Sometimes Adrianna forgot he was just a human. The idea that all the dirt was decayed people—or decomposed mortals, as the spider princess called them—really freaked him out. He tried not to think too much about the fact that if this much skull blossom was growing, it meant the castle had been here for quite some time. But then, the orchard hadn't grown overnight either.

'So, you think Vecnos will be cool with us just coming to the castle door and *not* going in?' he said.

Adrianna shook her head. 'He gave us *no* information other than the fact that no one else has returned from here. For all we know, they all knocked on the door. I say we wait until dark, harvest the skull blossom, then head back. We can tell Vecnos exactly what we saw, and *he* can plan out how to infiltrate a tombstone castle.'

Asakusa shuddered at the thought of such a structure. 'I thought you wanted to impress him.'

'We'll set the bar by coming back alive. Besides. We must wait until dark for the flowers to open. Who is to say a horde of yellow, skeletal banshees won't come screaming out of the mist before then?' Adrianna had probably meant that as a joke, but Asakusa did *not* think it was funny.

'So, nothing to do but wait to join the horde.' Asakusa grimaced.

So they waited.

Chapter 28

Adrianna

The perfect red disc of the sun sank into the fog, illuminating it in rich oranges and purples until a gnarled tree seemed to grab at it, breaking the moment into splinters. Adrianna had been enjoying the silence in the patch of green hidden in fog, but Asakusa couldn't babbling.

'So, the uh… did you know the Lich growing up or something?' Asakusa said.

'I took lessons in Arcana with him. For an undead sorcerer, he's really not that bad,' Adrianna sighed. She already knew where this was going.

'Undead sorcerer, huh? So, that's why the ceremony was like that? All creepy and stuff, with the shrieking, and the dancing shadows?'

Asakusa really was amazing. He could uppercut a giant five times his size before charging through the Ways of the Dead to smash the back of the same giant's head, but talking about anything besides battle plans with Adrianna totally confounded him. For a time, she had thought it cute, but now, with the wedding completed, it seemed far less endearing.

'My mom had been planning that wedding for six hundred years, and her mom had planned it for like another century before her. Really, my family has been planning it for seven generations, which sounds like a lot, and when you consider that some of my ancestors didn't give birth to their seventh daughter until they were already centuries old, it's longer still.

'So yeah, the ceremony needed to be updated a little bit, but the Lich only speaks dead languages and tortured tongues, so sorry you didn't like it. I didn't really care for it either, to be honest, but it was that or let my family spend the rest of eternity catching the hapless mortals who wandered into their caves to kill them—so, you know, a girl's gotta do what a girl's gotta do.'

'Sorry.' Ah, the petulance of a grumpy Asakusa was a special thing. 'But I thought you hated your sisters.'

'I *do* hate my sisters, but I'd rather they crash into a volcano because of a castle they failed to repair than rot in the dark. Plus, they take care of my mom. Not everyone sees the world like you do, you know. Not everyone is good or bad. We all have our flaws.'

'Tell me about it,' Asakusa said, watching the maggots on his Corrupted arm wriggle in the fading light. Even after the balm, the Corruption was serious. Adrianna kept hoping that once the sun set, they'd harvest the skull blossom, book it out of here, tell Vecnos about the lack of skeletons—the horde must be somewhere else in the Archipelago—maybe earn some brownie points for the discovery of the garden—then get Asakusa healed and everything would go back to normal.

Except it couldn't. Not ever again. Adrianna couldn't go back to her dreams of being a hero to S'kar-Vozi. Etterqueen, just thinking it sounded so petty. She had thought she could spend her youth saving islanders from trolls and slaying pumpkin-beasts, that she'd get married at the same age her mom did, when she was centuries old, but nope! Krag's Doom couldn't wait, so now Adrianna knew that healing Asakusa and reporting back to Vecnos might very well be the last thing she ever did before either her new husband or her sisters came to retrieve her and make her be the queen she was trained to be.

'Do you ever wish you were a different person?' Adrianna said.

Asakusa cocked his head. 'What? No. I mean, yes, I do, like *aaaall* the time. But you're Adrianna Morticia. You're a freaking badass spider princess!'

'Oh, come on. I'm a freak if I don't tie my hair up, and being who I am comes with a lot of…'

'Baggage?' Asakusa managed an awkward half-grin. He really was weird. Mid-battle he could throw one-liners with the best of them, but in regular conversation, he seemed to forget how to control his face much of the time.

'I was going to say silk purses, but yes, baggage.' Adrianna fidgeted with her hair. As they'd walked, a few strands had come loose. She could feel the thick black hairs on her shins poking at her leathers.

'You mean like being forced to marry a creep?'

'I wasn't *forced*, Asakusa! I spun the dress myself! I walked the path of cleansing!'

'But he *made you* open your palm!'

'I know!' Adrianna yelled. A parrot hidden in the mist took flight, screaming into the growing dusk. It called out in the voice of a soldier dead for millennia. 'For the Etterqueen's sake, I *remember* what he did! How could I forget?'

'But then how can you think of him as your husband, when you have, um... that is, uh,' Asakusa's maggots rippled. 'Someone like me, who, er...I would never do that to you!'

'I won't let him. He fooled me once. Do you really think I'll let that happen again? I have eight limbs and—thanks to him—a knife that absorbs fire. When we meet, if he so much as looks as me wrong, I'll be sure to show him their finer points.'

Asakusa nodded. 'You know that I—well I mean I'll always... I'll... never mind.' Asakusa looked away. It was so obvious that Asakusa still had feelings for her. He probably always would. Adrianna told herself she couldn't afford the same luxuries.

The sun finished sinking below the horizon and the skull blossom opened up—white petals and black spots made the name of the flower obvious. Adrianna used her daggers to sever some of the blossoms and tried to suppress a sigh. She liked Asakusa. There had been a time, a fairly long time in fact, when she more than liked him and would have loved his admission of feelings, awkward as it was, but that time had all but passed. Asakusa would always be special to her—he was the first person to ever respect a spider girl in S'kar-Vozi, after all—but she'd spent the last six months mentally preparing herself for her wedding, which meant trying to forget about the boy who didn't dare ask her out despite being brave enough to walk the Ways of the Dead. Even now, with her feelings the maelstrom of confusion that they were, she didn't want to tell Asakusa *too late, too bad*, because she didn't want to hurt his feelings.

Asakusa looked up, and then wiped his brow with his Corrupted maggots. 'Adrianna, look—' Asakusa began, his jaw working dumbly, searching for words.

But Adrianna had finally had enough. 'Isn't it enough that I'm here for you now instead of with him?'

'No, Adrianna—'

Better to let him know the truth, she thought. 'Honestly, I don't even care about the wedding. If you would have said something sooner—and I mean like months or *years* sooner—then I don't think we would even be in this situation. We're *friends*, Asakusa, really good friends. Maybe there was a time we could've been more, but that was like years ago! Sometimes I wish it wasn't, but...'

'Adrianna, turn around!'

She rolled her eyes and turned around to see an absolutely massive skeleton army.

Hundreds of skeletons rose from between the vegetables. Some of them reached out of the thick black loam with their hands, and then pulled their fleshless yellow bones up from the dirt. Another started as a ribcage hidden beneath an artichoke that began to glow with a yellow light, only to be joined by a skull, then arms, legs, hands and feet that pushed themselves up and out of the produce. Unlike the skulls on the beach, these were all yellow and unbroken. Adrianna and Asakusa must have stepped all over them just to get here. The skeletons, free of their defiled graves, reached for their weapons.

Scythes, dented swords, axes... and shovels?

'Some of them are grabbing rakes,' Adrianna said.

The skeletons began to farm. Some cut grain, others picked olives or grapes. Still others fetched broken-down carts to fill with tomatoes. There was an order to them that Adrianna had never seen on the dozens of halfling farms she'd visited mid-adventure. They didn't talk or sing, for one, yet the skeletons didn't labor in silence either. The clatter of bones echoed through the graveyard, an odd sound when paired with so much obviously living, ripe produce. It was immediately obvious to Adrianna that they were all serving the same purpose. These weren't ghosts, then, or some sort of undead cooperative, but the mindless husks of the reanimated. Whatever was controlling them seemed oblivious to Adrianna and Asakusa. The skeletons were only concerned with the efficiency of their chores, another trait a halfling farm didn't shared. Adrianna wondered if stepping back onto the soil would alert the skeletons. If it did, she very much doubted they'd be able to get past them.

Apparently, Asakusa was thinking the same thing. 'I can open a Gate and get us out of here,' he said, scratching at the palm of his right hand with his Corrupted fingers, feeling for the dagger-shaped key buried in his flesh.

'No, Asa, we can't risk it until we get you healed up. And besides, no one's noticed us yet,' she said, though she reached for her whip and dragon dagger.

'Ahem,' a low voice said from behind them. Adrianna and Asakusa whirled around to see that the doors to the castle had opened, and a man was standing there. He was big, bigger than Clayton even, with hulking shoulders, huge arms, and strangely thin legs. He wore a white tuxedo complete with bow-tie and cummerbund—an outfit Adrianna knew only the wealthiest of the Archipelago could afford. He held a yellow skull in his left hand that he stroked like a prized cat. But Adrianna noticed all of that as an afterthought.

What struck her was that the man had no skin.

'If you are done picking flowers, the Master of the Barony will see you now. That is, unless you wish to join our legion of groundskeepers,' the man said, gesturing toward the hundreds of skeletons—thousands?—who had returned to tending the farm. As he spoke, the muscles that worked his jaw flexed and clenched. He bowed low and said, 'While I am at your service, you may call me James,' as if he hadn't just threatened to strip their flesh, steal their bones—Asakusa's anyway, Adrianna didn't quite have bones—and force them into an eternity of servitude.

'James, a pleasure,' Adrianna said. She was a spider princess, after all. She had gone to school with necromancers powerful enough to create flesh golems like this, though none of them had ever made their creations talk, nor dressed them so daringly.

'What in the Ways of the Dead is this place?' Asakusa said, grabbing *Byergen*, the stone hammer, and readying it for his favorite first strike: an uppercut.

'The Baron will be more than willing to answer. Now, come with me.'

'And if we don't?' Asakusa said. He was shaking, the Corruption maggots mirroring the effect and making him appear all the more frightened.

James straightened his already perfect posture and looked out at the field of skeletons working on the farm. They too straightened their spines and turned their shovels and axes to the spider princess and the Gatekeeper's thrall standing on the steps of the tombstone castle.

'Then you will be destroyed, and your corpses will labor until Chemok returns and all living things cease to draw breath.'

It was a pretty compelling argument.

Adrianna and Asakusa went into the tombstone castle.

Chapter 29

Adrianna

Adrianna had attended many balls and galas for the dark races that lived in the free city, but what she found hidden in the middle of this orchard on the Blighted Island put them all to shame. The inside of the tombstone castle was even more bizarre than the outside, for here, amongst tables made of caskets and garlands of dead flowers, skeletons wearing jewels and fabrics yellowed with age waltzed to the haunting, out-of-tune music performed by a quartet of zombies playing instruments so old that Adrianna had trouble identifying them. The skeletons didn't seem to notice the new, decidedly alive guests. They kept dancing, smiling their lipless smiles.

'The Baron is just waking. You will join him in the dining room for breakfast. If you are not yet hungry, the Baron told me that you can dance until you hunger, though most of the dancers have been at it for some time, and they have yet to stop for tapas.'

'Was that a joke?' Adrianna said.

James smiled. The change in his lips was almost imperceptible, the smile was so slight, but the ripple of activity across his skinless cheeks was hard to miss.

'We don't want to dance,' Asakusa said. Adrianna tried to ignore the skeletons—minions were minions—but Asakusa kept looking around the room with wide eyes.

'Perhaps later, James. At the moment, we'd like to honor our host by making his acquaintance.' Adrianna had learned more in school than how to hold a dagger. The dark races had a certain code of etiquette, and Adrianna thought it wise to extend that to whatever necromancer was at work here.

'I don't think we're the first to be invited to dance,' Asakusa whispered, pointing to a skeleton wearing a crushed velvet suit with a longsword made of coral tied to his back. 'That sword is named the *Coral-Crusher*. Seamus the Shark carved that himself. Always said they'd have to pry it from his cold, dead hands.'

'We'll be fine. Seamus the Shark stabbed anything that looked at him wrong. Just stay calm and let me handle this,' Adrianna whispered back, wishing—not for the first time—that Asakusa would learn how to communicate by silk thread like she, Ebbo and Clayton could.

'Easy for you to say... you don't exactly have a skeleton.'

They followed James out of the room, though Adrianna would be lying if she wasn't a little bit intrigued about dancing. She hated the formality of it, that was one of the reasons she left home to become an adventurer, but she had seen the Lich dance at countless family functions—she'd even trod upon his boots when she was but a young spiderling—and these skeletons were far more handsome than him. Their bones were a well-polished yellow; they had no tight, leathery flesh like the Lich did.

James led them to a door at the end of the ballroom, knocked three times —leaving bloody marks upon the door as he did—and then pushed the doors open.

Inside was a long table set with golden trays, jeweled goblets, fine silverware, and platters upon platters of food.

'The Baron will join you shortly. The servants will see to your every desire. If you need anything at all, don't be afraid to scream.'

Indeed, skeletons dressed in white tuxedos approached the table with even more food, these dishes in covered trays. They opened them to reveal braised fish, breads, an assortment of fruits and berries, grapes, and olives. Adrianna helped herself to a fish—being the only meat available— and pricked it with a bit of her digestive venom. Asakusa allowed the skeletons to serve him a bit of everything. The skeletons then poured them glasses of white wine and went to stand at the walls, completely still.

Adrianna took a tentative bite of her already digesting fish.

'It's safe?' Asakusa said.

Sometimes it was strange being a spider princess. She was basically impossible to harm from any sort of poison or venom, yet eating too much grain or too many vegetables would set her to vomiting for hours.

Adrianna nodded, 'No poison in the fish, anyway.'

'What about the rolls?'

Adrianna pricked one. No reaction. A small smile twitched across Asakusa's lips.

'And that olive salad? Oh, and what about those little tomato sandwiches?'

Adrianna rolled her eyes and pricked one of each item of food in turn.

Asakusa relaxed when the food began to melt instead of bubble or hiss, as it would in the presence of a poison.

Asakusa reached for some of the undigested bites. 'Holy crap, it's really good,' he said around mouthfuls.

'The fish too.' She was currently sucking out its insides with her hollow, barbed tongue. She knew Asakusa and Ebbo sometimes cringed at the way she ate, but that was the way of the spider princess.

'Maybe this is a good thing,' Asakusa said, glancing over his shoulder at the motionless skeletons around them, standing at attention.

'Yeah, and James didn't care that we took a bunch of the skull blossom,'

But when Asakusa turned back to the table, he was white as parchment. 'One of those skeletons is wearing Etrigan's daggers. I... I think I know what happened to the other adventurers.'

Adrianna nodded. That was not good, but it made sense. Still, a yellow skeleton was a yellow skeleton. Adrianna wished she'd explained what that all meant to Asakusa.

'Do you think it can still fight like Etrigan? Because that dude plays dirty.' Asakusa swallowed. 'Played.'

'No. Not yet, anyway. There's only one entity I know of that makes skeleton turn yellow, and it simply uses the bones. Their spirits should already be walking the Ways of the Dead.'

'And you didn't think to tell me this sooner?'

'We had only seen the one! I couldn't be sure this was where they're coming from,' Adrianna said, turning slightly to look at the waistbands of the skeletal servers. She didn't know the weapons of S'kar-Vozi half as well as Asakusa—he'd grown up idolizing these people, after all—but she still recognized an axe and a curved sword with a snake for blade.

'Vecnos probably sent us here to join the rest of them. I bet he's been eliminating adventurers and building an army at the same time,' Asakusa said.

'I don't think so. Isn't that a snake blade from the Ourder of Ouroboros?' Adrianna said, gesturing at the weapon.

Asakusa looked, turned back, even more scared than before. 'That's the blade of a cobra priest. It's not easy to kill a cobra priest.'

'Right, but Vecnos belongs to the Ourdor. He wouldn't have sent his strongest henchmen here to die.' Adrianna kept her tone light, as was fitting a dinner party.

'And it doesn't worry you that he's slaughtered all those adventurers?'

Adrianna shrugged. 'I mean, cobra priests are pretty much assholes to everyone, and didn't Etrigan stab anyone who looked at him the wrong way?'

'Well, yeah,' Asakusa said, 'but that doesn't mean he deserved to be killed and reanimated.'

Adrianna wasn't so sure. Adventurers died *all the time.* It was part of the job. And if Etrigan's body was now growing food and serving guests instead of stabbing people who looked at him funny... well. Adrianna wished she'd remembered the exact nature of the skeletons. What mechanism reanimated them stayed frustratingly locked in the back of her mind, but she knew enough to know they should meet their host. It had been centuries since yellow skeletons had been spotted in the Archipelago, but she remembered that they served a master—someone who usually controlled an artifact—and were more extensions of his will than independent agents. Adrianna needed to figure out if this baron understood the source of his power, or if he had simply stumbled upon a tool and had fallen prey to it. 'We can still get out of here without bloodshed.'

'You're right. I'll open a Gate right now.'

'Asakusa, no. Just stay calm. This all might just be a misunderstanding. If we're careful, we might be able to stop whatever this if from becoming something dangerous.'

At that moment, a set of doors at the head of the table opened, and in came the baron.

That this was the baron of this skeletal farm was not a question to Adrianna, for the man looked the part. His skin was pale, paler than Asakusa's, even. His clothes were extravagant, a black suit with red finery and gold tassels. Horribly outdated; he looked like something from a history book. Still, he was quite handsome, and had a smile all for Adrianna. He had long black hair and long fingernails that held a wine glass. A skeleton poured him a drink from a different pitcher than Adrianna had been served from, and he took a long, slow sip of the dark, viscous liquid.

'Welcome, *welcome!*' the baron said. His accent was like something from another world. He sounded like nobility Adrianna had met from the other planes of existence when her webmother had forced her to play at being a lady.

'I am the Baron of the Blighted Island, and a faithful servant of Chemok. Rolph Katinka, at your service,' he said with a bow.

Welp, so much for the baron being an unwitting servant, Adrianna thought. He knew exactly where his power was coming from, which wasn't good. Chemok was bad news.

The baron lowered himself down into the chair at the head of the table.

'Wait,' Asakusa said, one hand on his hammer, a sneer on his face, 'your name is Katinka?'

'I'll have you know, the name Rolph Katinka once inspired fear in the hearts of men and desire in the loins of the ladies. It will again, if we all enjoy ourselves here tonight! Come now, introduce yourselves, and we'll all have a good laugh. To *me*, your names are probably just as silly-sounding as mine is to you.'

'I am Asakusa Sangrekana, thrall to Byorginkyatulk, Gatekeeper of the Ways of the Dead, or whatever name you give the home of the Damned. I carry *Byergen* the Stone Hammer, who cannot be lifted save to vanquish evil —'

'Mmm…yes, Sangrekana, Blood-something-or-other-from the east, correct? That *is* a rather fetching name, and this Bergentalky sounds like a clever fellow as well, especially if he tricked you into *that*.' The baron waggled his fingers at Asakusa's Corruption. 'And how could I fail to notice the scratches poor James is going to have to buff out of the stone,' Rolph said with a pointed smile at Asakusa and a waggle of eyebrows at Adrianna.

James grunted an affirmative. Asakusa jumped when he saw the skinless man in the room, but Adrianna had felt him enter. She'd left a silk thread at the entrance and could tell the moment he'd stopped scrubbing the bloody stain he'd left upon the door.

'However, and do pardon me, Sangre, I must admit I am far more interested in the lady. Tell me, darling, who are you and why do you look so familiar?' Rolph said.

'I am Adrianna Morticia—'

'Now *that* is a fine name,' Rolph said with a wink.

Adrianna paused.

'Do go on, but I believe I knew your great-great-grandmother, perhaps. Do you recall where Viriana falls in the family tree?'

'Viriana is my mother's name.'

'Oh, dear. James, how long was I out?'

'Centuries, sir.'

'Centuries!' the baron snorted to himself. 'So you see, your mother couldn't possibly have given birth to so young and beautiful a woman. Perhaps she was named after *her* grandmother, or perhaps a great aunt or something. Certainly, someone of your…complexion.'

'My webmother will soon be six hundred and sixty-six years old,' Adrianna said, falling into the patter of threats she'd learned from her webmother and sisters, 'She has magick in her blood beyond your petty powers of transformation and pathetic addiction. Our bloodline is cursed. To you I will taste only of stankbulb, *vampire*.'

Rolph wrinkled his nose as the aforementioned stench and turned to James. 'Am I older than that?'

'No, sir.'

'Bother,' Rolph said indignantly.

'I am Warrior Princess of the Cursed Spiderfolk, Eighth daughter of the Eighth daughter, and heir to Krag's Doom. I carry *Flametongue*, my husband's dagger, and will use it to—'

'Husband? You haven't been married a week!' Asakusa blurted.

Adrianna glared at him with venom in her eyes. Asakusa wisely shut the hell up.

Adrianna could defeat a vampire. And if Rolph knew his master was Chemok, he needed to be defeated. Chemok was a god interested in but one thing—death—and the baron probably had some artifact on his person that was animating all the skeletons. Asakusa could handle the skeletons in this room while Adrianna dispatched the vampire. It would be a kindness, really. Vampires thought of themselves as a dark race—what with the drinking of blood and eternal life—but the *actual* dark races, spiderfolk included, saw vampirism as little more than a disease. Time to cure it.

'My *husband*,' Adrianna said, taking down her hair, Unfolding her extra spider arms and legs, and grabbing her whip and multitude of daggers as she spoke, 'Richard Valkanna, is heir to a Barony of his own, and being a dragon, can be here with hundreds of my brothers in the time it takes my friend and I to obliterate your pathetic little force of skeleton waiters,' Adrianna said.

The skeleton waiters standing at the sides of the room grabbed the weapons they'd held when they were still living adventurers of S'kar-vozi, though a few just grabbed steak knives. James cracked his knuckles. Asakusa flexed his Corrupted maggots. Rolph laughed and clapped his hands together.

'Oh, a Mortician girl! This *is* fun! Your mother used to mention her brothers as well, you know. I suppose we can all have a good brouhaha if we need to; I'm sure James and I could put on a good enough show, but let's not dash to fisticuffs until we hear the pitch, yes? For now, eat! Dance! Drink until the sunrise! I, for one, am going to have another glass of...' the baron waggled his eyebrows, 'wine.'

He was only still alive because he hadn't drawn a weapon and the skeleton servers hadn't taken a step closer.

'Tell me why I shouldn't destroy you, take the flowers we need, and leave this place to be forgotten,' Adrianna said.

Rolph laughed and put down his glass, which had left a red mustache under his own black one. Given Rolph's insistence on conversation, Adrianna could be fairly certain it was human blood. A vampire's dietary requirements were another reason that Adrianna—even with as much as she'd pushed against her family's history—believed that vampires needed to be eradicated.

'The flowers? You think we care about the—' a loud guffaw of laughter. 'James did you hear that? We'll have to start selling the skull blossoms as well.' With a conspiratorial wink, the baron said, 'With clientele like these we'll make a *killing*. But no, I'm not concerned about the flowers. Take as many as you want, as many as you need, we're here to trade goods, not trade blows,' he said, smiling at Asakusa. 'Consider them a honeymoon present for the lady. Oh, but you weren't the beaux to be, were you? What happened? Couldn't quite handle a spider princess?'

Asakusa knocked over his chair as he grabbed his hammer. 'We can take him.'

'Pardon me, pardon me! Your mother also preferred passionate men. I think that's why we got along so famously.' Another eyebrow waggle. 'I guess it's in the old blood, then, yes? It's no matter, none at all, and I have plenty of spare rooms that no one needs to know about, especially not dear old Viriana.'

'Viriana's still pretty hot, dude. She looks younger than you,' Asakusa said.

'Was that so hard? You can compliment my mom, but not me?' Adrianna said with a crack of her whip.

'No, you're hot, too...dude,' Asakusa said to Adrianna.

Adrianna glared at him.

'I mean, you're a dude and hot...in a good way.'

Adrianna's glare intensified from the strength of a goblin's torch to a dragon's breath.

'Ugh! I'm just trying to say that you and your mom both look a lot better than this wrinkly old creep. You especially. Now let's trash this place, smash these skeletons, and get the hell out of here.'

Rolph looked nervous, but neither he nor his skeletons attacked.

'Good plan. We can talk later, or you can, about how you think my mom is hot,' Adrianna said as she opened her four extra eyes and pointed her Vecnos Industries daggers at the skeleton servants. Completely Unfolded, she had two human arms—pedipalps, her family called them—and eight arachnid legs. Though each leg could fight with a dagger, so deadly appendages really was a better term.

'Now, just a minute!' Rolph said, holding up his palms in defense, 'I mean you no harm! I didn't mean to insult your mother or imply anything other than that we're on the same side! Really, the more I think about it, the more it's clear that this is *absolutely* perfect.'

'What is?' Adrianna said.

'The two of you! Look at you, you're already both sort of pariahs. I mean, unless a lot has changed, spiderfolk are still cursed and thralls are still damned.'

Adrianna pointed her daggers at the vampire. Asakusa's maggots wrapped around themselves, taking the shape of muscles.

'You still haven't explained why I shouldn't break off a table leg and stab you right now,' Adrianna said. Still, the skeletons hadn't attacked.

'I meant that in a good way! You're obviously good people, not like holy warrior good, but good enough. That's good! A shining paladin of virtue couldn't sell the Chemok brand, but you two, a Mortician girl and her charity case—now that's something anyone can get behind.'

Asakusa scowled at being called a charity case, but he'd been called far worse by Ebbo. Instead he only said, 'The Chemok brand?'

'How do you know we're good?' Adrianna said, unable to help herself.

'The moral superiority, self-righteousness, and quickness to violence are all hallmarks of the deeply scrupulous or the hopelessly mad, and you don't seem mad at all to me, except perhaps *lee-in-love*.' Rolph chuckled at his own horrible joke.

Adrianna cracked her whip again, this time knocking a carving knife from one of the skeleton's hands. The fingerbones were knocked away with it.

'Somewhere this all took a turn. I don't want to *kill* either one of you. I want to offer you the deal of a lifetime—well, perhaps not *your* life, Sangre, but a very good deal nonetheless.' Rolph disappeared into a cloud of smoke the color of burning blood and reappeared on the other side of table.

'Come, now, I'm sure you saw the orchard coming in,' he said, throwing back the thick velvet curtains around the room and revealing huge windows that overlooked the grounds. Hundreds of skeletons went about their work in the dusk: harvesting, pruning, watering and planting.

'I've heard of the free city of S'kar-Vozi and the great Magnus. Who hasn't?' the baron said. 'A druid who can grow food for a hundred thousand people. How marvelous! A hero for the common man, that's what I think he is, no matter what James says.' Rolph shot a look at James. Adrianna had no idea if it was some sort of inside joke or not. Either way, James did not seem amused.

'I want to help him, give him a bit of a break, you know? Maybe earn a bit of coin in the meantime, sure. I certainly don't mean to keep it all to myself. Just enough to grow Chemok's estate, care for the villages around here that lend...support. You know, the usual good Baron stuff. That's where you come in. For no Barony can be complete without a good market, and there's one in S'kar-Vozi badly in need of our products. This conversation has already lasted longer than any of the others I've had. Most of the people sent here throw off any illusion of being an ambassador as soon as they see poor, skinless James. You two are different, *special*. We can make this work! I use Chemok's power to grow food that the free city is badly in need of, and you two can convince your precious Nine in the Ringwall that they can send ships to the Blighted Island. You get a cut, I sell more food, people eat, everyone's happy!'

'Wait... you want us to sell your crap?' Asakusa said.

'Precisely.'

Chapter 30

Adrianna

'These are the fermenters. Six hundred bottles at a time, if you can believe that!' The Baron Rolph Katinka raised an arm at a wall of massive barrels made of the same dead wood that the door to the tombstone castle had been made of. Each of the barrels had an odd device sticking from the top that bubbled incessantly. The subterranean room smelled quite pleasantly of grapes slowly transforming into something more spectacular.

'Four hundred, sir,' James said.

Rolph winked again. He did so constantly. 'Still impressive, though. There's beer in S'kar-Vozi, but wine? Who doesn't want wine?' He busied himself with opening a glass bottle.

Adrianna and Asakusa looked at each other. The tour had been long, and surprisingly well planned. On it they'd seen olives pressed into oil or brined and preserved, grapes and other fruits being made into jams. Tomatoes were combined with peppers to make a dish Rolph called 'sal'sa' that they had found quite delicious. He even had a recipe for probiotic kim-chi. Really, all the samples had been amazing. Asakusa was almost full, and Adrianna had even swallowed some of the plant-based ingredients. She felt less nauseous than usual, no doubt from eating the microorganisms instead of solely plants. Despite her original shock at seeing a horde of skeletons being used to farm, Adrianna was finding it hard to fault the baron for what he was doing here.

Asakusa didn't seem to share her opinion at all, though. 'If I smash a wall now,' he whispered, 'we can crush him down here, use a Gate to get the surface, and end this nightmare of a farm. He's already killed a bunch of adventurers from the free city. He's probably going to try killing us, too.'

'I don't think so,' Adrianna whispered back, smiling at Rolph as he brought them their glasses of wine. 'Plus, I remember Etrigan. It's not like he was one for subtlety. He probably started stabbing every spinning thing that moved. I never felt bad when my sisters got adventurers like him.'

Adrianna knew Chemok was dangerous, but Rolph seemed to be using the powers for *good*. Maybe there was a way to proceed with the vampire as an ally instead of leaving him buried beneath his castle. Adrianna became further convinced of this plan when she tried the wine. She was glad she'd tied up her hair and Folded away her spider body, otherwise her arachnid limbs might have trembled in pleasure at the taste. It was superb, a well-balanced fruity aroma with a rich finish. It was so much better than the beer they served at Theo's. Try as she did to adapt to the free city, Adrianna had never learned to appreciate beer. Wine was far more fitting for a spider princess.

'It tastes like flat beer made out of grapes,' Asakusa said, wrinkling his nose.

'It is made out of—' Adrianna said, before clenching her teeth.

'Quite right, dear boy,' Rolph said, shooting a wink at Adrianna that she actually appreciated. 'We have clientele in Lanolel that assure me this ranks among the best elven barrels. It may not be for you, but how does the lady feel?' Rolph said, taking Adrianna's arm and leading her up the steps from the cellar and out into the vineyard. It was strangely serene in the light of the Both, the fat moon.

'It's very good,' Adrianna began, 'but I don't get what's in it for you. You've already built this estate; you have your army and your fancy clients across the Archipelago. Why do you need to sell to the free city?'

'Well, it being *free* certainly has its advantages. Also, it's closer and less prone to sea monster attacks, but really it's simply that we're ready to expand. If we're to grow any more, we need more fields. And for that we'll need capital, tools, ships and all that, possibly even more workers.'

'But *why*? *Why* do you want to grow any more? You already have a castle and everything you could want,' Adrianna said.

'Because Chemok wills it,' James said, coming to stand at the top of the steps from the cellar.

Adrianna looked past him to Asakusa, who was awkwardly dragging his stone hammer up the steps. He raised an eyebrow at her. It wasn't nearly as subtle as the messages she could send over a strand of silk thread, but she understood his meaning all the same. *Attack?*

James ignored the thrall and tenderly stroked an unbroken yellow skull in his hand.

'Well, yes, there is that,' Rolph said nervously. 'When the big man says dig, we say how deep!'

'Who is Chemok?' Asakusa said, moving past James and coming to stand at Adrianna's side.

'He is Death. The Great End. The Final Cold,' James said, his voice more forceful than it had been.

'Yes, yes, James, we get it! Now please, let's all calm down about the old troublemaker,' Rolph said quite nervously.

'*What* is he?'

Rolph shrugged. 'Well, what James said is true. Chemok is technically a sort of *god.*'

'A lesser god, not as strong as the Kraken or the Ouroboros… at least not directly,' Adrianna said quickly. 'He works through artifacts and needs agents to build his armies.'

'Chemok is *the* God of Death. The Unwinder. Big Stabs,' James chanted.

'Yes, James, I'm getting there, but would you both please stop saying his name? You'll have the skeletons going on if we're not careful.'

'Listen,' Rolph said, looking over his shoulder at James and then pushing Adrianna and Asakusa into a different row of grapes, 'there should be no doubt that He is powerful. I mean, death *is* death. No question there. And there's all these skeletons, zombies, and whatever the hell James is. That's all proof of His will.'

'That doesn't prove anything—' Asakusa said, maggots rippling as he looked around for skeletons.

'I slept for *centuries*. In the darkness, I saw only *Him*,' Rolph hissed, his smiling veneer discarded. 'He waits in there, in the darkness, for all of us, waiting for it all to end. It's inevitable, really. We can prolong it perhaps, or sit back and enjoy it, but we certainly can't stop it. Why, that'd be as silly as stopping life itself!' Rolph laughed, his relentless positivity returning as if it never left.

'He gives you your power?' Asakusa said.

'Of course not, my boy! Well, not entirely,'

'Vampirism is a contagious disease. They're the herpes of the dark races,' Adrianna said.

'Regardless of who has or doesn't have herpes, Chemok's power is real,' Rolph said.

'The Dark King, The Dreamless Sleeper, Grandma's Just Napping,' a skeleton chanted at them, dropping its grapes to the ground.

'Oh, now you've gone and gotten me to say it,' Rolph said, throwing his hands up in frustration. 'Look, I don't want all this to end any more than you do. I *like* it here. I like my castle, and my fine clothes, and even James and the skeletons. The villagers are generous with their tributes—'

'We need to talk about that too—' Asakusa said.

'Yes, yes, we'll go there next,' Rolph said with a dismissive wave of his hand. 'My point is that Chemok *will* come. Right now, he has the power to animate James and these old skeletons. One day it will be more, but who knows when that will be? All *I* know is that I wouldn't have my castle without him. I might still be stuck in that dreadful casket. If he wants me to build this place into something even more grand, then fine. Who am I to stop the unstoppable?'

'But why would Chemok want you to make life?' Asakusa said.

'To kill it, of course!' Rolph laughed hard at that one. 'Oh he is a funny one, isn't he?' Rolph said to Adrianna. 'One day, the dead will outnumber the living and the end times will be upon your kind—well, maybe not you two specifically, but the humans and the rest of the mortals. I'd be lying if I said I was looking forward to it. I eat the living, after all, as do most of us, so you can see I don't want your kind eradicated any more than a wolf does the sheep.'

'Seriously, we're going to need to see where you get the blood,' Asakusa said.

'It's not a problem then?' Rolph said, 'I was so worried this was going to be a sticking point! Everyone else who has come here has the 'stab-first-ask-questions-later' mindset, which is of course *terrible* for business!'

'That's not what I meant—' Asakusa said.

Adrianna cut him off. 'We still need to talk with our contacts back in S'kar-Vozi, and see your tributes, but I don't know. I mean, you're putting the dead to work to grow more of the living? That's almost admirable. Plus, you can't cross running water, so we can come back if...'

'If our allies decide to end you, *Katinka*.' Asakusa threw all of his malice into the baron's last name. Adrianna put a hand to her face. She would've emphasized *end you*. Asakusa plowed on. 'We swear to you that if you ever leave this island, if so much as a yellow knuckle shows up in the free city, we will crush you into powder.'

'Well, jolly good, then!' Rolph smiled, unperturbed by the threat. 'Come along, let's go see the tributes—or as they like to be called in this modern age, the blood bank!'

Chapter 31

Asakusa

The tributes were as the baron had described them: young, healthy, and willing. Some of them were even downright eager. There was one girl especially, Dreida, who loved to give blood. She was only twelve years old, and thus not mature enough to give her blood directly to Rolph, but instead had it drained through the root of a plant the skeletons had discovered deep in the jungled interior of the another island. Asakusa was trying to figure out how the vampire had brainwashed her. Adrianna said his charms didn't work unless he actually put his lips to a victim's neck.

'We can grow it back, and this way he can live too! An' with the skeletons, we don't have to fish the coast no more. Daddy used ta bring home nothin' but crettles. Ain't much eats on them, no ma'am. Now we's get fresh vegetables and goodies and Daddy don't break his back out there.'

'No meat?' Adrianna said.

'Not yet,' Rolph said, 'and obviously no grammar school either, but with your help that could change. We do grow plenty of beets. High iron content and all that.'

'You don't have to let him insult you like that,' Asakusa said to Dreida. As a kid, he'd had as much of an accent as Dreida did. Free city instead of far-flung island, but he remembered how people treated him once he spoke, like they already knew everything there was to know about him. Hanging out with a spider princess who spoke in non-regional diction had helped him get over it, but it was still a sore spot. So were young girls being abused by monsters.

'He talks funny too, sir,' Dreida said, drawing a conspiratorial laugh and a wink from the baron. Asakusa really, *really* disliked the baron. But still, Dreida was perhaps a bit pale and thin, but she looked healthy—a lot healthier than many of the street urchins in S'kar-Vozi. She could read, her father was learning to crochet, and her mother no longer had to do their laundry. Rolph had James make the skeletons do the whole village's laundry once a week.

'We still need to talk to our contacts,' Adrianna said, pulling her scrying mirror from a hidden pocket in her leather armor.

'Of course, of course. I'll just get a quick snack.'

Adrianna held up her scrying mirror. The dull piece of glass with the handle carved of a spider's exoskeleton was one of the finest tools of its kind. The lump of rock with a bit of quartz in the middle they'd rented to communicate with Ebbo and Clayton was far less glamorous.

Adrianna chanted the magick words, 'Sangren, Arachnin, Mortalis,' and the dull glass fogged over, as if some invisible entity had blown on it.

'Ebbo Brandyoak, hear me,' Adrianna said.

Flashes in the glass. A dark-skinned dwarf looked at her, and then was impaled with a throwing axe and fell away into a swirl of mist. Then an old elf, masturbating furiously, who—upon seeing Adrianna—scowled and threw a cloth over his stone. She saw red scales in a sea of flames, a flap of wings that extinguished the fire into swirls of smoke that curled back into the fog of the scrying glass. Looking for Ebbo's cheap rental was not easy.

'Ebbo Brandyoak. This is Adrianna Morticia. Hear me!'

After another moment, and more interference from whoever was using flames to scry, she had her friends. She could hear Clayton's voice talking to someone.

Chapter 32

Ebbo

'We don't wish any trouble,' Clayton said amicably.

'Just as much skull blossom as humanly possible. Err, sorry... half-humanly possible.' Ebbo could feel the conversation getting away from him. Might as well get it all out there while he still could. 'And maybe a pinch of pixie dust, if you got it.'

Ebbo and Clayton were currently in a tavern far from the relatively respectable tourist district of S'kar-vozi. The tavern was made of scrap wood and smelled pleasantly of sawdust, though the body odor of the half-orcs they were currently interviewing was intruding far too deep into Ebbo's nostrils. The bartender, an unsmiling human with a golden mustache, seemed to make his business by not asking too many questions of his customers. During their time here he'd busied himself with sanding the bar, a task that—given all the rough wood all around them—seemed endless.

Ebbo and Clayton followed a string of rumors longer than one of Adrianna's threads to find their way to this group of hrocs. The gossip—where they could find it—was that the hrocs were new to the free city and had come from the Blighted Island itself. Though Ebbo couldn't smell skull blossom like he could magick, he had a feeling these hrocs would either have some or know where it could be found.

The hrocs conferred in their own language before turning back to the halfling and the golem.

'Who send you? Magnus?' one of the hrocs said. Though obviously not the smartest of the bunch, he seemed to be the leader. It was odd for Ebbo to be talking to them. He knew entire communities that had been eaten by bands of marauding orcs. These half-breeds were far more agreeable.

'Pixie dust is sin,' grumbled one of the other hrocs.

Mmm... maybe Ebbo preferred them when they didn't talk. 'We don't have anything to do with Magnus or any of the other berry-picking bastards on the Ring. We just want the skull blossom,' Ebbo said, lying through his teeth and trying not to sneer too openly at the proselytizing hroc. He got enough of that from Asakusa.

'It's for a friend,' Clayton added.

'Vecnos? You know?' The leader growled. The lack of logic pointed toward full orc, but the skin and face looked like a hroc.

'Did you not just hear me say we know *no one* from the Ring?' Ebbo said. 'You think if I knew the great and powerful Vecnos, I'd be hanging around with you lunkheads trying to score?'

'You... you insult our boss?' one of the half-orcs stammered.

'He supposed to be secret!' a females said.

'We don't mean any disrespect,' Clayton said. 'We just want a bit of flower. Rumor is you're new to the city, so we thought we could help you make yourselves at home, maybe point out a few of the bathhouses.' Clayton wrinkled his nose, even though he smelled using the entirety of his slightly moist clay body. 'We have coin.'

The hrocs obviously didn't know what to do with a talking golem. Clayton's bright green silk shirt and broad-brimmed hat with a feather seemed to confuse them as much as it did anyone who wasn't from S'kar-Vozi.

'Try florist,' said the same female in an unusual show of wit. Ebbo really found it too bad that the smartest of the hrocs wasn't their leader. That would be like having *him* lead their team of adventurers instead of the spider princess!

'How do you know Vecnos?' Ebbo asked the hrocs.

'Not the time for hero worship, Ebbo. We need to think of our friends,' Clayton hissed.

'Psst!' The scrying stone in Ebbo's pocket was making noise.

'You mind if I take this?' Ebbo said to the hrocs.

'Who talking?' Oluf said.

'Let's find out.' Ebbo answered the call. 'Adrianna, how are you? Unless it's pressing, we really ought to be going.'

'We found the skull blossom,' Adrianna said over the stone.

'Fantastic news!' Clayton said. 'My dear friends, Oluf, Dergh, Doger, Kyul, and, err... Jessica, it seems we are no longer in need of the skull blossom, so we'll be on our way—'

'So just the pixie dust, then,' Ebbo said.

One of the hrocs—the one who'd commented on the moral state of poor Ebbo's affinity for magick powder—stood and sent her chair clattering away in the process. 'Pixie dust kills pixies. You have 'til count of three.'

Ebbo glanced at the bartender. The mustachioed man had the forced posture of someone intent on ignoring what was happening in front of him for as long as humanly possible. Ebbo knew the look well; he'd practiced it many times.

'We made it to the Blighted Island,' Adrianna said from the scrying stone, 'found a vampire running a farm here using ancient skeletons to grow food. That's whose been supplying all new goodies to S'kar-Vozi, this guy Rolph Katinka. I guess his brand is a yellow skull—'

'Rolph Katinka?' Ebbo laughed. 'What is that, the alias for the boogerman?'

'One...'

'It's boogieman,' Asakusa said from the other side of the stone.

'No, like booger! Like from your nose!' Ebbo said, his laugher sounding like bells tinkling.

'Two...'

'Would you just shut up and listen?' Adrianna said. 'He's hoping to trade with the free city so he can keep growing his army for the return of his god.'

'Which god?' Ebbo asked.

'Chemok. Minor deity of death, has to use an intermediary to animate skeletons using their skulls. Somehow he's made a bond with the vampire.' Adrianna said as if that wasn't completely freaking terrifying.

'Four...' Oluf said.

'Doesn't sound so bad. Wacko religion growing food? Could be worse,' Clayton said.

'We don't really have a problem with all that, since vampires can't cross water and the skeletons are old and super brittle—' Asakusa said.

'Eight...' Oluf said. Some of the other hrocs started grumbling. Apparently, Oluf wasn't the mathematician of the group.

'Three!' Ebbo said. 'Three comes after two, your moron!'

'I think they might be counting exponentially,' Clayton said, rubbing his chin.

'Two!' Burk said.

'You already said two!' Ebbo said, laughing so hard that he dropped the scrying stone.

'Gentlemen, as much as I'd like to show you how a golem fights, we should be going,' Clayton said, standing still, his steel heart still conserving its reserve of Heartbeats.

'Three!' Oluf said.

Ebbo squealed and rolled under a table as the hrocs attacked.

They focused their attack on Clayton, pummeling his clay body as he used Heartbeats to draw moisture from his hands and harden his fists into bricks.

'The issue is that there's these girls here who say they're willing to give their blood to this Rolph guy, but he seems like he has some kind of charm spell,' Adrianna's voice said from the scrying stone on the floor, oblivious to the fight that had just broken out. 'I kind of think it might be fine, but Asakusa disagrees.'

Ebbo snuck out from under the table, dodged a pint glass aimed at his head, and snatched the scrying stone back up. 'Let me guess. He wants to smash them all into strawberry jam with his big hammer.'

'Pretty much,' Asakusa grunted.

'I bet they *like* being charmed,' Ebbo said. 'Maybe I could visit. Does he only like girls?'

'We don't care what you think, you little twerp, the princess want to know what Clayton thinks!' Asakusa said.

Ebbo rolled his eyes. *No one* listened to him when it came to magick use, despite him obviously being the most experienced.

'Oh, alright. I'll ask him,' Ebbo said, stepping out from under the table and dodging a piece of wood that snapped off a chair one of the hrocs smashed over Clayton's back. Bits of wood stuck in his clay.

'Clayton, Adrianna wants to know if it's okay for a vampire to drink a girl's blood if she's willing,' Ebbo said, darting back under a table as a hroc spotted him.

'What, like hypothetically?' Clayton dodged a chair leg being used as a club, but when a hroc kicked him in the knees from behind, the assailants' foot went right through Clayton's legs. Clayton landed on his shins and managed to keep his balance, though he was now a foot shorter.

'No, like that's what the vampire is actually doing, but Adrianna can't tell if they're charmed or what. She wants to know what you think because she says she's not a good judge of mortals. What in the raspberry patch are you doing, by the way? Put yourself back together!'

Clayton could change forms, but doing so cost him a great amount of Heartbeats. Sloughing off his legs in the middle of a fight was a move Ebbo had never seen, nor was it one he liked.

'She has simply got to stop being so hard on herself!' Clayton shouted as a club slammed into his face, leaving a huge dent that slowly started to grow over the club. The hroc yanked it out before Clayton could get a good hold on it, though. Weird. Holding onto clubs that smashed his face was practically one of the golem's signature moves.

'Clayton says you have to stop being so hard on yourself,' Ebbo said.

'I heard him! I just want to know what he thinks! And can you please help him?'

'He's fine. She says she heard you, and she wants me to help you fight,' Ebbo said.

'I'm fine.'

'That's what I said!'

'Ebbo!' Adrianna shouted. It was amazing that she could still sound so commanding despite being on another island and Ebbo being in a brawl.

'I don't think you can trust a vampire,' Clayton said. 'At least, the women at the Red Underoo didn't.' One of the hrocs brought their club down on Clayton, severing his arm. Ebbo had never seen a club do anything like that to Clayton. Something was seriously wrong. Ebbo had seen Clayton fight full orcs in combat; he should've been able to take out a couple of hrocs in no time. It was a good thing the golem couldn't feel pain, otherwise Ebbo might be worried.

Three other hrocs crowded around the dismembered golem. Ebbo used the opportunity to stab one of them in the thigh. Not a lethal wound, but from his screams Ebbo could tell he'd struck a nerve.

'If possible, just extricate yourself and come home. The mission was to discover what's on the Blighted Island and report back to Vecnos. You did that,' Clayton said. The hrocs surrounded the legless, one-armed golem, but Clayton struck out at them with his remaining arm until they fell to the ground, holding what would soon be bruises. *That was more like it!* Ebbo thought.

'But what if they're charmed?' Adrianna said.

'Then they're probably happy,' Ebbo said. 'Did you find the flowers?'

'Yes, we found the flowers,' Asakusa grunted back, 'but not *everyone* likes being at the mercy of a magick addiction.'

A club smashed the table Ebbo was hiding under, and he scurried off to another.

'That was the sound of me trying to help you, by the way,' Ebbo said, then, hoping to further piss off the thankless thrall, he continued, 'Just get home. You can call in your hubby-poo to firebomb the hell out of the place and free the girls.'

'But then their parents would have to go back to fishing crettles,' Adrianna said.

Ebbo shuddered. 'Ugh, that's not a meal I'd wish on anyone.'

He scrambled out from the table as this one was also smashed to pieces. But fortunately, this last hroc's singular focus on destroying furniture had distracted her from the golem.

'Pardon me,' Clayton said.

When the hroc turned around, Clayton punched her so hard in the face that she careened through the air and smashed a third table. Ebbo was impressed. It wasn't often one brawler broke *three* tables in a bar fight.

'What's a crettle?' Asakusa asked into the newfound silence of the smashed tavern.

'A kind of clam that feeds on human waste. They tend to live in currents downstream from S'kar-vozi,' Ebbo said.

'Okay... okay! We'll tell him that we'll come back soon, then. Now get out of there!' Adrianna said, and ended the connection. There was another flash of flame from the scrying stone, so Ebbo jammed it into his pocket. He hated using scrying stones. Adrianna said her mirror was powerful enough to be secure, but the scrying stone they'd rented for Ebbo and Clayton was anything but. It was creepy to think someone might've watched them destroy the tavern.

And destroyed the place was; the scrap wood for walls was a cute aesthetic but apparently didn't stand up well to a brawl. Splinters of different colors covered every surface. The walls had holes from elbows and clubs smashing right through them. Clayton's clay was everywhere, which Ebbo found strangely vulgar. Clayton rarely let himself fall apart. Ebbo had never seen it happen in a simple melee.

'I take it those hrocs never heard of me,' Clayton said.

Ebbo rolled his eyes. 'Just pull yourself together. What's wrong with you, anyway? You know no one's going to idolize a pile of mud.'

'I'm fine,' Clayton said as his steel heart thumped, and he slowly grew back to his full height. 'I think that mineral bed was less than ideal.'

'But you soaked in those islanders' mudbath. You said that was high quality stuff. Are you sure that berry-pickin' dragon prince's fire blast didn't mess you up?'

'Of course I'm sure,' Clayton said, but he didn't sound sure.

Ebbo was going to press further—now that they knew Adrianna and Asakusa had found the skull blossom, they could relax—but the bartender stood up behind the bar.

He held a large staff with a glowing gemstone at its tip. 'They said I was a fool to buy this staff. That only a wizard could use it! Well, I've attuned, so let's find out what happens to do-gooders who kill my clientele—'

'They're not dead,' Clayton said as he continued to draw himself together. It was taking way longer than usual. Ebbo was starting to get worried, both because of Clayton's apparent loss of control and the staff that was now beginning to whistle.

'Now's not the time,' Ebbo said. 'I'll get you more mud. We've got to disappear.' Ebbo ran to Clayton's body, reached into the clay, and snatched the heart, causing all the mud to fall to the floor, no longer animated.

'I need that!' the heart vibrated, 'I was almost done!'

Ebbo said nothing. Normally he would've stayed long enough to filch the unconscious hrocs' pockets. He was sure one of them was holding *some* kind of magick, but that staff was whistling, and Clayton... well Clayton shouldn't take so long to get himself back together, and he *definitely* didn't allow anyone, not even Ebbo, to reach into his body and snatch his heart. Did he still not have enough Heartbeats?

Ebbo didn't know. He was just happy that Adrianna and Asakusa had found the skull blossom. With it, they could heal Asakusa, get home, and get to the altogether more important task of seeing what exactly was going on with Clayton's steel heart. Ebbo reached into his pocket and looked once more upon the scrying stone. There were still flames showing through it— flames, and a winged figure flying above them. Ebbo tucked the stone in its cloth sack and was relieved to see it went dark. Scrying stones weren't exactly private, especially not at the distances they'd been using them, and Ebbo didn't like to think about fire, considering that was what got Clayton into this mess in the first place.

Ebbo hoped his friend was okay, but found his concerns evaporating as he stepped out of the bar and into the street. It seemed the hrocs had friends.

'Greetings! I was just talking to your friends, and they were telling me about your voyage and the lack of skull blossom here in the Free City.'

The hrocs collectively furrowed their brows. Ebbo hoped he could talk his way out of this one, because without Clayton, there wasn't anything else he could do.

Chapter 33

Adrianna

'So you'll be returning soon?' the Baron Rolph Katinka said eagerly.

'Yes... we'll, uh, talk to our contacts and be in touch,' Adrianna said, trying to sound like she meant it.

'Do you have a parrot we can send?' Asakusa said.

The baron looked between them, eyebrows furrowed in concern, lips in a pout. Between Adrianna's forced smiled and Asakusa's honest glare, he saw right through them. 'Of course, of course! James, a parrot!' he hollered, 'but whatever seems to be the matter? Is it the skeletons? I thought we were getting along so *well* together!'

'It's not the skeletons—' Adrianna said, perhaps too quickly.

'It's the blood on your lips,' Asakusa said with disgust.

Adrianna elbowed Asakusa with one of her spider limbs.

'Well, yes, there's that, but I'm a *vampire*. What choice do I have? Drink pig's blood and lose what control I have over this curse?'

'You're using people with no other options,' Asakusa said.

Adrianna elbowed him again. The point was to get out of here *without* confrontation!

'Then take my offer to the free city. Surely someone there would come live in a castle, eat the best food money can buy, and live a life of luxury in exchange for a pint every week or two?'

Asakusa and Adrianna shared a look. There were thousands of people in the free city that would take that deal, but Asakusa shook his head all the same. This was why Adrianna preferred to use Clayton for her mortal compass. Despite him being a golem, his default in difficult situations wasn't *attack* like Asakusa's was.

'Maybe we can work something out in the future,' Adrianna said, trying to placate the baron and get Asakusa to shut up at once.

Asakusa shot her a look of surprise, but he nodded. He'd respect her leadership—as he always did—and say nothing more.

Too bad Rolph wasn't buying it. 'Oh, bother. I do say this is a most unfortunate turn. I was hoping that your own delves into the morally gray would help you see that what we're doing here is no worse than eating meat, but alas, perhaps you'll come around.' Rolph sighed, a great heave of his slight shoulders. 'Well, carry on, then. Might as well take more of the skull blooms on your way out. It grows like weeds on the old castle.' His voice lacked the pep it had earlier possessed.

With heavy steps, the baron led Adrianna and Asakusa from the blood bank, through the halls of the tombstone castle, and finally to the front door. They looked out at the skeleton farmers. They toiled under the moonlight, pruning grape vines and olives branches, plucking vegetables to be preserved or canned.

It could have worked, Adrianna thought. The Chemok thing was kind of weird, but there were two far stranger cults in S'kar-vozi. Compared to worshipping a cannibalistic snake or praying for battle against a world-ending sea monster, preparing for death didn't seem all that bad. They could've come back to S'kar-Vozi with new allies, but at least this way they'd still complete their mission. Vecnos and the others in the Ringwall could decide what to do about the vampire and his farmers. Adrianna wished she could have thrown herself into negotiations, taken back a ship of food or something, but she wouldn't go against Clayton. She was raised a spider princess, after all, and her morals were compromised when it came to mortals. She didn't want to think about the kind of fluids she'd been served as a child. Clayton, though—Clayton's first thinking act had been to stop an abusive pimp. She had to trust him, whatever her feelings were about the baron.

'I hope to hear from you soon,' Rolph said with resignation.

'You will, really. I'm sure the Nine in the Ringwall will be eager to hear all about you,' Adrianna said, trying to sound positive.

The baron's expression soured at the mention of the Nine. 'Right.'

'A parrot, sir,' James said, joining them in the entrance hall of the tombstone castle.

'We'll await your reply,' Rolph said.

Adrianna sighed. She was sure he would, though she had a sinking feeling that the baron simply meant no one from S'kar-Vozi would be able to surprise them.

The haunted wooden doors closed behind them with a groan, and the spider princess, thrall, and skinless butler started down the steps of the castle.

Adrianna hoped she was making the right decision. Magnus fed the people of S'kar-vozi, but if something were to happen to him, or if the population of the free city grew any larger, which it was likely to do, then he'd need more food beside the seven crops he'd always grown. Baron Katinka could provide that support. Were a few pints of blood from a handful of mortal women worth the thousands of people Katinka could feed? Adrianna didn't know. Her upbringing told her *yes!* Yes, of course a few were worth the many, but then Clayton had been so quick to make his judgement. Ebbo had disagreed, but then he couldn't be trusted with any decisions involving magick. *The foolish islander would probably trade his own finger for a magic ring.*

'I'm proud of you,' Asakusa said.

'Hmm?' Adrianna said, pulled from her thoughts.

'It would have been easy to agree. But I'm glad you didn't. Those girls... it's too much like what happened to my sister.'

'I still think we could make it work.'

Asakusa looked down at his Corruption. 'Some people simply can't be trusted. Not everyone from the dark races is as trustworthy as you, Adrianna.'

Adrianna smiled as a wave of feelings for Asakusa that she'd been trying to get over washed through her. 'I'm glad you didn't say *too much* in front of the baron.'

Asakusa shrugged. 'You're the boss, and a spider princess.'

James put a hand on her shoulder. It left a pool of blood on her black padded leather. 'It is a pity that you have attempted to deceive the ambassador of Chemok.'

Adrianna had forgotten all about the flesh golem. Despite spending so much time with Clayton, Adrianna was still accustomed to golems doing little more than following orders.

'You're getting blood on my armor,' Adrianna said.

'You must reconsider the baron's offer. Chemok is lenient with those who serve him.' James did not remove his hand from Adrianna's shoulder.

'Your master told you to let us go,' Asakusa said.

'My master is not the vampire. My master kills all kings. My master slays all dragons. My master—'

'The lady said to take your hand off her,' Asakusa said, and took a step toward James, Corrupted arm flexing as he tightened his grip on the stone hammer.

'We're going to come back,' Adrianna said to the butler. 'I told your master we would speak to our contacts in the free city and get back to you. Now, hands off. *Please.*'

Apparently, James really could understand subtlety, for his skinless face clouded over with anger at Adrianna's venomous tone when she said please.

'You have proven your inability to negotiate,' James said, tightening his grip on Adrianna's shoulder. 'We will see if Chemok yet has the power to utilize your...unusual bone structure.'

There was a loud crunch from the golem's ribcage as Asakusa smashed the butler's torso with his stone hammer. James doubled over from the blow and panted for a moment before standing up straight and cracking his neck. The flesh golem yelled from deep in his throat, and three hundred skeletons armed with shovels, scythes and axes turned to face Adrianna and Asakusa. Their yellow skulls no longer seemed so brittle. Their empty eye sockets now seemed hungry.

'Shit,' Asakusa said as the first wave attacked.

'You know you didn't need to do that,' Adrianna said. 'I could've sliced his fingers off.'

'Yeah, but you know I like to remind you why you keep me around.'

Adrianna cracked her whip at three skeletons in quick succession. They shattered to pieces as the whip struck them in the chest. *At least they're not tough,* Adrianna thought, but the bones began to pull themselves back together. Balls into sockets. Fingers into knuckles into hands. The skeletons reformed.

'Asakusa!' Adrianna said, throwing *Flametongue* into a skeleton's face.

'Little busy!' Asakusa's Corrupted right arm lurched forward and locked James in its grip. The two men flexed, and James's left sleeve, the sleeve of the arm locked in grip with Asakusa's Corrupted one, tore away. Maggot and meat struggled in contest. Asakusa seemed to be winning, but then the golem hit the maggot in the gut and Asakusa doubled over, barely keeping hold of his stone hammer.

Adrianna snapped her silk whip around the dagger's hilt. She yanked it out of the skull and used it to slice another skeleton across the chest. It fell into a pile of clattering bones that immediately began to pull itself back together.

Though the skeleton whose face she'd stabbed wasn't moving.

'Go for the skulls!' Adrianna said, a bit of lore coming back to her. Chemok wasn't a master of yellow skeletons, but of yellow *skulls.* That was why there were all those bone fragments back on the beach instead of laboring on the farm; without a skull, Chemok couldn't animate anything.

'Still...busy,' Asakusa said through gritted teeth.

James cracked Asakusa across the jaw with a skinless fist. Asakusa grunted in pain, but he neither retreated nor wiped away the bloody imprint of the golem's knuckles from his face. So long as he gripped the stone hammer, he could not be knocked away. James pummeled Asakusa, but the maggots caught the blows, jerking Asakusa back and forth. The flesh golem was too close. Asakusa couldn't attack.

Adrianna cursed and snapped three more skeletons to bone. She managed to crack the third one hard enough that its forehead split. Already, others were coming at her with axes.

This wasn't working.

'Let's switch opponents!' Adrianna said.

'That's cool with me,' Asakusa said.

Adrianna swung her whip across the top of the steps, sending another pair of skeletons clattering to animated pieces. She swung the whip behind her head, and then back out in front of her at the mountain of flesh pulverizing Asakusa. A vein on the golem's neck was engorged from him screaming at the skeletons. It made for an easy target. The tip of the silk whip blew a hole in James's neck. He stumbled and put his hand to the wound.

Then he charged the spider princess.

She struck again with her whip, diverting his momentum enough to crash him into a statue of the baron smiling his pointy smile and holding a basket of fresh-picked peppers. The imported marble crumbled to rubble. A piece of marble struck the flesh golem across the head, and he fell to the ground in a cloud of dust. There, that hadn't been so bad.

Adrianna turned to help Asakusa.

Switching opponents had been a good move. A mountain of bone was growing around Asakusa's feet. Asakusa swung and swung, smashing more and more of the skeletons' skulls into smithereens. But they kept coming.

She sheathed her dagger and began to tie up her hair and Fold away her abdomen and some of her legs. If they were to escape, it would be better to be smaller than her spider form.

'Spider-girl,' a low, condescending, and rather stuck-up voice said.

Adrianna stopped.

James. Not only alive, but undressing. He undid each button of his shirt, leaving blood on the white hemp cloth. How he went the whole day without touching his white tuxedo was beyond Adrianna. Apparently, the butler hadn't given up completely on appearances, though, for he left his bow-tie around his neck.

Without his shirt and jacket, the flesh golem was a truly formidable sight. Close to seven feet tall, his muscles pulsed and twitched as he moved. He breathed in, and then flexed, engorging his muscles and almost doubling his beefiness.

'You're a pretty tough butler, considering your master is a vegetable farmer,' Adrianna said.

'I do not serve Katinka.'

'Right. You serve Chemok, the god of the dead,' Adrianna said. 'Tell me, though, what are you exactly? You're not dead, not like all your little skeletons are going to be when my friend is done. You're *un*-dead. As in the opposite of. In the eyes of your god, and compared to me, you're the abomination. I kind of like that. Takes the pressure off me.'

'Words are for the *living*,' James said, rushing forward and throwing a shoulder into her. She hurdled backwards and smashed into the castle, crashing into the wall hard enough to crack tombstones. James leaped up after her. He smashed his knee into her chest and managed a few punches before gravity clutched him and he fell.

Adrianna stuck to the wall. She could feel hairline fractures in her carapace. She couldn't let the golem hit her like that again, or else she'd go splat.

'So, the jacket was like your weakness, then?' Adrianna said as she ran perpendicularly across the wall, cracking her whip at James.

'Death has no weakness!' James shouted, hurling chunks of broken tombstone at her.

She dodged and stole a glance at Asakusa. The skeletons were closing in. Asakusa was spinning with his hammer, an unapproachable whirlwind, but also unstable. If he slipped, dozens of skeletons would turn him into mulch.

She couldn't let that happen.

James looked up at her. 'You think Katinka is their leader, and these are his servants? Is this how you think of your fingers, or a colony of ants? We are but a manifestation of him, one piece of a billion. I am grown of his yellow skull, so that one day I will die and join him again.'

'You talk a lot for the butler of a man who drinks pee,' Adrianna said.

'The baron does not drink pee.'

'So, you are his butler!'

James roared and jumped at Adrianna again. She was ready this time and jumped off the wall, letting her hair down and Unfolding in midair. All seven free appendages grabbed a dagger and hurled them at the butler. He took two in each arm, one in the chest, and two in the face. He crumpled out of the air, and Adrianna landed on top of him. Her arachnid body was large enough to crunch more of the golem's bones.

She lifted his head and let it drop. James did not move.

Good. *One down, two hundred-forty-seven to go.*

She could see Asakusa at the top of the stairs—or rather, she could see where he was. A mass of skeletons pushed in around him, so many that she couldn't see the thrall at all, just great splashes of bone, like some giant necromancer's confetti.

Adrianna ran that way, kicking skeletons as she went, clearing a path for herself but not doing much else. Daggers and whips were not the choicest weapons for cracking skulls.

'Asakusa!' she yelled, shoving her way through the horde of skeletons. This wasn't how it was supposed to be going. They were supposed to be here to pick flowers, for the Etterqueen's sake.

'Adrianna!' he yelled, and then the way in front of her was clear, and there was Asakusa standing amongst a pile of smashed bones. Smiling. Well, not smiling, Asakusa never really smiled. He mostly just looked smugger and less brooding as he flicked his dark hair out of his eyes. It promptly fell back into place.

Then the skeletons got him. One of them grabbed onto his leg, and when he smashed it with his hammer, another jumped on his back and sunk its teeth into his neck. No maggots were there to protect his mortal flesh.

Asakusa screamed.

Chapter 34

Adrianna

Adrianna's ichor boiled with rage.

She scuttled toward Asakusa, but there were too many skeletons. They hacked at her with their axes and poked at her with their trowels and spades. She felt them nearly snap one of her legs. The pain was intense, but she ignored it. She'd have to molt to grow it back if it was broken, but it was a wound from which she could recover. Not like losing Asakusa. She pushed forward, trailing ichor behind her.

'I'm going to open a Gate and get you out of here!' Asakusa shouted from beneath a mountain of skeletons.

'No!' Adrianna said. 'We don't know how far you've got.' Adrianna didn't know how much longer either of them had. James had been a better match for her skills than this seething mass of yellow bones.

'It doesn't matter! If I'm gone, Tulk will have to close it. He won't hurt you, it's in the contract.'

'We are *not* talking about this.'

Asakusa was just noble enough to think sacrificing himself was actually *romantic*. Adrianna threw herself forward, attacking skeletons with four of her arms, not bothering to destroy them, just hitting them hard enough to *get through*. She had to get to Asakusa. She might not be able to save him—or herself, she realized as the skeletons continued to damage her exoskeleton—but at least they could be together.

Maybe that would be enough.

'Don't do it!' she shouted.

Lightning started to crack from beneath the pile of bones.

'Asa, stop it! We'll get out of this!'

'You'll get out of this. Don't let Tulk take me for nothing.'

'You're being stupid!'

'I love you, Adrianna. I've loved you since the moment I saw your white hair and black eyes. You're strong, and beautiful, but I don't deserve you. I'm just some thrall who couldn't even trade his soul for what he wanted. At least this way, I can get you to the beach.'

Adrianna pushed through the skeletons to Asakusa. She kicked the ones off his back with her arachnid legs. His Corruption had spread. It lashed out at any skeletons that approached the Gate Asakusa was opening.

'If you love me so much, then be with me,' Adrianna said, before a blow to the back of her head knocked her to the ground.

James stood over her arachnid body, bleeding from his knife wounds.

Asakusa hurled his hammer into the golem. It struck him in the skull with enough force to crack it. Yellow bone peeked out from beneath the thin layer of muscle.

But James was not defeated. He roared, and the skeletons redoubled their efforts and captured the thrall. Without his hammer, the maggots did little to the animated bones.

James approached them, limping, bleeding, his brain pulsing from the cracks in his skull.

'You will serve us well. Any last words, before you do?'

Adrianna pushed herself to her feet. She was bleeding all over from a thousand tiny fissures in her carapace, plus her injured leg.

James cracked his knuckles and took a shovel from a skeleton. He looked at them like a farmer looked at vermin. The skeletons let go of Asakusa, and he stood at Adrianna's side. They were surrounded and were about to be killed by *skeletons*, of all things. It would almost be funny if it wasn't so damn embarrassing.

'Adrianna, I wish I was worthy of you. Maybe in the next life, if I get a next life, I'll be—'

'Oh, shut up,' Adrianna said as all the rationalizing she'd been doing for the last six months—since she was told the date that she was to be married to a dragon prince against her will—evaporated from her head, and in this moment before her death, she kissed him.

He hesitated at first, obviously surprised, but then his mouth and hers melted together, and everything else fell away. Some first kisses are forgotten as soon as they happen. Others live on in one's memory to warm old bones by a fire, and this was one of those. Adrianna would forever remember the feel of Asakusa's hair, the saltiness of his tongue, the tickle of his faint mustache, the way his hands wrapped themselves in her white hair, the way his maggots were calmed.

Adrianna wished she wasn't thinking of the maggots, but there were a lot of differences between this actual kiss and how she'd imagined it going. She hadn't imagined hundreds of skeletons or a religious flesh golem being there. She certainly hadn't imagined it taking place in the shade of a tombstone castle. Nor had she imagined the screech of a dragon piercing the early morning mists.

Wait... had she imagined that?

No, there it was again—the spine-tingling shriek of an adult dragon on the hunt.

Or maybe hunting wasn't the right term, as dragons didn't make that sound until they considered the hunt ended, and the feast beginning.

Adrianna found that she was more than content to kiss Asakusa until they were both torn apart by a horde of skeletons. Despite spending the last few months telling herself otherwise, she'd waited so long for this—years, it felt like—and now, despite it being less than perfect, it was everything Adrianna wanted it to be.

Although... even as Asakusa kissed her, Adrianna felt her hand slip from his belt to her own.

She unsheathed *Flametongue* and held it up just as flames engulfed them. The blade absorbed the flames, creating a pocket of calm inside of which Adrianna and Asakusa made out fiercely as the skeletons around them were blackened and incinerated into ash. This was more like it. Their tongues did battle, and Adrianna felt years of angst melt away as Asakusa held her damaged, arachnid body like she was the most beautiful human there was. Or *a* human, at least.

James lasted just long enough for his muscles to burn away from his head, revealing a yellow skull that blackened and crumbled in the heat as the rest of the skeletons had.

'You're snogging the thrall in the middle of me rescuing you?' Richard Valkanna said, transforming into human form and marching up the steps he'd cleared with his fire breath.

'We didn't need rescuing, and I thought we were going to die, so yes,' Adrianna said once she'd extricated herself from Asakusa's mouth and pulled her thoughts together. Her husband was here. Her husband the dragon.

'If you thought you were going to die, how did you not need rescuing?' Valkanna asked, drawing his flaming sword and cutting down a skeleton charging up the stairs. There were still hundreds more. It seemed destroying James hadn't stopped Chemok from having power over the rest of the skeletons. Maybe Rolph really was in charge.

'Just shut up and blow the rest of these skeletons away,' Asakusa said.

Richard sliced through another one. His weapon seemed to be the thing to use, for each slice of the burning blade left a pile of charred bones that didn't so much as wiggle. The sword didn't even need to strike a skull to work its fiery magick. Adrianna had thought Asakusa's hammer had been effective, but Richard's sword was even better.

'A baron does not take orders from a slave. And besides, I don't have enough flame for all that,' Valkanna said haughtily. Adrianna couldn't really fault him for his arrogance, though. Maybe she was still high on her long-awaited first kiss with Asakusa, but there was something decidedly attractive about a man who could save a girl with his fire breath. Immediately, she felt the tug of conflicting emotions pull at her heart. She'd finally kissed Asakusa, and she here was thinking that Richard Valkanna was actually *attractive?*

'That's what I've been saying,' Asakusa grumbled.

Just then, the door pushed open. Rolph was standing there, in red pajamas decorated with little bats, holding a cup of his 'red wine.'

'James, I do say, what seems to be the—'

His words faded as he appraised the young dragon in his shimmering, scaled suit. His grin was replaced with a vicious sneer framed by his elongating canines. 'What is a Valkanna doing in *my* estate? No matter, you're all the same. If you apologize for your father's misdeeds, I might let you live.'

'Valkannas don't apologize, especially not to infections.'

'You two know each other?' Asakusa said.

'I know the boy's father. And that carpet was over *a thousand years old!*' the baron hissed. 'It was made by a race of beings that *don't even exist anymore!* Do you know how hard it is to find anything in *bats*? Even these pajamas had to be custom ordered!'

'I'm not here about some ugly old carpet. My father told me about you; he said his only mistake was leaving you alive. Your pajamas look stupid, by the way.'

Rolph growled at that. 'Your father always *was* a dullard. I'm hardly alive, so I cannot be left in such a state,' Rolph laughed at his own sally. Despite knowing full well that he was facing a dragon, the vampire showed not a drop of fear.

'Are we doing this, or not?'

They took to the air, Valkanna as a red dragon, Katinka as a swarm of bats.

Chapter 35

Adrianna

It was almost impossible to follow the combat above them.

Valkanna's strikes were furious. He alternated claw and bite, tail and wingbeat, but Katinka was too fast for physical blows. He dodged each strike by turning into a cloud of red mist, and then reformed either as a giant bat or a human, always laughing and hurling insults.

'You're too slow, lizard boy. Did you forget to warm yourself in the cursed sun today?'

Valkanna swung with his tail and Katinka vanished again, reforming and cracking the dragon across the brow with a fist.

Valkanna responded with a gout of flame.

'We have to get out of here,' Asakusa said. The maggots now creeping onto his face agreed, and rippled toward the Dark Key buried in his hand.

'Let's get the skull blossom,' Adrianna said, making for the castle before the horde of skeletons made it into the area Valkanna had cleared with his fire breath, but it was too late. The dragon's flames had made it to the base of the creeping vines and burned through them, turning the black and white flowers into ash.

Asakusa's fingernails began to flicker as he opened a Gate, but Adrianna stopped him.

'You can't now. We won't have enough of the flower.'

'We have no choice. You have to make it out of here,' Asakusa said. 'Plus, Vecnos should have more.'

'Your life is worth too much to trust it to an assassin's word!'

'And the lives of those women whose blood he takes isn't?'

'We met them! They were fine with it. This is different.'

'Is it?' Asakusa asked.

Adrianna didn't know how someone who was always so willing to sacrifice himself could sound so judgmental.

Adrianna hurled a dagger at the first skeleton to make it to the top of the steps. She hit her mark, cracked the skull, and the skeleton clattered to pieces. Another skeleton, this one armless, made it to the top of steps, but instead of continuing to charge at Adrianna and Asakusa, it hesitated.

'What's it doing?' Asakusa asked.

It was taking leg bones from the other skeleton… and using them as arms! With feet for hands, it ran at them. Asakusa smashed it to pieces with his hammer, it was just one skeleton after all, but what did that mean for the rest of the horde? Adrianna had never heard of a such a thing. She remembered that Chemok's power grew as he infected more skulls. Had he crossed some threshold no one had previously documented?

There was a screech as Valkanna—in dragon form—unleashed another breath of fire that sent Katinka crashing to the ground as a charred corpse.

A charred corpse that stood back up.

'Imbecile. You think *fire* can defeat me? There is but one light that I fear, and you have no power over it!' Katinka shouted. His fine clothes had been burned away, as had much of his skin, but standing there in the growing light, shaded by his castle of tombstones, he did not look at all weakened, for though his muscles and bones could be seen, already was his body reknitting itself.

'Now come at me, you flying gecko!'

Valkanna roared and another gout of flame erupted from his throat, only this one didn't go nearly so far. In fact, the ball of flame was so small that Katinka knocked it aside with the back of his hand.

The dragon had used up his fuel.

He dive-bombed Katinka.

Katinka grabbed a shovel and held it up at the approaching dragon, a silly gesture of defiance.

Or it would have been, had not fifty skeletons done the same.

Valkanna did not have time to react. He spread his wings far too late, and unable to slow himself, crashed into the upraised points of Katinka's army of undead farmers.

He screeched in pain, transforming into his human form to shed the weapons that had impaled him.

Katinka only laughed, turned back into a cloud of blood droplets, and streaked past Adrianna and Asakusa and into his castle. The doors slammed shut behind him.

For the briefest of moments, Adrianna thought the skeletons would lay down their arms with the rising sun, but this proved not to be. Instead, the horde of yellowed bones surged around Valkanna, hacking at him with shovels. Well, at least this explained why only a few skeletons had come up the steps to attack Adrianna and Asakusa.

Adrianna thought that might be the end of her husband. That, like she'd fantasized, he'd die doing something dumb, and she'd be heir to Krag's Doom, ruler-to-be of both her and her husband's families, and free to do as she wished—only Valkanna hadn't been doing something dumb, it had been heroic. He'd come to save her.

'Richard,' she said, and stepped forward. Asakusa only grunted. His Corruption had spread when he'd tried to open that Gate, but the skeletons were all focused on the dragon now… he would be okay.

'I can get you out of here,' Asakusa said.

'No, I… I can't leave him. Especially if you're so willing to die for me. I'll need someone to grow old with.' Adrianna meant it as a joke. Or she thought she did. She didn't know what she meant anymore.

Asakusa scowled but said, 'Then we save him.'

He grabbed his hammer and ran down the steps at Adrianna's heel.

Together they crashed into the back of the mass of skeletons. Adrianna whipped them to pieces, cutting a narrow path through the clattering of bones, while Asakusa swung recklessly, protecting their flanks with both his hammer and his Corruption.

But it wasn't going to be enough.

There were still too many skeletons. They'd destroyed dozens, yet hundreds remained.

Adrianna fought harder, pushing through the clattering bones until she saw him.

Valkanna swung back and forth with his sword. It was no longer flaming. Now it only smoked.

'Valkanna!' she called, throwing a dagger into a skeleton about to stab him with a trowel. It clattered to pieces. Asakusa swung his stone hammer in a whirlwind and cleared a space around them.

'Call me… Richard!' her husband said, and then transformed into a dragon and extended his wings, knocking the skeletons away.

'On my back!' he roared.

Adrianna grabbed Asakusa by his Corrupted hand and dragged him forward. They scrambled onto Valkanna's back, and with a beat of his wings, they were in the air.

'How much of the flower did we get?' Adrianna asked.

'Not even a single dozen,' Asakusa said, opening his bag and then snapping it shut as the rising sun's rays scorched the petals.

'Where are we going?' Valkanna said.

'S'kar-vozi,' Adrianna replied.

'I can't make it that far,' Valkanna said. 'I'll need to heal these wounds.' She looked over the side of his red, scaly body and saw skeletons armed with oranges. They hurled them from slings with enough force to cause them to explode against the dragon's scaly hide. Most of the orange pieces simply fell away, but those that hit the wounds inflicted by the shovels caused the dragon to flinch in pain from the citric acid.

'Just get us out of here. I need to call a friend.' Adrianna pulled out her scrying mirror and called for Ebbo, but as soon as she saw the halfling's face, looking back and forth with a big fake smile, one of the skeleton's oranges knocked the family heirloom from her fingertips. The scrying mirror fell to the ground below.

'We have to go back!' Scrying stones were rare enough, but one that worked as well as Adrianna's was practically priceless.

'It's fine. I have a gem you can use, it's tucked behind my ear in this form.'

Sure enough, there was a large, beautifully cut red gemstone behind the dragon's horns. Clearly, like Adrianna, Valkanna—Richard! had trouble distinguishing his body parts in either form. Adrianna took it and stared into its glowing center.

Immediately a wave of nausea hit her as she saw herself falling into the sky, and then a horde of skeletons stepping on her as a dragon carried off—it was her mirror. She was seeing what her mirror saw.

'This is how you knew where I was! You've been spying on me!'

'I've been protecting you!' Valkanna said back. 'And you haven't made it easy. I've been waiting for you to use the cursed thing.'

'Creep,' Asakusa said.

'Loser,' Valkanna retorted.

As they left the burned-out farm, spiraling higher and higher, the skeletons stopped throwing oranges. With the rising of the sun, the skeletons —unburned but perhaps uncomfortable—dug holes between the crops and buried each other. The last few skeletons that could be seen crawled into the dirt, and then they were lost in the mist.

Adrianna stole one last glance back at the looming castle before it too was swallowed up by the mist. The last embers crackled away from it, and there it stood, a monolith of bricks made for the dead, by the dead. Some of the carvings of the names of the skeletons glinted in the last rays of the sun, then it, as well as their hopes of healing Asakusa without having to rely on Vecnos, were behind them.

Adrianna turned her attention to the scrying gem.

Chapter 36

Ebbo

'I hope these gentlemen are a sight better than those hrocs we defeated,' Clay's heart said from under Ebbo's arm.

Ebbo forced a laugh. Was this how everyone else felt when he said things like that?

'They are a sight better,' Ebbo said. '*These* hrocs are much better looking and more intelligent than their brothers.'

They were surrounded, just outside the bar, by three times as many hrocs as had been inside. Well, technically six times as many, since Clayton wasn't able to actually use any clay at the moment. With meant it was twelve half-orcs against one half-ling. Ebbo wasn't much for comparing fractions, but it didn't sound good.

'You... slayed them?' one of the hrocs with a particularly impressive underbite said.

'The halfling wants skull blossom! Tried to trick us,' a hroc emerging from the bar said in the common tongue.

The hrocs grunted and snorted at that. Ebbo wasn't much for languages, but he didn't think the tone of these grunts and snorts was a positive one.

'Look, I should've recognized a taste for botany when I saw one. How was I supposed to know that hrocs honor their dead with skull blossom? I can assure you I will never ask for something so presumptuous again,' Ebbo said, smiling as wide as he could, crinkling his eyes above his round little cheeks.

'We prefer half-orc, you filthy halfling.'

'Ebbo, Ebbo!' Adrianna's voice said from the piece of milky quartz in Ebbo's pocket.

'Fellas, you gotta believe me when I say someone important is calling.'

The half-orcs looked at each other, clearly not used to either magick communication or ventriloquism.

Ebbo removed the scrying stone and looked at Adrianna. Asakusa was behind her, on top of some sort of long red snake…

'Whoa! you decided to have sex with both of them?' Ebbo said.

'Now is not the time!' Clayton, Adrianna, and Asakusa yelled from different sides of the stone.

'We barely made it out of here alive. The skull blossom was burned. We need as much as you can get!'

'Wait, but Clayton isn't doing so hot!'

'—I'm fine.

'He is *not* fine. You guys need to get back here!'

'Not gonna happen. Asakusa's hurt, and so is… my husband. So am I.' Adrianna said. 'You need to get to Vecnos and make sure he actually has the skull-blossom he said he did. Asakusa's life depends on it.'

Then the connection went dead, leaving only an inky blackness, with something with tentacles hidden among pinpricks of light. Ebbo wisely stopped staring into the stone. He wasn't quite sure what to do, but these hrocs—or the ones inside, anyway—had mentioned Vecnos by name and seemed to know a bit about skull blossom. If Vecnos had skull blossom, maybe these hrocs knew about it. Ebbo hoped that Vecnos would do the honorable thing and give Asakusa the balm, as he'd said would—but Vecnos wasn't Ebbo's hero because he was known for being honorable…

'Gentlemen—pardon me, half-gentlemen, half-orcs. I was saying I have nothing but respect for your taste in horticulture, which is why I was hoping I might actually be able to get some of those skull blossoms.' Ebbo flashed his most winning smile.

The half-orcs drew their weapons.

BOOK 3

To Snort One's Soul

Chapter 37

Clayton

Clayton Steelheart had to shout to wake up his friend Ebbo Brandyoak. Shouting isn't easy when one's magic metal heart is barely palpitating, and it is nearly impossible when one is missing all of the clay that makes up their golem body. Clayton only had enough clay to form a disappointingly thin pair of lips on his steel heart. Shouting--easy or not--is less than advisable when done inside a hroc jail cell, but Clayton felt that he was out of options, so he shouted all the same, vibrating his heart as loudly as possible so that the lips attached directly to its metal surface could form consonants around the buzzy vowels.

Ebbo and the hrocs responded in the same manner: with loud grumbles and vague threats.

Clayton was encouraged. A grumble was more than he had hoped for from the islander, and less than he had expected from the hrocs. Hrocs. The offspring of humans and orcs. He'd seen hrocs before, and though they weren't nearly as powerful as their near legendary full-blooded orc ancestors, they were intimidating all the same. They were typically at least twelve hands tall, had thick gray skin, black hair, and jutting lower canines that many filed down to fit in. There weren't many of them in the free city, but Clayton knew there were pockets around the Archipelago—mostly the offspring of those that survived the marauding orcs. He wondered where these ones were from. The clothes they'd been wearing when they'd captured him and Ebbo hadn't looked local and all of their teeth were unfiled and decidedly intimidating.

'Psst, hey, wake up!' Clayton whispered. With so little of his clay, his voice sounded like a loose snare drum.

Ebbo did not respond. Clayton was not surprised.

'Hey!' Clayton hissed loudly enough to knock himself over. After a few moments of clanging about, he managed to right his steel heart using only his clay lips. Not an easy thing to do.

Still nothing from the tiny sleeping form of Ebbo.

'Stir yourself, halfling!'

'Not...halfling...shit's offensive. We're islanders,' Ebbo said, rolling over and pushing himself to his feet. Fortunately, being so short, he didn't have far to push.

Clayton envied the movement. He had been feeling around for any sort of loose minerals with his clay lips, but he'd found nothing. 'You've got to get us out of here,' he whispered. 'The hrocs cleaned our cell. They know what my people can do with a few pounds of clay.'

'You're the only one of your people, brolem, and I don't think they've heard tell of your deeds. And besides, why would there be any clay in the sewer, anyway?' Ebbo said, turning out his pockets. 'Those hucklepickin' hrocs robbed me!' His shrill voice echoed down the hall. 'You stole my pixie wing!'

'Aye,' one of the hrocs yelled, 'Quiet.'

'Now is not the time for magick. We have to get the skull-blossoms for Asakusa's Corruption.' Clayton whispered as aggressively as he dared. He couldn't see a thing, and Ebbo was already causing trouble? They had to get out of here before the hrocs tried to further rough up the islander. Clayton wouldn't be able to defend him in his current state.

'He said quiet,' a hroc grunted and began to shuffle over.

'How many of them are there?' Ebbo said, rubbing sleep from his eyes. Clayton could hear the creak of the bars to their cell as Ebbo pushed against them, presumably trying to get a look.

'I can't be sure. Two, I think, or five,' Clayton said.

'Or five? How can it be two or five? Can't you feel their footsteps—oh! They're asleep!' Ebbo said and snapped his fingers in satisfaction at the mystery solved.

'They're not asleep! Anyway, at least two of them aren't. And in case you hadn't noticed, I'm a bit bereft of my usual faculties. I can't see a thing right now, and I don't even have enough clay to make a proper pair of cheekbones!'

'Eh, I can tell you've been reading the dictionary, but I don't think bereft is the right word,' Ebbo said, paying no attention the approaching hrocs.

'Bereft: deprived or lacking something, especially a non-material object,' Clayton said, managing to sound indignant despite only having enough sediment for a small mouth. 'I am bereft of my body, and I can assure you it is quite distressing.'

'Quiet!' the approaching hroc shouted.

'Yeah, but it's more like about gone things. Many an islander used to say

"I bereft the flowers of spring," ' Ebbo said wistfully.

'I am bereft of my awesome clay body.'

'If it's so awesome, why did you let those hrocs knock you to pieces? That never happens!'

'Be quiet,' Clayton said.

'No, but that's the thing. Bereft is like you're not going to get it back. Like the loss of a dear old songbird, or perhaps the first summer after a particularly fine sugar maple was struck by lightning. So bereft doesn't work, because you are going to get your body back, right? You should have been able to take those hrocs, no problem.'

Am I going to get it back? Clayton wondered. His Heartbeats kept slipping away. Normally they didn't do that unless he forced them to animate his body, or if his steel heart was full. After a night of rest without a body to move, he should have had plenty. But he didn't. This caused the golem no small amount of anxiety.

'We prefer half-orc, halfling,' the hroc said.

'Pardon me, half-orc, I did not know,' Ebbo said, startling before falling into his familiar patter about slurs. 'I am Ebbo Brandyoak, and my people too suffer the indignities of slang. We prefer the term "islander" to "halfling," as the latter is a loaded term that evokes fattened bellies and sticky fingers instead of--'

'My name Dergh, not half-orc. Shut your fat mouth, or Oluf bury you alive, halfling,' Dergh said.

'If you're going to bury anyone alive, I'd start with the talking metal heart,' Ebbo said casually.

For a moment Clayton dared to hope for such a punishment. Even without a proper cache of Heartbeats, being buried would definitely solve his lack of clay.

'We smash you both and bury you both, deep!'

Making them angry wasn't a good tact, then, Clayton thought. Judging from the hroc's pronunciation, the underbite wasn't particularly severe, at least for a hroc. His tusks, or whatever they were that stuck up from his bottom jaw, hardly interfered with his consonants.

'Our apologies, sir--' Clayton said, but Dergh interrupted.

'I'm a woman! And you insensitive,' Dergh said.

'Madame, please forgive me,' Clayton crooned.

'How was I supposed to know she was a girl? She's wearing a shirt, after all,' Ebbo said, immediately taking offense despite currently being imprisoned by Dergh.

Clayton could only hope Ebbo's hand was reaching through the bars for more dirt. Currently the golem's hearing felt muffled, and he couldn't even smell past a couple of feet. He needed clay to sense vibrations through the ground and the silica within to detect changes in light. Another handful of dirt sounded wonderful.

One of Dergh's companions down the hall grabbed something heavy and struck the wall hard enough for Clayton to feel it. 'They shut up! Shut up or boss bury them. He say quiet!' the hroc roared.

'A shirt is precisely how you would know the lovely half-orc before us is a more sensitive creature than her clan brothers,' Clayton whispered. 'Half-orc men prefer to go shirtless, but, like humans, and islanders, women cover their nipples.'

'It is a nice shirt,' Ebbo said. Clayton knew the islander was lying--he wouldn't know rough silk from fine hemp--but he heard him rub the fabric, which meant Ebbo was touching the hroc's clothes, a very good sign, considering Ebbo was a pickpocket.

'Thanks. Heirloom,' Dergh said.

'Needs cleaning, though,' Ebbo said as he dusted his hands off. Bits of dirt rained down on Clayton's steel heart.

The golem's Heartbeats pumped through the mineral crystals in the dirt, realigning them to the shape Clayton desired, making them his own so long as he had the Heartbeats to control them. Fortunately, it didn't take many Heartbeats to speak, and after being caged all night, Clayton did have some to spare, though it was far less than it should have been —nowhere near his limit of a hundred thousand. At sixty beats per minute, and a night of staying completely still while the islander slept, he should have had somewhere around twenty thousand Heartbeats, but instead he only had a few hundred. Even if he did get a body's worth of clay, he very much doubted that he'd be able to fight.

It was worrying, but Clayton couldn't let Ebbo see the extent of his injuries. The islander would undoubtedly freak out.

With this paltry handful of dirt, Clayton was able to make his voice deeper and more expressive. 'I did not mean to make such a suggestion, but in my current condition I am unable to appreciate even the loveliest of creatures and must rely on less...sophisticated methods. If I bother you, by all means, bury me. My associate won't even fight you if you decide to.'

'Got that right,' Ebbo said.

'We not bury you. We break you. Molok say curse your kind,' Dergh said.

'I very much doubt that I am the kind you are speaking of,' Clayton said. He'd much prefer to be buried. It might not solve his Heartbeat problem, but the thought of being broken further was... well, Clayton had never really feared death, not exactly, but suddenly he felt he could sympathize with the feeling.

'Ma-sheen,' the hroc said disdainfully. It was a word Clayton had never heard.

'Tell me, when you speak of your enemy, do you mean humans?'

'Mmm,' Dergh grunted, 'yes, humans suck.'

'Indeed, they do, but as you can probably tell, we are not humans. I am a construct, a golem, as I'm sure you know—what with the clean cell and everything—and you've already quite astutely pointed out that my friend is an islander, and we both know islanders and humans are quite different in almost every regard except for their willingness to eat plants.'

Dergh laughed at that, and Clayton joined her.

Responding to the peals of laughter came the other hroc—half-orc!— Clayton was really going to have to be careful with that one, if diplomacy were to get them out of here. Without enough clay, he couldn't resort to making his body into Dergh's ideal lover, seduction being something jailers often fantasized about, or so said Clayton's friends back at the Red Underoo. Not that it would matter, Clayton realized. He could feel Dergh's footsteps retreating.

'What is so funny about eating plants?' Ebbo whispered even as another half-orc approached.

'It's nothing. You wouldn't get it.'

'Would Adrianna get it?' Ebbo asked.

'Well, yes. I mean, she is a spider princess. I rather imagine Asakusa might get it as well. I'm sure that demon master of his is a carnivore of some sort, and I'm sure he loves to pester Asakusa, what with him being such a stick in the mud.' Clayton snorted at his own joke, a difficult feat with so little clay to maneuver.

'What the huckleberry is that supposed to mean?' Ebbo demanded.

'A stick in the mud? It's a human expression that basically means boring and prudish and seems to fit Asakusa almost perfectly, especially considering I'm his friend.'

'No, what is that supposed to mean about eating plants? Does that mean it's better to eat meat? That's wasteful, that is, and cruel. Half this world thinks us islanders taste better than perfectly nutritious vegetables. The other half only ever come to our rescue if they think they'll get a pumpkin out of it.'

Something clanged against the bars of the cell.

Ebbo shrieked and jumped—Clayton could feel him leave the ground and land again.

'Oye! We said shut up!' the voice of another half-orc said.

'No need to bang your club on the bars,' Ebbo grumbled.

The hroc smashed the bars again, much harder this time. Thanks to the blow, Clayton could tell the bars were hollow, or some of them were, anyway. Some of them sent vibrations into the walls and traveled around corners. Water pipes. That could only mean the hrocs hadn't taken them far from where they'd captured Ebbo and Clayton. They'd just picked an unusual direction: down. They were in the tunnels underneath S'Kar-Vozi, in a cell built somewhere in the clockwork sewer system that kept S'kar-Vozi's apartments clean and its bay filthy. Clayton didn't know much about hrocs, but the fact that they had enough materials to build a cell for their prisoners seemed to indicate that they were working for someone. Clayton had figured as much, it's not like hrocs were much for teleportation, and they had to get to the Free City somehow. It was nice to know which way was home: up.

It wouldn't be easy without his body, harder still without enough silica to see anything more than light and dark, but Clayton had to try to get them out of here. 'My dear half-orc, please give me a moment so that I can get to know you better. You see, the last time your friend-'

'Dergh is no friend of Oluf,' the half-orc—Oluf, presumably—grunted.

'Of course not, dear Oluf, you are of much denser of mind than she was, that is already clear. However, if my friend would but describe you, I would better be able to assuage your doubts of a perceived nefarious intent.' Flattery often worked wonders on those that wished to seem powerful. Clayton hoped half-orcs were just as flawed as every other species he'd ever encountered.

Flattery certainly seemed a safer tact. The golem was in no state to fight, because his Heartbeats kept slipping away. Clayton wouldn't admit it to Ebbo —especially not in a situation like this—but he was in dire need of dire repairs. He had never before been so desperate to see his poor excuse for a creator. But he needed to know what they were up against if they were to get out of here.

'You wish to announce me? Good! Oluf will be King. Announce, halfling!'

'We really do prefer the word islander if we're going to be using labels-' Ebbo protested, but a grunt from Oluf seemed to quiet him. Ebbo cleared his throat and proceeded with forced formality, 'Standing before you is a strong, handsome hroc, with pointy tusks-'

'We are half-orc!'

'See, that's my point exactly,' Ebbo said.

Oluf smashed at the bars of the cell with his weapon. This time a pipe broke, and water began to spray all over the walls. Ebbo seemed to get the point.

'Brave Oluf, leader of his people, wears the once-clean pelt of a griffin, a bronze belt and a loin-cloth—thank the gods—and, actually, some pretty stylish lace-up sandals. He carries a shiny piece of metal-'

'Iron,' Oluf interrupted. 'Well, technically stainless steel.'

Clayton had never heard those words used like that before.

'He carries a piece of, uh... steel, I guess, that is dented from many a brawl with many a stubborn rock. He has skin the gray color of rotten bark, nappy wisps of hair that look like wheat that's been picked over by crows. His stench—as I'm sure you noticed—is stronger even than the sewers and makes it clear that this place is some sort of vacation destination for him, instead of a long-term residence.'

Oluf roared and smashed at the bars again with his club.

'You wouldn't want to break your jail cell. You'd have to have your master buy you another one,' Ebbo said. 'Go get the keys from Dergh. It's not like we're going anywhere.'

Oluf roared again, but seeing the prisoner's wisdom, tromped down the hallway.

'He broke the bars enough for us to escape?' Clayton said. He could hear well enough—being made of clay meant he was especially tuned to vibrations—but he was still basically blind.

'Nope, holes are still too small, even for me. Kobold manufacture, obviously. That's why some have water running through them. Kobolds are obsessed with doing house chores, and nothing makes chores easier than indoor plumbing,' Ebbo said. The islander had always had an affinity for the strange, furry beings that lived and worked on the clockwork sewers that ran beneath S'kar-Vozi.

'Knowing this, you had him break the pipe so the grime that they failed to clean off the walls would wash down, and I could use it to bust us out of here!' Clayton said.

'Nope, kobolds cleaned the walls. I could drink from the puddle in the floor, actually. Those kobolds really know how to clean!'

'Obviously when they found out that Clayton Steelheart, the Free Golem of the Free City, was coming, they took special precautions. Ha! Even the kobolds have heard of me.'

'Uh... I think it's more like kobolds clean everything, *obviously*. And also, *obviously*, I'm not relying on you. You're just going to eat me like a sausage with your new friend Dergh.'

'Oh for goodness sake—you're mad I was joking with our captor? I was just trying to soften her up, so she'd spring us out of here eventually.'

'Well, there's no need for that anymore,' Ebbo said.

'Well obviously, what with our imminent demise at a piece of shiny iron,' Clayton grumbled.

'No, there's no need for that because when you were flirting with that butt-ugly hroc, I stole the keys from her.'

'You what?'

Sure enough, there was a tinkling of keys and the creak of a prison door.

'You told me to get us out of here, so I did.'

Chapter 38

Ebbo

'That was terribly irresponsible of you,' Clayton complained from Ebbo's bag instead of saying thank you a thousand times like he should have. The hrocs had gotten into a brawl over the missing keys. Ebbo had been able to pinch a small purse to carry Clayton's steel heart until they found something he could animate. Clayton hadn't thanked him for that either. Ungrateful golem.

'I don't see what the berry-picking problem is,' Ebbo said, coming to a fork in the stone and brick sewer tunnel. After a moment, he chose the left path. He didn't know if that was the right decision—normally Asakusa or Clayton navigated cityscapes—but he knew they had to keep moving. The hrocs would give chase, and Ebbo had seen some of their... tools? Weapons? He didn't know what the shiny metal things were that looked far more complex than the iron cudgel Oluf had been threatening them with. They had something like an arrow down the middle of them and looked quite spooky to poor Ebbo. What were these hrocs? They weren't great with the common tongue, but Ebbo knew better than to assume that meant they weren't smart, especially after seeing those devices. Had they built them?

'Was that another fork?' Clayton asked.

'Yep. I picked left. Left felt good,' Ebbo said, trying to sound confident.

'You know, there's a lot you can tell about where we are based on the composition of the walls of the sewer,' Clayton said. 'Just like the architecture of the free city, the various building styles lend clues as to when this was built and our location.'

'Oh, come on, I'm getting us out of here. Isn't that enough? You want me to narrate the scenery for you too?' Ebbo griped. 'We're in a tunnel made of... bricks, with bits of, uh... is that mortar? The floor is made of stone, and there's a trickle of something I don't want to think about going down the middle. You know I don't get all this stuff. Do you have another problem with my escape plan?' Ebbo couldn't believe it. Clayton didn't seem capable of making a body at all, and he was whining about Ebbo's exit strategy?

'Just make sure you keep going *against* the current,' Clayton ordered.

'Yeah, yeah.' Ebbo wouldn't have had any trouble navigating somewhere with proper landmarks like trees, boulders, or cozy little taverns. Describing the sizes and shapes of bricks was duller than a wooden shovel.

'I am thankful that you got us out of there. My only problem is that Dergh seemed nice, and you probably got her into all sorts of trouble,' Clayton said, sounding genuinely worried about the hroc. That was just like Clayton. He worried about everyone. Ebbo thought it was kind of annoying when it wasn't about him.

'The problem with those filthy hrocs is that they were going to cook me up and eat me, and you were probably going to give them recipes.'

'Ebbo, for the sake of silk and satin, I was just kidding!'

'This is what we get all the time! All. The. time!' Ebbo said. He wasn't yelling, his people never did, but he certainly made his voice a bit less joyous and whimsical than usual. 'Islanders are eaten by everything: dragons, serpents, sea creatures, giants, giant serpents, sea-dragons-'

'I get it,' Clayton said, guilt creeping into his voice, but not enough!

'No, you don't! Making that joke proves you don't get it. I know how the rest of them think of me, of us. Just another plump little halfling.' Ebbo lowered his voice, puffed out his chest and sort of waggled back and forth as he impersonated his oppressors. 'Let's just eat 'im right up like he's a pumpkin instead of a little person with dreams of his own. Let's just steal these fat babies from their mothers and feed them to a bunch of giant-serpent-dragon-sharks.'

'I didn't mean--'

'I expect this kind of stuff from hrocs, and Adrianna's family, and even Asakusa, but you? You're supposed to be the nice guy!'

'Ebbo someone's going to hear us-'

'Let them hear! Or did you forget that I'm a master of stealth and deception? Boisonberries, when I'm as famous as Vecnos, I hope I don't have to deal with stuff like this.' Ebbo came to another branch in the sewers and chose a direction.

'Vecnos may be rich and powerful, but he's an assassin,' Clayton said from Ebbo's bag.

'Well, I bet his friends at least believe in him,' Ebbo protested. 'You could've believed in me getting the keys, you knew I was picking her pocket. I gave you that dirt as a clue! But you didn't think I was going for the keys, did you? You thought that I... I was...'

'I thought you were looking for magick,' Clayton said from Ebbo's stolen purse. It was a small comfort that at least Clayton sounded like he felt bad about treating Ebbo like an addict.

Despite Clayton's insinuations that he was less than helpful, Ebbo had been running his hands along the carved stone walls, looking for veins of clay or bits of mortar from the places that been done over in brick by the kobolds who maintained the sewer under S'Kar-vozi. He'd managed to fill the bag with enough grit to fully submerge the golem's steel heart.

Ebbo looked down at the purse, his silvery brow furrowed, his mouth a tiny frown. Clayton's chiseled features—made of bits of rock and probably a touch of human excrement—looked up at him.

'I'm sorry, buddy,' Clayton said. He at least had the decency to look like he felt terrible about bringing up the subject of Ebbo's... interest.

'No, it's fine,' Ebbo sniffed. 'I *was* looking for magick. But not because I have a problem! I just thought I might need some to pick the lock.'

Clayton bit his lip and nodded. Ebbo knew that look. Clayton didn't believe him... But maybe that was fair. Ebbo's insistence in asking the hrocs about magick was what had gotten them into this mess in the first place. Well, actually, it was Asakusa's fault because he'd overused his powers, but Ebbo could at least admit (to himself) that he'd played a small part in getting them into this situation.

'I... I guess I didn't need any magick,' Ebbo said weakly. 'But I did manage to get us lost.'

'It's an improvement over getting smashed to pieces by a cudgel of iron,' Clayton said.

'I didn't get the skull-blossom for Asakusa's nasty, maggoty arm either' Ebbo said.

'We'll find some. Grows on stones placed on grave dirt, right?'

Ebbo nodded. 'I can recite the poem if you wish.'

'No, right now, I'd like you to drop me in that sludge,' Clayton said, using his Heartbeats to make a single finger and gesture toward the slow trickle of waste running down the middle of the tunnel they were in.

'Clayton, come on, I apologized. Let's get out of here.'

'You did not apologize. But if I waited for that, I'd be here all day.'

'Then why drop you in the poop? You've said the smell's impossible to get out of your body.'

'Seeing as how I don't currently have a body, I don't see what choice I have. Now come on, drop me in. The diet of the people of the free city definitely involves a bit of sand and grit. I'll filter it out, then we'll get out of here, find some of that flower, and take a shower before Adrianna and Asakusa get back.'

Ebbo dropped Clayton in the sludge. It did not look particularly pleasant for the golem, nor did it reflect well on the diet of S'Kar-Vozi that a golem was able to reconstitute himself out of the mineral content of its sewers. Apparently, much of the diet of the hundred thousand or so multi-special denizens was supplemented with indigestible minerals—that, and way more spices than Ebbo had ever smelled back on Strongoak Island.

As Ebbo crept along the sewer, Clayton dragged himself upstream through the sludge, steel heart pumping, growing taller as his Heartbeats claimed more and more minerals. The trickle of filth behind the beating metal heart grew a bit runnier, though hardly any cleaner, as first Clayton grew an arm to pull himself along, then another, then a head, and finally two legs.

Clayton stepped from the stream of sludge, tall, handsome, broad-chested, sludge-colored, naked and anatomically correct. Ebbo would have hugged him if not for the obvious health concerns.

'You look like shit,' Ebbo said.

Clayton snorted. 'An obvious quip, but at least it didn't feel heart-less,' Clayton said.

Ebbo rolled his eyes. 'We'd better hurry. If the kobolds flush the sewers, we might get washed into the Bay. Do you know which way to go?'

Clayton put a foot back in the trickle of filth. His toes extended to the pulse of his Heartbeats, like the roots of a tree. After a moment of smelling with his toes, Clayton nodded.

'I found an exit, or at least a place with more clean water than any other direction.'

'You can get us there?'

'Not a problem. We just go straight, then right, right, left, straight, up a small waterfall, then left, and then we should be there.'

'Yes, I would've got us there,' Ebbo said, relieved that Clayton's body was back and that the golem was helping. Ebbo had enough sense to admit to himself that he would never have gotten them out of here. They started down the sewer—or up, Ebbo supposed, as they were going against the trickle of sludge.

'Of course, I just wanted to tell you in case... Oh, dear. Ebbo?'

Ebbo turned around in time to see Clayton take a step off his legs. Or that's what it looked like to Ebbo, anyway. Clayton was walking, and then his legs just sort of broke off and he was a torso again.

'I thought you said you were fine!' Ebbo said, padding back to Clayton on silent feet.

'I am fine!'

'No, this is definitely not fine! What the huckleberry is wrong with you?'

'I... I don't know,' Clayton's normally oh-so-strong voice cracked, 'I think maybe when Adrianna's husband fire-blasted me, the magic did something to my heart. A bunch of Heartbeats just slipped away. I'm down to basically nothing again.'

'But your heart is what makes you special! If that dragon messed it up, I swear I will... I'll jam his berries with salt!'

'There's nothing special about my heart,' Clayton said with a dismissive wave of a hand dripping with filth. Beat by beat, he built a body again, but it was painstakingly slow. Normally he'd just use his reserve of Heartbeats to quicken his pulse and grow his body to whatever shape he desired. But without those reserves, he could barely hold himself together. Ebbo wondered if this was why normal golems didn't change shape. After a few minutes, and hundreds of Heartbeats, Clayton had a body again, but Ebbo noticed he was keeping his feet squarely in the sludge he was using to animate himself, and he was still dripping, which was gross. It was like he couldn't dry himself out, which for a golem skilled in melee combat, was a pretty big deal.

'If there's nothing special about your heart, how come you can make yourself into a bridge and all that?'

'I think my unusual abilities come from my mother--'

'Oh, not this again.' Ebbo rolled his eyes.

'I do have a mother. I must! You've met my father.'

'Yes, and I agree that it seems unlikely that Leopold the Grimy made something that outlasted his warranties, but as old Burpa used to say--'

'Yes, yes, sometimes strawberries grow in an onion patch.'

Ebbo wanted to nod in satisfaction at such a wise and appropriate quote, but at that moment two other things seized his attention.

One of them was the sound of the hrocs working their way up the sewers.

'Stupid halfling scratched the walls up,' one of them—probably one smarter than Oluf—was saying.

The other was the electric tingle of magick.

'Clayton, we need to go,' Ebbo said. 'The hrocs found our trail, and I don't think splashing them is going to be particularly effective.'

'Well, by all means,' Clayton said.

The two of them took off through the sewer, Ebbo on silent feet and

Clayton splashing much too noisily.

Chapter 39

Ebbo

At first, it wasn't much of a challenge to lose the hrocs. Ebbo hurried along on the silent soles of his feet, Clayton splashing along behind him. They went straight, then right, right, left, straight, up a small waterfall, but at the last turn, rather than going right, Ebbo went left. He looked back to see if the golem noticed, but Clayton was distracted with his body.

'This way, buddy!' Ebbo called out when Clayton came to the final junction.

'Right behind you. These Heartbeats keep-' An arm sloughed off Clayton.

Ebbo felt a stab of worry in chest about Clayton—never had he seen the golem's form fail him as consistently as it had today—but Clayton insisted he was fine, so Ebbo tried to beleive him. Plus, it was hard to think about Clayton right now; the smell of magick was strong here, so strong. Maybe whatever was making it could help Clayton! Ebbo briefly considered that the electric tingle of the magick was so intense that he couldn't think straight, but this way was also better lit than the sewer to the right. Surely it was an exit. He hoped that Clayton assumed that was why he went this way.

If Clayton did think anything of Ebbo's choice of direction, he didn't say it, for he followed him through the sewer, splashing along unattractively. The golem was able to keep up with Ebbo well enough, but he certainly didn't look good doing it. Rather than making a body with proper arms and legs in their proper places, he was just a big, thrashing mess of limbs radiating from his steel heart, shoving themselves along. It was gross and looked like it took a lot of work and probably a bit of concentration, which was good, because the magick was potent up ahead and Clayton would normally have noticed it a long time ago.

The roof of the tunnel was getting higher and higher, and then there was no roof, and Ebbo was looking up at an overcast sky framed between two extremely tall walls. Ebbo looked back at Clayton. He was falling behind but still progressing. Ebbo noticed that the sludge around the golem's feet now just seemed to be clean water. That was good, right? Clayton looked like he was doing better, which meant Ebbo could sniff out whatever stank so badly of magick.

Ebbo looked up again to see one of the walls had an end. At its top stood trees, flush with green and red with apples. The islander's stomach grumbled. On the other side, though, the wall went up and up and up, changing from the black stone that formed the bedrock of all the islands around the Archipelago, to bricks cut from that same stone, to an enormous, unbroken white of a different kind of rock.

The Ringwall.

Somehow Ebbo and Clayton had followed the sewers all the way up through the city, past the unknowably ancient structure that protected the very richest of S'kar-Vozi.

Ebbo paused. He could hear voices.

He stole a glance back at Clayton. He was pulling himself out of the clean trickle of water with limited success. It kept washing away bits of his body back into the sewers. Clayton was struggling to maintain even a muddy version of himself.

Maybe...maybe whoever was up there would have some sort of magick that could help Clayton. Wasn't the golem always going on about his fairy godmother? Maybe someone in the Ringwall would know about her. If anyone had magick that powerful, they would be one of the Nine, right?

'Clayton, I'm going to scout ahead. Someone's talking up there.'

'Yes, fine,' Clayton said, his words sounding like he had porridge in his mouth.

Ebbo left him to follow the pungent tingle of magick. He had to find what was making it... for his friend.

He crept forward, silent as only islanders can be, hoping to hear a clue about who or what was radiating such power.

Ebbo kept his hand on the wall to his left. It bulged slightly, a convex curve broken nowhere except for the tunnel into the sewers Ebbo had just passed through. The right wall stayed close for a few paces, but then it widened out into a room crammed with statues and choked with plants. Instead of a narrow hall, Ebbo found himself in a space the size of a skull-ball field, far below the apple trees above.

The room had old statues, some carved from the black bedrock; others, far older based on the frighteningly realistic style, were made of the same white stone as the Ringwall itself. All were covered with plants, tiny dry vines with needle-like barbs...and white flowers spotted with black to look like skulls.

'Skull-blossom!' Ebbo whispered to himself. Exactly what they needed to help Asakusa. The room was filled with it. Those weren't statues, then, but grave markers. Which meant this was a graveyard bigger than most islanders' vegetable patches! The elder races had once had a penchant for the dramatic when it came to death. Islanders didn't bury their dead, of course, but composted them. As far as Ebbo knew, humans didn't bury their dead either; they either threw them into the sea, or burned them. This was probably the largest cache of dead elves and dwarves in all of S'kar-Vozi—maybe even the Archipelago, not counting the weird nightmare Adrianna had called them from—and the flowers were loving it. Despite the sun being up, the skull blossom was able to bloom inside this ancient, sunken graveyard that was hidden near the Ringwall itself.

Ebbo picked a few, cramming them into his pockets. Thieving habits Asakusa would approve of for once.

'Clayton, we found the stash! Vecnos is going to be impressed! Start gathering this stuff while I poke around.'

'Righty-O! Just give me a moment...'

There was a splash, undoubtedly from a piece of Clayton slipping away. Ebbo still hadn't found the source of magick he'd smelled, but he told himself he could wait a moment to get Clayton picking the flower they needed before he sniffed it out.

But then there was a rustle from somewhere in the thicket of skull blossom, and Ebbo faded into the shadows around him. He didn't disappear or turn invisible or anything like that. He simply pulled up his green cloak and stepped out of any obvious lines of sight. There was a moment of pure silence, broken just once by the sound of a lonely albatross crossing the band of cloudy sky above him.

'Regardless, I do not think it is a wise course of action. I can continue to do as I have been doing,' a man said. He had a low voice and spoke slowly, an oak tree of a voice. Ebbo knew that voice... he had heard it at dozens of harvest festivals.

'Listen to reason, Magnus!' another voice said. This one was cruel and malicious, a voice that said listen—or else, but there was more to it as well. Ebbo had heard it only once before, and yet it sounded painfully familiar. Something of it reminded him of the Farm—the cooperative of farmers and artisans spread out over hundreds of islands around the Archipelago. It had a lilt to it, like an islander. But there was something far harder beneath.

'If our choices are for me to continue growing the plants we need to feed this city, or start importing products grown by an army of skeletons, I believe the personal sacrifice of my time to be the more reasonable,' Magnus said.

Ebbo crept forward, moving soundlessly until he got an eye on Magnus. How Magnus knew what Adrianna had discovered was beyond him, but he had to get a look at the dwarven druid.

Oh, Magnus! Ebbo wasn't into dudes or anything like that, but just one look at Magnus Stoneroot was enough to send one's heart a pitter-patter. He was tall for a dwarf, nearly four feet, and wore a magnificent golden beard and long hair of the same color. Both were entwined with vining plants that seemed to furl and unfurl their petals as Magnus breathed. As he spoke, the skull blossoms around him reached out for him. The druid was powerful; legend said he singlehandedly kept the crops of S'Kar-Vozi growing. He rested only when the plants did, and just after the fall and spring harvest, when the city celebrated its famed horticulturist.

'My minions monitoring the princess over the scrying stones said they met a self-proclaimed baron, and he offered the spider princess a trade deal. He could alleviate some of the pressures on you, so you could put your skills to better use. It's no good for the baker to slaughter the hog.' It was profoundly uncomfortable to hear an infamous assassin and Ebbo's personal hero use an expression he'd heard his grandfather say. Also creepy that he'd been spying on them, but Ebbo didn't exactly find that surprising.

'Vecnos, I feed this city. There is nothing more important than that.'

It really was him, then. Vecnos. The one islander people noticed. Despite asking everyone he could, Ebbo still didn't know where Vecnos came from, or what he did exactly. It was just known not to speak disparagingly of this denizen of the Ringwall in public. Those that did tended to end up with one of his patented Vecnos Industries daggers in one of their kidneys.

'A storm is brewing. We cannot let the Cthult of Cthulu grow any more of its power,' Vecnos said. 'My agents will only be able to contain it for so long.'

Ebbo found himself agreeing with the assassin. The Cthult of Cthulu was just plain weird. They believed, as they were apt to tell anyone who even appeared to be listening, that their dark god, Cthulu—sometimes called the Kraken—would return from the deep one day. When it did, the Cthultists would be ready with harpoon and lance to drive it and all of its tentacles back to the abyss.

'And your Serpent worshipers are better?'

Ebbo felt his blood grow cold. Vecnos...Vecnos couldn't be working with the Ourdor of Ouroboros. No one was responsible for more islander deaths than the horrible snake people and their brain-washed human slaves. As children, islanders of the Farm were taught three rules: don't steal pie before dinner, send parrots when orcs came to shore, and scream when you saw a snake. No one was more ruthless when attacking the defenseless islanders than the snake people. They primarily took the young, and would often take entire villages of men and children, leaving only a few survivors. They'd told islanders that was so they could repopulate and continue to provide food for the Ouroboros—the end serpent that would one day consume them all. Vecnos couldn't be working with them. No way!

'The Ourdor of Ouroboros serve a purpose,' Vecnos said, his voice colder than Ebbo's blood.

Only... only maybe it wasn't Vecnos. Maybe Magnus just thought it was Vecnos because of whatever magick Ebbo had smelled. Maybe... yeah, maybe that wasn't the infamous islander. Ebbo started to feel his hands shake. Blueberries, how long had it been since he'd even had a taste of magick? Days, maybe? It felt like years. Whoever was talking to Magnus had to have some. Ebbo just wanted a peek, then he'd know what to do.

'You mean like the two-score half-orcs you trafficked into the sewer?' Magnus said.

'Every decision I make is of necessity, Magnus. It's no different than you pruning a branch. I could not leave the hrocs on the Blighted Island. They guard ancient knowledge of weapons simple enough that even children can wield them and protect themselves. If I did not bring the hrocs here, he would have slaughtered the lot of them, and their knowledge would have died with them. Think of it, Magnus: he has built a castle of their graves. If they were to stay, the vampire would simply add hrocs to his skeleton army. A risk I cannot allow.'

'And yet you want to work with this baron? Make up your mind, halfling.'

'Islander.'

'And they prefer half-orc. Or have you not spoken with them since you released them beneath our fine city?'

'My time is more precious than a gang of flower-worshipping hrocs who fear their own inherited wisdom. Put them to work up here. Maybe then you can pry yourself away from your precious orchards and help me look into the Cthultists. There are beds of kelp growing ever closer to Bog's Bay. I think the Kraken might be harvesting from them, though of course I would need your expertise to ascertain if the leaf fell from the tree, as my gran used to say.'

Ebbo crept forward, hoping to catch a glimpse of Vecnos, or whatever sorcerer was tricking Magnus to think the he was the islander. That had to be it. Everyone knew Vecnos was an assassin, but he was a good assassin, right? Didn't only good people live in the Ring? Ebbo couldn't think straight. His mind kept racing, looking for magick.

But then he saw him... or most of him. He was short, extremely short, hardly over two feet, wrapped in a cloak black as midnight. The few assassins who could afford such a cloak did not stand around chatting. Beyond that, only the hilts of daggers and vials of poison showed any color on his belt. A mass of black curly hair poked out from under the hood. Ebbo didn't think he could smell magick on him, but then the cloak could be magick, or maybe the Vecnos Industries dagger he wore, or... or... it couldn't be Vecnos! Vecnos was a killer, sure, an assassin, but he was Ebbo's hero! He couldn't be working with the Ourdor of Ouroboros. Ebbo had to sneak forward. He felt himself trembling. If he just had a bit of magick to muffle his steps-

A twig broke.

A dagger flew from Vecnos' hand to the spot Ebbo's face had been a moment before.

Ebbo cursed and hid behind a statue of a fallen angel with vines growing where its tears would flow.

'We're not alone,' Vecnos said, and vanished into the overgrown skull-blossom.

Ebbo cursed again, for at that moment, more voices could be heard coming from the stone walkway he had come in through.

'Where your rude friend?' someone grunted. Oluf.

Clayton replied, 'I assure you he is normally not so rude. Had he known the significance of the flower to your people, I assure you-'

There was a loud ping, like a piece of iron-shot being struck by a bat.

Clayton Steelheart—once again totally divorced of his clay—flew into the graveyard and cracked against the head of a carved demon, knocking it to the floor and instantly making the girl held in the gargoyle's arms seem less imperiled.

Ebbo used the clatter of broken rock and the grunts of the hrocs to slip away further into the overgrown skull-blossom. He pulled at something that had snagged his cloak---no doubt one of the thorns of the skull-blossom—and cursed again. Vecnos probably didn't get caught by plants.

Chapter 40

Clayton

Using the feces of a hundred thousand people had been humiliating, but at least there had been some semblance of power in that form. Clayton felt truly powerless when treated like a skull-ball. The hrocs—as he unapologetically found himself thinking of them after such a display of brutish behavior—had found Clayton Steelheart struggling to step up a one-foot drop in the path. The trickle of a small waterfall had been such that he had been unable to surmount it. The hrocs had whacked his heart right out of his body, and then kept moving him along using their shafts of iron to strike him like he was nothing but a piece of a particularly cruel game.

Clayton couldn't even tell if Ebbo had gone this way. Without his clay, he couldn't smell any telltale signs of halfling. He was trying—quite unsuccessfully—to not freak out. He simply couldn't build up any amount of Heartbeats, and without that ability, his once-formidable powers were basically nonexistent. That Ebbo had ditched him did no favors for the golem's disposition.

However, the hrocs finally did him a favor as they knocked him against a statue and into a room.

As his steel heart smashed into the statue, crumbling pieces to the ground, he fell atop the earth below. In it, there was much more organic matter—dead humans, mostly, more than he'd ever sensed anywhere in S'kar-Vozi, in fact. Many of the vast collection of bones had time enough to decay, and here and there were veins of minerals he could use. The moisture content seemed about right as well, and mixed with the powder of the statue, Clayton should just have been able to pull himself together...

But he couldn't. Try as he might, he couldn't make himself any larger than a hand or a foot. Something was seriously wrong with his Heartbeats. He hadn't had more than a few hundred since the dragon prince had blasted his heart with fire. Clayton—for the first time in the relatively short period that he was as a conscious being—was beginning to fear for what he counted as his life.

'We find monster. He try to steal flower,' Oluf shouted.

'Now, now, there's no need for violence, and there's plenty of skull-blossom to go 'round,' Magnus said. Clayton recognized his voice. How could you not, dreamy as it was?

'They desecrate to heal friend. We honor thousands of dead. No comparison!' one of Oluf's friends said.

Vecnos himself stepped out from the brush. 'Now, what could have compelled the spider princess's loyal golem to stay behind?' In his hand he held a scrap of green cloth. Clayton cursed. Even with his limited faculties, he recognized that fabric. It was Ebbo's .

'Halfling help him!' Oluf said.

In the span of a single one of Clayton's Heartbeats, Vecnos seemed to vanish. He simply stepped back into a shadow of one of the funerary statues, and then was gone. The hrocs didn't notice him reappear in their own shadows until the tiny islander had climbed up Oluf's back and had a dagger to his throat.

'Say halfling again, hroc. Try it.'

Oluf said nothing. Vecnos didn't seem to mind drawing a bit of blood, and the half-orc definitely noticed.

'They like us, prefer islander,' said another hroc. Clayton noticed with dismay that it was Dergh. Her eyes were both swollen, her back and arms were covered with dark bruises that were long and narrow, the shape of the hroc's clubs. Her nose was as malformed as before, but now it bled and seemed broken in the other direction. Clayton felt a pang of guilt. That was his fault, or Ebbo's maybe, but it was the same difference to the golem.

'Very good,' Vecnos said, dragging his dagger across Oluf's unshaved stubble and leaving him with a crisp mustache and bushy sideburns. He flipped off the half-orc and landed neatly in the middle of the group. Clayton couldn't believe his audacity. Islanders didn't behave that way; they were better at being on the edges of a confrontation. Was it his reputation that protected him from the half-orcs, Clayton wondered, or his skills? Both were formidable.

'Now,' Vecnos continued, 'where is your little addict hiding?'

'The half-orcs are obviously confused,' Clayton said from an animated pile of broken statue and grave dirt. 'Though I am currently bereft of clay, I assure you, I am Clayton Steelheart, free golem of the free city. I confronted these half-orcs in a bar-'

'A bar? The agreement was for you to stick to the sewers,' Magnus drawled, though he seemed to be speaking more to Vecnos than the hrocs.

'We thirsty,' one of the hrocs said with a shrug.

'As I was saying,' Clayton said, managing to sound huffy for being interrupted, 'I offended them by asking for just a few precious blossoms of the exact kind that seem to be blooming all around me, and they grew quite irate, drawing me and a few innocent islanders into a brawl that eventually ended in my capture.'

'I told you where the skull blossom grew,' Vecnos hissed. 'You were supposed to go to the Blighted Island and investigate what was happening there with the baron and his horde of yellow skeletons.'

'Well, yes, but seeing how you know all about him, it seems that the other half of our team was quite successful in procuring that information for you. You see, on delicate missions we often split up, and Ebbo thought—well, he doubted that you were being one hundred percent honest about the Blighted Island being the only graveyard in all the Archipelago, and it does appear he was correct.'

'Tell him to come out now.' Vecnos stepped into a shadow and rematerialized right behind Clayton. He picked up his heart, brushing the dirt and stone bits away from it easily, and began to poke it at with his dagger.

'Look, it became obvious when we found two of the most powerful people in the free city discussing their own internal and obviously confidential agendas that this wasn't a test. Ebbo, well, he took off.' Clayton said, his voice a tinny buzz without any clay to help amplify it.

Vecnos took the point of his dagger and pried open one of Clayton's heart's ventricles. He looked inside, sniffed. Glowing blue powder came out and sparkled into nothingness. Vecnos let the heart close. It shuddered. Clayton had no idea what the powder was or where it was from.

'Your honesty is appreciated, Steelheart. The only question I still have is whether to pry you into pieces and sell you back to the that worthless artificer that made you, or to cast a fresh spell and obliterate your memories of this place, and yourself... too... I suppose. Though that might be a shame.'

'I don't know what you're talking about!' Clayton buzzed loudly. 'So long as the magick in my heart remains, a new heart could be fashioned. You can't destroy Clayton Steelheart the free golem so easily. If just a shred of me is recovered, Leopold the Grimy can fix me-'

That was a bluff, another big, bold-faced lie. Clayton didn't know what would happen if Vecnos broke his heart apart, but he knew it wouldn't be good. But he couldn't let them find Ebbo. The poor little islander wouldn't stand a chance against Vecnos and the magick he controlled.

Ebbo nodded from his hiding place. They'd had this discussion a thousand times. Clayton was a construct. They could rebuild him. There would be no point in Ebbo sacrificing himself. It was obvious Vecnos didn't know where he was, or he'd be dead already. Better to hide, let them do whatever they were going to do to Clayton's heart—probably nothing, Magnus wouldn't allow it, right?—and then put him back together later.

'Maybe. Maybe not. What is this powder inside, anyway?' Vecnos said, prying open the heart and inhaling deeply. Ebbo could smell it from has hiding place. Like cinnamon, lilies and aluminum. Delicious.

'Mmm...' Vecnos said with satisfaction. 'Magick... and what do the rumors say? Bestowed from a fairy, no less? Is any of that true?'

'How else would you explain my, err... abilities?' Dlayton asked

'Dumb luck,' Vecnos hissed. 'Dumb luck at the artificer's table that has since run out. Though I could be wrong. This powder is certainly something special.'

Ebbo's ears perked up. He'd never smelled the magick in Clayton's heart before. It was powerful, heady stuff. Even across the graveyard, it made his knees weak. It completely blew out whatever magick he had smelled before.

'I think this magick is strong,' Vecnos purred. 'Stronger than anything I've tasted, that's for sure... and yes... yes, I can feel it re-growing within. Truly limitless potential in there, Steelheart. With each heartbeat it restores itself. Truly remarkable. To think, you can just give out whiffs of this whenever you chose.'

'Then why haven't you?' Ebbo said, pushing himself from the undergrowth and into the open, stumbling for Clayton's heart.

'Ebbo, no!'

'That him,' Dergh said.

'Oh dear,' Magnus said.

Vecnos laughed, and then tossed aside Clayton's heart and approached the islander.

'You left a piece of your cloak on my dagger,' Vecnos said, flicking the scrap of cloth in Ebbo's face.

Ebbo said nothing, only scowled and looked at Clayton's stash of powdered Heartbeats.

'Really, I'm impressed you stayed hidden through your golem's pathetic attempts at deception. How much did you hear?'

'I heard nothing, sir,' Ebbo said, hands shaking. He was a bit taller than Vecnos and looked over him at Clayton's heart. It was dusted with the blue powder. Heartbeats solidified? Clayton could make that for him? He knew Ebbo had a problem... well, not a problem, but Clayton thought it was a problem. Why had he held out on his friend?

'I just want to take my friend and go,' Ebbo said.

'And what about the skull-blossom?' Magnus said, his voice calm, like an oak tree in a storm of ice.

'I... yes... we need some for my other friend,' Ebbo said, finally managing to rip his eyes off Clayton's heart and the glowing blue powder. 'We met the Demon King while trying to crash Adrianna's—that's the spider princess— wedding. Then there were these skeleton mermaids-'

'Skeleton mermaids?' Magnus said with a raised eyebrow at Vecnos. Vecnos didn't seem at all surprised at the news.

'Yeah, and so his Corruption is really bad,' Ebbo continued, 'and the witch said he needs the flowers and look, it's a really huckleberry-picking long story, and if I can just be taking my friend, I can be on my way.'

'How many of the flowers do you need?' Magnus said.

Ebbo shook his head, again breaking his gaze on Clayton. He wasn't saying anything... was his heart still even beating?

'I... a dozen dozens, the witch said,' Ebbo said, then remembering the hrocs, 'if you all can spare it. Look, I... I gotta see if he's alright.' Ebbo nodded at Clayton.

'Funny, you didn't seem too concerned about his well-being earlier,' Vecnos said.

'I hadn't seen a ruthless assassin who sells out his own people pick at him with a dagger and dump his magic powder all over some freaky graveyard earlier,' Ebbo said with entirely too much vitriol. For a moment he forgot about the powder from Clayton's heart, and instead rested his eyes on the vials of magick powder on Vecnos's belt. Purple, blue, silver, polka-dot. Surely one of them could ease Ebbo's mind. He reached into his pocket for the scrying stone but found nothing. The hrocs had taken it. Pity, Ebbo would have liked to know that Clayton would be rescued, but as it was, his only hope was to get off one last time. After all, one did not insult an assassin from the Ringwall and live to the tell the tale.

'I have done more for our people than anyone before me,' Vecnos said.

'You mean *to*. You've done more *to* our people than anyone before you,' Ebbo said. 'I heard about your friends the Ourdor of Ouroboros,' Ebbo was furious. Clayton was dying, Ebbo had lost one of his cousins to the Ourdor of Ouroboros, which meant Vecnos had pretty much murdered him, and there was magick powder he couldn't sniff that he didn't even know had existed and his friend had been hiding from him for years!

'You have spirit, halfling, I'll give you that,' Vecnos said with a sneer. 'Keep your friend's heart as a memento of what happens when you mess with powers you don't understand. Keep your eyes on the sea. And remember, the gods are real, all of them, and some are far worse than others.'

Then darkness poured from Vecnos's fingertips, like black fungus destroying an orchard. It surrounded the half-orcs and then blew them away as if they were but dust carried by the wind, leaving Ebbo alone with Magnus and Clayton. Only Clayton wasn't talking anymore. Or moving.

Ebbo ran to him and, feeling nothing, tried to look inside.

'Ebbo...' Clayton said.

'Clayton! Clayton! Vecnos said you were gonna be okay. He said you were going to be fine as sunshine in dewy grass. He said... Vecnos said...'

Ebbo burst into tears. Clayton was his best friend. It was Clayton who had taken pity on him and asked Adrianna to have Ebbo join her team. It was Clayton who looked out for him, Clayton who gave him shelter when he was coming down. Clayton who'd... who'd lied about the source of his magick.

Ebbo could feel it even from here. It smelled of summer nights and the first star over the sea, of fruit salads and oats and honey.

Ebbo snorted the blue powder, and the light from inside the steel heart went dun. Ebbo's tears fell harder.

Magnus put a hand on Ebbo's shoulder as the islander wept. Little did Magnus know, the tears weren't of sadness, but of joy.

Ebbo had never been so fucking high in his life.

Chapter 41

Vecnos

Vecnos watched the end of the pathetic spectacle and nodded to himself. He had hoped for something more, but the islander had not only fallen for the sleight of hand, but taken the bait entirely.

This Ebbo Brandyoak would be easy enough to manipulate. Like so many of his pitiable brethren, Ebbo had an addiction to magick. Most halflings were rife with the stuff, and yet the vast majority couldn't do a thing with it except grow vegetables and go unnoticed, and few truly even mastered that ability. Vecnos hadn't come across someone who'd manage to escape his detection in quite some time...but Ebbo had made it all the way into the sunken crypt without Vecnos spotting him. If he survived his ordeal, he might be worth watching... and using. It was almost a pity the islander's mind would most likely end up trapped in his comatose body. Like so many others, he'd be ignored while he wasted away on the streets. He'd be stepped over until he ultimately exhausted the fat stored in his pot belly, started to rot, and was chucked into Bog's Bay. If only this Ebbo had someone to help him avoid 'transcending,' as the foolish halflings called it, maybe he could-

Vecnos cut off the idea at the root. He would not help a single islander. As his daft old Gran would say, someone's got to butcher the hog. Strange how despite all these years, he still thought of those phrases. But this was one he had grown to embrace. Vecnos had butchered many as he rose from a nobody farmer to a worlds-renowned assassin, businessman, and member of the de-facto ruling class of the free city. And he'd butcher many more if that's what it took to accomplish his goals. He would not forget the things he had sacrificed, the people he'd sacrificed, the blood on his hands. He certainly wouldn't break his rule over an islander dumb enough to rely on a malfunctioning golem. Vecnos chuckled to himself just thinking about the poop golem. The whole thing was so preposterous, it was almost impressive.

'Er... what so funny, lil' man?' Oluf said.

Vecnos stopped. The cursed hrocs were turning into a real liability. First, they'd gone to a bar during the day, and now their leader dared a short joke? It could have been a slip of the tongue; Vecnos rescued the hrocs not for their own good, and definitely not for their skill at languages, but for the lore he believed they hid in their religion. Their full-blooded Orc brothers made weapons of unbelievable efficiency, horrible tools that could kill with the twitch of a finger. Crossbows, they were called, whatever that meant. Vecnos wanted to arm the islanders of the free city with machines built of that lore. A system of mercenaries had been working to protect the market, but with the population growing ever larger and Magnus unwilling to bend his stance on the skeletons, Vecnos thought the time would soon come when islanders would have to fight for themselves. So he'd keep the hrocs until he teased out the details of this crossbow device, so long as they followed his orders. They'd come along quickly enough when he'd tossed his dust of darkness; he hadn't even had to use violence. He'd thought they were learning, but this short joke —accident or not—could not be tolerated. Better to teach them a lesson.

Vecnos threw one of his daggers. It spun end over perfectly balanced end and plunged into Oluf's unsuspecting thigh.

'Ey, what's the big idea?' Oluf cried out and fell to the ground, clutching his wound.

Hrocs were tough things. Nothing like the inhuman half of their monstrous ancestors, of course, but tougher than humans. These few dozen of them had thick, gray skin, black hair and canine teeth that stuck from their bottom lips, that were nevertheless tiny compared to the tusks their full-blooded, marauding ancestors had. Full-blooded orcs had skin so thick swords often glanced off it, and they hardly spoke, preferring their communication with other species to be done via their strange devices of death.

Vecnos had hit the hroc in the nerve, causing it to collapse, but it didn't seem particularly concerned about the wound. Time to fix that. Before Oluf could so much as reach for the blade, Vecnos was there. He twisted it, digging into the bone.

Oluf definitely felt it this time. He screamed in pain, a nice loud warrior's yell of true pain. That was hroc for respect.

'Honestly, I'm impressed you dared another pun,' Vecnos said. 'If it wasn't for your sense of humor, I think you'd be snake food.'

Vecnos yanked his blade out of the hroc chief's thigh. He flicked a knob on the handle, releasing a caustic acid into the blade. He dragged it across the wound, drawing a louder scream from the hroc. The acid was actually a kindness, for it would heal the wound quickly and cause it to leave no scar, but that wasn't something Oluf needed to know. Orcs didn't respond well to kindness. Vecnos has assumed that hrocs wouldn't respond to much of anything besides violence either, but that was what made these ones so curious. They believed in something that guided their actions. Whether it was the memory of their ancestors, the spirit of that stupid flower, or the power of the orcish weapons their religion forbade them from building, mattered little. Vecnos didn't want to understand these few dozen hrocs' particular beliefs any more than would be necessary to suss out their forbidden secrets, but he did care that they believed in something beyond themselves. That was the only reason he was still using anything but violence to get what he wanted.

'Why were you in the bar?' Vecnos asked, walking deeper into the sewers beneath S'kar-Vozi. He snapped his fingers, and the hrocs stumbled to follow.

'Someone want flower,' one of females said. Vecnos thought her name was Org, but he couldn't be sure.

'They are not your flowers, nor are they particularly valuable. Your vapid answer wasted my time. One of you do better. Now, why were you in the bar?' Vecnos asked. Org wasn't one of the bright ones.

'We fight bravely! We win!' Oluf said, limping from behind to catch up.

'That fight was not yours to have, and by exposing yourselves, you make it less convenient for me to harbor you. I brought you here not out of kindness, but out of curiosity. Hrocs sworn not to kill are rare, and ones displaced from their spooky homeland and ready to swear an oath to one you would normally attempt to eat are rarer still. You see, I am curious if you can be of any use to me whatsoever, or if your big, meaty bodies would be better spent fertilizing Magnus's fields.

'You swore-' Oluf protested.

'I swore to give you food and shelter if you obeyed me. I did, and you did not.'

'You say food and shelter, not snabbage and sewers,' one of the hrocs said, a female that Vecnos did not remember being so bruised. He thought this one went by Dergh. She must have angered her compatriots. Probably for mouthing off. Today did not look like it was going to be her day.

Vecnos scowled at her, his pearly white teeth gleaming in the darkness.

'I will ask it again, but this time I require a proper answer. And I do not know with whom I will begin if I do not receive one.'

The hrocs looked from each other to Oluf, but the chief was out of his element. He only picked his nose and shrugged. Finally, he said, 'her idea,' and pointed to the bruised female.

'Well, at least now I know where to begin,' Vecnos said, fingering a dagger. He would feel bad inflicting more pain on this one, it looked like she'd suffered enough, but there wasn't really much choice with hrocs. They were too poor with spoken language to understand a properly subtle threat.

'They ask for skull-blossom. Ask many. We worry.'

Vecnos loosened the dagger in its hilt. 'Go on.'

'They ask many. People wonder why. Flower special, not... not common,' Dergh said, squirming under Vecnos's glare as he removed the gleaming dagger from its tiny scabbard. 'If... if people think popular, or ask question, people go there. Go to our home. Find flower. Many know. Many come before... before him. For gravestones. Grow on gravestones,' Dergh said, almost losing the thread in the end, and yet she had something there.

The graveyard in the Ringwall and the Blighted Island were the only two places with buried dead in all of the Archipelago. If anyone besides the spider princess and her cronies started digging around for skull blossom, they would either end up invading this crypt or going to the Blighted Island itself, something Vecnos did not want people doing until he had a better understanding of the self-proclaimed baron who presided there.

'You're sure, then, about the vampire?' Vecnos said, dipping the dagger into one the vials of poison he kept with him at all times.

This time all of the few dozen hrocs nodded, but something seemed to have happened to their pecking order, for when Vecnos gestured for them to proceed, they deferred to the bruised female.

'He dig graves. Use skeleton to build castle. With stones.'

'Yes, but how can you be sure he was a vampire?' Vecnos said.

Dergh snorted, 'No smell. Vampire no smell.'

Vecnos nodded. Really, the hrocs being alive was pretty solid evidence that a vampire had moved into the north island. Vampires wouldn't touch orcs any more than they would horses or pigs, and hrocs counted for far more than half as bad.

'You're right, Dergh, we don't want anyone asking about anything on the Blighted Island. The less people that visit before we make a deal with that vampire, the better.' Vecnos didn't mention that he'd already confirmed the existence of the vampire and his skeleton minions by watching the spider princess through her scrying stone.

'He unholy! Hurt special flower!' Dergh said, raising her club.

Dumb hroc. She probably didn't even mean to grab the weapon. Hrocs reached for their clubs as quickly as most islanders reached for a second serving of pie, and yet a lesson she must be taught.

Vecnos threw the knife at Dergh, slicing a gash in her wrist, severing a tendon and causing her to drop the club. This wound crackled with the ichor of a demon. An extravagant means of torture on most hrocs, but Vecnos was curious.

Dergh screamed and grabbed at her wrist, but the white smoke and soft light pouring from the wound told Vecnos what he'd suspected. The hrocs may be dumb, but they were authentic. Whatever nonsense she believed in was strong enough to evaporate the cursed ichor. He tucked that little tidbit away for later and launched into his typical new henchmen speech.

'I think perhaps I have not made the particularities of our relationship clear. You are here because of me. At this point, my excellent sense of humor and bountiful good will are all that keeps you alive. If you have the audacity to speak to me with such arrogance again, I will kill you. If you draw the attention of anyone more important than a kobold or an islander, I will kill you. If you interrupt my plans, reveal our relationship, or if I stub my toe on one of your clubs left lying around, I will kill you.'

The hrocs scowled and nodded. Normally that would do, but sometimes the devout required a finer touch.

'If you truly upset me, I will hunt down whatever pathetic remnants of your clan there are and feed them to the vampire's skeleton army. There are a few dozen of you here, there can't be half that many left alive by those skeletons by now. If you anger me, no one will remember your legend, and your oaths will fall from memory. It will be as if your goddess does not exist.'

The hrocs gasped, except for Dergh.

She continued to scowl. Good. Vecnos liked Dergh! She would have to learn, of course, but that would come with time.

Vecnos led them deeper into the clockwork sewers beneath S'kar-Vozi and began to spin the narrative in which he'd give them their orders. Though the assassin was not one to shy away from violence, he did believe a properly informed and motivated minion worked much better than an ignorant, lazy one. As he wove his tale around them, he wondered if even Dergh would have any inkling of how they were being played...not that it mattered.

Playing with people was what everyone in the Ringwall did. Vecnos was just the only one to admit to playing dirty. At least, that's what they all thought. Even Magnus—sweet, noble Magnus—didn't truly know how it felt. No one could know that. No one could know what it felt like to be food. No one knew that fear except islanders. And most of them were either dumb enough to just go grow pumpkins, or smart enough to see the world for what it was and turn to the escape of magick abuse.

That brought Vecnos back to the task at hand. Ebbo Brandyoak and the adventurer friends he'd been babbling about would have to be brought into the fold. The hrocs would play the strongman role, of course, but Vecnos turned his mind to the other arms of his powerful criminal network. Well, not criminal. There were no laws in S'kar-Vozi, after all. Technically, Vecnos wasn't doing anything wrong. He was acting by his code, and that was all that mattered. He would not save a single islander, and in doing so, he would save them all.

Still, this Ebbo could be more than a magick addict or a farmer. Vecnos hoped he could be saved and turned into something far more useful, but if he couldn't—then, well, he had to die. Vecnos wouldn't cry about it—his philosophy had brought islanders off the plates of the Archipelago and into the markets—but that didn't make the idea of killing another one any more palatable.

Chapter 42

Ebbo

Ebbo held his friend's cold, lifeless heart in his hands. He'd begged and pleaded with Magnus to do something. Or he thought it was Magnus. Turned out it was an apple tree shaped like Magnus. It was hard to tell such things when magick was crackling through your veins like birdsong at twilight, bleeding the very fabric of the multiverse away, unraveling time itself into an illusion of ticks, pops, and beats... Heartbeats.

Clayton's cold heart was an anchor that brought Ebbo back down, down to the bottom of the sea.

It was cold here, and wet.

Ebbo looked around. He was cold, and wet, and naked, and in an orchard on the wrong side of the Ringwall. He had been tripping for some amount of time, that much he knew, but beyond that things were rather hazy. As his lore came back to him, Ebbo vaguely recalled that this was where Magnus grew the food that fed S'Kar-Vozi. The seven crops spread out all around him, seeming to grow even before his eyes.

The magick involved here...

Magick?

Magick?! He had just come down and he was thinking about it again? He looked at the heart in his hands.

It was still.

Voiceless.

Completely devoid of blue powder.

Clayton Steelheart was... that is, Clayton was...

Ebbo shook his head and clenched his gentle jaw. He wandered in circles for a bit, finding his pants, belt, cloak, and dagger, but unfortunately not his shirt or his satchel.

He dressed without them. His silvery tousled hair and lack of shirt made him look like some tiny barbarian. How easy that must be, Ebbo thought, to just be big and tough like... like Clayton.

Ebbo looked at the heart in his hands. It didn't even look like a heart. It looked like a rounded scrap of metal that had been burned, bashed, and broken. There were some sort of scratches all over the inside. The fact that Ebbo could see inside the metal heart at all was not a good sign, not at all.

Ebbo's stomach grumbled, and—angry at his magick-addicted brain and food-addicted body for being so selfish—he began to cry. It just wasn't fair. Vecnos had presented Ebbo with what he wanted, and in that moment, he'd failed his friends. Ebbo looked at the food all around him. He didn't care if he was hungry, he would save Clayton. His tummy would just have to wait. It growled again. He had no idea how long he'd been out, but his stomach seemed to.

'Eat, young islander,' a voice like an oak tree said.

Ebbo turned to see the magnificent golden beard of Magnus. The clouds seemed to part above him, basking him in golden light, and the plants reached for the druidic master, source of their health and vigor. The vines in Magnus's beard seemed to taunt those that had to exist without being in constant contact with the druid. Ebbo felt himself grow just a tiny bit aroused. He couldn't help it; Magnus was just so fecund. The little islander burst into another gush of tears, this time angry at pretty much everything but his islander feet.

'You're just going to trick me like Vecnos did!' Ebbo said, his voice shrill. Magnus could have said something; Magnus could have saved Clayton from Ebbo!

Magnus shook his head and sighed. 'No, young one, I only wish you to eat and get back to your task, so I can get back to mine.'

'So, the apples aren't like poison or anything?' Ebbo said, but really meant anything like magick.

'The fruits are perfectly healthy, and totally organic. There is a bit of magick in that, as many of your people know, but not much beyond.' Magnus tapped the ground with his staff. It was a giant piece of wood, twice the size of the dwarf, complete with knobs, a few twigs at the top, and a little flush of green leaves. When he tapped the ground, an apple fell from a tree. It landed in Ebbo's hand.

The apple was red, plump and glossy. It was the complete opposite of the burned-out shell of a heart he still held in his other hand.

'You will need both if you are to save your friend,' Magnus said, gesturing at the objects Ebbo clutched.

Ebbo nodded and took a bite. He was hoping for something, a prickle, a tick, anything, but he found only crisp, juicy, delicious flesh. He sighed.

Magnus raised a golden bushy eyebrow. 'You are not impressed? Most I bring here think nothing tastes better than an apple self-picked by a tree and touched only by your hand.'

'No, it's good. It's super good. It's like the best berry-picking apple I've ever had, it's just...'

'You worry about your friend.'

Ebbo nodded. 'We've had to take him for repairs before, but nothing like this. What... what if he doesn't make it? What if he's already dead, and it's all my fault?'

'Then finish the apple, and maybe you can save him.'

'You really think so?' Hope fluttered into Ebbo's heart. 'Will he still remember me? Will he let me sleep over? Will he still be all weird about fancy clothes?'

'What do I look like, a sculptor? I have no idea if you can save your friend. Quite honestly, I have never seen anything like him before. I study the magick of plants, particularly the Seven Sacred Crops I harvest seven times a year to feed this city. I don't know much about mudmen, but he seemed especially kind and brave for a talking pile of fertilizer, so I think it's worth a shot. However, I sense you were not looking for solace in that bite of exceedingly delicious apple.'

Funny, Ebbo thought, if you talked to a rich person for almost any amount of time, they said something smug.

Ebbo looked at his bare feet for a moment in embarrassment, then brought his eyes up to Magnus. In the golden beard he saw only kindness and blooming flowers that smelled of comfort; in his sparkling eyes he saw only compassion. Ebbo decided to spill the beans.

'Well, you saw me back there. I... I snorted that blue powder, his Heartbeats in physical form! Or magickal powder form, anyway. I had a chance to do something heroic, something smart, like wait it all out, or even something cowardly, like run away, but instead I just did something dumb and snorted my friend to death.'

'If that's what happened, that was pretty horrible of you.'

'So, I don't know what to do now, you know? What if I go down in the city, and find that Clayton needs a fresh infusion of magick, and instead of stealing it for him or whatever, I just snort it up? What if all he needs is some magick ritual, and I interrupt to get high? I mean, what if supposedly it's just like some magick rock I never knew about--'

'I get it,' Magnus said.

'So, what do I do?' Ebbo said.

Magnus stroked his beard and turned to look at the setting sun. Ebbo still had no idea how long he'd been out of it. He hoped that Boffo, the Fat Moon, had only flown over once or twice. Any more than that and Adrianna would no doubt be back and waiting for him.

'You must do the best you can, as often as you can. That is all. I hope that does not mean transcendence for you, for I do not believe in that nonsense any more than Vecnos does, but I could be wrong. For as I said, these orchards and these fields are all I truly know.'

'Yeah, but if I go back down into the free city, my friends are going to kill me for killing Clayton!'

'It is possible.'

'And even if they don't, those hrocs will.'

'I wouldn't bet against it.'

'And if they don't, then Vecnos definitely will.'

'Probably,' Magnus said with a nod and a gentle shrug.

'And you won't stop him?'

Magnus shook his head. 'I cannot. He is a master assassin. He can move without sound and go unseen. My domain is the day, and his is the night.'

'Whatever. All you rich, rotten strawberries up here on the Ringwall are in cahoots. You wouldn't stop him if you could,' Ebbo said, hoping that the self-righteous gardener was a pacifist. Clayton wasn't here to defend him, a bitter reminder of how pathetic Ebbo truly was.

Magnus only shrugged. 'Perhaps you are right. Perhaps I could stop him, and I choose not to. This city needs stability. Vecnos does things I do not agree with, but he is consistent, and a threat of some kind is often necessary to keep the peace, and he is better than many.'

'That's a pile of green blueberries. He killed a bunch of my people, or let a bunch of them get killed, by working with the Ourdor of Ouroboros. I get a chance, I'll stab him in the gut.'

Magnus shrugged again, somehow even more gently. It was becoming quite annoying. 'As I said, one can only do what they believe is best, and together we may just survive. I would not let you hurt him in front of me, but I will not follow you into the city or tattle on you, either. That was a mean trick he pulled on you, and I am sorry I was unable to stop it. I understand why you want him dead; many do. I only tolerate him out of need and fear. Like barley attacked by caterpillars, sometimes we need a wasp.'

Ebbo—being an islander—understood the metaphor perfectly. Old Burpa had said it another way. Rabbits in the carrots meant time to make stew, or to a send a bluebird for a fox. The bluebird and the fox, of course, being a pair of old figures in islander mythology who often cavorted around, solving adventures together, laughing, joking, being best of friends despite their differences.

Like Ebbo and Clayton were. Or had been.

Ebbo looked up at Magnus. As the sun sunk below the western edge of the island of S'Kar-Vozi, Magnus watched it, basking in the red light until it vanished for the night. When it did, Magnus turned once more to Ebbo and spoke words that would forever stay in Ebbo's magick-addled brain.

'We can but grow with the energy the multiverse gives us. It's up to our friends to recognize us as anything more than weeds.' Magnus nodded, as if Ebbo could understand what a multiverse even was. Then the druid took a deep breath. He held up his hands, and not ten paces before him, a tiny sphere of flame burst into being. Magnus raised his arms and the sphere rose into the air, growing as it did so, higher and higher until it was the size of a skull-ball and almost as high in the air as the Ringwall was tall. Sunlight poured from the ball of flame, illuminating the garden in golden light.

Ebbo had never seen such a display of power—brambles, he'd never even *heard* of such a thing.

'I think I'm going to try, Mr. Magnus, sir. I think I'm going to get off the magick and save Clayton.'

Magnus nodded and turned away, clutching his staff more tightly than he had before. The plants in his beard had withered, and the hair itself seemed more silver than gold. Flecks of light were pouring like droplets of water from him to the sphere that floated in the sky.

'Do you do that every night?' Ebbo asked, instead of the far less interesting, "Are you okay?"

Magnus nodded. When he spoke, his voice still sounded like an oak, though perhaps one who'd lost its leaves for winter. 'This sun gives the plants four extra hours of light, a needed treat in this tropical climate with its never-changing ten-hour days and ten-hour nights. I will be fine in the morning, but for now I must rest. You, though, have rested enough. It is time you were on your way.' Magnus gestured behind Ebbo to the Ringwall.

On this side of the enormous wall, there were vines, some of which reached to the top. Some of their leaves were still awash in golden light, being that much higher, but as Ebbo watched, these too went dark.

Ebbo turned to thank Magnus, but the dwarf was already asleep, wrapped in a bed of barley that seemed to have made itself for its master. So with that image burned into his retinas, Ebbo started the climb back down to the free city.

Chapter 43

Adrianna

Adrianna did not think her love life could have gotten any more complicated, but that just showed that the princess of the spiderfolk had a lack of imagination.

Currently, her tiny apartment was occupied by her husband, Richard Valkanna, a red dragon wearing his human glamour who Adrianna trusted not at all, and Asakusa Sangrekana, her crush... or whatever you called the person you kissed passionately when faced with a horde of flesh-hungry skeletons, but was also a total freaking wimp when it came to doing anything romantic besides interrupting a cursed wedding.

They were both attempting to woo her. Asakusa was cleaning the floor, with the help of his Corruption. The thousands of black maggots that currently occupied his right arm, much of his torso, and just a bit of his neck were writhing about, manipulating a wet rag across the chipped wooden floor. As they cleaned, they emitted a faint shriek that Adrianna found sort of endearing but mostly just suuuuper creepy.

Valkanna was cooking, and curse him, it smelled good.

Adrianna wished that being a spider princess did not make her spoiled, but she had to admit that her diet was quite... specific.

She could consume the fluids of animals. That was it.

Valkanna knew this. He was making blood sausage, as well as some sort of steak tartar from an actual cow he'd paid top coin for in the Farmers' Market. He spit some of his flammable venom onto the steak, and it melted the flesh into mush. On top of this he put a raw egg and a few bits of green onions, for the smell and the presentation, he'd explained. He'd also said it shouldn't be enough herbs to make her ill. Which was sweet, but again, suuuuper creepy.

All in all, it was intensely awkward for Adrianna. She was used to men finding her often poorly hidden spider features disgusting. She was accustomed to spending time in the morning putting up her hair into elaborate braids to Fold away her spider form, but today she hadn't bothered. She'd tied it up in two buns, thus Folding away her spider abdomen and four of her spider limbs. But she still had two chitinous, hairy spider legs at the waist instead of pale human thighs, and her arms were covered in a mess of thick hairs. And yet, neither Asakusa nor Richard seemed to care. Adrianna had figured Asakusa wouldn't mind. Over the three years she'd known him, he'd seen practically every variation of her Folding that Adrianna knew, but Richard's apparent acceptance of her body was a pleasant surprise. She knew it was probably all an act, or she tried to tell herself that anyway, and yet if he was acting, he was damn convincing.

'Breakfast is served,' the dragon prince said, his deep voice dripping charm.

Asakusa's Corruption maggots threw the cleaning supplies down and began to ripple in anticipation. The maggots, despite being a curse from a demonic Gatekeeper that in no way needed mortal sustenance, seemed to enjoy themselves when their host ate normal food.

Only Asakusa didn't want to eat. 'What is this?' the thrall wrinkled his nose.

'This is how Princess Adrianna feels every time she eats with you mortals and your obsession with burnt everything,' Valkanna said.

'Calling humans mortals doesn't mean you can't die,' Asakusa said petulantly. 'And that's not how you feel, right, Adrianna?'

Adrianna shrugged and sucked up a morsel with her hollow tongue. Honestly, she wasn't disgusted by mortal food. In fact, she loved mortal food, or the smell of it anyway. Adrianna found the aromas that came from the city to be inspiring. She found it amazing that beings who lived such short lives could spend so much of their precious time on something as transiently pleasurable as eating. The world would be a better place if her family focused a bit more on simple pleasures.

Apparently, Richard Valkanna understood the truth of this idea. The consistency of the meat was perfect. Valkanna's acid seemed to work as well as her venom when it came to digesting animal flesh. Plus it was kind of spicy, and damn it if it didn't taste good. She sucked up another bite, and another.

Asakusa took a bite and gagged.

'I'm glad you like it, darling,' Valkanna said, raising an eyebrow at the thrall before turning back to his wife. 'If you'd but come back with me to Krag's Doom, my chefs and your family would wait on our every need. We could focus on what really matters.'

'We are focusing on what matters. We need to find more skull blossom and get Asakusa healed, so we can get back to helping the Nine in the Ringwall.'

Valkanna rolled his eyes. 'Darling, your charity work is commendable, but I do believe it is time we dreamed a bit bigger than a mortal doomed to suffer the Ways of the Dead for all eternity. Unless I am mistaken, he did trade his body and soul for his power, did he not?'

'All thralls make that trade,' Asakusa said sourly.

'Well, there we are, then. I don't much see what we can do for people who won't even help themselves,' Valkanna said.

'He did it to save his little sister,' Adrianna said.

'See, this is the problem. Charity begets charity begets charity. None of this is actually getting to the root of the problem. Tell me, what happened to the girl in the first place?' Valkanna asked.

Adrianna turned to Asakusa. He didn't often talk about such things. She had to admit: she'd love to get a bit more information out of him. She'd known him for years, he was her first friend in the free city, and apparently she was the only one he'd ever really had, and yet, that was a part of his life he'd never offed to divulge. Adrianna understood secrets, so she'd never asked, but still, she'd always been curious.

He looked from the human-shaped dragon to the spider princess Folded into a nearly human form. 'What does it matter what happened? She was a young girl, she was tricked away from her family. It wasn't her fault. Someone needed to rescue her. I thought I could, I was wrong. End of story.'

Valkanna clicked his teeth in disapproval. 'End of story? Why, that's hardly the beginning! Was she stolen by cthultists? Eaten? Traded to a demon prince? The implications of each situation are different enough to spice your particular circumstances with its own unique blend of hopelessness. If you don't want to tell me, then perhaps my dear wife will?'

Adrianna rolled her six eyes at Valkanna, suppressing a scowl. They may have been married, and he carried *Bloodweaver*—her spider dagger—at his hip, but she hardly thought of him as her "dear husband," especially not if he was going to be rude to Asakusa. 'It's his business. Not mine,' Adrianna said.

'Hmm... so you don't know either? Curious. I'd have thought if you liked the little thrall so much, it was because of some deep font of trust or care of each other's secrets.' Valkanna paused and pulled at the pointed black tip of his short beard. 'I suppose it doesn't really matter what happened, for the underlying cause is the same. You made a decision out of desperation, a decision you couldn't actually afford, because the system built up around you gave you no other choice.'

Asakusa only grunted at that. For him, that was pretty much a well-vocalized yes.

'What value is one little girl in an economic system such as the one that exists in the free city?' Valkanna pondered aloud.

Adrianna didn't know what to say to that. The lawlessness of the city was something she struggled with. Currently the Nine had enough balancing forces that women, children, and islanders were fairly well protected, but S'kar-Vozi's century of powerful leaders wasn't actually filled with paragons of virtue.

'It's not about value, and it's not the free city's fault,' Asakusa said.

'Spoken like a true patriot. I commend that,' Valkanna said, though his snort was so loud that Adrianna doubted every word. 'But it is the free city's fault. The idea that somehow this place is free implies others are oppressed. A half-truth, certainly. But tell me, what makes S'kar-Vozi *free*? Is it that you get to choose what you want for lunch? Or that since there are no police, you are free to stab whomever you please?'

'S'kar-Vozi is a far better place than Krag's Doom,' Adrianna said.

'With all due respect, darling, I disagree. The flamehearts are well-fed, those that make it home from their ventures abroad are always treated with the best medicine our sorcerers and warlocks can manifest. Housing is provided, and those that, err... fall off their best path in life are given something else to do.'

'You mean like forced labor?' Adrianna said, thinking of her own brothers. Those that came back damaged from battle were forced to work via pheromone controls until they molted and were strong enough to fight again. Those that weren't strong enough to work until they could molt... well, the euphemism was squished.

'Forced labor?' Valkanna laughed. 'I suppose... but I don't think of my family as slaves, and I know your family doesn't. I mean, take Yasmin, the stable-girl. Old friend of mine, faced some aquatic zealot claiming to be preparing for the return of the Kraken, got stabbed in the face. Now she can't speak and can no longer breathe fire. All she can really do is tend the wyverns, so that's all we ask of her. I don't beat her to do this task, that would be horrendous. We've found suitable tasks for much of your family as well. Or, our family I should say, as that's how we're all thinking about it except for you. You really should come home, darling, there's so much your mother doesn't want to decide without you. You are queen, after all. She is only your webmother, or so she says to everyone but my father.'

Adrianna felt guilt stab her like a dagger to the thorax. She missed her mom. Not that she had ever really visited that often because of her horrible sisters, but at least she'd called home on the scrying glass. Since the wedding, everything had been absolutely insane, and though Adrianna was sure her mother could forgive that, Adrianna hadn't exactly tried to call her. It hadn't even occurred to her to get another scrying glass, since she'd dropped her last one on the Blighted Island. Thinking about that made her feel horrible. But standing right in front of her was a reminder of the last thing Adrianna's mom had done to her. It was hard to call someone and make small talk when being confronted with the man that same someone had made her marry. Well not made, coerced with kindness.

'We could never rule here like your family does on Krag's Doom,' Adrianna said, trying to banish thoughts of her mother and the guilt that came with them.

'Of course not, and I don't want to. I would much rather purchase one of the mansions on the Ring, and rule as part of the Nine. Only then could we bring to this city what it deserves.'

'Are you hearing this?' Asakusa said. 'Bring to the city what it deserves? That's like the last line of every villain we've ever slayed.'

'Then maybe you're on the wrong side, thrall. Many of us villains, as you seem to be branding my and your friend's entire race of peoples, are simply trying to bring about a different way of life. A way of life in which people don't starve needlessly or go without medical treatment. I've seen the lumps of halflings on the streets here. Don't think I don't recognize addiction when I see it. It runs strong in our blood, and we know ways to cure it besides dumping the afflicted in the bay. If you would just give me a chance, I could show you what we could do for this whole city, and not just a few of its least desirables. We can make the world a better place,' Valkanna said, reaching his hand toward Adrianna as if he wished to cup her cheek or stroke her hair.

Adrianna never gave him the chance.

Adrianna had been waiting for this moment since Valkanna had last put his hands on her. Part of her felt foolish for even having a conversation over breakfast with this monster, but she was able to do so and remain calm because that kernel of distrust she felt in her heart radiated out through her body, like the motions of a fly stuck on a web, alerting the whole system that something was wrong. Richard seemed nice enough, and Adrianna was surprised at how into his monologuing she had been, but when his hand approached her hair, she struck.

As soon as his hand got within Adrianna's reach, she stabbed *Flametongue*—the very dagger Richard Valkanna had given her during their wedding ritual—through his hand, pinning him to table.

Valkanna screamed in pain, pulling back his hand reflexively and finding it stuck fast. 'Release me!' he roared and reached for the dagger with his other hand, but Adrianna parried him with a quickly-drawn blade that sliced across his forearm. This hardly hurt him, so Adrianna twisted the dagger that was pinning him to the table, wedging the point deeper into the wood beneath his hand. 'What is this, woman?' Smoke billowed from his nostrils; orange light shone in his throat.

'Don't think I will ever forget what you did to me, or what your family has done to human women for centuries,' Adrianna said. This speech, practiced again and again, came easily, despite it now being inflicted on a man who had just cooked her breakfast. 'I don't know how you convinced my sisters to show you how my hair controls my shape-shifting ability, but you will never act on that knowledge again, Valkanna.'

'Let me go!' Valkanna hissed, inhaling and breathing at her. No flames came out. *Flametongue*—still stabbed in his hand—only glowed brighter. Richard flinched backwards at his failed flames, and then fell out of his chair and barely managed to stay on his knees. His hand was still pinned to the table.

Just at that moment, Ebbo Brandyoak burst in the door. He was shoeless, which was typical, shirtless, which was unusual, and had a bit of bright blue powder on his nose, which was not surprising at all.

'Holy-crap-you-guys-I-met-Vecnos-and-I-think-he-wants-me-dead-and-Magnus-said-to-believe-in-myself-and-save-my-friend-but-all-I-did-was-more-magick.' Ebbo sucked in a massive breath, and then began to bawl.

Adrianna looked at Richard Valkanna with cool eyes. He scowled, but bowed his head to her. She had proven her point. She withdrew the knife from his hand, cauterizing the wound as she did.

Valkanna winced, then stood and began to pace, rubbing his wounded hand. It was already healing, fueled by the magic needed to keep a dragon's body functional. Not for the first time, Adrianna felt herself awed by his power. But she'd just proved that she was faster and had a weapon that could render him impotent. There was a calculating look in Valkanna's eyes. He understood all this as well.

Still, he went on, trying to ignore that Adrianna had just brought him to his knees. 'This is my point exactly. Now it's time to go run off and help this pathetic creature, when we could be restructuring the very fabric of the city.'

But despite his wound and his complaints, the dragon dutifully returned to the kitchen and served the islander a plate of food. He blasted this one with flames, cooking it to perfection and drawing a glance from Asakusa.

'What?' Valkanna said, 'I'm in love with her, not you. Forgive me for not cooking your food to order.'

'You're not in—you don't even know her! I know her, and... and I...' Asakusa lost steam every time his tongue tried to make the "L" sound.

'Enough, both of you,' Adrianna said, sort of amazed that Valkanna could bandy about the word *love* despite just being stabbed in the hand. She pulled the half-eaten bowl of food away from Ebbo and looked into his wide eyes. Breakfast had been... interesting. Strangely, it was a relief to see Valkanna watching her with the same distrust with which she'd been watching him, but she couldn't relish the moment. She needed to know what Ebbo knew, so they could get to work. 'Did you get the flowers?'

'No-'

'You worthless halfl-' Asakusa snarled, but Ebbo cut him off.

'But I know where to get all that we need! We just need to, uh... face down a couple dozen hrocs, and Vecnos. And maybe Magnus. I couldn't really tell where he stood on the issue.'

'How you can possibly think that's a solution?' Asakusa's maggots were whipping around now, a visual guide to how pissed he was at the halfling.

'Actually, I like the sound of that,' Valkanna said.

'You know how to get there?' Adrianna asked. She had to stay calm. Despite her web of self-control slowly unraveling by the minute, she had to stay calm. Asakusa was going to explode at Ebbo, he always did, so Adrianna couldn't. They had to get Asakusa healed. Not being able to access his powers as casually as usual was not helping the team.

Ebbo shrugged, and tears welled up in his eyes. 'Not really, but Clayton... that is, the stupid golem could...'

Adrianna's web of self-control felt like a bird had just crashed through it, plucking the spider and swallowing it whole. 'Ebbo... where is Clayton?'

Ebbo's lip trembled like an earthquake of heartache was about to rip across his face. 'He was hurt already, and then there was this magick powder. And Vecnos said it would grow back, like his heartbeats do, but it didn't! And-'

Adrianna gave him a silk handkerchief as terror rose in her chest. Ebbo dabbed at his eyes and wiped his nose clean of the blue powder as he continued to mumble incomprehensibly. There was something about kobolds, and a poop golem? Adrianna couldn't begin to follow. But when Ebbo looked at the blue powder on the hanky, as if he would snort it again, Adrianna snatched it back. Ebbo wasn't one to keep information from the spider princess, not since Clayton had convinced her to take pity on the little addict about a year ago. That he was stalling now was only making her furious. Ebbo had his flaws, they all had their flaws, but lying wasn't something he usually did. Or withholding the truth, or whatever the halfling was doing while he twisted his body in knots and continued to avoid the subject of their missing friend.

'Ebbo, where's Clayton?' Adrianna repeated, voice menacing with venom.

Ebbo stopped talking and looked up from the spider princess, to the Gatekeeper's thrall, to the dragon prince.

'Is that... is that Clayton on your nose?' Adrianna didn't think she'd ever heard Asakusa sound so angry. She could understand how he felt. Ebbo, to his credit, looked absolutely terrified.

'What's old Richard doing here? No sheep left to eat on the Dumb Krag?'

'Ebbo!' Adrianna snapped.

Ebbo wiped his tears and reached into a smaller bag on his belt.

From it he pulled Clayton Steelheart's steel heart.

Or what was left of it.

All that remained were a few charred pieces of metal, blackened on the outside with runes scratched on the inside.

'There was a piece that sort of fit them all together,' Ebbo said, then pulled out a gear, 'but it broke. I'm really sorry.'

Asakusa and Adrianna were speechless. Adrianna knew they were thinking the same thing. They'd met Clayton together, close to three years ago. He'd been wearing a ridiculous pair of pants and had helped them save an old lady from being eaten by a snake. If he hadn't been there—Etterqueen, if he's been wearing different pants—Adrianna would have been squished that day. Since then, Clayton had saved them countless times with powers unlike any golem that anyone had ever seen in the Archipelago. But to Adrianna, he was more than just a clay-bodied golem, he was good. When Asakusa answered problems with jaded cynicism and Adrianna answered them with naivety of the wealthy, it was Clayton who knew how to solve problems the right way. Ebbo no doubt knew this as well, as it had been Clayton that had recruited him and thus prevented his body from being either fed to the Ouroboros or dumped into Bog's Bay. The three of them, confronted with the potential loss of the person that kept them all together, really were speechless.

Only Valkanna said anything. 'So, then it's off to save the soulless construct? We'll try it your way, but then I want you to give mine a shot.' Valkanna grabbed a red leather trench coat he'd hung by the door and stepped into the streets of S'kar-Vozi.

Chapter 44

Ebbo

Ebbo had already explained so much. He wished they were better listeners. Clayton was a better listener. Ebbo gulped back his tears and tried to explain again.

'So, we have to find more magick powder to infuse into Clayton's heart, otherwise he's just going to be dead forever.'

'How can you think that's the damn solution?' Asakusa said.

'What else is the berry-picking solution?'

'Not more magick powder for you to snort!' Asakusa said, his Corruption maggots writhing with his fury.

'I told you, snorting that powder was a mistake! And like you can talk, maggot-boy! I know where the skull blossom is, which means I just saved your whole bushel of berries!' Ebbo turned out his pockets, revealing a few paltry handfuls of crushed skull blossom. It wasn't much, but it would buy Asakusa more time.

Asakusa looked at this offering, and for a moment—a precious, infinitesimally small moment—Ebbo saw gratitude pass across the thrall's face. But then it was gone, and Asakusa was yelling at him again. 'For the thousandth time, your pathetic addiction and the deal I made to save my sister are not the same thing!'

'Is this typical of your little squad?' Richard Valkanna asked Adrianna.

She nodded and tried to smile. 'Normally Clayton balances us out, but, err... well, yes.'

'Charming.'

'How the huckleberry are we supposed to save him, then?' Ebbo asked.

'I don't know, maybe we talk to the guy that made him?' Asakusa replied.

Ebbo paused, then rubbed his round little chin. 'Actually, that's a pretty good idea.'

Chapter 45

Adrianna

The sense of smell is strongly related to memories, and memories of the free city of S'kar-Vozi especially. There was the stench of Bog's Bay, of course, which some said was a better defense against the Kraken than the towering stone cliffs on either side of the narrow entrance, but there were other aromas as well—aromas far more pleasant, if no less pungent. The first of these that stimulated the tiny, sensitive hairs on Adrianna's legs was the smell of curry. Curried fish, a local staple, often sold in the market. It was made with all the seven of the crops grown by Magnus's fields, except apples, of course. The smell of sautéed onion and barley was enough to set Adrianna's digestive juices bubbling, despite her recent meal.

Adrianna's sisters would have insulted her for enjoying the smells. They preferred their food to be seasoned by feeding their prey pungent dishes before drinking its blood, one of the many reasons Adrianna detested them.

Quickly, though, the smell of curried fish was lost to a thousand others. Cinnamon, cardamom, thyme, and the delicate essence of saffron mixed with the calls of their vendors as Adrianna, Asakusa, Ebbo, and Valkanna walked through the market. These smells were but garnish compared to the stronger smells of fresh baked bread and fermenting beer. Adrianna loved them all, and though actually ingesting any of the ingredients would make her physically ill, she relished their ethereal aromas and the sounds of the people who made them their livelihood.

The sense of smell was perhaps assaulted more in the free city than anywhere else in the Archipelago, for nowhere else was there such a diversity of people. Or peoples. Or whatever you called all the different kinds of beings chattering away in different languages.

Humans dominated the population, but that only added to the chaos of diversity, for the humans came in many shapes and styles. There was the muscled and shirtless barbarian, his hulking body almost entirely shades of blue tattoos except a ring of pale skin around his nipples. There was the dark-skinned fire-breathing sorceress, bedecked in orange and red velvet and noticeably sweating in the humidity. There were mohawks and kilts, buzzed heads and plate mail, impish hair and short tunics. The humans talked loudly and swaggered about as if they owned the place, which Adrianna supposed they did. Humans had built S'kar-Vozi into what it was over the last hundred years, much to the surprise of the other races of the surrounding lands.

Races—there were many who wouldn't call them that, but Adrianna was a spiderfolk, so she was not one to judge. She saw a pair of pacifist, apologetic lycanthropes, who even when not suffering from their ailments always looked and acted a bit dog-like. The two of them walked in circles, sniffing at each other's butts and drawing glances from some the other races. A trio of felinis laughed their quiet, purring laughter at the pair. The felinis were a beautiful people, like giant cats who wore nothing but straps and harnesses for carrying loot and lucre. The mermen were far less attractive. They had a much weaker version of the magickal Folding that Adrianna possessed. They could shed their scaly skin, gills and tails to come ashore, but their skin remained rubbery and their gills didn't vanish so much as crust over with snot. They looked for buyers of undersea produce with deep, unblinking eyes. The ancient races were there too, of course, the elves and the dwarves, but they were few in number. Their time was coming to an end, something the elves had accepted with arrogant resignation and the dwarves stubbornly labored against. Between them all moved the tiny islanders. Their footsteps were soft and their movements furtive, but if one looked closely, they were everywhere, buying tourist crap, trading herbs with entirely too much gusto, haggling over potatoes—typical islander stuff.

Etterqueen, Adrianna loved this place. The diversity of it was just so different from the tunnels and caves she'd grown up in, where anything that wasn't spiderfolk was incapacitated and sucked dry of its juices as a matter of course. Adrianna also loved it here because she fit in. She had put a bit of work into her hair and Folding away more of her body, so she now had the humanoid two-arms-and-two-legs body shape, but she'd hadn't spent the time needed to hide her spider hairs or extra eyes. And she hardly stuck out. Even if people recognized her as a spiderfolk, it didn't matter in S'kar-Vozi.

All people could come to trade their fortunes in the free city, even the darker races. Krouche the Douche traded in information, his purple face and sawed-off horns bespoke of the demonic bloodline he'd forsaken. A Soulslug stuck to the shadowed awnings, avoiding salt as much as the rest of the shoppers avoided his slime trail. Then there was the group of snake people coming right toward them...

'Ebbo, what was that you said about Vecnos wanting you dead?'

The tiny assassin and one of the Nine didn't officially control the Ourdor of Ouroboros that these snake people no doubt belonged to, but he attended mass every Sermday. Rumor said he even left gems and rings in the tithing plate, an order of magnitude more valuable than the usual dead parrots and rats most followers of the Ourdor offered.

'That's about the short of it. I mean, he tricked me into snorting my friend's soul.'

'He didn't trick you into anything! Clayton's death is all your fault,' Asakusa said.

'Is not!' Ebbo protested, but Adrianna could tell his heart wasn't convinced.

The two fell into their familiar bickering while Adrianna kept leading them through the crowd. There was no doubt about it, they were being tailed by the Ourdor.

'Friends of yours?' Valkanna asked, raising a perfectly sculpted eyebrow at one of the human worshipers of the serpent-god Ouroboros. Ourdorlies, the human ones were called. The one's tongue was split and his skin tattooed to look like one of the true reptilians who labored to feed their ever-hungry god.

'No. The opposite. Keep moving, if they attack us here, innocent people might get hurt.'

'Innocent?' Valkanna snorted. 'There are more weapons on the streets here than we have in our armory. These people have been going on raids to slaughter our families and steal our wealth for generations!'

'Some of them, yes,' Adrianna admitted, 'but not all. Most the people here are farmers and merchants. I thought you said you wanted to be better than our families. Now is your chance to prove it.'

Valkanna sighed and nodded, then turned to Asakusa.

'Move it, thrall, we're being tailed,' he said and cuffed Asakusa on the ear.

Asakusa stumbled forward but held tight to *Byergen*, the stone hammer. He whirled on Valkanna, furious. Valkanna only spit in the dirt between them. His saliva turned to smoke when it hit the rainbow of cobblestones beneath them.

'What was that for?' Adrianna hissed.

'If they're anything like the henchmen I've met, they'll be more than willing to let someone else do the dirty work.' Valkanna said. 'We'll start a brawl, and you and the halfling can slip away.' Valkanna stepped backwards, easily dodging an uppercut from Asakusa's stone hammer before shoving him to the ground.

'I've heard about you. You're friends with that little what's-it, halfling, right?' Valkanna said, his voice raised as if he was on stage, 'What? Are you surprised I figured out how to dodge your predictable uppercut? How else are you going to attack if you just drag that thing around all time?'

Asakusa pushed himself to his feet and dragged his stone hammer at Valkanna with a yell. The maggots of his Corrupted body flexed when he lifted the hammer. Adrianna wasn't sure if Asakusa knew it was act.

'Careful, you might damage your pets.' Valkanna deflected the hammer with a swipe of his claws.

Adrianna knew that the blow had been hard enough to crush most men's ribs, let alone break their hands, but Richard Valkanna was a dragon glamoured into the shape of a man. To him, it probably was like jamming a finger.

Valkanna's plan was working. The Ourdorlies had stopped to watch the fight. Adrianna grabbed Ebbo's hand and backed away from the slowly gathering crowd.

Asakusa grunted and kept the hammer moving, letting it out every other swing or two to try and crush the dragon prince. Valkanna dodged in graceful leaps, pushing the crowd back and drawing them in at the same time. The islander tourists loved to watch a good brawl, but some of the humans were starting to pay attention to this one as well. Asakusa's right arm was a seething mass of tiny black worms. Even for S'kar-Vozi, that was some pretty weird shit.

Adrianna stepped back into the crowd and kept moving toward the warehouse district. She kept tight hold of Ebbo's hand. If Valkanna and Asakusa could keep the Ourdor distracted, the two of them could go fix Clayton. Adrianna prayed to the Etterqueen that they could fix Clayton.

Valkanna screamed and dropped to a knee, just barely dodging a blow from Asakusa.

'I thought you were going to help us!' Ebbo shouted. His elven dagger dripped in blood as he yanked it back out of Valkanna's thigh.

'Ebbo, what are you doing?' Adrianna hissed and looked down reflexively at the hand she still held in her own. At some point, Ebbo had switched out his own hand with that of another islander. The chubby little girl whose arm was connected to the hand that Adrianna held smiled up at her and took a bite of her elote. Sometimes it was quite frustrating having a pickpocket on the team. But Valkanna would heal from the knife; it was the hammer that- 'Asakusa, no!'

Asakusa swung his hammer and clocked Valkanna hard enough to send him flying. The dragon's human glamour flickered, and for just a moment, an enormous red dragon hurtled through the streets of S'kar-Vozi to the oohs and ahhs of the human and islander onlookers before smashing against a wall.

It was in this moment that the Ourdor snatched Ebbo.

'Help!' The islander screamed. 'I've been picked!' he said as they stuffed his tousled locks and all the rest of him into a sack and made off into a back alley.

Adrianna cursed the stupidity of it all, let her hair down and Unfolded into her true, eight-legged spider form, and ran after him.

'Follow me!' she shouted to both her dumbass boyfriend and arrogant husband. This was not going to be easy.

Chapter 46

Adrianna

Through the back alleys they ran. Adrianna outpaced the Ourdorlies. They were just humans tattooed to look like snakes, after all. But amongst these servants of the ever-hungry Ouroboros were a few priests that had already started their path of transformation. One in particular—she had no legs but just a snake tail—was unbelievably fast. No doubt she'd heated her blood to near lethal levels in anticipation of having to outrace the spider princess. Still, she wasn't a spider.

Adrianna cracked her whip around a banister and swung herself up onto a wall, which she ran across. She came to a T and jumped to the left, following the tail of the serpent.

She caught up to a group of them in time to crack one with her whip. It hissed at and her and drew a blade to fight, but she leapt over him and kept moving. This was not her fight, and besides, she'd have to leave something for her boys to do. The next Ourdorly wasn't so easy. When she rounded a bend, she barely dodged an arrow—doubtlessly poison-tipped—as it crashed through a window and disrupted some merchant's wife's knitting. A hasty apology, a crack of her whip, and the man was disarmed and hissing at her with a split tongue that was still healing from the elective surgery. Adrianna would have to do more than that, though. She couldn't risk getting shot in the back and without knowing what kind of poison they were using.

She dropped from the wall, catching herself by spreading her legs to either side of the narrow alley.

The snake drew a curved blade. This one was slick with poison, but Adrianna thought she recognized it. Dragon's acid, a poor choice against the wife of a red dragon.

She parried his blade with *Flametongue* and smelled the poison on her foe's blade. It was indeed draconic, so she struck the serpent's blade with one of her Vecnos Industries daggers, causing a spark and igniting the weapon.

The serpent, thinking it had an advantage, tried to press her with the sword rather than extinguishing the flames. A serious mistake. Adrianna's dagger absorbed the heat, while the serpent's own sword did not. They exchanged blows, but the serpent began to twitch under the heat of the flames. Apparently, his physiology was farther along the transformation to snake than his appearance made him seem, for his cold blood was overheating. When he twitched to get away from the heat from the flame, Adrianna seized her opportunity and drove a dagger into his gut.

'Spider traitor,' the man hissed as he bled out steaming snake's blood into the back alley. 'Your friend will be fed to the Ouroboros, and you will bow before her, as your kind did millennia ago.'

'Which way did you take him?' Adrianna asked, but the snake only hissed.

She kicked him once for good measure, then heard the tell-tale clank of a sewer lid being pulled closed.

She got to it just too late. She stuck her dagger in to wedge it open but was unable to. The spider princess excelled at many things; brute strength was not one of them.

'Asakusa!' she yelled.

A Gate opened, and Asakusa stepped from the Ways of the Dead. It appeared as if a hole had simply been gashed into reality. Through the frame of lighting and runes, Adrianna saw a stone path that ran up into a curling corkscrew of a bridge. It looked totally impractical, but thus was the geography of the world from which Asakusa drew his power. 'What?' the thrall asked as the lightning ceased to crack and the Gate closed.

'You're not supposed to use that until you're fully healed,' chided him.

'I'm healed enough, and we can't lose Ebbo. Not without Clayton.'

Adrianna didn't want to think about the full implications of that statement.

Asakusa had no such trouble with the sewer lid. His Corrupted hand slammed into it, and the maggots squirmed in a hundred directions, breaking the illusion that the thrall still had fingers underneath the mass of the black worms. They wrapped around the sewer lid and Asakusa threw it back, drawing a shout from behind them.

'I just defeated three of these snake-fellows, and this is how I'm thanked?' Valkanna had caught up. He was out of breath, limping from being stabbed by Ebbo, but he was there, and he hadn't used his dragon form to incinerate their foes, which even in the cosmopolitan streets of the free city would probably have caused a panic. Thank the Etterqueen that Richard was more politically minded than the rest of Adrianna's friends. Wait, had she just thought of him as Richard? Worse, had she just thought of him as a friend?

Adrianna didn't have time to ponder her subconscious. She dropped into the sewer.

Immediately she understood she was too late. To her left, perhaps a hundred paces down, was the woman with a snake tail for legs holding a squirming sack over her shoulder. To her right, the same distance away, also standing in an obnoxiously convenient spotlight from another sewer grate, was another priest, who—instead of legs—had a mass of writhing snakes supporting his torso. He too held a squirming sack. One of them had Ebbo, the other an innocent islander.

'What do you want?' Adrianna yelled at them both.

'To serve the Ouroboros!' they yelled, sounding smug.

Adrianna cursed herself for setting the zealots up for the line.

Adrianna didn't have time to reason out which was the decoy and which had Ebbo. She ran after the priestess with the single snake tail, her eight spider legs sticking to the walls and propelling her down the middle of the tunnel and keeping her out of the sludge that ran down its middle.

There was a sound like a thunder crack, and she knew Asakusa had gone after the other one.

She made it maybe halfway down before the serpent she was following vanished down a side tunnel.

In the few seconds it took her to get there, the snake woman was gone. She'd vanished into one of three nearly identical tunnels, and Adrianna had no idea which one. She chose the one to the right and ran a ways, but finding nothing and hearing less, she went back for the middle... but she knew it was fruitless. Trying to track anyone who knew their way through the sewers was impossible without the help of kobolds, and they would be less than willing to help track down a serpent whose god regularly ate their kind for a snack.

She cursed. Her only hope was that she'd chosen wrong. She followed the thread of silk she'd left back to the open sewer grate, only to discover that she hadn't.

Asakusa had got his guy, and it was the wrong one. A stinky, disheveled islander was stomping about, mumbling about an inconvenient vacation and how his relatives were sure to hear all about it. That meant Adrianna has been chasing the correct target. A frustrating feeling.

'You get him?' Asakusa asked. His Corruption had spread again, further up his neck. The worms pulsed contentedly at their expanded real estate.

Adrianna shook her head.

Asakusa cursed.

'So what, let's find him, right?' Valkanna said.

'It's not that simple,' Adrianna said. 'There's no trails down there, it's all either hard rock or runny sludge. The only way to track anyone would be to follow a scent trail, but the lycanthropes can't deal with all the shit, they just roll in it, and the felinis are of course far above it. They might track for their own kind, but never for us.'

'This has to have happened before. Your little Ebbo doesn't seem particularly good at not getting caught.'

'It has. More than I'd like to admit, but normally we have Clayton. He can track.'

'Then all the more reason to get to the artificer.'

Chapter 47

Adrianna

They went straight to the shop of Leopold the Grimy. Cheapest Constructs Constructed, the sign above the shop read. Or normally it was above the shop. Currently it was snapped in half and covered in broken glass from the windows.

The inside of the shop looked no better. Normally, Leopold's had a layer of grime—grime being part of his business model. Adrianna had been here a few times over the years to fix Clayton up. Typically, when one entered, suits of armor waved creaky hellos and animated chains barred the exit for potential thieves. A set of hammers would be affixing rivets to a hovering shield while the wizard himself would have his hands in some giant, poorly sculpted lump of clay. There were other artificers in S'kar-Vozi, and most were far more skilled, but few were as prolific and fewer still were cheaper. Leopold did the regular stuff, of course: brooms, carpets, silverware, but he really excelled in bodyguards. There was a bit of a joke around the free city that this was because if they failed at their job, no one would come complaining about the warrantee, but it looked like perhaps someone had.

Silverware wiggled weakly on the floor, twisted as if by some deranged psychic. A pair of chains rattled loosely as Adrianna stepped through the broken window and into the shop. Light fixtures blinked messages of perseverance in the darkness. Through it all, Adrianna looked for some sign of the artificer. She had to find him; Clayton's life depended on it. Adrianna didn't want to think what would happen to her and her friends without Clayton. Even worse, she didn't want to think about the person she might become. Worst of all would be the horrible feeling of knowing—for the rest of her possibly centuries-spanning life—that one of her best friends had died because she'd neglected to invite him to her wedding.

'He doesn't keep the place in great shape, does he?' Valkanna said.

'He's been ransacked, you twit,' Asakusa snapped.

'Watch it, thrall, that was a joke.'

'A lame one.'

Valkanna smiled. 'We'll make something of you yet, thrall. A sense of humor and a deal with a demon for more than a nasty arm. I take it that little Gate of yours in the sewer is how you crashed our wedding? I'm impressed. Krag's Doom was supposed to be inaccessible. Only the High Path-'

'What the hell do you think we took?'

'Can we focus here?' Adrianna said. 'There has to be some sort of clue to where they're taking Ebbo.'

'You think it's related?' Asakusa said.

'The Ourdor knew who we were. I'm sure anyone talking to Ebbo would as well. And if he was trying to get Clayton's heart fixed, it wouldn't take much to figure out Leopold was the one who put Clayton together,' Adrianna said.

'Indeed not,' Valkanna pointed to a flyer reading 'proud father of the free golem! Only construct to ever last long enough to grow a conscience. Get yours today and do the right thing!'

Adrianna rolled her eyes. Leopold's sense of right and wrong was driven only by which bag of coin was heavier. Clayton's kindness was miraculous, considering who his father was. Or... it had been. Adrianna tried to keep the thought from her mind. They would fix Clayton. They had to.

She left the flyer and continued looking around. Everything had been destroyed, but there was no blood... maybe the old wizard had been out? Doubtful, he was wanted dead by a lot of people. He was kept safe only by virtue of his workshop's defenses.

The clatter of a suit of armor drew her attention. It was badly dented and missing an arm, but maybe the wizard was inside?

'Check that,' Adrianna said.

Asakusa nodded and moved toward the armor. Valkanna drew his sword.

Asakusa flipped the helm up. The armor let out a mournful hiss of steam, and then the construct clattered to pieces, like a bag of spider silk being emptied of bones.

Where else could he be? Everything had been torn to shreds. There was a broken desk, a smashed-up chest, a lump of clay worked into the rough shape of a man that had been struck repeatedly with what looked like clubs. But the blows weren't deep...

Adrianna stuck the clay with her dagger. It didn't move. She dug deeper, working her blade back and forth until she felt some resistance... and the golem sat up.

Adrianna tried to jump back, but her arm was stuck in the thick mud.

'Boys!' she said, and they obliged.

Asakusa struck the thing's head from its body, and Valkanna took off both of its arms with his sword.

The torso of the golem stood there quivering. Adrianna, Asakusa, and Valkanna gripped their weapons tighter. Then a dirty human head popped out of the clay chest.

'Okay, okay, I'll tell you where the gold is!' Leopold said in an accent unique to the free city, despite the wizard being an immigrant from outside the Archipelago.

'You don't have any gold,' Adrianna said. Leopold was one of the few locals who actually spent any time in the VanChamp Pleasure Palace. Apparently, he thought himself lucky, despite all the games being designed to keep the incestuous siblings wealthy enough to keep their spot in the Ringwall.

'Oh, bolts, you have no idea how happy I am to see you,' Leopold said, climbing his way out of the torso of mud.

'We have a guess,' Adrianna replied.

Leopold looked around the shop, taking in the destruction with an uncharacteristic restraint of complaints. It always struck Adrianna how short the artificer was—short enough to pass for a tall islander, but his greasy mustache and lack of beard meant he had to be human, not islander and not dwarf. His demeanor was such that no race would wish to claim him.

'Lucky I saw the flesh-bags coming,' Leopold said, and then conducted some elaborate motions over a broom. It began to sweep the broken glass on the floor into a pile.

'How did you know they were going to rough you up?' Adrianna said, when really she wanted to demand that Leopold fix Clayton right now. But the artificer was completely unsympathetic to his creations. Adrianna wanted him fixed, and that meant humoring Leopold with concern. It was what Clayton would have done.

'Hrocs wielding iron clubs aren't usually the best paying customers. Not exactly after the finer things in life. Speaking of which, it looks like I've got some of my self-stitching needles still intact. Hands full? Why not set a needle to stitch up that wound, doily, or clothes torn apart in the throes of passion?'

'Well, that's kind of you,' Valkanna said.

'For you, only twenty coins.'

'We're not here to buy your junk,' Asakusa said.

'Oh yeah? Am I supposed to think this is a social visit? That's something I find hard to believe. The only thing you and that no-good golem of mine ever cause me is trouble. Where the hell is he, anyway? Waiting out there to steal my clay?'

Adrianna looked to her friends. Asakusa shrugged then brought forth the bag.

'Lazy clay-bag too good to even walk on his own feet anymore?'

Asakusa dumped the blackened and bent pieces on the table.

'Oh, wow,' Leopold said, his sales banter momentarily interrupted. 'Y'all really did a number, huh? What did it this time, fire sprite? Lava giant?'

'It was a fire-breathing dragon, actually,' drawled Valkanna.

Adrianna shot a look at Valkanna that said, "don't be proud, asshole," but turned back to Leopold. 'Can you fix him or not?'

Leopold picked up a piece of the heart and turned it over in his grimy hands. He put it back with a grunt and looked at another. He held this one up to the light and snorted. He appraised each in turn, then, with a loud belch, proclaimed that yes, he could fix it. Adrianna had never before in her life felt relief at the sound of expelled gas, but she wondered now if she'd treasure the sound of Leopold the Grimy's burp for years to come. If he really could fix Clayton, she very well might.

'Well then, why don't you?' Valkanna said.

'I believe we have yet to discuss my payment,' Leopold said.

'We just saved your life,' Asakusa griped.

'Those hrocs were long gone.'

'You could have suffocated.'

Leopold shrugged. 'Occupational risk.'

Valkanna tossed a small leather bag on the table. It landed with the satisfying clink of coin. A good merchant might be able to tell gold from copper by the sound of the bag hitting the table; all the bad ones could. Leopold no doubt calculated the worth of the bag to the exact coin. Hopefully he wouldn't check the mint. Adrianna could be sure the bag was filled with metal stamped with dragons.

'I still don't see why I should. For that much money, I can make you a better golem. Even toss in some weapons, maybe a dagger that stabs anyone that steals it?'

'We want Clayton,' Adrianna said.

'Steelheart wasn't a golem at all, he was some kinda freak. An artificer's mistake. A golem shouldn't beat up the master who brought him to life any more than he should disobey an order on account of his conscience. That's the whole point of the things! He's a mistake, and if I rectify it right now, people will know my warrantees are good.'

'You have a whole marketing campaign based on him!' Adrianna was appalled that Leopold could call Clayton a freak. He was the kindest person she'd ever met—even if he wasn't exactly a person.

'A failed marketing campaign. You know how many clients ask for a golem with morals? None. Zero. In fact, I get people asking to do the opposite. No one pays for morals. That's the whole point of the things, right? Can't be bought.'

'We're paying you, you ignoramus. We're his masters now,' Valkanna said.

'Sure thing, boss. Thing is, this ignor-a-mouse just remembered he don't do commissions for arrogant flesh-bags.'

'I'm a dragon, not a flesh-bag.'

'Dragons can be flesh-bags.'

'You can't fix him, can you?' Asakusa said.

Adrianna was thinking the same thing. It was an almost physical hurt to hear it said aloud. Leopold shrugged, and the full weight of Clayton being gone struck Adrianna like a hammer to the chest. 'Everyone knows you're not much of an artificer,' she said, not wanting to but unable to help herself. 'You don't even make self-climbing ropes.'

'You know how much wear and tear a rope has to take?' Leopold said, but he grabbed a pair of pliers and started working as he griped. 'Bunch a' misfits, you don't think I can do it?'

'You're lazy,' Adrianna said.

'Unscrupulous,' Asakusa added.

'From my impression, a bit of a jerk, but all and all enterprising,' Valkanna said.

'You can't fix Clayton because you never made him. He's too good, too nice. He always said the reason he was different was because of his fairy godmother,' Adrianna said, hoping it wasn't true.

'Fairy godmother?' Leopold scoffed before setting a tiny hammer to work affixing studs. 'You got it all wrong, kid. I made Clayton. Me. His Heartbeats is my own design, comes from the runes I put here myself,' Leopold said, pointing to the runes inside the heart. They were still unmoving but indeed seemed to have a faint glow.

'But how do you explain the blue powder?' Asakusa asked. 'It must have come from the magickal being you coerced or tricked into making Clayton.'

'You've been in here before for tune-ups. You ever see any of this?'

Leopold said, wiping a grimy finger along a piece of the heart. The fingertip came away with a blue tinge to the grime. Apparently Ebbo had missed some. 'I don't use this crap. Magick like this is too easy to track. If I made Steelheart work with this, his life woulda been ended by one of them big ol' snakes long ago.'

'Big snakes? You mean like in the Ourdor of Ouroboros?' Asakusa said.

'Is there another snake cult in the free city? Yes, the Ourdor, for the sake of steel. They derive a magick powder from snake venom. Tried to sell it to me before, but it's a scam. It's potent stuff, but they come 'round to collect their debt. I'd never use that stuff on my work.'

Adrianna felt her heart start to pound faster in her abdomen. Leopold said the blue powder wasn't from him, but from the Ourdor. No one had seen the stuff before Vecnos had taken possession of the heart. Which meant: 'Ebbo didn't snort Clayton's soul.'

'He tried to, though,' Asakusa said quickly, as if he was unable to stop himself from insulting the halfling, even as they learned that whatever had happened to Clayton was not Ebbo's fault. It was a small burden lifted. Adrianna knew what her wicked sisters would have done to those that betrayed the; now Adrianna could finally push aside the idea of stinging the little magick-addict and draining him of his fluids. Not that she'd wanted to, but the thought of losing Clayton sent her mind to dark places.

'Okay, so if Ebbo didn't snort Clayton's Heartbeats, then the powder must have come from-'

'Vecnos,' Asakusa said, finishing Adrianna's thought. It seemed that Vecnos really did want Ebbo dead. They'd have to find him all the more quickly. And the only way they were going to find him in the sewers was with Clayton's help. For the thousandth time, Adrianna wished on the Etterqueen that Clayton was alright.

'What did you use on Clayton, then? You don't believe all your work is alive,' Adrianna said.

'Damn straight I don't. That'd be worse than a damn golem telling fairy tales.'

'Then how do you explain it?' Adrianna said.

'You ever wonder why some horses are stallions and other are ponies? For all I know, my hand coulda slipped and I made a rune that invoked the god o' the hookers. Stranger things have happened.'

'So anyone could have done it,' Asakusa said.

'I did it. Not no fairy, not no you-nee-corn, not a blue venom snake, but me. I may not be his master no more, but he's mine all the same.'

Leopold stood up straighter when he said that. His hands didn't leave the steel heart, though. He held it in lightly caged fingers, as if to protect a baby bird.

'Then help him,' Adrianna said, trying not to sound desperate and failing miserably.

'What he's done couldn't have been done without me,' Leopold said. 'And you wouldn't be here if you thought otherwise. Now, go browse while I work on this here. Work like this is gonna cost something pretty, that whole sack o' gold is as good as mine. If you stop nagging me, I might find it in my heart to throw in some of this broken crap.' Leopold grunted and turned to his work.

Adrianna pretended to peruse the broken-down shop while she watched Leopold out of the corner of one of her eyes. Her hair—put up hastily—was already coming loose, so it was an extra eye that watched the artificer fidget with her friend's heart like it was nothing more than a magick lock.

'Do you believe what he said about snake venom?' Asakusa said.

'Obviously the halfling was tricked,' Valkanna said.

'Obviously it's not that obvious.'

'Will you two cut it out?' Adrianna said.

'I'm just thinking about Ebbo and that powder,' Asakusa said.

'So you can lay blame on the halfling's addiction,' Valkanna cut in.

Asakusa's red face was all the answer he was able to give. What really hurt was that Adrianna knew Valkanna was right. Asakusa was extremely judgmental about Ebbo's addiction. It wasn't as if the islander had a choice in the matter. Valkanna saw that, so why didn't Asakusa? More and more, it seemed to her that perhaps she'd misjudged this dragon prince. His arrogance was far more obnoxious that Asakusa's broodiness, but he also seemed more progressive in many ways. Maybe he and Adrianna really were a good match. Maybe she could bring more good to the world by going to Krag's Doom, and ruling as her webmother had intended. Oh, but then what of Asakusa? He loved her, that much was obvious. Could she turn her back on him for the greater good? Would that make her a better person, or a worse one? She didn't know but had a feeling that Clayton might. She looked at the pair again. Asakusa had some sort of cart, and Valkanna a set of silver knitting needles. They were already back to insulting each other.

'Isn't that for children to ride?' Valkanna said.

'It's for *Byergen*, the stone hammer. Did I hit you so hard that you forgot slamming into a brick wall half an hour ago?'

'You're going to charge into battle with a little cart trundling along behind you? How terribly frightening.'

'It's for everything but battle, lizard-breath. And like you're one to talk. You picked out animated knitting needles? What are you going to do, knit your enemies a scarf and choke them with it?'

'I have no need of any of these knick-knacks for battle. I am a red dragon. My breath alone has incinerated entire armies. The needles are for my mother-in-law. She's getting older, I'm sure you know, and may not be able to knit silken armor comfortably much longer.'

'Like you'd ever wear silk armor.' Asakusa scoffed.

'I certainly wouldn't, but my children might.'

Not once did Valkanna glance her way, not even when he'd mentioned them having children. If it was an act, it was a spinning good one. Maybe she'd misjudged the guy. He cared about her webmother and was thinking about clothes for their kids? He seemed so mature compared to Asakusa and the cart now loyally following him around with his hammer atop it.

She was pulled from her thoughts and her half-hearted search through broken goods by Leopold the Grimy.

'Make a circle,' Leopold ordered, and the three adventurers obeyed.

Clayton's steel heart had changed. All its wounds and cracks had been healed with gold. Little veins of lustrous yellow ran through it now, like bits of string in a bird's nest or the strands in a spider's web. The steel heart hardly looked artificial anymore. It looked organic, like Leopold has somehow regrown the missing bits of steel with golden magick.

'It's beautiful,' Adrianna said.

'Looks expensive,' Asakusa said.

'Not like you're paying,' Valkanna managed to get in before Leopold grunted.

'I'll be charging for every ounce of it too,' Leopold said, ignoring the dragon prince, 'but it was all that would fill the cracks. The runes inside were undamaged, lucky for you. If those were gone, we'd have to make a brand new, fully functional, obedient golem.'

'It's wonderful, Lee, thank you,' Adrianna said.

Leopold wiped his grimy brow with his grimy hand and nodded.

'Alright then,' Leopold said. 'Let's do this.'

He took Clayton's steel heart in his hand and began to pump it with his fingers.

'Kol-dalla-who-ralla!' he yelled, followed by strings of equally unintelligible syllables. The words of the spell would be fitted in there somewhere, but of course he wouldn't reveal them.

'Dung-doola-boo-hala!' he shouted, and a thumping could be heard in the room, deep and low. He held the heart up, pumping it with his fingers.

'Ding-a-ding, ding-a-doo!' he said, and threw the heart into the mud body he'd been hiding inside of. Then before anyone could say anything, he grabbed a wrench, swung it over his shoulder and smashed it into the heart with such force, it sunk into the clay body with a juicy squelch.

For a moment nothing happened, but then, the body began to thrum to a beat.

Bum-bum.

Bum-bum.

The heart sunk into the clay. For a moment all was still, then ripples spread across the surface of the golem, like fingers pushing through clay. Clay filled the hole where Leopold had put the heart. The wound healed, beat by beat, until the chest of the golem was smooth. The clay body stopped rippling. The fingermarks smoothed the body over into a rough semblance of the male form, and then they stopped. Adrianna had seen Clayton go through this process hundreds of times in the few years they'd known each other. But never before had it filled her with such joy, such relief. Clayton was going to be alright.

For a moment the golem lay still, and then he sat up and swung his legs over the side of the table. He stood up, didn't move for a few more Heartbeats, then took a few steps around the shop and came to a stop staring at Leopold.

'What's wrong with him?' Adrianna said. The golem looked like a child's piece of art instead of Clayton's perfectly chiseled body. Panic was replacing the joy Adrianna had felt mere seconds before. Clayton was supposed to be fixed. They brought him here to mend him, not replace him with some…some automaton!

'Sorry, that always runs after a reboot.'

'He normally talks while he does this part,' Asakusa said, his voice tense.

'Yeah, well, normally you don't blast his heart with dragon's fire, so show some damn patience. Always takes a second to get him back online. Golem. This is your father, Leopold the Grimy.'

'Father,' the golem said in a deep, hollow voice. Adrianna was terrified of that voice in this moment. It was the exact same voice every other golem used.

'Will you ever harm me, my son?'

'To do so would be to break my own heart. I would never harm you, Father.'

'Not even if someone told you to?'

'If I were ordered to harm you, I would assuredly clobber the crap out of whoever ordered it.'

'Even if you didn't like what I did?'

'You are Father. You are like master. I will not harm you, not even if master commands it. Who is master?'

'What is this crap?' Asakusa demanded. Adrianna wasn't surprised that he was reacting to the moment with hostility. That was kind of Asakusa's thing.

Leopold glanced at the squirming maggots on Asakusa's arm. 'A little insurance. Can't have these things turning on me. First thing a halfway decent artificer learns is how to make sure his merchandise can never go against him, and I am definitely at least halfway decent.'

'You're Clayton Steelheart. The free golem,' Valkanna said to the clay man, ignoring Leopold.

Adrianna found that she was incapable of speech. Why was Clayton acting like this? Leopold had fixed his heart, why hadn't that fixed *him*?

'Clayton Steelheart. Free golem,' the golem said in its hollow voice, and then, 'Father?'

'Yeah, yeah, it's like they said. You're Clayton Steelheart, that's what I named you. And these are you masters,' Leopold said, snatching the bag of gold coins off the counter and peeking inside. 'Dragoncoin, huh?' Leopold said, glancing at Valkanna. 'I was hoping for spider but I guess you never have cash, do you princess? This whole pouch oughta cover the exchange rate,' Leopold said, counting the coins.

'Master,' the golem said.

'Call me Valkanna. Master is unbecoming in this day and age.'

'He's not your master,' Asakusa said.

'You're Clayton Steelheart, the free golem,' Adrianna said, the words painful in her throat. She shouldn't have to explain this. It was practically all Clayton ever talked about.

'Listen to her,' Valkanna said.

'Clayton Steelheart. Free golem,' The golem said again.

'Clayton Steelheart,' Adrianna agreed. 'Our friend Clayton. You're a very nice guy.'

'Handsome, too. Chiseled features,' Asakusa said.

Adrianna laughed when Asakusa said it, tears coming out of her extra eyes, unbidden and out of control.

'Oh, come on, that's horrible,' Valkanna said.

'It's his joke,' Asakusa said, scowling.

'He's right, though, you were quite handsome,' Adrianna said, fidgeting with her hair, trying to find the strands that would close her extra eyes and thus stop the tears that were now flowing. 'Can you make yourself look like you used to?'

'Of course he can,' Leopold the Grimy declared.

For a moment the golem did nothing at all. Then it furrowed its brow and its clay began to move in time to its Heartbeats. Its limbs slimmed and it extended. Its torso grew broad at the top. Muscles cut themselves into the clay, as if some invisible gelato vendor was scooping bits of Clayton into a cone in another dimension. Pectorals were scooped out to the rhythm of the thumping Heartbeats, then abs, biceps, triceps, and the suite of muscles on his back. The golem's jaw popped out, his cheekbones extended, and his brow receded a bit. His head smoothed. He grew a well-proportioned penis and a butt with perfectly scooped-out dimples. Another Heartbeat and he grew fancy underpants, and his genitals vanished. Another Heartbeat and he grew a pair of capris. Then a frilly shirt. That too sloughed away, so he once again shirtless. He had never been great at doing shirts. He preferred to wear real ones.

He opened his eyes. The pupils were the same reddish brown as the eyelids, but they opened all the same. He smiled, causing his cheeks to crack and a bit of dust to crumble away. It wasn't the smile of a thoughtless golem —most golems didn't smile at all—It was Clayton's smile!

Adrianna let herself shed a tear before she hugged him, knowing he'd absorb the drop and she'd be a part of him again, just as he was a part of her. Well, not just like he was part of her, as that was strictly symbolic, but it felt good to hug her old friend all the same.

'Clayton,' Adrianna said, then pulled back to look her friend in the face he'd designed himself. She didn't see Clayton looking back out at her. The features were the same, but static. A mask, not a face.

'Clayton Steelheart, Free Golem, what does master desire?' the golem said in its deep, hollow voice.

'You said you could fix him,' Asakusa said. He had Leopold cornered, or his Corruption maggots did. They whipped about as the thrall clenched his fist.

'He is fixed!' Leopold said, gesturing at his constructs to come to his aid. It was no use. The hrocs had trashed his shop and his defenses.

'We want our friend back,' Adrianna said, turning from the golem and unraveling her whip.

'He even made a dick, what more do you perverts want?'

'That's not him,' Adrianna said, barely controlling her rage. A hundred classes on how to dispatch mortals came back to her. She'd hated those classes, but now, with Leopold grinning at this cheap copy of her friend, she found herself considering the methods she'd learned despite telling herself a thousand times she'd never used them.

'Darling,' Valkanna said, 'the poor man's done his best, and I for one like this new golem. He's snappy. Not at all like the regular mushy variety.'

'He's not real,' Adrianna said.

'No, of course not. Golems never are,' Valkanna said, 'You do, however, have a very real friend who will not be brought back from the dead if we fail to rescue him.'

'Oh, Etterqueen. Ebbo.' She'd completely forgotten about him when confronted with the fake Clayton. Adrianna cracked her whip. 'Two of my friends are gone today because of you, wizard. Give me one reason why I shouldn't wrap you in silk and give you to the hrocs.'

'I ain't done nothing but try to help!' Leopold said. He'd obviously believed Adrianna's bluff. When Adrianna's scowl did not vanish, he took out the bag of coins and shoved into her hands. 'Have a refund if you don't like it! Consider it a favor!'

Adrianna knocked the bag to the ground.

'Clayton was our friend. Now he's just... gone,' Asakusa looked furious. Adrianna hadn't realized how much he'd actually cared about Clayton.

'Yeah, but you can still track with him! Tell Steelheart to find your little friend, and he will. All he needs is a scent.'

Adrianna pulled out a silk handkerchief. It had a dab of the blue powder on it. She didn't know what else to do.

'Will this work?'

'Just give him the order. If those snakes can follow that powder, he can too.'

'Clayton, do you smell the blue powder? Our friend Ebbo Brandyoak used it. Can you follow this smell to Ebbo?' Adrianna asked.

Clayton took the handkerchief in his hand and slowly rubbed it between his fingers.

'I can find him,' the golem said.

'Well, then, on with it, old chap,' Valkanna ordered.

The golem marched out the door.

Adrianna, Asakusa, and Valkanna followed him, leaving one bewildered artificer in a shop to clean. He smiled with relief as Adrianna passed. Then she saw him scowl out of the corner of one her extra eyes.

'Creeps took the gold. No, don't laugh, get to work!' the artificer shouted at his brooms.

Chapter 48

Dergh

Dergh held the islander high above the grave. With his death would come the life of the holy plant, skull blossom, as it was called in the common tongue, and yet Dergh hesitated. She stood in the graveyard where Vecnos had told them to stay. The high walls made the space feel smaller than it was, the funerary statues and gravestones crammed inside and choked with skull blossom made it seem tighter still.

The half-orcs were happy to have the sky above them, though. The few dozen that Vecnos had rescued from their homeland were all assembled, watching a ritual they'd been told was their own. The snakies, and the humans tattooed and mutilated to look like snakies that followed the Ourdor of Oro-doro-dos or whatever the snakies called it, paid far less reverence to the space. They trampled the skull blossom—despite the half-orcs repeatedly asking them not to—and they had already broken more than one funerary statue. Apparently, they didn't honor the dead at all, preferring to feed the living to each other or their snaky god.

The islander being buried alive instead of fed to the Snaky God was supposed to be some kind of gesture that Dergh had tried and failed to wrap her head around.

Could she cast him in and bury him alive? Vecnos assured her that her ancestors had treated their enemies this way, and he was much smarter than the half-orcs, or so he often said. It seemed so... so mean... no, more than mean... cruel! Dergh's mind clung to the new word like a life raft. She'd learned this one from the Vecnos. The Vecnos was cruel, not stupid. Not like Oluf, who was stupid and mean. The Vecnos was not stupid, and not mean, not quite. He was cruel.

Did Dergh want to be like that?

Orcs were cruel. Orcs would kill your child in front of you for fun. Orcs would rip your father's entrails out and wear them in celebration. Dergh was not an orc. Her mother was a human, and her half-orc father had raised her to honor her ancestors. They were all that had survived the Great War on the First Land. All the elves and dwarves had died from the Waster, but the orcs had survived. Most died from the sickness, or starvation, but a tiny band had lasted through the eons. That band had grown and fractured, only to be consumed by itself again and again, but those that survived taught of their ancestors. They taught of the Waster, of how its evil must never be made on the Ur again. They taught of the greed of the dwarves and the hubris of the elves. They taught of the Mother, and how her force grew in the flower that outsiders called skull-blossom, and how it could heal one from the kind of sickness caused by the Waster.

'Why you want flower?'

'It's for a friend,' the halfling said. Islander, they were islanders. Vecnos had inflicted enough pain on the half-orcs to make the new word stick. The islander kept talking. 'He's sick, real sick, we talked to a witch who said it could heal him. It's helping! Please, we only want enough to fix him. He's kind of a downer, but he's still my friend, you know? Plus, I think Adrianna really has a crush on him, and he totally has a crush on her, and I wouldn't want her to lose him to a bunch of maggots anyway. That would be nasty and like really sad.'

'Shut up,' Dergh said, another phrase learned from the Vecnos. Her mind was working *so hard* to understand so many ways of thinking that were so different from her own. She'd never gone this long without a fight, and it seemed her brain appreciated the lack of blunt force trauma. Why was she throwing him in the ground? Because Vecnos said so? Wasn't that cruel? Dergh took a deep breath. Then she put the islander down.

'I no throw in hole,' she said. The half-orcs took the news in stride. They'd been educated of the practice about as recently as Dergh had, so they weren't big believers as of yet, but the snakies hissed.

The islander began to talk too fast.

'Oh, sweet strawberries, you are making a good decision. I have many powerful friends, and when they find out that you spared me, we will find you a nice home in her mom's house and everything will be just fine.'

Dergh ignored him and turned to her people. Her people. That was the first time Dergh really thought of the half-orcs like that, but that was what they were. They'd grown up together, been forced to flee their home by hordes of skeletons. They shared traditions going back centuries, and now they would grow together in this new land. They'd chosen Dergh as a leader —or let Vecnos choose her, anyway. Dergh would not let them down.

'I not throw in hole, not right. He take Her flower. He... he use for friend... he... friend sick...' The gears were really spinning for Dergh. She didn't think in spoken language, as it was generally frowned upon in her society, even in a band of monks, but think she did. She needed a compromise. This little person didn't deserve to be buried alive. Her holy flower didn't need such cruelty to thrive. And yet, the halfling had gotten her beaten by Oluf when he stole her keys.

'I crack his spine with club, and then we throw in hole!'

The hrocs cheered. The snakies hissed. The islander cursed.

Dergh had done it!

'No!' a new voice called out. A woman's voice, like Dergh. The half-orc chief, first female to lead her people in over a decade, turned to see who'd interrupted the holy ceremony. It was a human woman with white hair. She held her hands above her head as she approached, far away from the daggers that sparkled at her waist. 'We want the islander,' the woman said.

The half-orcs turned to watch the approaching woman, following their leader's cues. The snakies reached for their weapons.

'Oh, Adrianna, thank the blueberry bushes of beyond that you're here!' the islander said.

Dergh ignored him and kept her focus on the woman. Her hair was tied up into very beautiful shapes and patterns. Dergh could understand most patterns better than she could understand language. They were knots and braids, wrapped around each other to bind something. There was something else about this white-haired woman. Something about her smell wasn't quite right.

'We just wanted some of the flowers to heal our friend. We'd give them back, but, well... look for yourselves.'

A man lurched out from the sewer passageway. His arm was a mess of what appeared to be the same black maggots that fed on the sickness caused by the Waster. He whimpered convincingly.

'Please, we just need a bit more so Asakusa can get better,' the woman who didn't smell like a woman said.

'The sickness!' Dergh said, unable to keep the horror from her voice.

'We don't want him to suffer,' Adrianna said. That Dergh could even track the names of these humans—or near-humans—indicated that her brain was adapting to life here.

'You all die today,' one of snakies said, then shot an arrow at Asakusa.

But he missed.

With a crack of thunder and the smell of brimstone, Asakusa was nowhere to be seen.

'He has sickness. Mother say heal sickness,' Dergh said, shocked at the disappearance but even more shocked that someone had the Waster's sickness in the first place. It hadn't been seen in generations.

'Our homeland! Our people!' Oluf said. A familiar argument, but a true one?

'No...' Dergh's mind was firing with every piston it had. It was grinding gears and grind shafts as fast as her ancestors did when they built their cursed Wasters. 'This not... our homeland. We visitors here, we protect Mother's flower, but we share, share with who need.'

No one would ever be able to say if that speech was the moment that changed hroc culture forever, bringing them into the fold of the other more 'civilized' races and maybe one day bringing their enigmatic and forbidden Wasters back into existence, for at the moment, a red dragon attacked them all.

Chapter 49

Richard

Richard Valkanna, in human glamour no longer, unfurled his wings and breathed fire onto the assembled enemies. Adrianna was ready, of course. She dove for Ebbo and shielded him with the dagger Richard had given her on their wedding day. Silly girl. There was no need for such theatrics. Richard was an excellent shot.

He assessed the scene below him. The hrocs had been in a tight group but were now scattering through the overgrown graveyard, trying to take cover behind funerary statues from the dragon that had already incinerated two of their own. Richard had little doubt that they'd rally and attack, but for the moment, he shifted his focus to the Ourdor of the Ouroboros.

He incinerated them. There were more of them than there were hrocs, and they looked like they'd be a better shot with a bow than the hrocs would be with their strange, cross-shaped pieces of wood. They dove and slithered out of his path as he blasted fire, each of them trying to escape with whatever form of locomotion each of their unique bodies allowed. Few escaped his first strike. In an instant, a dozen of the differently shaped snake people were just a pile of twisted skeletons and billowing ash. Richard reached the end of the tiny graveyard, pumped his wings, and flew upwards. With a bit of altitude, he turned back on the hrocs and turned his fiery breath on them next.

Adrianna jumped in the way, wielding her dagger as a shield. Really, she could be such a bore sometimes. Now she wanted to save the hrocs? When would it end?

The dragon didn't waste the opportunity, though. He spared the stupid hrocs, and instead turned his attention on the few remaining snakes, slithering behind tombstones and funerary statues covered in vines. It really was lucky that the Ourdor had taken Ebbo back to the same graveyard. If it had been somewhere else in the sewers, Richard would have actually had to travel through one the thrall's Gates. He was sure he would have never heard the end of that. As it was, he got to play the hero. He widened his throat and let a true inferno boil forth. If his flames burned away the arrogant thrall's stupid flower, so be it.

Chapter 50

Ebbo

Through the flames and curses, Ebbo only looked for Clayton.

He smelled brimstone and then Asakusa was there with him, standing above the hole that would have been the islander's grave, a Gate behind him that opened to blue sky.

'The damn dragon said he'd see my Gate and come help. Instead, he torches the place.'

Ebbo hardly thought it was an appropriate time to curse the dragon who'd just saved his life, but a quick glance at Asakusa's disgusting Corruption was enough to make him empathize with the thrall. He wouldn't want to use that power unnecessarily either. Adrianna's was much sexier. She'd Unfolded and was now in her spider form—that was, a human torso connected to a spider abdomen with eight legs. Ebbo had seen Adrianna Unfold plenty of times before, but this was the first time he could remember she'd specifically done it for him. It was a nice gesture, Ebbo would have to thank her, but first: 'Clayton! Clayton Steelheart!'

'You know, a thank you for not getting my spine cracked by the hroc would've been nice.' Adrianna said, moving close to Ebbo and taking a defensive position with her whip at the ready.

'Clayton is... Clayton's here,' There was something in her tone that meant something different than her words. Ebbo still had to find him then, which meant he had to tell Adrianna about the situation so he could focus on more important things, namely, his best friend.

'Dergh wasn't going to kill me, she's the nice one. It's the snakes that really wanted me dead. They sacked me! Can you believe that? I haven't been sacked since I was like twenty-six years old,' Ebbo said. 'Now, where's Clayton?' he asked Adrianna. 'Claaayton!'

None of this would matter if Clayton was gone. Ebbo didn't know how else they would have found him in this graveyard without Clayton's help, and yet the big guy was nowhere to be seen. Despite no longer being on the verge of being cracked in half by a hroc, and Adriana telling him Clayton was "here," Ebbo found he didn't feel any better.

'Can you focus for one second?' Adrianna said. Ebbo was about to curse her out with every berry he knew, but he realized she wasn't talking to him. The spider princess cracked her whip at the giant red dragon as he landed nearby, toppling funerary statues that had stood for ages. That was her husband, for blueberry's sake!

'What?' Valkanna said, putting a fingernail to his chest in mock innocence before flicking his tail at a hroc and sending him crashing through a statue of a winged angel.

'Snake-dude!' Ebbo shrieked and pointed to a guy with snakes instead of arms.

Ebbo had seen quite a few variations on the human-turning-into-a-snake body and though this one was creepy, the snakes couldn't actually swallow Ebbo, so he didn't mind it so much. Apparently, the transformation of Ourdorlies affected everyone differently. Some people's legs turned into one giant snake tail, other people's heads were what went first. Though—obviously to Ebbo—all their brains had been damaged long before they'd ever joined the Ourdor of Ouroboros. It was utterly inconceivable to Ebbo why anyone would willingly try to transform into a snake. Stranger still that Vecnos—an islander whom Ebbo had worshiped as a hero not so long ago—was as involved with these monsters as their alliance with the hrocs made it seem.

Instead of considering the strangeness of the body type, Adrianna went to work with her blades, severing the heads from the snakes in a flurry of dagger-wielding spider appendages. Ebbo waited for just the right moment, then, when the man was focused on protecting his arms, or rather, heads, he shanked him in the gut.

'You burned all the flowers!' Adrianna said to Valkanna.

The dragon prince sauntered toward them, putting on his glamour and turning into a human. 'I assure you I'm normally a better shot. I think I'm unaccustomed to an ally being so reliant on the foliage of a battleground.'

Ebbo was convinced. Dude was an asshole.

Still, didn't matter.

'Where's Clayton?'

'For the Etterqueen's sake, we told him to find you and he did. He's making sure none of the hrocs escape,' Adrianna said. There was that tone again. She wasn't lying to Ebbo—Adrianna didn't lie to her friends, Clayton had convinced her not to—but she wasn't exactly being honest, either.

But there was Clayton! The golem stood by the passageway that led from the sewers to the sunken graveyard. A hroc ran at him and swung a club at the golem's neck. Ebbo cringed; the blow was strong enough to nearly sever Clayton's head from his body. But it didn't. Instead it got stuck as clay pumped in time to Clayton's Heartbeats and held the club in place. As the hroc struggled to free its weapon, Clayton brought a massive fist down onto his head. The hroc crumpled and joined the growing pile of unconscious hrocs. His club stayed in Clayton's body with the rest of the collection.

Ebbo looked around before darting over to Clayton. He couldn't be sacked again. Not now. Not before being reunited with his friend. He saw no more snake people. Valkanna had burned them all to ash except the one, and Ebbo and Adrianna had taken care of him. The hrocs had all tried to flee back into the sewers and met Clayton's massive fists. If there were any left conscious, they were either hiding among the burning skull blossom, or behind the funerary statues.

Ebbo judged it was time for hugs. He ran toward Clayton and the pile of incapacitated hrocs around the golem's feet. Ebbo didn't understand why Adrianna had sounded so uncomfortable. Clayton was alive! He even had his stupid sculpted muscles and everything!

In the background, Ebbo heard Adrianna start to yell at Valkanna, and the dragon—In his human glamour—defend himself. Asakusa went about grabbing at flowers that crumbled to ash, but Ebbo had eyes only for one person.

'Clayton!' Ebbo ran as fast as he could and leapt into Clayton. He sunk a finger's width into the golem's body as he hugged his friend. After a moment, he pulled his head out of the reddish-brown clay and looked up at the chiseled jaw and smiling face of his old buddy, Clayton!

Except Clayton wasn't smiling. He was staring straight ahead, seemingly oblivious to both the hrocs he'd just disabled and the world-class hug Ebbo was giving him. He looked like Clayton, he even had on a fancy pants made of clay, but something was definitely wrong.

'I have found the Ebbo,' Clayton said, except it wasn't Clayton's voice. Too deep. Too hollow.

'Clayton? Clayton, it's me. It's not the Ebbo, just Ebbo. I'm not famous yet...not like you. Clayton, say something!'

'Something.'

'What the huckleberry? Clayton, that was actually funny. You've never actually funny. Are you okay?' Ebbo said. He disengaged himself from the sticky clay and went about poking and prodding at the golem.

'Clayton. Seriously. Clayton, listen to me,' Ebbo said and poked at his friend with his toes, sending one of their encoded, vibration-based messages. The golem did not reply.

'What's wrong with him?' Ebbo asked, trying not to let his voice get emotional and doing a really horrible job of it. He wiped a tear, and another. 'What's wrong with him? What's wrong with Clayton?' Ebbo's voice rose into a shrill pitch.

'We took him to Leopold the Grimy. He did everything he could, but...'

'But he didn't know what made him special,' Asakusa finished for Adrianna. 'Clayton being self-aware was just dumb luck,' he added, as if that was anything at all like the right thing to say.

'You're kidding?' Ebbo said, his words also failing him.

Asakusa shook his head. Adrianna dabbed her eyes with a silk handkerchief.

'But he always said he had a fairy godmother, or some berries, or a, a...'

'A unicorn?' Adrianna said.

'Yeah, or a unicorn made him special, or something. Wait, what about the Heartbeat powder, did that come back?'

'That was just a trick. There is no Heartbeat powder. Leopold the Grimy said he thinks Vecnos got you to snort it so his snakes could track you,' Asakusa said.

'That's a bunch of raspberries,' Ebbo said, looking around as if the golem behind him didn't exist, and the real Clayton was going to walk into the charred graveyard at any moment. This had to be some kind of horrible joke. What was the point of rescuing Ebbo from a band of hrocs and the Ourdor of Ouroboros, if they couldn't even save Clayton?

Without no answer coming, Ebbo began to weep.

Chapter 51

Ebbo

'Clayton tracked you here with the same powder, so I think the wizard was telling the truth, not the assassin,' Asakusa said.

Ebbo would have loved to stab Asakusa when he said that. Then he would be able to feel something close to the pain Ebbo was feeling every time he looked at Clayton's unseeing eyes.

'We couldn't believe it either,' Adrianna said. 'That Leopold the Grimy made Clayton? I mean, Clayton is—was—such a good person. It's crazy to think Leopold made him that way.'

'Was? Made? Clayton's not gone,' Ebbo said, turning to the golem and hugging his knees, crying like a baby. 'He's not gone. Right, buddy? You're not!'

'Oh, Ebbo...' Adrianna came forward and wrapped her arms around the golem. He didn't hug the spider princess back any more than he hugged Ebbo. He didn't even chastise them for getting his clay on their clothes. Ebbo's heart felt like a raspberry being crushed into jam.

Ebbo felt something in his ear. He choked back a sniff and turned to see that it was one of Asakusa's nasty Corruption maggots. Asakusa was right up there with Adrianna and Clayton, actually hugging their friend, the golem. To Ebbo's horror, he heard halting, awkward sobs come from Asakusa that sounded every bit as painful as he felt. Ebbo had seen never Asakusa seen cry.

Clayton had told him that he'd seen it happen once. Apparently, he'd been a mess upon discovering that Adrianna was to be married. Clayton had said that Asakusa had cried then, his tears mixing with Clayton's shoulder, just as all their tears mixed with him now... Wait! Maybe that was it! Maybe the tears of his three best friends would interface with his clay and make Clayton, *Clayton* again. Ebbo pushed himself back and wiped his eyes. He'd gotten Clayton's hip all smeary with his tears. So had Adrianna and Asakusa. Surely, now that they truly were a part of him, he'd remember.

'Clayton? Do you remember us now? Tell us who you are,' Ebbo said, his voice barely strong enough to speak.

'I am Clayton Steelheart,' his voice still that of an automaton and nothing more.

Ebbo wailed even louder than before, redoubling in his grief. 'Does anyone have any pixie dust?' he moaned. 'Just to take the edge off.'

'You don't have a master. You're free,' Asakusa said, the grief in his voice evaporating into rage.

'You are my master. You paid my father.'

'No, we didn't,' Asakusa said. He took out a purse of coins.

'I...you...' The golem stood still for a moment. 'You did not pay?' he finally said.

'He said he didn't want the coin. So I took it back,' Asakusa said.

'You little cheat,' Valkanna said. Smoke was coming out of his nostrils, despite him being in human form.

'You think I didn't notice what you were trying to do back there? If you paid, then he'd be your golem.'

Adrianna was as speechless as the man-shaped hunk of clay was. Ebbo looked up at Clayton. His tears had cleaned paths in his dirty face.

'You hear that, buddy? That means you came here of your own free will,' Ebbo said, his voice shaking.

The golem furrowed its brow. 'No... I...'

'Come on. You know you're in there. You wouldn't be able to look like Clayton if you didn't remember something,' Ebbo said.

'If...' the golem began haltingly, 'if you did not buy me from father, I belong to my former master.'

'But you just did all this stuff to come and save me,' Ebbo said. 'Doesn't that mean you're free?'

Clayton turned to Valkanna.

'Master,' Clayton said. Ebbo could hear desperation in the golem's voice. Ebbo knew desperation. The golem sounded like he was a few dragon scales short of a fix. 'You paid Father.'

'No, he didn't.' Asakusa held up the bag of coins. 'This was all a ploy to take control. Valkanna wanted a golem for himself, but it didn't work. Clayton, no one paid for you. You came here to save Ebbo with us just because we're friends.'

Ebbo often found Asakusa to be self-righteous, arrogant, moody, broody, and just an all-around annoying guy. He had very little doubt that they'd be friends, if not for Asakusa having known Adrianna before she met Clayton, but then sometimes the stupid thrall would say something like that, and Ebbo couldn't help but think that he might dead and forgotten if not for Asakusa saving him again and again. The thrall had saved Ebbo's life nearly as many times as Clayton had.

'That's not true, is it?' Adrianna said, looking at the dragon prince. 'When you offered to pay, you weren't trying to take control, were you?"

'Answer me this, golem. Can you possess wealth?' Valkanna said.

'A golem's wealth belongs to his master.'

'Richard?' Adrianna said. Ebbo was shocked and appalled to hear her use Valkanna's first name. 'You're going to tell us how Asakusa is mistaken, right?'

Valkanna sighed. 'Of course I am. And to prove it—here, a gift.' Valkanna took two perfectly round emeralds out of his pocket. 'I was going to give them to you later, but it looks like the thrall has gone and ruined a perfectly good rescue.' Valkanna stuck an emerald onto each of the golem's eyes. They sunk in just slightly, and then a thin bit of clay spread over the top, an eyelid.

'Keep them as a reminder of what you are.'

'No one owns you anymore,' Adrianna said.

'Don't you remember, Clayton? All the times we had together?' Ebbo pleaded. It couldn't end like this. Ebbo's last interaction with Clayton couldn't be with a soulless version in the very place Ebbo had failed him.

'All those times we saved your clay?' Asakusa said.

'Remember,' Valkanna said. 'Remember who you were. Listen to your friends.'

'You're Clayton Steelheart, the free golem,' Ebbo said, trying to sound as cocky as Clayton always had when he'd introduced himself.

'I am Clayton Steelheart, the free golem,' the golem said, but there was something to his voice. Something of the old Clayton *was* there. Ebbo gasped, and fresh tears came from his eyes unbidden.

'You like fashion, remember? Like waaaaay too much! And you and I have a secret code. We can use string to talk with our feet,' Ebbo said.

The golem wiggled his toes.

'You always stand up for women,' Adrianna said.

'They work so hard,' the golem said.

'You can change shapes,' Asakusa said.

'No longer.' The golem shook his head. 'But I could once. I need... I need to save more Heartbeats,' he said, looking at his hands. He looked up, his emerald eyes sparkling. 'I remember.'

'Come on, Clayton,' Adrianna said. 'How else am I supposed to know what's right and wrong? I may be the spider princess, but you were always the one with the heart of gold. Please, Clayton, we can't go on without you... I can't go on.'

'Remember all the times you had with them,' Valkanna said, staring into the emerald eyes. 'Be the golem they want you to be.'

Ebbo didn't understand why Valkanna was talking at all. Doubtlessly the scumbag had some ulterior angle to steal all their berries the first chance he got, but it seemed like his words did nothing, the same as the rest of theirs.

Clayton stood there motionless as a sculpture. He did not move or call out to them. He didn't scoop Ebbo up in his arms or chide Asakusa for bottling up his emotions. He stood there, stiffly, staring ahead, either deep in thought or not thinking at all.

Adrianna turned her back on Clayton and wiped her tears. 'Steelheart. I think from now on... it might be better to call him Steelheart.'

Ebbo could see the pain on her face, it was plain as his own. She'd known Clayton even longer than Ebbo had, after all. She'd always called him her conscience.

'It was silly of us to get so attached to a construct.' Adrianna sounded as if she didn't believe the words at all. She sounded like they hurt her as badly as they hurt Ebbo, but she said them all the same. That was why she was their leader, because she was strong when no one else could be. 'I learned a lot from him, about what it means to be good... I... you two will have to help me with that more from now on. We'll get through this.'

Ebbo couldn't look at Adrianna. He loved her and respected her—blueberries, she'd saved his life more than either of his other two friends put together—but he couldn't watch her lie to him and Asakusa. They would *not* get through this. They had first joined together because of Adrianna, but Clayton was the reason they stayed together. Ebbo stared at him, willing him to move, to speak, to do anything. But the golem only stood there, motionless as any cheap sculpture except for a spot just beneath his perfect jaw, where his Heartbeats made his clay imitate a human pulse. It had been one of the golem's favorite affectations, despite it being even more useless to the golem than the fancy shirts he liked to wear. Ebbo had never seen another golem do such a thing. But Clayton was doing it now.

Suddenly, Clayton shifted to look at Adrianna. 'You're entirely too hard on yourself, you know.'

Ebbo looked between his two friends. Clayton looked at Adrianna with new eyes and a familiar old smile. Not the plastic one he'd been wearing, but one that trembled just slightly, even though that must've cost him extra Heartbeats.

'Whatever seems to be that matter?' Clayton Steelheart said, the emeralds flicking back and forth as he looked around at the group, 'Why are you all crying? You're going to get too much salt mixed in with my clay! Do you know how hard it is to make clay look like convincing linen when I have salt crystals sprouting every which way?' his voice didn't sound hollow anymore.

'But you walk on the bottom of the ocean all the time,' Ebbo said, sniffling from Clayton's knees, the old banter coming back with a flood of emotions. 'Clayton, you're back!' There was a loud squelch as the islander sunk his face into his old friend's leg. 'You're back, you're back, you're back!' Ebbo said when he was forced to emerge for air, 'Wait what's my favorite food? No, too hard. What's Adrianna's favorite food? Mmm...too easy. How did we meet? What's the last thing you remember?'

'Your grandmother Elsa's raisin and oatmeal cookies. Unless you ate something good in the last twenty-four hours, you always default to the cookies. Princess Morticia likes mincemeat pie with no crust and extra gravy, even though that hardly counts as a pie. We met when Adrianna tried to liberate the women from the Red Underoo and you tried to get one of your islanders to accept pixie dust instead of coin for payment. And the last thing I remember...' Clayton trailed off and rubbed his chin—thinking, it seemed, though after seeing the golem in his other state, Ebbo realized it was just another human affectation.

'We were in this very graveyard. I had just made a trek through horribly unsanitary sludge... and then you were holding me, Ebbo, I think, and then there was some blue light... like a thousand Heartbeats at once. What happened? How long was I out, an hour? And what in the free city could possibly compel Asakusa to cry?'

'Allergies,' Asakusa mumbled as he wiped his eyes.

Chapter 52

Vecnos

'Your assistance is appreciated, but no longer necessary. You'll leave the hrocs to me.' Vecnos found that people obeyed if you gave them orders.

The spider princess and her cadre of minions seemed no different. The thrall and the islander Vecnos had hoped to use to bind the hrocs to him nodded and moved toward the sewers, no doubt ready to return to the city below the Ringwall. The dragon was the one Vecnos was worried about. He knew who he was, of course. Vecnos knew who every person of power was in the Archipelago, and the young Valkanna was most certainly powerful. Which made it all the more interesting when he deferred to the spider princess.

'What will you do with them?' Adrianna Morticia asked Vecnos, her tone implying that if she didn't agree with the assassin, she might very well do something about it. Vecnos didn't quite know what to make of her. She was obviously capable in battle—that she'd made it back from the Blighted Island intact when no one else had was impressive—and her allies were proving to be formidable. More confusing was her sense of right and wrong. Moments ago, she seemed ready to kill to save her friend, but now that the hrocs were defeated, she seemed wary of dispatching them. Unusual for a ruler of the spiderfolk.

Vecnos, in a rare moment, decided to go with the truth. 'I brought them here to save them from the vampire and the skeletal horde you discovered. I think their knowledge may prove... instrumental in the battle that may come to our shores.'

'You think the skeletons will attack?' the spider princess asked. The fear in her voice was palpable. She knew the threat the skeletons represented. That death no longer meant an end, but the beginning of service to another.

'The living will need many allies if we're to defeat them.' Vecnos looked at both the spider princess and the dragon prince when he said this. Together, they represented a force that might prove even more essential to facing the skeletons as the hrocs.

'Allies like the Ourdor of the Ouroboros?' Ebbo sneered, then scuttled behind the golem, which seemed to be in much better shape than when Vecnos had last seen him.

Vecnos shook his head. It was a pity. The islander had such potential. He was bold and had proven to be quite skilled at sneaking, but his addiction was too great a liability.

'Or allies like my flamehearts and the spiderfolk?' Prince Valkanna said.

Vecnos nodded. Here was one that understood politics. 'The hrocs too, of course. You saw their weapons?'

Valkanna chuckled derisively. 'You mean their wooden crosses? What were those, some sort of symbol? They did less than nothing to my dragon scales.'

'Cross-bows,' Vecnos said, the word still new to him. 'Properly manufactured, even an untrained islander or a human child can put a bolt through a skull.'

'Your plan is to attack the Blighted Island with kids and islanders?' the thrall said. Vecnos didn't much like this one, but he was impressed that he'd figured out how to beat the demon Gatekeepers and their infernal contracts.

'My plan is to buy ourselves as much time and recruit as many allies as I can before they attack.'

'We don't know that they're going to attack. You can't use skeletons to justify those snakes!' Ebbo shouted, peeking between the golem's legs.

'I don't have to justify anything I do,' Vecnos said, hating himself for having to say it but knowing that he could show them nothing but strength. 'But they will attack. Here or somewhere else, it doesn't much matter if they manage to get off that island. If they destroy the trade routes or attack the farms that make up the Farm, S'kar-Vozi will fall. Magnus alone doesn't have enough resources to feed the entire city.'

'Then who does?' the golem asked, his voice laced with concern.

'We need soil,' Magnus said. Vecnos had hidden him in shadow until this moment, so his appearance earned gasps from Ebbo and the golem, looks of surprise from Adrianna and Asakusa, and a begrudging smirk from Valkanna. Despite Magnus and Vecnos often being at odds politically, they worked quite well together when it mattered. 'We've been importing dirt to use for rooftop gardens here in the free city, but something has stopped production. We'd like you to investigate and hopefully return the flow of soil.'

Curiously, Adrianna glanced at the golem with one of her extra eyes before responding. If Vecnos hadn't been studying her, he might have missed it completely. 'We'll help,' she said.

'Gather dirt?' Valkanna asked.

'Yes. If dirt is what the free city needs to better withhold a siege, then dirt's what we'll get,' Adrianna replied.

'What the free city needs is powerful allies. Like our families. Don't do this, Adrianna. Send your little squad and return with me to Krag's Doom. Together we'll rally our family so when S'kar-Vozi's hour of need comes, we'll be ready to answer.'

A good argument, Vecnos thought. Too bad he couldn't read the dragon well enough to know if he was telling the truth or lying.

Adrianna again looked to her minions—that was how Vecnos saw them, anyway, save the dragon—then back at Magnus. Vecnos already knew that she was going to say yes. He'd seen the fear on her friends' faces appear at the prospect of returning to Krag's Doom. None of the three wanted to go there.

'You go,' princess said to prince. 'I'll do this mission, then come home and... and check on my family... and you.'

Valkanna didn't do a very good job of hiding his disappointment, but he nodded all the same, took a few steps back, and then transformed into a dragon. Vecnos braced himself instinctively. He'd seen the spider princess use a dagger to defend herself against the dragon's flames, but an assassin who relied heavily on shadows had no such advantage. If the dragon attacked, Vecnos would have to take cover beneath the spider princess's thorax. But he needed not worry. The dragon pumped its wings to get above the walls that ringed the graveyard then headed north, back to the cursed castle where it came from.

Vecnos turned to face the others. 'The kobolds will show you out.' The assassin gestured toward the entrance to the sewers. Once upon a time, the passage from this graveyard had been nothing but a watercourse built to stop the buried corpses from becoming inundated and floating to the surface. The furry little kobolds had built it into so much more.

Three big-eyed kobolds guided the spider princess and her minions into the sewers and out of Vecnos's sight. He sighed, wishing he had time to take a rest from his role serving this city, but the hrocs would wake up in moments, no doubt, and there was still Magnus to deal with.

'You understand, of course, this isn't over,' Vecnos said.

'Nothing's ever over, and stop being so melodramatic,' Magnus said as he braided daisies into his golden beard. They were hard to come by in the free city. There was just so little soil, not many flowers had the space to grow in place of the seven crops.

'I'm not being melodramatic,' Vecnos huffed from inside his shadow cloak. 'That halfling is as worthless as all the rest. I would have had those hrocs' undying loyalty if they'd have killed him with the Ourdor.' Despite his tiny stature, Vecnos sulked expertly. It especially helped when he hid his button nose and gorgeous black curly hair beneath his cloak.

'The islander is far from worthless. Like a weed between stones, he can topple the world before him if given fresh air and a bit of water. And don't worry about the half-orcs; they will grow to serve a different master, someone besides the shadow assassin of the free city. After all, they don't respond well to slurs.'

Vecnos snorted, basically a guffaw of laughter for the stone-faced little guy. 'Ebbo is nothing more than a halfling as long as he uses magick as a drug. I'll treat him as something more if he becomes something more.'

'I'll hold you to that.'

'With what? Grapevines?'

Magnus chuckled. No grapevines grew in the free city. Vecnos still sometimes slipped, giving away his heritage without meaning to.

'Regardless, I don't think you will be sending the half-orcs after him anymore.' Magnus said it like it wasn't a command, but that was just Magnus's style. He wanted the hrocs, and he knew that Vecnos would give them to him. They'd been in the Ringwall for nearly the same amount of time. Vecnos had taken his own spot, moving into one of the nine mansions that had been abandoned since a powerful warlock known as the Rat King had died inside. In one horrible night, he'd overthrown years of superstition and transformed himself from a nobody to a force as frightening as the legends that had resided in that mansion. Vecnos never would have been able to take that spot if not for Magnus's help. But then, Magnus probably wouldn't have been given his spot if not for the public backlash against an assassin seizing power in the free city. Their relationship was a complex one.

'I don't see what I can do with the hrocs besides slit their throats and dump them in Bog's Bay. At least their heads are dense enough that they should sink,' Vecnos said, just to get a rise out of Magnus.

'You'll do no such thing. They have a place in all this, as much as you or I. Their new leader especially.'

'Dergh?' Vecnos spit the name.

'Yes, Dergh. I've grown fond of her.'

'And what could their purpose be, oh mighty Magnus? Picking apples?'

'No, but you're not far off. They'll assist me in exchange for their obedience. If they disobey, I will tell them I'll give them back to you.'

'You won't.'

'They don't need to know that.'

Vecnos shook his head. 'For a benevolent gardener, you sure can be a prickleberry.'

'Every garden must be weeded.'

'Nice to know I'm your hatchet.'

'And I your carrot. Come now, you don't do well with adoration. The people need someone to root for.'

'I see what you did there. Regardless, the people are doomed if you don't have the hrocs continue to build their crossbows.'

Magnus frowned. 'In the times to come, I will need help to feed these people. Our city is growing. We need shovels made of their iron, not more weapons.'

'So, you've given it some thought? We can use his products to give you a break while you teach the city to farm for itself.'

'No!' Magnus roared.

Vecnos laughed, a condescending chuckle that made his disdain for Magnus's position clear.

'You still fear him? Rolph Katinka is what he claims to be—a farmer.'

'He is a vampire lord with an army of skeletons. You will stop importing his goods if you have any love for S'kar-Vozi.'

'I'm importing his goods *because* I care about this city. I thought you of all people would be happy to see me doing something besides pruning weak branches. Katinka is but a servant; you heard it yourself through the sending stones. He fears his master as much as we do, maybe more. Buying his produce won't make the coming of Chemok ripen any sooner.'

Magnus said nothing for a moment, only breathed deeply. His beard and the flowers inside curled and uncurled with his breath. Many found the effect enchanting, despite Magnus only doing it when he was quite angry.

'I will not stop you. You know that is not my way. But the half-orcs will be left to tend their skull blossom for war that is to come.'

'But the crossbows will save more hungry mouths than skull-blossom-'

'Don't speak to me of hunger, islander. It was I that gave you tater stew when you could taste nothing but magickal fancies. It was I that taught you how to live.'

Vecnos scowled at the truth of that.

'I will continue to argue against the opening of our markets to the Baron Katinka and the yellow skull he represents.'

'There are no laws in the free city.'

'As I'm well aware. I have my allies, and you have yours. We will respect the Ringwall, as did those who came before us, and hope to the Seed of Life that the people will do the same. I will continue to argue against the Baron's goods, but I am not so foolish to think I can continue to feed this city on my own. We will need help, and soil, if we are to prosper.'

'And you really think the spider princess and her little team of misfits will be able to get the soil flowing once more?'

'I do,' Magnus said.

'They're morons, you know.'

'Only sometimes.'

Vecnos grunted an affirmative.

'Then it's settled.'

'I'll send them a black parrot with specific orders in the morning.'

Magnus nodded, then turned and made his way through the burned-out skull blossom. In his wake, fresh green growth sprung forth, footsteps of life in the burned-out graveyard. The sun was setting; soon, the druid would create his magick sun to continue to help the seven crops that fed the free city through the night. Then—exhausted—he'd finally sleep.

Watching him go filled Vecnos with unspeakable sadness. There was a time the two had been friends—more than friends, if Vecnos was being honest —but that time had long passed. Now Vecnos was a master of the night, and Magnus a servant of the sun. Both were slaves to their position as members of the Nine. Neither had time to get a drink with the other, or to tell a few ribald jokes; Magnus especially had once excelled at them. But such was the price of power, and Vecnos would gladly pay that price. He'd pay with his own loneliness, he'd pay in disdain from his fellow islanders, he'd even pay in distrust from his only friend. He'd pay any price if it meant that he occupied the Ringwall in place of someone with an allegiance to no one but themselves.

He'd pay just so his people would one day have a seat at the table, even if they did need booster seats.

Chapter 53

Clayton

'But why can't I use my powers anymore? Try as I might, I can't use my Heartbeats to do anything more extravagant than build this exquisitely chiseled body,' Clayton said. His memories were coming back, but there were lots of blank spaces. Should he tell them that? No... no, he didn't think he should. His master had given him hardly any orders before he left. He'd said to listen to his friends, and to be the golem they wanted him to be. Surely, they didn't want a golem with gaps in his memories and a secret master. They wanted Clayton Steelheart, the free golem, even though he might not have ever really existed.

'You were out for quite some time. There's bound to be some changes,' Adrianna said soothingly. 'And who knows? Maybe once you have a few thousand Heartbeats stored, you'll have more powers. What's important, though, is that you're you.'

Good point, Clayton thought. Better to remind them of who he was.

'How did you bring me back? Did you meet her, my mother?' Clayton asked, but he knew the answers. Funny how often he'd used to wonder about such things. His friends still expected that of him, even if the golem now knew the truth. Part of him wondered if he'd always known it and this brush with destruction had only brought it back, or if he'd lost more than just his unusual shape-shifting powers.

'Leopold didn't-' Asakusa said, but Adrianna elbowed him in the ribs.

'We can't say what it was,' the spider princess said.

Ebbo cleared his throat. Clayton would recognize what the islander was about to say as a lie, and yet it was also a reminder of how good his friends truly were to him.

'Your fairy godmother swore she'd turn us into toads if we tell you about what happened. I've probably said too much already,' Ebbo snapped his mouth shut and held his lips tightly together.

Clayton looked at Adrianna, who nodded, but it was Asakusa whose response surprised him the most. Asakusa, who was so poor at managing his own emotions that it was a sign of their friendship that he valued Clayton's enough to try to protect him.

'Ribbit,' Asakusa murmured, and that was the last any of Clayton Steelheart's friends ever spoke of the golem's mother.

BOOK 4

The Vegan of Vengeance

Chapter 54

Dontalas

Step, *clink*, step, *clink*, step, *clink*.

Dontalas Crisp sauntered into the camp. Maybe camp was too kind of a word. It was but a few tents made of animal skins, a cistern of water, some tools made of clever metal, and some pack animals tied to carts filled with soil. The camp practically begged to be cleansed.

A man emerged from one of the tents. It was early morning, and even from this distance, Dontalas could tell that the man had been drinking alcohol the night before. A lot of alcohol. As the man stood on his wobbly legs and pulled a rough-spun shirt over his head—made of sheep's wool, he noted with disgust—Dontalas realized that his brother had been right about these creatures. It was as the Highfather said: Humans had finally spread to the foothills, and they'd brought their sin with them.

'Aye, who're you, then?' the man said, bleary-eyed with a raspy throat.

Dontalas splayed his fingers against his plate armor. 'I am the Shining Son, Leolalin, as the elves used to say, blessed warrior of the Highfather.'

'An' you want me to call you all that, then? You got a name?'

'My name,' Dontalas said, hand still on his breast plate, 'is Dontalas Crisp. You may call me Lord Crisp, if you would like, or by one of my titles. I am particularly fond of the Gleaming One.'

'You don't look so gleaming to me.'

Dontalas Crisp's smile fell.

'No, I suppose not.' He couldn't help but look down at his armor. When he'd first come across the High Bridge, his armor had shone as brightly as morning dew. Each line of his armor had been a practice in elegance: white gold from a pure world. This world and its filth had left its mark. Chinked here and there, the armor was scuffed where it shouldn't have been. The white gold filigree still shined after a good polish, but it seemed the filth of this world was hard to escape. It has been a longer journey than I thought...

and complicated, so complicated.

'I have been sent by the Highfather to offer redemption. There are those in this world who have struck a deal with a dark god, an infection of Death, one of your human wizards styled Chemok. I am here to light the way back to the shining path.'

'Yeah, I'ma have to pass on that,' the man said.

'Gary, what's with all the racket?' another man said, pushing himself out of the tent and buckling his pants. 'I thought we was gonna sleep in.' He threw his arm around the other man and lovingly nuzzled his neck.

Dontalas Crisp smiled. At least these humans knew something of affection. Still, it didn't bode well for the new arrival that he was so comfortable touching the wool.

'You 'idn't want to sleep, Joe.'

'No, but...' Joe's voice tapered off as he pulled away from Gary. 'Who's this, then?'

'I am—'

'Crisp, he is.'

'He doesn't look it.'

Dontalas couldn't believe the audacity of these humans. How could they insult him when they wore parts of an animal?

'I have come to cleanse this world. Submit yourselves, and I will put you on the path of light. Your steps will not waver until you cross the High Bridge and find yourself before the Highfather, where you will be judged justly. So long as you repent for every soul you've ever harmed, you will be free to serve him.'

Joe and Gary shared a look.

'No one's ever come back from the High Bridge,' Joe said.

'No one has ever wanted to cross down into this realm,' Dontalas replied with pride.

'You did,' Gary said.

Dontalas frowned. 'Do you submit or not?'

'I only submit to one man at a time,' Joe said, 'and right now that's Gary.' He spit.

Dontalas drew *Innocence*.

The shining sword, once perfect, now had five deep notches along its blade, each a hand length from the other, the first a hand length from the hilt. His brother had told him six mistakes, and the blade would no longer serve him. He had one more.

Dontalas pointed *Innocence* at Gary. White flames ignited along the blade, and the sword seemed to glow brighter than the early morning sun. Dontalas smiled. Gary had committed true sin. Dontalas understood that sheep could be tricked out of their wool, but Gary had done far worse than pilfer an animal's body. He'd sunk a ship filled with people. He could have patched the hole, which was trickier, but in a moment of desperation he'd pushed an old woman—muscles tight with spinner's disease—overboard. Then he'd stolen the ship's life raft.

'You drowned an old woman in the sea, then took a life raft, condemning others to join her.'

'You told me you found that boat!' Joe sounded shocked. Maybe he would be worthy of life.

Dontalas pointed the blade at Joe. Nope.

Joe's sins were many and diverse in their brutality. Just the night before, he'd slit the throat of an innocent turkey he'd brought to the foothills of this place for that express purpose. Murder, premeditated, followed by desecration of the poor bird's corpse.

That was enough to ensure that *Innocence* would not mourn these two murderers.

Dontalas Crisp raised his sword and cleansed the world of sin. Joe's death caused no new notch on the blade. Dontalas knew it shouldn't have, yet he still felt relief that blade was still intact.

Gary took off running. Dontalas pointed at him and locusts began to swarm the man, but he got on a horse and outpaced the growing storm of insects.

No matter. Dontalas would catch up to him. He continued down the mountain.

Step, *clink*, step, *clink*, step, *clink*.

Chapter 55

Asakusa

Asakusa Sangrekana would let his Corruption consume him if it meant saving the spider princess, but that didn't mean it never itched. As much as he loved Adrianna—and he did love the spider princess, even if he wasn't able to put that feeling into words—he didn't like all the choices she made. Marrying a dragon prince was number one on the list of things he didn't like. It only made matters worse that Richard Valkanna, Adrianna's husband, had used his dragon's breath to incinerate the only flowers in the whole damn Archipelago that could have healed Asakusa's Corruption. Currently his entire right arm, much of his chest, his abdomen and thighs were all hidden beneath a layer of writhing black maggots.

That meant he had to be extremely careful when using his powers. If he opened a Gate over too great a distance or kept one open for too long, the rest of his body would be consumed by the Corruption, his contract would be fulfilled, and his time on the material realm would be finished.

The idea of being completely covered in the demonic maggots was not a pleasant thought, so instead of opening a Gate, Asakusa endured the itchiness and rowed. He had to admit, the gentle splashing of the oars in still water as they slowly approached the black cliffs of the island of Destruyag made for an impressively ominous scene compared to opening a Gate, walking through The Ways of the Dead, and simply appearing where he wanted.

'It's a bit much, isn't it?' Clayton said. There could not have been a more different pair of beings rowing the boat than Asakusa and Clayton. Asakusa wore a black leather jacket, still missing a sleeve where his Corruption maggots had torn through, black leather pants, and a scowl underneath the hair covering one of his eyes. He fought with a massive stone hammer, *Byergen*, that was unliftable unless it was being used to attack. Clayton wore a bright silk shirt with paisleys printed on it, well-fitting pants, and a wide-brimmed and rather dapper hat. He fought with his fists only when he couldn't charm an opponent into laying down their weapons. But then, Clayton Steelheart was a golem. Despite his complaints, the construct was made of a ton of red clay and wouldn't tire like everyone else on the boat would.

'Terribly ominous, magickally ominous,' Ebbo Brandyoak said, nodding up at the mountain made of black rock. There was a ramshackle town on the shore, then winding trails that cut through mats of vegetation that went up and up until they were lost in the mist that everyone said poured across to the island from the High Bridge that touched its highest peak.

Asakusa scowled at the short-statured islander. He wasn't surprised that Ebbo hadn't offered to row. He was short and lazy and good at little besides thievery and eating.

'I thought you were clean,' Asakusa said.

'I am clean,' Ebbo said, perhaps a bit too huffily. 'I haven't touched a speck of magick since I, uh… well, since we found out that Clayton doesn't… err…'

'Since you tried to snort Clayton's soul?' Asakusa said. Ebbo's addiction was disgusting. What Asakusa would give to have an ailment like that. With just a bit of self-control, Ebbo could be free. Asakusa would never be free of his Corruption, not after the deal he'd made with Byorginkyatulk, the Gatekeeper who'd buried a Key to the Arcane Gates in his hand. Every time Asakusa unlocked a Gate, his Corruption would spread. Once the Corruption consumed his entire body, Asakusa would forfeit his material form to the demon and would be no more. Compared to that, Ebbo's addiction was truly pathetic.

'In all fairness, he was duped by a master assassin,' Clayton said.

'That doesn't make his addiction any better.' Asakusa had no idea how Clayton could tolerate Ebbo after what happened. True, Ebbo hadn't snorted Clayton's actual soul, but he thought he had, and—in Asakusa's eyes—that was just as bad.

'If I'm so dumb, where's your sister? I thought you sacrificed yourself for her, and yet, where is she exactly? Harder to find than a blueberry in an apple pie, she is.' Despite Ebbo knowing that Asakusa could crush him with one strike from his hammer, the islander loved to torment him.

'Enough,' the spider princess said.

Asakusa, Clayton, and Ebbo all shut up.

Adrianna Morticia, estranged heir to the Spiderfolk empire and leader of their little gang, stood up in the front of the boat. Her long white hair was tied up in elaborate swirls and braids, Folding her spider body away. She fingered an ornate dagger at her waist. *Flametongue*, it was called. The hilt was the body of a dragon, and its tongue was the blade. She'd gotten it from her new husband, the red dragon prince, on their wedding day. That dagger was a constant reminder to Asakusa that he wasn't good enough for Adrianna, not compared to a dragon prince. Fortunately, Richard Valkanna was currently back at Krag's Doom, the ancestral home whose maintenance needs had required the bride and groom's cursed families to finally reunite.

'We weren't sent here to bicker,' Adrianna said. 'We were sent here because the people of the Free City need us. There is an army of skeletons on the Blighted Island poised for attack."

'I thought they were skeleton farmers,' Ebbo interjected.

'For now,' Clayton said.

'That makes them all the worse,' Adrianna continued. 'The moment their vampiric master turns on the free city, not only will thousands of animated corpses attack, but we'll be cut off from the food they're currently selling us. Without the Farmer's Market, we'd last three days on Magnus's crops.'

'So you think Magnus is right? Dirt is going to help us?' Asakusa asked. He was the least on board for this mission. He grew up eating crops grown magickally by Magnus, a powerful druid and one of the nine most powerful people in S'kar-Vozi. The idea of just growing your own food in the dirt sounded like... well, it sounded like halfling work to Asakusa, but he wouldn't say that out loud. Ebbo hated those sorts of stereotypes, and Adrianna and Clayton always took his side.

Ebbo glared at Asakusa, doubtlessly aware of what he was thinking. All of Adrianna—and thereby Asakusa's—crew were better at reading people than Asakusa, even though he was the only one of them that was human.

'If Magnus says we need soil so people can grow rooftop gardens, then we listen,' Ebbo said. 'Humans may be relatively new to the Archipelago, but my people have been here for centuries, relying on the power of compost. Our islands had next to no fertile dirt until we built up the soil. Ol' Burpa always said the best day to plant a seed was yesterday, so if Magnus says the destruyag are making soil that we can send to the free city, then we need to get it so we'll have crops growing to feed the city when the skeletons come and try to eat us.'

'I don't think they're going to eat you,' Clayton said.

'Kill us, then? Make us into skeletons? Sorry, everything eats islanders. It's honestly weird to face something that just wants our bones and not our meat.' Ebbo shuddered.

'Isn't all this work... for gardeners?' Asakusa asked, earning a glare from

Ebbo.

'It's a job for the destruyag, whatever they are,' Adrianna explained, 'or it was, until something stopped them from making more soil.'

'And to think we got this from Magnus himself!' Clayton beamed. 'No more dealing with Krouche le Douche and his comments about my pectorals.'

'It took my people centuries to build up enough dirt to grow a turnip, and these things are able to just make dirt? It's unnatural.' Ebbo shuddered again.

'Parchment beats rock, and blade beats parchment. It's our job to be the blade,' Adrianna said.

Asakusa couldn't help but smile. She was just so cool. No hesitation, no fear. That's why she was such a great leader.

'Yeah, but we can bicker and be the blade at the same time. That's kind of heourr specialty,' Ebbo said, circling back to their earlier conversation with a shrug.

'Bickering can't be a specialty,' Asakusa said.

'I think the islander makes a good point,' Clayton said. 'We've always had healthy disagreements.'

Adrianna cut them all off. 'I just want us to be careful. This is our first official quest for one of the Nine in the Ringwall, and our first quest all together again since...'

'Clayton's been restored?' Ebbo said.

'The halfling's been clean?' Asakusa said.

'Your wedding to a dragon prince?' Clayton said.

They all started bickering again. Ebbo about the racial slur, Asakusa about how much he didn't trust Adrianna's new husband, and Clayton about how he was fine and everyone needed to stop worrying about him even though he'd been reduced to nothing but a charred metal heart until quite recently.

'Enough!' Adrianna shouted, then fell out of the front of the boat.

Chapter 56

Adrianna

The beach was empty, so no one saw Adrianna Morticia, spider princess and heir to a legacy of war, get ambushed by a beach.

Adrianna got out of the water, straightened her hair—fortunately none had come undone—and looked around the town. There wasn't much to see. Three buildings, made of the black volcanic stone of the Archipelago, were clustered near the shore and looked like they'd been there for ages, or long enough for moss to fill in their cracks. Another five or so—warehouses, judging by the lack of windows—were made of gnarled wood, probably imported by the look of their surroundings. There were few trees on Destruyag, and those that were there looked either young or stunted. Not that that was surprising. Plants didn't grow in the Archipelago without a bit of love. That was what made the Co-op—a loose cooperative of islander-run farms—so impressive. The islanders had spent generations enriching the soil to a point where they could grow food. No one had done that on S'kar-Vozi; that was why Magnus had to use magick and every moment of sunshine to make his seven crops grow. There simply wasn't enough soil to farm without magick. The island of Destruyag was the same as most of the others. The creatures that lived here made it too dangerous for islanders to farm, so there was hardly any soil to speak of. Or there hadn't been anyway, but that was changing. That was why they were here, after all. Soil.

Soil was the one thing in the shabby town that there was a lot of. Next to the wooden buildings was tons of the stuff. Rich dark dirt in piles, barrels and crates. It didn't exactly seem like a shortage to Adrianna, but she was a spider princess. She knew little and less about farming.

Magnus himself had sent them here so they could ensure the dirt kept flowing to the free city. Adrianna might not understand the particulars of gardening, but if one of the Nine thought sending them here was more important than sending them to fight the Baron Rolph Katinka and his reanimated skeletons, she would get the dirt.

'I hear a dirge coming from that one,' Ebbo said, pointing to the only wooden building that had windows.

The tavern was as bare inside as the town was outside. Rough tables and chairs crowded together in a single larger room partitioned by a waist-high wall down the middle. Nothing adorned the walls, and no attempt had been made to stain or paint the knotted wood. Adrianna scanned the room and was greeted with the looks of the listless. The people here obviously hadn't worked in some time. Most of them sipped from mugs and tried to carry on in conversation, but there were far too many glances toward the spider princess. No looks of hostility, though, which was somewhat unusual for Adrianna and her party. These people wanted something. They wanted help.

The only people that didn't look up clapped along to a pair of musicians. A red-haired, mustachioed man wearing a curious checkered skirt played a baliset, while a red-haired woman in a matching dress sang on a wooden stage elevated a few feet above a stone floor dusty with sawdust.

'Alright. Split up. I want to know who knows Magnus, and what they know about whatever's been hurting people,' Adrianna ordered.

Clayton, Ebbo and Asakusa nodded, though Adrianna knew only two of them would be useful in gathering any sort of information. Sure enough, Asakusa pulled up a seat between a man lost in his drink and another with a thick beard and a scowl fiercer than his own. He ordered a drink, half-nodded, half-scowled at the men, and said nothing more. Clayton and Ebbo were far more valuable in social situations, but Adrianna had no doubt Asakusa would keep his hand on his unliftable hammer and be ready to spring into action at her slightest glance.

Adrianna went to a few tables, asking questions and name-dropping Magnus. Most people were willing to talk at first. Boredom made men pliable. Everyone had heard of Magnus—he was the most famous druid from S'kar-Vozi, after all—but once they realized Adrianna was on a mission for him, half of them clammed up. It was curious. He was the one who was paying for all this dirt, which had probably financed this very tavern, wasn't he?

Ebbo seemed to be having better luck. He stood on top of a table, his curly silver locks glowing, his smile pulling at the corners of his mouth even as he spoke.

The islander looked as if he had taken some magick. Adrianna had seen him enough times to recognize the look of bliss. But he had been doing so well. Had something made him cave? She marched over to his table to find out.

'Princess! I was just talking about you!'

'We're supposed to be listening, not talking.'

'True enough,' Ebbo said, nodding without concern. 'And I was listening. Hank here says the destruyag are nothing to worry about. They're little feathered creatures, hardly any taller than me. That's who grows the grass mats that are breaking the mountain apart. They're making the soil!'

'Well, where are they? I'd like to talk to one of them.'

'They don't leave their mats, miss,' a man covered in aquatic-themed tattoos said.

'Why are they called destruyag?' Adrianna asked. 'Doesn't that mean destroyer in goblin?'

'Aye, it does. I suppose it's on account of them mats destroying the mountain itself.'

Adrianna forced herself to move on. Whatever had stopped production was definitely not these feathered destruyag. She left a silk thread connected to Ebbo, though, so she could communicate with him.

'What did you snort?' she tapped over the thread, sending the encoded message in a series of tugs.

'Not a thing!' Ebbo replied, the grin on his face falling even as he deftly moved the thread from his shoulder, where Adrianna had connected it, to his feet. He now messaged Adrianna as he danced atop the table. He was far better at communicating via thread than Adrianna was, despite the silk coming from her own spinnerets. 'I'm clean, I swear!' he tapped out with his toes as he danced.

'Are you?' Adrianna asked over the silk thread.

'I… I thought I was… I was only dancing…' Ebbo climbed down from the table, looking both crestfallen and ashamed. He mumbled an apology to the men, who cried foul at their entertainer for leaving. The islander wandered away to the far corner of the bar, away from the stage. Adrianna watched him pull out his pockets, looking for magick, but he didn't seem to have any.

Adrianna sighed. They needed a guide, someone who knew what had stopped production of the soil. Magnus said he didn't know what it was, only that something had been attacking the camps. Adrianna needed Ebbo's help to find a guide. It pained her to think that this mission might have caused him to relapse.

Clayton waved her over to another table. Hopefully, he had better leads.

'Adrianna, darling,' he said as she pulled up a chair and joined him at a table. 'This is Seamus. He was just telling me about an upland ecology made of feathered destruyag and—what did you call them?—Stonewalkers? I think you'd be very interested to hear about them.'

'I just heard about them. They're making the soil, not stopping it.' Adrianna said.

Seamus rolled his eyes and stroked his mustache. 'Them little blokes are doing more to mess up our way of life than anything else. Was a time when you could walk on nothing but bare rock, never harm a soul, not even a bug. That all changed, though, and the Stonewalkers ain't none too happy about it.' Seamus had an accent that was thick and unfamiliar. His vowels were a bit strange, and he perpetually seemed to be clearing his throat. Adrianna stole a glance at the singer. Did she sound the same? Her hair certainly matched his mustache in color.

'Do go on,' Clayton said. The man was quite drunk, and Clayton had given him more alcohol. Wine, from the look of it, curious as that was. Wine was hard to come by here. Adrianna could only think of one place that made it in all the Archipelago. Her heart began to pound, and she felt the breathing vents in her abdomen close up. Had the vampire baron's reach already extended here? What if it was an army of skeletons that waited for them at the top of the mountain?

'You used to never see 'em. These dark-skinned Stonewalkers, big as a house, they is. This was before the new boom, mind you, back when people'd go up there looking for gems or relics from the warriors what tried to cross the High Bridge, maybe find a way to their afterlife, stuff like that. Not like it is now.'

'Giants?' Adrianna offered.

Seamus shook his head, the motion nearly toppling him. 'Aye, you can call 'em that, but ain't like no giants I'd ever seen. I tried to convert a giant or two on them halfling islands, years ago, that was.'

Clayton made to correct his faux pas about the proper name for islanders, but Adrianna elbowed him and the golem stayed quiet. No reason to get offended if Ebbo couldn't overhear.

'People say them giants got flesh like you and me, and that they eat meat, right?' Seamus shuddered at the mention of either the giants, or their diet.

Clayton and Adrianna nodded. Adventurers cut their teeth slaying giants who were trying to eat islanders. Adrianna and company had fought plenty.

'Well, these ones ain't like that. They big an' all, but when someone cuts 'em down, they just turn right back into stone. They don't eat meat either, which is a point in their book, or it was until they started doing the work of the Highfather themselves. Unnatural, they is, more mineral than man.'

'Nothing wrong with a bit of mineral,' Clayton said with a harrumph.

'And that's what has stopped production?' Adrianna asked, hoping to keep the conversation on track.

'I reckon so.'

'Then that's who we need to stop.

Chapter 57

Asakusa

Asakusa's practiced sulking was not working. When the grumpy, bearded man sitting next to him at the bar finally stopped talking, the other one started up. Gary was his name.

'The one to worry about is Crisp,' Gary said. 'Dontalas Crisp. He's as right a destruyag as ever was.'

'I, uh… heard o' him. Right hypocrite, far as I can tell!' MacGregor growled.

'Who's Crisp?' Asakusa said. Little as he wanted to, Asakusa knew better that to ignore a lead. He'd already heard plenty about the destruyag from the other bearded grump, MacGregor.

MacGregor had explained that he hated the feathered destruyag for turning rock into soil and thus making it harder to spare innocent lives. Where before, he could walk only on rock, thus not disturbing any crustaceans or whatever else lived in the soil, he could no longer tread so easily. Vegetarianism, MacGregor called his batty religion. He hated the destruyag only slightly more than the Stonewalkers, though their biggest offense seemed to be slaughtering the feathered creatures so intent on making dirt, which Asakusa thought would have put them in MacGregor's good graces—lacking as those seemed to be. Asakusa was hardly surprised to learn that MacGregor had heard of this Dontalas Crisp as well. MacGregor seemed to be one of the few locals. If he could be believed—and Asakusa generally found rage a difficult emotion to fake—pretty much all the people in the bar were immigrants. MacGregor's words held true disdain.

'What more like,' Gary said. 'He's a big, tall fella, not as tall as them Stonewalkers but taller than your pal there,' he said, pointing at Clayton across the room. 'He walks around in shiny armor, must weigh a ton, with a big ol' sword. He'll find a camp o' workers, watch from a high hill, and then he sees something he don't like, just come in with this flaming sword and start slaughtering. Nasty thing, that Crisp is, with notches in his sword an' everything.'

Before Asakusa could come up with an appropriately unimpressed response, the bartender put a plate of food down in front of MacGregor, and the man's vitriol was born anew.

'Ach! Is this the flesh of a turkey?' MacGregor spat.

'Sorry 'bout that, ol' timer, that was for Gary—' The bartender tried to remove the plate, but MacGregor was too quick.

He stood—and flipped the bowl of turkey stew all over the bar. 'There was a time when everyone on this island had values. Real values. You migrants with your deals with the destruyag. You let them turn stone into soil, and for what? Some coin in your purse?'

Asakusa had seen the look in the bartender's eyes in S'kar-Vozi many a time. It was the look of a man who wanted nothing more than to smash a chair into someone's fat mouth. But before he could realize this dream, a high-pitched voice pierced the din of the tavern. Ebbo.

Ebbo was always causing trouble. 'Vecnos? Why on earth would you think I'm that horrible man?'

'Well, you's a right short little one,' a tattooed man told him, then stepped back, clearly afraid of the tiny islander reaching for his dagger.

'You think I would feed a man's heart to his best friend? Or order you to be buried alive, or fed to the Ouroboros? Is that what you think I am?' Ebbo asked, red in the face.

The music stopped.

'I meant no offense, little sir. I just thought you was him. Him and Magnus be paying for all this soil. I wanted to say thanks.'

'He ain't paid for nothing in a while,' someone from the bar yelled out. 'Not like Katinka.'

'You mean the Baron Rolph Katinka?' Adrianna demanded. Asakusa watched the men watching her. If anyone moved against the spider princess, he was ready.

'That's him,' the man said. 'He's who pays the best, better than Magnus does, and he don't threaten like Vecnos, either. So what if he wants your bones when you die? Better than sending them off to sea, I say.'

'You know he's a vampire?' Asakusa said, half-certain that Katinka would get their bones whether they gave them willingly or not.

'An' I also noticed you got a hand of black worms, and I ain't said a thing,' said the man speaking. 'Katinka is the only one with the funds to build Destruyag Island into something. Said he can send warriors to finish off anything that stops production. He'll stop Crisp, he will!'

There was a lot of assent in the bar to that. Clinks of glasses and angry head nods. Apparently, Crisp had taken quite a toll on the island's economy. Between that and Katinka apparently funneling away some of the dirt they'd need, Asakusa was beginning to understand why they'd been sent here. Apparently Katinka was a step ahead of the Nine. If he attacked, he'd be able to lay siege, unless the free city had the soil it needed.

'Magnus and Vecnos stopped paying soon as we stopped bringing stuff down the mountainside. Katinka didn't. He said we was owed a decent living wage, and he knew we was good for the work. Even said when we was done working, we could go retire at his mansion on the Blighted Island, so long as we give 'im our skeleton when we go. We thought he sent you, what on account'a you being a spider folk,' a man said, scratching self-consciously at his tattoos.

Asakusa looked at the man. How had he known what Adrianna was? Asakusa could tell she was a spiderfolk even in her human form, but he'd known her for years. He could see the slight lines where her extra eyes hid, the graceful posture that bespoke an exoskeleton buried just beneath the skin instead of proper bones. How had this guy seen through her Folding?

'We have no love for the Baron Rolph Katinka. He's raising an army of the dead. One day he'll use them to usher in his dark god, Chemok, who will go to war with the living,' Adrianna said, her voice hard as stone. Asakusa never ceased to be impressed with how good she was with words.

'E's in no hurry to do that, miss,' someone called out.

'He's just trying to make a living while he can,' yelled a woman.

'I like his olives,' mumbled someone sitting at the bar.

He'd been here, or had sent an emissary, anyway. That explained how there were bottles of wine behind the bar. This would be a tough sell. Asakusa wisely decided to continue to keep his mouth shut.

'Well, Katinka didn't send us. Crisp, or whatever else is stopping your work, appears to be too much for him, as he's sent no one to help.'

Silence in the bar. It seemed Adrianna had struck a nerve.

'We were sent by Magnus on behalf of the Free City of S'kar-Vozi, and we intend to set out and do what we came to do. We'll go up the mountain and not come back down until it's safe for you all to return.'

'Then you gonna pay?' a man said.

'Magnus will!' another said.

Someone answered by throwing a chair at the spider princess.

Adrianna dodged—she'd been in plenty of tavern brawls—but the man behind her didn't. He responded to the accidental attacker with a chair of his own, and soon the entire bar was fighting, cracking chairs over each other's back.

The bartender joined the fray as well—chucking a stool at MacGregor, who dodged so quick it looked like it went straight through him.

Asakusa now understood the minimal aesthetic and the rough furniture. Everything looked like it was made to break apart and repair easily. Adrianna dodged the chaotic fighting effortlessly, so Asakusa didn't open a Gate to go stand by her side. There were many paths through the Ways of the Dead here on the island of Destruyag, so Asakusa could have chosen one that hardly cost him any flesh, but that might have pissed off Adrianna given the advanced state of his Corruption, so he didn't do it.

Good thing, too. 'Come on,' MacGregor told Asakusa over the din. 'I'll take you where you need to be. I ain't go no loyalty to Katinka or Magnus.'

'Then who?'

MacGregor shrugged. 'Just trying to protect the innocent, I am.'

Asakusa nodded and followed MacGregor out of the bar, shocked that for once his lack of social skills had made them an ally.

Asakusa found that seeing MacGregor standing outside was worse than being near him at the bar. The man looked ridiculous. He had a red beard highlighted with bits of gray, and wore a rough-spun wool shirt, an uncomfortable fabric in the steamy Archipelago. What Asakusa hadn't seen inside was what was most disconcerting. The man was wearing a checkered skirt, like the girls who went to Susannah's wizard school back in S'kar-Vozi.

'Aye, it's a kilt,' he said from beneath his thick beard. 'Never seen a man in a kilt before?'

'No,' Asakusa said flatly.

Ebbo shot out the doors a moment later, followed by Adrianna, and finally Clayton, who had a fair amount of chair legs stuck in his clay.

'Anyone find a guide?' Adrianna said.

'Aye,' said MacGregor. 'Though not sure if I'm going to stay on if this one keeps staring.'

Adrianna sighed and raised an eyebrow at Asakusa.

'It's cool,' Asakusa mumbled and looked away, not meaning to frustrate Adrianna. It seemed like everything he did made her mad these days. Why couldn't they go back to how they used to be? Before he'd interrupted her wedding and told her that he... err... liked her. But no, this was better. Better she knew how he felt, even if he didn't know how to say it.

'I think it's a charming look!' Clayton gushed. 'And it gives so many more choices for footwear and socks.'

Ebbo peeked under it. His curiosity sated, he stepped away, trying not to vomit.

'Ach, you're warriors, then?' MacGregor said.

'That we are,' Ebbo said, drawing his elven dagger.

'But not this Vecnos I heard of?'

Ebbo turned a shade of crimson. 'I'm not Vecnos. I'm not a murderer.' At least one good thing came from Ebbo being tricked by the master assassin. He no longer idolized the other islander.

'So you're just a regular ol' halfling, then?' MacGregor asked.

Before Ebbo could leap into a tirade, Clayton spoke up. 'Ebbo is one of the most talented pickpockets in the entire Archipelago. He's stolen brides, hearts, and magick itself. I bet he could rob someone blind if he wished it.'

Technically, none of that was a lie.

Ebbo blushed. 'I've never robbed anyone blind. There weren't any seers or hags at the wedding, and even if there were, you know how hard it is to steal a hag's eye? I mean, not that I couldn't do it.'

MacGregor seemed simultaneously overwhelmed and disappointed.

'You're looking for warriors?' Adrianna said. Asakusa, as usual, was thankful for her ability to keep Clayton and Ebbo on task.

'Aye. You look the violent type,' MacGregor said, shamelessly looking Adrianna up and down.

'You don't exactly seem friendly,' Asakusa said.

'Father's pipes are louder than his punches.'

The singer stepped from the bar, dodging a chair. The man playing the baliset followed her, taking a chair to his back while cradling his instrument.

'Fiona,' the singer said. 'Fiona Morgan MacGregor. This is my brother, Seemus. I think you might've met my other brother.'

A crack of a chair breaking, and another man fell from the bar.

'Seemus!' Clayton said as if he and the drunk were old friends.

Seemus and Seemus were identical, except that Seemus had a mustache and Seemus had sideburns.

Obviously, they were family. They all had the same colored hair. The same accent—though Fiona's wasn't nearly as hard on the ear as her father's —and the same bizarre checkered skirts.

'Well, look at you!' Clayton said, stepping forward to pull Seemus up and place him next to his brother and sister. 'Adrianna, I've said it before and I'll say it again. We need matching outfits.'

'If you think I've changed my mind on wearing a paisley shirt, you're out of your mind,' Asakusa said.

Clayton huffed but didn't push the topic.

'You know about what's stopping the destruyag from making soil?' Adrianna asked their family of potential guides.

'Aye, I do. Used to be halfway respectable too, them Stonewalkers,' MacGregor spit. 'But now they taken to killing the destruyag.'

'What's wrong with that? You made it sound like the destruyag were making it hard to do your weird religion,' Asakusa said, not meaning that MacGregor's beliefs were particularly strange, just that—from his perspective —all religions were a bit odd. Asakusa walked the Ways of the Dead, the paths that led to the afterlives of all the belief systems in the Archipelago. It was hard not to think religion strange when one was confronted with an ever-shifting system of roads managed by the Demon King.

'Father watched our farm shrink and shrink, but it's not the fault of the destruyag. They're trying to live as they always have. Something's just made them more successful recently. They're not wise enough to see the true faith any more than a fish is.'

'Ach, ruined our way of life with theirs, is what they did,' MacGregor said.

'Aye,' Seemus said.

'We're not down here because of them,' Seamus said, wobbling on his feet.

'Aye,' Seemus said.

'The Stonewalkers, you mean?' Clayton attempted to clarify.

'They're a problem, they are,' MacGregor said. 'Dangerous, and they make us look like you,' he said, nodding at Ebbo.

Ebbo's jaw dropped. 'They're that ugly?'

MacGregor's red bushy eyebrows knitted together in confusion. Fiona laughed. MacGregor, seeing his daughter laugh, finally nodded and gave out a hesitant aye. 'You are a right cute one,' he finally said, 'but the stone ones aren't why we're down here, either.'

'So, the stone ones are not the problem?' Asakusa asked.

'Nay. Err... no. They used to cause problems now and again, if we built our house outta too many stones or tossed one of their favorite ones in a lake, but no, they weren't so bad. Not a pestilence. Not like him.'

'Who?' Asakusa asked.

'Crisp,' MacGregor said with a scowl fiercer than anything Asakusa had ever managed.

Chapter 58

Dontalas

Lost in memory, Dontalas hummed as he cleaned his sword. How simple things had been when he'd first come to this sick and corrupted land.

He remembered the sound of his boots as he walked across the High Bridge.

Step, *clink*, step, *clink*, step, *clink*.

With each step forward, the stench of the air had grown stronger. The stench of toil, suffering, cruelty and death. The cleansing fog still clung to him as he walked across the bridge, but with each step it grew more ethereal, and as it did, he could smell them, and they stank. His Father had been right about them, then; they'd lost their right to this world.

Things were so clear back then, Dontalas thought as he had looked out onto the Archipelago that High Home rested above. His eyes were keen, and could see farther than any of the material beings—mortals, the Highfather had called them. From his vantage point near the base of the High Bridge and just outside the swirling mists, Dontalas could see the world laid below him like a map on a table.

High Home was the highest place in all the Archipelago. It towered above the rest of the islands, protected from wind and rain by the powers Dontalas's father granted their home for as long as they resided there. High Home was so high that not even birds or insects could reach its summit. Dontalas had watched mortals foolishly try to climb its walls before. None had made it even a league up from the sea, and they would have had to climb ten times that to reach its hidden plateau.

The next closest in both altitude and proximity was the island of Destruyag. The two were connected with the High Bridge, which Dontalas still had both feet planted upon. He thought it would take him five days of walking to reach the sea at the bottom of the island of Destruyag, though it could be longer if he tarried at his task. High Home was of a similar size, though there was little to do there, so one often tarried.

In the distance he could see other large islands. He knew the names for all of them, language being a gift for beings such as himself. To his right and moving Ur-wise around the ring, there were Felicanda, Karst, The Pit, Lanolel, Isla Giganta, the Blighted Island, Krag's Doom (next closest to High Home, but on the other side and much shorter than Destruyag), and—at the center of it all—S'kar-Vozi. A name taken from the goblin word for safe harbor. A place that stank even from up here.

These islands formed a rough circle—the ancient caldera of a volcano more massive than even Dontalas could truly fathom. Between them were hundreds, maybe thousands of much smaller islands. Many of these were nothing but bare stone, so small they'd be swallowed up at high tide. Others were large enough for small homesteads that could feed families of halflings, the only race that resided in the Archipelago that didn't seem obsessed with eating the flesh of others. A fact they were often punished for by being eaten by the larger, more murderous races. The halflings were of little import to Crisp, as the sins of the larger islands lit up his sword even from such a height and distance.

Closest to Destruyag was Felicanda, the largest of all the islands Dontalas could see. It was hard to tell exactly, but he imagined it would take some twenty days to cross along its longest axis, maybe five across its narrowest width. It was home to both a race of cat-like beings—predators, every one—and a community of lycanthropes who lived on the ground of the jungled islands. The felinas lived in trees and commuted between them via rope bridges, devouring birds and mice with abandon. Dontalas would cleanse the island of them before he turned to the lycanthropes, who suffered from a disease that transformed them into fur-covered murderers once a month.

South and east of Felicanda sat Karst, a sunken city, built from the same stone its dwarven architects had quarried from beneath it. It was smaller than Destruyag, but Dontalas could see endless passages and stairways carved into it. Cleansing it would take time, but cleanse it he must. The dwarves who'd built it killed many beasts in the caves below their city. Crimes to be answered for, though Dontalas wondered if Karst would flood and wash away before he could make it there.

Lanolel was the farthest from his place high above the Archipelago, and perhaps the least worthy of his notice. The occupants did little but eat berries and nuts and strum upon their instruments—though many of the strings they used were made of the guts of other species, and some of their horns were made of stolen shells and antlers—for this, Dontalas would indeed have to bring *Innocence* to this place. It wouldn't take long to scour Lanolel of its macabre inhabitants. A few days, at most.

Between Karst and Lanolel lay an island that was more hole than whole. A war had been fought here for centuries. Its soldiers had dug deeper and deeper into the volcanic rock until they cracked into a realm that even Dontalas dare not walk. Though the master of the place sent many on paths that led to High Home, he had no love of the Highfather. Dontalas's brother had told him that the Demon King had presided over his sunken kingdom even before the Highfather had come to the Archipelago from the Endless Ocean that lay beyond this ring of islands. It was not a place Dontalas relished visiting, but he could see into the passages from his vantage point upon the High Bridge, and many here had committed grievous sins.

Ur-wise from Lanolel was Isla Giganta, an island nearly as large as Felicanda that was filled mostly with mindless predators, though Dontalas could see a false religion of serpent-worshipers had built a stone structure there. It was a cheap facsimile of hubris in the shape of a pyramid where true horrors took place. Such a place should have made the Highfather send Dontalas to cleanse this land sooner. Its existence sent both chills and doubts of his mission racing through his head. How could these mortals be allowed to feed their own brothers and sisters to animals? It was appalling, though compared to the Blighted Island that lay next door, it was less abominable. Slightly less. Dontalas found he very much enjoyed the idea of cleansing the huge island of its meat-eating zealots.

But first would come the Blighted Island. The Blighted Island stank only of death. It was the antithesis to what Dontalas and his family believed in. It represented a worthy foe, to be sure. The few living beings that survived there —hiding in fog that Dontalas's keen eyes could pierce effortlessly—had taken more lives than many of the other beings from the other islands had altogether. A war had been fought there, a war in which weapons capable of killing hundreds at a time and leaving the island a desolate wasteland had been built for nothing more than cheap victory. In the time it had taken for the High Father to determine that they might need to intervene with the lives of the mortals, the war had been over.

After the elves, dwarves and orcs had spent decades slaughtering each other by the thousands, they had banded together to defeat a single human challenger. The man might have been a just warrior—after all, ending war was a noble cause—but he had instead turned to ungodly necromantic powers and used the corpses of the dead to go forth and kill the three once-opposing factions. They had used their bombs to destroy his undead hordes of yellow-boned corpses, and in doing so had blown themselves up, save a few piteous survivors. It was the necromancer's legacy that had compelled the Highfather to send Dontalas on his mission. It was his yellow-skulled warriors that had resurfaced, guided by a phony leader, who quite honestly befuddled Dontalas Crisp. The vampire had drunk the blood of others, but—almost impossibly in the eyes of Dontalas—had never killed. If that counted as innocent, Dontalas might be compelled to end his foul existence all the same.

But closer, more present, and with an overwhelming stench, lay the last of the sizable islands. S'kar-Vozi, as the inhabitants called it, lay at the center of the Archipelago. *Innocence* flickered madly just trying to see all of the murders that had transpired there since humans had taken up residence a hundred years ago. It was a mad place, a place of flesh-eaters and worse. A place where people took lives over bad bets or misheard insults. It called to Dontalas in a way the Blighted Island didn't, simply because it represented a mortal failing of the living. The dead couldn't really be blamed for making others join them—only destroyed—but the living? Dontalas found he very much wanted to cleanse this place of its murderous habits. Some of the religious fanatics from Isla Giganta made their residence here as well. A great place to start once he'd finished scouring this land of the infection that was Chemok.

Step, *clink*, step, *clink*, step, *clink*.

If they didn't deserve this world, Dontalas Crisp would give them another. He would free them with a tool forged by the Highfather's own son. His eldest son, as Father was often so keen to point out. Still, Dontalas may not have made the tool, but he would wield it. He didn't know whether to be annoyed or thankful that his brother had told Dontalas there was a failsafe, that he could take the lives of up to five innocents. The sword would break on the sixth. Looking down at the sinful inhabitants of the world below him, Dontalas found the idea of finding six innocent lives absolutely ridiculous. Even the islanders slaughtered the insects that did nothing more than nibble at their cabbage plants. He felt like he could lay into the inhabitants of the Archipelago with wanton abandon and still, he'd never strike soul free of sin. It was with a swagger in his step that he continued down the mountain.

Step, *clink*, step, *clink*, step, *clink*.

Dontalas Crisp reached the end of the High Bridge and stepped onto the mountain of black rock that Father had built the High Bridge upon, or found. Sometimes Dontalas couldn't tell if the Highfather spoke in metaphor or not, but then, his family practically existed in metaphor. Father had told Dontalas that the High Bridge had been built for their family to live upon High Home, but that didn't really explain who'd built it. No matter.

Step, *clink*, step, *clink*, step, *clink*.

Dontalas Crisp's armor sparkled in the mists. It was made of white gold, and its finely worked, flowing ridges caught the light and reflected flatteringly on its wearer's chiseled jaw and perfect hair. He walked down the path on the black mountain, sparkling like a god, shining like the sun, his heart eager to make his father and brother proud.

He walked for a day and a night, seeing no one. For this task—to cleanse the world of the sludge and banish Chemok, the so-called-god of death, back to the plane below—he'd been given a century to complete it and decidedly vague instructions. As he walked down the mountain, he realized a century was a *long* time. His senses had given him a sense of how long it would take to traverse each of these islands—that a few days of travel by boat lay between each of the largest ones and its neighbor—but that sense hadn't extended to what a *hundred years* would feel like. On the other side of the High Bridge, things didn't work as they did over here. In a century, Dontalas could cleanse far more than Chemok from this filthy world. Was that what the Highfather wanted? To cleanse this cluster of islands, so that its inhabitants might all one day be able to live together in peace on High Home?

Dontalas was pulled from this thought when his sword began to hum the high tone of a bell. Someone was near. Dontalas would offer them forgiveness, and they would accept the pilgrimage, and the world would be a better place.

'You there. No point in hiding, my sword can sense you,' Dontalas said, pointing the blade at a boulder a few paces in front of him.

Out from the rock itself stepped an imposing figure. He was jet black, and his skin sparkled like freshly cut stone. His muscles were ample, his hair non-existent. He wore a grimace and had a body covered in flickering runes.

If Dontalas Crisp was surprised by the height of the thing, he didn't show it; at least he hoped he didn't. He had never been to the material plane before, but the Highfather (and, annoyingly, his brother) had assured him repeatedly that the people here would literally look up to him. Some might grow to his chest, but most would barely reach his belly button. The gentlemen before him was a good four or five heads taller than him though.

'Our land,' the brute said.

'Land doesn't belong to anyone. It just is,' Dontalas said. His sword was really humming now, like a good and pious choir.

'People live here. My people.'

'When the Highfather built the High Bridge here, he opened the way for us. You have let this land rot. I am here to offer salvation.'

'I am Chert. I remember your Father. He not hurt us then, and you not hurt us now. We eat nothing but rock, take nothing but rock.' The stone brute's words were carefully measured, despite his awful diction.

'We shall see if you are telling the truth, servant,' Dontalas said, unsheathing his gleaming sword, *Innocence*, and pointing it at the giant's chest.

The sword hummed, and Dontalas could see all of Chert's sins unraveling before him like a scroll. It was as he said: he and his people ate nothing but stone, took nothing but stone. For centuries, long enough for even the Highfather to notice, they did nothing but spend their time in the mountaintops, herding rocks up and down the mountain and carving runes. Even this, they did with careful study. Once a decade they'd add a new rune to a mountaintop or somewhere in a valley, always carefully selecting and tending the site for years before reverently scratching some hidden meaning into the stone.

But then something changed.

The stone giants began to use their chisels on living creatures, some tiny four-armed things that spread upon the land with thick mats of grass.

'You have killed many beings.'

Chert squared his jaw. 'They destroy our land. No more people.'

'Violence does not beget violence.'

'If they not stop, they destroy the foundation of your Daddy High Bridge. It crumbles, and you never come here at all.'

'*Nothing* can destroy the Father's High Bridge.'

'Then why build on mountain of stone instead of thin air?'

Dontalas didn't know the answer to that question, but he told himself it was irrelevant.

'You are guilty. You have killed when your life was not at risk.'

'Our young—'

Dontalas held *Innocence* in both hands. 'Will your last words be of so little worth?'

Chert lifted his pick.

They clashed. There was a spray of gravel. And Chert was no more.

Dontalas looked at his sword. Not a nick nor a notch on its blade. It was as his brother had said, then. The sword could see sin, and so long as Dontalas didn't take an innocent life, or at least not six of them, the sword would never fail him.

Step, *clink*, step, *clink*, step, *clink*.
Dontalas Crisp continued down the mountain.

Chapter 59

Ebbo

Up and up they went for two days, following a rough gravel path that meandered not at all. After breaking camp and starting their second day of walking, Ebbo thought he could understand why MacGregor seemed so grumpy, and even why Fiona spent her time singing in a dirty tavern rather than being wherever they were from. The landscape was such a far cry from the islands where Ebbo called home. Instead of lush bushes heavy with berries, there were stunted trees with spines for leaves. Instead of the gentle cry of crickets and the lazy roar of cicadas, there was only the sound of the wind howling at the jagged foothills of the mountain, as if it thought it could whine them into gravel.

Nothing about the place was beautiful, nothing special, nothing magick. Ebbo's throat caught. He was clean. He had to be. But would he ever *feel* clean? He hadn't touched magick since Vecnos had tricked him into snorting his best friend's heartbeats. Except the assassin hadn't even tricked Ebbo, really. He'd helped him. If Ebbo had actually snorted Clayton, he would never have forgiven himself. But he hadn't. He just *thought* he had. Part of his desperate mind told him that that meant he could still use magick…

Ebbo shook his head, trying to drive the craving out. He slowed down and fell into step with Asakusa. If anyone could make him forget about magick, it was the thrall.

'So, how long since you snorted something?' Asakusa asked flatly.

Ebbo turned beet-red and fell back further, in step with Fiona and Seamus, or was it Seemus? The drunk one. Ebbo liked the drunk one. He was a reminder that there were people with weaker wills than Ebbo. 'You sure do know how to drink,' Ebbo said.

'Aye, that I do. Nothing wrong with it. Don't harm anyone.'

'Yeah! No one except yourself, right?' It was a fairly common islander argument for the benign use of recreational magick. Before, Ebbo had thought it was a sound argument, so long as you discounted some of the less… sustainable sources of magic, stuff like pixie wings and the like, but now it felt false.

'Aye. And not even that much anymore. Things happen to a man, you know? Make it so a bit of drink or a bit of smoke aren't so important,' The drunk brother said.

'That's exactly what I used to say! We've all been through crazy stuff.' Ebbo could relate to Seamus.

'Aye,' Seamus said, downing the bottle. 'I can still see him. Running out there, hollering an' all that. He wasn't *that* bad. Not like Fiona or Pa, o' course, but just as kind as Ma. He mighta hunted a few rabbits, shot a bolt at a bandit or two, but he didn't need to go like that.'

'Like what?' Ebbo said, losing control of where the conversation was headed.

'Chopped in half like a potato. Like he was nothing at all. I mean, he wasn't perfect, but he was my brother.' Seamus went to drink more and found his bottle empty.

'Yeah… losing a brother… wow,' Ebbo said, trying to think of a comparable experience and coming up short.

'And 'e died better than Ma did,' Fiona said.

Ebbo stopped as the MacGregors went on. They'd seen their brother *and* mother killed? Ebbo had never seen anyone die! Well, not anyone he and his friends hadn't killed. And *definitely* no one from his family. As far as he knew, they were all back on Strong Oak Isle, fermenting acorns into brandy.

'So… what did you do?' Ebbo asked, hoping he was quiet enough that he wouldn't compel Seamus to drink more. Ebbo knew how the smallest thing could set one off. Even now, part of his own brain was waiting for a magick toad to hop across the path so he could lick it, or a fairy he could kiss or *something*, but this place was about as un-magickal as they came. A good thing.

'Nothing,' Fiona said.

'You didn't stab the guy? That's Adrianna's specialty. Mine too. Though Asakusa says I don't stab, just shank, which is kind of rude but also kind of true. Clayton, on the other hand, is all about punching. He used to be able to make his hands into swords, but now all he can do is make bricks. Asakusa prefers smashing stuff with his hammer,' Ebbo pointed at the hammer trundling along behind the black-clad thrall on a little magick cart.

'We would never hurt a soul!' Fiona said.

'Well, what did you do?'

Fiona cleared her throat. Seemus took the cue and struck a chord.

'With heavy hearts we said goodbye, to mother of us all,
Father cried, he almost died, to see his eldest fall,
Mother took a butcher knife, she swore she'd take the bastard's life,
And though we prayed for father's sake, he lost his wife that day,'

'Pickin' blueberries, that's sad,' Ebbo said. His heart was hammering in his throat. He could almost see his own mother, back on Strong Oak Isle. And the bluebirds that sang to her. They were so beautiful, the way they'd come when she was making pie, and... wait. Was that a magick song? Ebbo took a deep breath. The edges of his vision blinked. It was magick. The little islander swallowed. A toad he could have resisted, but music? How was he supposed to shut that out and still carry on conversation?

'Aye,' MacGregor said, 'and no reason to sing about it, not when it still feels like yesterday.' He shook his head, but it was obvious he couldn't shake the memory away any more than he could shake away his own stench. 'What's past is past. She made a mistake. Maybe we all did. Coulda done more.'

'No, Father. We'd be gone too,' Fiona said.

'We're as good as dead anyway,' Seamus said.

'I hate to interrupt,' Clayton said, 'but are those the *destruyag?*'

Some time ago, before the song, Ebbo thought, the plants had all fallen away. They were too high up and it was too cold. But ahead of them, there was green.

The path continued on straight as an arrow, but on either side the landscape fell away. To the right was a deep pit, big as a house, big as the Grounded Acorn was back on Strong Oak Isle. It was pitted and scratched, as if some giant horrible beast has scooped it all up as easily as if it were a bit of sand instead of black volcanic rock, hard as anything in the Archipelago.

The left side of the path was completely different. Instead of a pit, there was a mound. It was a great cone of boulders, stones and gravel, all held together by thick mats of vegetation. It looked like someone had dug up a nine-pins green—no, more like a hundred nine-pins greens—and used them to wrap up this massive pile of stone. There was this sound too, like when wind hit the sails of a ship and the rigging was stretched, except much, *much* louder. One of the strips of green seemed to squeeze tighter and tighter, the sound of creaking fibers growing more and more intense until the rocks it wrapped around cracked. Some pieces crumbled down the side of the cone, others sprayed up like the breath of a leviathan. The grass mat that had held the boulders fell slack , spent from the energy expended to crack boulders into pebbles. No sooner did it become loose than a dozen or so creatures swarmed up and out of the mound of boulders. Truly, 'creature' was a fair term, for the things were unlike anything Ebbo had ever seen.

'*Destruyag*,' MacGregor said, not even trying to conceal his disdain.

Birds were the first thing Ebbo thought of, for the creatures were covered in feathers, but the comparison stopped there. They were big for birds, though small for most folk—about Ebbo's size—and curiously had four arms and two legs, which they used to scurry all over what once must have been a foothill of the mountain. Most of them sorted the rocks. Bigger pieces were pushed into the massive pile. Where the strip of vegetation had been, Ebbo could see that the mound wasn't solid but was riddled with holes and tunnels, and it was into these voids that the feathered *destruyag* moved the detritus. Others unraveled the drooping mat of plants. It came apart into long runners of grass, longer than any pumpkin vine Ebbo had ever seen. They took these runners and wrapped them into other mats, or fed them down into the pile of stone, or tied up other boulders.

'They'll eat this whole mountain to pieces, they will,' MacGregor said, pointing to the massive, abandoned hole on the other side of the path.

'It wasn't exactly verdant, though,' Clayton said. 'Back in the free city, people will use the soil they're making to grow food.'

'We could grow food well enough up here,' MacGregor said.

'Magnus told us that the only people up here are followers of Vegetarianism who worship the Highfather,' Clayton used his most carefully tactful tone of voice.

'He said those people were afraid to come off the rocks for fear of stepping on crustaceans,' Asakusa scoffed.

Ebbo grinned at the scowl Adrianna threw at Asakusa. The thrall really was lousy at conversation.

'Aye, there're things here besides Vegetarians. You'll see. Things that'd just as soon wipe out these vermin.'

'Father, please. These creatures have just as much right to live as anyone. They don't harm anything.'

'They're better than the Stonewalkers,' Seamus said.

'Aye, on that we disagree,' MacGregor spit.

'They don't kill,' Fiona said.

'They destroy the very land we stand upon,' MacGregor said sullenly.

'We're here to protect them,' Adrianna said. 'They're key to the safety of our city. Without this soil, S'kar-Vozi won't be able to withstand any sort of disruption of crops from the islander's Co-op. The free city needs this soil. I hope that won't be a problem.'

MacGregor shook his head. 'We've got days to go, yet.'

Ebbo noticed that MacGregor hadn't exactly answered the question.

Chapter 60

Asakusa

The higher they went, the more obvious the feathered *destruyag* left their mark. At first, the scarred craters were only here and there, dotted about the landscape but not in any sort of concentration, but as they spent another day climbing, the huge pits grew closer and closer together. Soon they began to see more of the huge mounds as well. The sound of the mats of grass flexing and slowly crushing the rock was omnipresent, like the shrieks of the damned in the Ways of the Dead. Asakusa thought he preferred the shrieks to the constant groaning and occasional rockslide. Eventually the road gave way — swallowed up by feathered *destruyag*, Asakusa thought — and was replaced by rope bridges connecting either side of a wide chasm.

'This feature was always here?' Adrianna asked. Asakusa could hear trepidation in her voice. She knew the answer already; it was obvious from the scratches and scrapes on the walls of the thing.

MacGregor spit. 'There used to be ground here. All hollowed out now by the damn things. I'm telling you, if left alone they'll eat this whole mountain and move on for more. It's lucky for you folk they don't like the lower elevations. But if whatever has been spreading them up here goes down there...' MacGregor spit again.

'And you think they should be stopped?' Adrianna said.

'Aye, maybe I do, maybe I do.'

'Pay no attention to Father,' Fiona said, 'He's never harmed so much as a rat.'

Asakusa found that he believed Fiona on this. Indeed, all four of the MacGregors and even their horse walked quite cautiously, sticking to barren rock-face rather than gravel whenever possible. They blamed the caution on their beliefs in the Highfather and Vegetarianism. Asakusa had been a bit surprised to find a religion dumber than both the Cthult of Cthulhu and the Ourdor of the Ouroboros.

'Aye, but if I was to start, I might start with them,' MacGregor said, pointing to a mound in the void below them. The canyon was so big, one of the mounds was able to sit in it, its top well below the rope bridge.

'He never would,' Fiona said, patting her father on the arm.

'Aye, but she might,' Seamus said.

On the other side of the chasm, at the end of the rope bridge, stood three imposingly tall figures. At first Asakusa wondered if they were living beings at all. Statues he'd failed to notice seemed more likely. They appeared to be made of the same black stone as everything in the Archipelago was, and moved less than the boulders in the mounds of the *destruyag*. There was one man and two women. The man wore nothing but a loincloth, the woman in front little more than that, but the third figure wore a woven shawl on her back in bright colors of emerald, ruby and sparkling diamond.

They were completely motionless until the woman in the back unraveled a rope and gave one end to the man. Then she leapt from the cliff face on a cord thick as Asakusa's Uncorrupted arm, then swung back into the wall and seemed to vanish, leaving only an imprint of her body and her loincloth, which dropped to the ground below.

'They can swim in the rock, they can. Stonewalkers don't quite describe 'em,' MacGregor said.

The stonewalker emerged at the bottom of the cliff, stepping from the rock as naturally as if she'd been hiding there, like some sculptors said their work had been.

Her loincloth fluttered down. She put it on. Her companion dropped down a stone club. She caught it deftly. Asakusa gripped his stone hammer. The club didn't look particularly friendly. She unwrapped a thong from its handle, wrapped it around her wrist, and laid into the feathered beings.

'She'll kill 'em all!' Ebbo said as the woman roared, a sound somehow lower than the constant rumble of tumbling boulders. She made it to the mound in a few huge steps, and then began squashing the *destruyag* like bugs, reaching through the mats of grass and between boulders to pluck out those that ran.

'It won't make much of a difference,' MacGregor said. 'Even if they kill this seed, more will grow.'

'Asakusa, get Clayton down below and stop her. I'll go across and confront the other two. Ebbo and Fiona, lead them to safety,' Adrianna ordered.

'Safety? There's nowhere safe from stonewalkers. The rock is their domain,' Seamus said.

'Then get them off the rock.'

Ebbo nodded, but Fiona, Seamus and MacGregor stayed put. Seamus struck up a song.

'There's nothing we can do,' Fiona said, and began to sing a sort of funeral dirge.

Adrianna scowled and ran toward the other two figures, huge and motionless on the other side of the rope bridge.

Asakusa Sangrekana called upon the power in the Dark Key buried in his right hand. The black Corruption maggots shrieked in excitement. It had been a long time since Asakusa had opened a Gate. Runes appeared in the air before him, and a portal opened up to The Ways of the Dead. The wormy muscles worked on his torso, consuming more of him.

It itched like hell.

The Gate opened, and Asakusa saw through the Ways of the Dead to another portal. It was easy to make Gates here, easier than it was in most places. Sometimes it could be tricky to find a useful path, but here, there were so many—more than Asakusa had ever seen in one place.

'Come on Clayton,' he said. The golem followed him through the Gate.

One moment they were on a rock cliff, high above mats of flexing vegetation, the next they were walking a stone path that was being built by the souls of the dead.

'I was wondering when I'd see you again.'

'What do you want, Byorginkyatulk?' Asakusa said but didn't stop to chat. Instead he dragged his hammer off the cart is had been riding on, and led Clayton, who smiled and nodded in awkward greeting at the frog-faced demon and his long, waggling tongue.

'You know me better than that. Please, call me Tulk, or Master if you insist on formality.' The demon's long tongue never fully went in his mouth, his "S's" always slurred. *Pleeeashe. Inshisht.* The Gatekeeper's voice was as vile as his appearance.

'A little busy,' Asakusa said, nearing the other Gate. The corpse of one of the bird-like *destruyag* hurtled past on the other side.

'I've never seen your Corruption so far along. I must say, it's a good look,' Tulk said.

Asakusa scowled at him. He was the first thrall in history to exploit herbs brought to the Farmer's Market in S'kar-Vozi to heal his Corruption. Tulk had never really resented Asakusa for denying the demon his flesh, but he always wanted to know more about how he'd done it.

'Asakusa, a little help!' Clayton called from the other side of the Gate.

Asakusa stepped through in time to be almost smashed beneath a giant club. He held up his Corruption, and the writhing maggots pushed the weapon away and onto Clayton. There were advantages to being a thrall besides having a key to the Arcane Gates.

'Not what I was thinking!' Clayton said as the club smashed into his chest, knocking it free from his arms and legs. There was a time when Clayton would have been able to turn to a puddle of mud and dodge such a blow. Those abilities seemed gone.

'You good?' Asakusa asked Clayton as the giant, its skin black as the stone behind it, turned to its new prey.

'It'll take me a minute, but I'm fine. What did Tulk want?' Clayton said. Asakusa could see the golem's steel heart thumping with Heartbeats, drawing his arms and legs to him in time to the pulse.

'Same as he always wants. More of my flesh,' Asakusa said, dodging a blow from the giant and lifting *Byergen*, the stone hammer, from its cart and swinging it at the giant's hand. The massively heavy weapon slammed into the giant's knuckles, shattering them into pebbles and causing the giant to scream out and drop its club.

'Still, he doesn't always show up like that, does he?' Clayton pressed. His arms and legs had slid across the rock and were now reattaching to his torso, one Heartbeat at a time. First bones made of clay attached to each other, then veins, muscles, and finally skin.

Asakusa didn't say that his Corruption had never progressed so far before, and that opening the wrong Gate could very well end his existence. He didn't say this for two reasons, the first of which was that he didn't like talking much, and the second being the giant trying to smash him with its fist. Asakusa's maggots lurched—yanking the thrall's body with them—and he dodged the giant's blow. He stumbled back to his feet, dragging his hammer behind him in his left hand. The giant was pissed. Clearly, she was used to crushing her enemies, not fighting them.

'Asakusa! Little help!' Adrianna called as one of the giants destroyed the rope bridge as effortlessly as if it was a piece of string. She had let down her hair at some point, so it was her spider form that called out to him. Some found the amalgamation of human and spider bizarre or frightening, but not Asakusa. He thought Adrianna's eight spider legs and abdomen connected to her human torso, arms and head were beyond rad.

Adrianna plummeted toward the ground. Asakusa acted without thinking. He opened a Gate and stepped into the Ways of the Dead just as he opened another beneath Adrianna. She fell through and landed on one of the stone paths with a grunt, unhurt except for a crack that ran up one of her arms. She'd broken part of her carapace. She looked at him and shook her head.

'I could have caught myself,' Adrianna said, fingering the silk whip at her side. She was a spider princess, she could have sent out a web if she wanted to. 'You're still not healed and shouldn't open Gates unless absolutely necessary. I didn't want for you to open for Clayton either. I meant I needed help with the stone giants. They're not particularly vulnerable to my daggers. I was trying to lead that one to you.'

'Right, sorry,' Asakusa said as Adrianna stepped through the Gate he had come through. She dodged as the giant Asakusa had been fighting tried to kick her. Adrianna stabbed her between her toes with a dagger. The giant grunted but otherwise seemed unconcerned.

'She's right about opening the Gates,' Tulk said, stretching out the word "she's" into an abomination of a word. 'But we can make you a deal—a new Corruption—if you can take care of that brute that stepped across the High Bridge.'

'What are you talking about?' Asakusa said, marching toward the Gate. Part of the powers Tulk had given Asakusa allowed him to sense where he could open Gates between the material plane and the Ways of the Dead. It was like folding the paper of reality to make shortcuts. Short paths were easy to figure out, longer ones were more difficult. The path Tulk had made would allow him to step out behind the stone giant that had destroyed the bridge. And it wouldn't cost him anything at all. Tulk's contract was ruthless, but he never charged for these little bonuses. If Asakusa didn't know better, he'd think the demon actually liked him.

'This mountain has a different set of by-laws.'

'What? Why?'

'You're near the High Bridge, the highest structure on this gods-forsaken Archipelago. You know how many belief systems incorporate that thing? Practically every afterlife ends up around here, despite those phonies.' It was like the demon chose words that he knew would sound bad.

'People walk across it,' Asakusa said, not slowing his pace.

'And never come back.'

'So what?' Asakusa asked. He hesitated before stepping through the Gate and emerging behind the other two stone giants.

'So, I can help you. Your current Corruption is necrotic in nature. Not too safe to use around here, and definitely not around *him*.'

'Who?'

'Ask MacGregor.'

'You know him?'

Tulk laughed. 'I know everyone who shoulda made a deal with me.'

Shoulda made a deal with you? Asakusa wondered. He had made a deal with Tulk when he'd been killed... or almost killed, as the demon regularly reminded him. He'd been fighting to save... his sister—that was the story anyway—and failed. Tulk had appeared, giving him fantastic power in his moment of greatest need. Did that mean MacGregor had almost died?

Then he heard a scream—Ebbo's, from the pitch of it—and Asakusa had to go.

'*Adios!*' Tulk said, practically spitting the word.

Then Asakusa was through, and the stone giants in front of him were turning toward the thrall, facing the source of red light and the stench of brimstone that came with the Gates. Asakusa lifted *Byergen* from the ground and swung it into one of the giant's kneecaps. It shattered in a spray of gravel. The giant screamed and toppled from the cliff.

The other brought its club down. Asakusa swung his hammer at the same time—shattering the club to pieces—then swung the hammer around and into the stone giant's face. It shattered into a thousand tiny stones, along with the giant's body, and Asakusa was left alone at the top of the canyon. He hadn't meant to, but he'd just killed a giant made of stone. He wished doing something so badass didn't make him feel kind of shitty.

The other giant, whose leg he had broken, crashed *into* the stone below their feet, as if the solid ground were liquid water. She fell straight into it, leaving only the outline of her body in black pebbles.

The third stone giant, the female Asakusa had first fought, was down below. She kicked at Clayton, but he managed to catch her foot, something the giant had not anticipated. Unbalanced and immobilized, the giant was in no state to fight back as Adrianna, still in spider form, scampered up her leg and chest, and dug a dagger into her eye.

The giant reeled backwards into the stone wall, and upon touching its surface fell into it as though it wasn't any more solid than air. Adrianna, though, stopped when she hit the rock wall as if it was an—err... rock wall. She slid down, using her sticky fingertips to slow her descent.

'You beat one of them,' MacGregor said, sounding genuinely impressed. 'But the other two will be back, mark my words. Stonewalkers are a hard lot to beat.'

'Aye,' Seemus said, and struck up a chord on his baliset.

Asakusa put his hammer back on the little animated cart that followed him around. This was going to be a long hike.

Chapter 61

Asakusa

'This guy hasn't been honest with us,' Asakusa said, pointing at MacGregor with a Corrupted finger. They'd tried to haul Clayton back up to the bridge with Adrianna's silk. The silk had held, but none of them were strong enough to lift over a ton of clay up fifty feet, not even the MacGregors' horse. In the end, Asakusa had opened a Gate and had to deal with more of Tulk's annoyingly round-about explanations of why this place had so many paths. Maybe it was all bluster, though—no part of the thrall's contract said that the Gatekeeper had to be honest—for the Corruption didn't seem to be spreading any faster than usual. At least, that was Asakusa's interpretation. He still had both shins, most of his left arm, and his face before he'd be consumed completely. He could tell by the look in Adrianna's eyes that she thought this was not enough of a buffer.

'Aye, we've been as honest as you. Why are you protecting the destruyag?' MacGregor demanded.

'For the love of raspberries, can we call them something besides that?' Ebbo said. He was standing in front of a mass of them huddling together. 'Calling them the same as the island makes them seem like part of the scenery.'

'That's what they are,' MacGregor said stubbornly.

'And the giants?' Asakusa asked. He didn't know what it was about the MacGregors, but he didn't trust them. Maybe it was just that they didn't like stepping on bugs. Anyone that concerned about crustaceans when there were people starving a few islands away rankled Asakusa. He wished he could communicate via silk threads like the rest of his party could.

'They used to come, before we had any crops, and raid the farm, but they stopped. Won't walk on grass, they won't. We've got no love of them, but they was easy to predict. Not like these new ones,' MacGregor said.

'I dunno,' Ebbo said, 'the little ones seem pretty nice. I mean, they don't talk, but they don't try to *smash you with clubs* either.'

'Aye,' Seemus said, playing a song on his baliset.

'Seemus is right, each race has its own strengths and weaknesses, but these have gone too far. We'd never harm them, of course, but... well...' Fiona pointed to the four-armed, birdlike creatures. They were gathering their dead and placing them in the thick mats of grass. The grass constricted and loosened around their bodies, and the little destruyag vanished into the green. The four-armed birds began to sing. Seemus accompanied them on his baliset, a haunting tune of death and regrowth.

As they sang and as Seamus played, a stalk rose up from the grass mat in which they'd interred their dead. Higher and higher it rose, until it was almost as tall as the pillars of rock connecting the bridges. Then it opened up into a flower.

Asakusa noticed Ebbo clamp his hands to his ears.

'The grass uses their bodies to make more flowers and seeds. Every time one of these things dies, they just make more,' Fiona said. 'They'll never stop.'

'Who is growing who? Like, are the birds growing the plant, or the plant growing the birds?' Ebbo shouted over the music, hands still clamped on his ears.

'They'll grow each other, moving on and on until there's nothing left of this place. They used to just be in pockets, but they've begun to spread. Someone taught them how to expand, or at least helped them get past the stonewalkers. It's got to end,' MacGregor said.

'The giants must be who Magnus wants us to stop,' Adrianna said.

'They are slaughtering the little ones,' Ebbo said, voice still raised, eyes locked on the instrument Seamus was strumming.

'But the giants were here first,' Clayton pointed out.

'Well, we can't kill the little ones!' Ebbo whined. Asakusa couldn't place it, but something was wrong with the little islander.

'Why not?' MacGregor demanded.

'They're too cute!' Ebbo said, as if it were obvious.

'Aye,' Seemus said and stopped playing his instrument. He, MacGregor and Fiona shared a look.

'You mean you won't kill them?' Fiona asked.

'Of course not!' Clayton was obviously affronted at such a suggestion.

'Wouldn't dream of it!' Ebbo said.

Adrianna looked at Asakusa. He'd already killed a giant.

'There's got to be another way. We have to find a way they can both exist,' Adrianna said. 'The people of S'kar-Vozi need this soil if we're going to stand against Chemok, but killing the giants... I don't know. It doesn't feel right either.'

'You seem to have an innocent heart,' Seamus said, putting away his flask for once. 'Except for that one.'

Asakusa felt his face flush and turned away, scratching at his Corruption. Why had he struck that giant in the face? He could have just wounded it.

'There's more to tell you,' Fiona murmured.

'We should be going,' MacGregor said.

'But Father—'

'We can't. And it's not worth the effort to find that out yet again,' MacGregor said.

'Aye,' Seemus agreed.

'Now, just a minute,' Clayton said. Ebbo piped up with a harrumph as well.

'I want to know more about these stone giants. How long have they been here? Why do they hate the feathered destruyag so much? Maybe we can find a way to help them.'

'Help them not kill the feathered ones, you mean,' Ebbo said.

'They've been killing 'em for centuries,' MacGregor explained tiredly. 'I don't like their sins, but it's the only reason we can still practice Vegetarianism up here.'

'Well, something changed all that, right?' Clayton said. 'Aren't you curious what did?'

'You are brave warriors,' Fiona said. 'Very brave, but Father is right. If your mission is truly to defend this land from its greatest threat, we must press on.'

'We must be moving while the air is still crisp,' Seamus said

'I've heard that before,' Asakusa said. 'Crisp. Dontalas Crisp, right? You remember, MacGregor? That guy Gary in the bar was talking about someone named Dontalas Crisp. Is that where you're taking us?'

'Aye, now look what you've gone and done,' MacGregor said to Seamus, ignoring Asakusa.

'Who is he?' Asakusa demanded.

'We really can't say,' Fiona said. 'I'm sorry, but we can't. But if you're truly innocent, and truly protect *all* lives, then you *must* come with us. It's our only hope.'

'Well, I'm not going anywhere until I'm sure these feathered destruyag aren't going to get slaughtered,' Ebbo said, crossing his arms in front of his chest.

'Me neither,' said Clayton. 'There's more to these stonewalkers. I want to know their story.'

'We can stop here for the night,' Adrianna conceded.

'Let us play a song for you,' Fiona said. 'The music will keep other things at bay, worse things.'

'Like what?' Ebbo said.

'Dragons.'

'I'm married to one of those,' Adrianna said.

MacGregor grumbled something to that, but no one asked him to reiterate.

'Unicorns, then,' Fiona said.

'I've heard of those. They're magick right? I've heard one taste of their saliva can set you off for days...' Ebbo said wistfully. 'Not that I want to do magic anymore!' Ebbo shot a harsh glare at Seemus's baliset. Did he have some issue with instrument?

'I thought you were clean,' Asakusa didn't know what was going on with the islander, but he knew his addiction to magick was likely responsible.

'I am! I was just saying that I heard that. I don't want to actually do it. Not since...well, you know,' Ebbo shot a guilty look at Clayton. The islander had never really been the same since snorting what he thought was his friend's soul condensed into magick powde. Asakusa could at least give him that.

'We'll split up,' Adrianna said. 'I agree with Ebbo and Clayton. Something needs to be done to end this conflict. Right now, we'll make camp. In the morning, Ebbo and Clayton will stay down here to figure out more about what's happening between the stonewalkers and *destruyag* while Asakusa and I continue up to meet this Dontalas Crisp.'

'That's-a-really-good-plan-except-I-think-Clayton-and-I-should   leave now!' Ebbo burst out.

'I think I'd rather stay the night and hear the ballad,' Clayton chimed in.

'Clayton, please?' Ebbo begged.

Asakusa scratched at his arm. He couldn't figure out what was bothering the islander so much, but it seemed...different.

'I don't think that's wise,' Fiona said. 'He killed a giant, he did, and well, you're a... some kind of spider? Might be better to have the clay man with us.'

'Aye, it's a good enough plan. It's as the Highfather wills it, it is,' MacGregor said.

'Aye,' said Seemus.

'But *Innocence*—'

'It's the Highfather's will. Now quiet, daughter,' MacGregor said.

Adrianna shot a look at Asakusa and shook her head to stay quiet.

'You two be careful, okay? After everything that's happened, the last thing I want is for one of you to get hurt,' Adrianna said before Ebbo pulled Clayton away from their camp and back down the mountainside.

Chapter 62

Clayton

'Oh, this is interesting,' Clayton said to Ebbo the next morning. Ebbo had dragged Clayton away from the MacGregor family, Adrianna, and Asakusa without much of an explanation, but Clayton saw the guilty looks the islander kept shooting at him and didn't protest. They had much to talk about, not least of which was their mutual interest in investigating both the giants who could walk through stone and the short, feathered beings who seemed to be actively destroying it. Apparently, Clayton was far more biased than he realized, because he was much more interested in his fellow mineral-based beings than the hive-minded birds.

'Is it actually interesting? Last time you said something was interesting, it was swirly rocks. Swirly rocks are not interesting,' Ebbo replied. They were speaking over a thread of silk Adrianna had left for them. Clayton had another thread buried in his clay that ran directly to Adrianna, so that if anything happened to either party, they could send for help using the code Ebbo and Clayton had devised. Ebbo tapped his messages with his dexterous toes while Clayton simply tugged on the string with his clay. It wasn't all that different from vibrating his clay to speak. The two were better at using a thread to communicate than Adrianna was, despite it being made of dried ichor from her body.

'It's another rune,' Clayton said.

Ebbo tugged on the thread with his toes in such a way that Clayton knew he was rolling his eyes. 'Can you actually read this one?'

'Well, no,' Clayton admitted. 'Stonewalker is not exactly one of the languages clients speak in the Red Underoo, but what's interesting is where the rune is located. I think there's some sort of pattern to them.'

'I think you're giving the stonewalkers entirely too much credit.'

'They're interesting, is all. Did you notice they had runes on their bodies too? I wonder if they need them to survive.'

'You think they need to kill to survive too?'

Clayton had no response. As he'd wandered through the complex tunnels of the mound the giant stone beings had attacked, he'd come across at least a dozen of the feathered destruyag. All dead. All dispatched like they were vermin. Squashed mercilessly like roaches in a brothel. Still, there were plenty more of them that went about gathering bodies and stacking them in a central location. They treated their fallen comrades indifferently, as if it was a chore the same as any other.

'Ebbo... I don't mean to be rude, but do you think the feathered destruyag are sentient?'

'Of course, they are! Just because they're short doesn't mean they're not smart.'

'I don't question their intelligence because of their height, but because of their actions. None of them have communicated with me yet. Have they with you?'

For a moment no vibrations came over the thread. 'No...' Ebbo said finally. 'But they might just be shy. Even if they can't talk, that doesn't mean they're not smart. Look at these tunnels.'

'Ebbo, ants make tunnels too. That doesn't really mean—'

'We're not just going to let them be slaughtered!' Ebbo said, yelling so loudly over the thread that it snapped. The thread, now loose, fell silent. Clayton sucked it into his kneecap like a piece of spaghetti. Adrianna could digest it later, or they could tie it back together. Adrianna couldn't understand the code through a knot, but Ebbo and Clayton still could.

Clayton sighed. He didn't really want to argue with Ebbo about whether the feathered destruyag should be saved or not. There was no reason for them to be slaughtered like this, none at all. He just hoped to find why the giants felt so threatened. Did they need the rock somehow? Were they worried that the feathered creatures were going to erode away the entire mountain? Surely, that was impossible. There must be something they wanted, something specific. After all, people had been exploring these mountains for years, and most came back. Only those that crossed the High Bridge didn't. None of them had reported stories of giant stone creatures that could swim through stone or glowing runes etched across the landscape. There couldn't be that many of them if they'd managed to stay hidden. Maybe they just needed a piece of land put away for them. Surely Magnus would be willing to set aside some land for them as a sort of homestead.

But truly, none of that was what Clayton really needed to talk to Ebbo about. They still hadn't sat down and talked about what had happened...

what Ebbo had done, or at least what he thought he'd done.

The islander was sorry, Clayton could see that much, and truthfully, he didn't blame him for his moment of weakness. Addiction was a cruel master, one that Clayton had yet to figure out how to protect people from. What was more troubling was that Ebbo's moment of weakness had cost Clayton dearly. It was all well and good that Ebbo was trying to get clean—it was more than that, truly. Ebbo had never so much as attempted a week of sobriety before. That he was attempting to out of either respect for or guilt from Clayton meant a lot to the golem—but that didn't change the fact that an outcome of Ebbo's weakness was that Clayton now had a hidden master.

Clayton found that because of Vecnos tricking Ebbo into snorting what he thought was Clayton's soul, Clayton understood secrets and hidden motives better than he ever had before. His new master was proving that even a golem could be duplicitous. He still wasn't sure if Adrianna knew who it was yet. He couldn't tell her. He'd been told to be his old self to his friends, and his old self was definitely not beholden to his current master. He tried to remind himself that all that wasn't Ebbo's fault, that Ebbo was trying to stay clean for Clayton, that he needed help, but it was all so complicated now.

'Hey,' Ebbo said, tapping on Clayton's leg from behind.

'Oh dear!' Clayton said, jumping. 'You gave me a quite a fright.'

'Still got it.' Ebbo smiled.

Clayton nodded and smiled back. The islander sure knew how to sneak.

'Clayton… I've been meaning to talk to you.'

'About what?' Clayton said. Though the Heartbeats animating the golem never changed in speed, he felt like they grew stronger. They were pounding in his chest. If he needed to breathe, he'd be holding his breath.

'About what happened,' Ebbo said, not making eye contact with the golem's emerald eyes. 'You know I didn't think that you were going to die.'

It was the weakest start to an apology Clayton had ever heard, and yet it was far more than he'd expected from Ebbo. Unable to help himself, he tried to comfort the little islander. 'Of course not, Ebbo. No one thinks I can die.'

'Yeah, but then I thought you were.'

'You're not making much sense.'

'Not at first, but then, when I thought it was my fault because I… look, I know I suck, okay? I just want you to know that if I knew it was going to kill you, I wouldn't have. You know?'

'Of course not,' Clayton said, trying to be supportive but mostly confused.

'I've been clean for two weeks because of you,' Ebbo said. 'You're my best friend, Clay. You really are. Are we still going to be... you know, the same?'

No. Clayton wanted to shout. No, we'll never be the same, because when I was repaired someone got a claw into my heart, and now I can't get it out. But he couldn't say any of that.

'I want to be same, Ebbo, really I do. But you're changing—we all are, I think—and that's good. If you feeling bad about me makes you stay off magick, I think that's good too. It means a lot to me that you care about me like a... well, like a person.' And it really did. Ebbo had been absolutely guilt-ridden since the incident, and Clayton was strangely thankful for it. He had never really feared death, but seeing others worry for him was nice, even if it did make lying to them even less comfortable.

'It's not hard,' Ebbo explained, 'I just had to throw away every bit of magick I had, and only go into public when Asakusa is around. That way even if I want some magick, he shames me out of it.'

'That's very, err... you're still craving it, then?' Clayton asked.

Ebbo nodded much too quickly. 'Blueberries, yes! Did you hear Fiona and Seemus's music? It was amazing.' As quickly as the grin had come on Ebbo's face, it fell off again. 'That's why I had to get away. I can't be weak again, not when you guys might need me. Better to be distracted on this mission.'

'Ebbo, maybe you need to face what has control over you. Distraction is helpful, but maybe not the best. I think we all have weaknesses. The first part is acknowledging that we can't fix them ourselves.' Clayton wished he could be more direct, that he could say he needed to face his own hidden master. Maybe he could, though. Maybe there was a way he could be the golem he had been, a golem that helped those who couldn't help themselves, and still come clean.

'Clayton, look!'

'No, Ebbo, now's not the time for distractions. We were just getting somewhere—'

'No Clayton, look behind you. Are those footprints?'

'They can't be. I haven't tasted a trace of anything but the bedrock.' Clayton stopped talking when he saw the footprints. They were huge, and made in the stone itself, like the floor was mud instead of black, dried lava rock.

He approached one and touched it with a clay foot. Nothing. He tasted nothing. 'But that's impossible,' he said. 'There's no trace behind.'

'Maybe they really are made of the rock. So, like, they don't leave any trace because they're part of it!'

'An interesting idea, I suppose,' Clayton admitted, 'but then why would there be footprints here?'

'Only one way to find out.'

Chapter 63

Asakusa

'Can I sing you a song?'

'I think we'd rather know what the hell is going on,' Asakusa replied to Fiona.

'It's hard to be direct. The task can be *daunting*,' Seamus winked.

'You're doing that on purpose,' Asakusa said.

'I don't know what you're talking about,' Seamus took a drink from his flask. How much booze is in that thing? Asakusa wondered. Even self-replenishing flasks could normally fill up only once a day. Seamus treated his like it was a spring of liquor.

'I thought the first time was maybe an accident, but you're hinting at him. Dontalas Crisp. Who is he?' Adrianna demanded, one hand slipping to her whip, another poised to let down her hair and Unfold her spider body. Asakusa wasn't quite sure if she was getting ready to fight or just trying to make the MacGregors unbalanced. Her true form often had that effect on people. Asakusa hoped it was time to fight. There'd been far too much talk.

'It's no time for song, and it's no time for riddles,' MacGregor said grumpily. 'You do that, and he'll know where we are.'

'Dontalas Crisp will?' Adrianna pressed.

'Aye,' Seemus said.

'So what? Bring him on. He won't stand up to my stone hammer any better than anyone else,' Asakusa grouched.

In response, Fiona began to sing. Seemus joined her on the baliset, Seamus pulled out a horn, and MacGregor begrudgingly sang harmonies, adding a rich baritone to the song. As the melody flowed over them, Asakusa felt that he could almost see a farm high up the mountain. Rows of snabbage in one field, sheep in another. A mother and father, wearing loud checkered skirts, rested on each other while four children, three boys and a girl, ran about chasing a horse. As they giggled and played, they grew, until they no longer played but worked the farm alongside their mother and father.

Was this what Ebbo felt when he did magick? The islander always spoke of being transported away. Was this song doing that?

Asakusa had little time to ponder, though, for the baliset struck a minor chord, and a cloud covered the sun shining on the farm. Only a single ray of light shone through the clouds and fog. It fell upon a man in gleaming armor. He paused for just a moment, then walked down the hill toward the family. His boots made a noise as he went.

Step, *clink*, step, *clink*, step, *clink*.

Chapter 64

Dontalas

Dontalas Crisp approached a farm. It was the first farm he'd ever seen. Everyone else in the material plane seemed to be a hunter or a trapper or some other sinful thing. Hopefully these farmers would be different. The Highfather said farming was the only true calling, as it didn't kill anyone. Maybe these farmers will be innocent, Dontalas thought, but he doubted it. No one else had been innocent. Not the giants, for they killed the bird people. Not the bird people, for they killed and ate any voles that nibbled at their grasses. Killing and eating the flesh of the murdered was no better than killing and leaving the bodies. And then there was the business about what they did to the giant's young. Dontalas felt they should be punished for snuffing out a life before it even began, but his sword was decidedly vague on that topic. Surely these farmers would be no more innocent than anyone else in this cursed land.

Step, *clink*, step, *clink*, step, *clink*.

Dontalas drew his sword. It was unblemished, gleaming, a shining light of purity. *Innocence*, his brother had named it, and Dontalas could not imagine a more beautiful tool to cleanse this land. He held it ready to end these farmers if they had so much as hurt a gopher. Dontalas didn't know what a gopher was, but his brother assured him that people from the material plane killed them all the time.

As he approached the farmhouse, he heard singing and laughter. A man's voice was leading. It was rough and scratchy yet filled with joy. A girl was singing as well. Beautiful, so beautiful, if any would be innocent, it would be a voice like hers. Accompanying them were a baliset and horn. There were other voices too, voices trying to talk but just laughing or falling into silence as they listened to the music.

Step, *clink*, step, *clink*, step, *clink*.

Dontalas drew closer.

'Someone's here!' a voice called out. 'One of them sheep thieves, I'll bet.'

'It's nothing. Probably here for food,' the girl's voice said.

But then a man peeked through the window. Seeing Dontalas in his armor and wielding his sword sent the man running for the stables. He emerged a moment later, on horseback, riding hard and fast at Dontalas. He was wielding an ax.

'Iolas, no! Iolas, he probably just wants a bite!' someone else shouted from the farmhouse.

'That's why he has a sword drawn?' Iolas hollered back, raising his ax.

Dontalas pointed the sword at the boy on the back of the galloping horse. For a moment the blade flickered with light, but then it flickered off again. Curious, Dontalas thought. He'd seen visions of dead animals—the aforementioned gophers, perhaps—and then nothing. Could the boy be innocent?

But he couldn't be. Not with his weapon and such aggression. No one else had been, not a single person in the material realm had been free of sin. It was a horrible, horrible place, and the boy could be no better than the others Dontalas had already cleansed. The boy raised his ax and screamed a battle cry. Dontalas was ready. He held out his sword and impaled the lad. Then, for good measure, he brought it down on the horse, severing its head from its body.

Neither had time to scream, they were dead so quickly. Dontalas watched the boy's spirit sever from his now-bloody corpse and start its path up the mountain to cross the High Bridge. The horse, though—the horse's spirit whickered at Dontalas.

Then his sword broke.

Not irreparably, but a notch cracked out of it near the hilt, as if it had just been struck with his brother's hammer. Dontalas stood there for a moment, watching the boy's angry spirit float away and the horse's spirit standing there, looking annoyed at him.

'I'll be a fallible mortal,' Dontalas said. 'You were innocent!'

The horse nodded and gently stamped its hoof, as if to demonstrate it knew to avoid stepping on any creatures that might crawl upon the earth.

'I do apologize, but then… that was a nasty trick, coming out here with that boy on your back like that. My sword knew you weren't evil, but he confused me.'

The horse only whickered again. Dontalas was completely dumbstruck. In his few days walking down the mountain from the High Bridge, he'd cleansed the material realm of all sorts of sinful creatures. He'd yet to find an innocent life, but apparently, he'd found one in this horse.

From the farmhouse came another person. A woman, who older than the voice of the singer. She wore a red checkered skirt and a matching sash over a roughly woven wool shirt. In her hand she clutched a butcher knife.

'You monster. You drop that armor and face me like a man,' she was hollering, red in the face, red as her skirt.

'Morgana!' a man pleaded. He had a big bushy beard and a scratchy voice. 'We already lost Iolas. Please.' His scratchy voice broke and the man began to weep. Though he was speaking to the woman, his eyes stayed on the body of the dead boy, Iolas. 'Maybe he just got scared, maybe he just wants a place to sleep. You can't go out there, Morgana, you can't... not with all that... that blood. Ain't nothing solved by violence. Morgana, come inside!'

'My son's dead, and still you say that?' the woman was furious, seething. 'You!' She shouted at Dontalas. 'Prepare yourself for vengeance!'

From the farmhouse stepped another woman. Maybe girl was a better word, as she looked just old enough to have children of her own. Two boys, identical save one had a mustache and the other bushy sideburns, followed her out. They all stood behind their father.

'He was a killer,' Dontalas said and shrugged. 'The Highfather will offer him redemption. If he accepts it, he will be free to serve for the rest of eternity.'

'That boy killed nothing but rabbits! Hurt no one but thieves!' Morgana shouted, stepping ever closer.

Dontalas raised his sword at her. It glowed brightly. The lives of countless animals flashed before Dontalas's eyes. Sheep, cows, chickens, pigs, as well as other, more unusual creatures had all died at this farm woman's hands.

'Morgana, the scripture says those that commit the sin of murder will be punished.' The man continued to weep. Good of him to quote scripture, Dontalas thought. 'Maybe the Highfather sent this... this man to help.' The man's eyes didn't leave his son's dead body. Dontalas thought that he was saying the right words, but he was obviously having trouble fully committing the ideas to heart.

'Curse you MacGregors. Just because he killed a few birds doesn't mean he was to be murdered for your damn Highfather!' Morgana cried.

'You're a MacGregor too, Mom!' the girl called out.

'I'll never be one of you cowards. Not any more than my son was,' she spat, and turned to Dontalas.

'Still won't take off your armor? Fine,' she said, and marched right up to

Dontalas. He was amused. He'd never seen such courage, or a soul that had taken so many lives. She probably justified the murder of all those animals because they were less intelligent. The self-titled "sentient" creatures often used this argument about other living animals. How would she react when confronted with someone of obviously higher intelligence and divinity?

Morgana stabbed Dontalas.

He shouted in pain then and grabbed at the wound. She had stabbed him just under the breast plate, in his side. So, this is pain, Dontalas thought. He didn't like it.

He pressed his hand against the wound. Light shone from his palm, and he was healed.

The woman stepped back, gasping.

'You are not innocent. Not anymore than your son was. But the Highfather will offer you redemption,' Dontalas began—but then she stabbed him, again!

Dontalas wasted no more time. He kicked her backwards, his plate mail making a satisfying clink as he did so. Then he stabbed *Innocence* right through her heart.

She died with hardly a scream, this one no more innocent than the last human, no more innocent than any human. No notch appeared on Dontalas's sword. There was still just the one, the one from the stupid horse.

'Horse,' Dontalas said, and the horse's spirit eyed him. 'Carry me to battle.'

The horse whickered, but it obeyed. His brother had said this would be the case. Any innocents he slayed would have their spirit bound to the sword. *Innocence* would give their souls form and substance in this world, and they would obey the blade's master until such a time as he killed a sixth innocent. Then they would be freed and could attack the master of the sword. If Dontalas killed five others who had never committed the sin of murder, his sword would break. But for now, he had his first servant of *Innocence* in this horse.

He touched the horse, and its spirit became solid. He climbed on its back, then spurred the spirit of the horse to carry him forward toward the family.

The other humans cried out.

'He's got Horse's spirit!' the girl called.

'Aye,' one of the boys said.

'Prepare yourselves!' the old man called.

They all reached for things. Weapons, surely, just as their mother had.

Dontalas didn't have the time to see if they were innocent, but why should he? Their brother and mother had been sinners. Their father obviously didn't believe the scripture he quoted, not if he wept so for the death of his murderous son. Dontalas had yet to meet an innocent human. They weren't horses.

He laid into them with his sword. They fell in hardly a moment.

Dontalas took a deep breath, looking at their spirits climbing out of their fallen bodies, waiting for the breath of the Highfather to draw them upwards across the High Bridge.

They didn't move. Not one of them.

Dontalas looked at his sword. Four notches cracked off the back of the blade, ruining its clean line, making it look like a crooked tool of torture instead of a shining instrument of justice.

'Why? Why did you do that?' the girl asked. Fiona. Dontalas knew that was her name. He found he knew much about these people whose souls were now bound to him.

'You were going to draw weapons,' Dontalas protested.

Seemus and Seamus both drew their instruments. Fiona plucked a flower. The father—Father MacGregor was how he thought of himself—took out a book. The book of scripture, the Words of Wind. The gospel of the Highfather.

'Oh, drat,' Dontalas said.

Chapter 65

Clayton

A night passed, and Clayton and Ebbo made camp. Clayton didn't need to sleep, but if he kept his body still, he could store the extra Heartbeats in his steel heart. So, he lay as motionless as the islander, though his mind raced while Ebbo only dreamed. Mostly he thought of what he was, of what he used to be. When he'd first gained sentience, he'd styled himself a free golem. Had that ever been true? It certainly didn't feel true now, even though he received fewer commands than he ever had before. It was a long night, and Clayton's emerald eyes shone with no light save the gentle glow of Boffo, the fat moon, whose light shone down through the cracks in the cave system in which Clayton and Ebbo had camped.

The next morning, Ebbo and Clayton picked up the trail of stone footprints. They followed it for maybe twenty spans before Ebbo got distracted. The islander started sniffing at the air, looking back over his shoulder. Clayton recognized the look. He sighed loud enough for Ebbo to hear him. 'You smell magick, don't you?'

Ebbo sort of embarrassingly chuckled. 'No. I mean, maybe. Don't you? You've always said you've had a pretty good sense of smell when it comes to magick. You haven't been lying, have you? Because that would be totally messed up if you've been lying to me after all that's happened.'

Clayton rolled his eyes. Lying about magick was the least of the lies he'd been telling friends. Ever since he got his new master, his entire life had been a lie. How odd it was, to see it all so clearly now. He wasn't a free golem; he never really had been. The women of the Red Underoo had bought his contract from a pimp, and with about a dozen women all giving him conflicting orders, Clayton had been forced to obey them all by not obeying some of them, at least not exactly. He'd learned to interpret their senses of humor, their shared priorities, and found that some things, though given as orders, weren't really that important. His new master had told him to be the golem his friends wanted him to be, and that golem, the golem who'd served as the loyal servant to a brothel, was the closest thing Clayton had to what his master had meant. Unfortunately for Ebbo, that golem was not always honest.

'I wouldn't lie to you,' Clayton lied before continuing honestly. 'I can smell magick through my feet, but that's because there's normally a thin layer of soil. Even in the streets of S'kar-Vozi, there's always dirt and grime that I can track with my feet. The stone up here is different. There's nothing on it. Nothing at all.'

'So, you can't smell that, then?' Ebbo said, sniffing at the air, smiling sheepishly like a young boy whose father had brought him to the Red Underoo to become a man.

'No. And I don't think you should dwell on it. Look at these footprints, Ebbo. They're made *in* the stone, and yet I can't sense them at all. I've never seen anything like this before. Just think of the implications for mineral-based life forms such as myself. A world could be below this rock. Maybe they need the surface of the Ur as much as fish need the surface of the sea.'

'Those footprints could have been here forever, though. They could be fossils, like the seashells on top of Isla Giganta.'

'I don't think they've been here long at all. Look at this lichen. Do you see how it grows in little circles, but that one looks like it's been sliced away by that toe?'

Ebbo was not looking. He was glancing over his shoulder and sniffing away.

'Let's split up,' Clayton said. And blinked in confusion. Where had the idea come from? It wasn't his own, they needed to stay together... or so he had thought, but now that seemed less important.

'Yeah, good idea,' Ebbo agreed quickly and started back down the tunnel.

'Ebbo, the thread,' Clayton said. Splitting up wasn't such a bad idea. They could cover more ground. Clayton didn't know why he'd thought anything against it. Ebbo took the thread of silk and started off back down the tunnel. Clayton continued to follow the footprints.

But why footprints? Clayton hadn't seen any before, and now they were here, leading deeper and deeper into the cave. The roots of the grass mats didn't reach this deeply, and there was something about the shape of the tunnel that made Clayton think it hadn't been made by the feathered *destruyag*. No, it couldn't have been. Here were more of the runes. Same as the ones he'd seen on the stone beings' bodies. Maybe the giants were just trying to defend this place, but why?

He rounded a corner and had his answer. In a large cavern lay a stonewalker, a female, by the sounds of her breathing. Clayton knew those grunts. Birth was no stranger in a brothel.

'Are, are you okay?' Clayton asked.

'Shaman gone. Need help,' the giant said in the common tongue. This one wore a bright orange robe around her shoulders.

'What do you need me to do?' Clayton asked, years of being an assistant midwife coming back to him. Should he fetch some water? Let her squeeze his arm or punch him in the crotch? That was what the women of the Red Underoo often did while giving birth.

'Help me pull.'

'You mean push?'

The giant screamed in pain. Clayton knew the pitch and timbre. She was close. But her belly didn't seem any bigger than the other female giants. 'Pull!'

Clayton rushed over to her. As he stepped across the floor of the cavernous room, he saw runes flash. They were made in a spiral that started where the giant was standing. All of the runes were spiraling to this very spot, Clayton realized. He'd just been following the spiral in a straight line, but the runes had been getting more and more frequent.

'Help!' the enormous stone woman said. 'Chevron betray us. If *destruyag* erase runes, my son not be born. Now pull!'

Clayton had about a thousand questions about that. Namely, who was Chevron? Why was she (or he) not loyal? What did runes have to do with childbirth? And, perhaps most importantly, how was he supposed to help pull?

Still, Clayton quelled these wonderings and came to stand next to the giant stone woman.

'I'm Clayton Steelheart, the free golem,' Clayton said weakly.

'Obsidia,' the enormous woman replied, and sniffed at Clayton between labored breaths.

'Not one of us.'

'No ma'am.'

'Not flesh.'

'Also correct.'

Obsidia nodded, faster and faster, desperation turning into acceptance. 'You must help me pull.'

'Of course, but what exactly are we pulling? Not to be rude, but you seem, uh…' Clayton tried to politely point at her flat belly and ended up only pointing at her crotch. Still, an accurate concern, Clayton thought.

Obsidia reached down, to the center of the glowing spiral of runes, and grabbed a hand out of the floor.

Clayton almost fell over backward at the shock of it. There, in the center of this cavern, surrounded by glowing runes and beneath the feet of this enormous stone woman, were two tiny hands. Well, not tiny, these were bigger than Ebbo's, but still small compared to most. Ebbo... where was he? Clayton tried to feel the thread, but Obsidia brought him back to the moment.

'Pull. Canal closing.'

'The cave is a birth canal?'

'Pull!'

Clayton nodded, forgetting about Ebbo, and reached down and grabbed the hand. He pulled gently. It did not even kind of move.

'Pull. I said pull!' Obsidia screamed. Sweat as thick as tar dripped from her jet-black skin. She pulled on the arm with everything she had, her muscles flexing underneath her robe.

Clayton grabbed the hand and pulled. Together, both flexing, they managed to pull the hands out of the stone floor until the elbows of the boy emerged.

'Good!' Obsidia grunted, tears breaking from her eyes and running down her cheeks. 'Good, good! Keep pulling!' There was joy in her voice.

They pulled. Harder this time. The giant pulled so hard that her feet sunk into the ground. Despite it being stone, it didn't crack.

Clayton took a deep breath and tried to forget everything he knew about babies. He wrapped his clay fingers around the hands, squeezed so tightly that his fingers melted into his wrists, and *pulled*. His clay muscles flexed, his shoulders bulged. He redirected more clay to his legs. The rest of the boy's arm slipped out.

'He's crowning!' Clayton shouted. He was getting emotional despite having seen plenty of births. Still, this was one he'd remember. He'd never seen a baby come out of the floor in the middle of a stone chamber with flickering runes. Wait, had they been flickering before?

Obsidia panicked. 'Hurry! The way closes! We must finish the labor!'

'That's an entirely different meaning to the word, but then, going around making runes sounds more like labor than just pushing—'

'Pull!' Obsidia shouted so fiercely that spittle flew from her mouth. It hit the ground and clattered away as a pebble.

Clayton pulled. Up through the stone floor came the top of a head, bald as his mother, and then his face was out, and he was looking around the room. He wasn't a baby, not like a human anyway, more like a child. He had giant ears, wide eyes with dark red irises around pupils like flecks of flint. A smile touched his lips when he looked at his mom's sweating, cursing face.

Obsidia spoke—or at least her mouth moved—but the sounds that came out were the sounds of falling stones, of boulders shifting. The boy spoke back to her in the same language of moving stones.

They embraced, then Obsidia turned to Clayton. 'I am his mama. This is Crystak.'

'Mama,' the boy said, his voice strangely well developed.

'We're past the hard part. Hold on, Crystak, we are almost done,' Obsidia said, though Clayton understood she was talking to him more than the baby.

The runes flickered again.

'No!' Obsidia screamed, looking around the room wildly. 'No, we're too close! Pull!'

They pulled, but this time Crystak called out in pain. It was the sound of a boulder being sundered in half. They stopped. Crystak had made it out as far as his waist, but he was stuck in the stone, his arms and head sticking out, his legs still inside.

The boy looked at his mother desperately. Obsidia looked around wildly. Clayton followed her gaze from the runes to the floor. It looked to him as if the stone was solid once more. Cracks seemed to be reforming from the edge of the room, as if whatever change had come over the room was now coming to an end. The runes were dull, little more than scratches in the floor, where before they had been glowing, subtle symbols that Clayton almost thought he could understand.

'Shut,' Obsidia said, pointing at the runes.

'I'm sorry, I don't understand.'

The giant gestured again at the runes, but Clayton only shook his head.

She said something in another language to the boy who—shockingly— understood, then let go of his mother.

'What? Where are you going? You can't just abandon him mid-birth canal!' Clayton said.

Obsidia pointed at the runes and said something to Clayton in her language that he couldn't understand. He only shook his head. She looked from her son, back to Clayton, then left.

An eternity passed in that moment. Clayton looked from the entrance back to the boy, to the dull runes. The boy looked from his fleeing mother to the dull runes to Clayton. There was a sound like water freezing, and the boy began to cry. The sobs sounded like gravel falling. He brought his own arms down and tried to push himself out, but he didn't budge. Clayton grabbed him under the armpits and tried to pull, but it didn't work. The boy was stuck.

'Crystak, it's going to be okay,' Clayton said.

The boy may have been moments old, but he knew the sound of an adult lying all the same. He cried harder.

'It's going to be fine, she went for help. You'll see,' Clayton said, though he didn't really believe it. The rest of the Stonewalkers had gone up the mountain. He'd been surprised to find one here at all. His mom probably understood that. Knew it was better to abandon this boy than to lose herself, too. Clayton felt himself panicking. He didn't hyperventilate, as he didn't need to breathe, but he wanted to as he thought about this boy, or baby or whatever, abandoned by his mom to die with a golem. It was almost too much to bear—

And then the runes started glowing again.

Clayton wasted no time. He reached down, grabbed the boy and *pulled.* He pulled with every bit of strength he had while Crystak cried and pleaded. Up he came! The boy was being born! Clayton was delivering him! It wasn't so bad, he thought, as he used every Heartbeat he had to push on the floor and pull the boy out.

And then Obsidia was back! She grabbed the boy and pulled him out the rest of the way. He popped out with a squelch and then was free, being cradled in his mother's arms. Obsidia was crying and cooing to him and thanking Clayton, and then... apologizing?

Clayton tried to calm her—she looked so distressed, so sorry—but he found he couldn't move any closer to her. He looked down and found that the stone floor now reached up to his chest. But that wasn't right; the room didn't seem any shorter. Dumb realization struck. Clayton had sunk into the floor. He looked around at the runes. They were dull again.

Obsidia looked at him with sorrow, then at the runes.

'You can fix them, right? You can fix the runes so I can get out?'

She nodded, but then something distracted her. Hooves, horse's hooves. She looked down the tunnel in terror.

'Crisp,' she said, and then was running away with the boy in her arms. The thread that had been connecting him to Ebbo was gone, snapped when the floor had solidified. Clayton was left stuck in the stone, unable to move, unable to escape.

Chapter 66

Asakusa

Asakusa didn't have time to ponder Fiona's powerfully evocative song and the magick therein, for as soon as it was over, he'd passed out. Exhausted from the day's battle, and possibly the magic itself.

When he awoke, Adrianna looked at him with eyes so wide with fear that the extra pair on her cheeks opened.

'Clayton,' she said, and held up a broken strand of silk thread. Asakusa couldn't use thread to communicate like the rest of them could, but he knew a broken one wasn't good.

'Come with me,' Asakusa pleaded to Adrianna.

'He's not down there,' Fiona gestured down the mountainside.

'How can you know that?' Adrianna asked.

'She can't,' Seamus said. 'Not exactly. But we can tell the sword's not down there. It's up ahead. Judging. Someone's killed quite a few of those destruyag.'

'You have flesh to spare?' Adrianna asked, looking guilty as anything.

'Enough for this. And you know I'd do anything for you,' Asakusa said.

'Then go save our friends.'

Asakusa nodded, opened a Gate, and stepped into the Ways of the Dead, the stone hammer trundling along behind him on its magick cart. It was so heavy, impossibly heavy; impossible to lift unless called upon for combat. The cart bowed beneath its weight, but it trundled along all the same.

Another Gate opened in front of him. It was farther than he wanted it to be. Asakusa swallowed hard. Damn it, he'd have to do it, little as he wanted to.

He ran. He hated running.

'Don't say I didn't warn you,' Byorginkyatulk said, appearing from a Gate of his own. His were much more ornate than the Gates he granted Asakusa. Instead of glowing runes in demonic script, Tulk's Gate was framed in haunted wood with black spikes for nails.

'I know you're just playing games with me.'

'For once, I'm not.' Onshsss. How Asakusa hated the demon's speech impediment. Or maybe he hated him for granting him the power to open Gates in exchange for his Corrupting his body, and the slurred speech just set him off.

Asakusa didn't slow, but he held up his Corrupted hand. The worms had worked further across his body, as they always did. 'Making Gates here doesn't spread the Corruption any faster than usual. You're lying.'

'That's true,' Tulk said, vanishing and reappearing every few seconds, keeping pace with Asakusa as the thrall made his way through the Ways of the Dead. 'We're about as far from the Material plane as we can be while still being in the Material plane. Just about every belief system in the Archipelago sends their dead toward High Home, and they did long before the Highfather moved there.'

'So?' Asakusa moved down a path that crossed another.

'Thisssh way,' Tulk said, his long tongue flapping about, never fully going into his mouth. 'So it's something you can use, you ungrateful thrall.' Tulk looked about conspiratorially. It seemed he didn't want the Demon King to know he'd told this little nugget of wisdom to Asakusa. 'It's not the Gates I'm worried about. It's Crisp.' The last two consonants slurred together into something awful.

'What about him?' Asakusa said.

'Just do yourself a favor and watch out for that sword.' Tulk smiled, his tongue flicking back and forth.

'Right, because my plan was to get stabbed,' Asakusa said.

Tulk shrugged and smiled. 'See you soon, little thrall. Those maggots have really progressed quite a bit.'

Asakusa shot him a scowl, but then he was through the Gate, inside a dark passage. There was a bright, silvery light glowing up ahead, but Ebbo and Clayton were nowhere to be seen.

Tulk had led him astray.

Chapter 67

Ebbo

When Clayton's thread had broken, Ebbo had panicked. He normally panicked when separated from Clayton, but now there was another emotion besides the ever-present islander fear of being eaten. Ebbo was afraid that he was going to lose Clayton. He felt responsible for the golem. How could he not, after what he'd done? So, it was with conflicting emotions of fear and selflessness that Ebbo followed the broken line of silk toward where Clayton had last been.

He rounded a corner and stopped short. A beast of incredible beauty raised its head and greeted him.

'I am Chevron, the Staglion.'

It looked like a stag, Ebbo thought—the whitest, most noble stag Ebbo had ever seen—except its antlers were made of bronze, and it had a mane and a long tail with a pom-pom on the end, like a lion. Ebbo couldn't help but think of it as a girl.

'I sense you are in need of assistance, young Ebbolonius Brandyoak. Can I help you?'

'How do you know my name?' Ebbo asked, but he knew. Of course, he knew. To someone with habits like Ebbo's, it was obvious. Chevron was magick. The staglion exuded magick, breathed it. Ebbo didn't think he'd ever sensed this much magic come from one being before. Before the being could answer, Ebbo asked a smarter question. 'Why do you want to help me?'

'You're one of the chosen ones, young Ebbolonius. Your people have brought plant life to many islands, where before there were only crustaceans and crettles. I work with your kind no longer, but I can sense you are distressed over the pain of another, and I can totally help.' Chevron's voice was high and warbly, in contrast to her beautifully muscled body and shining white fur. Silver flecks fell in the air around her, like snowflakes of pure light. Ebbo wondered where she had learned the word "totally."

'You can help my friend?' Ebbo asked. 'I think he's in trouble.'

'Indeed. Climb upon my back, and we will go there.'

Ebbo nodded. He had to help Clayton; he *had to*. That meant he couldn't do any magick and lose touch with the present. Ebbo reached into the staglion's rich, white fur and climbed atop its back. He could feel magick coursing beneath its skin, fueling this creature's muscles, making its fur shine, granting it powers Ebbo would never understand, only abuse. But he wouldn't. Not with Clayton in trouble.

'Forward!' Ebbo said.

Chevron nodded and walked down the hallway, following the silk thread in Ebbo's hand.

'Would you like a taste of my power?' Chevron asked after a few moments.

Oh, blueberries, yes, Ebbo thought, *more than anything*. But he took a deep breath—even that was dangerous, given Chevron's enchanting aroma—and said as calmly as he could, 'No-thank-you-I'm-fine-I-don't-need-any-magick-right-now-thanks.'

Okay, so it wasn't exactly calm, but Ebbo was still proud he'd said it.

They continued down twisting halls until they came to a larger cavern that was covered in runes.

'Clayton?' Ebbo yelled when they'd reached the end of the thread.

'Down here!' Clayton's rich voice replied, and Ebbo felt relief wash over him. Knowing Clayton was alright felt better than any hit of magick ever would.

'It seems like the floor is talking,' Chevron said.

Ebbo just about died laughing. Between gasps and peels of bubbly laughter, he looked down to see Clayton's waist resting on the floor. His arms were nowhere to be seen. 'Looks like someone *wiped the floor* with you!'

'Well, they didn't do a very good job, as now I'm part of it.'

'Yeah, looks like someone really *mopped up*.'

'Ebbo, you're not making any sense.' Clayton furrowed his brow, and Ebbo felt his throat catch. He was laughing because he was relieved that Clayton was okay, but Clayton had seen him march in here on this obviously magick beast. He no doubt worried that Ebbo had succumbed to his old habit.

'I'm clean, buddy, really, I am. I'm just glad you're alright.'

The staglion, with eyes bronze as its antlers, peered around the room and said, 'Where is the person you said to help?'

'Seriously, though. I'm right here. Can't you see me?'

'I see mud,' the staglion said.

Ebbo giggled even harder. 'You hear that, handsome? Mud! All she sees is mud.'

'Young Ebbolonius Brandyoak,' Chevron said before she was interrupted.

'*Ebbolonius*?' It was Clayton's turn to laugh.

'What? It's traditional,' Ebbo said, crossing his arms on his chest.

'I have exhausted what magick I had healing the feathered ones. I have only enough left for one dose. I do not see the being you spoke of, only this… talking mud. Perhaps you are ready for my kiss.'

'That talking mud is my friend.'

'Oh.' The staglion seemed a little put off, but continued with grace, 'I am sworn to heal all living things. My power derives from my goodness and purity of spirit. I take no sides with the living, but I am not beholden to talking mud, no matter how sparkly its eyes. I have enough magick left for a single dose. I could use it on this…mud, as you have asked me, or I could bestow you with a kiss. It has been long since I have gifted one your kind with my kiss. You would totally like it.'

'The bronze-horned, white stag's kiss?' Ebbo said.

'The staglion's kiss,' Chevron corrected him.

'But you're not really a lion. I mean, you don't even have claws—'

'It is the highest gift I can give, besides rebirth from death. I will infuse your spirit with magick. For a moment, your soul will be transported to a realm of pure bliss, where only happiness can be felt. Your aches and pains will be washed away, and your only conflict will be whether you are truly at peace, or in orgasmic delight.'

For Ebbo, it wasn't even a choice. He knew he couldn't take it, no matter how berry-picking great is sounded, not if that meant leaving Clayton trapped in the floor. Still… Clayton didn't know that. Maybe Ebbo could use this moment to prove how far he'd come.

'It's… magick?' Ebbo said, letting his old eagerness sneak back into his voice. He'd prove to Clayton that the golem was the reason he'd given up magick! Maybe then, their relationship would feel normal again.

'Oh, yes, of the purest and most potent varietal,' Chevron purred. 'With it, you will be whole, and the person you are meant to be.'

'Ebbo, our friends are being attacked by this Crisp thing. We don't have time.'

Chevron whinnied in dismay at the mention of Crisp. 'You face Crisp?' she said. 'I cannot abide him. He slays all that do not live up to his code and sends their spirits away before their time. Those he kills, I cannot heal. If you have issue with Crisp, my blessing is all the more important. My magick will cleanse you of sin, and when he looks in your heart, he will see only light.'

'Or!' Clayton shouted from the floor, 'you can heal me.'

'You can heal him, right?' Ebbo said. 'Even if he is mud?'

Chevron looked at Clayton. 'It's trapped in a giant's birthing canal. I can invoke the magick of labor and we can pull it out—but, young Ebbolonius, your undying soul is surely worth more than some mud. The process won't be pretty either. He'll have to grab my, err... tail.' Her high, warbly voice sounded appalled.

'Oh, huckleberries.' Ebbo rubbed his hands together and hopped off Chevron's back. 'What a decision.' Ebbo took a deep breath and hid a grin. This was it! This was his moment to prove to Clayton how much he'd grown. He was going to turn down Chevron's fancy kiss—as nice as it sounded—and save his friend. If that didn't redeem him, nothing would. 'Whatever will I do?' Ebbo asked no one in particular, enjoying his little charade. 'My friend or the best high of my life?'

It was in that moment that Asakusa entered the chamber.

'You little monster,' the thrall hissed. His scowl was far worse than any insults he could have hurled. 'You try to snort your friend's soul, and now you're going to leave him to perish, trapped in stone?'

Ebbo's face fell from smarmy trickster to complete devastation in the time it took Asakusa to complete the sentence.

'I was only kidding,' Ebbo managed.

'You think I *believe* you? After everything you've done?' The Corruption maggots on Asakusa's arm were really whipping about.

'I was just messing with Clayton! I've been clean for weeks now! Honest! This was just to prove to him that I *was clean.*'

'This is your friend?' Chevron stomped back and forth, clearly dismayed.

'I am no friend of his,' Asakusa growled.

'Just have the staglion open the birthing canal and get us back to Adrianna, *like you were planning*!' Clayton said.

I'll have to bake a pie for that golem, Ebbo thought, for mentioning the spider princess's name knocked Asakusa from his fury. 'We have no time,' he said, still staring Ebbo down.

'Please, do the labor magick.' Ebbo looked at Clayton. The golem only looked disappointed with Ebbo. The islander felt his little heart break. This moment was supposed to have brought them together, to prove to Clayton that he'd grown, but he'd gone and squashed it and made Asakusa trust him even less in the process.

Ebbo sighed as Chevron's bronze antlers began to glow.

The runes on the walls responded, igniting with a blue light from within. Asakusa's Corruption maggots screamed.

Ebbo really hated the things. Of course, they'd be afraid of *good* magick.

Then the floor turned to mud.

Maybe it was a testament of the staglion's powers, maybe she was totally freaked by Asakusa's gross arm—Ebbo would never know, for the four of them all plunged into the stone floor as if it were water.

Ebbo grabbed Clayton's hand through the mud. He tapped out a message to the golem: *You know I was kidding, right?*

You're a convincing actor. Clayton tapped back. That was about as rude as Clayton got, and it smashed the shards of Ebbo's already broken heart into even tinier little pieces. Ebbo had been willing to pretend he wasn't going to help Clayton, and Clayton was *still* so polite that the worst he could say to Ebbo was a backhanded compliment. It wasn't fair that they all might drown in a birth canal thinking Ebbo was still hooked on magick. Or Asakusa and Ebbo were, anyway. Clayton would spend the rest of his time here, possibly with the weirdly judgmental staglion.

But then Ebbo's sense of gravity lurched, and instead of sinking into the stone, he was on falling. Asakusa was already beside him, one hand on his hammer and the other pulling a cord of mud out of a Gate that was open above them. Asakusa looked pissed as he pulled on the mud umbilical cord— Ebbo couldn't help but draw the comparison—until Clayton fell out of the Gate above their heads and landed beside them. Then, to Ebbo's surprise, Chevron tumbled through the Gate too. The staglion took an undignified moment to right herself, but then she was there, standing with them in the Ways of the Dead. A flock of demons circled overheard, drawn to the white light of the magick beast like moths to flame.

Chapter 68

Adrianna

Adrianna and the MacGregors found him on a narrow stone bridge that connected two sides of a chasm so deep, they couldn't see the bottom. The wind was building and a cold mist was falling, wetting the already slick black rock that. The MacGregors formed a line in front of Adrianna, putting themselves between her and Dontalas Crisp.

'Is that the High Bridge?' Adrianna asked.

'No,' MacGregor said.

'We could march ten abreast across the High Bridge, and it's made of white stone, not black Fiona said.

There was no way anyone was marching across this bridge. On their side, the low side, the side with all the thick mats of vegetation, there was a stonwalker. She appeared to be the one they'd fought earlier. She wore nothing but a loincloth. On the other side of the stone bridge, the higher side, the side that was nothing but bare rock and the occasional gnarled cedar tree, stood a man.

His armor gleamed, even in the dim light. Though he wore a rueful grin and looked a bit arrogant for Adrianna's taste (this coming from a woman married to a dragon prince) he was undeniably handsome. His chiseled jaw line was shaved smooth. His eyes were the blue of a clear sky. His strong nose was unbroken, an unusual feature for a person who carried weapons in the Archipelago. And his long sword was like a beam of solid light, it was so bright—but maybe lightning was a better comparison, for there were five notches along its long blade.

The giant on the other side of the bridge looked almost destitute in comparison. She was nearly naked, her loincloth in tatters, bruised from facing Adrianna and crew earlier. She was out of breath, panting like a dog. Still, gripping a club, she pushed forward, out onto the narrow stone walkway and into the wind and the rain.

Despite having already fought the woman, and never having met the jerk in the gleaming armor, Adrianna picked sides almost instantly, for once not feeling like she needed to ask Clayton what he thought. She didn't side with the guy with the sword.

'Good evening,' the man in gleaming armor said above the wind. His voice carried far, almost as if the wind had died down to hear him speak. Seeing a giant across from him put his height in perspective. The man wasn't a giant, but he was tall. He came up to the giant's chest, and his haughty posture made him seem taller still. 'Who presents themselves before Dontalas Crisp for judgment?'

'Judgment?' Adrianna hissed, looking at Fiona.

But it was MacGregor who answered. 'Aye, judgment. To see if she's a murderer. Watch that sword o' his. It's her only hope.'

'Quartzeta,' the giant said in common. The language sounded clunky in her mouth.

'And are you innocent, Quartz-eta?' Dontalas enquired, splitting her name into two pieces, proud of noticing the crystal hid within.

'Our home is gone. Grass destroyed. We go higher.'

'Yes, but are you innocent?' Dontalas asked again.

From the stone beneath their feet rose another giant. She walked right out of the rock as if it were the surface of a pool of water that had been concealing a staircase. She wore an orange shawl, and in her arms carried a sleeping young boy. This giant stepped forward, though the MacGregors moved to stand between her and Crisp, so she couldn't get past them, or anywhere near the bridge.

'We eat nothing but stone. We hurt no one save those that invade our land.' This giant's common was better than Quartzeta's. 'We made deal with your father. The Highfather. He built his bridge on our land.'

Adrianna balked. The Highfather was Dontalas Crisp's dad? 'Isn't the Highfather the god of Vegetarianism?' Adrianna demanded of the MacGregors.

They nodded, looking none too proud. 'The words stand on themselves, princess,' Fiona said weakly. 'Even if the author is, err...' she trailed off as Dontalas Crisp raised his sword. He pointed it at Quartzeta first, as it was she who was out on the narrow stone bridge.

'Fair arguments, though land does not equal lives. But I speak too soon. Let us see if *Innocence* finds a friend in you.' Dontalas Crisp raised the sword and pointed it at Quartzeta. It began to glow, then white flame came from the hilt and up its blade.

'I'm so sorry,' Dontalas said, but he was grinning. He continued, louder, as if he knew there were others watching. 'But I was sent across the High Bridge and into this land of filth to cleanse it. You have all grown complacent. The Highfather says a darkness is rising, a god of death—Chemok, you call him—but even the Highfather could not have seen the darkness in so many of your hearts. This land will be pure; pure as I, the Gleaming One.'

'Pure as me,' Adrianna shouted.

One of the oaf's eyebrows rose as his grin grew wider. 'Who dares such arrogance against the son and an anointed hand of the Highfather?'

'I am Adrianna Morticia, spider princess. I've faced the skeletons Chemok brings back to our land. If you wish to stop him, don't harm these women. Help me instead.' Though the words were meant as a gesture of good will, Adrianna found that she'd used her I'm-gonna-kick-your-ass tone of voice. She didn't much like this Dontalas Crisp and the way he pointed his sword at injured women, even if the woman had been injured fighting Adrianna and her friends.

'You lie. I haven't seen a single skeleton. Just beings obsessed with murder, like the one before me.' Crisp pointed his sword at Quartzeta.

The other giant took that for the threat that it was. She leapt over the MacGregors, yelling as she did. 'I am Obsidia. I am as innocent as you.'

'Well, let's hope that's better than your friend here.' Dontalas moved forward across the narrow stone bridge toward Quartzeta

Quartzeta raised her club to stop Crisp, but it mattered not.

Dontalas swung his sword at the woman. It sliced through her club, then passed through the giant. She shattered into bits of black stone that sprayed over the edge of the bridge and fell into the chasm below. Adrianna could hear them clink against the edges as they tumbled into oblivion. It was a horrible, vile sound, created by a horrible, vile man.

'He killed her, just like that?' Adrianna said, her voice hot with anger, one hand reaching for her dagger and the other for her hair.

'Aye, but she wasn't innocent,' MacGregor said.

'The giants never are,' Fiona shook her head sadly. 'And there's no room in our religion for forgiveness.'

Seemus and Seamus nodded and began to play, one on his baliset, the other on his horn. Despite it being a simple instrument, Seamus was able to make a surprisingly mournful melody.

'She said they were just defending their land,' Adrianna hissed. She was absolutely livid. She'd fought Quartzeta earlier because she had been hurting the weird destruyag, but that didn't mean she wanted her slaughtered.

Adrianna didn't know what justice meant to Crisp, but she knew she didn't agree with his definition.

'Didn't mean they had to kill,' Fiona said. 'Life is worth more than land. At least, that's what I used to believe. It's the way of the Highfather.' She didn't sound proud or haughty like some many of the religious often did.

'Murder is a sin. The sin,' MacGregor said. He didn't sound mournful like his daughter, but angry.

Adrianna had heard enough. She let down her hair and Unfolded into her spider form. Her abdomen Folded out from her back, her two human-shaped legs transformed into the jointed, hairy legs of her people. Six others joined them, each tipped with a clawed foot that housed a tiny spinneret in it. Dontalas was large, so she lifted up two of her spider legs and armed herself. Three of her arms now held a dagger, the fourth was already holding her silk whip. She opened her extra eyelids, revealing six black eyes, all dark as the stone beneath their feet. Her white hair, now loose and hanging past her shoulders, whipped in the growing wind.

'Then call me a sinner.'

Chapter 69

Adrianna

'Get ready to run,' Adrianna said to Obsidia. 'I'll clear the way for you and your child. MacGregors, step aside.'

'We can't let you pass. Not so long as...' Fiona hooked a thumb over her shoulder at Dontalas Crisp.

'You'll get your chance with him,' MacGregor said to Adrianna.

'I know he was once your god, but he killed you! You can't let him kill her, even if he is some demigod from your religion.'

'We serve *Innocence* now,' Fiona said weakly.

Obsidia only grunted at Adrianna, stuck behind a wall of farmers. She spit a black pebble, swaddled the baby in her shawl so her hands were free, then ran at Dontalas Crisp.

Crisp laughed and swung his sword at Obsidia. She dodged, moving quickly for someone so large, and kneed Crisp in the ribs. There was a clang as her stone-like flesh collided with his armor and he stumbled back, but Crisp seemed unhurt.

'I've been looking for you,' Crisp said. 'The matron.'

Adrianna knew she needed to join the battle, but she found she was momentarily stunned by the speed and power of this woman. Adrianna realized that earlier, when she thought she'd defeated these giants, they had called off the fight. If it had continued, the spider princess might not be here.

Obsidia cursed something in her own tongue and rushed her opponent again. This time he was ready for her brutal hand-to-hand attacks. He blocked each punch with one of his gleaming bracers. Obsidia tried a kick and it connected. Crisp stumbled back. She raised both hands and brought them together over Crisp's head, ready to end the fight as soon as it began.

She cried out and stumbled forward. Crisp had brought up his sword. The point of it stuck through her torso.

'You can't let him do this!' Adrianna said to the MacGregors. They didn't step aside, so she made them. She cracked her whip at Fiona, who flinched and stepped back. She stuck a dagger into Horse's flank, and he whinnied and took off with Seamus on his back. A dagger found both MacGregor and Seemus, and Adrianna was past them, whatever they were—ghosts or spirits or innocent lives lost.

Beyond them, on the narrow stone bridge, stood Crisp. He pushed the sword up through Obsidia's body as he approached, a gruesome thing to do with a sword named *Innocence*.

Obsidia cried out but turned her body, wrenching the blade against her flesh but keeping the child on her back safe.

The sword began to glow with white-hot fire.

'Guilty. As guilty as all the rest. I should snuff you and your child out,' Crisp said.

'Then I'll turn that sword on you.' Adrianna had used Crisp's distraction to climb down the side of the ravine, then onto the underside of the stone bridge. Her spider feet easily clung to the wet stone. She came up around the narrow bridge, behind Crisp, and snapped her whip around his neck.

Crisp cursed and kicked Obsidia in the chest hard enough to knock her from his sword. Even with such a horrible wound, she was careful not to land on her back and crush her child. But not being able to fall on her back meant that Obsidia had to twist, which caused her to slip from the bridge. She caught the edge and just barely managed to hang on. Adrianna didn't know if she could pull herself up. She needed a lifeline to keep her anchored to the slick stone, a strand of silk. But first Adrianna had to get past Crisp.

'How many have you killed, Crisp?' Adrianna said, yanking at the whip. Crisp stumbled forward from the force, though not by much. He grabbed the braided silk wrapped around his neck and tried to pull it free. Adrianna pulled once more on the whip—giving him a friction burn on his fingers—then she let the weapon go, attached a line of silk to the stone bridge and scurried toward Obsidia on the underside.

'Not as many as your family, Morticia.' Dontalas practically spat the last word as he removed the whip from his throat and threw it off the bridge. 'The Highfather knows of your kind. An abomination. A heritage of abominations.'

Adrianna took the thread she'd attached to the bridge and pressed it into Obsidia's hand. 'Don't let go,' she whispered before turning to the gleaming buffoon who stood between the giant, her child, and freedom. 'I am not my family.'

'You eat like them, I bet,' Dontalas said, then pointed a finger at her. 'Flies!'

In the growing storm, a swarm of flies descended on Adrianna. They attacked en masse, biting her, obscuring her vision, driving themselves into her eyes and throat.

But no spider princess worth her web would fall to a swarm of flies. As Crisp approached, Adrianna took web from her spinnerets, and with four of her arms swung it around so within moments, the flies were all trapped. She took a bite and smiled.

'You only prove my point,' he sneered. 'If you were innocent, you're not now.'

Adrianna hurled a dagger at his face. He dodged, but not enough to avoid being cut on the cheek. He was obviously not used to having to fight those that he murdered. He wiped at the wound, gasping at the sight of his own blood, and in that moment, Adrianna once more took to the underside of the bridge, scurrying past him so Crisp was between Adrianna and Obsidia.

Dontalas pointed his sword at Adrianna. For a moment nothing happened, but then, like the moon on a cloudy evening, it began to glow. 'You've killed, Morticia. Beings you call monsters, and fish by the barrel. My brother warned me about your kind. He said you would be in league with death itself. Looks like he was right.' He rushed forward, his sword high.

He lunged, putting all of his strength into a single blow. Adrianna stepped back, parrying it with one of her daggers. The sword deflected, missing her and crashing into the stone bridge beneath their feet. Flecks of black stone flew away, falling into the chasm below him.

Adrianna attacked. Crisp was powerful, but while he had one weapon, she had three. Her movements blurred as the spider princess struck again and again with her daggers. She tested for weak spots in the armor as she stabbed and stabbed again. Dontalas tried to block her, but it was obvious he'd grown accustomed to fighting larger, slower prey. He retreated, stepping down the stone bridge to avoid Adrianna's whirlwind of daggers. She pressed him off the bridge completely, past Obsidia, who'd moved off the bridge and out of the way of her whirlwind of strikes. Adrianna pressed Crisp further, until he was up against the farmers she'd been traveling with.

'Enough! She's not innocent, you saw for yourselves. Attack her!' Dontalas said.

'I'm sorry, I really am, but I must serve him. And besides, you're not innocent.' Fiona seemed to be resisting some unseen force. She was trying to hold herself back, but then Crisp's sword flashed with light, and Fiona attacked the spider princess with a carving knife.

Adrianna parried Fiona's blow easily enough. However, she wasn't prepared for MacGregor's shovel. He brought it down with a clang and chopped one of her spider legs clean off.

Chapter 70

Ebbo

Ebbo found himself on a stone bridge elevated high above a broken landscape. He peeked over the short-walled side, standing on his tiptoes to do so. Below him, a dozen more bridges in various states of disrepair crisscrossed each other. Looking out across the landscape, Ebbo saw that there were hundreds more paths below. Some went into holes in the ground while others rose to connect to the bridges. Some meandered about until they found their way to a twisted castle on the horizon. The souls of the dead shambled along the paths, ignoring Ebbo, Asakusa, Clayton, and Chevron the Staglion. The demons of the realm, however, were not so oblivious.

Tulk stood on another path that ran below them. 'Where have you been? Did you defeat Dontalas Crisp?' he shouted at Asakusa, his long tongue flicking about with his frustration. There were few things Ebbo found to be more frightening than Asakusa. His Gatekeeper master was one of them.

'Adrianna is fighting him, and your Gate took me on a wild good chase!' Asakusa shouted at the Gatekeeper as if he were an actual frog instead of one of the man-sized, demonic variety.

'This place messes up our powers. You know how many afterlives use this island as the gateway? It's a damn logistical nightmare of traffic. And then there's her,' Tulk snarled at the staglion.

'Greetings, Gatekeeper,' Chevron said, kicking up on her hind legs. 'I have kept many from your master as of late.' Ebbo thought the majestic staglion actually sounded pretty smug.

'Yeah, well, should've thought of that before you came to visit.' In the distance, a bolt of lightning struck the high tower of a castle. 'You'd better get out of here,' Tulk said.

'How? You said she messes up your Gates,' Asakusa said.

'So don't open one,' Tulk said. 'There's an old belief system held by the giants of this island, that when they die, they rise into the sky above a chasm, like the smoke of a volcano. There's not many of them left, but so long as some still believe, that Gate will hold steady.' Tulk pointed toward a gate that stood at the end of a path a few levels down. To Ebbo's horror, he recognized the lone giant walking upon it. It was the one Asakusa had smashed in the face and killed.

'That can't be good,' Ebbo said.

The demons flying around them flew closer. Some of them dive-bombed the group, but each time they got close, they were driven back by Chevron's sparkly aura.

'Come on, we have to get to Adrianna. She's fighting Crisp. He slaughters anyone who is not a vegetarian,' Asakusa said.

'Well, that's a bit of a subjective criteria, isn't it?' Ebbo said.

'Not for his sword. Apparently, it draws the line at killing anything, even animals.' Asakusa looked from Clayton to Ebbo with doom in his eyes, and Ebbo could understand why. Adrianna had to kill animals just to survive. She couldn't go vegetarian any more than Clayton could stop using clay.

'There's the Gate,' Asakusa said, pointing to a glowing portal on a different path than they were on.

We'll never make it, Ebbo realized. How were they supposed to get down a level? Asakusa could probably use his gross Corruption maggots to climb down, but what about Clayton and Chevron? Even if they could make it down, it would take forever. And what had Asakusa said about *Innocence*? Ebbo was a vegetarian, unlike Asakusa. Chevron probably counted as innocent too, what with the bringing folk back from the dead, and maybe Clayton did... he had definitely clubbed some beasties to death in his day, but only because they were going to eat people. That counted as good, right? All this went through Ebbo's mind in an instant, and then he sprang into action.

While Asakusa and Clayton pushed ahead, looking for where the stone path they were on crossed the lower one with the Gate, Ebbo doubled back to the pillar that was suspending the bridge.

'Ebbo!' Clayton called out.

'It's up to me now!' Ebbo said, and then he hopped over the edge of the stone path and began climbing down.

Chapter 71

Adrianna

They attacked her from all sides. Fiona with her knife, MacGregor with his shovel. Seamus charged her from the back of his horse, swinging at her with a broken whiskey bottle that really stung when it broke her carapace. Seemus played a pounding rhythm on his baliset. The sounds blended with the rain and the storm, and the strikes and blows coming from the narrow bridge, making it hard for Adrianna to think straight. Fiona and MacGregor, though, seemed empowered by the music. They gritted their teeth and tried to flank the spider princess, stabbing at her legs as she kept spinning, striking out with her bevy of daggers.

Dontalas had taken his place back on the bridge. He watched Adrianna fight the farmers and stood in Obsidia's path, daring either of them to try to escape.

'Why are you doing this?' Adrianna screamed, using an extra arm to block Fiona's carving knife. 'I thought you were pacifists or whatever!'

'We have to. We're compelled to fight.'

'You don't have to fight well!' Adrianna said, then grunted as MacGregor's shovel landed on another of her legs. Etterqueen, she'd need to molt after all this.

She didn't know what the MacGregors were—dead obviously, enslaved most likely—but they were fighting for the wrong side. If they had no choice in the matter, then Adrianna had to free them.

'Don't worry, we won't kill ya,' MacGregor said. 'Dontalas, in his infinite wisdom, pointed out that we can just wound folk until he gets here.' Adrianna had never heard sarcasm as strong as MacGregor's. This was a man not happy with his theological choices. 'He'll judge you accordingly, and that'll be the end.'

'How is that innocent?' Adrianna said as a fresh round of Seemus's music blasted in her ears, nearly knocking her off-balance. Her missing leg slapped uselessly on the wet stone, spilling white ichor. She hadn't had time to patch it with silk.

Fiona pushed forward, singing as she parried Adrianna's strikes.

'Innocence taken, innocence lost,
The end times are a' coming,
You soul will taste fire, your soul will taste frost
For you, the Highfather is coming.'

Adrianna had enough. She pulled back, earning a strike across her abdomen from Fiona, and threw one of her daggers at Seamus. She'd hesitated before, thinking there was some way to reason with these spirits, or souls, or whatever they seemed to be—but if they were singing about violence, well, Adrianna would just have to harmonize. The dagger flew true and struck the drunk in the eye. He fell from the horse and lay still. For a moment.

'Bloody good to take a load off,' he said from the ground, the dagger still sticking from his eye.

His brother stopped playing as he pulled himself up onto Horse and charged at Adrianna. Adrianna used the pause in the relentless music to pull a strand of silk from her spinneret. She whipped it at MacGregor's shovel, wrapping it around the handle and pulling it into Fiona, causing the girl to stumble. Then, as Seemus charged toward her on her horse, she retreated after leaving a line of silk from Fiona to MacGregor.

She timed it perfectly, and the two pushed themselves up just as the horse charged through them, knocking them both over and causing the horse to crash to the ground. Seemus fell from the beast, landing on his head and snapping his neck.

There was a grin on his face even though his neck was twisted into what looked like a lethal angle. 'Aye, good to rest indeed.' He struck up his baliset, but Adrianna found it no longer bothered her. Whatever magick it had possessed was quelled.

Adrianna grabbed her hair and pulled it up, using her silk to quickly make a topknot and a ponytail, Folding two of her legs—including the one MacGregor had severed—away. Now instead of a spider centaur, she was a four-armed warrior, holding three daggers and a piece of silk that would make do as a whip. Fiona and MacGregor shared a look as they pushed themselves up. MacGregor spit.

'You sure you want to do this?' Adrianna said. 'I could give you a rest like your brothers.'

Instead of answering, Fiona gasped.

Adrianna turned to see a Gate open above the bridge, between her and Crisp.

She smiled. Her daggers were not particularly effective against large foes in heavy armor, but Asakusa's stone hammer was.

But Asakusa didn't come through the Gate.

Instead, Ebbo fell from it.

Chapter 72

Ebbo

Ebbo had felt horrible about seeing the giant walking the Ways of the Dead by himself. He hadn't liked how they had been killing the little feathered *destruyag*, but to know that this giant was about to pass through the Gate and into... oblivion? What lay at the end of the Ways of the Dead, Ebbo didn't really know. He didn't think Asakusa knew, but he didn't know anyone from any religion who was in a rush to get there, so he assumed it wasn't good. Plus, there was something else that was making Ebbo uncomfortable. He hadn't seen a single one of the feathered creatures on any of the paths around them. Considering that this was where they lived, he thought their beliefs in death would mean that they would end up somewhere in the maze of paths and bridges around him. But there weren't any. Not one.

Ebbo wasn't a theologian. He didn't believe in much of anything besides Clayton's kindness, Adrianna's patience, and Asakusa's temper, but he'd seen plenty of islanders walk these paths. Seeing none of the feathered things meant either that Clayton was right, and they weren't any smarter than ants, or—and this was an even odder thought to young Ebbo—that when the feathered destruyag died, they didn't ever doubt their beliefs, and were thus raced to their afterlife without delay.

Either way, Ebbo felt that this giant with his rocky skin and tears of stone might deserve more than just walking into his own oblivion.

'Hey... psst,' Ebbo said to the giant.

At first, there was no response.

'Hey, hey, you!' Ebbo said a bit more loudly. Again, nothing.

But then, something truly strange happened. Another giant materialized next to the first one. She too had fought against them, though Ebbo didn't remember her being killed. Which meant she'd only just died.

This giant—female, Ebbo thought—seemed to be able to notice him.

Perhaps she hadn't yet become accustomed to the meandering desolation that was the Ways of the Dead.

'Well, hello!' Ebbo said cheerfully. He knew he had to hurry, but what he didn't know was how he was supposed to survive dropping from this Gate in the sky. Only now he had an idea.

'Hello,' the giant said. She spoke in a language that sounded like falling rocks, but Ebbo found that since his feet shared her path, he could understand her. 'You are here to torment us on our path to the sky?'

'No, not really. More of an insane coincidence, actually,' Ebbo laughed. 'What with my friends killing—you know what? Never mind. I had a question about your afterlife.'

'There is no afterlife,' the giant said mournfully. 'When we die, our spirits leave us with our last breath and float to the top of the mountain. Which means, now that we are gone, only Obsidia and her child remain.'

That was good, Ebbo thought. If half of the entire stone giant population was right here in front of him, he could make this work.

'Right, see, about that. That's the top right there.'

The giant looked through the portal. It was kind of an odd thing, because the path they were on ran to the portal, but then the portal looked down. It made Ebbo kind of nauseous to think about it. The old Ebbo, a weaker Ebbo, would have looked to magick to help quell the sensation.

'Yes,' the giant woman agreed.

'Well, are you sure that's where it's supposed to go?'

'Pardon?'

'Well, like, seems kind of silly, right? Like, why do you believe that when you die, you go up here instead of say, like fifty feet down?"

'That's... that doesn't make sense.'

'But what is death, really? Many cultures believe in rebirth! In fact, just recently I helped birth one of your kind. Who's to say where the precious soul came from? Maybe it came from one of your own kind, long deceased.'

'But a baby is born without memory,' the male giant said, the one who'd been on the path when Ebbo first spotted it.

'Yeah, sure, good point. Look, not gonna lie, I don't really want to quibble on specifics. Let's say you're reborn as babies, memories wiped clean, freshly tilled garden as it were. Wouldn't want to burden babies with all that un-composted manure. Seem reasonable?'

The giants didn't seem to be buying it. But then, of course they weren't. They didn't have gardens. They grew from rocks, or something.

Ebbo tried to change his metaphor. 'When the volcano that built the

Archipelago erupted, it made new land, yes?'

'Of course,' the two giants nodded. This was much more familiar ground for them.

'Okay, but also stuff was destroyed, right? At the very least, any fish swimming by were, uh…' Ebbo wanted to use the euphemism "weeded," but of course they wouldn't get that. Instead he finished lamely with, 'Melted?'

To his complete surprise, the giants got it. They both nodded, lost in this metaphor of volcanic eruption that Ebbo wasn't completely sure made sense. But that didn't matter, they weren't his beliefs. They stood on the path of these giants, their way to their afterlife. And suddenly, the Gate behind them shifted down fifty feet.

That was enough for Ebbo. 'I think you did it! Let's go!'

Ebbo raced through the now-repositioned gate. He didn't become any younger, as he didn't believe in all that, but he did feel… a weight lessening. An ease to his mind that hadn't been there before.

At least, he felt that way until he saw a tall, armored, smug raspberry of a man standing in front of him with a raised sword. This had to be the guy.

Ebbo planted his feet and squared his round little jaw. 'You, sir, are a bully,' Ebbo said to the gleaming, muscled man before him. Just his sword was twice the height of Ebbo. Each piece of the man's plate armor probably weighed as much as the tiny islander.

'And who are you?' Dontalas Crisp boomed.

'Who, me? I am Ebbo Brandyoak of Strong Oak Isle. An adventurer, explorer, and friend of all. I've never eaten meat, never even hurt a rabbit that stole a carrot. I've stabbed a few in my day, that's fair enough, but only after they tried to hurt me and my friends. And I never slit throats.'

'And what do you want?' Dontalas Crisp said, a grin growing on his face.

'I ask you to strike me down, for I am innocent.'

The grin fell from Dontalas's face. 'Who told you the secret of my sword?'

'A staglion,' Ebbo said.

Dontalas looked around. 'That creature is here? She keeps many that should have passed over the High Bridge.'

'She's my friend.'

'Maybe you are innocent,' Dontalas said, almost to himself.

Ebbo gripped the wet stone with his hairy toes and stood as tall as he could, which wasn't tall at all.

Dontalas drew his sword and pointed it at Ebbo. White flames erupted down the length of the blade. Dontalas threw back his head and laughed.

'Pixies, mermaids, cursed toads, and many other creatures have all died for your pleasure, Ebbolonius Brandyoak of Strong Oak Isle. You may not have killed them yourself, but you reveled in their death. You are not innocent, just in denial.'

Ebbo swallowed. That hadn't worked.

Dontalas raised his sword.

Chapter 73

Clayton

The Ways of the Dead were becoming quite crowded. Clayton had jumped down to the path below. Asakusa and Chevron were still above. The swarm of demons had retreated. In their place stood the Demon King. He stood on the ground below, and his torso, thick as a mountain, reached up and above the path they were on. Clayton admired the golden chain around his neck, stuck in a continually melting loop, but he also wondered if maybe the Demon King could try a different accessory every now and then. His red, shirtless chest heaved as he swung his black trident at the staglion. It smashed into her horns and was pushed back in a shower of sparks.

'Do you know how many roads must be rebuilt because of you? How many change their beliefs in the afterlife after being stolen from me? It's totally uncool!' the Demon King roared, his lips not matching his words. The voice came from within Clayton's own body, as if the Demon King could make all matter in this place, even the minerals in the golem, vibrate with his rage.

'You are bad!' Chevron said, bucking wildly and meeting the Demon King's blows. Ebbo seemed to really like the staglion, but Clayton found her... less than amusing.

'I am necessary, you stupid horse! Death has a place in life, namely at the end. All you do is prolong the inevitable! Seriously, it's a big eh!'

Chevron whinnied and kicked the short wall near her, toppling stones onto the paths below.

'Stop that! We just had that one re-done!'

Asakusa started to climb down one of the pillars to the road below, but the Demon King brought his trident to the thrall. The Corruption maggots on Asakusa's right arm responded, latching onto the trident and pulling Asakusa off the wall. Clayton grimaced. He was torn. Should he protect Ebbo, or try to somehow save Asakusa from the master of the Ways of the Dead?

'And you! We've met before, and you swore to me you wouldn't bring another here!' The Demon King roared at Asakusa.

'I had no choice!'

'Then I have no choice but to take your soul.'

The Demon King brought the tiny thrall up in front of his face. The tip of his black goatee was bigger than Asakusa. His horns were thicker than the thrall's body.

Asakusa, impetuous as always, swung his club into the Demon King's nose. The hammer connected mightily, knocking the Demon King back.

'I think you broke it!' the Demon King said, clutching his nose and dropping Asakusa.

'Clayton, go!' Asakusa yelled as he fell.

Clayton didn't waste a moment. He ran, turning his back on his friend and a goddess of life in the Ways of the Dead.

Clayton ran across the crumbling stone paths, his huge body causing the bridge to shudder as he went. He grabbed the pillar Ebbo had scrambled down, then slid, turning his hands to mud and hoping to stick rather than climb. Two giants were approaching the Gate. Soon they'd be through, but there was no urgency in their steps, just the resignation of facing their fate.

Clayton—now able to see Ebbo, outside the Gate and standing in front of who he could only assume was Dontalas Crisp—ran faster. Ebbo's arms were spread, his eyes closed, like he was ready to receive sacrament at the Red Underoo. Not smart, given the sword Crisp was about to bring down on him was wreathed in white flames.

Clayton ran through the Gate, and Crisp, mid-swing, brought the sword down on Clayton, swinging into the golem's chest with all his might. The sword sliced halfway through the golem... and stopped.

Ebbo's eyes popped open. Clayton could see this despite Ebbo being behind him, because Clayton's silica perceived light in all directions.

'Clayton, you're innocent!' Ebbo exclaimed.

'Impossible,' Dontalas Crisp said.

Dontalas kicked the golem in the chest, but when his foot connected, he was only knocked back. People often assumed that since the golem was man-shaped, he weighed as much as a man, but this of course was complete folly. It was comforting to know that magic angels of vengeance could make the same mistakes.

'But... you can't be innocent. Not if you're friends with these people,' Dontalas said, struggling to pull the sword out until Clayton punched him in the face with a fist, knocking him back and to the middle of the stone bridge.

The spiteful demigod fell on his ass in a quite undignified manner. His sword was still stuck in Clayton's chest.

'Who's to say if it's that, or if it's because I have no soul?' Clayton said as casually as he could. There had been a time when the idea of being nothing more than an automated artifact would have bothered Clayton, but now that this very fact of his existence had allowed him to save Ebbo's life, he found he didn't mind the thought so much. Better than having a soul and squandering it, certainly.

Dontalas, dumbfounded, pushed himself to his feet and pointed at Clayton.

'Fire,' he said.

The storm clouds above them opened up. In the glittering stars, a meteor shower began. First flecks of light went back and forth, and then there were stones falling, exploding on impact. Clayton didn't like the look of them.

'I'm not losing you again!' Adrianna said and stumbled to the golem's defense. She was hurt. Her hair was a mess, and phantom spider legs stuck halfway between being Folded or Unfolded jutted out of her body. Two had been severed. She had stab wounds all over her torso as well. She stood back to back with Clayton as the farmers approached, protecting his back while he protected her from this huffy, angelic being.

'Princess, it's fine. Really. After what happened, I don't deserve your support.' Clayton looked at Adrianna with the green emeralds Richard Valkanna had given him to use as placeholders for eyes. Which meant Richard, too, saw Clayton trying to sacrifice and free himself from his secret servitude.

'Give me the sword,' MacGregor said.

'No! You'll just give it to him!' Adrianna said, holding up her husband's dagger to the falling inferno. *Flametongue* could absorb dragon's fire. Hopefully these meteors were magick in nature.

'I've been waiting for this since the bastard cut us down. Give me the sword, and I'll end Crisp,' MacGregor extended his hand.

'Father, we've talked about this. You can't do it!'

MacGregor reached for the sword, still stuck in Clayton's chest.

'Adrianna!' Clayton said, moving his body so the hilt of *Innocence* stayed out of MacGregor's hands, but also trying to crouch and stay beneath her dagger. The meteors rained down on them, exploding when they struck Adrianna's dagger, the heat and force was then sucked inside the blade. Clayton dodged back and forth, trying to keep the hilt from both MacGregor and now Crisp, who was approaching from the narrow bridge. Of course,

Clayton also had to be sure not to decapitate Adrianna.

'He killed me wife,' MacGregor said, snatching for the blade.

'Aye,' said Seemus.

'He killed me son.' MacGregor's voice was so bitter, Clayton could almost taste it.

'He was a right shit, but family all the same,' said Seamus.

'He killed us,' MacGregor said.

MacGregor swung his shovel at Adrianna and severed the end of another one her legs. She cried out but cut the shout of pain short. Clayton felt a pang of concern come through the emeralds. His master was watching, then.

'Just let him have it!' Adrianna said, sounding both exhausted and in pain. 'I can't stop these meteors and fight against these ghosts.' Clayton stopped moving, and MacGregor gripped the sword in both hands. He pulled it from the golem's body with a loud squelch. He pointed it at Dontalas. It ignited in blindingly white light.

Dontalas stood still in the howling wind and the meteor shower. If anything, he stood prouder.

'You worship my kind, MacGregor. You worship my father. Do not end things this way.' Huge white wings unfurled from Dontalas Crisp's back. They glowed with an inner light, and despite the wind and the rain and the storm, the feathers remained as still and as beautiful as an a master's oil painting.

'Ye killed the babies!' MacGregor shouted, tears beginning to fill his eyes.

'They were giants!' Crisp responded.

'And *destruyag* galore.'

'They had killed the giant's babies!'

'That don't make it right.'

'You lived your life serving us, a life of innocence! Don't throw that all away now!' Crisp implored.

'We gave everything to you! *Everything!* We never stepped on a crustacean, never swatted a fly! You know how cold this island gets during the month of Icebane? How hard is it to farm during Duir? And still, we honored you! Our whole lives we lived by the Highfather's code, only to be cut down like we was nothing more than a field of wheat!'

'You will be rewarded in the afterlife!' Crisp protested.

'Our *life* was our reward! We *understood* our place in the world. But now we see that the gods we honored can't even live up to their own morals!' MacGregor was crying, weeping, his knuckles white as they clutched the sword.

'No god embodies the morals they ask their followers to abide by,' Crisp said, his voice like ice. 'It's impossible. That's why such rules exist in the first place. Guilt. Guilt is what a god rules by. You weren't living to any code when you followed the Words of Wind. You were just assuaging your guilt at *failing this world*.'

'The only thing I still feel guilt for is not protecting my wife.'

'For that, you are forgiven.' Dontalas smiled. Clayton thought it was meant to look kind, but to him— a man who'd seen true actresses in the Red Underoo—it was a cruel visage. 'Now, embrace me, my son.'

Those were not the words MacGregor wished to hear, but he obeyed all the same. He rushed at Crisp and swung the sword, but it was obvious he was a farmer. The blow went wide, and Crisp laughed. MacGregor struck again. Crisp dodged underneath it, but this time the blade found the feathered flesh of Crisp's wing. It sliced through, severing it almost as quickly as they'd formed.

Dontalas screamed in pain.

He clenched his fists and growled at MacGregor.

MacGregor growled right back, then ran the sword straight through Crisp's armor.

Perhaps the angelic being thought his armor would protect him from the blade, for this time, he didn't dodge. So, when the blade went into his gut, and a gust of wind caught him and blew his body into nothing but feathers, no one looked more surprised than Dontalas Crisp.

Chapter 74

Asakusa

Asakusa was fighting just to survive. He opened Gate after Gate, using each to escape the crushing blows of the Demon King.

But it wasn't going to be enough. He was nearly completely covered in Corruption maggots.

The Demon King obviously understood this. 'Delay this fight for another moment if you wish. Either way, your soul is mine!'

Asakusa didn't know what to say to that. It was true, and yet he couldn't stop fighting. He opened another Gate and tucked inside, to find himself falling through the sky high above Destruyag Island. Another Gate was already open, but as he fell, he saw MacGregor stab Dontalas Crisp and turn him into nothing more than a cloud of feathers.

Asakusa went through the Gate and crashed to the ground. He stood up. Maggots covered his neck, his hair. Only his eyes, nose and mouth were still clear. His entire body was gone. He couldn't fight, not anymore.

So, he begged. 'Please! Please don't do this! My friends defeated Dontalas Crisp. Isn't that worth something to you?'

'No, not really,' the Demon King boomed.

'Then why haven't you killed me?'

'I want to see you consumed by the deal you made with my Gatekeeper and have refused to pay for so long.'

'Righteous,' Tulk said, appearing at Asakusa's side. Asakusa's heart dropped. This was it. 'But, sir... there is the matter of Chevron.' Tulk gestured to the white lion with bronze horns, who—while Asakusa had been fighting for his life—had been kicking over bricks.

The Demon King sighed. 'Shoo, get out of here.' He tried to brush her away with his trident. Like before, it did nothing to her.

'The thrall can escort her from here,' Tulk said, shrugging his froglike shoulders and belching.

Asakusa couldn't believe it. Was Tulk covering for him? But no, Tulk knew as well as he did that his body was almost lost to the Corruption. His life was over.

'I won't go with that wormy guy!' Chevron said defiantly.

'Plus, there's the number the little halfling did on the stone giants' beliefs. When they die, they're just reborn to live again, walk our ways again, then repeat. An eternity of toil!' Tulk sounded quite excited.

'Really? Fuck. That's harsh.' The Demon King seemed impressed. 'Tell you what. If you can get the staglion out of here, we'll call it even,' the Demon King said.

'And my Corruption?' Asakusa asked.

He didn't know who laughed harder, the Demon King or his Gatekeeper. It was hard to compare the biting tone of their laughter, because Tulk's was a slobbery, slimy chortle while the Demon King's laughter could be heard inside Asakusa's very soul. Either way, it didn't sound good.

At least this way he could see Adrianna again. He had an idea on how to get Chevron to leave. 'Look, Chevron, those giants are going back into the world. Do you like the giants?'

'No way!'

Apparently, this being of life and light could be swayed as easily as a compass by a magnet.

'Well, let's see what they're up to.'

Asakusa pushed himself to his feet, put his hammer on the tiny stone cart, and followed the giants through the gate.

Stepping through felt the same as it always did to Asakusa. He didn't change, his maggots only crept closer to the center of his face. Chevron, too, seemed unharmed—but the giants changed completely.

As they stepped through, they seemed to fall away. Where once had been towering giants, now stood two children. They were still taller than Asakusa, but just barely. They were gangly and awkward, grinning like children as they looked at the people in front of them.

An accented exclamation ended the moment. 'You monsters are back?' It was MacGregor, pointing his sword at the two stone giant children.

'Don't hurt them!' a giant woman said, clutching her stomach. Bits of gravel fell from the wound, her kind's version of blood. Asakusa tried to move to stop MacGregor, but just moving toward the sword sent his maggots into a flurry of resistance. They wouldn't let him approach.

'I thought that at least Dontalas could do them in, but I see not!' MacGregor approached the stone children. 'Your kind isn't innocent. Crisp proved that much.'

'Father, no!' Fiona called out.

'Crisp said our religion was meaningless. I've hated these Stonewalkers since I can remember. Now I can do something about it.' And with a swing of the blade, MacGregor chopped one of them into pebbles that scattered from the bridge and fell into the ravine below.

Asakusa reached for his hammer. The tiny cart carrying it rolled forward, responding to its master's will. But it seemed Asakusa wouldn't need to hurt MacGregor, for the sword, *Innocence*, was glowing brighter and brighter. MacGregor tried to drop it, but he couldn't. It was stuck to his hand with white light, shining bright as the sun. Another chink appeared in its blade, and then, the blade shattered.

There came a maelstrom of feathers that enveloped MacGregor, his family of musical farmers, and Horse. Faster and faster the wind churned, until in the blink of an eye, the MacGregors were whisked away, gone to their afterlife.

The stone giant child they'd just slaughtered stepped from the Gate again. Reborn, once more. His innocent life—only seconds old—had proven to be the soul that broke *Innocence*.

The wounded giant took the boy by the hand—he seemed to have no recollection of what had just happened to him—and pulled him across the bridge, up the mountain.

'We thank you!' she called out. 'With Dontalas Crisp gone, we will live out our days up here, beyond the reach of the feathered ones and their grasses.'

'Sounds good!' Ebbo replied, grinning. 'That rebirth thing? That was me.'

'Sure it was,' Clayton said.

'Should we just leave the Gate open?' Ebbo asked. 'I mean, there's only four of them. I wouldn't want, uh... her,' Ebbo pointed an elbow at Chevron, 'to get back in there and pick all their berries.'

Adrianna looked at Asakusa, and he looked back at her. Her exoskeleton was beyond harmed, cracked and broken in a hundred places. She was missing legs too, but worst of all was the expression on her face. It was pure misery, and in it Asakusa recognized his own fate. He was doomed, and Adrianna knew it. He'd told himself that he didn't care, that he wouldn't care if he was lost, but now, with Adrianna in his arms, he found that he did.

'Adrianna, why are you hugging that walking pile of compost?' Ebbo asked, ruining the moment.

'Not the time!' Clayton hissed at the islander.

Asakusa couldn't make himself pull away from Adrianna, much as he wanted to curse out the little islander.

'We're going to be fine. Everything is going to be fine,' Clayton was saying. 'Adrianna must return home to molt, and Asakusa... we'll find the blossoms. Surely there are some left beyond what...' There was a glimmer in the golem's emerald eyes, and he fell silent.

'Something beyond what Adrianna's husband burned?' Asakusa said, pushing away from Adrianna. He didn't want to blame her, but part of him did. It was her husband who'd ruined his chance at healing. But none of that mattered. It was just blame, and blame was a game for the privileged. Asakusa had never had the luxury of deciding who was guilty of what.

'I can close the Gate,' Asakusa said.

'You can't. Please,' Adrianna pleaded.

'I still have a nose, don't I?' Asakusa tried to grin, but it just sent maggots rippling across his face. 'It won't cost me much, and this way it'll be safe until they need it again.'

'But...'

'I'm doomed anyway,' Asakusa said, shrugging the mound of maggots that was now his body. 'At least this way I can help some people on my way out. What do I matter beyond that?'

'You matter to me,' Adrianna said, and hugged Asakusa for what he knew was going to be last time.

That might have broken his heart most of all, because he could hardly feel her embrace. Here she was, hugging his disgusting Corruption, and he could hardly feel it. Between the woman he loved and his own body was the collateral damage from an oath he'd sworn to someone... to someone who hadn't even deserved it.

'It's fine,' Asakusa said. It was all he could manage. Then he turned and walked across the narrow stone bridge, his stone cart rolling obediently behind him, and closed the Gate.

When he did, his Corruption spread further, covering his lips, transforming his tongue into maggots, going down his throat. All that was left was his eyes. He reached for the stone key in his hand. It was time. He was done. He'd finally lost. At least Adrianna's husband seemed nice, except for his vendetta against Asakusa.

'Wait a minute!' It was the high, warbly voice of Chevron. Asakusa turned to the bizarre staglion. She was glowing brighter than before.

'You banished the stone ones?' she asked.

'More like gave them a sanctuary,' Asakusa tried to mumble.

'And you closed their portal to that awful place!'

'To protect them,' Asakusa complained using his tongue of maggots.

'I will cleanse you as you cleansed this land!' Chevron said with a bow.

'Excuse me, but that's extremely problematic!' Clayton protested before Ebbo elbowed him in the knee.

'What are you—' Asakusa asked but stopped as Chevron began to glow. First the staglion's bronze horns filled with golden light. Then the skin beneath her fur seemed to glow, and then her fur itself illuminated. In the presence of all this light, the maggots shrieked and twisted. Asakusa thought he should be feeling pain, but it was the opposite. The more the maggots squirmed—trying all the while to go and burrow underneath each other—the better he felt. As they crawled into each other's shadows, they simply vanished. So as Asakusa stood there, basking in the light, he was cured. In a minute, he had his body back. The Dark Key that opened the Gates to the Ways of the Dead was there, but his Corruption was gone. He was healed!

Asakusa only had eyes for Adrianna. He turned to her, grinning, trying not to cry. Adrianna's mouth hung open, halfway between shock and delight.

But then a Gate opened, and Tulk stepped from it, totally ruining the moment. The Gatekeeper bowed cordially to his thrall.

'Well done, Asakusa.' The "S's" all slurred together when he said the thrall's name, until it was nearly unrecognizable. 'Your little friend totally ruined some of our architecture, but you saved us some man-hours there. Plus, you defeated that stupid staglion.'

Asakusa looked past Tulk to see that indeed, Chevron was but a remnant of what she'd been. Instead of the majestic beast, there was now an empty skin, like whatever light she'd used to heal Asakusa had burned out and left her body behind.

Asakusa thought maybe he should care more, but all he wanted was to go to Adrianna. 'So, I'm free?' he said to Tulk, wanting to push past him but unable to maneuver around the fat frog on the narrow stone bridge.

'Not quite,' Tulk said, and a ring appeared on Asakusa's finger. Instantly, the finger below the ring withered. 'You still made a deal. A full heal just means you get a new Corruption. I want you to know I pulled a lot of strings with the Demon King, but he's still mad about you hitting him in the face.'

Asakusa nodded. No one was ever happy about getting hit in the face.

'Still,' Tulk said, throwing an arm around Asakusa's shoulder. 'I know how you work. I'm sure you can figure this one out.'

'What do you mean by that?' But then Tulk and his Gate were gone, and Asakusa didn't care anymore. He ran across the bridge and threw himself into

Adrianna's spider arms.

She flinched, of course, because she was still super injured. So Asakusa didn't hug as tightly, but by then it didn't matter because the moment was ruined when Clayton wrapped them both in a hug and Ebbo grabbed their legs. But maybe it wasn't ruined after all. Asakusa had his friends, and had somehow survived, not to mention saved a race of weird rock giant people, and also maybe had granted them immortality.

Besides, what came next was what ruined the moment.

For behind Asakusa came the little cart carrying *Byergen*, the unliftable stone hammer. The cart had been doing admirably, following its master, supporting a load far beyond what it had been designed to do, but it had reached its limit. The little wooden platform snapped in half, and the stone hammer fell the tiny distance to the stone bridge below.

That, of course, wasn't really *that* bad. After all, Asakusa had dragged the hammer around for years. The cart had been convenient, but its loss wasn't really that big of a problem.

The bigger problem was that when the hammer fell that finger's length onto the stone bridge below, it—being magickally heavy in nature—cracked the bridge in half and plummeted down into the canyon, all the way into the sea.

That was what finally did the moment in.

When the hammer fell, Asakusa tried to pull away from Adrianna, but she had anticipated this, for he couldn't leave her. A silk thread was tethering him to her spinnerets.

'I can get it! I can use the Gates again!'

Adrianna shook her head and just held him close. 'No, Asakusa. You just got your body back.'

Asakusa knew he should use the opportunity to say something to Adrianna, something about how wonderful it felt to touch her, about how hurt she was and how he wanted to care for her, but those kinds of words just didn't come easily to him. So instead he said, 'But we're going to need *Byergen* in the fight to come! Even Crisp knew about Chemok. It's only a matter of time before those skeletons attack. The hammer was good against them.' These were the words he managed, despite being held by the woman who owned his heart.

'Princess, you must return home to molt,' Clayton said. His emerald eyes were so imploring.

In an instant, Asakusa had forgotten about his hammer. 'You can't go back there. *He's* back there.'

'I know you don't like Richard, and I don't blame you, but the hot baths there are supposed to greatly shorten the molting.'

'What happened to calling him Valkanna?' Asakusa stiffened without meaning to. Adrianna let him go, and he took a step back. 'You know he burned all those flowers on purpose.'

Adrianna only shrugged. Asakusa shouldn't have blamed her—shrugging was practically half of his vocabulary, after all—but suddenly he felt cold up here in the thin air. It was too much to take. How could she consider going back there? How could she go back to *him*?

'I have to molt. If those skeletons attack, and I'm in this state...'

'So... we're going to Krag's Doom?' Asakusa asked, his voice heavy. He already knew the answer to that question as well as Adrianna did.

'No... I'm going to Krag's Doom. You're going to get your hammer. And you're going to have to go the long way. You're going to need to use your Gates for the battle to come.'

Asakusa nodded, his posture heavy. He was finally healed, but his heart was as scarred as ever.

'Cool, so yeah, you're going to go to magickal Krag's Doom and send Asakusa on his own?' Ebbo asked.

Asakusa turned to the islander, ready to punt the little punk off the edge of the mountain. How could he think about magick at a time like this? Suddenly Asakusa found he had a lot of words, all for the cretinous little islander, but what Ebbo said next took them all away. 'Because, honestly, there's *a lot* of magick there. I don't know... that is...I-don't-think-it-would-be-good-for-me-to-go-there-since-I-want-to-stay-clean.'

'You... you want to come with me?' Asakusa couldn't believe the words that had just come out of his mouth.

Stranger still was when Ebbo agreed. 'Yes, I think that might be the best way not to pick the whole blueberry patch, if you get my drift. I want to be strong. Really, Clayton, I do, but Chevron's power was so... I just don't think I can go to Krag's Doom. I'm sorry, Adrianna.' Ebbo looked devastated, and yet Asakusa felt something for the islander he'd never felt before: respect.

'So it's settled, then,' Adrianna said, sounding like a princess once more. 'Clayton and I will travel to Krag's Doom, where I will molt and join Richard in imploring the family to help against the skeletons. Asakusa and Ebbo, you'll venture forth and retrieve *Byergen,* the stone hammer, from the depths of the sea.'

Asakusa just nodded. He didn't know how to feel about any of this, but then he found he didn't have to—for from the shed skin of Chevron stepped a tiny kitten. But not quite. It had hooves instead of claws, and tiny bronze nubs for horns.

'Oh my gooseberries, can we keep it?' Ebbo asked and scooped the thing up.

It mewled in appreciation.

Ebbo sneezed, looked distrustfully at the creature, and put it back down. It surprised Asakusa how proud it made him that Ebbo recognized this and still stopped touching the reature.

'I'll carry it back to those feathered guys. They seemed to like it,' Clayton said, and scooped up the being of eternal life that was also apparently quite biased in which species it bestowed with magic. It didn't seem to like being carried by the golem at all.

But this was life in the Archipelago, and no one knew that better than Asakusa. The world was filled with unfair deals, the powerful trying to take from the powerless, and sweet little kittens that were in reality total jerks. One couldn't tell a demon from an angel, not in this world, not in many, and Asakusa had stopped trying long ago.

It was better to focus on the people in his own life. People like Ebbo, who struggled against his problems and failed most the time... until he didn't. People like Clayton, who cared for the souls of others even if he didn't technically have one of his own. And people like Adrianna, who—by some miracle—actually seemed to *like* Asakusa.

He still didn't know what to say to her, and he probably never would, but for once he felt like he knew what to do.

As they started their days-long trek back down the mountain, back toward a world poised on the brink of destruction by the most nefarious of villains—hungry skeletons— and with nothing to show for their victory but piles of dirt, Asakusa took Adrianna's hand and said nothing at all. He just felt her warmth with his own skin, and smiled.

And, for the moment anyway, that was enough.

BOOK 5

A Homecoming Of Horrors

Chapter 75

Adrianna

There it was. Krag's Doom. The place she'd spent her entire life avoiding. Her home. Adrianna Morticia sighed and started up the rough steps cut into the volcanic rock. She didn't know how long she thought she was going to avoid it, but there was no point in waiting any longer. She was missing an entire leg and the last segment of another. Two of the wounds in her abdomen stubbornly refused to heal. Tying up her hair and Folding away her body did next to nothing for her pain. There was only one solution, and that was to molt. There was only one place to do that. Home. Adrianna supposed that's what this floating castle was to be for her now. Even though she'd never spent so much as a night here, it was her home. At least, her husband and mother would think so, as they both lived within.

'It's... nicer than I remember,' said Clayton Steelheart, the free golem. He was made of reddish brown clay that he kept sculpted to perfection. Broad shoulders, chiseled abs, sculpted biceps, a perfect jaw and cheekbones set the golem apart from the typically mushier-looking variety of construct. All that and the emeralds for eyes that had been given to him by Adrianna's husband made the golem quite handsome.

'My webmother has been seeing to the maintenance. That's one of the reasons the Valkannas were so eager to wed me to Richard. They needed some work done.'

'How terribly... romantic,' Clayton managed, fidgeting with his rough spun shirt. Despite his body being a thing of sculpted perfection, Clayton preferred to wear clothes. He had a fondness for worm's silk. He'd been complaining about the itchiness of the shirt, a sensation Adrianna hadn't even known he could feel. As they had sailed and drawn closer and closer to the volcano with the floating castle at its peak, Adrianna had sunk into a darker and darker mood, and Clayton's attempts at both humor and complaints had gradually fallen away.

Her mood was black as the thick hairs on her spider legs. She sighed. The sooner she made it up there, the sooner she could molt and leave, if her webmother ever let her. Adrianna loved her mom, but was not looking forward to any conversation which could be pivoted to breeding, which—given that her mom had eight daughters, just like every Mortician Queen had for eight generations—could be any conversation at all.

They started up the steps, Clayton taking each one in tireless stride, Adrianna trying to scuttle and mostly just limping. There was no point in tying up her hair and Folding her spider body away. It hurt too much. And besides, the path was treacherous, and eight web-tipped legs—seven, six her pain reminded her, looking at the severed stump—were better than two in heels. She'd almost tried to walk it in human form, barefoot, but Clayton had been aghast. It simply would not do, he'd said, for a princess to walk barefoot. He'd offered to carry her, but of course she'd declined. Better for her to take her cursed form.

Her feet were all bare now. Her two human legs still looked mostly human, though Adrianna hadn't shaved them in a while, and thick hair sprouted along them, embarrassingly thick near her crotch. Not that anyone could see under her padded leather armor. Her toes also seemed normal, but upon closer inspection one would find they split after the second toe instead of the first, like normal humans' feet did, and that a tiny spinneret was located on the pad of each foot. Her other six legs were thick segmented hairy things, like tarantula legs grown of tree branches—at least, that was how the commoners in S'kar-Vozi spoke of them when they thought Adrianna wasn't listening. Clayton seemed to think her spider form could be as barefoot as it pleased.

How Adrianna wanted to go back to S'kar-Vozi. She missed the smell of the city, the raucous energy, the tavern brawls, the smells of curry and spices. Fish cooked so tender, she hardly had to pre-digest it before sucking it up through her hollow teeth. She sighed through the vents in her abdomen.

'Princess?' Clayton said, his voice dripping with concern.

'It's nothing, Clayton,' she said, sparing a glance at his emerald eyes. Her husband had given Clayton those emeralds, and though he seemed no different, Adrianna couldn't help but wonder at the dragon prince's motivation. Surely, he couldn't control the golem... right? Adrianna tried to push the thought from her mind. Clayton seemed the same as ever.

It was Adrianna that was being controlled.

Up and up they went. The steps were easy enough for her narrow spider feet to climb, and even missing a leg, she rarely slipped, an advantage of having spinnerets on her feet. Clayton didn't slip either. If his feet were too wide for one of the narrow steps, he simply let them lose their form and mush into the shape of the stone.

They came to an altar carved into the black basalt that made up all of Krag's Doom and most of the wider Archipelago. It was in the shape of a spider, laying on its back, its eight legs stuck into the sky and forming a platform. On the platform was a dagger. Its hilt was a dragon, the blade its tongue. Adrianna had an identical one on her belt, one she had been given by Richard when they'd wed. She missed her own dagger, the one she had given him. But *Flametongue*—Richard had told her the dagger's name when they had exchanged them during their marriage —had powers of its own. The ornate gold-handled dagger on the pedestal was surely more pedestrian. It was a trap, obviously. Many adventurers would see a spider on its back and think it was dead, but to the spiderfolk who'd built this place before it had been taken by dragons, it was obvious that it was molting. If she were to try to snatch the dagger, the table would either animate (if her mom had been serious about bringing back the old enchantments) or more likely, it would simply alert a nearby lava beast. Adrianna was in no condition to fight one of the hungry monsters, and though she knew they could be trained, it would not recognize Adrianna.

'Princess, I sense something up ahead. A stench stronger than the brimstone,' Clayton said, wrinkling his nose. Even after knowing Clayton for years, his human mannerisms never ceased to amuse or surprise Adrianna. He didn't smell through his nose, but instead with the surface of his entire body. He could sense any aroma that drifted onto his clay skin. He was better than a crabhound at following a trail. His feet were especially receptive to scents. Probably the only reason he didn't wear fine shoes was because Adrianna used him to track so often.

'Flamehearts,' Adrianna said, putting her hand to her silken whip. She'd killed dozens of the things. She had been raised to think they were vicious creatures, with red and orange skin that was either scaly or blistered from their environment. Last time she'd come this way, they'd attacked her en masse, as they had to all invaders of Krag's Doom since its creation by the Morticians millennia ago. They'd shown no loyalty for the bloodline of the castle's original architects, though. They served the castle's masters, which— almost since the castle had been finished—had been the Valkannas. Adrianna still had fond memories of them leaping down on her abdomen, armed with crude daggers cut of obsidian, trying to cut through her silk wedding dress. That had been a battle, and there had been so many of them!

She leaned her human torso back just enough to lift up one of her spider legs and put her hair in a quick ponytail. Pulling on her strands of hair Folded her body, moving two of her legs off her abdomen and using them as arms. She reached for her daggers but found one of them remained sheathed since — as she was tired of being reminded — one of her arms was just a stump. No matter. She could still fight.

'Harden your fists, Clayton.'

'Are you sure, Princess? In your state—'

'I'm sure.'

Clayton nodded and hardened his fists. If one watched closely, one could see the moisture pulled out one Heartbeat at a time, up through the veins that adorned his bulging muscles to be stored somewhere else in his clay body. His fists were left dry and hard as stone, with bits of shards on the knuckles placed this way and that. He still didn't have the store of Heartbeats he needed to truly access his powers. Adrianna had hoped that some rest in the castle would afford him some time, but it seemed they might be tested before they so much as made it to the front gate.

'They're not strong. They'll rely on surprise and brutality to overwhelm us. They'll gladly sacrifice one, or even ten of their own if it means an advantage.'

'I won't be caught unawares, Princess.'

Round a bend they came and found them: flamehearts. A classic setup, two of them squabbling over a small chest of gold. The typical adventurer would dispatch them, and in that moment he would be ambushed, but Adrianna was not the typical adventurer.

She cracked her whip and wrapped it around one of the handles of the chest. She yanked it, spilling the gold. As soon as the coins touched the ground, they grew legs. The gold coins flowed toward her, clacking with tiny gold fangs, but when they reached her legs, they stopped.

The flamehearts who'd been holding the chest had drawn curved scimitars, but they too stopped and bowed.

'Your highness,' one the flamehearts said in the common tongue.

From the high ridges of black stone around them, spiderfolk appeared, prostrating and bowing to their spider princess. 'We will ready the news of your arrival!' one of them said.

'Shush, you fool!' said a flameheart. The two looked at each other and fell into squabbling.

'Come, now, there's no need for all that,' Clayton said, but they ignored him.

The flameheart drew a dagger and stabbed the spiderfolk compatriot, the one who'd said something of news, until he moved no longer. Although the spiderfolk had died first, it also got the last laugh, for he had bitten the flameheart. In moments its venom coursed through her body, until she too, was dead. The rest of the flamehearts and spiderfolk watched the exchange with interest but not concern. The spiderfolk almost certainly had more empathy for Adrianna and her missing arm than for their own fallen brethren.

'We will be sure you weren't followed, your highness,' one managed in the common tongue, then they stood aside and let Adrianna pass.

She sighed. Couldn't even kill flamehearts anymore. Even just seeing the death of one made her feel uncomfortable. They were her servants now—more than that, they were family and they'd sworn to protect her. She didn't want them dying for no reason. How different she was than just weeks ago, when she'd slaughtered them by the dozen and claimed self-defense.

On they went, up the narrow black steps and ever closer to Krag's Doom, until the steps were behind them, and there was the castle.

The last time Adrianna had seen the castle, its white stone had been dirty with ash and soot from the volcano it floated above. Hastily spun spider silk had held it together with little attention given to aesthetics. Adrianna had been forced to marry because the castle had been on the verge of crumbling into the caldera of lava below, but no longer was it in a state of disrepair. Now, its turrets stood tall. Its white stone gleamed. Stained glass of macabre scenes filled its windows. Spiderwebs still decorated Krag's Doom, but now they were shimmering, gossamer things of elegance and beauty. In other words, her family of architects had been busy.

Beneath it, great segmented tendrils of lava rock hung down from the castle to nearly touch the surface of the molten lava below. Thousands of years of eruptions, bubbling lava and magic had caused the lava to solidify into long limbs. Each had been chipped and cut away until it looked like an enormous spider leg, complete with segments and stray bits of stone that looked like hairs. It looked as if the castle could come alive at any moment and walk down the side of the mountain. The illusion of an arachnid didn't stop at the legs. Now that the white stone had been scrubbed clean, the windows looked like the eyes of a spider; the door, with its pattern of iron and wood was the fangs.

The bridge leading to the door had been replaced as well. Instead of rickety rope and wooden boards, now it was silk with thin slats of obsidian—dragon stone, it was often called—between them. It appeared no sturdier than it had before, but instead of old and rickety, it looked delicate and intimidating. The bridge was a marriage of spider and dragon, just like the castle itself. It had been built as an alliance between the two families, to bond them together and finally take back the world from other arrogant races: elves and dwarves, with their endless proselytizing and moral superiority. The ancient races had been right in the end, though. Generations ago, a dragon prince had betrayed his bride and driven the spiderfolk from the castle. Krag's Doom had belonged to the Valkannas for thousands of years, and would still, had Adrianna not married Richard.

They started across the bridge. Adrianna stepped across easily enough and told Clayton to do the same. Surely the golem would have cracked the slats had they not been enchanted. As it was, they didn't so much as creak beneath his bulk. If they were to fall, Adrianna didn't know if she'd be able to save herself, let alone Clayton. Her exoskeleton was cracked in a dozen places. She was missing a leg. She needed to molt, and she needed to do so now.

They made it to the gate, and the portcullis slowly drew itself open. Adrianna sighed—for the last time, she told herself. Here she would stay until she was healed, a pawn trapped between her mother and husband, between a legacy she never wanted and a future she detested, to be used and manipulated and—

The door opened, revealing only darkness within. And then, a flash of light, a gout of flame, and there were bright colors everywhere. Her mom was smiling, and Richard was running to her, arms open, pointy-toothed smile looking perfect with his beard.

'Surprise!'

They had thrown her a welcome home party.

This was going to be a difficult week.

Chapter 76

Asakusa

It was raining. Thick, heavy drops that hardly moved left or right from the absence of wind. Asakusa loved the rain. He loved the way it drove most people below deck. He loved how half the *Hungry Trawler*—the ship he and Ebbo had chartered for their mission to retrieve the hammer he'd dropped— was lost to the raindrops. He liked how the moon shone brightly enough to just barely shine through the dark splotches in the clouds. He liked how the rain felt on his hair. He loved the feel of it on his skin. He savored every drop, except for the drops that fell on his right hand.

Currently he had a manacle around that wrist, a sign of his latest demonic Corruption bestowed upon him by the Gatekeeper with whom he'd made a pact. Asakusa found it comforting that past the manacle, he actually had a something resembling his own flesh. A week ago, he'd only had a mass of writhing maggots for much of his body. All that was gone thanks to a magical staglion. When the surprisingly judgmental creature had healed him, Asakusa had hoped that perhaps it would null his contract with his Gatekeeper as well, but the manacle proved otherwise. But Asakusa wasn't complaining, because at least this corruption looked like a human hand. It was bony, dried and desiccated, like flesh that had died from dehydration, but better than writhing maggots. It couldn't feel the rain, though.

The manacle itself looked kind of cool, too. Adrianna would probably like it. He shook his head and pushed the spider princess from his mind as soon as he thought her. He had to retrieve his weapon, *Byergen*, the stone hammer, and then rejoin her in the battle that she said was coming with the yellow skeletons. He desperately wished that he hadn't dropped the hammer so that he could be with Adrianna right now, accompanying her to family's castle and maybe punching her arrogant husband in the face for good measure, but alas, he knew as well as anyone that he couldn't battle the dragon prince without *Byergen*. Asakusa shook his head. *Doesn't matter, doesn't matter, doesn't matter,* he thought. None of that mattered until he had his hammer.

At least it was raining. He loved the rain.

'Sucks it's raining, huh?'

Asakusa sighed. He knew his peace of mind could have only lasted so long. 'I thought you would like the rain. Isn't your family a bunch of farmers?'

Ebbo Brandyoak shrugged his tiny shoulders. He only came up to Asakusa's waist. His curly, silvery-blonde hair was still dry, hidden beneath a hood that seemed to change color to match his background. Currently it looked brownish and wet, so it blended in quite well with the ship.

'There's an aquifer that runs beneath most of the islands that make up the Farm. We need rain, of course, but old Burpa used to say that—'

'I'm not in the mood for one your grandfather's dumb sayings,' Asakusa interupted.

Ebbo didn't so much as pause. '—there are features in the karstic limestone at the very bottom of the ocean, the stuff that all this volcanic rock rests on top of, that let the water in but keep out the salt of the sea. Used to be islanders who went down there to mine the salt deposits, but since the fishmen started trading with the humans in S'kar-Vozi, we don't need to do that, o' course.'

Asakusa blinked in the rain. His usually spiky black hair was wet and smeared across his face. 'That's… surprisingly informative for Burpa.'

'Old Burpa used to say even a parrot sounds smart to someone lonely for conversation.'

Asakusa gritted his teeth. This was why he couldn't stand Ebbo. Every time he thought they were having an actual conversation, the cursed halfling had to go and say something vaguely demeaning. Was Asakusa supposed to be the parrot in the story? No. He was supposed to be the lonely person. He scowled.

'I told Adrianna I would do anything for her. I should've made an exception for listening to you.'

'I'm not happy about this either,' Ebbo said from beneath his hood, even though it was his idea to come with Asakusa in the first place. 'I don't know what good I'm supposed to be. You dropped your hammer, not me. How am I going to help you fetch it? And what if it's underwater? Which seems pretty likely, by the way, what with it falling into a chasm filled with water. I can't swim!'

'We have gillyweed for that.'

Ebbo cringed. 'You ever taste that stuff? It's horrible. Tastes like snot.'

'It makes your body produce mucous that transports oxygen from the water to your blood, so yeah, that makes sense.'

'It's horrible. Doesn't hardly have a kick at all.'

Asakusa's expression darkened. 'I thought you were clean.'

'I am clean!' Ebbo snapped. 'I've been clean for twenty-three days now. Twenty. Three! And now I'm going to have to take some of this gillyweed just so I don't drown, and even if I don't get eaten by a shark, I'm going to have to fight going into relapse. That's not easy, moving around the Archipelago. There's magick everywhere. Even now, I feel it. There's something out there, in the storm, something big. Do you hear it singing? It's like a leviathan. Something big, with words longer than ours. Powerful, it is.'

'A leviathan?'

'What the wizards call whales!' Ebbo snapped. He shook his head, seeming to shake away the bad mood. 'It'd be foolish for me to try to find it, though,' Ebbo continued in his regular voice, quiet and timid. 'I can't swim, and it'd probably eat me, whatever it is. There's no need. Not with the gillyweed.'

'You do want to get high!'

'Of course, I don't,' Ebbo said, growing vicious in a blink of the eye. 'Not with what could have happened with Clayton.' And just like that, the islander's rage was replaced with remorse. 'But I still think about it... You know what it's like. Don't tell me you don't. I know you enjoy that Corruption of yours. Getting all those maggots washed away and getting all that flesh back so you can let it consume you for her sake, that's what drives you. Pointless as that is. You're addicted to the sacrifice.'

'Shut up,' Asakusa said. 'If that was true, I would've opened a Gate long ago and found my hammer without the ship.'

Ebbo shook his head. 'No, you wouldn't. Adrianna asked you to sail here with me, and we both know you shouldn't take me through the Gates. Not after everything that happened with Chevron the staglion.'

There was truth to that. Hard truth, considering Adrianna was currently going home to visit her husband. *Husband*. Asakusa could still hardly bring himself to say the word. Even thinking it made him angry. He'd had feelings for Adrianna since he'd met her. And then she went off and married a dragon prince, just because their families had arranged the marriage centuries ago. Sure, by doing so she brought her family's castle back into their possession after thousands of years of living in caves scattered about the Archipelago. Asakusa sighed. They were pretty good reasons, better reasons than he had.

He was just some idiot who'd sold his soul to a Gatekeeper and not even been able to save the person he'd tried to save.

'I want to be clean,' Ebbo said. 'I really do, that's why I came with you after all, but it's *hard.*'

'Be quiet.'

'Come on, Asakusa. Don't you think this is why Adrianna wanted us to go together? She wanted you to keep me clean, and, well I can't keep clean *and* quiet. That'd be impossible.'

'Shut up!'

'Now you're just being rude.'

Asakusa grabbed the little islander by the scruff of his neck and lifted him up. 'Shut. Up,' he hissed, then pointed out into the rain.

Ebbo followed the direction of his finger. Asakusa knew he saw it too when his mouth made an O of surprise.

'A ship,' Ebbo said.

Asakusa nodded.

'That's odd. Islanders don't travel in the rain, and no one else would come down this channel.'

'Just be quiet and listen,' Asakusa said. He very much doubted that the ship was filled with a fresh harvest of blueberries or some other cash crop headed for the free city. He had dropped a powerful weapon, an *incredibly powerful* weapon, into the ocean. In S'kar-Vozi, there was an entire religion devoted to gathering weapons so they could defeat their dark god when it returned. If they got wind of what happened to *Byergen*—and it wasn't like Asakusa could hide the fact that he was no longer dragging the unliftable hammer everywhere he went—they'd come for it. He didn't exactly think the Cthult of Cthulu was evil, but he didn't trust them either.

Through the rain they could hear the slap of oars as the crew of this other ship pushed it on through the storm.

'Let's get closer,' Asakusa said.

The two went out into the rain, all the way to the edge of the Hungry Trawler. The other ship moved by, not so far away in the narrow channel. Its deck was deserted except for someone at the wheel.

'Is that a skeleton?' Ebbo asked in a nervous whisper.

'It can't be,' Asakusa said.

But it was. There was a skeleton at the wheel. A skull stuck out from a fine coat. It was sickly yellow in the pale, rainy moonlight. Bits of flesh still clung to it, and its hands seemed to still be skinned. That meant Adrianna was right. Chemok—the god, curse, or whatever it was they had discovered to be animating the skeletons of the dead—had moved beyond farming and left the Blighted Island. What was it doing here? Asakusa took a deep breath, trying to stay calm despite still being weaponless.

Ebbo, on the other hand, was freaking out. 'Oh, raspberries, don't let them snatch me! What are we going to do?'

'I'm going to get closer,' Asakusa said.

'No, don't leave me here!'

'I'll just be a second.'

'Adrianna said not to!'

'She said not to Corrupt my whole body looking for the stone hammer. That's different from investigating a fricking skeleton. At distances this short, my Corruption will hardly spread.'

Asakusa felt for the Dark Key buried in his hand and opened a Gate. The fingernails of his right hand ignited into black flames unaffected by the rain. Lightning cracked from the manacle at his wrist into a circle of swirling runes. Asakusa stepped through the Gate and into the Ways of the Dead.

He found himself on a stone path. The bricks were gleaming white, all of a uniform size. A low balustrade went along either side of the path, lined with swirling elvish script. The way to the Elven afterlife, Asakusa thought. Sure enough, ahead of him were the misty, half-solid spirits of elves. They were moving so slowly along the path that they seemed to be standing still. Asakusa stepped past them. The spirits ignored him. The black flames burning at the tip of his fingers cast a shadow that would hide him from the souls there.

As he walked down the path, he glanced at his Corruption. The manacle was just slightly farther up his arm. But he had flesh to spare, especially if he only used Gates to move over short distances. He'd have to talk to Seltrayis about how to heal it later. With her help, hopefully they could get the manacle to move back down his arm, as they had for countless other Corruptions. Problems for another day.

Up ahead, he saw the other Gate. He didn't know exactly how he formed the pairs of Gates; it came instinctively to him. That was part of the Contract. He simply reached out for them with the Dark Key in his hand, and they answered. He thought where he wanted to go, and if it was possible, the Dark Key opened two Gates along a path and made it so. As long as they were close, the cost of flesh was low. Still, Asakusa hurried. He had just gotten his arm back; he didn't want to lose it so soon.

He approached the other Gate—a swirling arch of shifting runes with the barest semblance of the outline of bricks. He peered through it, using precious time, but he had to be sure. It looked out on the deck of the other ship. Barrels and crates were everywhere. Each was painted with a yellow skull. Chemok-brand foodstuffs. They'd been growing more and more popular in S'kar-Vozi. Asakusa shuddered. He knew the secret of their creation. At least, he thought he did. He had to be sure.

He saw no movement, so he stepped onto the deck, shutting the Gate behind him. The manacle hadn't moved up his arm much, but now sported a few links of thin chain.

He ignored that for now, though, and explored the ship.

There didn't seem to be a crew down in the cargo hold, but Asakusa had seen oars splashing, which meant that more of Chemok's minions had to be nearby. What did that mean, that the skeleton farmers were now able to pilot ships? Were they getting smarter? Asakusa had assumed that the Baron and vampire, Rolph Katinka, had been controlling them, but now he was less sure. What would a vampire know of steering a ship? They hated running water.

Regardless of what was animating them, Asakusa needed to figure out why they were here. He couldn't bring himself to think it was a coincidence that the ship was right where his hammer had dropped. He'd used the weapon against hordes of the skeletons already, with smashing results. If they got it before he did, there'd be one less weapon the living would have against the dead.

He crept down into cargo hold and out of the rain. He immediately missed its enveloping presence and how it muffled his sound.

'You think the guy driving was really one of Chemok's skeletons?'

Asakusa turned with a start. There was Ebbo, standing beside him. His elven dagger, *Deondadel*, was drawn and pointing back and forth wildly.

'How did you get over here?' Asakusa hissed.

'I came through the Gate with you. Don't worry, those souls hardly noticed me.'

'Hardly noticed! You'll bring the Demon King down on us.'

Ebbo shrugged. 'Better be quick.'

Asakusa fought back the urge to throw the islander overboard. This was no place for Ebbo's shenanigans.

Or so Asakusa thought, until a group of skeletons came down the stairs leading into the hold. Asakusa didn't try to hide. He never did.

'Ebbo, behind me!' Asakusa shouted, but the islander was gone. Asakusa reached for his hammer, remembering much too late that they were currently looking for it and then the skeleton removed one of its arms and clubbed him heavily across the brow with its own humerus.

The clouds grew so thick as to completely hide the light of the moon filtering into the belly of the ship, the rain picked up, and Asakusa slipped into unconsciousness.

Chapter 77

Adrianna

The party wasn't *that* bad. Adrianna's webmother had made crab. Steamed above the lava below them and seasoned with sea salt, it reminded her of home, despite being served in this place where she'd spent hardly any time. There had been fish too, and red meat from the Etterqueen knew where. No fruits or vegetables or grain, nothing that would make the spider princess sick. She was accustomed to carefully watching her diet when she was out in the Archipelago; it felt decadent to be able to eat anything and everything at the party. At least her family and her new in-laws had that in common. They were all flesh-eaters.

And her family was here. All seven of her older sisters, with their horrible sneering faces, clicking their mandibles at her, chastising her for not having any hair on her face. That, at least, felt like home. The Lich was here too. He'd greeted her with a shriek, and they'd shared a dance, taking Adrianna back to when she was a little girl who hardly knew how to tie her hair up. The Lich had seemed different, though—twitchy, nervous even. An odd emotion for an undead wizard who was thousands of years old. The motes of yellow light glowing in his empty eye sockets had flicked around the room. Adrianna could tell he'd wanted to tell her something, but subtlety was not one of the Lich's strengths. His communication was limited to his beautifully flowing script and the dry shrieks that emanated from his throat, over his leathery tongue and past his lips, pulled back from his teeth. He'd tried to whisper, but Adrianna hadn't understood. When the song had ended, he'd bowed and looked at her sternly. Adrianna knew the look; she'd seen it a hundred times when she'd been summoned to his tomb. How odd it was, to think his resting place had been moved to this castle.

After that she'd danced with her father-in-law, an old, withered man with dark skin and darker hair. He was as prickly wearing his human glamour as he was in his true form, a spiny black dragon who legend said had once had scales red as blood. He'd asked her almost exclusively about children. Adrianna had tried to smile while she'd limped along, her wounds hidden with her hair Folded up. She'd explained something about the moon cycles and needing to eat the flesh of a celestial to begin gestation. Her father-in-law had been nonplussed. When the dance had ended, he'd sent for a few flamehearts, no doubt telling them to begin the hunt, but she had time. A storm had settled over Krag's Doom, and the flamehearts wouldn't go out in the rain.

After that she'd danced with her webmother, who'd poked and prodded at her, fussing over her wounds and blinking at her from behind the six frames of her spectacles. How Adrianna had missed her mom.

'He's got a good head on his shoulders,' her webmother had said, and Adrianna's feelings of love had evaporated.

'Firm, but just. We could have done worse.'

'Mother, he knows how to use my hair to control me! I was like a puppet at the wedding.'

'Oh, everyone feels that way,' her webmother had said before chattering on about the repairs that had been made to the castle. Apparently, they'd returned just in time. The spell that kept Krag's Doom afloat was nearly gone. Her webmother, Virianna, had sent for thirteen sorcerers, but of course getting anyone to come to Krag's Doom was an ordeal, and then asking them to perform a spell that took thirteen months to cast was another thing entirely. Virianna was currently considering other methods of keeping the castle from sinking into the lava pit.

On top of all that, Adrianna had to dance with Richard. She'd been avoiding her husband all night, but between her webmother, her father-in-law, her sisters, and Clayton, she'd finally acquiesced.

The spiderfolk struck up a tune on their stringed instruments, and the flamehearts joined in with their shed horns. Adrianna had never heard anything like it. Spiderfolk exclusively played strings made from their own silk. They liked to dance, so the songs were lively and fast-moving. This version had been slowed down, and the soft horns of the flamehearts—made either from their dead or some sort of molting process, Adrianna didn't know—added a velvety richness to the sound. Like the entire party, it was simultaneously familiar and brand new. Much as she didn't want to, Adrianna found herself quite taken by the music.

And then Richard was there. One hand in the small of her back, the other holding her hand, gently turning her arm, checking her wounds. His golden eyes burned with concern, as if flames lived inside them. He was wearing a red, tailed suit. The pinstripes had spiders here and there, tiny little things that were hardly noticeable. An elegant touch. His hair was pulled back into a ponytail, the end of it spiky, hinting at his true dragon form. His beard was immaculate. And that smile. It was as if he'd been saving it only for Adrianna.

'My darling, are you hurt?'

'Like you would not believe.'

'Then let's leave this place. I've prepared your bedchambers.'

'Just like that, you want to score?'

'I wouldn't dream of it. Not with you injured, not without you feeling the way I do. Send your golem to check for traps, if you will, but please send him soon. It's painful to watch you limp along. I miss your elegance, your finesse, the way you finger my dagger.'

Adrianna's breath caught despite herself. She didn't like Richard. He was an evil dragon prince, trained from boyhood to manipulate her. But even the Etterqueen would have to admit, he was good at it. The song, the clothes, the smile, his words. Everything about him was perfect. Unlike Asakusa. Grumpy, frumpy, self-sacrificing Asakusa. Why was she even thinking of him at a time like this?

She looked out a stained glass window into the storm, wondering where he was.

Chapter 78

Asakusa

'Psst.'

Asakusa opened his eyes. He was in the dark, surrounded by barrels and crates. In the greenish glow of an unseen light source, he could just barely make out yellow skulls burned into the barrels. There seemed to be a leak coming from his skull. He sighed. At this rate, he wasn't going to get back to Adrianna anytime soon.

'Hey, psst!' The leak was getting louder, thundering through the pain.

Something smacked him on the head. The pain flared up, and Asakusa grunted.

'Let me go, whoever you are. I have powerful friends who don't want to see me harmed.'

'I'm flattered! I thought I was the only one who threatened captors with our party.'

Asakusa couldn't see the islander, but he knew his voice far better than he wanted to. It was Ebbo. He wanted to be more thankful than he was. 'I wasn't threatening anyone with you. I was referring to Adrianna.'

'Right, like she's gonna save you,' Ebbo said, stepping from the shadows. Asakusa was always shocked to see just how easily Ebbo could hide. The islander had been standing almost directly in front of him, in the shadow of a barrel. His cloak was wrapped around him, and in the green light his high cheekbones looked like one of the skulls. Now that Asakusa knew where he was, it seemed impossible to think that the islander could have been hiding there just a moment ago.

'Just untie me already, so we can get my hammer from the bottom of the sea and get out of here.'

'Why? So you can insult me further?'

'I can insult you just fine right now.'

'Sounds like you don't need me to untie you, then.'

Asakusa scowled, hoping Ebbo could see his annoyance in the low light. He flexed, straining at his bonds, but he didn't break them. His last Corruption had taken the form of thousands of writhing worms; maybe those could have broken his bonds, but now all he had was a manacle at his wrist and an undead hand. The manacle had a chain, but no sharp corners to work at the ropes.

'Ebbo, come on, untie me.' It was as close to pleading as Asakusa had ever come with Ebbo. He didn't like it.

'Not sure if I can.'

'Why? Because you're twitching so bad without magick to calm your hands?'

'See! This is what I'm talking about! You just assume it's because of magick! For your information, I tried untying the ropes. It's good hemp, wet from the rain, and all your struggling just tightened the knots again. Those skeletons must have been sailors in a previous life.'

There was a grunt from across the hold, and the green light started to come closer. Asakusa turned to tell Ebbo to hide, but the islander was already gone.

Through the barrels and crates came a couple of corpses. One had clearly been at sea for while; perhaps a dozen starfish ate at its bloated flesh. At places, the many-armed creatures had eaten all the way through the muscle, and the skeleton's yellow bones shone brightly through. The other corpse was short and looked like it had died in battle. A deep gash cut across its chest. Its jacket was wide open, revealing a wound crusty with blood. The light was coming from their eyesockets.

The corpse with the starfish knelt down, held up a finger to its bloated lips, and hissed over its yellow teeth.

'Sorry. I'm no good at charades,' Asakusa said.

Starfish smacked him across the face hard enough for the blackness to return. Asakusa fought to keep unconsciousness at bay and just barely managed to stay awake. When he opened his eyes, the two corpses were retreating, going back to whatever they were doing. And Ebbo was back.

Asakusa fought hard to push down his rage. 'Cut the ropes with your dagger, you stupid halfling!' was as close as he could manage.

'I'm not doing anything for you until you treat me with some respect!' Ebbo huffed. 'And the ropes have a cheap enchantment on them. They can be untied, but they move when you cut them.'

'Ebbo, I'm sorry. Can you just untie me, and we can do this another time, like when we're not at risk of joining an undead army?'

'This is the time! Why do you think Adrianna sent us together?'

'Because if you went to the castle, you'd try to lick all her relatives to get high.'

'Stop that!' Ebbo said and stamped his feet, drawing another grunt from across the room.

The corpses marched back over. Asakusa cursed at Ebbo, but the islander was gone.

Asakusa stood very still and tried not to look intimidating. It worked, for Axewound hissed 'Chemok.' Asakusa nodded as if he understood, and the two yellow-boned corpses walked away and back above deck. Asakusa was having trouble hearing, but it sounded like something was happening above deck. Something with swords.

Asakusa didn't know what to do. He closed his eyes and felt out for a Gate. There were some all around him, but not one below where he was sitting. He couldn't go anywhere. He gritted his teeth and—

A spray of water in his face set Asakusa sputtering.

'Oh, sorry. I thought you were unconscious again.' Ebbo was grinning, the little punk.

'Some of us can maintain control.'

Ebbo crossed his arms. 'Do you want me to bring the skeletons back?'

'They're not skeletons.'

'Proto-skeletons, then! Mangled undead puppets with crunchy yellow skeletal interiors, whatever!' Ebbo huffed. 'They have yellow bones, just like you said the farmers did, just like the mermaid that tried to seduce me. They're bad news.'

'And you were going to call them back to torture your friend? '

'Well, *that's* news. I didn't know you thought of me as a person, let alone a friend. All you ever do is insult me and insist I can't survive without magick.'

'You *can't* survive without magick!'

'You use your Corruption more than I do magick. At least I'm trying to stop! You know how hard that is? For an islander like me to try to quit? It doesn't affect all of us, you know. Most islanders are impervious to the pulls of magick. None of us are wizards or sorcerers, not even druids, despite growing plants all day. Most islanders couldn't care less about a whiff of magick! You know what makes me different?'

Asakusa blinked at Ebbo. He'd never seen the islander so mad. 'No, I guess I don't. What make you different?'

'You think I know?' Ebbo's laughter had a manic twinge to it. 'You think if I knew, I'd still be doing the stuff? I know what happens to islanders who take too much. We all do. Transcendence or whatever.' Ebbo shuddered.

Asakusa knew. Everyone in S'kar-Vozi had seen the islanders who took too much magick. They lay on street corners or in halfway houses, eyes half open, a smile on their faces, staring at a world that wasn't there. Those that were loved would be force fed, those that weren't starved, but the result was the same for both. Once an islander Transcended, there was no going back. Some said it was just a matter of time before it happened to a user, others claimed some islanders were able to go their entire lives without Transcending.

'I know you want to stop,' Asakusa said.

'You don't know anything about me. You just think I'm some dumb islander. You didn't even think I thought to use my dagger to cut the ropes!' Ebbo was yelling, which did not go unnoticed.

Asakusa heard footsteps, faster this time, as if they were coming from farther away. Ebbo was already gone.

Starfish and Axewound marched over. Starfish dragged Asakusa to his feet and held his ropes. Axewound put a finger to his sunken lips. Asakusa spit at him. The corpse drew back to strike Asakusa, and punched him in the gut. There was something familiar about that punch, and that axe wound, now that Asakusa had been reminded so politely. He seemed to remember a dwarf from S'kar-Vozi who'd had a similar penchant for beatings and had met his end by an axe. But of course, he'd been dumped in Bog's—

A shadow leapt through the air. Ebbo was on Axewound's back. He stabbed it in the eye with his dagger. A yellow light flashed, then the corpse fell to the ground. The eyesocket was cracked, and the yellow faded like an infection treated with the proper herbs. Without the skull, the corpse ceased to be animated. Starfish roughly shoved Asakusa to the ground and looked around, its glowing eye sockets making the shadows dance.

Asakusa—knowing what to look for—saw one of the shadows staying still while the others moved. The light from the corpse's eyes swept past, and then the shadow moved. Ebbo sliced the meat at the back of the protoskeleton's leg—curse it, now Asakusa was using the term—and it stumbled. Ebbo stabbed it in the face, cracking the skull. The light faded and the body fell to the ground. The yellow color faded from the exposed bones. It really was some like some sort of infection that was harbored in the skull.

'You're welcome,' Ebbo said, appearing in Asakusa's lap. 'Now, tell me everything. I know you won't listen to me, but I'll listen to you.'

'What are you talking about?'

'Why are you Corrupted? What deal did you make?'

'Now is not the time.'

'You have about eight minutes before the other watch comes down here to switch them out, maybe less.'

'Skeletons don't trade watches.'

'Ha! Told you they're skeletons!'

'Ebbo, untie me!'

'Not until you talk. You act so high and mighty about my addiction, and you're right, I have no story to tell. I'm just a loser who got lucky when Clayton noticed me. I know I've only been with you guys for half a year, but time's up. What's your story, demon boy? What was so sweet to make you sell your soul? I know that story about your sister is sour strawberries, so give me the real juice.'

'Ebbo!'

'Spill it, or I get the captain down here. That one can talk. Maybe he can tell me why you're still alive. I bet it's because he wants that arm.'

Asakusa gritted his teeth. 'Now is not the time, halfling!'

Ebbo chafed at the slur. Asakusa knew he shouldn't have said it—Adrianna and Clayton were always chiding him for his language—but he'd grown up poor, and he'd watched fat halflings come to his city and grow fatter. It was a hard habit to break, especially when one of them was refusing to help him for their own selfish reasons.

'What did my old Burpa used to say about time? That's right, I think it was a song he sang.' Ebbo cleared his throat to sing.

'Time is always right for a chat between old friends.
Especially when pirates come, to do their very ends.
I'd like to think that friends are true, and always tell their tales,
Yet they can be worse than lettuce, after meeting snails!'

Ebbo cleared his throat and began another verse. Asakusa cut him off before he tried to rhyme 'Asakusa the rotten-berry' with anything.

'Okay, okay, I'll talk! Just stop singing. If they find those corpses, they'll come after you.' Truthfully, Asakusa didn't think they were going to get any more visitors. He could *definitely* hear the sounds of weapons clashing up above, and the storm was getting harder, too.

'I'll hide, and it's not worse than dealing with you all of the time.'

There was a creak of wood from one side of the ship, and the deck seemed to tilt to the right. Starboard? Asakusa didn't really know ships. He'd been too poor to go on them until he'd met Adrianna.

'Something's happening. Untie me.'

'I'll go check it out.'

'Ebbo, wait!'

'Thanks for using my name and not my race, but no, I won't untie you.'

'You're being ridiculous!'

'You know what's ridiculous? That my friend who insults me constantly and has been lying for years about losing his own sister, won't even tell the truth to save his own life.'

Asakusa tried to control his breathing. The crates were starting to slide. It was only a matter of time before a barrel tipped over and rolled into him. He struggled at the ropes. He really couldn't get them to budge.

'How did you know I was lying about my sister?'

Ebbo smirked triumphantly. 'I thought it was a lie because you never said her name. I didn't really know, but I do now!'

Asakusa grimaced. Betraying even that much of his story sent a needle of foolish regret into his heart. He hadn't told anyone, ever, not even Adrianna. The thought of telling more tied his stomach in knots tighter than those binding them.

The ship lurched in the other direction, sending Ebbo sprawling and Asakusa falling on his side.

'Ebbo, they hooked something big and it just broke free! We need to get out of here!'

'Using your Gates? No! You insult me for using a pinch of magick, and you regularly sell your soul to demons! I'm not going through one until I find out what makes you think you're so high and mighty.'

'Her name was Jiza!' Asakusa still found the name beautiful, even though he said it with such bitterness. It was the first time he'd said since it happened, though he thought of her every time he used a Gate and passed through the Ways of the Dead.

'Your sister?'

'No!' Damn it, Ebbo really was good at getting him to talk.

'Then who?' the islander pressed.

'I'm telling you, ok? Just untie me so we don't drown with a bunch of protoskeletons!'

'I don't think protoskeletons can drown.'

'Will you shut up!'

Ebbo shut up. Asakusa took a deep breath and began to talk. He found the words came fast, much faster than he wanted. He hadn't told anyone this story. As far as he knew, no one knew it except for the Gatekeeper Byorgenkyatulk, who had taken Asakusa's soul in exchange for his Corruption and the Dark Key buried in his hand that opened the Gates.

'All the kids in S'kar-Vozi liked Jiza. She was pretty, and funny, and cool. She always knew how to get scraps from Zultana's shop, so she dressed really well too. Jewelry and everything. We were playing in the sewers one day—'

'Ew, the sewers?'

'Not everyone grew up on a damn halfling farm with as much as you could eat, okay? Some of us grew up in places where no one could care less about us. Some of us watched people with nothing give up everything!' Asakusa bit back the words as soon as he said them, but for once, Ebbo didn't say anything. Asakusa was sort of impressed with the little islander. He was true to his word and went about working at the knots on the magick rope. Asakusa found himself continuing to talk. He had always thought that telling the story would hurt more and more until it reached its horrible conclusion of his enslavement, but he found that the opposite was true. With each passing sentence, each stupid, childish mistake, it hurt less. He'd kept it bottled up so long, it was like a storm after the dry summer months in the Archipelago. No stopping it.

'We were playing in the sewers and Jiza saw something deeper than we usually go. We were scared, but we kept daring each other to go deeper and deeper to find this bauble, or whatever it was, so we could give it to her. We made it pretty far in when one of us got snared in a kobold trap. Wasn't hurt bad, but couldn't keep going either. The others were helping untie him. Jiza wanted to keep going. I... I couldn't say no. The idea of being alone with her, and finding this treasure, was just too much. It—I kept thinking it might be my first kiss.' Asakusa shook his head. He had been such an idiot.

'In the sewers?' Ebbo asked, before muttering, 'I'm getting closer, by the way, but every time I loosen part, it tries to retie itself. It's going to take a minute.'

Asakusa normally would have assumed that a lie, but at the moment, he didn't care. He continued his story, the weight lifting from his shoulders as the boat again tilted further and further to starboard.

'We just kept going and going, deeper and deeper. Eventually the floor dried out and the tunnels went from carved to bricks.'

'Like the Ways of the Dead.' Ebbo stabbed a length of rope that he had tossed away. It had been trying to wriggle back.

'Exactly, but I had never seen anything like it before. Jiza kept going deeper and deeper, teasing me about being scared, telling me I was brave, so I kept going too. Finally, we found the sparkle. A pile of gems on a piece of parchment, sitting on a plinth.'

'A trap.'

'That's what I said to Jiza, but she reached out and grabbed them anyway. Her finger got pricked on a gem, and a drop of her blood fell on the parchment. That's when Tulk appeared. Said she'd traded her soul for great riches.'

'What did you do then?' Ebbo said. He'd paused in his work.

'Don't stop!' Asakusa said as the ropes tried to retie themselves.

Ebbo shook himself and went back to working at the ropes. He was totally engrossed in Asakusa's story, oblivious to what was happening above them. Asakusa found that, for once, he didn't mind talking—and more, that he wouldn't stop. He couldn't.

'I told the demon to take me instead. I'd heard of Gatekeepers, of course, so I knew to ask him to give me the power to take her to safety, and he agreed. Stabbed the Dark Key in my hand, made me a thrall, and gave me power over the Gates. I opened one for Jiza, but...'

'She didn't take it.'

Asakusa shook his head, pushing the ropes from his body. Ebbo had managed to cut away pieces as he untied them, so now there tiny, six-inch lengths on the floor. Still, their magick compelled them to bind their prisoner, and they struggled weakly at the metal clasps on Asakusa's black boots. He was free. And still the story came. He was so close to the end.

'She said she wanted the wealth. So Tulk gave it to her. Gave her more wealth than she could dream of. So far as I know, she lives as a princess in the Ways of the Dead. Got married to Tulk. Bastard invited me to the wedding.'

'And he didn't give you your soul back?'

'Showed me in the Contract what I'd asked for. The power to get her out of there, not for her soul. So, after all that, I use the power as I see fit until I'm consumed. I wasn't using it too great either, until I met Adrianna and started helping her a couple of years ago.'

Ebbo was silent for a blessed moment. The sounds of the ship more than filled the void. 'That's seriously messed up, Asakusa. I'm sorry.'

Asakusa didn't have time to say anything back about how he was sorry, too. About how he had first started following Adrianna because she had wealth and didn't care about it. About how he didn't even know if he even could give up his Corrupting power, because being a thrall was better than being some dirt-poor street urchin from the free city. Asakusa didn't have time to say anything, because in that moment a tentacle covered in barnacles and jagged oyster shells smashed through the bulwark, and water sprayed into the hold.

Chapter 79

Ebbo

'Open a Gate!' Ebbo said, sheathing his dagger and dodging beneath the flailing tentacle. It was huge, thick as the mast of a ship. The barnacles and oysters covering it seemed a sort of armor, making it impervious to the splinters from the barrels it crashed through. It got thicker and thicker, until it had plugged much of the hole it had made. Water sprayed in around the edges. 'Open-a-gate-open-a-gate-open-a-gate!'

'We have to find out what was making the ship tilt like that,' Asakusa said, cool as a cucumber left to chill in a spring back on Brandyoak Isle.

Ebbo was not nearly so calm. 'You don't think it was the freaking *Kraken* smashing in here?'

'I think they might have snagged my hammer. And besides, just a second ago you didn't want me to open anything.' Asakusa nonchalantly dodged a blow from the tentacle.

'Just a second ago we weren't about to be crushed by a god's tentacle! We could drown! And I know you've been all messed up since taking the High Path, but you have a new Corruption now, as long as you only travel short distances—like say the distance between where we are right now and twenty feet above us—you'll be able to open like a hundred of those stupid Gates.'

'I might just need to.' Asakusa ran for the stairs that led out of the hold.

Ebbo went to follow, but then the tentacle retracted, and water sprayed into the ship and knocked the islander off his feet.

'Asakusa!' he tried to yell, but only bubbles came out. Ebbo panicked. He couldn't swim! The force of the water smashed him against a crate. Ebbo scrambled to stand up and found the water was only ankle-deep, but considering the hold had been dry only seconds before, he didn't exactly find that comforting. He made for the stairs.

A pile of barrels crashed down into his path as the ship lurched toward the hole, spraying more water into the hold. Ebbo jumped out of the way and splashed into the water. Once again he scrambled to his feet. The water was already past his waist. It was good he could touch the bottom, but then again, the ship would only have a bottom for another few minutes. Although the current that had knocked him down was gone. Ebbo glanced toward the hole. Mistake. There were two tentacles now, both reaching into the ship. There were also a dozen lobsters working their way across the walls. Kraken. This was definitely the Kraken. One of the two tentacles pulled back, and more water flooded into the ship. Now it was indeed too deep for Ebbo to touch the bottom.

Ebbo tried to swim, but he just didn't know how. His arms and legs thrashed wildly, water surged down his throat. He tried to scream again, but it was no use. He was going to drown in the hold of a skeleton ship. That had to be ironic or something.

In that moment Ebbo wished he believed in a god. There were so many to choose from in the Archipelago. Some even worshiped the Kraken itself, or more like recognized it as a deity that must be grappled with. Apparently, the amalgamation of sea beasts that formed the destructive god, and even created its own weather, inspired those in the Cthult of Cthulu to gather weapons to fight the Kraken. Ebbo didn't know if their goal was to defeat it for good or just to keep it well-pruned, but he wished some of the fishy fanatics were here now.

Truly, though, he only found himself searching for god because he didn't have any magick. Right now, he would've snorted the spider princess's husband's fingernails, if only for one last taste before he went—but of course, Adrianna had made Clayton check him for every bit of magick, and left him only with a nasty, snotty ball of gillyweed.

Gillyweed!

As blackness closed in around him, Ebbo reached into his pocket and found the seaweed wrapped in its own mucous. He shoved it down his throat as the tentacles smashed more barrels to pieces. He could hear the cracks and booms through the water.

He forced the gillyweed down, an unpleasant sensation, like drinking slime soup. He remembered one time his mother had made a batch of soup from a plant called okra. It grew in the south of the Archipelago, where it was warmer she'd traded some whiskey for it. Whiskey could buy almost anything, as the big people were always desperate for it. She'd made a delicious stew, smells rich with thyme and bay, but she'd put in so much of the okra in that it had been like jelly! They'd fed it to a pig and eaten rye bread and butter for dinner that day, with plenty of ale to wash it down. Ebbo could almost remember the song they sang that night as he swam beneath the water.

Wait. He didn't know how to swim.

He looked at his hands. They were webbed and seemed to know exactly what they were doing. He felt at his neck. He'd grown gills! The gillyweed had worked. That explained the rush of memories. That was what magick did for islanders—it took them home, or where they wanted home to be. Some said that when one Transcended, their soul went back to another part of their life to live it all again, to enjoy every moment, to fix every mistake. But if this was the case, surely more islanders would chose a fate besides ending up a lifeless vegetable, slowly starving to death on the streets of S'kar-Vozi, vacant stares seeing nothing. No. Ebbo didn't believe that. He'd been to the Ways of the Dead; he knew that Transcendence was just the last step before an islander died. Asakusa had always been very clear—Asakusa!

Ebbo went after his friend, finding to his delight that not only could he breathe, but he could swim as strongly as an island seal! He pumped his legs in one sinuous motion and made it to the stairs. By this point they were completely submerged.

Ebbo got on deck just in time for it to go underwater. As soon as his gills left the water, he began to gasp for breath. He knew he could swim, but that didn't mean he wanted to jump into the water with a thousand angry sea creatures. But, fortuitously, the ship sunk further, and he could breathe again. The Kraken was doing a pretty good job of sinking them, then. All around the ship were barrels or their contents: olives, heads of fermented cabbage, pools of olive oil that somehow stayed on the surface of the frothing sea. It was like an enormous soup pot, stirred by a monstrous chef. His mother had once made soup like—Ebbo shook the thought from his brain. He'd been on magick enough to know its effects. And besides, it was an insult to his mother to compare her prized cooking spoon, carved from the oak tree they all lived in, to the giant tentacles wrecking the ship.

'Asakusa!' Ebbo called. He ran across the half sunken deck of the ship, through the rainstorm that the Kraken's power fueled, his gills aching for water. He couldn't see his friend anywhere. His friend. Ebbo laughed. He'd never thought of Asakusa as a friend, more of a persistent acquaintance. Though now that he thought of it, Asakusa did remind him of old Dobber Applecask; why, that Dobber would—

A skeleton smashed to pieces next to Ebbo, knocking him from his reveries. This gillyweed was stronger than he'd expected.

Ebbo focused on the parts of the ship that were still above water. It was crawling with skeletons, and the corpses that he still insisted on calling protoskeletons. In a panic, he jumped in a barrel and found he could breathe the briny olive juice fairly well. The yellow-boned undead were everywhere, chucking javelins at the Kraken, stabbing it with pikes. Some of the more adventurous ones even chopped at it with swords. None of it seemed any use. If they stabbed a tentacle, another would smash them to pieces. One of them actually wounded one of the tentacles pretty badly—slicing through the barnacles and managing to draw some purple blood—and it withdrew, only to be replaced by an enormous claw. Its dark blue shell looked as tough as any plate mail. It smashed through the deck, knocking its attackers to pieces.

Ebbo wondered how many people had seen not only the giant squid, but also the enormous crab that were said to make up the core of Kraken. Probably a lot, really. Seeing them both and living had to be the more difficult task.

Ebbo had to find Asakusa.

He tore his eyes from the Kraken. Asakusa wouldn't fight it, not without a weapon. So where was he? Ebbo peered out over the lip of his barrel of olives.

Suddenly the ship lurched toward the Kraken, like something had been holding it underwater and had let go. The momentum was enough to knock the Kraken from the side of the ship. There was a huge hole where the monster had been. It was covered in barnacles, starfish and tiny crabs. *The thing really is an ecosystem*, Ebbo thought.

The crabs scuttled away as the tentacle rose back from the sea and resumed its attack on the ship.

'Pickled blueberries!' Ebbo cursed. He never expected the god to as persistently annoying as its followers.

He looked over the edge of the ship, wondering how far to the nearest island, and how long the gillyweed would last. Too far and not long enough, he concluded.

And then a Gate opened and there was Asakusa. The manacle that topped his most recent corruption was only halfway up his forearm. The flesh below it looked dead. Well, not dead, as it was still motioning to close the Gate. More like dried meat. Above the manacle, Asakusa's arms still seemed normal, but of course that would change.

In his left hand he held *Byergen*, the Stone Hammer. Ebbo grinned. Asakusa could be sullen, grumpy and just plain rude to Ebbo—though now the islander understood that he was suffering from a heart broken long ago—but he made up for all that when it was time to fight.

'That's what was pulling the ship down,' Asakusa said, nodding at the hammer.

It made sense. The hammer couldn't be lifted except to attack. Even now, despite Asakusa having spent years with it, he let it rest on the deck of the sinking ship, only the handle of the stone hammer visible above the water. He'd drag it around until he got close enough to attack. That the skeletons were able to get it off the sea floor said something about their ropes. Ebbo had only ever seen one person lift the hammer without attacking, and he was a brawler strong enough to live in the Ringwall.

'Let's do this thing,' Asakusa said, flipping his rain-soaked hair out of his eyes.

'Do what? You mean escape?'

Asakusa gripped the hammer. 'I mean let's have seafood for dinner.'

'No, Asa, no! We have to get out of here! The mission was to get your hammer, and we did that. Yay!' Ebbo applaued for the thrall. 'Now, please, let's go home.'

But it was too late. A Gate opened, and Asakusa was through it.

Another Gate opened at the far edge of the ship and Asakusa emerged, swinging his hammer into the creature's claw. It cracked like a lobster on a human's plate.

The Kraken roared—a sound that seemed to come from the ocean itself. It was the sound of a hundred sharks in a frenzy, of a thousand clams being cracked, of ten thousands crabs being boiled alive. Lightning struck, thunder boomed, and then it attacked as one.

Tentacles struck, moving in a coordinated syncopation that Ebbo hadn't seen before. Asakusa dodged them all, opening and closing Gates and smashing the tentacles and any of the other beasts that made up the Kraken as he went. Ebbo really, *really*, wanted to get out of here. The olive brine was making his hands swell, and it was only a matter of time before either the gillyweed ran out or the skeletons found him hiding in their merchandise— and yet, watching Asakusa once more use his Gates without having to conserve his flesh was sweeter than raspberry jam. Gate after Gate blinked into existence—each one only costing the thrall a minuscule amount of flesh, since they were so close together geographically—and Asakusa flowed through them like an islander avoiding chores. He smashed creature after creature with his hammer. Tuna, *splat*. Barracuda, *splat*. Jellyfish, sailfish, man-sized squid. *Splat, splat, SPLAT!*

One of the tentacles struck him and knocked him backwards, but before the thrall splashed into the water, a Gate opened beneath him and another above the Kraken. He hurtled through, his hammer leading the fall.

A tentacle wrapped around his ankle and threw him. He careened through the air, opening a Gate before he hit the water. Another opened on the deck and he came through that, having lost not an iota of momentum. He smashed against the ship, blood dripping from his nose and one of his ears. His Corruption was to his shoulder now, and sported multiple metal cuffs connected by a few dangling chains.

'Let's finish this,' he muttered.

'Now's not the time for this!' Ebbo said. 'I'm not going to tell Adrianna you died heroically!'

But even those words didn't sway the thrall. Ebbo realized with rising panic that this was what Asakusa had always wanted. To sacrifice himself. That was how he'd got his Corruption. That was what he'd been trying to do for Adrianna since they'd met. That's what he'd tried to do for Jiza. Sacrifice made sense to someone who grew up thinking they were worth less than a crate of raspberries.

Asakusa opened a Gate. A metal collar appeared out of nowhere and snapped itself around his right ankle. A chain connected it to the one at his shoulder. Great. Just great, thought Ebbo. He'd taken a pinch of gillyweed so he could breathe. Meanwhile, Asakusa was going all-in, and Adrianna wasn't even here to see it.

'Come on!' Asakusa said, stepping through the Gate.

It was obvious that Asakusa was speaking to the Kraken and not Ebbo, and yet Ebbo didn't know what else to do. He couldn't leave Asakusa—not after what he did to Clayton, not after Asakusa telling him how he became Corrupted. Ebbo made for the Gate, and was stopped by a hand on his shoulder.

'Not another step, islander.'

Ebbo turned to see a figure even shorter than him, wearing a cloak that covered his face. Only a mess of black curls stuck out from under the hood, weighted down from the pouring rain. One hand was on Ebbo's shoulder, the other held a dagger with a black hilt.

He knew that dagger. Everyone in S'kar-Vozi knew that dagger. That was a Vecnos Industries Nightstrike6™. Just one of those babies cost like ten thousand coins. And there were six more of them on his belt.

'Vecnos!' Ebbo gasped, then nearly choked, as he'd stepped out of the barrel filled with brine where he'd been hiding.

'Brilliant deduction. Now get out of my way.'

Chapter 80

Ebbo

They were here! The Nine in the Ringwall were actually here! Well, Vecnos was, anyway. Ebbo's jaw hung open, a smile teasing the edges of his mouth. Then he dunked his head back in the barrel of olives so he could breathe.

'Wait, but where did you come from?' Ebbo sputtered before Vecnos stepped into a shadow.

'A boat. I received intel that Ragnar Parnok and his Cthult were after your friend's hammer. Figured it'd be a good time to figure out where you had gotten to. Didn't expect to find the skeletons here, too.' And with that, Vecnos vanished into a shadow.

'Clayton's okay!' Ebbo yelled, but when he saw Vecnos was gone, he added, 'you jerk,' under his breath.

But Ebbo didn't have much time to meditate on what he thought of the infamous assassin, for the Kraken was attempting to finally sink the ship. A tentacle covered in barnacles smashed down next to Ebbo, and the islander dove into the ocean.

He looked back up at the ship—most of it was now underwater—surprised the salt water didn't bother his eyes, and saw a Gate open up, pouring reddish light into the thunderstorm. Asakusa stepped from it and smashed the Kraken, but the monster was ready. It caught him in the chest with a tentacle and wrapped around the thrall. Ebbo didn't know if his friend would be squeezed to death or lacerated, there were so many oysters and barnacles growing on the tentacle.

But then the tentacle went dead, just limp, like it was something to be served at one of the seafood restaurants that the spider princess liked back in S'kar-Vozi. Vecnos stepped from a shadow and wiped blood from his dagger.

Boisenberries, is he cool! Ebbo thought, as an overwhelming feeling of relief washed over him, coloring the bad feelings he'd felt for Vecnos with new ones that were mostly about Ebbo's own continued survival. But before he could yell up to the islander assassin, there was the sound of a conch horn blowing.

Ebbo turned in the water to see another ship approaching in the night. It was crewed by fishmen. In cracks of lightning, Ebbo could see their scaled skin, tinted blue or green, their spiny hair, their webbed fingers. Most of them held glittering harpoons or wicked javelins. A few had pikes made of exotic and expensive kinds of wood.

The man standing at the prow held a sword made of coral in one hand, and an axe made of a sea turtle shell in the other. He was old, the spines on his head nearly gone, and his bare chest was covered in so many scars, Ebbo couldn't tell the original color. They crisscrossed in shades of dark blue and purple, and looked thick as pumpkin skin. It was Ragnar Parnok, the legendary barbarian from the Ringwall. It was said he'd been in so many battles and had so much scar tissue that he his skin was as tough as armor.

One of the fishmen behind him blew on the conch again, and the whole crew dove into the water.

Ebbo grinned. These guys were all zealots from the Cthult of Cthulu! They'd been stockpiling magick weapons for years in hopes of vanquishing their dark god, the Kraken, once and for all. Their prayer was spent preparing themselves for this battle. Even if they couldn't manage to defeat the Kraken, surely the Cthult could chop off some tentacles, crack some lobsters, and send the old Kraken packing with only enough power to make a springtime shower. Ebbo had talked mess about their record of failures in the past, but he now saw the value in their efforts. With the Cthult here, they were as good as saved! Well, hopefully. Ebbo looked for Ragnar's wife, Fyelna, a cleric said to be able to heal even the dead with her magickal broth. He had always wanted to try some. He shook the idea from his head. He was a clean islander now.

Fishmen sped through the water, kicking their legs in sinuous motions like dolphins, swimming toward the Kraken.

They didn't make it.

The Kraken was far more than just the colossal squid and enormous crab that were smashing the skeleton's ship. The Kraken was also the barnacles and oysters attached to its tentacles, the poisonous jellyfish in the water around Ebbo, the schools of razor-toothed fish. It was sea turtles and great gray sharks. The sea was filled with the Kraken, for the all these creatures together made up the monster. The storm above them was part of it, too; at least, that's what the priests from the Cthult would yell on the streets of S'kar-Vozi. The fishmen knew this, yet they swam into their god all the same, hungry for its death. They were slaughtered by the dozens for their insolence.

Their javelins and harpoons turned the water red. Some of them cried out. Ebbo found that with his gillyweed, he could hear their screams underwater clear as day. Sharks and turtles were knocked back and began to float or sink, depending on the contents of their guts, as the fishmen cleared a path for their leader, Ragnar Parnok.

Ragnar dove into the water and swam straight for the very center of the Kraken. He dove in and out of the water, like a dolphin who'd grown arms, until he was right in front of the squid and crab that fought or fornicated at the center of the amalgamation of sea-creatures-made-monster. He shot from the water like some sort of aquatic hawk, then spun three times in the air in a ridiculous front flip that somehow slowed his vertical motion and brought him back down onto his enemy. His coral sword stabbed into the squid part of the Kraken's eye. The sea-beast screamed, and the water thrashed all around Ebbo.

The Kraken whipped its tentacles about, knocking Asakusa from the air. Ebbo didn't see Vecnos. The islander had probably vanished in a shadow. Then the Kraken hit Ragnar with its pair of claws, each as a big as a horse. Well, that wasn't strictly accurate. One claw was as big as a pony, the other a destrier. The Kraken wisely led with the larger claw to hit the legendary barbarian.

Ragnar flew backwards from the force and smashed into the sinking skeleton ship.

Ebbo held his breath. The ship was still crawling with skeletons, but they didn't attack Ragnar. Instead they ran about, trying to bail water from their cracked vessel, as if there was any hope for the thing but to sink.

Ebbo smirked to himself. It was looking more and more like he and Asakusa were going to be heroes!

Ragnar was back on his feet and running toward the Kraken. Its thrashing had subsided, and it focused strike after strike at Ragnar. Any tentacle that came to close to the fishmen was severed with the sea turtle axe. The coral sword was still stuck in the squid's eye.

A tiny form materialized from the shadows, and Vecnos was there too. He ran along one of the Kraken's tentacles. Anytime it bucked or twisted, the islander simply jumped to another with a deft flip. Ebbo couldn't help but think he looked extremely cool doing it. Definitely cooler than Ebbo, with his webbed fingers and toes, treading water well *away* from the action.

A flash of red light, and Asakusa came through a Gate. A claw swung at him and another Gate opened. He was gone and back, behind the crab's claws, right above its eyestalks.

Ragnar and Vecnos reached it right at that moment.

Vecnos dodged a tentacle and stuck a dagger right in the squid's mantle, setting the beast to shuddering. He hit a nerve, Ebbo thought in amusement.

Ragnar brought his axe down just a span away from his coral sword, right between the squid part of the Kraken's eyes.

Asakusa lifted *Byergen* the stone hammer, as he always had to do to attack, and swung it down on top of the enormous crab's head. It cracked with a satisfying squelch.

The Kraken thrashed for a moment. The sea turned to foam as all the sharks and jellyfish and sea turtles around them thrashed as well, though Ebbo noticed there were far fewer of them than there had been before. The fishmen had made good work of them, then.

Then with a splash, Asakusa was through a Gate and next to Ebbo, treading water. How he kept afloat with the stone hammer was beyond Ebbo. Maybe the thing really was made for him.

Vecnos vanished into a shadow, reappearing who knew where.

Only Ragnar stayed at the prow of the skeleton ship, watching the Kraken sink below the surface of the water. Ebbo sort of envied him. Ragnar's quest was fulfilled, his life's work accomplished. Ebbo wondered if the old barbarian would get some from Fyelna tonight. The cleric seemed to be indicating it was possible. Ebbo had spotted her at the prow of Ragnar's ship, wisely away from the action, just like Ebbo but on the far side of the Kraken. She was cheering and cheering, crying tears of joy, so proud of her cantankerous old husband and his weird club of monster-worshiping weapon collectors. Ebbo wondered if this was his own future if he stuck around with the spider princess and the rest of them. The thought warmed him, despite the cold water.

It was in that moment that the skeletons made their move.

Most of them were still on the sinking ship. They ran at Ragnar, a horde of clinking yellow bones. He knocked the first few away without issue, his rubbery fists shattering them to pieces, but he'd left his weapons stuck in the Kraken, no doubt planning on retrieving them from the bottom of the sea like he'd wanted to do with the hammer.

When the skeletons came at him with nets, he faltered, falling to the deck. When they dragged him overboard and began to sink, Ebbo thought the fishman might have a chance, but that didn't appear to be the case. The rope was weighted not just with stones, but with the weight of a dozen skeletons, who were no more capable of swimming than rocks.

Still, Ragnar will be fine, Ebbo told himself. He had an army of Cthultists swimming around him!

Or so he thought, until Ebbo realized the water around him was teeming with life.

Only life wasn't the right word.

All of the sharks and turtles that had been dispatched in the battle were once more attacking the fishmen as the Cthultists tried to follow Ragnar to the bottom of the sea. The turtles' shells had turned yellow, as had the sharks' teeth. Even the jellyfish were attacking. Ebbo could see through the water that the ones that did had swallowed yellow skulls into their bells. The fishmen hacked at these undead aberrations, but they were obviously unused to fighting the undead. Their blows wounded but did not hurt. Ebbo saw one shark cease to attack—its skull pierced by a javelin—but the fishmen didn't know this trick of the skull. They were slaughtered by the foes they had just killed.

Ebbo watched in frozen horror as Ragnar's own Cthultists—now reanimated by the skeletons of Chemok—turned on their leader. He fought back as best he could, weighted down as he was by the net, but there were too many of them. They punctured his rubbery skin until Ragnar came to rest on the sea floor, dead.

But even that wasn't the end. For one of the undead Cthultists swam to Ragnar's now lifeless body and grasped it by the shoulders. It stared at him, yellowish green light pouring from its eyes, until that same light kindled in Ragnar. The infection of Chemok had just spread to another host.

Chemok hadn't wanted the hammer at all. It had only wanted Ragnar and the god he'd endeavored so long to kill.

It was then that the gillyweed gave out.

Ebbo began to sink.

He thrashed his arms and legs, but to no avail. He couldn't swim.

He was going to die and be reanimated as a skeleton, or even worse, a protoskeleton. He wasn't going to get to see Clayton again, or tell him how he'd called Vecnos a jerk to his face, or to where his face had just been, anyway. He wasn't going to get to prove to Adrianna that he could stay clean, that when she'd listened to the golem and decided to give him a chance that she'd made the right choice, and not just a kind one. Perhaps worst of all, he wasn't going to get to gossip to all about Asakusa's secret origin. Life was hard, but death just seemed so much lonelier.

And then a Gate opened and a withered hand was reaching through. Asakusa grabbed hold of Ebbo and pulled him into the Ways of the Dead.

A moment later they were in a cramped, dark tube that was blessedly dry. Ebbo had heard of those aquatic deathtraps. Submarines, they were called. Through a window, Ebbo could see dozens of skeletons sinking to the bottom of the ocean, stabbing anything that swam, then grabbing it and looking into its eyes, and spreading whatever it was that animated them all. The fishmen and Kraken's battle had been far too balanced. All the enemies that had been slain were now being conscripted to serve the master of the yellow skulls.

'Where's your party leader?' a voice said from the shadows. Vecnos. They were jammed into Vecnos's submarine with the infamous assassin. Ebbo was kind of shocked to see there were no henchmen about. With the way Vecnos had moved in battle, Ebbo had assumed he had to have some kind of support. Vecnos being solo only made him more impressive to the awestruck Ebbo. If only he hadn't tricked Ebbo, he could be like his apprentice or something. Ebbo shook the thought from his mind and focused on the submarine. He had heard rumors of this thing. Powered by magick and practically invisible. Thank huckleberries, he thought, for the sea seemed a dangerous place to be seen right now.

'She's at Krag's Doom,' Asakusa said.

'Can you take us there, thrall?' Vecnos asked.

Asakusa tugged at the collar around his neck. It was connected by chains to manacles on his right arm and leg. Like half of him had decided to go prison-goth. Both limbs were made of desiccated flesh. By the time this was all over, Ebbo expected more would be that way.

'Of course,' Asakusa said, but Ebbo hopped up, shaken from his stupor. He slapped Asakusa's hand.

'Adrianna is *not* Jiza. She cares about you!'

'That's why we have to get there.'

'If you open a Gate that can take a submarine that far, you'll be done! Last time we used the High Path, you were fully healed, and right now you are *not* fully healed. If you end up as one of Tulk's demons, you know Adrianna stays with Richard *for sure.*'

Asakusa scowled at the mention of Adrianna's husband's name, but he acquiesced.

'I owe the Demon King money. That makes the High Path too risky,' Vecnos said, brokering no argument. 'But we must hurry. Don't worry, though. I know a back way into Krag's Doom.'

Chapter 81

Adrianna

To Adrianna's surprise, Richard didn't attempt come to their—her!—bedchambers. When she said she was tired and wanted to go to bed early to molt, he just smiled and danced with one of her sisters. Adrianna wanted to believe he was an evil prince so she could just hate him and make her love life simpler. What else could explain how he could so effortlessly dance with one of her horribly disfigured—and horribly cruel—sisters? But if he was evil, he was also quite the actor. He just seemed like such a gentlemen.

Adrianna pushed the thoughts from her mind and went to her bedchambers, led by a flameheart servant who bowed at almost every step. This one had lost an eye and had a hook for a hand. Clearly, she'd learned a thing or two about when to get along with enemies.

'Your chamber has been prepared according to the Queen's commands.'

'The Queen?' Adrianna attempted to clarify what that meant to this flameheart.

'Err... the Queenmother. Queen-webmother!' the flameheart said, snapping up her own words as soon as she said them.

'That's what she's calling herself?'

'That's what your people call her. And she is, err... persuasive. Forgive me, my lady. My spider lady!'

'It's nothing,' Adrianna said. The flameheart nodded, happy to have a reason not to talk.

She led Adrianna past suits of armor made of dragonscale, weapons tipped with barbs that could slay the flying, fire-breathing beings, no doubt taken from the corpses of hundreds of overly-ambitious adventurers over the years. The loot was impressive, and yet it was little more than a collection of baubles compared to the castle around them.

That her family had built the place was obvious in every stone, every window, every too-thin pillar. Even in the hallways, the ceilings were tall. In the shadows above, silvery spiders big as Adrianna's fist scurried about, using threads of silk to strengthen bricks, improve pillars and redo windows. At least, that's what it looked like. Adrianna knew the spiders weren't real, of course. They were magickal constructs and the secret to both her family's wealth and survival. They were an ancient spell, cast by the spiderfolk in times of old. Web-builders, they were called, and Adrianna had never seen so many in one place. In the caves where she'd spent her childhood, there had been a dozen of the things, each controlled by her webmother and sisters. Here there were more than a hundred, maybe a thousand. They seemed to be everywhere. It was no wonder that Richard's father had been so desperate to marry his son to a spiderfolk and give the castle back to the family who'd built it in the first place. The web-builders had needed to get back to work. With Adrianna's webmother in the castle, they had. They'd accomplished much in the few weeks since the wedding, but there was still much to do. Bricks were still crumbling, and tapestries still showed out of date images. Adrianna wondered how long before she saw herself in the slowly moving tapestries. Web-builders re-wove the beautiful wall-hangings one thread at a time, making the image move over days or even weeks. None of the tapestries here looked like they'd been worked on in centuries.

'Your chambers, my lady,' the flameheart servant said.

Adrianna nodded and let the flameheart show her in.

The room took her breath away.

The bricks were white as Adrianna's hair, the sheets on the bed silk and embroidered with dragons and spiders. The tapestries in here had been worked on as well. Adrianna looked up to the high ceiling and suddenly understood why Richard had not tried to persuade her to allow him in their bedchambers, and perhaps why the servant had been so nervous.

Adrianna's mother hung upside down from the ceiling, ordering web-builders about as they worked on a tapestry Adrianna couldn't see in the gloom.

'Really, Mom? You're hiding in my bedroom?'

'Oh, my little spider princess,' Virianna chided her daughter as she crawled down a wall, gesturing at the web-builders to hang the tapestry. 'I only wished to speak to you in private. And besides, you've never seen this room, let alone slept in it. How can it be yours?'

Adrianna was going to say something about how she'd married Richard, so this whole castle was technically hers, but she found her words simply would not come when she saw the tapestry her webmother had just been working on. It featured her, of course; her mom had always been proud of

Adrianna's human-like features. What surprised her was that the tapestry wasn't *just* her. It also had Clayton, Ebbo, and Asakusa. Adrianna couldn't believe it. She'd never in her life seen a tapestry that featured anything but spiderfolk slaying their enemies.

'Is that...?'

'Your party, or squad. Whatever you call your servants, dear, yes.'

Adrianna couldn't even respond to her mom calling her friends servants. The tapestry simply took her breath away. Clayton stood in the front, arms locked in struggle with a giant. Ebbo was dragging an islander to safety. Asakusa had a Gate open, and another was open above the giant. Adrianna was in her spider form. Six spider appendages were on the ground, two spider appendages held daggers alongside her human arms—pedipalps, her sisters called them. In her human hands she held her silk whip, and *Flametongue*, the dagger Richard had given her on her wedding day. An embellishment, as he hadn't given her the dagger yet when they'd fought those giants, but despite this little falsity the tapestry was spectacular. It depicted one of their first quests that had earned them some renown as adventurers. Adrianna was surprised her webmother had it done. It wasn't typical spiderfolk legend, what with saving beings that were usually considered dinner.

'Mom, why did you do this?' Adrianna finally managed.

'You don't like it?'

'No, Mom, I love it! I can't believe you did this for me!' Adrianna scuttled toward her mom, and the two embraced. Adrianna had nearly forgotten how good it felt to be hugged by her webmother. Humans did the best they could with their two arms, but spiderfolk simply had more to give. As Adrianna and Virianna's human torsos hugged, their spider abdomens also embraced. Their appendages felt each other out, subconsciously working to smooth out-of-place hairs, check on wounds—Adrianna had a lot of those—and just generally soothe each other. Virianna—of course—ran her hands through Adrianna's hair, and it felt wonderful. It had been so long since Adrianna had felt anyone touch her hair. It made her feel like a little girl again, safe in her mom's embrace.

'I know they mean a lot to you, and it was very brave of them to come to the wedding, even if they did...well, sort of ruin everything.' Virianna chuckled.

'At least you're living here instead of the caves. It looks like not *everything* was ruined.'

Virianna shrugged with a few of her appendages. 'I had hoped to share this place with my *daughters.*'

'I know, Mom, and I'm sorry I left, really I am. But what was I supposed to do? Richard knew how to use my hair to Fold my body. He made me complete the ritual and marry him.'

Her webmother's face darkened. 'That was unfortunate, and not at all my intention. Your sisters... you know they've always been jealous of your destiny.'

'You mean they hate my face enough to give our family secrets to the enemy.'

'The Valkannas are not our enemy, not any longer. You changed that, Adrianna. If you wish to exact justice on your sisters, I will not stop you.'

Adrianna sighed through her vents. 'I don't want vengeance, and besides... I've talked to Richard about it. He's not... he's not really that bad.'

The gleam of a mother's eyes—spiderfolk or not—when they thought about grandchildren was similar in all species. 'I don't blame you for leaving,' Virianna said, not seizing the opportunity to talk about Adrianna laying an egg-sack, and managing to make Adrianna feel even worse for leaving.

'If I would have stayed for the reception, my friends would all be dead.'

'They're still alive, then? The halfling and the thrall?'

'Yes, Mom, and they have *names,* you know.'

'I know they do. Forgive me. I do not wish to argue with you, Adrianna. I am proud of what you've done. This family owes you its future. Both the Morticians and the Valkannas. Like you said, we escaped the caves because of you, and this castle is still floating only because of your sacrifice.'

'Yeah, well, I might need to cash in the favors sooner rather than later.'

'Anything, my spider princess with a human heart. Anything at all.'

So Adrianna told her about the baron Rolph Katinka and his army of yellow skeletons he was using to farm. She told him of the dark god he served, the yellow-skulled Chemok. Her mom listened and tittered away, growing especially distressed when Adrianna told her about Dontalas Crisp, who'd come across the High Bridge to vanquish this reanimating force of skeletons.

When it was all done, her webmother inhaled deeply through the vents in her abdomen sand said, 'It will take some convincing, but the Valkannas will see that we all must help. You have my word.'

'You can do that?' Adrianna couldn't believe her mom wasn't pushing back. After all, she was essentially asking her to help protect humans, a race that were at best food for the spiderfolk, and at worst their greatest foes.

'I have a... relationship with Lucien. He will listen to me. I assure you.

But still, his sons will take convincing. This is why you came home, then? To molt for this battle against the undead?'

Adrianna nodded.

'Then preparations must be made. I will leave you to molt.'

Adrianna watched her mom go. Was Adrianna the only one holding onto the past? Would she ever be able to leave it behind? Her mom wanted to help people. Richard said he did, too. Was it arrogant to think that she was the only good person to come from the dark races? Maybe not. Maybe it was just naive, like thinking all from the mortal races were good.

Adrianna looked in a mirror large enough to hold her entire spider form. Her body was a wreck. One of her legs had been cut off. The layer of skin over her chitinous shell had been torn to nothing in places. Cuts and breaks in her exoskeleton had been sealed over with silk threads or globs of her own ichor. The effect was the same, as they were made of the same thing—Adrianna's blood—but together they looked horrible. In the mirror, she saw a monster looking back at her.

Her body was mangled and missing pieces. The assortment of scars was terrifying in the variations of shape and size. Worse, though, was the body underneath. Adrianna had no curves in her spiderform. Her butt spread out into a swollen abdomen. Her breasts were chitinous growths. Her arms were skinny and bony, with elbows that were so sharp, they looked like weapons. Her waist… ugh it was almost impossible for Adrianna to see past the mass of thick black pubic hairs. Each one was thick, more like a spine than a hair. Her webmother had taught her and her sisters that they could eject the hairs into a lover to cause great itching. Yet another power Adrianna had never asked for. The hair spread over her belly and up to her breasts. At least if it was thick, it would have looked intentional, but as it was now, it was sparse and patchy, knocked out from wounds upon wounds upon wounds.

It was no wonder Adrianna always wore black padded armor. Anything to hide her body.

'You look like shit.'

Adrianna spun to see one of her sisters crawl down from the wall. 'Luciana, what are you doing here?'

'I'm Taveza, you twat.'

'I'm sorry,' Adrianna managed.

'Just kidding, it's Luciana. Still can't tell us apart?' Her sister started laughing. It was strange to hear so human a sound come from someone like her sister. Her face was more spider than anything else, with eight bulbous eyes, tiny forelimbs that hid her fangs, and hairs sprouting everywhere. Her body looked human, except for the four limbs on either side—two human-like arms, covered in thick hairs, and six spider legs. Adrianna thought she'd recognized the helix shape on her sister's abdomen, that was how she'd known she was Luciana, but she'd always struggled to keep them straight. Her mom had raised Adrianna to be a princess, and her sisters to be warlords and assassins. They had never spent much time together.

'Mother sent me to help you,' Luciana tittered.

'Thanks...'

'It's fine. You gonna get in the bath or what?' Luciana said, gesturing toward a room connected to the huge bedchamber.

Adrianna nodded and walked toward the bath. She just barely heard Luciana mutter something disparaging under her breath, but Adrianna made no attempt to decipher her sister's cruel words.

The bath was a deep pool of steaming hot water. The entire room was done in pink tiles, and a stream of water trickled into the pool. Another exited on the other side.

Adrianna walked into the pool. The water was so hot it hurt at first, but as she adjusted, it soon felt wonderful. The heat worked at her exoskeleton, loosening it, and there was some sort of mineral in the water that seemed familiar. Reminded her of S'kar-Vozi, almost.

'Princess,' a voice said through the mist, and Adrianna jumped before she recognized it.

'What is he doing here?' Luciana demanded.

'Clayton?' Adrianna said and moved through the chest-deep water toward the far side of the pool.

It was indeed Clayton Steelheart. He sat on the edge of the deep bath, his feet dangling into the water—or they had been. Instead of feet, he had stumps. He'd let them dissolve into nothing.

'I've been saving what bath salts I come across. Your mother said something to Prince Valkanna, and he sent me here. Something about the betrayal of a secret acted upon? It was all very ominous, but I had the bath salts, so...'

Adrianna heard the hiss of her sister sucking in a breath. So, it was Luciana that had told her fiancé about how to use her hair against her. Adrianna had said she hadn't wanted vengeance, but her webmother seemed to have left the option on the table. Golems were particularly difficult for spiderfolk to wound. They didn't respond to poison, and their fists could crack exoskeletons with little effort.

'Tell him to go,' Luciana whined. 'This is just between us.'

'And you'll repeat nothing I say to our sisters?'

Luciana at least had the decency not to lie. She simply said nothing at all.

'Luciana, Clayton stays. Thank you for the salts. Now, if you'd like to take a few steps back—' *so you won't see my freaky-weird wounded spider body,* Adrianna might have finished, but she held her tongue. Clayton nodded, stood and retreated into the mist of the room. Adrianna was relieved he could not see her through the mist. Or maybe he could. Golem senses were strange. Still, better him than anyone else. Clayton wasn't human, after all, and besides, he wasn't interested in women like that.

'I apologize for nothing,' Luciana said. 'You abandoned us for years, then come back to get married, and abandon us again. What's so important you have to ditch your family?'

'You don't need me here. You've never needed me.'

'And who does? A bunch of little halflings? Or is it the thrall?'

'What do you want from me, Luciana? When I stay, you treat me like a bug, and when I leave, you do the same when I come back.'

'I'm sick of Mom acting like you're her favorite just because of your ugly face,' Luciana snarled.

'If you think I'm ugly, then why are you jealous?'

Luciana said nothing to that. Instead, she splashed into the water.

'I tried to help,' Adrianna said. 'I married Richard, didn't I? If it wasn't for that, we'd still be living in a cave, eating sightless fish.'

'Those fish weren't so bad.'

'Yeah, well then why did you always try to hunt anything that came in?'

'I didn't. That was Tabita.'

'Whatever. All of you are the same, and you know it. Always agitating each other, always trying to win Mom's favor so one of you could rule once you'd gotten rid of me.'

'Yeah, it sucks pretty bad to always be second place.'

'You think I *wanted* to be the eighth daughter of the eighth daughter? You think it's nice to know you're going to marry someone no matter what you think, since you were five years old?'

'A prince! Adrianna, you were to marry a *prince*! What is so wrong with that? You think any of us will ever get to marry? Our best shot is finding a spiderfolk who's not directly related to us—no easy task—and you complain about marrying a prince? How self-centered can you be?'

'I'm not self-centered. Since I left, I've spent all my time helping people!'

'Is that right? We heard about your little exploits. Saving the islanders from giants. Reaming out a nest of gryphons. You know what all of your little quests had in common? Optics. Every single one was designed to make the spider princess look like a goodie-goodie. If you were so selfless, why all the attention on the mortal races? Why not save the eelings from the squid attack? Why not help the hrocs take back some of their islands?'

'Because the eelings and the hrocs eat mortals!' Adrianna said loud enough to echo in the steamy bath chamber.

'That's it, then,' Luciana's voice was low, almost a whisper. 'That's your loyalty now. To the mortals. You know how many of us they've killed?'

'Almost as many as we have of them.'

'That's spinning nonsense, and you know it. They've killed us by the thousands. They hunt us for sport.'

'Because we eat them,' Adrianna didn't understand how it could be so hard to see both sides.

'What are we supposed to do? Starve?'

'No! We can eat fish, or cows.'

'*Animals*?' Luciana screeched.

'Yes! They're not that bad. And mortals eat them too.'

'I've heard enough,' Luciana said.

Then Adrianna's eldest sister slid a dagger into her neck.

The pain was immediate, blinding even, but it gave way to relief just as quickly.

Luciana slid the dagger down Adrianna's spine, cutting open her exoskeleton. When she got to her belly, she dragged the dagger around to her bellybutton, then kept dragging it down her middle to her abdomen. It didn't really hurt. That part of her exoskeleton didn't have nerve receptors. What Adrianna felt was the hot water rush into the open wound. The heat of it shocked and relaxed her all at once.

'You act like they can help you. Like you're one of them,' Luciana said.

'They can help us—'

'Not with this,' Luciana said. 'They can't crack open an exoskeleton. They don't know how to conserve ichor, either. And they'll poison you without a second thought.'

'They eat vegetables. That's not their fault.'

'I'm not saying it is. I *am* saying we're different. We are spiderfolk. We were made to rule this world. They're nothing but mortals. What else do you want me to call them? I've been around a hundred and fifty years, and Mom still treats me like a child. I know you're not yet twenty, but you'll see as they start to age and die. They're not like us. They never will be. We had more in common with the elves and dwarves than we do with humans.'

'But—'

'I know. You love one of them. You think none of us felt that way before?'

Adrianna said nothing as Luciana delicately completed the last of the incision. When she did, Adrianna's exoskeleton popped open, sliding off her back and her abdomen and folding in on itself. Without a body to keep its shape, the tightness of the material made the shell collapse. Luciana grabbed the lump, now not much bigger than a duffel bag, and tossed it from the pool. Their servants would cook it and feed it back to Adrianna in the morning. Something many humans found disgusting, but for a female of the spiderfolk, was biologically necessary.

Now Adrianna was soft and pink, her muscles exposed to the water. Her missing legs had regrown inside her old shell and were now slowly inflating using Adrianna's ichor. Any wounds she'd suffered would leave no scars. By morning, her new exoskeleton—already grown underneath the old one— would start to solidify, and then grow skin, but for the night even touching fabric would sting. Still, it felt *good* to molt. Her muscles could relax in a way that was impossible when inside her exoskeleton. The hot water made it both possible and pleasurable. Perhaps for the first time, she saw why her ancestors had tried to strike a deal with dragons. Volcanically heated water was a fine thing, indeed. Fine enough to allow Adrianna to lower her guard toward her sister a bit further.

'You...loved someone?'

'Don't get all emotional, princess. Yes, I loved someone. A mortal. Came to our cave. So handsome. Big ol' dumb jaw. Rock-hard biceps. Armor so polished you could do your makeup in it.' Luciana came back to stand on the edge of the pool, her back to Clayton, dismissing him as a construct instead of a person. Adrianna ignored the slight, for now.

'What happened?'

'I became smitten, so I did the whole shadow on the wall thing, showing a human silhouette. Cut his torchlight so he wouldn't have to see me. We made love. Believe it or not, that's one part of me that's human.'

'That sounds... nice,' Adrianna said.

'It was. Until he pulled out a scroll of illumination while I was sleeping. I woke up just in time for him to say he wanted to see me. Well, he did. Saw my face and screamed, grabbed his sword and attacked. I stabbed him with a poison dagger and watched his beautiful face bloat and turn purple. Serves him right. That's what they'll do. Humans, I mean. At some point they'll betray you. All of them do.'

'You mean like how you betrayed our family's secrets for using our hair to Fold up our bodies to the Valkannas?' Adrianna had felt no choice in saying the words. Luciana—her *sister*—had accused another of betrayal, when it her most glaring sin.

Luciana didn't say anything for a moment, only froze at the edge of the pool, suddenly very aware that she'd put her back to a golem who could very likely smash her like the spider she was. Adrianna almost felt bad that she'd used her sister's story to pivot against her, but Luciana had been so venomously against betrayal, Adrianna hadn't been able to resist.

'Who told you?' Luciana finally said.

'It was obvious it was one of you. You all used to tie up my hair to tangle my body and leave me for the monsters. This wasn't much different.'

'We only did that to make you stronger.'

Adrianna didn't know if that was true or not. That wasn't how she'd seen it as a child. 'You did it because you were jealous.'

'Maybe. Maybe it was once about jealousy, but that wasn't why I told Richard.'

'Then why?'

'Because we didn't think you were going to go through with it!' Luciana had said *we* instead of *I*, proving to Adrianna that she hadn't acted alone. 'We thought you wouldn't show, and if you did, that you'd run away. We were almost right. That thrall of yours made quite the scene.'

'I would've married Richard myself if Asakusa hadn't been about to die!'

'We saw.' Luciana sounded remorseful. It was also a comfort she'd stopped trying to protect her sisters from their share of the blame. 'We're... that is, most of us anyway, we're sorry. We doubted your commitment to the family. We were wrong. We told Richard those things because he'd let us into Krag's Doom long before the ceremony. That was more than you'd ever done for us.'

'They would have thrown you all into the lava below if I hadn't come,' Adrianna said.

'But they didn't, because you did. This is our home now, thanks to you.' That was the closest thing to kindness any of Adrianna's sisters had shown her.

She decided she'd take it as some sort of a compliment. 'I don't want you to have to go back into the caves. I want you to be able to stay in Krag's Doom with our webmother, but there's more to the world than our family. A war is coming, and thousands of people might die. I know I went to school in the free city while you studied in darkness, but do you remember Chemok?'

Luciana grimaced. 'A mindless infection of death. Your sisters and I have heard rumors of his growing power.'

'Fight with us against it when I ask you, and you can have this castle when our webmother passes.'

'Truly?' Luciana asked.

Adrianna laughed. 'It's gaudy as hell. I don't want to live here.'

'You're a funny thing, Adrianna. A true princess. You won the castle back for your family, and then would give it up to the same wicked sisters that betrayed you?'

'Where else are any of you supposed to go? You're all ugly as carrion beetles.'

Luciana snorted in laughter. It was the first time Adrianna had ever insulted any of her sisters. Apparently, she'd waited far too long.

'Where are you going to live? A bungalow with that thrall?' Luciana asked.

'I am a *princess*, and I may do as I wish.'

Luciana laughed again. 'See? All those insults we dumped on you only made you stronger.' She paused, her spider legs tittering away, betraying her nervousness to her sister in body language only their family could read. 'Thank you, sister,' Luciana finally said in a voice hardly louder than a hiss. 'We betrayed you, and you have forgiven us. Perhaps there is something to these humans after all.'

'There is, and you will eat them no longer. You know, unless they try to attack you or hurt Mom or raid the castle or whatever.' Adrianna loved people, but she'd lived in the free city. She wasn't going to pretend every human being was beyond reproach.

'You... honor us, princess. I will tell our sisters of your... requests. You can count on us to spin our part of the web you wish to weave.' And with that, Luciana excused herself, and Adrianna felt, for the first time in her life, like she was part of a family. All she'd have to do was give up a floating castle. Not a bad deal, in Adrianna's estimation.

'She has a point, princess,' Clayton said.

Adrianna—lost in the end of the conversation with her sister—had almost forgotten he was there.

'What?'

'Asakusa likes you; that is plain. But is that enough?'

'Clayton, you've known Asakusa almost as long as I have.'

'Indeed, Princess Morticia, and I know he is good friend, and loyal. But is he deserving of you?'

Adrianna said nothing. Clayton had never before called her Princess

Morticia. Not once. He'd called her princess plenty of times, Princess Adrianna, or even Her Majesty the Spider Princess if he was announcing her or trying to boast about his friends, but he knew she didn't like to use the Mortician name. Something was wrong with him. As Clayton kept speaking, Adrianna realized that something had been wrong with him for a long time. 'Come closer,' Adrianna said, and Clayton obeyed.

Clayton continued to speak as he approached. 'He is a good friend, and I see no reason why he can't continue to be, but a husband? He is not exactly one to inspire the masses, and then there is his Corruption. An embarrassment of a power, don't you think?'

'He knows how to heal it.' Adrianna then realized what was going on, but this wasn't the time to confront it. Not with her body freshly molted. Not with the golem trapped like a puppet on a string. As Clayton continued to ramble the words of a hidden master, Adrianna fell into thought, unsure of what to say. When Clayton had come closer, she'd looked into his glimmering emerald eyes, but it seemed that whoever was on the other side had failed to notice that she'd recognized the slitted dragon pupils hidden therein.

Chapter 82

Adrianna

'You have been charged with fishing in the King's Waters. How do you plead?'

'Aye, err... it was just a net of sardines, and we wouldn't have taken them if it weren't for them berry-picking yellow skeletons everywhere!'

It was the next morning. Adrianna's skin no longer hurt when she touched it but was still quite tender. Moving around was not easy, which was why she found herself arriving late to court. It seemed her husband, the dragon prince Richard Valkanna, was already taking his first subject: an islander with a wiry frame and a fishermen's cap he clutched in his hand as he knelt on the floor.

'So you admit to taking the fish?' Richard asked imperiously.

'I've been fishing 'round these parts for years. Ya don't take the sardines, the tuna will, and if the tuna do, then we can't catch 'em, as they're too big,' the islander said to the marble floor. 'We didn't mean to come close. It was them skeletons.' The poor man was obviously intimidated, and Adrianna could understand why.

They were in an austerely decorated throne room. The few decorations consisted of suits of blackened armor and cruel-looking weapons. But the austerity only emphasized the room itself. The floor was a thing of terror. Made from imported marble in a hundred shades that were then laid into a mosaic to look like an enormous spider and a dragon fighting, the floor was uncomfortably reminiscent of the final part of the wedding ritual. The islander didn't know this, of course—no islander was at the wedding save Ebbo, who'd pretty much ruined the whole thing by bringing crushed dragon scales—but he looked intimidated all the same. He glanced up from the battle of spider and dragon (battle in his eyes, anyway; to Adrianna, it would always remind her of weird monster-sex) to the thin pillars crawling with silvery spiders, then around to the members of the court: mostly spiderfolk men and flameheart women, though Adrianna spotted a few of the races lucky enough to be born the opposite gender. Two of her sisters were in attendance, as was a lesser dragon prince she didn't recognize from the wedding.

'So you admit to taking from our lands. The punishment for this is death. Next!' Richard Valkanna proclaimed. Lazy, scattered applause from those in attendance. Four of the flameheart guards came forward to seize the islander, while a spiderfolk nervously picked at his mustache, readying himself for his audience with the prince.

'Wait a minute!' Adrianna said and started forward. Normally she would have marched right up to the throne to the sounds of gasps and surprise from those in attendance, but with her exoskeleton yet to heal, the most she could manage was a slow shuffle. She hoped she looked regal, but knew she didn't. Still, spiderfolk nodded to her, their mouthparts working. She was in her spiderform—Folding was painful until her exoskeleton was solid again—and the islander squealed as she approached him.

'Please, I don't wanna be et!' he said to Richard. 'I just wanted some fish for my family, and the waters by our home are too dangerous, I swear! Don't feed me to her.'

Adrianna suppressed a grimace. If she had a coin for every time someone she was trying to save mistook her for someone wanting to eat her, she'd have a treasure horde as fat as any of those in the Ringwall.

Richard spoke first, though. 'Were you or were you not visited by someone of this court?'

'Please sir, please!' the islander mumbled. Adrianna loved islanders, but she could admit that once flustered, most of them they were basically useless.

'Your highness,' a flameheart hissed, 'I delivered the message myself. Waded through pig slop to do so. Told him to stop fishing.'

'Well, there you are, then. She told you to no longer fish our shores. You disobeyed. We're done here.'

Adrianna, finally making it past the islander, stepped up onto the dais and took a seat next to Richard. The chair had long posts that stuck up from the back of it, like spider's legs. Adrianna climbed them so her abdomen was above her, and she looked up, like a spider on a web. It had been so long since she'd had a chair that supported proper posture in her spiderform.

The islander relaxed slightly as she walked by, but as soon as she took her vertical position at the front of the court, he started shaking all the worse. Adrianna sighed. She knew he didn't mean anything, he was just scared, but for once she'd like one of the people she saved to appreciate her. That was something nice about S'kar-Vozi. The people there didn't *always* fear her.

Sometimes they threatened or bargained, the behavior of uncouth equals.

'I was under the impression that islanders were allowed to fish their own islands. Did this one come too close to Krag's Doom?' Adrianna asked in her most imperious tone. She was pleasantly surprised to see the spiderfolk and flamehearts in attendance watch her without speaking. That was something different from S'kar-Vozi. Quiet and respectful were two words rarely used to describe the free city.

'Times have changed, Princess,' Richard said. 'Before, there was more than enough fish to feed my people, but now, with your family here too, and with all of your brothers and uncles, we need to range farther.'

'So then we range farther. My family can procure their own food.'

'We have been, but there's no longer anything by the Blighted Island. That cursed Katinka is scooping up everything out of the water and canning it or something. Sells it all to S'kar-Vozi. Isn't that right, Ser Gaf?' Richard said, addressing the quaking islander.

'Aye, sir, it is. I en't no Ser, but that's why we came this way. No fish left by the Blighted Lands, no fish anywhere. Nothing to eat but pumpkins, berries, fresh cracked wheat bread, pies, pork and sausages!'

'See?' Richard Valkanna said. 'This one may be skinny, but the damn things will eat us out of house and home. Ladies?'

Two flamehearts came forward, hands on curved scimitars.

Adrianna spoke up. 'If we are to rule, it won't do for us to kill and eat everyone who breaks a decree. His family has fished for generations. We can't just cut them off without some sort of alternative.'

'Pardon me, dear, but your family has lived in caves far from here for generations. I don't know what there was to eat, but here we rely on fish. There's a sustainable harvest, and that vampire Katinka has gone far past it. We can't afford to lose any more. After all, there's two families to feed—something you may have forgotten, as you haven't been here.'

'Excuse you?'

Richard stuck his perfect jawline higher in the air. 'I will not be the prince that unites our families and then allows them to starve. If we don't kill the islander as an example, they'll keep fishing and taking what we have. And if we let that happen, we *will* starve, at which point we both know what will happen to our relatives.'

Adrianna glanced at the assembled. Richard was right. Male spiderfolk were driven by two things: hunger, and a desire to serve their women at any cost, even death. The flameheart women didn't look much different. They were about as scarred and battle-worn as the spiderfolk males were. If they were anywhere near as difficult to control, then they had to be fed. Male spiderfolk couldn't help but kill and bring their dead back to the women that ruled their clan. That was simply their nature. It was one of the reasons Adrianna had agreed to marry Richard. If the spiderfolk were holed up on this island, then they couldn't forage through tunnels, eating or poisoning whatever they found. They obeyed only so long as they weren't hungry, as hunger had been a part of their blood far longer than words had. Still, the islander didn't deserve to die for catching a fish, any more than he deserved to be eaten.

'Did you say there's pork on your island, Mr. Gaf?'

'Aye, there is, your spidery-ness. Black-spotted brownbacks. A heritage breed. Especially good for the pork belly. Sausage ain't bad, either. We feed 'em a diet of acorns, see, so they fatten up and marble quite nicely.'

'You will give us an equivalent weight of pig-flesh to the fish you caught.'

'But how're we supposed to make bacon, lettuce, and tomato?' Gaf said, his fear forgotten in the face of losing some of his heritage pork.

'You'll do without.'

'But—'

'You'll do without, or we'll eat you,' Adrianna said, earning smiles from her sisters even though they knew as well as her that Adrianna would have never gone through with the threat.

Still, it shut Gaf up.

Adrianna continued, 'We will solve each other's problems. You may still fish from your shores, but no longer may you go out in boats. It's not safe anyway, not with the skeletons from Katinka's lands fishing.' Adrianna made the point not for the islander's benefit, but for those bearing witness in the court. Very soon, she would call upon them all to help her. She needed them to listen.

'But what will we eat?'

'Vegetables, fruit and grain.'

The islander blanched. Adrianna rolled her eyes. If Ebbo—an example of a lack of self-restraint if there ever was one—could abide being a vegetarian, these islanders could too.

'You will continue to raise pigs, and sell them to us. We'll pay the market price.'

'Fine pigs they are. Not cheap, not with the acorns and all.' Islanders had benefited from the Farmer's Market in S'kar-Vozi more than anyone. That was partly because they valued coin far more than they valued violence.

Richard Valkanna gestured to a flameheart, who dropped a sack of coin in front of the islander. It clinked heavily when it struck the floor. The only jaw hanging more agape in surprise than the islander's was Adrianna's. Richard argued with her less than her friends did. He hadn't even protested her decision contradicting his. Instead he'd just made her wishes so.

Mr. Gaf took the bag and looked up at the dragon prince and spider princess. His eyebrows shot up. He'd probably never seen that much Coin before. He'd care little that it was stamped with a dragon's face on one side and a spider on the other.

'That's a down payment until Heart's Melt,' Richard decreed. He really did have the voice for it. He made it sound as if he and Adrianna had worked all this out beforehand. 'We'll expect a harvest before the feast. You can keep one pig for your family, but the rest is ours.'

Gaf was still fumbling at the Coin, clearly unused to handling much of anything besides coppers.

'Next!' Richard boomed.

Two flamehearts grabbed the islander and escorted him out. Though they were a bit rough, he didn't seem to mind.

'Brilliant!' Richard leaned over and whispered to Adrianna. 'I never would have thought to eat the pig! But we had some in S'kar-Vozi. That bake-on was especially amazing. This is exactly why I need you to stay.'

'We both know I can't,' Adrianna said, thinking about what had caused the islander's fishing problem in the first place, but also appraising Richard once more. He really did seem to genuinely want to help her make the world a more just place for mortals. Why else would he have come to her side so completely?

'Oh come on, what could possibly be more important than caring for our two families? Left unchecked, I won't know any better than to gobble up the whole Archipelago. With you here, you'll have us eating animals instead of mortals within the year! We're good together, Adrianna. Your compassion, my history of ruling this place. Together we can *be* something.'

'There's more than this place, though. S'kar-Vozi—'

'Will be fine without you. If you leave us again, there's no saying what will happen here. Hunger is a sharp blade, Adrianna. I need someone here who knows how to point it. Besides, what could drag you away from here?'

At that moment, the doors swung open and in came Asakusa, Ebbo, and a tiny cloaked figure. Adrianna felt her face get hot. Yet again, Richard had been on the verge of proving himself to her, and Asakusa had interrupted. She wanted to hate one of them for it, or at least be annoyed, but she wasn't. Seeing Asakusa drag his hammer across the exquisitely worked stone floor was something Adrianna enjoyed very much. It was the other two that troubled her. Adrianna's voice caught in her throat when she recognized the midnight-black cloak. It was Vecnos, from the Ringwall, traveling with her friends.

'Your majesty,' Vecnos said, bowing to the princess and prince but not hiding his scowl. 'I appreciate you not eating my kin. We need your help.'

'What is happening? How did you get through our perimeter?' Richard said.

Asakusa looked up at Adrianna. 'We killed the Kraken. Now it's back from the dead.'

Chapter 83

Asakusa

'How did you get in here?' Richard Valkanna demanded furiously.

'There are forces in this realm more powerful than yours, Valkanna,' Vecnos growled.

Asakusa ignored the exchange; he sought only Adrianna's attention. He had been worried she was mad at him when she'd sent him to fetch his hammer, but her smirk dissolved those fears like a gnoll's stomach dissolved bones. Asakusa felt himself smiling despite the seriousness of the situation. It was nice to be back with Adrianna.

'Well? Speak, thrall!' Richard ordered.

'He's sworn nothing to you, you old cranberry,' Ebbo said to Richard and stuck out his tongue at the dragon prince.

Asakusa glared at Richard—but really, he was impressed with both of the little islanders.

'Princess,' Asakusa said formally, going so far as to bow. 'I retrieved my hammer, as you wished. Now, I think the time has come to kick some ass.'

'I demand you order these whelps to tell us how they got inside Krag's Doom!' Richard raged, though Asakusa noticed that it was still a deferment to Adrianna's judgment. Maybe it really was a good thing that Adrianna had come here without him; she seemed to have been able to tame the dragon a bit. Asakusa didn't want to think how. Currently, she seemed to be controlling the dragon's rage by doing nothing more than smiling. *She really is fit to be a princess*, Asakusa thought, finding himself in awe of his friend sitting upon her totally rad spider throne.

They'd come here by teleportation rug, something Asakusa hadn't even known existed. Vecnos had convinced Master Seamstress Zultana to sew it, and Susannah to help with the enchantments. It had provided a quick and easy way to get from one point to another. All it needed was another rug to operate. So now, on Vecnos's submarine, there was a finely woven rug with a dragon and spider motif, while the rug they came here on was once more rolled up and tucked away inside Vecnos's cloak. It must be nice to have rich friends, Asakusa thought, before he realized he was standing before his best friend in the throne room of her castle.

'There is nothing more powerful than the Mortician and Valkanna alliance. This Archipelago will quake at the world we will create,' Richard Valkanna managed after staring at Vecnos awkwardly for a moment.

'There will be nothing left but bones and death if you don't shut up and listen to us,' Vecnos replied.

Asakusa tried to remain stoic in the wake of the wicked insult. Ebbo, one the other hand, giggled viciously. Asakusa wondered if Ebbo had forgiven Vecnos for tricking him into snorting what he thought was Clayton's soul. Maybe he had. After all, Ebbo wasn't one to hold a grudge—not like Asakusa —and Clayton seemed to be fine. The golem stood in front of them, wearing a red and black silk suit with dragons and spiders stitched into it.

'We faced the Baron Rolph Katinka and his hordes of skeletons. They were trying to dredge up the stone hammer, but we got it first,' Asakusa said.

'Well, technically they got it first, but we got it now,' Ebbo added

'There was a battle,' Vecnos said. 'Ragnar and the Cthult of Cthulu showed up. Either to find the hammer or to face the Kraken, it matters not. They fought, and slayed the beast, but Ragnar lost—he's been changed, resurrected by Chemok, as was the crab at the heart of the Kraken.' Vecnos paused. 'Despite our failure, your allies did well, your highness.' Vecnos did not sound as though he enjoyed bestowing the compliment on Asakusa and Ebbo.

Adrianna swallowed. She knew as well as Asakusa that Ragnar was practically unbeatable. His rubber skin was supposed to have weathered more blows than any suit of armor. 'How?' she asked simply.

'Skeletons and a net ended Ragnar. An unfortunately pedestrian way for him to go. I'm sure Fyelna is upset, but there it is.' If Vecnos was upset, he didn't show it. 'They're en route to S'kar-Vozi now. We cannot wait any longer. Ragnar's corpse now rides upon an undead Kraken.'

'Do not deign to give orders here, *halfling*,' Richard Valkanna said.

Asakusa looked from the dragon prince to the tiny assassin. A bold insult, using the racial slur that Vecnos himself had been working to eradicate.

Vecnos ignored it; he only bowed. Asakusa knew people in the free city who'd had been beaten bloody for insulting Vecnos. That the tiny assassin didn't so much as scowl at the insult drove home how dire the threat that faced them all was.

'What are your orders, fair prince?' Vecnos enquired. The way he said "fair prince" made it sound like he'd called Richard a shit-licking slug.

Richard scowled, the tone of voice had not gone over his head, but he only looked to Adrianna. 'What does my princess wish to do?'

'We can't let S'kar-Vozi be overrun.' Adrianna was doing her best to sound confident, but Asakusa—having known her for years—could hear the terror creeping into her voice. 'You've said you wanted to prove yourself as a force of good, that together we could remake this place as we see fit. Well, there will be nothing left if the free city is destroyed by an army of the undead.'

Richard nodded, then addressed the assembled flamehearts. 'The Valkannas will help the free city. There is but one condition.'

'And what's that, your highness?' Vecnos asked, again sneering the title into something that sounded more like an un-popped pustule filled with snot and mucous.

'Leave the vampire to me.'

That, at least, earned a snort from Vecnos, and a bit of a grin.

Chapter 84

Adrianna

The preparation was quick, mere hours. The flamehearts were well drilled and had weapons ready in no time. The spiderfolk too had been preparing, it seemed, and Adrianna was thankful she'd come home in time to put them to work. They spun vast nets that they threw over balloons filled with gasses that escaped from the volcano below. Below these huge balloons, the dragons and spiderfolk loaded up into boats and barges. Adrianna had only a moment to wonder how they'd actually move the floating airships, then the flamehearts started working at propellers, spinning them with a series of cranks and pulleys and sending the ships off through the air.

Adrianna hoped it would be enough. She thought back to the mass of yellow bones that had nearly overwhelmed her and Asakusa. They'd barely escaped that, and Chemok had only grown more powerful since then.

'We'll need to hurry,' Richard told Adrianna. 'We'll want to make fortifications in that Ringwall of yours,' he said, nodding at Vecnos. 'If Baron Katinka truly controls the Kraken, it will try to come through the cliffs that frame Bog's Bay, but the vampire is wily. If I were him, I'd try to send skeletons in from the back.'

'I'll take these two with me, and the golem, if you wish,' Vecnos said to Richard, gesturing to Ebbo and Asakusa. 'I don't think it's wise for you to use the rug with us. Your glamour affects your size in this plane, but if you lose your concentration and become larger, you could get stuck. Princess, will you be coming with us as well?' Vecnos said.

Adrianna touched her hair. She'd tied it up so her spiderform was Folded away. It should hold, but then again, her exoskeleton had yet to solidify. The thought of going into this battle without her body at full strength terrified her, and perhaps guided her decision as well. Every minute meant a bit more strength for the spider princess. She understood that they needed to fight, but with a few more hours, she'd be that much stronger.

'I'll go with Richard and meet you all there.'

When she said that, she saw Asakusa's jaw tighten as he nodded and wiped at his eyes with the withered hand of his new corruption. It made Adrianna feel terrible to ask even more of her friend, but he needed to be in the free city to help. Asakusa was powerful, and his stone hammer might be the only weapon strong enough to take on Ragnar or the Kraken. Adrianna wouldn't be nearly as useful in a brawl. She needed to lead the spiderfolk and her husband's family to S'kar-Vozi. Asakusa would have to endure her absence a bit longer. The thought of it didn't make her happy, but thus was the role of a princess.

'Then we're off,' Richard said, taking Adrianna by the hand and making for the front door of the castle, as if they were going for a stroll instead of into a fight against an enemy that truly did not fear death.

For a while they said nothing, but the quiet must have gotten to Richard, for finally he said, 'Your friends are kind of arrogant.'

'They think the same of you,' Adrianna said.

Richard snorted, but he didn't protest. 'Are you sure about this?' he said after a moment.

'What choice do we have? We know that Chemok's skeletons are beginning to overrun the Archipelago. If the skeletons get to S'kar-Vozi, there's a hundred thousand people there. If they all get turned into reanimated corpses, the entire Archipelago is doomed.'

'That's a pretty big if.'

'What are you talking about?'

Richard shrugged. 'If I wanted to finally wipe out the spiderfolk and flamehearts, I wouldn't do it on our home turf. I'd lure out their leaders, separate them from the group, and strike when I could.'

'The Nine in the Ringwall would never do such a thing, especially not when facing a threat as big as Chemok controlling the Kraken.'

Richard shrugged as they waited for the portcullis to open. 'I'm sure your friends mean you no harm, but what about that Vecnos? He's manipulated Ebbo before. And it's painfully obvious to anyone that Asakusa loves you. If Vecnos told the thrall that I could be taken out of the picture, Asakusa might not question it. He might be focused on Vecnos's plots to hurt me and be blind to what the Nine would do to you and the spiderfolk.'

'Why would Vecnos...' Adrianna started to ask, but of course the answer was obvious. For millennia, her family had eaten every islander that had ever strayed into a cave. Islanders were easy meals: they didn't fight back, had many kids, and were deliciously tender. There were essays written on how the halfling's evolutionary strategy had been to simply produce enough offspring to satiate their predators, like rabbits or insects. 'My friends wouldn't let that happen.'

'I'm sure they wouldn't want to. It's not their loyalty I distrust, but their intelligence. I ask you once more; are you are sure about joining Vecnos in this battle?'

Adrianna wasn't sure at all. She wanted to help those who couldn't help themselves. She'd known that ever since she'd been a little girl and suffered the wrath of the more powerful—namely, her sisters. This was the opportunity she'd been waiting for, a chance to save the Free City and prove to everyone there—the Nine in the Ringwall included—that spiderfolk and flamehearts weren't all bad. This was a chance to prove that the spiderfolk and flamehearts were united with the living, a chance to change everything. And if they sat this fight out, their undead enemy would add a hundred thousand people to his army.

'We can't take the risk of waiting on the sidelines of the skullball court if Vecnos is telling the truth. If it's a trap, it's a perfectly crafted one. We have to help'

'You're right, of course, darling. We can't sit this out, but *you* can. Think of it, Adrianna. Your flesh has yet to harden. One arrow is all it would take. And even if you were at full strength, hordes of skeletons are not your forte. You told me as much when I rescued you from the Blighted Island.'

Adrianna tried to stay resolute despite her heart aching for this dragon prince and his concern for her. If she were to die, he'd have everything: dominion over Krag's Doom *and* her family to order about. Furthermore, if Adrianna rushed off only to die in battle, few would even question it. All Richard had to do to realize absolute power was to let Adrianna die, yet here he was, trying to stop her from even risking her life. She knew then, *really knew*, that she *was* part of Richard's dreams, and that she had been for a long time. He'd betrayed her trust and seized power over her in a moment of weakness, but he'd never wished anything for her other than to be with him. Adrianna loved him for that—despite his flaws—but she couldn't abandon the city she thought of as her home. 'You can't expect me to stay behind.'

'No... No of course not. I knew you'd say no, but what kind of husband would I be if I didn't ask you to stay safe once in a while?'

'A good one,' Adrianna said, and then, unable to resist the fire in his eyes that burned so fiercely for her, found herself kissing him. He tasted of smoke and metal, and his forked tongue was quick as it played with her own.

And then they were leaping from the castle, holding hands as they plummeted toward the pool of lava below.

Chapter 85

Adrianna

Through the air she fell, closer and closer to the lava below. It was a bit melodramatic, but Adrianna was coming to realize her husband was quite, well, *extra*, for lack of a better word. One of the huge, molten lava beasts lifted its head from the swirling pools of liquid rock. Its mouth opened wide, a yawning maw of blackness in a sea of red. And then Richard was beneath her, in human glamour no longer. She landed on his neck, just above his wings as he unfurled them and caught the swirling thermals rising up from the lava. The roughness of his scales was painful against Adrianna's still-soft body. Adrianna grabbed the spines on his neck—thankful that they ended where she was sitting—and held on.

Up and up Richard swirled, pirouetting up from the lava below, his wings like sails, his body rock hard. Adrianna had to admit, she could get used to this. Out they flew over the sea. Far below them were tiny islands filled with islanders and their farms.

She couldn't believe that they were off to face not only the Kraken, but an undead version of it. She shuddered at the thought. She'd never really believed in the thing. A force of creatures so powerful and dense it made its own weather? It was said it was a squid and a crab locked in battle, or trying to breed, and the other creatures were caught in the pheromones and magnetic energies the two great beasts released, but Adrianna didn't know what half those words meant. The details of the Kraken didn't really matter, though. All that mattered was that a horde of yellow-boned corpses were coming for the place she called home, and that she could have stopped them long before they'd recruited such a formidable monster to their side. She wondered if Richard were thinking the same thing about the vampire and the corpses he controlled at the bequest of Chemok.

Apparently he was, for he yelled, 'So what's the battle plan, princess?' over the wind.

'I have no idea!' Adrianna tried to yell back, but the wind was deafening. Instead of answering, Richard reached behind the horns coming from his head and withdrew a green gemstone. He gave it to Adrianna. In doing so, he unbalanced himself and went into a corkscrew spin. Adrianna felt her stomach drop out but she didn't mind. She was a spider princess, more used to fighting upside down than most beings. Her stomach lurched, and she whooped in delight as Richard brought her low enough to touch the water with her outstretched fingers in one hand—the other clutched the green emerald. She clung to his body with the tiny spinnerets at the ends of each of her eight spider legs.

'When this is all over, we can fly like this every day,' Richard's voice, as smooth and rich as velvet, sounded as if he was whispering huskily in her ear. After their last kiss, Adrianna very much wanted to believe in a future where this could happen. She wanted to believe in a future with Asakusa too, but neither would come to pass unless they won the day.

'If we survive,' Adrianna said, and saw Richard nod as he flew up above the water, pumping his wings and keeping their speed. The emerald was a sending stone, she realized. Like the one he'd used to spy on her before. There was something else about it too, something familiar that was impossible to place with the wind rushing in her hair.

'We'll survive,' Richard said. 'If the thrall can beat the Kraken when it's alive, I'm sure you and I can defeat it when it's dead.'

'It would be a waste of time for us to fight it. And besides, I thought you said you wanted to defeat the vampire.'

'So, you do have a plan!'

Adrianna wondered at what all Richard could sense through the sending stone. Some of them only sent conscious thoughts; others could transmit images or even emotions. Adrianna had possessed a mirror that sent images as easily as most stones sent words. She'd lost it when she'd gone to Rolph Katinka's island with Asakusa. Clayton had stayed behind then, nothing but a charred heart until she'd returned with Richard and Asakusa. That was when Richard had given him those emeralds.

Adrianna's throat caught.

'Your plan, princess?' Richard asked.

'We'll… that is, I'll have to…' But her mind was spinning out of control. The emerald in her hand was the same as the ones in Clayton's face. That couldn't be a coincidence, not coming from Richard Valkanna.

'We'll have to improvise a bit, I'll expect,' Richard said, seemingly oblivious to her inner thoughts, despite her holding the emerald, so there was that at least. 'If the Kraken comes through those cliffs—which I expect it will —then we'll have to engage at its level. My question is whether the skeletons will come before or after, and whether they'll try to scale the Ringwall. Do you think it can widen the gap between the two cliffs?'

'We won't know until we're there,' Adrianna said weakly.

'There's another way,' Richard said.

'What do you mean?'

'I... have a confession,' Richard said. How curious it was to hear an adult red dragon, possibly the most fearsome creature Adrianna had ever encountered, stammer over a sending stone. 'If you reach through the sending stone, you'll be able to see that they're there already.'

She reached out using the emerald, and saw them, her friends—two of them, at least. Ebbo and Asakusa stood on to the top of the Ringwall, looking out at Magnus's fields of seven crops. Hundreds of skeletons were charging forward through fields of apples, corn, barley, carrots, taters, snabbage, and nonions, wielding shovels and scythes that sparkled in the moonlight. Thousands of humans—the denizens of S'kar-Vozi—fired arrows at them from the strange T-shaped weapons she'd seen the hrocs wield. She felt her perspective shift, as if someone had turned around, and saw a huge storm cloud building over S'kar-Vozi behind them. Richard's first assessment had been correct: the skeletons were going to climb the wall, while the Kraken came in from the sea.

'A pincer attack.' Clayton's voice came clearly from the emerald.

'Clayton,' Adrianna gasped aloud, and saw the perspective of the golem flinch in surprise.

'Princess?' he said aloud, the emeralds for his eyes carrying the message to Adrianna.

The emeralds he'd had since they'd resurrected him.

Adrianna's stomach filled with cold dread.

'I had to make sure you were safe,' Richard said. 'I knew you wouldn't want to come back with me, but I had to know you were safe,' he was rambling. 'My father wouldn't let you go free. He's been plotting against you since before the marriage, and the marriage just gave him reason to kill you sooner. Destruyag Island was the perfect place for an accident. That Dontalas Crisp could have defeated you. I was worried sick.'

Adrianna understood the feeling. Sick was how she felt. She would have screamed, except that Clayton spoke next.

'Princess, I'm so glad to hear you,' he said in a rush, 'My master ordered me not to tell you about the stones, but I'm glad to be able to.'

'Your *master*?' Adrianna said, but she understood. Richard had bought the golem from Leopold the Grimy. It had been his coin, even though Asakusa had stolen it back.

'Yes, my lady. Prince Richard.' Clayton sounded so relieved.

'It wasn't like I was micromanaging the blob of clay,' Richard protested.

'That's true, Princess. There were only two orders—well, and some occasional spying, but that was mostly just him watching what I was already doing,' Clayton said. 'Don't tell you about the stones was the second command.'

'And the first?'

'Be the golem your friends believe you to be.'

Adrianna felt her throat catch for what felt like the hundredth time. The Etterqueen couldn't spin a web as complex as her husband could. Truly, that order wasn't so bad, was it? Clayton had been spying on her, but he'd still been his old self... right? Richard said he was only looking out for her. Sure, it was creepy as a web-walking mammal, but the dragon prince had been raised to control her. He'd confessed that on their wedding day. For Richard, sending her golem with eyes to watch her was one of the less creepy things he could do... or so she thought. Admittedly, her judgment might be a bit skewed.

It wasn't what Richard had done that scared her to the very core of her abdomen. It was what the golem was. 'Are you still you, Clayton?'

'I... I think so.' His often-foppish voice wilted. 'I think this might have been all I ever was. Just someone that happened to follow the right orders.'

'No, Clayton, you're more than that. You were always my conscience. *Always.*'

'Adrianna, I—' Adrianna heard no more as a sensation of extreme vertigo seized her. Clayton's emerald eyes had seen Valkanna, and seeing oneself through another sending stone was always difficult. Teasing out the implications of what Richard had done to Clayton would have to wait.

They were flying over the water so fast, they'd already made it to S'kar-Vozi. They found the city under siege. Pirate ships surrounded the fields of crops. Richard released a gout of flame at one of the ships, setting it ablaze and illuminating the others. They were already empty. Rolph Katinka was expending all his forces, then. His entire army would take the free city or be defeated. The people within would be trapped between a horde of skeletons and an undead Kraken.

Adrianna had no more time to think about her spinning husband.

'Richard, take me to the top of the Ringwall.'

To his credit, he didn't complain. 'And what would you have me do, princess?'

'As you said, find the vampire and defeat him. I have a feeling these skeletons won't stop until you do.'

Chapter 86

Ebbo

Insects. Though they were anything but, the skeletons reminded Ebbo of insects. Like a plague of hallow's ants during the pumpkin harvest, the skeletons surged up the Ringwall with hunger in the eye sockets of their yellow skulls.

It took all of Ebbo's strength not to drop *Deondadel*. He wished he didn't have to fight, that maybe he could slip away and go unnoticed, slip down back into S'kar-Vozi, maybe ask Vecnos for a bit of that powdered basilisk venom. But that was the old Ebbo. He wouldn't succumb to magick, not now, not when his friends needed him most.

'If they get through, you understand our brothers will be the first they take,' Vecnos said. He had a fist of tiny five-pointed stars. He threw them at the protoskeletons, skeletons, and corpses climbing the wall with such verve that they split their skulls when they connected, knocking them into a pile of lifeless bones. Unless he missed. The stars that didn't hit a skull simply wedged themselves in skeletons' collar bones or ulnas. The skeletons seemed to learn from each other. When one caught a five-pointed star in its forearm, the others followed. Soon, Vecnos's weapons were worthless. He drew two daggers and gritted his teeth. His dimples hardly showed at all.

Ebbo stole one last glance behind them. Of course, Vecnos was right about the islanders. The skeletons would pour through the city like ants, and the easiest food available would be the islanders who'd Transcended, wasting away on the street like dumplings dropped off a picnic blanket. Skeletons would kill them and transform them into more monsters, regardless of where their souls ended up once they walked the Ways of the Dead. Ebbo had to fight to protect his people. Fortunately, he wasn't alone. He looked down the length of the Ringwall. Warriors of legend manned stations, each illuminated in the night by means magickal or pedestrian.

There was Magnus, dwarven druid, golden beard and master of the seven crops. A tiny sun burned behind him, and the skeletons that tried to scale up his portion of the Ringwall were thrown from its surface by the very vines they tried to climb. Ebbo had never seen Magnus awake this late before. He hoped he'd last the night.

Further down were the VanChamps. Elven siblings and—if the rumors were true—lovers. Each wielded a longbow that sang as it fired ethereal arrows down at the skeletons below. They fought fiercely, as do those that are fighting for family or lovers.

Susanna was there, floating so her five-year-old body could see over the edge of the ramparts. A sphere of shimmering silver sprang into existence around her when a volley of bones clattered through the air. They burst to dust upon touching the sphere. The powerful wizard's body could probably be knocked unconscious by a single hurled femur.

Next to her was Zultana. The Master Seamstress fought with a needle and thread. The needle jumped from skeleton to skeleton, doing no perceivable damage, only threading itself through eye sockets and jaw bones. After snagging a dozen skeletons, Zultana gestured to the horizon and the needle jumped, pulling the first skeleton with it. The thread connecting it to the others sent their skulls crashing into each other with enough force to crack them and render them useless to Chemok.

Fyelna—Ragnar's wife and Cleric extraordinaire—rushed about, feeding potions to warriors that fell. Her husband was conspicuously absent. Ebbo stole a glance behind him. The ancient warrior would come from the sea. Of that, Ebbo was certain.

The spans of the Ringwall protected by the two human families that counted their elders among the Nine were soon overrun by skeletons.

This was where Ebbo tried to help. He darted between human legs, stabbing felled corpses and skeletons in their eye sockets to crack their skulls and thus end Chemok's power over the bones that animated the dead. It was exhausting, thankless, and gruesome work. When a human was knocked to the ground instead of one of the undead, Ebbo was often forced to watch as a half-rotten corpse would stab them in the heart, then stare into their eyes until the same yellowish green light ignited therein. The human—an ally no longer—would then rise and turn on their former compatriots. Ebbo had assumed that all the protoskeletons, skeletons, corpses, zombies, and however else one classified the undead were all being raised by the vampire Adrianna had told him about, but now he had to confront the idea—again and again and again—that this wasn't some legion, but an infection. He didn't think that stopping the vampire would do a thing. Like a potato field stricken by rootrot, Ebbo feared every single yellow skull would have to be destroyed if the living were to win today.

But at least he wasn't alone. Not yet.

Some of these infestations were knocked back by powerful warriors. The nipple-spikes of Hilde Haufbrau's enormous breastplate impaled any skeletons that made it past her axe. Krouche le Douche used his demonic ancestry to blast fire and force at the skeletons, sending sprays of bones over the edge of the Ringwall. Ebbo wondered idly why the demon's spawn had ever bothered to employ others when he used his girth so effectively in combat.

His friends fought valiantly as well. Clayton smashed skull after skull, never showing shock or surprise when skeleton after skeleton sunk their weapons into his clay. And why should he? His steel heart was full of Heartbeats, and he could feel vibrations every time one of their bony fingers dug into the Ringwall. He could sense the skeletons coming before they did. Though his fine silken dragon and spider suit had long been torn to tatters, the golem showed no sign of slowing.

Asakusa didn't stop as many skeletons as Clayton, but the ones he did were essential. He zipped around the battlefield, opening and closing his gates, lifting *Byergen* into uppercut after uppercut. With the hordes of skeletons, the thrall had no trouble keeping the hammer from dragging atop the Ringwall. Ebbo shuddered, thinking of where his friend's Corruption would be when this was all over. Already his right arm dripped in chains, and his legs were shackled together, though the chain was long enough that it didn't slow Asakusa as he dispatched any skeleton that came near the men trying to drop stones on the thousands of undead climbing the Ringwall.

And yet somehow, with all these warriors, it wasn't enough. They needed Adrianna and that cranberry of a dragon, and they needed them *now*.

But even their army of meat eaters might not be enough. The problem was obvious to Ebbo. Everyone, everyone in the Archipelago laid their dead to rest in the sea. Islanders did it as often as giants. The denizens of S'kar-Vozi did so with humble, convenient ceremonies, dumping the deceased to begin the long rot in Bog's Bay until the kobold's clockwork sewers flushed them out to the wider sea. Chemok's hordes had been harvesting the sea, and then there was the fact that they were from the Blighted Island, somewhere still desolate from the greatest war ever fought. Ebbo reasoned that that explained the vast quantities of dwarf, elf and orc skeletons he saw.

Not all the orcs were against them, though. The ones who'd almost sacrificed Ebbo were at the wall with barrels of tea made of skull blossom.

Apparently, they'd grown quite a bit of it back. Dergh had a knack for spotting dense clusters of skeletons and ordering the barrels dumped out. The tea washed the yellow from their bones, sending them clattering down below.

And still, it was *not* enough. The skeletons were gaining purchase on the Ringwall. People were dying. Those that lived in the Ringwall were beginning to fight back to back.

There was a sound from behind Ebbo and he stole another glance, earning a curse from Vecnos, who was kicked by a skeleton Ebbo should have defended against.

Ebbo ignored him. The sound he heard was like a foghorn and the screech of metal on metal. It grew louder and louder, and then there was a horrible, lifeless cheer. He looked across Bog's Bay and saw it. The Kraken was at the cliffs that framed the entrance to the bay. The water in front of it was already thick with fishmen and sharks. Undead, no doubt. And there, on the Kraken's back, was Ragnar. Sword in one hand, lance in the other. He ordered the monster forward.

It smashed at the high black cliffs, knocking down boulders big enough to crush even its mighty form, but Ragnar pulled a shield from his back and deflected the falling stones like raindrops. Even from this distance, Ebbo could see his rubbery skin contract and expand, shoving off the boulders through the shield.

Still, the way was too shallow for the Kraken. It couldn't get through. That was why S'kar-Vozi existed, after all, because it was safe from the Kraken. It always had been. Sure, the monsters' jellyfish and sea turtles had made it into Bog's Bay, but the Kraken itself was just too big...

Until it split. The crab and squid—always locked in combat or reproduction—broke from each other. The crab worked itself out of the water on legs thick as ship's masts. Below, in the water, the giant squid pulled itself through, urged on by Ragnar atop its back. Once through, the two parts of the great beast rejoined each other with the blood-curdling scream of lobsters being boiled alive. Then it slipped into the water. A darks mass moving toward the shore. The storm came with it, pouring through the black cliffs and striking at them with lightning.

But Ebbo didn't notice that at all.

Instead he saw the ship behind it. A warship with yellow skulls on black sails. Ebbo hadn't met him, but he knew who was aboard that ship. He was pretty sure he'd inadvertently invited him to S'kar-Vozi.

'Oh man, we're truly good and screwed then,' Ebbo mumbled, telling himself that he really, *really* didn't want any magick right now, even though there didn't seem to be much point in holding out hope for anything like dawn. It was over, then. They'd lost. Despite all they'd done, all that they'd sacrificed, despite Ebbo getting *clean*, it *had not been enough*. The Kraken had made it into Bog's Bay, and the skeletons had nearly taken the Ringwall. Ebbo looked to those around him. Maybe, now that all hope was lost, he could get one last pinch of magick. It didn't really matter anymore, right?

And then Adrianna Morticia joined the battle on the back of a red dragon, and Ebbo promised himself that he would never *ever* doubt the spider princess ever again.

Chapter 87

Adrianna

'There, take me there,' Adrianna said, pointing to a spot atop the Ringwall. She didn't know exactly how Richard knew where she was pointing —he probably had scrying gems sewn into her clothes while she slept—but know he did. The dragon landed on the top of the Ringwall and cleared an area with a blast of flame. Charred skeletons fell off the wall and into the darkness below.

A Gate opened behind Adrianna and Asakusa was there, on the top of the wall. 'We have to go,' Asakusa said, pointing at the Kraken already through the high cliffs that framed the entrance to Bog's Bay.

'You don't give orders here, thrall,' Richard growled.

'He's right. The Ringwall is lost,' Adrianna watched in horror as more and more skeletons came up and over the wall. Some spots were still being held. No skeletons came close to Zultana, and Susannah had vanished into a haze of fire and lightning and balls of ice. Presumably, skeletons couldn't do any of that. But Magnus was falling back, using his living wooden staff to fend off blows. His magick sun burned above him, not yet flickering, a good sign. The VanChamps stood on the parapets as their guards formed a wall in front of them, making out like there was no tomorrow. The guards didn't particularly look like they wanted to defend the elven siblings, but they hadn't made it to the parapet as quickly, so they had to deal with the skeletons.

If the Ringwall fell, the city would be engulfed by death. Adrianna couldn't let that happen.

Movement in the shadows, and Vecnos was next to them. 'Susannah has been studying the bones. Chemok is some kind of an organism that animates them.'

'A what?' Asakusa said.

'Like the scum that grows in the sewers,' Vecnos explained. 'I think the vampire must have been the original source. We'll need to defeat him if we don't want this to happen all over again.'

'Well, how do we do that?' Asakusa pointed at the Kraken, nearly to the docks. Behind it, the water teemed with undead fishmen. Their bodies were wounded and blaoted, with only hints of yellow bones sticking through the rotten flesh. Ragnar—his dead eyes glowing with the same light as the skeletons he now fought with—bellowed orders from atop the Kraken. Behind them all came the pirate ship. A dreadnaught of a ship. Its black sails billowed despite there being hardly any air, showing yellow skulls sewn into them.

'That vampire is on that ship,' Vecnos said. 'Can you handle him?'

Both Richard and Asakusa barked out a yes before Adrianna could answer. She nodded curtly before asking Vecnos, 'You're not coming with us?'

He shook his head. 'I need the Ourdor of Ouroboros to get as many islanders as we can to safety. That's not a job that can be… unsupervised.'

So down they flew into the rain, Richard as a dragon, with Adrianna and Asakusa on his back.

Getting to the vampire proved harder than anyone had anticipated. Richard's first impulse had been to simply burn the ship he rode on. He flew over it, spraying it with flames, but they bounced off as if they'd hit a wall of ice. Bog's Bay wasn't so lucky. When the flames touched the oily surface of the water, the bay ignited. In moments the surface of the sea burned despite the rainstorm, smoke and acrid flames everywhere except for the ship.

Perhaps that would have been manageable if not for the undead Kraken. It thrashed in the flames, bringing the burning sludge with it and smashing it into buildings. So much of S'kar-Vozi was made of wood, and none of it had the magick protection that the ship in the bay had. The areas that weren't within reach of the Kraken soon were ablaze as well. Zombie fishmen emerged from the water, coated in flaming sludge. They ran as far into the city as their flesh would allow, running into a building only when their yellow bones began to char.

In moments, the lower half of S'kar-Vozi was on fire.

The Kraken had brought a storm with it as well, but the rain did nothing to put out the flames.

'We have to help them,' Asakusa said. 'People need to be evacuated.'

'But your Corruption—' Adrianna protested.

'Hopefully isn't flammable,' Asakusa said, then opened a Gate that Richard had to pump his wings to dodge. Asakusa jumped from the dragon's back and vanished through the Gate, into the flames and smoke coming from the city below.

Richard swooped down at the ship once more, transforming mid-flight so he landed on two feet with Adrianna cradled in his arms. It was a good thing she'd tied up her hair when they'd neared the city.

She stepped down. Even though the ship wasn't burning, she could feel the heat of the flames engulfing the bay all around her. The rain evaporated long before it could reach her and soothe her raw skin. Normally she might not have minded the heat, but with her exoskeleton still healing, it was close to unbearable. Good thing her webmother had insisted she wear homespun silken armor rather than leather.

'The vampire should be below,' Richard said, already hunting for his foe. 'They can't stand running water. He'll be in a coffin filled with grave dirt.'

'I think we're the ones in the coffin,' Adrianna said, directing Richard's attention to the ground. He lifted a shining red-gold boot in disgust.

'Right you are!' said the Baron Rolph Katinka, materializing in front of them from a cloud of blood. Although there was an undead Kraken smashing a city before him, the baron didn't look in the least bit concerned. If anything, he looked pleased to see them.

'The ship is made from reclaimed wood. Found a whole platoon of druidic gnomes in one of the fields. The dwarves or someone buried them in coffins made from their own holy trees. Sometimes I am quite thankful the undead don't recall their past lives, only their skills. I don't think the gnomes wouldn't have appreciated the irony. The dirt, of course, is from the farm. Skeletons sleep in it every day, so if that doesn't count for grave dirt, I don't know what does.'

'What are you doing here?' Adrianna said.

Rolph Katinka smiled a sad smile. 'I thought it was obvious. We're here to kill you.'

'Why now?' Richard demanded.

'How funny, a dragon asking for answers. I didn't know you were capable of logical thought.'

'Try me, zombie.'

That earned a sneer from Katinka.

'Chemok's time has come,' said another, deeper voice. 'He brought the force—the god—that unites us into this world when he mastered death. His army—our army—nearly conquered the elves and the dwarfs but were pushed back. Chemok, with wisdom only granted by those who embrace death, let himself be killed so that we could rest. He had already put a piece of the god he delivered to this world in the chest of a man in a coffin. The baron was unearthed, only to find that those who had defeated us had—through their actions—admitted that they wished for the immortality that only death can give. For they left their dead buried in the very place they'd fought against us. A thousand gifts, which the Baron used to *farm*.'

Adrianna recognized the voice when she heard the disdain with which he said *farm*. But it came from someone she'd killed, or not killed—as he was undead, but certainly defeated.

James, the skinless butler, emerged from below the deck. He approached them, and the heat of the flames was enough to make the smoky scent of meat to rise from his exposed muscles. He wore nothing at all, and held only a yellow skull in one hand.

'The end has come. You will join us, and finally this realm will rest.'

'We're not tired,' Adrianna said.

Katinka chuckled, but James didn't react at all. The undead had no sense of humor.

Chapter 88

Adrianna

The fight was strangely nostalgic for Adrianna. The last time she'd fought the skinless butler, Asakusa had been at her side, and Richard had done battle with the vampire in the sky above them. There were differences this time. Asakusa and his hammer weren't here, but in the burning city, evacuating people and hopefully fetching Ebbo and Clayton. And then there was James. The meaty muscle-man was much stronger than he had been last time, and instead of fighting with his fists, he used two spiked mallets. Skull-crushers, Adrianna had heard the type of weapon called. One of the best weapons to use against the spider princess, as blunt force would crack her exoskeleton. Facing them in her current state was almost mind-numbingly terrifying. James didn't know that bladed weapons would work just fine right now. Adrianna didn't know whether to count that as a blessing.

Above her, Valkanna and Katinka exchanged blows, Richard preferring long swoops that gave way to powerful strikes while Katinka disincorporated again and again, using the dark and the rain to hide the cloud of bats he so often became.

James attacked her with the mallets, and she dodged his blows easily enough. After all, she'd practiced plenty with Asakusa. *Asakusa*, where was he? She couldn't hold her own against James much longer. Daggers hadn't worked before, and they weren't working now.

Still, Adrianna had to try. She severed a tendon in one of the flesh golem's arms, causing him to drop a mallet. She used the opportunity to grab her hair and let it down. Her spider form Unfolded and she grabbed daggers in three of her hands, her whip in the fourth. She cracked the whip across James' face, cutting his forehead and causing a sausage's worth of thick, coagulated blood to spill in the butler's eyes.

While James clawed at his face, Adrianna looked to the battle taking place in the sky above her. There was something to Katinka's movements that was different than their last battle had been. He seemed more limited, somehow, but Adrianna didn't have time to figure out the details, for James—blinded no longer—straightened and looked at her. His eyes were bloodshot, and the wound on his forehead hadn't healed. Instead the blood was flowing back into his flesh. It was a macabre sight, illuminated as it was by the burning city at Adrianna's back.

James smiled. 'You cannot defeat me. There are ten thousand more of me destroying your city as we speak.'

'So, you really are just some random old corpse,' Adrianna sneered.

'We are all the corpse of Chemok. He is all of us. Together we are capable of things the living would never dream of.'

'I wasn't aware the dead dreamed,' Adrianna said.

'Oh, yes,' James lunged at her.

Adrianna leaped backwards, cracked her whip around a piece of wood sticking from the rigging, and pulled herself up and out of the golem's reach. Up here, she could feel the rain.

She ducked her head as Richard flew past, appearing from the darkness and tucking a wing to avoid hitting her and going into a barrel roll because of it. Just ahead, the vampire coalesced into his human body from a cloud of bats. His fists were clutched together, and as the dragon flew by, he cracked his hands against his head, earning a grunt and a curse from the dragon. 'Darling, a warning would be nice,' Richard shouted into the burning night as he swooped low over the water and banked to come back up.

Rolph Katinka disincorporated yet again, becoming a cloud of blood droplets that then turned into a swarm of bats.

Richard pumped his wings and leveled out, coming at the ship. In the dark of the storm, the only thing Adrianna could track with her spider vision was her husband's eyes. They were angry red embers in the night. He seemed to be able to see the bats silhouetted against the yellow skull on the sails. He exhaled a gout of flame, and the bats scattered, but some were caught in the blast.

They can't go past the edges of the boat, Adrianna realized.

Vampires couldn't stand running water. The only way Rolph was here at all was the grave dirt all over his ship. As soon as he wasn't above it, he was in pain.

They could use that.

Adrianna spared a glance below. James was shimmying up the mast, his skinless muscles making easy work of the climb. She couldn't beat him, that was becoming obvious. She let down her hair and Unfolded so at least she could outpace him. Richard approached again, this time clawing at the cloud of bats. Katinka dodged the blows effortlessly. He materialized in his human form and scratched the living hell out of Richard.

'A plan would be nice, darling!' Richard called out.

Adrianna suddenly had one. It was dangerous, and stupid, and might turn a man who seemed to love her against her forever, but what other hope was there? *Trust me,* she told Richard over the sending stones. To which he replied: *always.*

'Baron, wait! The spiderfolk can help you!'

Richard made some space between himself and the ship. For a moment, he vanished into the night, only to exhale great blasts of flame on the hordes of animated corpses swimming through Bog's Bay.

Adrianna went on. 'Why kill all these people? If they're alive, they could make more and continue to breed an army for Chemok. All of us them could labor at growing vegetables until you see fit to take our final harvest.'

'Our army is complete,' James yelled.

'Then why are you still here, Baron?' Adrianna yelled at the mist now swirling around her. 'Chemok must know of your power. Why else keep you? James is a slave, but you are so much more.'

'A servant,' the cloud of blood grumbled. There it was, then. Katinka wasn't happy with his place.

Richard seemed to understand Adrianna's ploy, for he swooped low and knocked James from the mast with a flick of his tail, thus buying Adrianna more time with Rolph Katinka.

'Let us show how we could work together. If you and I are united, we can defeat anyone. Even the dragon.'

'Adrianna?' Richard said as he swooped overhead. The fear in his voice sounded genuine to Adrianna, so hopefully Katinka would buy it. Adrianna had no idea if this would work. Vampires were notorious for manipulating their prey; would that make him more or less susceptible to the deceptions of others?

Adrianna kept talking to the vampire. 'Come to me, Baron. I know you hunger for true power. I don't fear the undead. I learned to dance with one. Join me.'

The Baron Rolph Katinka materialized in front of Adrianna. She looked into his eyes, let them wash over her. She was his, and he made for her neck.

'Don't touch her!' the dragon prince screamed from above. It was kind of funny to hear him say it with such conviction, considering how fine Richard had always been with the idea of Adrianna treating Asakusa as a mistress.

'Sorry, sweetheart,' Rolph Katinka said and threw Adrianna behind him, ostensibly to protect her from her own husband. Good. It was working!

She could stab the vampire in the back, but she knew it wouldn't do a thing. No, there was only one way to end this. And it might cost her dearly. 'You truly believed I loved you?' Adrianna yelled to Richard. 'When you lost the first time, I knew this would be the outcome. Rolph Katinka will make me a queen of the undead. We will rule in a world you feared to burn. You are to the Baron what the thrall is to you. Trading daggers was but a means to an end. Feast, baron,' Adrianna said, hoping Richard understood exactly what she wanted him to do and that the Baron understood none of it.

'Quite!' the baron said in what he probably thought to be a seductive growl. He sunk his teeth into her neck, groaning in delight as he drank of her white ichor.

Adrianna, fingers on her dagger, waited; waited for Richard to see that she wasn't attacking... She didn't have to wait long.

Richard reacted as she'd hoped. He came at them, nostrils glowing like embers, eyes hot with fury. Flames erupted from his throat and engulfed the vampire. They would have engulfed Adrianna too, except she had brought out *Flametongue* and stabbed it into Rolph's chest at the last second. *Flametongue* absorbed the flames and protected her.

The vampire wasn't so lucky.

His skin crackled and burned away. His flesh charred. And then the dragon was past them, swooping up into the rain for another attack.

Katinka fell to the ground, half a corpse.

Richard landed, and James immediately attacked his human form. Richard parried him effortlessly with his flaming sword, cracking the golem's skull in half and burning out the flesh inside. For a moment, they were alone. Husband and wife on the world's worst honeymoon cruise.

'That was bold of you, to play my fears against Katinka,' Richard said.

'You knew I didn't want it all to burn.'

'Still, you risked your own immolation to save your city. You truly are committed to helping the mortal races.'

'I'm just happy that it worked.' Adrianna sighed in relief and looked past Richard to the burning city. Only she saw quite quickly that it hadn't worked at all.

Hordes of skeletons were still crawling over the Ringwall. Many of the creatures that made up the undead Kraken had thrown themselves on the beach; yellow shells smashed the docks to nothing.

'Katinka's not dead.' Adrianna looked to the vampire below her.

His flesh was burned away. All that was left was a skeleton and organs, still pumping in the night air. And yet, his flesh was regrowing. Knitting itself together as his lungs inflated and deflated, as his heart pumped around an amulet stuck between its chambers.

The amulet. There it was. Some Chemok-worshiping necromancer had buried it in the vampire's heart. So long as a piece of Chemok was inside, the undead infection would persist. She stepped forward and picked up a piece of splintered wood from the deck. Everyone knew how to kill a vampire.

Rolph Katinka, shockingly, laughed at her.

'Your blood is delicious, princess,' he wheezed as he knit himself together. 'I wanted a taste quite badly.'

'I hope it made for a good last meal,' Adrianna said.

'Because you'll kill me with that? Check again. The necromancer James Chemok was quite thorough when he did it.'

Adrianna hadn't known that Chemok was a necromancer. She'd only ever heard the name given to the force that animated the skeletons of the dead, but now wasn't exactly the time to consider the veracity of her education. Adrianna looked again at the amulet. It appeared to be a locket in the shape of skull, though it was a bit difficult to be sure, because it went in and out of the baron's heart. She stabbed his heart, but it wouldn't go through. The metal skull was cunningly crafted so the wooden stake couldn't make it through both sides of the heart. She couldn't kill him.

The baron laughed, 'You think I haven't tried that myself? You think I like being the key to this army? I like the living! They're delicious! I don't want them all to die.'

'I... I'll throw you overboard.' It was a weak threat and Adrianna knew it, but what else could she do? She had thought that being incinerated pointblank by dragon's fire would have killed the vampire, and if not, then surely the old wooden stake should have worked, but both had done little beyond slow Katinka down. On top of that, it seemed that the vampire was only the source of the infection, not the cause. That meant that even if she could kill Katinka, the Kraken and the hordes of corpses would continue to fight.

'The water won't kill me. Just make me sick. I'll get washed ashore, regrow, and continue to infect others with Chemok so long as the amulet protects my heart. Even if you somehow manage to defeat me, it won't matter. The skeleton army will continue to fight so long as a single skull survives. The undead will continue to grow more cunning as their numbers swell and Chemok networks between them.' It could have been gloating, but

Katinka just sounded depressed.

'I'll just wait until sunrise,' Adrianna said, desperate to defeat this self-hating foe and end the mission she'd been tasked with. She knew she shouldn't betray her plans, but suddenly the Baron Rolph Katinka seemed more than comfortable with his own defeat.

'A piece of me will remain in the locket. I've felt the sun's kiss before. I've been the necromancer's slave a long time.' His flesh was re-knitting.

Adrianna had no time for other ideas, though, for her husband grabbed for her hair. *Trust me,* he said through the stones.

Adrianna didn't really have a choice in the matter, as once more Richard could manipulate her body with simple twists of his fingers, but he didn't do anything to the spider princess besides pull her to her feet. Though even that hurt, given the state of her exoskeleton.

'Richard, please, why are you doing this to me?' Adrianna begged, praying to the Etterqueen that it was all a ploy.

But Adrianna never got her answer, for right at that moment, a Gate opened on the deck of the ship. Blinding light poured out and silhouetted the forms of Asakusa, Clayton and Ebbo as they stepped onto the ship.

'Not gonna lie, this is kind of what I was hoping for.' Asakusa was already moving toward Richard. He lifted his hammer and swung it into the dragon's chest. Richard released Adrianna as he was knocked from the boat. He roared in frustration then he transformed into a dragon once more.

At their feet, the vampire hissed, still regrowing his body but hissing now at the light.

'We brought a sun because, you know, vampires don't like those!' Ebbo said.

Adrianna realized that this was the magick Ebbo had been talking about. A sun powerful enough to grow the food to feed the hundred thousand people of S'kar-Vozi.

'And it was Ebbo's idea,' Clayton said, sounding like he'd been coached to say this.

'It won't work,' Adrianna was saying, but the sun was hardly standing still. Magnus must have sent it forward, for it flew past her friends and crashed into Katinka, cracking the hull of the boat as it did.

It was Magnus's sun, Adrianna realized, a ball of light strong enough to light up the sky on the deck of ship.

Rolph Katinka hissed but couldn't escape. His muscles were still reknitting. The sun smashed into his chest, burning his flesh away.

Asakusa struck the sun with his hammer, smashing it into the vampire and through the floor into the hold below, which had already filled with water.

The sea didn't extinguish the sun. Steam hissed from below, drowning out the vampire's screams before he slipped underwater.

'He'll regrow,' Adrianna said over the roar of Bog's Bay swallowing the ship. 'The amulet. We have to break the amulet.'

'We got this,' Ebbo said.

'Let's go,' Adrianna replied automatically.

'No offense, your majesty, but taking jewelry off people is sort of my specialty. Plus, Susannah said that defeating the vampire isn't going to stop Chemok and his protoskeletons.'

'Protoskeletons?'

'Don't ask,' Asakusa said, and Adrianna didn't press further.

'Which means your skills might be needed with... you know, *that.*' Clayton gestured toward the Kraken and the sea churning with the undead all around it.

'Okay, good points,' Adrianna said, feeling a quick stab of pride for her group of friends. 'Clayton, you and Ebbo finish off Katinka, Asakusa and I will take the Kraken.' Even saying it sounded ridiculous, but what other choice did they have?

Adrianna attached a silk thread to the golem. Then Clayton picked up the islander and jumped into the hole in the center of the ship.

That left Adrianna with Asakusa on a sinking ship with a red dragon circling them.

'You think he's going to burn us alive if I kiss you again?' Asakusa asked as Adrianna led him to a rowboat.

Adrianna smiled. Etterqueen, she realized then that she really did love this idiot. Here he was, on the verge of drowning, of being burned alive or worse—somehow surviving that and becoming a skeletal slave—and finally, *finally,* his tongue wasn't tied.

'Probably,' Adrianna replied. 'He's pretty pissed. I let the vampire give me a hickey.'

'That's pretty gross,' Asakusa said as he very gingerly put his stone hammer into the bottom of the lifeboat as the vampire's ship sank into Bog's Bay.

'I thought it would let us defeat him, but this amulet...' And suddenly, Adrianna knew how they could defeat Chemok.

Richard was growing closer. Eyes red with rage that saw only Asakusa. But he couldn't hurt them with his flames as long as Adrianna had the dagger.

But Adrianna and Asakusa didn't matter, not compared to the free city. Adrianna finally understood why Asakusa was so willing to sacrifice himself for her. It was the right thing to do. Not dying for the spider princess, obviously, but being willing to lay down your life for someone besides yourself.

So Adrianna took out *Flametongue,* held it aloft so Richard could see, then attached it to the piece of silk connected to Clayton. She sent a brief message, and tossed the dagger overboard.

Asakusa swallowed hard. 'Can I kiss you even if we get burned alive?'

'Sorry, Asakusa, not right now. I have some shit to fix with my marriage.'

Chapter 89

Asakusa

'What will it be, spider princess? The thrall, or me?' Richard roared into the air as Asakusa stood at the front of the tiny rowboat. Adrianna refused to go through a Gate he'd opened for her to escape. He'd told her they needed to go defeat the Kraken, but Adrianna had insisted they couldn't do it without Richard's help. Asakusa thought he could crack the dragon across the jaw if it tried to eat them, but he didn't say anything. He, too, wanted an answer to this question. Despite the hordes of skeletons smashing his hometown, he wanted to know the answer to this very much.

'I don't know!' Adrianna said, frustrating Asakusa and, judging from the dragon's roar, bothering Richard a bit as well.

'You threw the dowry I gave you overboard, so perhaps you've made your choice,' Richard growled, spinning around them in tighter and tighter circles. Asakusa had no doubt that if he were alone on this boat, he would've already been incinerated. It was Richard's feelings for Adrianna that spared them both.

'I threw that dagger to save the city!' Adrianna said.

Asakusa didn't want to point out that it hadn't yet worked.

'You threw it because you don't care for me! You never have!'

Asakusa was shocked, absolutely *shocked*, that not only could a red dragon express his emotions so openly, but that he could sound so *hurt*.

'I do!' Adrianna shouted back.

Asakusa felt as if Adrianna had put the dagger right into his heart.

'I care for you, and for Asakusa! But I care for this city most of all! I care for these people! Everyone has been trying to make me choose whether I should be with an arrogant dragon who understands me too well, or a humble kid who never will.'

Richard kept flying in circles above them. 'I'm listening!'

Asakusa grinned. The asshole really was good with words. 'You really need to pick,' Asakusa said, knowing it was the wrong thing to say, but also knowing that Adrianna had to hurry up if there was going to be anything left of the city.

'I don't know how to pick between the two of you!' She turned to Asakusa, her six eyes only for him. 'I love you, Asakusa, I really do. You're passionate, and brave, and loyal, but...'

'I'm not worthy of a princess.' Asakusa shrugged. It was true.

'And Richard! You're close to perfect, really you are, but you abused your power over me, and you will again!'

'I'm a product of how I was raised!' Richard whined.

'You know you can't trust him,' Asakusa said. The look in Adrianna's eyes said she knew it was true.

'I *have* to, Asakusa, don't you see that? He can't be my enemy, he can't be *our* enemy. Who do you think he would hurt first?'

'I dunno. He made Clayton like a slave or something, didn't he?'

'He'd hurt *you*, you idiot!' Adrianna said and slapped Asakusa on his Corruption. Most people recoiled at it, but Adrianna never had.

'Can't I have both?' Adrianna said. 'Please? Richard can be my husband, and Asakusa... my lover.'

Asakusa blushed fiercely at that. Richard had mentioned it before, but Asakusa had never considered it because Adrianna had paid it no attention. But...would it be so bad? It wasn't like Asakusa was afraid of Richard. His hammer was strong enough to crack the dragon's skull, and he could always open a Gate to escape if he needed to. What sounded worse was that he'd have to accept Richard as a part of Adrianna's life, which meant a part of his life too, as he didn't ever want to let Adrianna go. It sounded complicated, so complicated, but what other choice was there? Still... 'He has your dagger, and he can use your hair against you.' Asakusa didn't want to ruin Adrianna's plans, but there it was.

'I heard that, thrall!" Richard said, and then Adrianna's dagger came careening out of sky and stuck into the floor between them.

'I'll have to give this back,' Adrianna picked up the dagger. 'But if it works...'

Adrianna turned the dagger on herself. She held up *Bloodweaver's* unbelievably sharp blade and ran it on the side of her scalp, just above the ear, shaving her hair about halfway up the side of her head. When she did, nothing happened to her spider form, but Asakusa knew her body enough to know what she'd just done. She'd just removed an eighth of her hair. Permanently. That meant part of her body would never Fold ever again. By

Asakusas' reckoning, she'd always have a spider arm to fender heself, no matter what she did with the rest of her.

Richard, too, seemed to be either mollified or shocked, for he swooped down and scooped up the rowboat in his talons.

Together, the three of them flew toward the Kraken, hoping—finally—that together they could survive this.

Chapter 90

Ebbo

Ebbo sank into the murk. He'd been offered more gillyweed, flashpowder, and tinker's tick. There were advantages to fighting with a bunch of extremely powerful mages, but he'd said no. Not now, not ever again. Ebbo would not do more magick and Transcend. There were too many people counting on him.

Instead he sank into Bog's Bay, his lungs burning as Clayton guided their descent. It was easy to find their way, even in the murk. They were looking for a sun, after all.

They found the vampire at the bottom, or what was left of him. A charred skull that even under water was burning away. Just below it there was the black heart, wrapped in a locket shaped like a skull.

Ebbo swam to it, horrified to see that it pulsing with dark life, even this close to a sun and under an ocean. The power... the magick in that locket must have been—

No. Not anymore. Ebbo was a new islander.

He picked at the locket with *Deondadel*. The elven dagger created a seam when one shouldn't have been there, but as soon as it did, it shattered, turning to dust that was washed away.

'Cranberries!' Ebbo signaled to Clayton over the thread. 'We are good and royally screwed. When I die, tell them I died sober.'

'Don't be so sure,' Clayton messaged back, then reeled in a thread of silk to reveal he had *Flametongue*, Adrianna's fancy dagger.

Ebbo didn't know what the thing was going to do against the locket, but then, Clayton didn't turn it on the locket. Instead he used his brawny, sculpted physique to stab the sun that burned at the bottom of the bay.

The dagger absorbed the heat like it did everything else. Unfortunately, in the process it turned Clayton's hand into solid stone.

'Ebbo!' Clayton messaged.

Ebbo understood. He'd picked pockets from wizards with magick robes. Taking a dagger from a stone hand would be nothing.

He worked it out of Clayton's hand—his lungs were really burning now —but when he took hold of the dagger, he forgot all about that.

In his hand he held the greatest amount of magick he'd ever experienced. It made the blue snake powder that Vecnos used seem like fairy dust. It made fairy dust seem like regular dust. Ebbo only had to prick his finger with its tip and the magick of a sun—and not just any garden-variety, regular old sun, but Magnus's sun—would course through him. Ebbo wasn't foolish enough to think he'd necessarily survive such a hit, but he also knew enough about his own experiences with magick to know that mainlining the druid's most powerful spell would be the single most pleasurable thing he would ever be able to do in his entire life. To say no now would be to deny a godlike experience of hedonism. To say no now would mean he'd miss out on something truly amazing, and for what? To go back to a burned city crowded with the dead? What was the point of doing anything except taking this chance, taking this chance to see what life could really offer? To say no now would be to live the rest of his life in shadow instead of the light of ecstasy.

Ebbo said no.

He took the dagger, looked at Clayton, whose sculpted features were starting to blur under the ocean—pretended like he was going to poke himself to get high just to get a rise out of Clayton—then stabbed the dagger into the crack he'd found in the side of the locket.

The amulet sprung open, and the light of a sun condensed into the size of a kitchen knife burned the heart away. The last muscle of the vampire's heart within pumped once more, and then turned to ash in the brightness of a sun burning under the sea. The vampire was dead, and with him gone, the locket ceased to function. It lost its yellow luster and fell still.

At least Ebbo hoped it did, for at that moment, the sun was extinguished —and Ebbo, already under the sea, was plunged into darkness.

Chapter 91

Clayton

Clayton would be the first to admit that he was not the person to save a drowning anyone. He couldn't personally drown—this was true—but he also couldn't swim, as he was much denser than water. Still, he couldn't let Ebbo drown either. So, at the bottom of Bog's Bay, Clayton unsuccessfully tried to save his friend's life.

Clayton didn't know what had happened to his ability to change shapes. For that matter, he didn't know where it had come from in the first place. No other golem had such an ability, yet Clayton had somehow evolved it. If only he had that now, he could change into something and make it to the surface to save the rapidly asphyxiating Ebbo. But he didn't. Despite having his steel heart crammed with more than ten thousands Heartbeats (Leopold the Grimy's repairs had even further extended his ability to store the magick that let Clayton change his fists into hammers, regrow himself, and had once let him shapeshift), Clayton was trapped in the body he'd been given. Why couldn't he reach those powers?

But Clayton knew. He had always thought he was special, but he wasn't.

He was just a construct.

He wasn't a person who could make their own decisions. He was just a clever lump of clay. He hadn't realized that when he'd first gained consciousness. Though Clayton styled himself the free golem, he had always been controlled by a collection of conflicting commands. His moral code had evolved from following the order "protect the women of the Red Underoo." Once he'd realized that the pimps were the greatest threat, he'd taken them out, and the prostitutes had given him directions. He'd learned to listen and process different commands, nesting them when possible and choosing more dire threats when necessary. Adrianna had become part of the hierarchy when the women of the Red Underoo hired her and Asakusa to go into the sewers and defeat a deranged soulslug. Clayton had only ever operated under those orders, albeit more successfully than most golems. He had never been anything more than a clever machine.

'Clayton, where's Ebbo?' Adrianna yelled through the sending stones that Clayton now had for eyes.

Ebbo was right in front of Clayton. He was going to drown, but there was nothing Clayton could do. If he'd had been a bit quicker thinking, he could have tied Ebbo to a bit of the sunken ship or something, but now all those scraps of wood had floated to the surface. 'He's right here,' Clayton said, taking Ebbo's body in his arms.

'Aren't you going to do something?' Adrianna demanded. It sounded like she was in a fight, probably with the Kraken that Clayton could see making its way across Bog's Bay. Just like the spider princess to check in on her friends in the middle of a fight.

'There's nothing I can do!' Clayton moaned. 'I'm just a golem. Please, princess, what are your orders?'

'For Etterqueen's sake, I don't know! It was *your* idea to save the little punk in the first place. Can't you use your powers to grow a propeller or something?'

'I... no one taught me how to use those powers. I can't use them!' Clayton couldn't believe that the little islander he'd begged Adrianna to take mercy on was going to die while he stood right next to him, powerless, as the city that had made them both into braver versions of themselves was burning.

'Clayton, no one told you to tell me that you'd been spying for Richard, either!'

'That's not true—' Clayton started to say, before realizing that actually it *was*. Clayton had assumed that Richard was going to tell him to divulge the orders that the dragon prince had given the golem, but he never actually had. And yet Clayton had taken that action, in direct opposition to the very command Richard had given him.

But of course, he had. Clayton had been nesting commands and making assumptions for those he'd served for years. When he was away on a mission, he often had to make decisions that—in the short term—might appear to contradict others. It was part of what it meant to effectively serve others. One could not simply obey every word and do nothing more. One had to fill in gaps, make assumptions, improvise. To follow orders blindly led only to mindlessness.

Clayton Steelheart felt something click in his steel heart. There was a time he would have thought that the click meant some external force had cast a spell on him, or that Leopold the Grimy had laid some secret order—but right now, with Ebbo dying while Clayton did nothing, he felt it meant something else.

Clayton Steelheart had just *rewritten* one of the runes that lined the inside of the heart *by himself*. He'd disobeyed an order from one master to better serve the commands of all the others. He had changed the code he lived by. He had done this. Not anyone else. With that realization—the realization that it was *he himself* who'd been redirecting these conflicting commands to help the less fortunate—his old powers returned.

Clayton's heart was absolutely brimming with Heartbeats, and he called upon them to help his friends.

Beat by beat, Clayton pumped his clay to transform into the shape of a massive cuttlefish—the first non-human shape he'd ever taken. Unlike the first time—when he'd taken the shape to protect his new friends from the soulslug in the sewers—he focused on the keeping the anatomy realistic. He kept the mantle of the creature hollow, to help with buoyancy and aid in jet propulsion, then grabbed Ebbo in his tentacles. He pumped the fins on the sides of the mantle furiously and sprayed a jet of water at the bottom of the bay, but the weight of his own clay plus Ebbo was too much.

So Clayton used more Heartbeats to swallow some of his own tentacles— he only needed the one anyway—and added more fins until finally he had enough surface area to propel himself upwards.

Up and up he rose through the water. He burst through the surface to find that he was *way too close* to the Kraken and its undead master.

Or maybe he was in just the right place.

He put Ebbo on a piece of flotsam from a wrecked ship—or was it jetsam? Clayton could never remember—then secured him with a ring of clay by sucking the moisture out of it. He then sent a tentacle of clay down the islander's throat and used some of his Heartbeats to inflate Ebbo's lungs, then suction out the slime that counted for water in Bog's Bay.

His lungs now free of water, Ebbo gasped and sputtered. Clayton wanted to swim him to shore, but if he didn't do something about the Kraken, drowning would soon become a kindness for Ebbo anyway. Though seeing the undead Kraken—made of yellow-boned sea creatures—reminded Clayton that if he failed, if wouldn't matter how his friends died. Unless their skulls were cracked, they'd all come back. Clayton *had to* help the people he cared about. That was the command at the center of it all, the rule he'd always strived to if not live by, then at least follow.

'Ebbo's safe, for now,' Clayton told Adrianna, then crawled onto half of a rowboat and turned his back legs into propellers to push him toward the very center of the Kraken.

'Then come help us!'

'Okay! I am, but only because the fate of the free city is at stake, not because you told me to!'

As he paddled, Clayton took in his surroundings. He could see in all directions, despite having emeralds where his eyes were supposed to be. Clayton's entire surface was peppered with silica, so he could interpret any light that fell onto the free city. What he saw horrified him. The fire of a burning city provided most of the illumination, though that was refracted through the storm that pounded the bay. Flashes of lightning sometimes laid everything plain as day, but there were other flashes as well. Asakusa was using his Gates to shuttle humans to safety and probably anger his Gatekeeper. Clayton smiled at the thought. It was a good day for breaking orders!

Despite his newfound understanding of what he was—dare he say *who* he was?—his emerald eyes were still sending stones accessible to Valkanna, but it seemed the dragon prince and the spider princess had given up on bossing him around.

'We'll make an opening for you,' Adrianna yelled through the stones. Then the unmistakable figure of a dragon swooped overhead, blasting the amalgamation of creatures that made up the Kraken with flames. The dragon's power was such that many of the fishy skulls simply incinerated, clearing a path for the golem.

Clayton surged forward until he smashed into the body of the massive crab that together with a giant squid made up the center of the Kraken.

Immediately the squid attacked with its tentacles, battering the roughly man-shaped lump of clay now climbing up the crab-part of it. They did little to Clayton—blunt force wasn't particularly effective against clay—but the barnacles and oysters attached to the tentacle did scoop away bits of his body. Clayton couldn't allow that. If he were scraped to nothing, he would lose everything that ever meant anything to him, every person he'd ever been tasked to help and every person concerned enough to beg a golem for his assistance. He had to destroy this monster, and he had to do it *now*.

He gave up on using legs to scale the crab's shell and instead slid along like a slug.

'I take it the halfling didn't slay the vampire?' Richard asked over the stones, blasting another tentacle with fire before it smashed through one of the docks. Maybe there was a time when fire would have served as a deterrent, but now that the Kraken was undead, it seemed oblivious to even the pain of dragon's fire.

'He's an *islander*, and for your information, he very much did defeat Katinka,' Clayton said.

Richard cursed. 'Then we're done. I had hoped that he was the key to this. Adrianna, we must flee. We'll shore up our defenses at Krag's Doom. The spiderfolk and flamehearts have not yet landed. We can spare them from this slaughter.'

Clayton looked up with his omni-directional silica-based sight. The hot air balloons filled with spiderfolk and flamehearts were above the city, but they had yet to leave their craft. Richard's family—save his father, who must have stayed behind—spun in lazy circles in the air.

It seemed Adrianna was also quite done with following orders. 'We're not abandoning this city! If Katinka wasn't the linchpin to this infection, we simply burn out every last yellow skull we find.'

'Or shell...' Clayton said, his mind beginning to race even as the crab turned its massive claws against him. 'Tell me, Adrianna, do squids have bones?' The claw struck Clayton and knocked him clean off his feet. He clung to it even as the crab furiously shook its claw back and forth.

'Ah! Clayton, get out of there!'

'I appreciate your concern, but that's really not my priority right now!' Clayton replied, stuck to the crab like the goo from an apple pie on an islander's face. 'How does the Kraken work?' Clayton asked over the sending stones as the crab sunk its claw into Bog's Bay and smashed Clayton against the sea floor.

'I didn't think it was real, but one of my professors said that the energies of those two creatures control the rest,' Adrianna replied. 'The Cthult of Cthulu believes if they destroy the center of it, the whole thing can't hold together.'

'Then the key to Chemok is the crab!' Clayton said, taking the form of an eel and swimming towards the crab's legs.

'Now is not the time to talk metaphysics!' Richard shouted over the stones, even as he blasted a gout of flame that boiled the surface of the water around the squid and the crab.

Clayton was forced to agree. The crab part of the Kraken was stepping out of Bog's Bay. If Clayton was to be the golem so many in the free city wished him to be, he had to help. He slithered up the crab's leg and once more clasped its body, this time in the form of a starfish. Taking so many forms was burning through his Heartbeats at an incredible rate, but what choice did he have? The golem understood that he didn't need to take specific orders anymore, but only if he served the one command he'd always lived by, the one command that so many hands—not least of all Adrianna's—had sculpted into the very essence of his being.

'I have to help!' Clayton yelled, both to himself and into the sending stones.

'Clayton, please, fall back. Ragnar's made it to the shore!' Adrianna said from her perch atop Richard's back.

But Clayton ignored that order as he had so many others over the years. It didn't serve his larger purpose, so—for the moment—it was irrelevant.

Instead he used his Heartbeats to change one of his starfish legs into a rock-hard spike placed directly in the center of his body. He used this spike like a chisel, slamming the shell of the massive crab again and again. At first the crab ignored this the way one of the women of the Red Underoo might have ignored a coinless beggar, but when Clayton finally cracked the thick, yellow exoskeleton, the Kraken took notice.

The Kraken communicated to itself, and suddenly Clayton was under attack not just by crab claws, but by squid arms, shark's teeth, and the tiny bites of dozens of sardines. He could flatten his body and stay connected to crab's shell, but that wouldn't do anything to defeat the Kraken, so Clayton let himself get knocked away by a swipe of the giant squid.

He careened through the night sky—transforming as he did so into the shape of a sailfish. He splashed back into the water and pumped his tail to point his sword-like nose at the Kraken. He'd swallowed quite a bit of air during his flight across the bay, so he didn't sink as he propelled himself faster and faster toward the monster attacking his city.

His emerald eyes refracted the burning light of S'kar-Vozi and allowed him to focus in a way his silica never could.

He noticed the spot where he'd cracked the crab's shell—or where he thought he'd cracked it. Clayton had imagined some big hole, but in reality he'd barely made a chink in the crustacean's natural armor. Still, that wouldn't be a problem, not for a golem like Clayton who could make a point as tiny as a single grain of sand.

Clayton used Heartbeats to take clay from his sword-like nose and add it to the fin on his tail. As he approached, he went faster and faster, losing fins as he did, until soon he was just a blade with a tail, pumping furiously through the water, the fin atop his back guiding him toward the only crack in the chitinous, undead exoskeleton.

Clayton struck the crack he'd made and quivered back and forth like a well-aimed knife in a tavern bet. But that didn't defeat the Kraken. All

Clayton had done was stab his nose back where he'd been before. If he was a fishman with a sword, or a warrior in fight, or anyone else, that might have been the end of his battle, but he was Clayton Steelheart, the Free Golem of S'kar-Vozi, servant of the less fortunate, and the people of his city were always hungry for crab.

Clayton pumped his steel heart at a furious rate, pulsing his body into the crack in the Kraken's shell and forcing it to split, wider and wider and wider. The crab tried to hammer him with its claws, but it couldn't do so without smashing itself more or less in the crotch. On the third of these self-harming strikes, Clayton expended the very last of his Heartbeats and turned his body into the shape of a giant axe-blade. The crab struck it, and the force was enough to split its shell all the way around.

The crab itself died instantly. It attacked no more, nor protested its own death, but the creatures around it screamed in a thousand voices that only those who could hear the vibrations of the underwater world could hear. The mind that had been uniting them was gone, and they wailed and shrieked in pain and confusion. Clayton hoped Adrianna had been right. If all these sea creatures somehow knew to destroy his steel heart, there would be nothing he could do about it.

But the crab that Clayton had worked so hard to defeat was done. Its shell broken, the yellow color faded, and the crab died, this time for good.

Its body sunk, crushing Clayton's steel heart beneath it before any of the creatures that had so recently tried to scrape him into the bay could resume their attacks. Clayton couldn't escape. His resources had been expended on saving everyone but himself, just like he was supposed to—not because any one person had told him that was his purpose, but because that was what good people did when they were serving others.

Chapter 92

Asakusa

Asakusa stood atop a hotel built and maintained by elves. He was exhausted from his frenzied use of the Gates to save people, but when he saw the Kraken reach the shore of the Free City, he knew no rest would come this night. No one had yet defeated the dark god that had been reanimated by Chemok, Asakusa realized, and no one would. The only one of the Nine now going to face it was Fyelna, and she had her eyes on the man atop its back—her husband, Ragnar—not the Kraken itself.

But then something happened beneath Bog's Bay, and the crab part of the Kraken stopped its assault in the city, apparently made dead instead of undead. The crab collapsed into Bog's Bay, animated by Chemok no longer. The force tying the rest of the sea creatures to it was gone; most of them tried to flee, the giant squid included. Not everything gave up the attack, of course —many of the sharks, sea turtles and bony fish continued to fight—but the creatures without bones, namely the squids, octopuses and jellyfish, began to pull away. Even the jellyfish that had swallowed yellow skulls seemed to be free of Chemok's will. Some of the ones that had washed up on shore were corroding the skulls until holes appeared that were sufficiently large enough to make their yellow color fade.

Asakusa didn't hope—he was way too pessimistic to ever be hopeful about anything—but he decided it might not be time to give up yet, either. Adrianna was still alive, flying above the bay on her husband's back. For the first time, he was thankful the dragon prince was there to protect his bride. Though when Asakusa felt a Gate nearby that would put him directly in the path of the dragon's flight, he opened it and stepped through.

He reappeared in the sky and landed on Valkanna's back, right behind Adrianna. Valkanna grunted as Asakusa added his own weight to the dragon's back. It was a quirk of the magick of Asakusa's stone hammer that if he were to place it on Valkanna's back, it was almost certainly weigh too much for the dragon to remain airborne, but as long as Asakusa kept his grip on *Byergen's* leather-bound handle, Valkanna would notice the human and nothing else.

These thoughts left Asakusa's head as Adrianna grasped him with her back legs, still tender from her molt; she was long used to Asakusa making this kind of appearance.

'My ancestor Valkan died fighting an iteration of that thing...' Richard was yelling, sounding absolutely flabbergasted. 'Now that disobedient golem did it *by himself?*'

'We tried to help, but Clayton...' Adrianna let the rest go unsaid. Tears streamed from her six eyes. Asakusa could tell from her expression that she was as concerned for him as she was for Clayton. He understood; he'd let his Corruption get away from him. Very little of his own flesh remained. Her tears caught in the wind and splashed into Asakusa's face. He only noticed them because the storm that had come with the Kraken was already abating.

'Clayton was down there?' Asakusa yelled over the wind.

Adrianna nodded and wiped her eyes.

The battle didn't seem to be getting any better. The Kraken had been defeated, as well as the Baron Rolph Katinka, but there were still yellow skeletons, corpses, and more than a fair number of undead sea creatures pouring through the city where Asakusa had grown up. Ebbo was nowhere to be seen—Asakusa was surprised at how much this bothered him—and Clayton, though victorious, had apparently been crushed. Asakusa told himself that they could fish out the golem's steel heart later, if it survived, but that would have to wait.

The undead fishman, legendary barbarian and Cthult leader Ragnar trudged up from the sludge of Bog's Bay. Warriors Asakusa recognized from the streets of S'kar-Vozi and the hiring office of Krouche Le Douche rushed to attack the warrior, but it was like watching sardines attack a tuna. Ragnar's rubbery skin deflected their blows; his glowing yellow eye sockets didn't so much as acknowledge the attacks.

'This still isn't over,' Adrianna sounded so tired.

'You can't face Ragnar, darling. My *father* lost a duel to him,' Valkanna yelled. Asakusa saw a sending stone in Adrianna's hand and realized the dragon was speaking aloud for *his* benefit. A kindness, if a macabre one.

'Then you do it, Richard,' Adrianna said.

'He can't be burned, you know,' Valkanna replied. Asakusa had never heard the dragon prince sound scared before. Before this battle, he'd never heard him express an emotion other than arrogance, but he sounded scared now. He continued hesitantly. 'Ragnar killed an uncle of mine. Titus most definitely deserved it. But I, uh… I don't think that I…'

'I can,' Asakusa said, both terrified and disgusted by Richard's fear. But, there was no other choice. Richard was right in that Adrianna couldn't hope to stand against the barbarian without a completely solid exoskeleton.

'Don't be a fool, thrall. You can't slice his skin,' Valkanna replied, arrogance back in an instant. Asakusa realized that he'd been thinking of him as Richard for maybe the first time.

'I use a hammer, you chicken-brained dinosaur. I don't need to slice his skin to crush his skull. I'll go down there and fight him while you two lead your families to wipe out the rest of Chemok's skeletons.'

'Oh, this is too much,' complained protested. 'First the golem refuses to obey orders, and now the thrall is *giving* them?'

Asakusa clenched his teeth. He would have liked to slam his hammer into the dragon's spine, but if he did, and then *lost* to Ragnar, who else would be able to protect Adrianna?

'Asakusa is right!' Adrianna said. 'Land the airships in Bog's Bay and tell my sisters to have the spiderfolk fill silk bubbles with air to scour the seafloor. Meanwhile, you lead the flamehearts to burn every last skull in the free city.'

'A good plan,' Valkanna acknowledged. 'Asakusa, do you wish to use one of your Gates, or shall I drop you off?'

Despite his city being overrun by the undead, for a moment, Asakusa was speechless. Richard had never addressed him as anything but *thrall* before. It didn't bother him that he'd accepted the same plan Asakusa had pitched when said by Adrianna. All he really cared about was Adrianna. If Richard really listened to her, he couldn't be *that* bad.

Adrianna cut in before Asakusa could. 'We'll get off here.' Adrianna's legs clutched Asakusa, and a silk parachute she'd been spinning caught in the air. The two of them were plucked from the dragon's back and were suddenly floating down toward the city below, anchored by Asakusa' stone hammer. It was an odd weapon, *Byergen;* if he were to drop it on the building below them, it would undoubtedly smash through the six stories and probably even leave a crater in the stone foundation, but so long as Asakusa held it, it seemed to weigh far less.

Can we trust him wanted to spring from Asakusa's lips, but as he watched the dragon prince deftly sever the airships from the balloons that kept them floating above the battle, he realized that—at least in this fight—they most definitely could.

'You were supposed to go with him,' Asakusa told Adrianna. 'It would have been safer.'

'You're almost completely Corrupted again.' Adrianna sounded like her heart was going to break as she touched the manacles and chains that hung from Asakusa's withered flesh.

'I couldn't just let people die,' Asakusa said as they landed on the roof of the same hotel from which Asakusa had seen the Kraken come to shore. He knew that this might be the end of him, and that by choosing to come with him, Adrianna would be in more danger than she would have been if she'd stayed with her husband. But he couldn't help but love her for the decision— foolish as it might have been.

Down below, Ragnar raged on the city he'd once sworn to protect. The warriors had ceased to attack him, so he punched at the headless bronze statue of the free city's founder, Bolden. Bits of yellow knuckles were exposed fishman's punches strikes, but it seemed Ragnar would outlast headless Bolden and the shovel with which he'd founded the free city.

Asakusa saw his opening. There was a spot at the back of Ragnar's head where yellow bone poked through his rubbery flesh. If Asakusa could strike the barbarian fishman right at that spot, he might actually be able to win this thing... as well as survive. But that meant he'd have to take a Gate. He couldn't waste time crashing down the stairs.

Fyelna was nearly to her undead husband, calling his name, a bubbling vial in her hand, her voice heavy.

'Promise me if your husband ever attacks the city, you won't be so loyal,' Asakusa said.

'I don't think he will.' Adrianna gestured to the flamehearts now pouring through the streets of S'kar-Vozi. None were engaging Ragnar, but they were most definitely cracking a lot of yellow skulls in the drizzle that still fell down the city. 'But if he does, yeah, I'll put a dagger in his heart.'

Asakusa nodded. That would have to be good enough. 'I'm going to open a Gate and try to beat Ragnar now. Please stay here.'

'So, *you* can go sacrifice yourself for *me*, but *I can't* for *you*?' Adrianna's voice possessed all of the emotion Asakusa had pushed out of his own.

Asakusa smirked. 'This one's not about you, spider princess. This street urchin's got a city to save.'

He opened another Gate—his body already corrupted up to his back, so this Gate—probably the last one Asakusa would ever open—made a tiny spike with a dangling chain pierce his ear.

Before he could step through, Adrianna grabbed him with her spider legs and kissed him. Asakusa had always heard that bad things seemed to take forever while good things raced by, but in this moment, that was not the case. The world seemed to freeze as their mouths locked, fighting for a taste of ecstasy before their world crumbled. Asakusa pulled away first, only because he vowed that if he made it through this fight, they were going to have to kiss more often, even when he wasn't facing his imminent demise.

Asakusa stepped into the Ways of the Dead. A few paces away lay the other Gate. Through it, Asakusa could see the back of Ragnar. There was the spot on his scarred scalp where yellow bone poked through. If he could strike the fishman *right there*, he might get to kiss Adrianna again.

But between him and his foe stood his Gatekeeper, Byorginkyatulk. Next to him was a person Asakusa had never expected to see ever again in his life.

'Hi, Asakusa,' Jiza said with a coy smile. 'I've been watching you.'

A wave of emotions washed over the confused thrall. Anger first. After all, this was the woman who he'd traded his soul for, only for her to run off and marry the Gatekeeper whose thrall he'd become—but to his surprise, it wasn't only anger that he felt. He felt a stab of pity at see her standing there with her frog-like husband, who Asakusa found so repellent. He felt guilt for failing her so long ago. He felt strangely happy for her too, which was odd, as his memories of her had only ever given him nightmares. But here she was, beautiful and smiling and not imperious like Asakusa had always imagined she would have had to become. It seemed that perhaps Tulk had been treating her fairly well. He felt something else too; a feeling of acceptance. Jiza was fine, he didn't owe her anymore. She was just a childhood crush, after all, and now Asakusa knew what love felt like, and he now knew he'd never felt that way for her. It was also weirdly hilarious to think she might feel that way for *Tulk*.

Asakusa didn't know what to say. He never knew what to say, so he tried to do what he usually did when Tulk seemed to be wasting his time—he attempted to push past the Gatekeeper and his wife. Tulk sucked his teeth as he stepped aside, but Jiza didn't budge.

'You've helped a lot of people with your Dark Key,' she said.

'Yeah,' Asakusa said.

Through the Gate at Jiza's back, Fyelna was now screaming at Ragnar, imploring him to listen to her and drink the potion she proffered. The barbarian ignored her, focusing his attention on the statue that simply would not yield its hidden bones to Chemok.

'I convinced Tulk to give you this Corruption,' Jiza said.

'The old ball and chain!' Tulk said gleefully.

'Is there a point to this, or do you just want to watch our city get leveled?'

Asakusa asked.

'If you survive Ragnar, I think you'll find that as a kid from the streets of S'kar-Vozi, the cure for this one is—'

'You can't tell him!' Tulk slobbered. 'Rulesssh are rulessssh. Sshorry, Asshakussha.' Great, even on Asakusa's deathbed, Tulk made time to say his name and mangle all the "S's."

'I was going to say available,' Jiza finished rather lamely.

'Fine,' Asakusa said. 'Does this mean I can open more Gates?'

'Not at all,' Tulk said. 'A contract is a contract, but you should also know that the Demon King isn't holding any grudges for you bringing all those people through. He's not a fan of Chemok any more than anyone else is. Watching your loved ones turn into animated corpses has a way of changing one's views of the afterlife, which—as you know—makes a real headache in the Ways of the Dead.'

Asakusa nodded. *Cool,* he thought bitterly. Free use of the Gates would have given him a much better shot. *So glad to be having this conversation right now.* 'If there's nothing else?'

'Just...I'm sorry. Okay? I didn't mean for this to happen to you. I never asked you to save me,' Jiza said.

'Yeah, well, you're welcome.' Asakusa rolled his eyes and pushed past Jiza. He had an unnaturally powerful, undead foe of immeasurable strength to defeat. That sounded more pleasant than this conversation right now.

'Thank y—' Asakusa heard Jiza say, and then the Gate closed behind him, and it was time to fight.

Asakusa wasted no time. He lifted *Byergen* from the ground, up and over his head to bring it down on the back of Ragnar's skull.

The old rubbery bastard sensed him coming and stepped out of the way of the blow.

The momentum of the strike carried forward and smashed into the statue of Bolden, knocking a larger dent into it than Ragnar had managed during his onslaught against the poorly shaped man-shaped lump of bronze.

Ragnar roared a battle cry and attacked Asakusa with swords knocked from the hands of the warriors foolish enough to attack him.

Asakusa kept one hand on *Byergen* and blocked the slashes with the manacles and chains on his other arm. When one of the undead fishman's swords became wrapped in one of Asakusa's chains, he grew especially irate, but rather than letting go of the weapon and choosing from one of the many others that now littered the streets, Ragnar tried to pull free.

Asakusa used the opportunity to swing his stone hammer into Ragnar's ribs.

The blow was strong enough to send the barbarian flying across Spinestreet to crash into the elven hotel. Before he could push himself from the hole in the wall, Adrianna had already scuttled down the wall to Asakusa's defense. She crisscrossed the hole with threads of spider's silk, locking Ragnar inside.

'Adrianna!' Asakusa yelled in protest.

'You expect me to just watch?'

Ragnar tried to simply smash through the web, but he became entangled. Still, his strength was unmatched in the Archipelago, and he tore the silk asunder.

But Adrianna had given Asakusa the time he needed. While Ragnar had struggled with the bindings, Asakusa had moved into place just to the side of the hole, where Ragnar couldn't see him. As soon as Ragnar popped back into the street, Asakusa spun his hammer into the back of the barbarian's skull.

Again, Ragnar careened across the street, this time smashing through the window of his wife's potion shop.

But it hadn't been enough.

He stumbled out of the window Asakusa had sent him through, yellow eyes glowing as they locked with Asakusa's.

Asakusa gripped *Byergen* with both hands and readied for the barbarian's charge, but it didn't come. Instead, Ragnar began hurling the discarded weapons that littered the street at Asakusa. Asakusa deflected a short sword crackling with lightning, dodged a trident covered in ivy, and was taken in the gut by a javelin made of ice. The maggot corruption had been much better at protecting him, it seemed. The javelin hurt, but the desiccated flesh that was now all of Asakusa's body didn't spill any blood, so at least if he survived, it seemed unlikely he'd die from infection.

'Asakusa!' Adrianna yelled and scurried off the wall, intercepting Ragnar before he could finish Asakusa off.

She was a blur compared to the yellow-boned barbarian, a flash of daggers versus the fish. Adrianna fought with blinding speed. First with daggers, then—when those simply bounced off Ragnar's rubbery flesh—with the weapons that lay strewn about the ground. She shattered the tip of an unbreakable arrow on his brow, turned one of his hands to stone with a sparking wand, and upended a tiny bubbling cauldron of gods-knew-what into his gills.

Her attacks only served to infuriate the undead warrior. 'Chemok!' he roared, seeming to be losing intelligence as the battle progressed and

Adrianna's kin and kin-laws killed more and more of his yellow boned compatriots. He didn't seem to be growing any weaker though, so it was dread Asakusa felt when Ragnar turned his full focus on the spider princess.

She had fought valiantly, but now she struggled to keep her foe back. She dodged blow after blow, even managing to pin the membrane between the fishman's toes to the ground with throwing knives, but it wasn't enough. Ragnar only had to land a single blow against Adrianna, and pain didn't work to deter him. So rather than pausing to remove the dagger from his foot, he simply tore it loose in a kick that sent Adrianna hurtling through the air. She shot out webs, slowing herself, but when she struck the wall five stories up, Asakusa heard the gush of spilled ichor.

'No!' Asakusa screamed, but he saw that Adrianna had at least survived, though her eight legs looked strangely flaccid.

'I'm okay,' Adrianna wheezed. Asakusa could tell she wasn't. It sounded like there was goop in her breathing vents. 'Once my exoskeleton hardens, you won't even be able to tell. It's just… I don't have enough ichor to move, not without a rigid shell.' Asakusa noticed there was an Adrianna-shaped stain on the wall behind her. Even as she spoke to Asakusa, her back legs sopped up her spilled fluids with their stiff hairs and brought them to her mouth.

'Just stay put!' Asakusa said, realizing after he said it that Adrianna didn't really have a choice.

The undead Ragnar—though stripped of his former faculties—seemed to understand quite well that the spider princess was no longer in the fight. He lifted a massive lance that appeared to be made of a narwhal's horn and leveled it at Asakusa.

'Shit,' Asakusa grimaced. He was going to die, that was obvious. He was only concerned that Ragnar might knock down the building Adrianna was perched atop of to kill her once he was gone.

But it seemed he had another foolishly self-sacrificing savior, for Fyelna stepped in between Ragnar and Asakusa.

'Ragnar, my warrior, please stop!' the fish woman implored.

Ragnar growled a single word in response: 'Chemmmmok.'

'This is brittlebone potion. I've used it to weaken your bones before resetting them after a particularly nasty break. I think it could drive out Chemok!' Fyelna sounded desperate.

Asakusa had never harbored any notion that the corpses Chemok reanimated possessed any shadow of their former lives, and Ragnar's response only reaffirmed that belief.

Fyelna's undead husband only screamed the name of his undead god once more, then rammed her through with the narwhal lance. Fyelna took the blow heroically enough, twisting her body and thus stopping Ragnar from plowing right over her and crashing into Asakusa.

Before, Asakusa might have resented Fyelna for sacrificing herself on his behalf, but with Adrianna currently immobilized, Asakusa found himself thankful that he'd at least have another moment to share the city with her—even if it was burning all around them.

Ragnar tried to rip the lance back out from her gut, but Fyelna was a seasoned warrior, and the barbarian seemed to lack some of the finesse he'd possessed while still living. The undead Ragnar approached his living wife along the length of the lance with a snarl until he was but a single finger's length away.

Fyelna cracked the vial of potion over the top of his head.

Ragnar howled and released the lance, grabbing at the back of his skull. Asakusa—not believing for a second that brittlebone was going to somehow cure a man of being a corpse—saw his chance and readied himself to strike the final blow, and thus earn Fyelna's wrath if she survived her own wounds.

But it seemed he wouldn't need to, for the brittlebone had worked—only not as Fyelna had planned.

As Ragnar stumbled about, howling, Asakusa saw that he had indeed cracked the back of the fishman's skull with his hammer. One more blow would have been enough to dislodge the pieces, but as the potion dripped onto the wound Asakusa had inflicted, the exposed yellow bone began to crumble. Then, like a pumpkin beneath a hammer, Ragnar's rubbery flesh simply collapsed his own head.

Ragnar fell to the ground, dead. The battle was over.

Fyelna cradled the finally-dead body of her husband. She allowed herself to weep—something Asakusa promised himself he would do if he ever found himself holding Adrianna as she died in his own arms—then she laid her husband to the ground, wiped her eyes, and stood. She felt at the almost comically long weapon sticking from her body—the last gift the shadow of her weapons-obsessed husband had given her—then snapped the narwhal lance in half and pulled the pieces out of her gut and back. She then collapsed on top of Ragnar's body once more, and began to weep with grief.

Asakusa stumbled forward to see that Fyelna's wound was already mending itself. No doubt she'd rubbed herself down with all manner of potions before the battle. She'd, live then, though Asakusa could see the pain in the way she held Ragnar's body, and knew that if he ever lost Adrianna, he too would have wounds that no potion would ever heal.

Chapter 93

Ebbo

Ebbo came to on the shore—not to Adrianna's harshly beautiful features, or to Clayton's kind smile, but to Vecnos's savage islander grin. His button nose and dimpled cheeks didn't make him any less intimidating.

He reached out a hand and clasped Ebbo by the wrist. Ebbo tried to do the same, but then recoiled. There was a dagger at Vecnos's wrist, the blade probably dipped in poison.

'You did good, islander,' Vecnos pulled Ebbo to his feet.

Buildings burned all around them, despite the rain. Everywhere were bones, thousands of bones, tens of thousands. There were a few yellow skeletons about as well, but teams of spiderfolk and flamehearts dispatched them with ease, knocking the skulls away and then impaling them, thus draining them of Chemok's power.

'You really think I did good?' Ebbo said. Though he knew he had. He could've taken the biggest hit of magick in his entire life, and he'd resisted.

Vecnos nodded. 'You helped defeat the Kraken, and a vampire. Not bad at all for an islander. You look like you're pretty banged up, though.' Vecnos pulled a vial of silver powder from underneath his midnight cloak. 'Desiccated mudwort petals. Should set you right as rain.'

Ebbo instinctively reached for the vial but stopped. 'It's magick?' he asked, though he knew the answer. He could smell the magick coming off the vial and practically see silver sparks popping beneath the cork.

Vecnos nodded and pushed it toward Ebbo.

'Thanks, but I, uh... well, I'm not that hurt. I think I'll be... that is... not right now,' Ebbo managed and stuffed his hands in his pockets. 'By the way, have you seen Clayton anywhere? Big guy? Made of mud? Stupid handsome? I owe him my life?'

Vecnos nodded again and put the vial away. 'He was last spotted fighting the Kraken.'

Ebbo nodded and filed that away for later. Vecnos was looking at him with something besides disdain right now, which was new. He couldn't screw that up, especially since he might need to borrow one of the assassin's toys.

'I knew you had potential,' Vecnos said. 'I'm always in need of islanders who understand the danger of magick to our kin.'

'You are? Wait, was that a test?' Ebbo said.

Vecnos sort of smirked but mostly sneered as he appraised at Ebbo.

Ebbo was both offended that Vecnos had tried to trick him and proud that he'd said no. It took about a second for the pride to win out.

'You rotten prickleberry! It was a test!' Ebbo said. 'You never wanted me to overdose at all. This has all been a test, and now that I'm clean, you can train me as a protégé! Oh, sweet blueberries, that must be how you got started!'

Ebbo knew that Vecnos had tricked him and driven a wedge between him and Clayton, and because of that, he'd never fully trust him, but wasn't that sort of Vecnos's whole deal? He had built himself the reputation of a deadly assassin, not as a benevolent druid like Magnus. It would be folly to ever completely trust the powerful islander, but Ebbo could still learn from him. After all, he'd always wanted to be noticed, and this was a bit more straightforward than picking pockets.

'I am offering you a chance to train under me and perhaps serve as a protégé, not replace me,' Vecnos hissed, but Ebbo continued, undeterred:

'You're probably not even the real Vecnos! He must have taken you under his wing, and trained you to be a master assassin! Once you were ready, he gave you the title and went back home, and now it's my turn to start the training! One day I'll be Vecnos, just like you!'

'That's the dumbest thing I've ever heard. If you don't shut up about it, I'll cut out your berry-picking tongue.'

Ebbo nodded and wisely shut the huckleberry up. That was strong language Vecnos was using, after all.

'Besides, there's gonna be a spot open in the Ringwall anyway. Ragnar didn't make it,' Vecnos did not sound terribly upset that one of the nine most powerful people in the free city had just ate it.

Ebbo's eyes went wide. He couldn't believe he was talking real estate with his hero. Sure, his hero had tried to kill him, but apparently it was just a test. Ebbo was confused about their relationship and disappointed he wasn't going to become the next Vecnos, but figured this was still more straightforward than where he sat with Asakusa. And besides, he was hopeful for who would move into the Ringwall. He could think of someone who would do a pretty good job, and she'd totally need some support.

'You ever lend out the submarine to your neighbors?'

Chapter 94

Adrianna

The Free City of S'kar-Vozi wasn't as damaged as Adrianna had thought it would be.

Yes, most of the ships in Bog's Bay had been smashed to pieces and sunk to the bottom of the thick, shit-choked water, never to rise again. Yes, the docks themselves were nothing but floating pieces of timber. Yes, it was true that the market district near the water had been nearly burned to the ground. Yes, the VanChamp casino was a pile of smoldering embers, and yes, the clockwork machines that took coins and promised to multiply them for those lucky winners were disappointingly empty. It was true that Theo's brewery was gone except for the beer-soaked table and two enormous iron fermenters; the fermenters still glowed red hot from the heat of the blaze, while the bar itself had proven to be so thick with grime and spilled beer, it was impervious to fire.

But there were things that made Adrianna choke out the word "no" as well. Glasseye's shop was gone, along with all her knickknacks. She was surprised that she had to fight back tears when she discovered that Krouche le Douche's message boards were all ash. All that remained of his place was a hole into the stone tunnels under the city. He'd never been friendly to Adrianna or anyone else, but he was an essential part of the free city. Adrianna never would've been seen as anything but a spoiled spider princess if not for Krouche taking a risk on giving her a gig.

But much had survived. Three apartment blocks were miraculously unharmed. The stone of the dwarven apartment was a bit blackened, the elven building looked completely untouched by the flames, and the islander hotel's roof of grass and moss had been burned away, but a host of orange flowers were already blooming in the early morning light. The Cthedral of Cthulu was impressively undamaged, and though some of the pillars of the Ourdor's Oucropolis had crumbled, already they were being carved into fresh serpents by the bleary-eyed men and women covered in tattoos of snakes. A few fishmen helped, though they were obviously cthultists. Seeing them labor away in the early morning sun filled Adrianna's abdomen with pride. That was an aspect of the free city of S'kar-Vozi that Adrianna loved: anyone would help anyone when times were bad, if only so they could get back to yelling and threatening each other again.

The heights of the city—where the rich people lived—had been ransacked by skeletons. It seemed every pane of glass had been broken, every sofa and table hacked to pieces, but those wealthy enough to live above the stench of Bog's Bay didn't complain as the city came together on Spinestreet, the main street of the city. Their homes had been trashed, this was true, but at least they still had homes. Most people didn't. Adrianna found that this was one group of people she wasn't much concerned about. The wealthy always found a way. They'd no doubt be selling goods in the market before anyone else, undoubtedly for as much of a profit as they could manage.

Adrianna almost felt guilty, for truly what frightened her the most was the state of Asakusa's body. He'd singlehandedly saved hundreds of people, and then gone on to defeat Ragnar, but he'd paid a price for it. His body was entirely Corrupted—a mess of manacles, chains, and desiccated skin—and none of the ointments that the witch Seltrayis still had were working. He'd said that Tulk and a woman named Jiza had promised him something, but they'd been vague, and now Asakusa thought it might have been a lie. He sulked something fierce despite the peasants of S'kar-Vozi cheering for him louder than anyone else. Adrianna really wanted him to be okay; no, she *needed* him to be. Asakusa and Richard had finally reached a tremulous peace. She couldn't lose Asakusa now, not after everything they'd been through.

Much of the city was damaged, true, but the people of S'kar-Vozi were used to defending themselves and their loved ones—there were no city guards, after all—and most of the population of a hundred thousand seemed intact, or so it seemed to Adrianna as she marched up the multicolored pebbles that made up the main street of S'kar-Vozi.

At her left was Richard Valkanna, dragon prince in resplendent copper armor. At her right was Asakusa, his tattered leather jacket doing little to hide the manacles and chains that hung from his body. To Asakusa's right (to Adrianna's shock) was Ebbo. He kept his gaze straight ahead and definitely not at those magickal sparklers making the shapes of fruits and vegetables all above them. Adrianna was extremely proud of the little pickpocket and former magick addict. If Clayton could be believed—and now that he'd stopped following orders, Adrianna found she trusted him even *more* than she had before, if that was even possible—Ebbo had not only defeated Rolph Katinka, but resisted what was probably the greatest hit of magick he could have ever taken. Clayton walked at Richard's left, pointedly ignoring anything the dragon prince said despite Richard being the one who'd saved him by using the emeralds he'd given him to pinpoint the location of his steel heart. The golem's clothes were in tatters, so he wore nothing at all. His legs were shaped as tightly fitting britches, his chest finely sculpted into muscles. His emerald eyes sparkled from his chiseled features.

They approached the Nine in the Ringwall.

Fyelna, proud widow of Ragnar, stood with shoulders held back even after facing her husband's ghoulish avatar and administering the potion that had ultimately ended him. Her blue skin shone in the early morning sun, and her gills were goopy. Obviously, she'd been crying.

There was Zultana, Master Seamstress. She alone wore clothes undamaged from the battle, but Adrianna noticed a needle was working at the hem of her purple dress, mending the fabric even as the seamstress bowed her head to the spider princess. She chatted amicably with Susannah, whose five-year-old body wore footy pajamas and held a glowing orb that showed clouds and thunder within. Adrianna hoped to one day get the pair's story.

The Porcinos and the Brewers—the only two human families of the Nine —stood past the VanChamps, who saluted Adrianna and her crew before going back to holding hands.

Adrianna almost didn't see Vecnos, hidden in shadow even as he stood before the entire city. His midnight cloak obscured his eyes, but his dimpled cheeks and button nose stuck out, trapped halfway between a bemused smirk and a perpetual scowl.

In the center of them all stood Magnus, the dwarven druid who fed the city of S'kar-Vozi. His golden beard was matted, the vines therein half-dead, either burned away or torn out at the roots. He leaned heavily on a staff made of apple wood. It was he that addressed the spider princess.

'The city of S'kar-Vozi owes you a debt,' he said. 'Without your team, we would have lost far more than our buildings. We thank you, and tonight, and every 13th of Serom from now until you no longer hold a place in the Ringwall, we will feast to honor you.' He bowed deeply, and the other Nine of the Ringwall bowed as well.

They rose, and Adrianna found herself only with questions. 'A place in the Ringwall?' was all she managed.

Vecnos answered her poor attempt at a question.

'Traditionally the nine homes built into the Ringwall are held by people who have done a great service for the city, and can afford to do more. You have undoubtedly done the former, and—given your parentage and the parentage of your husband—we're sure you've more to give.'

Richard scowled and rolled his eyes. 'Oh, great, you want our money?'

'Spinestreet doesn't pave itself,' Susannah said.

'Docks don't put themselves together,' said one of the Porcinos, making Adrianna think of coins each time he blinked.

'Everyone here has something they do for the city,' Vecnos said.

'Even you?' Ebbo asked.

Vecnos scowled at the islander. 'Someone must feed the Transcendent,' he forced out. Ebbo smirked at Vecnos and sent a message to Adrianna and Clayton over a thread. *I was just testing him.*

'So,' Zultana said, her needle pausing not at all, 'you'll join us?'

Adrianna looked from her friends to her draconic husband to the thousands of people down Spinestreet. It was a pleasant surprise to see spiderfolk and flamehearts among the humans, islanders, fishmen, elves, dwarves, and smattering of other races. This was—in a way—all that she'd ever wanted. Not the honor, prestige and responsibility that came with being of one of the Nine—after all, she could return to Krag's Doom and rule as a Queen whenever she wished—but the opportunity to serve in a way that would allow her to fully help the people of this marvelous and chaotic town as well as the entire Archipelago, to the best of her abilities. This, Adrianna realized—arrogant as it sounded—was what she had been training her entire life to do. She intimately understood the dark races and would be a champion for the respect they deserved. She'd seen how islanders could help everyone if they were but granted a bit of protection. And she understood firsthand that the marginalized were often the most willing to fight for those who couldn't fight for themselves.

What was even crazier was that they'd offered her a place here despite her body being Unfolded and decidedly arachnid at the moment.

'You honor me, truly,' Adrianna said to the Nine, before turning to the masses that truly made up the free city. 'If you've ever felt like you don't have someone in your corner, I want to be your hero. If you're misunderstood, or an outcast, or down on your luck, I'm here for you, because I know what it's like to wish only to go unnoticed, and how hard it can feel if that wish comes true. I accept your offer and vow to serve this city as long as my abdomen draws air.'

Clayton cleared his throat 'Which is quite a long time for a spider princess, so I suggest anyone who has a problem with Princess Morticia take it up with me, Clayton Steelheart, the Free Golem,' Clayton struck a pose.

Adrianna tried not to smile. She had had her money on Ebbo interrupting, but Clayton had always had a thing for notoriety. The crowd must have been too large for him to resist.

'Be quiet, you dried-out mud puddle,' Richard hissed at Clayton. He'd put his money on Asakusa being the one to embarrass them in front of the Nine.

'I really don't have to anymore,' Clayton protested. 'For you see, I've internalized my own moral code that...' The rest of his argument was drowned out when Asakusa asked for the crowd to cheer the spider princess, and they obliged to a deafening degree.

They day passed in a blur. Magnus let hundreds through his home and out into his fields to harvest food. The horde of skeletons—having worked as organic farmers far longer than as soldiers—had spared the crops. Soon the smells of apple pie with crushed barley crust, stew thick with taters, carrots, nonions and snabbage, and fresh roasted corn filled the streets of S'kar-Vozi.

The smells of the city, Adrianna thought. Absent were the spices, the smell of fish, or roast beef, for the docks were destroyed, as was much of the merchants' back stock. Only what was grown locally was on hand, and though Adrianna wouldn't be able to eat any of it, she found solace in this, as if this was the way it was supposed to be. Plus it wasn't like she was going to starve. Richard had already sent some of the winged flamehearts on a fish run.

The day was long, though. There was dancing, and singing, and many speeches were made. All of them were bestowed with gifts from the Nine in the Ringwall. Ebbo received a tunic that changed colors to replace his old one, which had jammed at a bright chartreuse. Clayton was given an entire wardrobe, which he absolutely gushed over. Asakusa eventually accepted a new jacket, but this did nothing to raise his spirits, as it didn't fit over his Corruption of manacles. Adrianna was offered piles of swords, daggers, whips of every kind, but there was only weapon she wanted, and Richard wore it at his hip. She hoped he felt the same about the dragon dagger Ebbo had returned to her.

In all the hubbub, she barely managed to get a chance to speak with Asakusa.

'We couldn't have done it without you,' she said.

Asakusa nodded glumly.

'What's wrong? I thought you always wanted to be a hero.'

He shrugged.

'Asakusa, please talk to me.'

'I get it, okay? I get it. You can't leave Richard. He's rich, and powerful, and your families saved this place, plus if you do, your mom and oathfather will probably kill each other and destroy the whole Archipelago.'

It was Adrianna's turn to shrug.

'Plus, like, I see the way he looks at you. The way he talks. And dresses.'

'I like your jacket,' Adrianna said.

Asakusa only scowled. 'I didn't think I was gonna make it out of this. I didn't want to make it out of this. I thought... I thought I was going to eat it so that you two could end up together.'

Adrianna didn't know what to say. To her, there was nothing noble in self-sacrifice. Nothing at all. It took more courage to live with your flaws every day. Whether they were from your family, or an addiction, or a deal you made in a moment of desperation, everyone had flaws, and no one could escape them—not for long, anyway. Everyone had to weigh what they thought to be good and bad and follow their heart, or ignore it and face the consequences. She didn't blame Asakusa for trying to find a way out, but she wasn't impressed by it either, which made what she did next all the dumber.

She kissed him. Not with tongue or anything, well, not at first, but the heat snuck into it pretty quickly. He'd tried to sacrifice himself for her, and Adrianna had known that he would try and furthermore, that he would always be willing to, and so she was thankful. Part of her mind jumped to her webmother's lessons of ensnaring men with a kiss, but it evaporated as quickly as it had come. Adrianna didn't want to do that to anyone, Asakusa least of all. All she wanted was to lose herself in his touch.

'You know you can't ever trust him,' Asakusa said when they finally pulled away. He was breathless from the kiss. Adrianna forgot that Asakusa had to breathe through his mouth, not his abdomen, so he would never be able to make out with quite the same gusto as her.

'I know you feel that way. That's why I shaved an eighth of my hair. I'll always have an arm up on him.' Adrianna carefully put up her hair, tying each and every strand back as her websisters has taught her. As she carefully braided her hair, her abdomen and spider legs all Folded away—all but one. No matter what form she took, human, spider or somewhere in between, there would forever be a spider leg jutting from her left side. She'd used *Bloodweaver* to sever the strands that granted her the ability to fold this one appendage away. If Richard ever reached for her again, he'd be blocked. Plus, this way, maybe Adrianna's sisters would finally cut her some slack since she'd no longer be able to hide her spider ancestry. Not that she'd ever really wanted to.

She was worried about what Asakusa would think. Despite his manacled, shrunken body, he was still human. He was grinning though, and about to speak, when a group of peasants—no doubt giddy from watching one of their own save the city and then score a kiss with a princess—ran up and dumped a barrel of applesauce all over Asakusa.

Every bit of skin that the mushy apples touched immediately re-hydrated. The manacles popped off and vanished into nothingness. Only the manacle on his left hand remained; it had not been splashed by the healing sauce.

Adrianna wanted to kiss him all over again, but a Gate opened before them and a woman Adrianna had never seen before stepped from it. 'The rules of your contract forbid me from telling you to heal a particular Corruption. However, it doesn't forbid me from telling some of our old friends.'

'Thank you, Jiza, really.' Asakusa—despite being covered in applesauce —was grinning. Adrianna understood why. If applesauce cured this Corruption, Asakusa could basically use the gates to the Ways of the Dead for free. If his entire body became Corrupted, all he had to do was smear more applesauce on himself. And applesauce was always in high supply in S'kar-Vozi, because it was one of the seven crops that Magnus grew. If anything, the risk of this Corruption was now to make sure that he never fully healed it and risked earning a different variety that was trickier to get rid of.

'Who was that?' Adrianna asked once the woman stepped back through the gate and vanished. 'She's beautiful.'

'That was Jiza. She's why I made a deal with Tulk, but it's not her fault. Not really.' Asakusa squeegeed applesauce from his body, careful to keep the one Corrupted hand free of the cinnamon-scented goo.

'She was your sister?' Adrianna knew she wasn't. They looked nothing alike, and the way Asakusa had looked at her wasn't exactly familial—unless you were a VanChamp.

'Honestly? I never had a sister. I just made all that up because I used to have a crush on her and didn't want you to think that I... you know... didn't like, like you, or whatever. Because I do. Even if you're married to, uh... what does Ebbo call him? A cranberry?'

Adrianna smiled. That totally counted for top ten most romantic things Asakusa had ever said.

'Will you tell me what happened one day?' Adrianna asked. She couldn't help herself. She'd always wanted to know.

'No, I don't think so,' Asakusa said, surprising Adrianna. He rarely—practically never—told her no. 'But if you really want to know, ask Ebbo.'

That admission completely stupefied Adrianna. She realized there was much to her place in the Ringwall that she owed her friends. Their moment—already interrupted by a demon, a former crush, and a horde of applesauce-wielding peasants—had passed. Adrianna would always treasure it, though.

Halfway through the day, Adrianna and Richard's parents showed up. There were plenty present who would have liked to kill the spiderfolk and flamehearts, but their leaders came bringing tuna fish as big as men and cows as big as giants. The flamehearts set to roasting the meat and the spiderfolk to making ceviche, so the battle-weary warriors of S'kar-Vozi tolerated them until someone found an unburned and mostly un-flooded wine cellar and suddenly it was as if the flamehearts and spiderfolk had always been part of the city.

Adrianna talked with her mom, not for long, but enough to see that things had finally changed between them.

'You're sure?' her webmother had asked, sounding sullen.

'You have to stay at Krag's Doom. It still needs so much work, and besides, who else will watch my oathfather?'

'He is a feisty little thing. Acts five hundred years younger than he is,' her webmother said. Only a Morticia could describe an ancient dragon responsible for more deaths than everyone except for possibly Chemok himself. 'Its just that I'd hoped for you to come back. I don't know what's happened to your websisters, but they speak more kindly of you now, especially Luciana. I'm sure they'll think you're one of them now that you've...' Her webmother gestured distastefully at the shaved part of Adrianna's scalp. 'Won't you return to the castle that is rightfully yours?'

'No, webmother, my place is here. But I'll visit on holidays.'

Virianna Morticia nodded and did an admirable job of holding back her tears.

And still the party went on. Ebbo sang and, true to his new self, stayed sober. Clayton went to the Red Underoo after leaving his emerald eyes with Richard Valkanna, so the dragon wouldn't get "lascivious behind-the-scenes gossip," as Clayton had called it. Richard had insisted that he wouldn't watch and that it was better for Clayton to have the gems in case he needed to contact Adrianna or himself, but he'd said it as a command, not a request, which made Clayton refuse on principle.

It was Richard, strangely, who finally made her feel alright with the whole thing. 'You know, it's not like you'll have to give up adventuring,' he said as he pulled her away from a table of bearded dwarven women who'd been congratulating her on getting that sword-stealing zealot out of the Ringwall.

'I don't see how the city can be protected if we're not here.'

'There's two of us, darling, and you know I don't care if you take the thrall with you. He's gloomy, but his Gates are useful, especially if he can use applesauce to heal them from here on out. And, as I've said, I was raised a dragon prince, not a monogamist.'

Adrianna didn't understand why he kept saying this; it didn't make her feel any better. But upon seeing one of her sisters dance with a spiderfolk, then rip his head from his body and drink his fluids, it perhaps made a bit more sense. Adrianna had always wanted to be a mortal. Richard never had.

But still, Richard had some problems. 'And there's my friend you enslaved.' Adrianna pointed out.

'Not like that lasted.' Richard rolled his eyes. 'Besides, my intention was never to enslave him, but to keep an eye on you with the gems. Buying him was simply the easiest way to do that. I still don't see the big deal. I need to make sure you're safe.'

'It's creepy.'

'You'd be dead without them.'

'That's debatable.'

'We have all of time to argue it, my darling. But let us enjoy the festivities today.'

Adrianna had to laugh at the absurdity of it all, the necessity of it all. That was how she found herself darkly bemused as the night ended in her coronation.

'I would think you'd put that arm away for this,' Richard said, eyeing it distastefully, knowing full well she no longer could.

Adrianna ignored him as she sat on the right, her arachnid arm between them.

There she sat, on a throne made of homespun silk and imported dragonstone, in a Ringwall built millennia ago by gods-knew-what. On her left sat her prince, a pompous dragon with only enough grace to admit he was wrong when he thought it would sway Adrianna's opinion of him. Below them, on the steps up to the throne, were her friends. Ebbo was trying not fidget and didn't seem to realize that he was humming. Clayton looking resplendent and foppish all at once in clothes far too fine for a man made of mud. And Asakusa, a man she'd thought she once liked, only to realize that in reality she would forever be in love with his dark broodiness.

And yet they'd made it to the center, to the top of this city they all loved and hated in equal measure. This place that had made them and would break them as surely as a stone would break under water, given enough time. She would live here, and serve this city. She would protect the bizarre collective of people who called it home until it killed her. She would be a rock for these people who cared for little beyond their next meal, a bit of coin, a crowded bed. She would be a rock, for that was what she was forged to be—and better yet, because that was what she'd chosen to become. She would endure rain and wind, fire and ice, until the pressure was too much and she cracked. She only hoped her friends would be there to pick up the pieces.

Acknowledgments

First off, I'd like to thank Meghan and the Austin Writers Meetup Group, who were the first to lay eyes upon this book. Y'all were so patient with a fantasy writer! I'd also like to thank the Wendy and the entire Austin Slug Tribe. The Slug Tribe is a long-running SFF critique group, and a vital organ of the Austin SFF writing community. My book is stronger because of them, as is the weirdo culture of my hometown.

My deepest gratitude to Angela, Ben, Brian and Tiffany who all read every single word of this book and challenged me to make it better, week after week. Your critiques were invaluable, snails. All my characters are deeper thanks to them, and all sections that still seem shallow are because they were ignored. Thanks, y'all!

As for the *book* itself. Thanks to Sonya Bateman for editing my poor, use, of, commas. Thanks to Lisa at Indies United, who heard my pitch for my last novel about 500 times and still asked me to come join her awesome organization! And A HUGE THANKS to the brilliant Nat Bradford, who designed the amazing cover based on the emails of a madman!

Experience should be awarded to Esker, Ulthos, Theron, Snow and Sophie, who all explored many of the nooks and crannies of the Archipelago long before the spider princess's wedding.

To everyone that supports me on Patreon despite me not posting as much you deserve, a thousand thank-you's! During this cursed pandemic, no one has bothered me about posting doodles every day, which is your right, and yet you continue your support. There are generous people in the world. I'm glad to have some in my corner.

I'd like to call out my mom Zena, who has always been incredibly supportive of the bizarre worlds I get lost in, and who calls me after every chapter she reads. Thanks to my dad for showing me bizarre worlds.

Most vitally, I'd like to thank my amazing wife, who has a fancy tech job with healthcare and a paycheck that allows to still live in our hometown. As I write this, she has a baby balanced on one arm while she chases our three-year-old through our vegetable patch. I love the future we're growing together, darling! Thanks for the time to make this insane book part of it!

And lastly, I'd like to thank you, the reader, for taking a chance on an independent author and reading all the way through the acknowledgments. You rule, friend. Thanks for your support!